Cleelok
(Chaos as defined by the limits of Eternity)

by

Sean Nuber

FRITTER AND
BOONDOGGLE

Contents

Chapter 1	Croy	Page 1
Chapter 2	Clerin	Page 32
Chapter 3	Vrric	Page 69
Chapter 4	Trela	Page 107
Chapter 5	Croy	Page 136
Chapter 6	Clerin	Page 162
Chapter 7	Vrric	Page 203
Chapter 8	Trela	Page 244
Chapter 9	Croy	Page 302
Chapter 10	Clerin	Page 347
Chapter 11	Vrric	Page 391
Chapter 12	Trela	Page 434
Chapter 13	Croy	Page 470
Chapter 14	Clerin	Page 498
Chapter 15	Vrric	Page 534
Chapter 16	Trela	Page 588
Chapter 17	Croy	Page 619

Chapter 18	Clerin	Page 651
Chapter 19	Vrric	Page 687
Chapter 20	Trela	Page 715
Chapter 21	Epilogue	Page 761
Appendix A	Races	Page 765
Appendix B	Magic	Page 768
Appendix C	Map	Page 775

Chapter 1

Darkness, emptiness, desolation. Croy knew that he was dreaming. He even knew the dream. When Croy was a child he had the same dream, night after night, for at least a week straight; and it had always started the same, in darkness. The end had always been the same as well: futile.

Movement… He could feel himself being flung through the emptiness. In the distance an object, appearing as a dot, came sliding into vision. The rushing continued, bringing the object to recognition. A wall. Faster it fell towards him, or faster Croy fell, he couldn't tell the difference. Then, with an involuntary flinch, Croy was flung through the wall. He could feel the wall sliding into his body. The sifting of sand through a sieve. More darkness as Croy slowed, the friction of rock tugged him back.

Light began again, as seen through a gauze at first. Then, as the rock thinned out towards the exit, the light became distinct. Still floating, Croy entered a spherical room, like the inside of a ball. There was a ring of torches around the edge of the room, and a pedestal in the middle. It was towards the pedestal that Croy floated. He came to a gentle stop about two rods from the pedestal. Levitating a full hand above the pedestal was a small wooden sphere. It looked engraved, but it was a puzzle sphere, like the ones Croy's uncle always used to bring him. You would drop it on the ground to shatter the pieces, then try to put it back together.

The air started to grow thick, butterflies erupted in Croy's stomach, his hands clenched involuntarily. The sphere fell in melted dreamtime motion. Everything blurred. There was a great crack! Like a tree being split by lightening. The pieces of the sphere laid scattered across the floor, the world began to shake. Croy was on his knees, weeping as a child would, as he was when he last had the dream. He forgot years of his life, his growth, forgot adulthood, forgot his wife. It was as if he had never aged, never left the dream, never left this room. The pieces laid scattered across the floor, mocking him. Pieces of the sphere, of his life. Croy, mutated teary vision, crawled across the still shaking floor, trying to pick the pieces up. Fear entered into Croy, fear that this would be like all the other dreams, fear that this was his life, that his memories were merely false fantasies that he had made to keep his sanity.

Always in the past he was unable fix the sphere, couldn't figure out the puzzle. A cloaked figure would enter the room and remove its hood. Croy never got to see the face, he always woke up before the hood fully fell away. He felt the fears from his childhood, fears he had assumed conquered, creep back to gnaw again on his spine.

Fumbling with the puzzle pieces, not really paying attention to them, Croy saw the figure enter. Brown cloak, flowing, floating, with boots of gray peeking from underneath. Cowl down, the faceless apparition walked straight to Croy and pulled a gloved hand from the cloak. The hand pointed to the puzzle. Looking down, Croy saw the pieces. They were the same shapes that they always used to be, he knew that they wouldn't fit together. He started to work the puzzle again, to try combinations that his broken memory told him would not work. They just wouldn't go together. Lifting his frustrated gaze to the figure, Croy showed the pieces to the figure again, hands raised in supplication. He waited for the hood, waited for the end, waited for the frustration to cease. The figure shifted uneasily. It began to raise its arms, the gloves reached for the hood. Behind a bootheel, never noticed before, never known before, lay another piece.

Shouting wordlessly, triumphantly, he snatched the piece and fitted it into the puzzle. The other pieces snugly slipped into place over the core piece. Light shot from the sphere. Smiling, ecstatic, Croy faced the figure, for the first time triumphant. The hood fell back. Eyes, glowing pinholes through the rift of dreams. Pure light pierced into the back of his skull. Screaming…

The sun beat down on a small unassuming Gaen, the derlian race that was born of the stone. He was short, even for a Gaen, only about one rod high. His rough wrinkled hands looked like they had served more than one lifetime of service. His stubby fingers grasped the grass as he awoke from his unrestful slumber. His chestnut hair and short beard bespoke of his younger age; these contrasted with the lines in his face. Croy stood and shook the last of the foggy sleep from his head. His pale gray eyes found the path down the mountain that his leather-shod feet knew by heart.

With the sounds of bleating sheep cascading down the mountain, Croy Sie'tin walked blissfully down the trail. He had a crook for a walking stick and moved it like it was an appendage. Croy had lived most of his life on the trails in these mountains. He was old enough now to remember sitting under most of the different trees he passed. While he was whistling his way back down to the valley, he was thinking of his absent wife, Ilana. She was away at Larelt, a school of sorts. The thought of her sent little shivers of pleasure down his spine, and had since he first saw her almost nine sun cycles ago. Looking off the ledge to his left he wondered if he should pick some wild flowers for her, to dry them out for her eventual return. Smiling to himself, he started to meander off the path, toward a rift in the south, occasionally watching the familiar plants float by on either side of his feet, looking for that special flower that he could take back to save for Ilana.

"Croy! Croy! Where are you?" The distant cry startled Croy from his reverie. He sighed and turned back towards the trail, thinking of what might have happened to the sheep now. Last year they had nearly lost seven of them down a steep ravine, only to spend all day hoisting the rebellious sheep back up and onto the trail with an ingenious set of pulleys and rigging. Chuckling to himself he wondered what predicament the animals could have gotten into this time, and why the rest of the Sie'tin could never seem to handle a crisis without him. He had just been married two cycles ago, and they had yet to have a child. There was no real reason that the older Gaens in his caste should ask him for advice; he was a mere thirty-three sun cycles into an average derlian life span of a little more than two hundred. There were even some that breached two hundred and fifty.

"Where have you been? We've been looking all over for you." Belg, one of the older of the Sie'tin, appeared in front of Croy. He looked as if he had been running uphill all day the way he was panting. Belg was a bit taller than Croy, with reddish hair and a beard that flowed midway down his chest. His usual calm brown eyes flashed with his small panic.

"I just went a little way off the trail to look around, can't the boys get the sheep in?" Croy blushed secretly about his quick nap. "What happened?"

"Come, look for yourself. The sheep are fine, Densal already has them in the caves and the shepherds are with them. There is trouble in the east. Look." With a stubby finger Belg pointed down a ridgeline. In the distance Croy could make out smoke coming from the forest line.

"Who else is here? Has anyone been sent to tell one of the 'jin about the smoke?" He used the general term for the warrior caste, without adding any rank. At the same time he was trying to figure out where the fire could be. It had to be several spans off in the distance, maybe a league or two. He looked up. The sun was halfway down from its zenith.

"Densal was going to right after he got the sheep and the boys back in the caves. He sent Nolt ahead to see if it was a wild fire. We spotted the smoke a little while ago, Densal said it must be coming from the forest, but Nolt didn't think so. He thought the smoke seemed to be coming from the lower meadow, not up in the trees. When he took off I thought it would be best to follow with someone, you never know, so I found you." Belg's giggle sounded a little odd, like it came from too high in his throat. He was usually more stolid than most Gaens. It made Croy a little uneasy that Belg should be shaken so, especially for just a little smoke.

The smoke was fading by the time they topped the last rise, giving the thought that it was going out. Croy was glad to see that it was thinning. Trotting ahead he went to the top of the hill and leaned on a tree. He checked the smoke hanging in the air one last time, then looked down onto the valley floor. Searching the land for the source of the wildfire.

Gazing down he heard a small curse and was shocked to realize it came from his own mouth. He dropped his crook and started running. In the back of his mind he wondered where Belg was, but he only stared ahead at the meadow in the valley. In the middle of the meadow were almost a hundred carts and wagons, all in dying flames. As he got closer, he could see blackened bodies lying in and amongst the burned-out husks of wood. As Croy ran along, finally reaching the valley floor, he heard Belg catch up from behind.

"Wait! You don't know what's down there. What if it's the Pyrans, or even a Yaven. Croy!" Belg's voice seemed shrill from behind Croy. It sounded out of place. All Croy could feel was the heat of the dying fire, and catch the occasional sound of popping wood. He could see the embers snaking across the ground, winding around bodies and the shells of wagons. He stared at the glowing red lines while he ran, he couldn't think clearly. The lines were spiraling outward and the pattern struck him as quite beautiful. Croy shook his head and tried to banish the thought, to think only of who was left alive, who could have done this, and if they were still around, looting amongst the carnage. He could feel wetness on his face and wondered why he was crying. As he reached the center of the meadow, time seemed to displace itself. To slow, stretch and lengthen, where every second tried to etch itself into his memory. He ran through the wreckage looking for someone alive, for someone who could explain the questions that danced through him. It was while he stared at a dead derlian with a child in her arms that he felt a hand on his shoulder.

Croy spun around, hands clenched, and half expected to see a Yaven staring into his face with eternal eyes. It was said that you could forget you had a soul just by staring into a Yaven's eyes. Instead he saw a derlian, a Gaen, someone he should know. He couldn't clear his head. The Gaen was about Croy's stature and age, wearing the same loose wooly shepherd's clothing that also adorned himself. With short dark straight hair and light hazel eyes, Croy felt a soothing familiarity for this Gaen, even without direct recognition. It was the soft but solid grip on Croy's shoulders that brought Nolt's name to his mind.

"Croy, you've come. I was hoping you would come. I can't find anyone. We should tell the 'jin, they will know what to do. We should go back soon, they're probably wondering where we are by now. They'll know how to handle this." Nolt stated all this hopefully and looked at Croy with furtive eyes.

Croy wandered silently and looked around, not answering Nolt. He watched a cloud of ravens squawk overhead. He watched a flame no larger than a candle's crawl along a wagon edge. He looked at the charcoal husks of the dead. He stared for what seemed like seconds, hours. He heard a noise behind him, like that of someone being sick, coughing and coughing. He whirled around, looking hopefully behind him. He saw Belg doubled over, coughing, staring at the ground where his lunch stared back up at him. Croy felt his own stomach clenching. Gasping he held himself tight, turning, staring, looking for a place to escape to. Maybe Nolt was right. He had been here longer, he would probably know. Croy chose a random direction and started to walk south through the meadow. He tried not to look at all the death, and yet was unable to help himself. He wandered aimlessly through most of the devastation before he heard a noise. It was almost imagined, the faint cracking of a twig. He headed in the direction it came from.

"Hello? Hello? Is there anyone here?" Croy heard himself repeat, repeat, repeat. He waited for someone to answer, walking and wandering. He followed his nose until he came to the edge of the meadow. He looked towards the trees and thought he saw something back in between their branches. Something moved against their silhouettes. He stumbled towards the forest and picked up his pace.

"Hello? It's all right. It's over. I won't hurt you. Who is there?" The words tumbled out of his mouth, one after another. He had not even noticed when he entered the woods. He squinted, trying to see between the branches. He heard a snap and whirled to his right, hands clenched uselessly.

Croy looked down at the roots of a giant birch and noticed a child. The child appeared to be wounded, though asleep. Staring, Croy did not move until he saw the child's chest rise, then fall, slowly, ever so slowly. The girl had long pale reddish hair, stringy with sweat. Her soft jaw line was outlined by an errant lock of hair. She was tiny, skin and bones that could only come from youth. Croy watched her eyes flicker back and forth under her lids briefly. He broke from his trance and bent down to check on the child, to make full sure it was alive. While his hand was held tentatively out, he stopped.

"Don't move Gaen! You touch her and your death will be slow and painful." The voice sounded different than Croy was used to. Still deep like a Gaen's but faster, more insistent. Croy lifted his head, without moving his hand, and looked straight into the eyes of a Pyran, those born of fire. Croy stopped, tensed. He noticed that the Pyran was bleeding and weak; he was leaning heavily against the birch, but the hand that held the sword pointed at Croy was as steady as a rock. He was wearing close-fitting black clothing with a purple sash across his chest. His hair was yellow, like the sun Croy thought. Tall and lithe, the Pyran looked dangerous, like a cat was dangerous. The eyes were a strange glow of green peering out from a smooth long face.

"I wasn't going to harm her. She's wounded, so are you. I just wanted to make sure she was alive." Croy spoke slowly, evenly, his chest tight. "I'm Croy Sie'tin."

The armed Pyran smiled, showing teeth with red streaks on them. "I swore to protect her, Gaen. I don't go against my word. If you don't move your hand I will remove it for you." Grinning insanely the Pyran shook his sword to show Croy that he could. "Not that I'd fear much from a farmer, eh? Of course, you could be lying to me. But you look simple enough. My name is Synde. I would probably be Cru'jin if I lived in a cave, but I'm bleeding in a forest, so it's just Synde."

Croy thought back to the Gaen caste rankings. Cru'jin would have many fighters under him. This Pyran was probably important in his world. Croy cleared his throat, so as not to seem threatening, and said, "I would help you if I could, but since you seem to have everything under control, I'll just be leaving." He smiled ingratiatingly and began to back away with his hands safely held up. None of the 'jin caste would strike an unarmed opponent and Croy was hoping that this Pyran had as much honor as he seemed to claim. "I should be getting back to my sheep."

"Stop! Wait. There is something you can do. I need water to cleanse the girl's wounds. If you will fill my waterskin, I will give you this ring for your kindness. I can't leave her in the woods alone, and I'm not sure how long I can walk, or where the nearest stream is. Please help us. The ring is priceless in my lands, I'm sure a farmer like you could live off of it for quite a while." Synde held his left hand aloft, and the ring on his middle finger shone like fire. There was one large red stone glinting out from a golden band. Croy thought he could live off that one ring for years if he were to sell it. Smiling to himself, he thought of the streambed less than a span south of there. "Please, look at the child, she's wounded badly. Her name is Trela, Croy. She's young and innocent. You are the only one who can help her." Synde's eyes were starting to unfocus as he talked, his voice dropped to a loud whisper.

"Give me the skin. There is a stream very close, I will be back before you know it." Croy smiled softly as he picked up the skin. "Keep the ring, I couldn't watch a girl bleed to death. You don't need to bribe me to fetch water." Croy wondered if most Pyrans had to be bribed to help a little girl. Giving an unconscious shudder, he started to walk down the trail towards the stream. Life is simple, life is beautiful, he thought to himself, not realizing that you should never forget what you have finally remembered.

As Croy walked he hummed a bit of tune and brushed the trees' leaves when he passed close by them. The leaves were soft and pliant, almost like moss hanging from the branches. He started thinking of what Nolt and Belg were doing; had they left, or were they waiting for him to return? He resolved that once he had filled and returned the waterskin he would leave Synde and go back to the caves as quickly as he could. He turned along the path and could hear the stream gurgle in the distance. He breathed inward and marveled at the feeling. He had smelled the greasy stench of burnt flesh for so long that he had thought it was stuck up his nose. It was good to be rid of that smell. The air was crisp and fresh, numbing the twinge of fear. Through the trees he could just make out the stream up ahead.

Croy knelt down and pushed out all of the dead air and the tiny bit of leftover water from the skin, then he put his head down and drank directly from the clear stream. Finally, he filled the skin and headed back to where he remembered Synde and poor Trela were. He caught himself wondering who Trela was and why she had a well-trained warrior to protect her. Was she Synde's daughter, or the daughter of a friend? Or maybe she was royalty? Croy laughed at himself. Royalty, indeed. His head was playing tricks on him. The girl was hurt, that was all. Croy never could get his mind to stay close to the task at hand. Always dreaming, that's what Ilana said. Ah, he should pick up some flowers on the way back with Nolt and Belg, to dry them out for Ilana's return bouquet. He grinned to himself as he returned to the birch.

Glancing down at the bleeding child, Croy's smile slipped a little. He crouched down and pulled the stopper from the skin. Still staring at Trela, Croy began to wash some of her wounds. There was a large gash across her chest, starting from her collarbone, down between budding breasts, ending in the upper hipbone. Croy wondered at the child's tenacious cling to life, not sure if he would have survived a wound so grisly. He ripped some of his shirt to wrap around the wound, almost making another shirt of bandages. While he washed a minor cut on her left cheek, Croy realized that Synde was gone. Synde had practically cut his hand off the last time he tried to touch Trela. Surely the Pyran's trust wouldn't run this far. After he washed all the wounds out and wrapped them with makeshift bandages, Croy stood. He decided to look for Synde. After all, an insane protector was better than none, and Trela would have to have time to heal before she should be moved. He glanced at the ground and noticed where the grass was matted down from the Pyran's clumsy pacings.

"Synde!" Croy's urgent whisper carried through the forest. "Synde, where are you? I've brought back the waterskin. You need to look after the child." Croy started to follow the depressed plants, wondering at how the Pyran could be so uncaring as to what he marked with his passage. Croy figured this Synde had probably never hunted wild game in his life. While looking at the well made path of Synde's course through the trees, Croy noticed blood on a tree.

Staring at the bark he saw that the smear came from someone's hand, grasping at the tree for support. Croy tried to think of how badly Synde was truly wounded. He could not remember seeing any major wounds, surely not anything like that gash across Trela's chest, but there were certainly many minor ones. Croy was not a good judge of wound severity, certainly not from a distance. He started to speed himself up, trying to figure out if Synde had thought himself well enough to go look for water by himself. Surely even a Pyran wouldn't have become impatient enough to try to find some water in the small amount of time that Croy was gone and just leave the girl unprotected. Following the trail as intently as he was and dreaming different possibilities that could have happened, Croy almost stumbled over a body lying on the ground. The amount of blood laying around the body was prodigious, certainly not all of that could have come from one being. The pool of blood was slowly being soaked up by the hungry plants.

Croy stood there for a second, staring at the back of a dead Pyran. Though both races were naturally muscular, he must have been a Pyran for he was much too tall to be a Gaen. Croy grabbed a shoulder and pulled him over, to look at the wounds. Staring back through blank glass eyes was a stranger; the snarl of the lip was unknown to Croy. He heaved a sigh of relief, for he had almost thought that the body was Synde's, and he dropped the body back down to the ground and glanced around.

Looking through the trees along the trail of matted-down vegetation, Croy saw several corpses lying up ahead. The forest seemed oddly quiet, and Croy strained to hear something, anything. Some of the corpses were lying face up. They were all Pyrans. A sudden chill went down Croy's back. Why would so many Pyrans come into the Gaen realm? Staring emptily back at the corpses, Croy began to methodically make sure that none of them were Synde. He wasn't even positive if Synde had gone through here, but it was the only trail he could find. It seemed to be getting harder to see into the distance. Glancing upward he saw the splattering of red across the sky, a beautiful sunset normally, but to Croy it reminded him of the blood splattered across the forest. Hurrying forward he wondered where the time had gone. In the distance he thought he could make out some sounds, not natural sounds maybe, but the eerie feeling was lessened somewhat when he thought of other derlians.

Croy rushed forward, hoping he wasn't making as much noise as it seemed. As he stared through the trees at the sun going behind the mountains in the distance, he heard the sounds becoming louder. Reaching a small dip in the trail, Croy slowed and crouched as he slowly came toward the rise in the land. The noise was recognizable now. It was a steady clashing, like near the 'cha section of the clan, the blacksmith caste, but it had a more sinister ring to it. Not one of making a master's idea come to life, but one of tearing the artwork in half—with a giant metal club. Croy felt his stomach drop toward his knees and he clenched his teeth against the feeling. He climbed the rise with suddenly wet palms and looked out over the land.

There was Synde, with his back against a tree, and there were four other Pyrans in front of him. All had their swords out. Staring at Synde, Croy noticed new streaks of red on him. Across his chest and legs, ribbons of red flowed down to feed the hungry soil. From the distance Croy was at, he could not make out what the other Pyrans were wearing. Their clothing looked different from Synde's garb, though he couldn't say exactly how. Croy felt himself begin to move forward, slowly, quietly, like stalking a rabbit, but he didn't know why. Sure Synde was intriguing, especially with a charge like Trela, but that was no reason to die. Still Croy's feet pulled him along steadily toward the fighting Pyrans.

Grabbing a large stick off of the ground Croy slipped off the trail and into the forest edge. In a low crouch, he quietly made his way around the path towards the fighting. Staring in between branches and twigs, Croy could see one of the Pyrans go down on one knee. Drops of blood fell from his mouth, sputtered out with each breath. With eyes clenched in pain, the Pyran jerked as Synde's sword flashed back out of his stomach. As Croy crept onwards he watched the Pyran slowly lean forward and topple to the ground. He was almost directly to the side of the Pyrans and, still crouched fearfully in the trees, he kept trying to figure out what he was to do. Every scene in his head ended with a sword flashing through his chest. He looked at the stick in his hand and almost laughed out loud. Looking at the forged weapons that the Pyrans handled so easily, he quickly realized his only real weapon was surprise.

"C'mon Synde! Give me your sword and ring and we shall let you live. You won't get that generous of a deal if we take you back to the King, his trials can be quite harsh as you know. Synde! You cannot just leave the Guard, you cannot just take warriors and run. What were you thinking? Your death is assured, there is no going back from betrayal such as this. If you don't give us what we want, we will just take it after we have killed you." The Pyran in the front chuckled assuredly, moving back from Synde's sword. He had the same purple sash across his chest that Synde did, and Croy noticed that those two were the only ones with sashes. The Pyran was smiling, eyes darting to the wounds on Synde and then back to Synde's face. "I just want the sword and the ring, Synde, that's all. No more death, no bloodshed. You have given up your old life as it is, what do you care? You have run from your duty, to be hunted down like a sick dog in a foreign realm. I promise you life and freedom if you will just hand me what I desire, otherwise your dying will take a long and painful time in arriving." A little spray of spittle flew from the Pyran's mouth, while his eyes glistened like a starving derlian who has finally found sustenance.

"You are a cowardly lying fool, Brycca! If you want my rank then you must slay me. You know the rules. If you fear my sword then let one of the others try me, or will you kill them for the ring? Where will it end, Brycca? Do you trust those around you to guard your back?" Synde's voice filled the silence of the glade. Even bleeding and leaning against a tree his body sung of a personal power. His eyes were feverish against the setting sun, almost glowing red. Croy had stopped, unseen, mesmerized, at the edge of the trees. Glancing at the other Pyrans, watching their chests heave in and out, Croy wondered if Synde needed him at all.

Glancing back at the other Pyrans, Brycca said, "Take him! You will never have a better chance at killing a leader of the Guard! Think of the glory! Your names will be sung for cycles!" The light in Brycca's eyes narrowed, became more focused, more intent upon their prize. Croy looked at the other two Pyrans, one was smiling, the other thoughtful. While Brycca leapt forward, swinging in a huge arc, Synde danced forward to meet him. Croy could feel himself moving, gliding through the trees, swinging his cudgel, and he watched as wood smashed into a smiling Pyran face.

Time slowed. Stopped. There was no sound.

He stared into the Pyran's face, unmoving, shocked. Croy watched as the derlian's face exploded red, as his head rocked back with the impact, at the blood droplets soaring freely through the dusk. He watched a thoughtful Pyran's back, at the steel punching through the back of the derlian's shirt, being pulled back through again with a sucking noise. And as if all the air were coming back into the glade, that noise brought all others. Hearing screams, Croy stopped swinging at the immobile shape on the ground in front of him. Staring toward Synde, he saw Synde sink to his knees, watched an unknown legend crash, watched a leader of the Pyran Guard fall to the ground. Screaming, Croy wished the noise had stopped permanently. Screaming, Croy leapt over a Pyran that would not think thoughtful thoughts again and, bringing the stick down on Brycca's head, Croy listened to the screaming. Seeing Brycca fall and bounce on the ground, Croy swung again with all his might. Watching the body lift a little from the ground, Croy swung with all his might. All to the constant howls that floated through the forest. Watching the stick break on Brycca's still body, the screaming slowed. Losing volume, Croy stood with mouth open for several minutes, hours, days. Finally the screaming stopped; the silence came crashing back, Croy almost wished the screaming had gone on. Almost.

Dropping the end of stick he had been clutching, Croy crouched over by Synde. Looking down at the body, Croy's eyes became wet. Watching the red bubbles come from Synde's mouth, he wondered why Synde's chest was still moving.

"Please, take Trela. Teach her what you can." The rasping that came from Synde's body convinced Croy that he was right and Synde was wrong. Synde had to be dead. The body was getting blurry, and Croy wondered why he could still hear Synde speak. "There is a necklace in my pouch. Give it to her when she leaves you. Prepare her for what must come, please." Synde's voice was dropping, becoming harder to hear. "When I was a child, my mother told me of the prophecies. I grew up with them, as all poor Pyrans do. We grow up with hope, only to get old and die." The voice became a whisper. Croy could no longer see the body behind the blur his vision had become. "She will unite us…she will lead us through the flames…she is the one…take her…teach her peace…she was born with war…" The voice flickered, died.

Grabbing at Synde's body, Croy felt for the pouch. Finding it he peaked inside. Through the blur he saw a pale necklace, so he tied up the pouch and put it inside of his shirt. Standing up, feeling ill, he lurched back toward where he came. Not thinking about the bodies, not caring about the dead, he left them where they were, to feed the forest and the animals. Nature was always hungry, Croy thought, always hungry.

Staggering back along the trail, Croy passed bodies seen before in a dream of life. He made his way back toward where Trela lay. Finally reaching the giant birch tree, he looked down at a peaceful child, sleeping in the arms of the tree, snuggling with its roots. Croy felt himself start to cry again. He tried to stop it, he had cried too much today, but did not even understand his own emotion. He sat down at the foot of the tree. For the first time in what seemed like a long while, he truly rested.

He could feel the warmth of the sun on his face, but there was no sound. Staring down into the forest, Croy watched the grass wave back and forth, the trees bend and warp to the flow of silent air. He looked around, glancing at the plants. They seemed too vivid. They glowed with life, pure life. Looking down at himself he noticed that he had that glow as well, that he was alive and at peace with his surroundings. Smiling to himself, Croy started to walk down the hill, out of the trees, and into the meadow. There were no dead here, no burnt husks of wood, no bodies. Just the grass, blowing and flowing, all to the silent wind. Laughing, Croy ran down the hill, stumbling, falling, rolling. Croy watched the sky turn green, into grass, to blue again, rolling down the hill. Watching the meadow floor come closer, Croy prepared himself for the jolt of stopping. He kept getting faster, rolling with more speed, his laughter began to fade. Everything seemed to blur, he couldn't slow his decent. Thinking he should have reached the bottom by now Croy started to feel the twinges of panic on the edge of his mind. All he could see was blue and green, blurring into one sliding picture. Suddenly, all was black.

Feeling sick from all that spinning, Croy looked for any splotch of color, any object to rest his eyes upon. Staring into the blackness, Croy felt the panic rising, like a clawing beast, trying its best to overcome his own mind. Spinning, looking, searching, becoming frantic, Croy saw a glimpse of light, like a candle in the middle of a giant cave. Croy tried to walk, but his feet felt no resistance. He tried to swim, but his hands had nothing to grasp.

Feeling out with his mind, he began to pull himself towards the flickering light. His stomach began to drop, like when he used to jump from a cave ledge into the great Serif lake. He could feel the movement of his body, but nothing else. Watching the flame flicker in the distance, he could feel something clawing at him, trying to drag him. Resisting it, resisting everything, Croy flowed towards the flame, his need to know starting overcome the panic and clawing. The flame was coming closer now, he could see that it came from nothing, it was placed in nothing, and it burned with a feverish light. He was close to it now, could look into its dancing flames. He could see what seemed to be a volcano, a giant broken mountain. He could see someone climbing up one side of it. He could see two other figures climbing after it. It seemed that the one figure in the front was trying to distance itself from the other two. Peering closer, the fire fading, Croy could see a bow on the back of the first figure. The figure was swathed in gray clothing and Croy couldn't tell if it was male or female. Only the mountain was contained in his vision anymore, with flame spurts shooting from crevices in the rock. Small rocks slid about and hailed upon all of the figures, making their passage that much more distracting. About three fourths of the way up the mountainside was a ledge with two statues on either side of a cave. It was towards this ledge that the figure seemed to be heading. The figure pulled itself up the ledge and lay there with its chest heaving. Croy wanted to call out, to alert the figure that the other climbers were close behind, but his voice was not working properly. Croy thought he heard something in the cave and turned to look. The statues looked to Croy like they could move, almost as if they had started while he was not looking, but that they had been unable get any further so they stayed frozen. They were so incredibly lifelike that they seemed to be stuck on the verge of movement. The one on the left had armor of stone covering stone skin. It had a helmet with a full faceplate, hiding its visage, and a staff of stone held in its hands. The one on the right had armor as well, but different designs cut into it. It too had a full helmet, but held a giant sword, point down, embedded slightly in the ground.

The first figure finally stood back up, face covered in cloth. Then the statues began to move, a slow deliberate movement. The figure glanced back at the two figures following it. They were almost upon the ledge. The statues continued their own uprooting from the mountain and began to move towards the figure. Glancing one last time down the mountain, the first figure faced the oncoming statues. They were speaking to the figure, walking onwards. Croy couldn't figure out what they were saying. The figure nodded, raised its hands, and threw back its cowl. Light seared into Croy's soul...

"Croy! Wake up! I've been looking for you forever. It's well into night, we should be getting back to the caves. I promised Belg I'd have you back before twilight." Nolt's voice sounded clogged. It took Croy a moment before he realized it was his ears that were clogged, they felt as if someone had stuffed wads of cloth into them, keeping the muffled world at bay. Shaking his head to clear his ears, Croy tried to remember where he was. "Are you all right, Croy? I thought you were dead when I saw you through the trees. You don't know the relief I felt after seeing your chest move. You aren't hurt are you? I think this is blood on your clothes. It's not yours is it?" Nolt's voice wouldn't stop. Its relentless sound beat upon Croy's head until all he could do was hold up his hands in a silent bid for a reprieve.

"Please, I need rest. I can't think clearly." Croy tried shaking his head again, but it just seemed to make it worse. "Is there a child under the birch over there? Make sure she is all right, will you? All I need is some rest." Croy felt like he had worked for several days in a row, without rest, never rest.

Nolt stood and walked towards the birch, knelt down beside the child. "She is fine, Croy. Sleeping like a babe. Which is what you should be doing I suppose." Nolt's smile came beaming through Croy's dim eyes. Smiling to himself Croy thought of when he and Nolt used to go looking through old caves, searching for hidden treasure. The world seemed to be getting darker to Croy. Nolt's voice jumped back into his world. "Belg will probably want to skin me alive, but there is no way we can carry a child with us tonight, not all the way to Serif. Go to sleep, Croy. I will make a litter for her and make sure no one comes snooping around. We can head back with the sun." Just hearing Nolt's voice made Croy sleepy. Closing his eyes Croy thought of a dream, and tried to recapture a volcano, but only peace invaded his sleep.

✳✳✳

Light. The brightness burned into Croy's brain, it sifted him through the layers of sleep until all he could do was to crush his eyes closed. The redness of his lids was a reminder that he could no longer hide. Slowly he turned over, hoping that his life was a dream, one that could fade with the coming of the light. Opening up his eyes, he looked toward where he knew the birch would be. There among the roots sat a young Pyran girl. She was chewing on some bluish berry, smiling up at Nolt. Nolt was describing searching through an unknown cave, using his thick arms to exemplify the fear and excitement of the dark. Croy smiled to himself, lying on a warm patch of grass, listening to Nolt tell his wondrous tales. Breathing in the crisp morning air, he could forget the blood stains on his clothes.

"We turn toward the last bend back to one of the main chutes, and there's this gorge that we have to cross. Usually this wasn't a problem, we would tie a rope around a rock, and throw it to the other side. You could usually get it to wedge behind a boulder or something and then we would cross one at a time. We had crossed this same gorge so many times in the past, that even I had stopped getting scared looking down. This time, though, I had forgotten the rope back in the cave where we had found those bones." Nolt's rich voice was well into the tale, one that Croy recognized since he had been there. Croy always enjoyed the way that Nolt told tales and he had heard this one many times before. Somehow Nolt's tales were different each time he told them, as if they evolved beyond his control. Chuckling under his breath Croy thought back to the gorge. He had been furious to find out that Nolt had forgotten their only rope. "How could you have left the rope?! Rope is only the most basic equipment you could want in a cave! What were you thinking? Obviously, you weren't thinking at all." Nolt had tried to switch the blame to Croy, since Croy was also there when it was forgotten, but Croy would have none of that. "I still have the water that I was in charge of, so now we can slowly die of starvation instead of dying quickly of dehydration!" Croy could laugh now, since the moment was funny in retrospect. And, after all, Nolt did go down into the gorge first. Of course, Croy had to climb back out of it first, but he enjoyed climbing up. It was down that was the problem. His favorite cave exploring memories usually happened with Nolt, and sometimes with Kraftig. They were inseparable as children. More often than not they got their punishments together as well. Croy couldn't seem to stop smiling in his reverie even though he was trying to appear sleeping.

"Halfway down the rift Croy starts tossing pebbles at me and saying how flaky the rock at the top seemed. 'It seems like it could all come tumbling down at any second. You had better hope you spot some rope at the bottom.' And he starts laughing! Here I am, clinging to the rock, wondering how my mother is going to react when they find my dead body, and Croy is laughing his head off. For a moment I thought he snapped, I wasn't quite sure if he was really angry about the rope, and maybe the rocks falling down would start getting bigger. So I yell back at him, 'Listen! If you want to be the one to tell my mother how I died, just keep it up! I'm trying to find a way down for us!' And Croy just laughed and said that the only way he would talk to my mother was if he was tied and dragged to her. My mother can be a bit strict sometimes." Nolt's voice was filled with mirth. His mother was known for being as stubborn as the rocks and she had quite a temper besides. Croy couldn't help but laugh aloud at Nolt's mild description of her.

"Ah, he becomes coherent." Nolt's glance said he knew why Croy was laughing. "You should bathe yourself before we set off. You are starting to smell like one of the sheep."

Croy grabbed Nolt's outstretched hand and stood. Wiping the sleep from his own eyes, he looked into Nolt's. "Thank you, my friend." Smiling, Croy turned towards the stream and tottered off to the sound of rushing water. Reaching the stream, he stripped and began to get the grime off his body. The caves seemed such a long way off, almost in another time. Croy wondered what they were doing back at home. Belg must have gotten back there by now and alerted the 'jin as to what lay in the meadow.

After stepping back to the land, Croy stood and looked at his wet clothing hanging on a tree branch. He had done the best that he could, but the clothes would probably have to be burned. The dirt had come out, but blood never wants to leave. Shaking his head, he put on his wet breeches, and carrying his torn shirt he walked back to where the birch was.

Nolt was showing Trela the litter, explaining that she would be carried back to the caves because of her wounds. "Why? I am not your concern. There is no need to drag me into a mountain. Synde will take care of me here. Where is Synde?" Her eyes gazed fully at Croy since Nolt had already explained he knew nothing. Her eyes were a strange yellowish color. They were haunting in their otherworldliness. Croy had never even heard of such eyes before, such that he was unsure how to even describe them. They were speckled lightly with green, but held that unnatural yellow. He wondered if she was jaundiced or ill. It was then that he noticed her jaw was only soft while she was sleeping. "Where is Synde?" Her voice was crisp, pronouncing each word distinctly. Croy wished she wasn't staring at him so hard. "He is my teacher and protector. He would never have left me alone with you unless he trusted you. Do you know him from his travels?" Croy could tell Trela was beginning to panic by the way her voice sped up at the end. He could feel her lack of air, could see her eyes get furtive.

"Synde asked me to help you. He had to go back for something, he should be back in a few moons. We will take you to Serif and let you heal. I will explain what happened later. Do you remember what happened? How you got here?" Croy couldn't bring himself to tell her. *Later,* he thought. *She needs some healing time.* It made Croy uneasy though, to lie like that. He knew he would regret it later, yet it was as if someone else was making him do it this way. Of course that someone could only be the cowardly portion of him. "Tell me how you ended up in Gaen lands, Trela. And who was chasing you." He felt he had to change the subject somehow.

"Well, I was born the Kriishan, you see," Trela said smiling.

Her pause was definite. Croy knew she was waiting for his recognition. "Um, that is wonderful. What exactly is a Kriishan?"

"Everybody knows who the Kriishan is! Well, I suppose every Pyran knows who the Kriishan is. It is the savior of the commoners, but it's much more complicated than that. There is one Pyran who is destined to rule over the realm every generation. They are the Kriishan, and the land flourishes under their guidance. The other rulers, known collectively as antoshan, are those that become rulers for their own gain and benefit. Synde told me that I was going to be a great warrior and unite the Pyrans under my sword." Trela's voice sounded far away and soft. This was her dream—to massacre. Croy couldn't believe it. He knew the Pyrans were violent, but this was a little girl.

"You see, most of the Pyrans that work the land do not own it. Some of the farmers are so poor that they cannot afford seed nor livestock; they are known as metayers. So, the landowner provides everything they need to get started and then they split the profits.

This is all well and good, for the landowner at least. However, the landowner is also the protector of the tenant. This would be all well and good also, but sometimes the task of defense raises a prideful feeling of power. Sometimes the landowners become insistent upon their own needs, feeling that they give so much to the poor metayers. In short, the Kriishan rightly protects the tenants from their own protectors, while an antoshan is only concerned about protecting the landowners if they are concerned about protecting anyone at all." Trela was trying to be serious now, to explain why a Kriishan was necessary. Croy wondered if she had noticed his look, but she had not been watching him.

"We are like that as well, except that we pay our guilds for our seeds and livestock. It's kind of a tax really, or a membership fee, but since everyone belongs to a guild, everybody pays. They don't have to protect us, because we have a separate guild for that. Plus our status in the guilds gets us special things. Like the ability to move to a nicer cave, and what not." Nolt was smiling at Trela while he got the litter ready for her.

"Wait, wait. It's not the same at all, Nolt. She's talking of oppression. We aren't oppressed." Even as Croy spoke the words, he knew they sounded too nervous, too bothered. But he didn't feel oppressed by his guild or its leaders.

"Wait, maybe you don't understand. Under the right ruler our system works very well, the king before Qizern, Rylco, was wonderful. The land flourished, the common folk produced excellent craftsmanship and there was plenty of good harmony. But then came Qizern. He killed Rylco and took his crown. Now more and more land is lost to the deserts each cycle, the food and equipment goes to the warriors through purveyance and tallages, the jewels and scattered wealth all funnel up to Qizern. He is greedy and evil, and to think, I am chosen to defeat him."

"How will you defeat this Qizern? He sounds like a nasty fellow. Can't you just overthrow him, or something? Get him dethroned without violence." Croy was looking at the slight girl being hoisted on the litter by Nolt and wondering how she could overthrow anything.

"Don't you know any of our customs? Has Synde told you nothing? The only way to become king, or even just to change kings, is to kill the old king in single combat. The random revolt is much too hard on the land. If the king is considered unfit by you, all you have to do is challenge them, and if you have enough warriors that follow you, they must accept or fall from honor. Unfortunately Qizern is a sword-master, a sect of warriors who live in the desert that do nothing but meditate on war and practice fighting. He killed his own teacher, they say." Trela was strapped down finally. Croy grabbed the litter at her feet, while Nolt, smiling down at Trela's face, grabbed the litter by her head. With an unconscious grunt, they lifted Trela and started to pack her down to the mountain.

"Please, please, go on. I have never heard anything of the Pyrans and find it fascinating. Was Synde a sword-master?" Nolt's voice held true excitement in it, and all Croy could do was flinch at the name Synde. Don't ask too many questions in that area, he thought to Nolt, for I can't answer any of her questions yet.

"No, Synde is a natural. He never received any formal training, but he has traveled everywhere. Each place he goes he learns a new trick. He says that is the secret to his success. The way he moves, it's like he's dancing. Or like cats, playing and rolling together. He has such a grace while fighting. I can't wait until he comes back and teaches me how to achieve that grace. That is what I will need to defeat Qizern. Grace." Trela's voice trailed off as she imagined herself victorious. She was lost to the world for a moment, and Croy silently sweated.

The silence was getting long and ate at Croy due to his own guilt. He either had to explain or to cover up. He wanted to explain, to say that Synde was dead, that his last wish had been that Croy should teach Trela peace. Peace before war. For some reason... Maybe because his mind had thought of a "clever" way out. Or maybe because he felt he should teach this "saviour" peace. Or maybe he thought he could avert some bloodshed by keeping her away from Pyran lands, especially her own bloodshed. Or maybe it was simply destiny. But Croy did not explain the truth...he lied and covered up. "My father always said that grace of the mind comes before grace of the body. Synde asked me to show you the ways of the great thinkers, the Gaen philosophers, before he will teach you the way of the sword. How will you rule once you've conquered this Qizern, will you be just? You say you will now, but power has a way of making adults forget what they promised to their destinies as children. For three sun cycles you will live with us in Serif, then Synde will continue your martial training." Croy felt flush and heady, but good. Like after a draught of good beer. He didn't even notice Nolt's frown burrowing into his back.

"I knew it! I knew Synde wouldn't just leave me with no reason. I will learn then, everything you will teach me. I will be like the sand, soaking up the rains from the sky. How long have you known Synde? Has he had this planned for a while? I wondered why he turned the caravan towards the Gaen realm, but I never dreamed it was because he had allies here. Is he going back to Pyran lands then, to set up Qizern's demise?" Trela just wanted to believe, wanted it more than anything. The wishful desire was loud in her soft voice.

Croy's mind raced. Not frantically, like it usually did when he lied, but smoothly, like a well-trained runner, pacing itself at top speed. Not deeper, he thought, mustn't get deeper into Synde. "I don't know Synde very well, but I owe him a favor. He saved my life once, in the forest. He had said that he would come to me with a package for me to take care of. It was several cycles ago and I honestly didn't think he would ever come back. But he did, with you, of course. He said that you needed to be hidden for a while, and that you should be educated. He had important business back home, and wouldn't be around for a few cycles. But I don't really know him. You should tell me about how you two met, he seems like a remarkable derlian. How did he know you were the Kriishan?" Croy thanked Gunzgak that Ilana would be gone for almost another cycle. Never in the world did he think he would be glad of her absence. He did not want to have to explain this to her right away. He needed time to figure out what to say. He needed time to figure out what he was doing.

"Well, when I was a very little girl..." Trela's voice was lost into a fit of coughing. The coughing got bad enough that they stopped jostling her and set her down for a moment.

"Maybe we should just let her rest, Croy." Nolt sounded almost annoyed. They picked her back up and walked for quite a while in silence. At first the silence was a little uncomfortable, Nolt's last words echoing through their minds. Then, after their second wind began to wane, they hiked with heads down, saving their breath. The silence turned into a kind of solace.

They finally came to the last rise before the trek through the foothills to the entrance to the cave, the entrance to Serif. "Hold up a second, Nolt," Croy said, slowing down and lowering his end of the litter. "Let's rest a moment in the shade." Nolt lowered his end of the litter. Looking towards his home, he wiped sweat from his brow.

"You're right, I don't think there's another tree from here to the cave." It was meant to be sort of funny, but just came out tired. Nolt arranged the litter slightly before he collapsed under a large tree. Croy gulped loudly from his waterskin. Sighing and wiping the sweat from his face, Croy offered the skin to Trela. Holding it for her, he let her drink from it. "It'll be nice and cool in the shade of the cave, Trela. The heat won't beat us down, like it is now."

"I like the heat." It was all she said, and she gave him a cute girlish smile. After she drank, Croy gave the waterskin to Nolt and began to wander towards the forest, looking for flowers.

"Hey, Croy! What are you doing?" Nolt yelled to Croy's retreating back.

"I'm picking some flowers for Ilana," said Croy's back. He kept close to them, however, well within hearing distance.

"You know, she'll be gone for some time still," Nolt yelled back. "They'll be all withered up by the time she gets back. He never listens to me." Nolt was half talking to Croy, half to Trela, and half just to himself. "You'll like Serif, Trela. It's the Gaen race's greatest achievement in my opinion. It has lakes, huge coliseums and stalagmite pillars that reach the ceiling, or maybe stalactite pillars that reach the floor. It has everything." Nolt's voice was of one who is almost home.

"I'm sure it's very wondrous, but I don't like caves. My brothers used to take me to the sand caves outside of Virkan, the village I grew up in, and get me lost. They'd leave me in the dark, laughing, and they would go home. I would beg the walls to show me the way out, crying with my hands bleeding, that they would finally release me to the light. I don't know if I can live in a cave, Nolt." Trela's voice suddenly became full of emotion; it sounded full of old tears.

"Don't worry about Serif, Trela. It's not the same. It's well lit and it has derlians within hearing distance, almost always. It's a city, Trela. Think of it as a city. Plus, you'll have Croy to look after you. He's as safe as a mountain." Nolt was trying his best to sound reassuring.

"Just say that you'll be my friend. I don't know anyone in there, and I want someone I can trust as my friend." Trela's voice was quiet.

"Of course I will, Trela. You are already my friend." Nolt's voice was stolid and enthusiastic.

"Look at these beauties! Have you ever seen a wild rose with so many petals?" Croy rounded the bush he was circling. In his hands were three pinkish-reddish roses, full of petals. And they were full of thorns as well. Croy's hands were bleeding slightly.

"Croy, how are you going to carry the litter and carry the roses?" Nolt sounded a little astonished. "And what are you going to do with them for so long?"

"Don't worry Nolt, I'll dry them. By the time Ilana gets back, our whole home will be covered in dried flowers." Croy was beaming with ingenuity. You could find your way out of a cave he was glowing so much. He carefully set the flowers on the litter at Trela's feet while she giggled.

"That's such a sweet thought, Croy." Trela was smiling up at Croy, and he didn't notice that her eyes were still a little wet.

"Well, are we all rested?" Croy took one last drink from his waterskin, stoppered it, and placed it over his shoulder. Then he turned around and took the arms of the litter in his hands and lifted with Nolt.

The last leg of the journey was swift. They were at the entrance to the cave in less than an hour. The gate was a massive twenty rods high at the center, covering the entrance to Serif—a giant gaping maw carved into the stone, waiting to swallow any foolish passersby. There was an open door within the gate, large enough for two derlians to pass through comfortably, side by side. Two of the 'jin class stood guard at the entrance, large pikes polished and shining in the sun.

One of the guards looked quite young contrasted with his grizzled companion. He was tall for a Gaen with his back straight and long. His hair was darker, with shoulder-length curls that framed his face. He seemed slimmer than the usually staunch 'jin class. Though, since his brown beard was so short, Croy figured he would probably thicken up with age.

"Croy, the captain wants to speak with you about the Pyran invasion. And you too, Nolt." The grizzled guard had a scar on the side of his face making it, Croy was sure, very difficult to smile. So to compensate the guard had, at some point in his life, decided not to smile anymore. The crevices in his face were drawn vertically along staunch lines, deep grooves of constant scowling. They were the same depth and shape of the scar, and Croy thought that maybe the guard had been trying to camouflage the scar with the rest of his face.

"Can we at least bring in the little girl first?" The notion that the 'jin class would take such an interest had not fully occurred to Croy. Foolishly he had been thinking that nothing would come of it except Trela. "She is wounded and has been travelling all day." At the same time Trela let a little cough escape her. Croy almost smiled.

"You can leave her inside. Greshcly will show you the way." The scarred guard turned and looked outward, signifying that he was done with them. Croy wondered what he looked for out there. Certainly they couldn't be afraid of an actual invasion.

"Follow me. I'll show you where to drop her off and then take you to Narst Dea'jin. He was quite agitated after your friend, Belg, told him about the carnage in the meadow. We've been waiting for you for some time now. And believe me ol' gnarl isn't much company. All he can talk about is the old civil wars. That's where he got that scar, you know. Oh, I could tell you the whole story, he's told it to me so many times." Greshcly's smile was beaming and he certainly seemed sincere.

They walked down a short tunnel and the light was getting a little dimmer, especially compared with the blinding daylight of outside. Though Gaen eyes were quick to adapt to large light changes, it was still a little disconcerting to Croy. And, as a farmer, he was part of one of the few guilds that regularly worked outside. The floor was smooth, with countless feet using this tunnel as the main entrance and exit to Serif. The walls were unfinished though, with the chisel marks still visible. The main cave of Serif was natural, but the main entrance was considered too easily accessible, so it was closed up with rock and new entrances had been made. The ceiling here, however, was of woven iron grids. You couldn't quite see through the slats of iron into the room above, but Croy knew what was up there. More guards, with the ability to pour hot oil and water, or stab their pikes through the slats. Every Gaen in Serif learned about how safe they were, that was part of their education. At the end of the hallway, there stood a massive oak and iron door. It was at this door that Greshcly stopped and knocked.

A little porthole opened up and a large furtive eye peeked through, then squinted into an one-eyed smile. "So they finally came back, eh Greshcly?" The voice was old and weathered, much like the eye. The door creaked with age as it opened, and a short, bent, old

Gaen waved them inside, smiling hugely. Croy tried to count the missing teeth, but decided it would have been quicker to count the teeth that were still there. He smiled and nodded as he passed and made sure to make eye contact with the weathered old derlian.

Then they were in the Great Hall of Serif. It was a gigantic open sphere, with the walls going up chiseled into walkways, so that it looked striped with dozens of levels and floors. There were five main pillars bracing the ceiling, laid equal distant from each other in a pentagon shape. Trela, lying on her back, stared at the ceiling. Croy stared at her, attempting to read her thoughts. At first she would have thought it was unfinished, there are so many bumps and ridges. But then they would come into focus, and she would realize that they were carvings. That the whole ceiling was covered in statues leaning out of the ceiling, trying to touch her. There were hundreds of scenes, of Gaens and sheep and Yavens and Pyrans and Fluens. She wouldn't see any of the air, though. There were no carvings of Luftens in Serif. She appeared duly amazed at the sheer vastness of what was the largest continuous carving in the world, at least the largest that Croy knew of. There, just to her right, there was a carving of some Gaens at the entrance to a cave, chisels held upright in their stony hands. And up above her there were Gaens and Fluens shaking hands with some parchment or document held between them. He watched her eyes follow the curve down, to where it sloped almost imperceptibly into the wall. There were some Gaens diligently chiseling the rock as she stared openly at them.

"Why are they still carving? It's so magnificent already." Trela's voice seemed small, so incredibly small. As if she was the tiniest echo in the gigantic hall. She tore her gaze from above and looked down along the walkways that striped the lower walls, down to the floor. There were hundreds of Gaens, all entering and leaving through the twenty or so doors and archways. There was a big group in the middle, sometimes a few of the entering Gaens would join them, and sometimes some of them would break off from the main pack and leave. It took Croy trying to see through Trela to realize what insects the Gaens appeared to be. They were like ants or bees, Croy thought; yes, like bees. Swarming together, dancing some incomprehensible communication, groups breaking off to become different groups. It was almost too much to fathom. It had always amazed Croy at how coordinated it all seemed, but never as much as it did now.

"The ceiling in the Great Hall is our history! Every major event in our communal lives is carved upon that ceiling. I could teach you all of our past just by pointing and explaining the various scenes. Isn't it magnificent? When I was a boy I wanted to be a sculptor, but I never really developed the skill, I guess." Croy's voice was at once proud and puffed up and, at the same time, a bit wistful of a dream never realized.

"This is where you get off little girl. Just place her against that wall. Don't worry we won't be long." Greshcly's voice sounded kind but gruff.

"But...but, what if something happens?" Trela's voice wavered slightly as she spoke. She looked up at them all and eventually nodded. They all smiled back at her to reassure her.

Croy and Nolt were soon at the entrance to the guardroom, nodding their way past soldiers. Croy felt odd. He had never entered a functioning guardroom before, and had wondered what it would look like. Images of swords and pikes along the walls, maybe a decaying head from an old enemy. Croy smiled unconsciously at his own childishness.

Instead what met his eyes was the largest collection of maps he had ever seen. Strewn over every available inch of the walls, on all four walls, top to bottom. He was amazed at the sheer magnitude of them; they looked like most of them were of Serif, and many of them looked like they were of the same areas. There were at least five along the wall opposite of him that had the Great Serif Lake in their center, and he wondered how efficient it was to have a bunch of the same maps connected haphazardly about a room. Before he had too long to contemplate it, though, the seven or so Gaens in the room walked around the table and closed in on both him and Nolt. With a slight feeling of claustrophobia he edged back and walked into Greshcly's suddenly hard chest. They wouldn't speak, they just tightened up.

"So. I hear that you wanted to talk to Nolt and I." He hoped his smile was not as ingratiating as it seemed to him or, if it was, that that was what they wanted out of a farmer.

Staring, grim faces. All of them scowling as if he had just been caught stealing the Guild Lord's crown. Croy obviously had not said the right thing, and so he decided he would just wait until they spoke. Maybe they would give him a direction to steer the conversation. A minute passed, Croy was looking as nervous as he possibly could, not because this was a plan of his, but merely because he was at such a loss as to how to look. Staring at the gnarled Gaens, Croy thought that he had never seen a scarier bunch of derlians in his life. They looked as if they had all killed their mothers just to join this illustrious club that they now belonged to, and the club was the only enjoyment they got from their lives. Not that they looked like they got much enjoyment from their lives. Their looks made him feel so incredibly guilty, if they had asked him to confess to murdering Nolt, he would have. Glancing at Nolt, since he had thought of him, didn't really help either. If it was possible to look more nervous and guilty than Croy felt, Nolt had found the way to do it. Another minute passed, or was that just the seconds ticking by?

Croy stared at the one on the left, maybe it was some defense mechanism that chose the left one—to turn his right face to the crowd—he wasn't really sure how he was making decisions now. The one on the left was a massive Gaen, not necessarily tall, but barrel chested. No, not barrel chested, but tree-trunk chested, and a large tree at that. He was wearing a leather jerkin with black wrought iron studs and buckles coming out of the jerkin. Croy wasn't sure if the studs were necessary to keep the garment together during battle, but they certainly gave a more ominous picture to the derlian. Croy started to look up at his face and then thought that might be considered rebellious or something, so his gaze shifted to the next chest in the line-up.

The second from the left Gaen's chest was covered in a beard. It was bright red and had five braids in it. The middle braid went all the way to the Gaen's belt, and as Croy followed it down he noticed that this Gaen had a similar jerkin as the last Gaen. This Gaen had a prominent axe tied to his belt, a huge double-sided half-moon axe. The amount of nicks and scarring along the blade showed quiet testimony to the axe's use, unless, of course, the Bearded One used it to carve statues out of rock. Noticing the weapon, Croy almost went back to the Studded One to see if he just missed his weapon or if it was just so much smaller than the Bearded One's. Almost.

He decided to continue his careful study of the enemy, or more correctly, his wide-eyed stare at a vastly meaner and much better armed enemy. And that was not even considering the chasm of difference in social status. His eyes moved to the right a little and beheld a chest of metal. Obviously the chests on the left were the scouts or something, because this chest was completely covered in steel. And the arms… and the legs. Even the gigantic sword hanging at the Metal One's hip was nothing compared to the sheer mass of steel binding his body. Croy decided not to look at this one too long.

So his eyes encountered the center Gaen. The chest looked small, in a leather jerkin, no iron or steel whatsoever. Croy was somehow relieved by this. This derlian didn't look like they could kill him by breathing on him, and his gaze was unwittingly pulled upward. He didn't want to and certainly didn't mean to, but he stared right into the Gaen's eyes. Except that the other Gaen had only frosty cataracts to stare back at Croy. It was so completely startling that Croy whispered "Great Gunzgak" under his breath. The oath was so quiet that Croy wasn't even sure that he had uttered it out loud. But the Blind One smiled.

"You must be Croy Sie'tin. We have only heard rumors as to what your reality has been. Please, sit down, enlighten us." The old Blind One's voice was soft, as the moss that grows on the water. Yet something in Croy tightened and coiled upon itself. Croy's inner voice, the one he usually ignored, said that this was the dangerous Gaen in the room. In those few times in Croy's life that he listened to that voice, it had never sounded as sure as it did now.

Croy was nevertheless grateful to be motioned towards something to sit on. "Thank you, you are most kind." He didn't want to be too obsequious, but definitely wanted to convey his respect.

Both Croy and Nolt salt down on two of the chairs in the room. Croy wiped his slightly moist palms on his pants, something that his mother had failed to remove from his list of habits. Nolt breathed a tiny sigh of relief, just this side of audible. Anything that happened now, Croy was happy that it would be happening while he was sitting. Standing straight at attention while warriors glared at you wasn't nearly as comfortable as slouching in a chair while warriors glared at you.

"I want you to tell us what happened to you, Croy, after you left Belg at the mountainside. I want you to be complete, honest, and detailed." The Bearded One's voice was deep and husky, full of resonance. He smiled, and Croy was sure that the smile was meant to be reassuring. It wasn't in the least, however.

Croy told them of the path down to the smoke, seeing the Pyran caravan, running amongst the charred ruins looking for anyone alive. They seemed relieved, and asked several questions to make sure that there wasn't a Yaven there. When Croy began telling of his encounter with Synde, the Blind One stopped him.

"What was his name, the Pyran you just mentioned?" The questioned stopped Croy and he wondered if it had been a mistake, to not filter his story. He was just prattling on, doing what they had asked, and hadn't even thought that Synde may be known to any Gaens.

"He said his name was Synde, that he was part of some guard, or something." Suddenly Croy wanted to be vague. He didn't want to seem like he was lying though, so he decided then that he would leave the smallest bits of information out, to try to forget them. Mainly about what Synde had said about Trela, the girl shouldn't be jeopardized, Croy thought.

"I know the name, Croy. I have even met the derlian, if you believe. He would have been fairly imposing if it wasn't for his impetuous demeanor. Attention span was the only thing I think he lacked to become a great general." The smile on the Blind One's face looked far away, even without the eyes to show it. Croy suddenly wondered if he had been blind all his life, or if it had happened to him this side of the veil. "Sorry to interrupt, if your story has more with Synde, then continue please. If not, I'll ask you about him later." Croy didn't doubt that the Blind One's attention span was long and sharp.

Croy explained when he had come upon Synde while fighting Brycca and the Guard. Croy even went into good detail of his own involvement in the violence. "I was beating on the dead body for quite a while, I think. I just couldn't stop." Croy's own voice sounded wounded and small to him. He had wanted it to sound big and brave. After all, he had survived combat. Something that had never before occurred to Croy to think he was capable of.

"You don't have to explain the battle-rage, Croy. All of us have been through that." It was a female's voice, still low and husky though. She must have been standing on the right of the Blind One when he was making his inventory of the room.

"Well, then, I went to Synde to see if he was alive. I figured I had saved him, you know. When I looked over at him though, he was bleeding out of his mouth and nose profusely. I shook him a little, then I thought I heard someone else, so I left him lying there. I ran back the way I came, or so I thought. I quickly became disoriented and lost. I was stumbling along, heading towards the sound of water, when I saw a wounded child. The one outside. So I bandaged her up, washed out some of her wounds with the stream water, seems I wasn't far from the stream after all. I was pretty tired by then, and so I lay down to take a quick nap, and that's when Nolt found me." Croy hoped it sounded good. He was just a farmer after all, what kind of retelling did they want? He smiled up at them, all of them, and waited for their questions. He had decided not to tell them anything else without questions.

"Would you show us Synde's body? Take us there?" The Bearded One was suddenly in his face with his beard.

"Be patient, Crydlak, we have yet to hear the rest of the story. There is also the question of what Nolt saw. I do agree, however. We will all have to go and have a look at the body. The dead tell some interesting stories." The Blind One's smile was broad and grim, with a touch of too much amusement for Croy's taste. "Is there anything more interesting in your story, Croy? Do you know why the caravan was headed here, or why they were butchered? Do you have any details of the destroyed caravan? Did you actually do anything for the day and a half that you were gone?" The agitation in the Blind One's voice was palpable, though very calm.

"I've already told you about the destruction of the caravan. I saw lots of burnt-up wagons and derlians. We went around the caravan on the way back. I couldn't stomach it." Croy was stammering and suddenly afraid of what was going on. Obviously the Blind One thought he was lying.

"Why did you say burnt-up derlians? Weren't they all Pyrans?" The Female's voice was taught, waiting for him to slip. Fortunately for Croy, there were only Pyrans that he knew of. So he wasn't even trying to hold anything back from that.

"I don't know why I said derlians, there weren't any Yavens or anything. And no there weren't any Gaens or Fluens either! I was just using a descriptive word." Croy heard his own voice, not as it's usual meek self, but getting angry and defiant.

"We will see that for ourselves, don't worry, we already have a team investigating the caravan. It's Synde I'm interested in. Why any member of the Guard should leave Pyran lands is confusing at the least. Now, what of the girl? Who is she and why did you bring her inside our walls?" The Blind One was losing some of his smooth patience. Croy just wished they would be done with him and he could stop annoying them.

"The girl's name is Trela. She was with the caravan when it was attacked. She was wounded and had dragged herself off into the woods. She's just a little girl. I promised her I would nurse her back to health and raise her. I think her parents were killed in the caravan." Croy hoped that they wouldn't interrogate her yet, he hoped with all his might.

"Are you taking full responsibility for the girl? You know what that means, don't you? Anyway, I think we'll talk to Nolt for a while. I want you rested to show us where Synde's body is tomorrow. We'll talk to the girl in a few days, after she has regained her health. That sounds like a good arrangement, yes? Good, you are free to go now. Soon we shall have to have you show us what you saw." The curtness of the Blind One's speech struck Croy as odd, as if there was something amiss. Greshcly took Croy by the arm and helped him up. He almost fell when he was pulled from his chair, but regained his feet while heading for the door. Greshcly opened the door and they walked out together.

"You had better be telling the truth, Croy. The Blind One can talk to the dead, and I don't think the dead lie that often. I'd get some rest, and maybe have somebody ready to take care of the girl if something happens to you. You do not have much time." Greshcly's whisper was quick and frantic. Croy didn't think that his eyes stayed still for the split second it took the say the message. Greshcly gave an odd wink, and turned around, entering the room again. Croy tried to see Nolt's face when the door was open, but only saw shoulders and backs. Well-armored backs, of course. Croy wondered briefly whether or not he could manage the stretcher by himself, and he decided to wait for Nolt.

Chapter 2

Clerin Toswin was more aware of energy now than at any other time in her life. Mainly her own energy, her blood pumping and making her heart pound inside her head, but also the energy of the others in the room. Some derlians would have called it nervousness, agitation, or maybe even fear. To Clerin, however, it seemed like she was more in tune with the world around her. That everything in the room, the room itself, was harmonizing at a certain pitch. Not only was she harmonizing alongside it, but she was the only one in the room truly aware of it. Clerin was a stunningly beautiful girl, though after today she would be considered an adult. She had pale blue eyes, like the color of the ice mountains far into the Clatsvol Sea, that seemed just a bit too large for her face which was framed by her pale hair. Her long body had never known strenuous work, nothing beyond practicing or training for some sport, just enough to keep it toned and supple. Her usual smile, pert dimples with enough white teeth to detract from the small eeriness of her luminous eyes, was replaced by a look of seriousness. She slowly contracted different muscles and then relaxed them, an old habit she had from childhood. Something that could take the edge off of being nervous without showing any sign of weakness. Her mother deplored weakness.

The room itself was small. It had a tall ceiling, with four arches curving together in the middle of the ceiling, with a small round of glass in the center to let the sun beam down upon the brow of the waiting initiate. Of course, with her luck, the clouds roiling above prevented the sun to beam upon her. The rest of the room was fairly cramped. An ancient rowan tree awash in red berries stood in the center of the room. The tests, or Tellings as they were called, were conducted every cycle for as long as that tree was fruitful. There were two doors, one facing the land, and the other facing the sea. They were in the center of Tureyn castle, far from being able to see the water, but the symbolism was still there. Clerin had entered from the door that faced the land. She would exit for her Telling through the door facing the sea.

She took a slow gaze at the others in the room with her. She wished to remember this moment, to be able to tell her children exactly how her first trial of public appearance went. She looked over her father—tall, lithe, and respectful. His white hair showing his age as it flowed past his waist. His crystalline blue eyes, those that had pierced through her so many times in the past, were now pensive. He was wearing white, as the parent of an initiate, even though he was royalty. Everybody obeyed the same laws when it came time to observe the life cycles. So he came only as a parent, with no symbols adorning him.

Clerin pulled her gaze over to her sister, to see what emotion played upon her face. Normally Clerin's mother would be here, but she was at the Fluen Temple, underneath the weight of the sea. There had been some harsh words from her aunt, for technically she should have been given the honor in Clerin's mother's absence. It had taken her father some doing to get her aunt assigned to another outpost before the trial. Her aunt had left without much grace either. There was something there that Clerin was not quite sure of, but she would rather have her sister with her anyway. Her sister, who had surpassed her own Telling just a few sun cycles before, was grinning from ear to ear. Her blue eyes, less electric than Clerin's but still haunting, were conveying all of the well-wishes that her voice could not. The family witnesses were not allowed to speak with the initiate, unless asked a specific question. Clerin could ask each of them three questions, any three she could come up with, and they had to answer them to the best of their ability. Clerin had taken a personal vow, many sun cycles ago, to not ask for help before her trial. So they waited, smiling and supportive, until the ten allotted minutes were used up.

Clerin could feel herself gain more and more energy as the seconds passed. It seemed not only to come from the room now, but to come from both her father and sister directly. It was as if she were pulling it right out of them, sucking it out like a leech. They both seemed oblivious to it. It seemed to get quiet outside of the chamber, a little too quiet. The background noise of derlians in hushed tones, the scuffle of leather-clad feet on stone, the occasional cough, had all disappeared. Clerin quickly tried to rerun the major points of the story in her mind, so that she should not forget anything while in front of everybody.

A loud trumpet blast. Two more in quick succession. The soft swish of fabric as her father walked towards the door. The small click of the door being unlocked, the vacuum woosh of the door being opened. Everything seemed amplified. More than amplified—clarified. Each sound was perfect in its distinctness, each motion was completely fluid. Clerin's smile was tremendously wide; she thought she must look like a beast. As she walked towards—and then through—the door, she managed to calm her hands and nod towards her father before she stepped out onto the stage.

The amphitheater was gigantic. She had seen it many times before but always from one of the benches. It seemed to grow tenfold when she was standing on the stage, staring out at all of those Fluens. They seemed to rise up into the sky and surround her on three sides. The vast openness had stolen her breath, so she continued to walk towards the front of the stage, beaming up at all of the derlians. She blinked once, stopped walking, blinked again. She drew a full deep breath, remembering the breathing techniques her tutors had instilled into her, and began her story. The story that is told every cycle of the sun, at every major Fluen city, and eventually by each Fluen. The story of their Creation.

"The tale I begin is not new. Nor is it as accurate as some would hope. I face several great difficulties in attempting to tell a tale such as this. The first one is language. The Yavens can speak our language, but rarely do. The Belegs cannot speak our language, since they communicate with thoughts more readily than words. These thoughts are very difficult to bring into words. It is with this onus that I begin." Clerin stated the ritualistic beginning with what she hoped to be excitement and enthusiasm. Every Teller of the Cycle began their story such. As every ending was also the same.

"We do not know the beginning of the Yavens. Even from our conversations with the great Beleg Lembin we do not know the beginning. So from the beginning of our story the four elemental kingdoms were already there. In isolation. They did not know that each of the others existed. The Void separated them, the empty starless blackness kept them apart. In each realm there was but one element. The Fluen realm is made up of only water and only Fluen Yavens inhabit it. Now the Yavens are a tricky sort, and it is here that we get our start. Our history." Clerin paused long enough to catch her breath and wet her lips. She hated beginnings; it was always the worst part.

"The Yavens are made out of their element. You could say that they are the element with Spirit infused. Each Yaven is physically the same, being made out of the same material. Each was as fast as the other, as strong as the other, as competent as the other. In fact, the only real difference was their spirit, their minds. In essence, it was their imagination that had begun to set them apart. For if a Yaven could think up something that none of the other Yavens had, well, that was where their advantage was. If you could surprise your opponent with something that they had never encountered before, you had the upper hand. Since Yavens live eternally, being able to be killed but never aging, the hunt for experience became the all-consuming passion for them. The more untried and improbable the better. They made different games, all dealing with manipulations of their specific element, and competed with each other. For uncountable cycles." Another slight pause as Clerin started to warm up to her audience. Some of the younger derlians were peering upwards with intent already, those that had heard this story only once or twice before.

"This aeon is what was known as the Age of Peace. In this time there was no language, no hierarchy, and hardly any death. The Yavens were able to mate, but at an incredibly slow rate. Their art of mating is incomprehensible to us as we live too short to understand it. Some mating rituals would take centuries, millennia, in our reckoning of time. Yavens are neither male or female. Or maybe they are both. We only know that it takes two of them to mate. Slowly, but ever increasingly, more Yavens were introduced to their elemental realms. It is with this increase that we begin to see change. The redundancy had begun to take its toll upon the Yavens. The experiences they were able to have were reaching a finite amount, surrounded by only one element. The Age of Peace is also referred to as the Infinite Age. There was no real way that the Yavens had been keeping track of the passage of time. And, truly, why should they?" Clerin had unconsciously brought her voice up a little high at the end of the last sentence. She silently cursed herself as she continued with her telling.

"It was not until the Age of Enlightenment that the Yavens began to accumulate time. It was during this aeon that the Yavens invented time, rulership, and language. Time gave each Yaven something to be coordinated about. It meant that everyone had to centralize and communicate with each other. There had never before been a single factor that the Yavens had had to keep track of, collectively. It was this collectiveness that began to socialize the Yavens. Soon afterwards came society, because every society has something in common to judge individuals by. For the Yavens, this became time. The older, more venerated Yavens began to clamor for special rights, for the need to differentiate not only younger Yavens, but also actions. The violence at the beginning of this cycle nearly destroyed the Yavens. Laying waste to your neighbor meant that you were that much older compared to the common pool of 'society.' Each disintegration of a fellow Yaven meant there was that much less competition. From this outburst, this uncertainty, came laws and language. The two are inseparable. The Yavens decided to give up certain rights for security. And in this they set the precedent that we now exist under." This last part was purely Clerin's. She had spent the last week thinking up unique ways of saying the same histories. Little additives of her own opinion laced around the known stories of the past.

"The rulers, however, would grow weary of time. Endless, infinite time. There was never an attempt at a coup during this next aeon, not that has ever been spoken to a derlian. The laws had done their job, the violence was stifled. There was only time to compete with, and, in the end, time always wins. The current ruling Yavens would grow to dislike the redundant cycles, just as they had before they were rulers. They would exhaust every possibility in their power. They would exhaust them again and again. Eventually they would step down of their own accord. In this way many of the ancient Yavens, for many of them are alive to this day, became rulers for a while. It was a gentle way to pass the time, especially since the spurt of violence was still heavy within the fore-memories of the Yavens.

"With the cycles of the different rulers came different specializations. Each Yaven would try to bring to the position something unique, something that would make them cherish reliving their memories. And to make other Yavens remember their rule as well. During the end of the Age of Enlightenment came the first real attempts at exploration.

"It was the organization, or the rulership, of the Yavens that truly enabled them to explore their realms with the utmost scrutiny. Without the organization, without the language, without the laws, they would have played on infinitely, without knowing what lay beyond. They began their exploration by having special volunteers memorize the entire realm, section by section. These Yavens would tell anyone who asked where anything they knew of was. It was a time of intense specialization. The Yavens worked as a cohesive unit like never before, though ever since. It was during this time that the wormholes were discovered." Clerin had wanted to build more up to that, the ultimate find. Her mind, however, kept charging ahead without telling her. She had to fight to reign in what she had retold hundreds of times to her relatives, to herself. It was as if her mouth was in a race to finish the story before she even had gotten her audience interested.

"The wormholes, as all of you probably know, are pinholes in the Void. Tiny punctures linking one realm with another." *As all of you probably know*, repeated in her mind. How could she sound so stupid? Heat rushed into her eyes, filling the bottom lids with its self-hatred. It was all Clerin could do to continue, without a wavering voice, without any sign that she noticed her own atrocity. "Through these tunnels between the realms sound can travel. Very faintly, and only if a Yaven was close by on the other side, could it be heard. Still, it was the most shocking discovery that ever could be. That of, 'We are not alone.' Not only that, but that of, 'We are surrounded.' " Clerin had added that bit of humor as well. It sounded so much better amongst trusted friends than it did now. She peered into the audience, their faces blurring together to make one vast organism, and saw a few heads slung back in polite chuckles.

"Once the wormholes were found, and there were not many, the Fluens posted Yavens around them constantly. The random sounds meant nothing to the them, though they spent an inordinate amount of empty cycles trying to decipher them. There were many rulers during the Age of Wormholes, many. Each tried different tactics to interpret the noises. It was not until Lembin that the idea of comprehending another's language was even considered. It was during another's rulership that Lembin became famous. She was one of the Fluens stationed outside of a wormhole. Instead of memorizing the noises, as the ruler had told her to do, she attempted to mimic the sounds. She took one noise that she heard countless times, and she practiced constantly until she was able to make a similar sound. She would not know this until much later, but she was across from the Gaen Yaven meeting hall. The sound she had stumbled across, from hearing it repeated so often, was 'Hello' in Gaen. She waited outside of that wormhole for ages of time saying 'Hello,' until, finally, she heard an answer. A Gaen on the other side of the wormhole had thought that he had heard a distinct noise from nowhere. Since it was a vague form of 'hello' he ignored it, considering the amount of Gaens that said that word in the vast hall. Still he lingered in the area for quite some time. Eventually he decided that it was not coming from any of the myriad of Gaens around him, and he began to speak back to the empty voice." Clerin started to feel as if she was beginning to gain some momentum, that some in the audience were actually becoming more interested in the story. "This Gaen had the same thought that Lembin had, that of mimicry." Since the Yavens were sexless, Clerin took the time-honored approach of assigning her own sex to Lembin during her telling. She left the pronouns for the Gaen as male just to make the distinction simpler.

"It took them quite some time before they were able to decipher more speech. They repeated each other's names back and forth. Then they realized 'I am called,' before the repeated name. They extended their greetings to one another to include 'How are you?' And began to receive different responses for them. Without any gestures, they could at first only understand emphatic words, those that voice inflection could accommodate, and therefore define. 'Long' and 'short' for duration, 'loud' and 'quiet' for volume. Some concepts went quickly, but vast majority did not. Yaven language is different from the derlian one in how it is transmitted. There is more of a melding of minds, of visualizations and emotions, that transfers more information than the mere speech of us derlians. It was certainly not easy, nor were they the only two to try to understand the incomprehensible. Once it was understood that there was a form of communication going on, the entire realm rallied to understand. The pace was agonizingly slow, with each element of Yavens convening and discussing what each had heard, and what each had deciphered. All the other specializations began to slow, to stop. Nothing else could contain the respective Yavens' eager minds. Eternities had passed with the slow pressing sameness, like gems forming from the pressure of the mountain that contains them. It all seemed to come to a head with this one great realization. That they were not alone." Clerin began to smile inwardly, now. The repetition of her crippled joke from earlier had earned it more smiles, more faces pointed towards her with attention. It was as if she had told it earlier for the sole reason of being able to say it now, when it was more tense, more engulfing.

"Each time a new word was realized, it was documented and shared between all of the other Fluen Yavens who were speaking across the void. After a great rift of time a communal language was being born. Some of the Fluens were speaking to Gaens, as was

Lembin. Some, however were speaking to the Luftens. In each realm it was the same. Speaking between two other Yavens, beginning to understand each other. No one had realized that there was another type of Yaven across the void. The Fluens could not communicate to the Pyrans, nor could the Gaens communicate with the Luftens. With their language skills being as limited as they were, they were unable to realize the truth. They began to speak of their politics and their games. Some of them were amazingly similar, which is partly why they could communicate them. It was the actual stuff that their realms were made of, that they, individually, were made of, that eluded explanation. You can teach a blind derlian to talk, to run, the objects that you are surrounded by, almost anything. But attempt to tell them about color, just try. You can talk of blue being cold, and red being hot. You can try to explain the green of the grass, or the yellow of the sun. You can spend your whole lifetime working diligently towards the same end. It will, however, prove impossible. So did the Yavens eventually find out that there were some things about themselves that just could not be talked about. There were some words that could not be figured out. For even the most imaginative Fluen cannot be made to understand stone or soil. Not without experiencing it themselves." Clerin wished for a moment, an incredibly brief moment, that she could go back and explain more. She had skipped their games, their way of life, their realms. She had explained nothing that the Yavens had not figured out about themselves. As the irony came crushing into her, she saw the audience's attention. The thickness of it was almost palpable, and into the gaping maw of silence she thrust herself. Her father had stressed the inertia of storytelling more than anything else, and it was against this inertia that she decided to leave the unsaid, unsaid.

"It was during this next age, the Age of Cooperation, that Lembin had begun to rule the Fluens. It was known widely among the Yavens who the first communicators in their respective realms were. Lembin was the first of the Fluens Many argue that she was of the first of all the Yavens to understand what communication was. It was with this experience that she was pushed into rulership. Not necessarily that she did not wish it for herself, though she is most humble, but that the other ruler did not wish to step down. It was a first for the Fluen Yavens, that one ruler did not wish to step down when another was beseeched to take control. The Fluens considered the importance of communicating with the other realms more important than the life of one of their leaders. Not since the violence of the beginning of the Age of Enlightenment was there ever such a rending. Though Lembin was not even present, the sheer weight of guilt still felt by her was enough to destroy a Fluen derlian in her retelling." This part had always amazed Clerin, that guilt could be lethal. She had, of course, never personally felt the telepathy that the Belegs used to communicate, but it seemed inconceivable to her that mere communication should have such dire consequence.

"The four realms each chose new leaders at about the same time. There was an excitement in the air, something that had been lacking amongst the oppressive eternity. All of the Yavens had the feeling that they were on the verge. Of what, no one was quite sure, but certainly on the verge of something. They each wanted to be best represented by those Yavens who had shown an inner knack for communication with the other realms. So Lembin was chosen to direct the next Age for the Fluens. She had a great structure built upon the clearest wormhole in the realm. It was made of deuterium and stands to this day. It was in this structure that she spent all of her time conversing with Yavens of other realms. Mainly she conversed with the other three rulers. She could not directly talk with the ruler of the Pyran Yavens, but through the other Yavens they would relay messages back and forth." Clerin had wanted to say some words to the effect of the coincidence of the four realms evolving along the same time line, and then add her own part about the non-existence of coincidence. She was finding, however, that the story seemed to flow better if she just closed the rational part of her mind, the part that had done all of the rehearsals and wanted everything that went well then to be incorporated into the speech today, and just lost herself in the story. She found that although she skipped a few things that in the past she thought would get a good laugh or might increase the tension in the audience, the audience seemed to feel her more this way.

"This went on for some time, and the communal language between the Yavens was finalized. At least that which they could communicate between each other was finalized. While all things such as language and what the other realms did and were, had been communicated to the other Fluens, they did not understand as much as Lembin did. She heard it first. She filtered it, whether consciously or not, to the others. They only understood part of what she would try to explain to them. It was in this way, unknowingly, that Lembin

began to outdistance the other Fluens in imagination. In power."
Clerin wanted to emphasize that, needed to. Derlians were different
in so many ways that it was difficult to imagine a type of being that
was only differentiated by imagination. To Clerin, it was the secret to
understanding the whole of their past, of their creation. It was the
secret to understanding the Yavens and, through them, the Belegs.

"It was the same with the other three rulers. Their power
began to grow exponentially compared to the learning that the other
Yavens gleaned from them. It was with this combined power that
the four Yaven rulers began the make a plan. There was no way to
travel through the wormholes, not to another realm of element. They
figured, or imagined, that there was a way to travel to the nothingness
that separated them. To the Void. It was the one realm that they
could all imagine, all hold in their minds. They began, as a team, to
attempt to widen the wormholes enough to slip them into the Void.
Into a pocket dimension that they could meet each other, see each
other, and know each other. It took time, of course, and time was
the one thing that the Yavens have always had. It has been their gift
as well as their curse. The continued communication and learning,
the solidifying of the communal language, all of these kept the other
Yavens satisfied, while the rulers spent the bulk of their energy
attempting to meet each other.

"Finally all of their energies came to fruition. They were able
to slip enough of their minds into the wormhole to see into the void.
There, they glimpsed the unthinkable, the unknowable. They saw,
for the briefest of moments, what another element was like. What
they each *were*. It was this one moment that gained them the most.
Though each was immediately thrust back into their home realm, the
image of the other elements, of the other Yavens, was burned into
their minds. They rested and recuperated. They gained in energy and
in strength. And then they planned the next meeting.

"The next time they attempted to meet each other they were
able to stay in the void for a full minute. Not much was said, merely
exclamations of astonishment. Each was briefly introduced to one
another, so that each individual look of each element came with a
name. Lembin stated her name and that she was the Fluen Yaven
that they had been speaking to through the wormholes. She made a
flourishing bow and smiled at her fellow rulers. She was doing her
best to look happy and excited at them. Her mind, however, was
racing to memorize their features, while at the same time trying to

hold back the natural repulsion felt at meeting something so foreign. We ourselves do not really know what truly foreign is. The closest feeling of revulsion we could feel would be to a grub or an insect."

Clerin could feel herself building up energy. She knew that she shouldn't overdo it, but it was intoxicating.

"Gunzgak introduced himself next, as the Gaen Yaven's ruler. So slow and regal was Gunzgak's self introduction that Lembin at first took it to be pompousness. It was Gunzgak who had talked to Lembin through the wormhole that first time, and so Lembin has always had a sacred spot held for Gunzgak inside of her. The next to introduce themselves was Gorbanax, the one that Lembin had yet to talk to, the Pyran Yaven. Though his grin was wide, his smile held something behind it. The voice seemed peculiar to Lembin, probably because she had yet to hear it. The last to speak was Linchon, the Luften Yaven. As for their appearance, well, we all know what the elements look like, do we not?" Clerin was looking down at the front row, where all of the younger derlians were gathered, smiling heavily upon them. Most of the older Fluens had probably seen a Yaven before, so the description would be amiss with them. Clerin figured if they knew that she was speaking to the younger Fluens, they would excuse her inaccuracies. For the meeting of a Yaven is so completely overbearing for most derlians that one derlian's description is completely unlike the next's. So she turned up the drama a notch. She lowered her head to take in the front rows, and swiveled it back and forth. This served the dual purpose of incorporating all of the younger ones as well as adding some comic menace to her visage. "Try to imagine a fire, a great roaring bonfire, in the vague shape of a derlian. Spitting pieces of itself into the starless blackness of the Void. Its eyes the bright yellow of the bottom of a flame, while its extremities the deep red of blood. Or the constant motion of steam and smoke, billowing about, this way and that. For the briefest moment you can catch a glimpse of the nothing behind the Luften Yaven, as the wisps of itself whip around. Or the solid mountain, moving with seamless joints." She smiled largely, and somewhat maniacally at the end, while she raised her arms outstretched dramatically. Then she stepped back two steps and continued with her story to the entire audience.

"They worked and wheedled at it until they were able to stay in the pocket Void for a sufficient time. It was a great era of learning for them and for the other Yavens. Every time the rulers would come back from the Void it was with greater knowledge of the other realms. This they shared openly, trying their best to use a limited language to describe what they saw and what they heard of the other realms. For though their vocabulary increased dramatically, explaining what fire meant to other Fluens was still exceedingly difficult. Lembin tried her best to explain the concept of fire, of liquid heat. Except that it wasn't a liquid and the temperature stayed almost constant in the Fluen realm. The rulers began to feel different from the other Yavens and, consequently, began to distance themselves from them. They spent more and more time in the Void, with the other rulers, amongst themselves. After they had exhausted the explanations of their realms, what little they could relate, they discussed their rulerships, what the other Yavens were demanding of them. Mainly more time, more experience. At least in Lembin's case they were clamoring for other Fluens to enter the Void, to experience at least a fraction of the other elements." Here Clerin took a moment to pause. She had heard this explanation several times, by other storytellers, each with their own slant. Their own opinion. Most seemed to think that Lembin was attempting to protect other Fluens from the trauma of experiencing the other elements, or that she thought that others would be unable to reach the Void. Clerin had her own ideas of what had happened, however. Though she knew that no derlians had died of shame during Lembin's first telling of this part of the story, she felt that Lembin's reasons were not entirely honorable. Her family, however, had attempted to curb her vehemence in this area, long before she was to take her first Telling.

"Lembin, however, refused. She gave the Fluens a myriad of excuses until they stopped asking her. She gave the Fluens promises and explanations, then she spent more and more time in the Void. It was similar amongst the other rulers, though we like to think that they were worse than Lembin." Clerin could feel the audience pull back slightly. Mainly some of the older derlians that had heard, and told, this same story countless of times before. She knew that this would be a sore point for most of them, as Lembin was considered their Creator. Many derlians thought that "Creator" meant infallible. Clerin felt slightly smug as she was telling them *her* truth.

"Their meetings grew longer, and their friendships tighter. Though they were each of a different element, and so each inexplicable to the others, they had many similarities. Most of these were in rulership. Each realm's Yavens were becoming insistent with the wish that others could share the elements. The four discussed their need to understand the unknowable for them. They talked of being able to feel the other's element. Not in the mere connotation of sensation. But of immersion 'til the point of comprehension. They argued and they contemplated. They shared the growing unrest of their Yavens with each other. They talked of everything they could think of to stall the inevitable. Then Gunzgak voiced his plan. I say his plan merely because he spoke of it first, gave it the courage of life. The others, Lembin at least, had the same thought but had not the will to breathe life into it by speaking of it.

"The plan was startlingly simple and yet, as we derlians hear it, impossible to duplicate. They were each of the four realms, working as a cohesive unit. It was only through their combined energies that this could work, so Gunzgak had to get the complete agreement of the other three rulers before explaining his plan in its entirety. Not just the agreement of their words, nor just of their heads. He had to be completely sure that each of the other Yavens would go through with it completely." Clerin had tried for several moons to come up with a good Gaen voice. Something gravelly and heavy. Yet she had been unable to make her mouth and lungs bring to life what was in her head. So she told the next part in the same rich voice as the rest of the story: her own. She stepped towards the audience, looking up into its darker depths, and began Gunzgak's speech.

" 'We have reached a point of stagnation, my friends. We have reached the pinnacle of our rule. There is nothing more to gain by way of these meetings. Our Yaven brothers grow restless, and rightfully so. We have deigned to rule for longer than most rulers. And, particularly, we have deigned to rule during such a time of complete discovery. This discovery, by all accounts, should be fully shared with the other Yavens. They plead me for it in my own realm and I am sure that they are vocal in yours as well. With all of the facts at hand, I can only see two distinct and separate possibilities. One is that we are honorable. We step down. We let other Yavens, one by one, feel the presence of another element. We do this until we are all equal and then decide what we do next. Whom shall the rulership of our Yavens fall upon? What other directions of exploration will be open to us? Yes, my friends, this is one of the options.' " Clerin stepped forward another step, her face still upturned towards the uppermost listeners. She tried to keep her voice stable while projecting it to the farthest depths of the listeners. Though she could not replicate a Gaen voice, she did not want to sound shrill either.

" 'There is another option open to us, however. I have thought long and hard upon this. Whether to even mention it, whether I actually wished it. The hardest thing for me to admit is my own selfishness. There are so many possibilities to this research that should be shared with the other Yavens. There are so many implications that should be gone over before an attempt like this should be tried. However, I know the passing of time. I feel the changes in my realm. My own research has come to a head. I feel as if I am almost compelled to speak.

" 'I have visited every wormhole in the Gaen realm many times. Both the ones that link the individual realms and those that link to the Void. I have studied their 'size.' I have pressed upon their elasticity, and I have come to one conclusion. The wormholes that exist from the Void to the other realms are at least five times as large and about three times as malleable. I have gone through my own wormhole as slow as possible, inspecting the 'walls' of it as I pass through. I believe, in the innermost depths of my being, that if several Yavens who have already tasted the other realms were to join energies and imaginations, they could travel into each separate realm.' " Clerin paused for the briefest of moments here. Not only to catch her breath, but also to regain her energy. She had been pushing her energy out at the audience for so long that she felt that she would need to rest for a week already. Knowing that she was not quite halfway through the story did nothing for her self confidence. She began to wonder what had happened to all that energy that she had felt before her speech had started, alone with her family.

" 'I have not been able to calculate the chances of our surviving such an ordeal. I know that when Lembin and Gorbanax touch there is intense pain to both of them. I do not know the damage that will occur to us if we attempt this. I am not very sure that we will be able to even survive a visit to an opposite realm. I do know, however, that to have this work correctly, each of us has to be in complete agreement. In no part of our being can we falter at the chosen moment. If we do, the wormhole will collapse. If this happens before we enter it, then one of us is stranded here.' " Clerin had heard many ideas of what would happen to them if the wormhole had collapsed during their travel through it. She had also heard the "original" story through her mother, who had communicated with Lembin herself. Who was communicating with Lembin right now. She had decided to leave the idea of the consequences of a collapsing wormhole up to the audience. For, truly, nobody knew for sure what could happen.

"The time it took for the other Yavens to agree was miniscule. The only arguments were about when they should go. They had all thought that this was the natural evolution of their rule. That they could each be the first to travel to the separate realms, not just the first to see a foreign Yaven. They were all especially excited that one of them had done some true research into such an idea, not just dreamed about it. They decided to go at the next meeting, rather than right then. That way they could leave instructions about what to do if they were destroyed. Detailed enough that their successor could find the Void, hopefully, and meet with the other new rulers of the realms. They did not feel fear. They did not feel foreboding. There was only the need to conquer more, to understand more, to be more. In this they were equal. And it is through this that they were able to gain their victory." Clerin smiled up into the darkened corners of the room. She smiled into the silence of her audience. She could feel the tide of energy shifting. Back towards her.

"They each went their separate ways, into their separate realms. They passed down their instructions, their secrets, their well-wishes for their *friends*." Most derlians spoke this as friends and family. It seemed to Clerin, however, that those were the same to a Yaven. She only hoped that the inflection in her voice could convey that concept to the audience. "Lembin spent much time with her *friends*, trying her best to explain what another element looked like, how they felt. In every way possible, not just physically. Lembin, though she felt an assured amount of companionship with the other three Yavens, especially with Gunzgak, was beginning to feel that she truly was a Fluen long before she was a Yaven. There are certain traits that separate the different elements, just as each element is different. This is the main idea that she tried to impress upon her *friends* before her leaving. Before her changing." Clerin let the final word hang onto the audience's silence. She let it wash over them and envelope them, leaving the kiss of mystery on their cheeks. She smiled at the children in the front as she paced past them. *I wonder which ones have yet to hear this tale?*, she thought to herself. She tried to read their faces as she swept by, but they blurred together too much.

"They met again for the last time as Yavens. They had each prepared themselves. They each carried an air of vibrant excitement. They traded grins amidst the Void." At this Clerin's own grin showed too much teeth, her eyes wide over her inflated cheeks, in a poor caricature of a Yaven's show of emotion. "They had already decided to travel to the Pyran realm first. Gunzgak had suggested it because it had the least elasticity of any of the wormholes and he was worried that they would gain in density during their travels. They had all agreed quickly wanting no argument to taint their excitement." Clerin had stopped her pacing, her head was slightly bowed as she stared at the wooden stage floor in front of her feet. Her voice was deliberately softer. "They now stood around the entrance to the wormhole, silent and waiting.

"The first to pass was Gorbanax, to make sure the room they were to pass into was clear. They had decided not to encounter any other Yavens the first time. Just to attempt to experience the other realms, the other elements." Clerin was beginning to walk towards the audience, down the center of the stage. Her voice was gaining volume in a slow crescendo. "Then went Gunzgak into the wormhole. Making sure his bulk would travel through the less dense realms. Then went Linchon, disappearing into blackness. Ah, the blackness upon the blackness. Seeing a wormhole in the Void is a skill to be learned, I am told, not just an experience to have. Lastly, hesitatingly, went Lembin." To increase the tension amidst the audience and to hold their attention taught, like an anchor rope, she had waited to explain the wormhole travel until now. She was at the edge of the stage, staring down into the front row. Her hands curled in front of her, parting an invisible veil.

"Lembin slid into the opening, as much with her mind as with her body. Forcing the Void to open around her and accept her passage. Like trying to bore through a mountain with only your mind. Such a feeble instrument for so great an accomplishment. Once Lembin had gained the wormhole, she felt the movement begin to tug at her. There is nothing in the wormholes, nothing. Even the Void might contain another Yaven, somewhere, anywhere. Even the Void may pass sound from one being to another. But in the wormhole, the blackness upon blackness, there was truly nothing. Except, of course, for Lembin. The feeling of motion came not from any wind, or even any outside influence whatever, but came from the drag on the interior of the Yaven. Like when you jump from a high place, your innards are following just a moment behind you. The drag increased with Lembin's apprehension. When they both were beginning to become unbearable, and Lembin's silent scream was tearing at her, she finally pushed through to the Pyran realm." Clerin's arms dropped back to her waist at the last word, her head raised slightly and she took two steps back. She smiled into the silence briefly before she took up the story again.

"What happens when fire and water meet? One must succumb to the other. What happens if both are eternal? The struggle is the same, but it never ends. The sheer full force of pain that Lembin has described to us is not translatable." After five translators died, Clerin was told, they had given up trying to pin down this experience. It was better to leave the experience as "unfathomable" than to lose more derlians. "Surely a being any weaker, such as one of us, would have died. And surely any mind weaker would have gone insane instantly. The fire has never left Lembin. It has never been soothed over or forgotten, though it has ebbed somewhat on a physical level. The Fluens have always been known for their patience, their peaceful attitude and their artistry. Now Lembin had new feelings, new emotions. She had fire coursing through her now, and unlike any other Fluen before her or after her, she truly understood why the Pyrans are so high-strung and quick tempered. For try as she might, these things had become a part of her and she could not quell them." Clerin's head had tilted upward, talking to the entire audience now. "This infusion changed Lembin completely and eternally. Her understanding of the other element grew a hundred fold, a thousand fold. She understood fire in a way that even a Pyran derlian can not understand it. For fire had ceased to be something to sense, but was now an integral part of her composition. And derlians are composed of mere flesh." Clerin had thought long and hard how to explain what had been explained to her. This was something that she could never understand, not fully anyway. The Yavens do not just sense their element, they ARE their element. The difference between experiencing something completely new and unforetold and having something as immutable as your spirit permanently changed was incomprehensible to Clerin. She had never even "spoken" to Lembin herself. Very few derlians had. So it was incredibly difficult to make this part of the story her own. She couldn't really add anything new to what she had always heard, nor could she leave anything out. It had been a sore point in her preparation for her Telling.

"Though Yavens do not truly breathe, the pain of compression, the slowly blackening consciousness coupled with the panic that comes with feeling close to death are similar to a derlian asphyxiating. It was with this foggy mentality that Gunzgak was heading back towards the wormhole at the same time that Lembin was reeling from her own stunning entrance. As Gunzgak disappeared into the wormhole, Linchon slipped past Lembin also. Gorbanax, meanwhile, just stared at Lembin, waiting for Lembin to reenter the wormhole back to the comfort of the empty Void. In his eyes Lembin thought she saw a calculating glance, along with the bewilderment and curiosity that Lembin expected to see from someone who could not feel the extreme reaction that his companions had just been put through. It was a glance that Lembin remembers still." Clerin was still planted in the middle of the stage, smiling into the crowd. She was trying her hardest to not let any frustrations show through. She was only halfway there, she kept reminding herself.

"When they had all reached the safety of the Void again, they rested. They rested for what seemed like days to Lembin and what surely seemed like eternities to Gorbanax. He had at first attempted to riddle them with questions but quickly eased up into silence. He waited as patiently as a Pyran Yaven can. For that was what he still was. The others, though, were feeling the change upon them. They had at first assumed that visiting each realm would give them experience, one of the necessary ingredients of imagination and thus greater power. They had all assumed that it would change their minds, a little at least. Change the way that they looked at their realms and their fellow Yavens. Now the full realization was dawning upon them. They did not, however, wish to speak of it with Gorbanax just yet. They felt, without communicating with each other, that he would find out what the true consequences were on his own. When they felt ready enough, one by one, they stood about before the wormhole to the Luften realm. They had begun upon their path and there was only one way to go. For what is a being made up of two elements? One element too much to be what it was, two elements short of being whole. Correct or not in their assumption, nothing, not even common sense, could deter them now." Clerin was never really sure if each of the three had already formed regrets or if it was just Lembin.

She had yet to meet any of the other derlian races, or to even make it out of the Fluen realm. She was not sure how the histories would be told in foreign lands. Maybe Gorbanax reveled in the experience.

"When they had prepared themselves to assay again, Linchon slipped into the blackened hole. Almost before it had sealed up behind him, Gorbanax dove in after him. Lembin looked upon Gunzgak and saw her own pain and exhaustion mirrored there. Gunzgak smiled to Lembin and said, 'We two agree, remember that.' As Gunzgak slid into the wormhole his words seemed to hang there in the Void. Shapeless they were, utterly unknown. How can others agree if they are not sure what has passed between them? Then again, how can you not agree with a statement of companionship like that? Either way, a small bond was placed between Gunzgak and Lembin at that moment. A gesture of mutual respect had passed between them, one that would be remembered later." The burning curiosity almost overcame Clerin. She had heard others tell the same story and they all agreed as to the words between Gunzgak and Lembin. She, however, could not fathom what they agreed upon. Nor could she see how they could understand each other with such little communication. She knew, *knew*, that there was something missing here. There were things missing throughout the story, to be sure, but this was such an obvious dangling thread that she wanted to shout it out to the audience. She wanted to stop her story and ask the elders probing questions. To strike up a debate about the inconsistencies and loose threads that abounded in the most repeated story of the entire realm. She had already tried, however, to talk to her family of this. And they had merely suggested that she pass the part quickly and spend more time on the parts that she liked, or at least felt she understood fairly well. As hollow as it made her feel, she could, in truth, not think up another solution. So she glossed over her curiosity and continued, seamlessly, to tell the story as best she could.

"Each realm was similar in the excruciating pain that three of them would feel. Each realm seemed to attempt to snuff out their spirit, through loss of sustenance. Like one of us trapped without any air. Or maybe dying of thirst. But it has never been described as the slow gnaw of starvation. Each realm also left a piece of itself living inside each of them. Before their experiment began, they had thoughts of spending some time in each of the realms, maybe exploring a little. After experiencing their first foreign realm, however, they each knew, individually, that exploring was out of the question. It was more a matter of survival. To be capable of visiting the realms was enough. To come away from each realm with that element permanently seething inside of them was enough. As they came back from the Gaen realm, they collapsed in the Void and rested for quite some time. Enough time that the Yavens of their realms became worried to agitation that they had not returned. This coupled with the fact that they had been rulers for much longer than any other Yaven led to their realms choosing different rulers while they were recuperating." Clerin had meant to draw this part out more, but found herself hurrying along as she meandered towards the water glass at the far edge of the stage. Pausing to take a drink, feeling more recuperated herself, she began again.

"The four stayed in the Void for a while after they had begun to gain their strength back. They talked. They took eternities attempting to describe what had taken mere moments to experience. Each had, basically, felt the same things, were feeling the same things, yet they could not stop talking about it. It was as if each new approach, each new telling of the same story gave it more depth, more meaning. More than anything they wanted to understand what had happened to them. Understand it to the point of acceptance. They kept trying to reassure themselves that what they had done was for their own betterment. As if repeating it would make them feel more comfortable in their own skins." As Clerin spoke the last idiom she inwardly cringed. Even the youngest derlian out in the audience knew that Yavens did not have skin. They were merely, or amazingly, their pure element. "As they spoke to one another they became more and more fond of each other. They knew something was different about themselves now. Something completely fundamental. Trapped deep within themselves, where they were unable to reach, something intrinsic had changed. The only ones who understood, the only individuals who could, were in the Void with them at that moment, talking to them. Each trying to salve the others' wounds." Clerin was hovering around the water glass, away from the audience. *Just one more drink*, she had kept thinking to herself. She finally moved back towards the center of the stage.

"When they felt that they were healed enough, in body, mind, and soul, they decided to leave the safety of the Void. Each slipping into their own wormhole, like a babe through its womb. The elasticity factor seemed to play little part in their capabilities to enter into their wormholes. When Lembin reached her own realm, the

Fluen realm, she felt refreshed and invigorated by the familiarity of it. She spent a while finding old *friends* and attempting to explain where she had been, what she had been doing. The loss of rulership did not bother her in the least. She had felt like stepping down for some time, anyway. It had been, mostly, her new foreign friend's ambitions and curiosities that had emboldened her to keep up the rulership. No, it was only the way her old *friends* looked at her, and spoke to her, that bothered her really. Physically she appeared the same, both to herself and to her *friends*. She had no outer markings showing the fire burning inside of her, or the stone weighing her down, or the wind whipping through her mind at random intervals. There was no real way to just look at her and notice the change. But talk to her. Now that was a quick and sure way to realize the difference. Just as she had always loved the way her old *friends* could see through her words into her meaning, now she was uncomfortable by their knowledge of her changing. Every time that she saw the look of confusion as she tried to explain some foreign concept. Every time she saw a look of pity as she lost track of the concept she was trying to talk about. Every time she noticed the uncomfortable way that Fluens acted when she was around. It was not quite revulsion, but almost. Lembin spent a lot of time physically visiting and reliving the far reaches of the Fluen realm, but her mind kept wandering to other things. Either she was pining for the times past that she was the same as the other Yavens, without this stigma that marred her, or she was thinking about the other three that had experienced the same tragedy, the same blessing. Either way, her mind was not very present. Though she stayed in the Fluen realm for quite some time she had decided early that she should go back to the Void." Clerin was moving slowly towards the front again. She had felt a slight withdrawal from her audience. Whether it was from her moving from the center and drinking, or if it was because the history was between peaks of interest, she was not sure. She did know, however, that she had to get some of that back before launching into the next crescendo. She was beginning to really enjoy building an audience's energy, easing up, and building it again. She felt that if she could keep in harmony with them that she could easily pass her Telling.

"Upon Lembin's arrival at the Void, she found herself alone. There she recuperated in the dark and quiet. Linchon was the next to appear. He had been 'overthrown' in his own realm. He had gone back and attempted to continue his old rule, only to be confronted by an angry conclave that had been instigated in his recent absence. Rather than attempt a coup, Linchon had decided to say his goodbyes and meet with his fellow outcasts. Though normally loquacious, Linchon seemed more reserved than normal.

"Next came Gunzgak, still excited by the recent changes in him. He was full of bluster and flurry. His talk was quick and had a different form of energy behind it. Not necessarily more energy just... different. There used to be a low rumble behind his words. Though each word was slow and deliberate, they carried a weight, a gravitas, that was unmistakable. Nobody ever really won an argument against Gunzgak, though you rarely argued with him. He had a habit of not speaking unless he had already thoroughly examined his position. Therefore his position was normally unshakable. Now, however, that he was 'complete,' as he put it, his words slid from his tongue lightly and easily. The rapid explanation of how he spent his time in the Gaen realm left Lembin somewhat taken aback.

"The last to re-enter the Void was a very agitated Gorbanax. His form spit bits of flame into the Void. They extinguished themselves immediately as they left their host." Clerin often wondered why the Four never changed physically. If they were now made up of four different elements, how come their appearance never changed in any of the stories? It was a fleeting thought that she refused to let take hold as she was barreling towards the Creation. "Gorbanax ranted and raved for quite some time about his realm. How they were waiting for him at the edge of the wormhole to return. How they attempted to imprison him. And of his final escape back through the same guarded wormhole. He seemed, rightfully so, frazzled and put upon. These feelings, though, did not stay as they had begun: self-pity and anguish at the 'betrayal' of *his* Yavens. No, they quickly morphed into anger and vengeance. So were the four reunited into their own tiny conclave. Alone in the Void, as they were alone amongst their old kind." Clerin knew that she was summarizing some of what had happened. She had, herself, sat through many an audience where the attack on Gorbanax was explained in great detail. Surely it was part of the story, an important part if you needed to understand what changes were happening in Gorbanax as well as the changes in the others. It seemed odd that by gaining other elements the Four seemed to have their personalities shift, sometimes even just back and forth. There seemed to be a long time when they went through serious dichotomies, or quadchotomies, with their changes in personality. This seemed at odds to Clerin, especially because they did not change, physically, at all. She knew she should spend more time upon the changes, rather than their consequences, but they seemed somewhat inexplicable to her. Cycles later, after much had happened to Clerin, she would understand better, but at the young fresh age of reckoning, performing her first Telling, she breezed by the difficult to understand and landed straight into the "reason" why the story was told every Cycle. The true beginning. The Creation.

"There were new emotions amongst the four Yavens. Things they had never felt before. That of separateness, that of alienation. For a Yaven, surrounded constantly by *friends* made of the same element, in an entire realm made of the same element, alienation was completely unknown. Yes, they had times when they wished to be alone. And times when those that they wanted to be with wished to be alone. Some had been ostracized before and there were even those who were exiled for a period of time. However, no matter how much they differed from their cousins, mentally and emotionally, they were still cousins. No longer, not for these four. They decided that they had become different enough, or evolved enough, to warrant a different category that they belonged in. They renamed their race, renamed themselves. They left their Yaven ancestry, as they had left behind their realms that had once encompassed them, and became Belegs." Clerin had struggled and practiced not saying the word Beleg too much too early. She had troubles with saying "the four" instead, since everybody knew who the Belegs were. Her father had impressed upon her, however, the fact that you should never call anything by name until you have named it yourself.

"As with the Yavens, the Belegs are impervious to time. We do not truly know how long each 'Age' or each season or aeon for them passed. We merely know the crushing weight of time, slipping unseen through the Void, not the actual knowledge of how long. The cycles that passed were enormous, that we can tell by the emotions of Lembin. The Belegs became very close during this time. They grew to understand their own nature together. They grew into their power together. They took their spirits and filled in any gaps, repaired any chinks, and smoothed out all roughness. This was the time that the Belegs spent maturing and gaining a segued grace that we cannot comprehend. As told by Lembin, it was a time that they truly were many wicks sharing a common tallow." Clerin was walking towards the front of the audience again. She was walking as unhurriedly as her speech.

"Enough time had passed that they began to grow weary of their Void. They had sealed the entrances to the separate realms. They had chosen a gate to seal the wormholes. This allowed sound to still travel through them, but not for any 'solid' element to filter through. Their first reason for this was fear, not undeservedly especially from the Pyran realm; the second was to give them the time to regroup and recover from their changing. The third reason—well the third reason is why most things get held onto long past their time. Habit. They had decided upon their defenses, and they stuck to them. Long after Yavens gave up trying to enter through the wormholes, the 'bars' were still in place. In fact, they are still there." Clerin was at the edge of the stage again, smiling warmly down upon the young Fluens' faces.

"Time, as it always does, eventually took its toll. The feelings of entrapment and alienation became too much for even the Belegs to bear. They grew restless. They began to plan again. They knew that the Yavens would remember them, and maybe none too fondly, either. They also knew that being around Yavens made them feel somewhat off center. It reminded them, too closely, of their own change from what they were. They had finally stopped thinking of it as an abomination and were attempting to exercise their atrophied powers. They decided that what they wanted was a place to be that had all of their elements mixed, like they themselves were mixed.

"In their restlessness and their insatiable curiosity, they hatched an incredible plan. They could envision what they wanted. They knew their dreams well. This, I am told, is the first secret to success." Clerin paused for a moment for the polite chuckles of some of the older Fluens in the audience. "They played with it in their minds. They brainstormed, they meditated, they imagined. They began to bend each of their considerable wills to the task at hand. To make a realm that contained each of the elements. To make a realm that contained every part of themselves. They knew they had to make it in the Void, to keep it separated from the other realms. Common sense, really. They also knew that they had to inundate the Void with perfectly equal amounts of each of the elements. They knew that they had to work in secret, that no Yavens could catch wind of their plan. And they knew that where they were, what they had already been doing, gave them each of these things. Throughout the entire process of imagining, they had only one real problem. Little known to them at the time, however, was that they also had the answer.

"It was Linchon who found the way past the most difficult section of the plan. They knew that they had to create a rift in each of the four realms, letting the raw element spill into the Void. They also knew they wanted a certain perimeter with the rifts. They wanted the flow of elements to meet at a central point, in the center of the rifts. They knew that they would have to remove the gates that sealed off each of the four chosen wormholes. They knew that they would have to seal them off again at exactly the same moment. They were not sure if the rush from the element entrance would cut off their communication or not. They had decided to time themselves, so that they could each seal off the wormholes at the correct moment, without communicating with each other. The entire process, the whole making, only took about three of our minutes, we are told. They would sing to themselves. Each had a song that lasted the required minutes, and each could keep the same tempo under various stages of duress. They practiced trials that sometimes approached the violent. They knew that they needed wormholes of the same size, and preferably tiny, as to keep most of the more *solid* portion of each element out. They learned every tiny aspect and detail of their plan. They were all simple logic. In fact, there was only one real hurdle in their plan. That was how to begin the flow of the particular element through the chosen wormhole. The Void was the Void because this did not occur naturally. They would have to instigate this through their own power, through their own individual will. It was this particular problem that Linchon had finally figured out." Clerin was trying to build up anticipation. So she again turned her attention to the front of the audience. To the most inexperienced part of the audience, those who may not of heard the story at the detail that must be told during a Telling.

"Linchon had found a way to direct energy *through* himself, not merely from or around himself. He was able to swirl energy into himself from in front of him, using both of what we would call his arms and head to move the energy. While the energy traveled through him, he shrank the spiral bands down until almost nothing as the energy left him. This had the effect of speeding up the energy flow as it was leaving him. He could then get the top of the funnel, as he called it, near an energy source, such as another being, and it would siphon some of their energy into its spiral. Using this method he could almost 'steal' energy from one of his fellow captive Belegs. They practiced this on each other until they felt they could all duplicate Linchon's findings. They were cautious to try it out on any of the other realms, however. They didn't want any extra elements floating around. So, instead, they chose to begin.

"They decided to find the smallest, most obscure wormholes within communication distance and centrally focused. Each took a post at their first original realm, at those tiny wormholes. They each waited for Linchon's countdown to begin. '5…4…3…2…1…Zero.' They decided to begin at zero, because as Gunzgak put it, 'Everything begins at zero.' There was a small pop as four different gates were removed at once. Each began their spiral, their siphon. They began to increase both the amount and the velocity of their energy at a slow measured pace. They air around them began to grow thick. Thick with fog, dense as a lightning storm with a massive thrumming energy. Each Beleg, with considerable force in their own individual right, began to hum with power. The vibration was almost imperceptible to begin with. A flicker of light from behind, a small noise in the distance. It took what seemed an eternity for it to become felt. For the queasiness, the heat, the rhythmic shifting of their entire bodies. Through the *essence* of them came what felt like the smallest band of molten iron. More thin than one wisp of smoke. Searing, freezing, slicing, bursting, straight through the *center* of each Beleg. Not so much as being filled up. But more like being pushed away from yourself through yourself. Like an empty reed swallowed, but one that gains in radius, inflating in size and taking you, stretching, around it." Clerin had switched to second person to better convey the alien feelings to her audience. She had always kind of wanted to be a translator. To be able to speak with Lembin directly. Empathetically. "Each Beleg could feel their element, their realm, passing through them. It began to flow. They continued to increase the amount of energy that they drew upon, that they spiraled through themselves. The flow was as thick as a fist and increasing. Scouring at their insides. Scraping and reaming their *being*. It increased until it was about the size of a full-grown derlian's head. A solid column of pure element screaming through you. Vision blurred because you could not stop your entire body from shaking. Vibrating apart at the seams, the bodies were misshapen from the columns passing through them. Backs were sickeningly rounded around the columns etching through, chests splitting open to accommodate too much power.

They no longer needed to attempt to 'siphon spiral' any more. They had truly created a siphon and the realms were pouring in as fast as the wormholes would let them. Their focus shifted from that of building power, to that of surviving such an incomprehensible ordeal. All of Lembin's energy, in the last half of the making, was spent on trying to focus on when she could close the gate. Just on singing and keeping herself together. But it was too much. Too much to continue. Screaming as loud as possible. Attempting to focus enough power into survival. Yet attempting to focus enough to grasp the gate. The singing stopped. There was too much to go around. Lembin's mind was having difficulty concentrating. The torturous column. It wouldn't end. More and more just kept pouring through. Must close the gate. The gate. Forgetfulness and lethargy. Lembin's arms were leaden. They were swimming through tar. They had weights tying them down. The column seemed to have knives attached to it somehow. It was definitely moving faster than it had started out. What seemed like eons ago. The screaming. The gate. Lembin could no longer think in language. Mere symbols trotting along her field of vision, through her clenched lids. The symbols seemed to be getting simpler to her. Or maybe she was getting more simple compared to *them*. Yes, that must be the case.

"SLAM!" Clerin jumped into the air, as high as she possibly could. She yelled on the way down. Her feet clapped loudly and lewdly upon the stage and her butt hit her heels in her final crouch. Her hair, as if sensing her mood, looked disheveled as she crashed to the ground. "But the screaming didn't stop. No, that continued for some time. It's not known how they managed to get the gates closed at the same time. Surely, by the end of the three minutes, none of the Belegs were still singing. Maybe as they closed it, it shrank the amount of pressure that each was exerting, making each gate that much easier to close. Lining their timing up along a funnel of lesser resistance. But they did do it. What was left behind, floating in the void, was our world." Clerin rose back up and walked slowly, with shoulders slumped, to the glass of water. She took two sips, set the glass back down, and walked back towards the front of the stage again. She was trying to *show* the audience the trials of the Belegs. She could only hope that it worked.

"As you might have guessed, there was a period of recuperation." The laughs from the audience cheered Clerin. She had been worried, and her father had been especially worried, that her performance would be too dramatic. That it would put the audience on edge and make them uncomfortable. She smiled back at the audience. "The first smiles and glows of creation are unconceivable. In a realm made of one element, you merely *shape* that element. Surely new designs come forth, but not true creation. As the Belegs gained in strength, they also gained in awe. They had vague thoughts of what their experiment would entail. They surely never envisioned this, though." With a large sweeping hand, Clerin encompassed all of the stage, the audience, the entire palace and the world outside.

"The Belegs examined the world that they had forced into being. The world was much different back then. Barren of life, with only the elements clashing back and forth. The molten rock would crash into the seas, sending plumes of steam roiling into the air. There was a constant shifting of balance. A violent interchange of strength and weakness. Every time an element lost ground somewhere, they would make it up somewhere else. Each element seemed bent on destroying the others, yet never could. They could just make them change states and shift to another region of that element's control. This Age happened for a long time while the Belegs regained their strength and gathered intelligence about what was happening to the world they had just created.

"This shifting constant, this dynamic static, might have endured forever. Never resting in its eternal struggle. Or, maybe, it would have found a peace with itself. Each element in its corner, separated by a thin skirmish line against the other elements. We will never truly know what would have happened if our world had been left alone. For it was never truly alone." Clerin smiled down upon the rows of children. "The Belegs immediately began to shift the balance. They made the shell of air, the islands in the oceans, and volcanoes everywhere. Too much fire, and the sun was made. Too much ground, and the moon was made. Too much water, and the clouds began to circulate. While the air was piled on top of everything. Every time the Belegs shifted the dynamic, it shifted itself even more. They continued on thus for many thousands of cycles. Their constant energy attempting to at least slow down the roiling elements. They worked together for much of that time, pooling their collective energy to confront the massive power that they had created. Not only did they create our world, but they had created Chaos unintentionally as well. Within each realm, made of one consistent element, separated from each other by the Void, there was only

Order. The elements are naturally repelled by each other, or at least opposed to each other. So they will separate themselves if left alone. When forced together, however, they stay in constant movement, repelled from every point at once. This movement is too small and complicated to be seen by us, maybe even by the mighty Belegs themselves. This is where all uncertainty stems from. The Belegs tried their hardest to shackle it down, but could not. It did, however, keep them quite occupied for some time.

"Things began to find their rhythm. Time became measurable again, for the patterns were becoming more regular. The Belegs got to the point where they felt they were able to sit back and enjoy their world. They did not rest for need this time, but for want. They took note of the patterns of cycles. They basked and glorified in the almost inconceivable notion that they had made a realm of mixed elements and had kept it together. They amused themselves with terraforming and element shaping. It took quite a while before they noticed one of the great consequences of Chaos. Even though the Belegs are the most powerful sentience we have encountered, they were preoccupied with playing with the larger aspects of our world, and missed the life that was forming here. To be sure it started very small. Lembin has spoken of life so small that we are unable to see it, or hear it, or feel it. It was this life that began to grow unbeknownst to the Belegs." Clerin felt very at ease and peaceful. She had slowed her speech down to a flowing rhythm. Though she was talking towards the front and center, her head was held high and occasionally purveyed the upper balconies. The tension she had felt building within her seemed to have left her after her crescendo at the closing of the wormholes. She knew that she would have to begin to slowly build that energy back up, towards her next peak in the story, but she felt unhurried by such thoughts.

"The Belegs wished to have things that they could relate to. Things made up of each of the four elements like themselves. They helped each life form along as much as possible. The different plants, the tiny animals. They nurtured each of them equally. They felt a great love for everything that existed in the world. The possibilities seemed endless. So, too, did their relief from boredom seem endless. There came a point where things seemed almost balanced. Completely unpredictable, yes, but balanced. The ebb and flow still had its highs and lows, peaks never before ascended, and troughs unheard of in their depths. Eternity, however, continued its crushing turn.

"The Belegs began to wonder if their own brethren could survive such a chaotic and violent world. For even the animal populations had their cycles. They began to discuss amongst themselves two distinct possibilities. One, of attempting to become *solid*. To gain a permanent physical structure on the world they had created. They had so far maintained a kind of ethereal quality. Flitting from one mountain range to the next. From one end of an ocean to the other end. Unable to directly experience the world that they had made, and yet able to direct it with their own experience. This was hotly debated amongst them. They saw how the animals died. How they constantly died. They saw the uncertainty and the violence that seemed to accompany Chaos unilaterally. They discarded the first possibility. Instead, they decided to attempt to bring a few Yavens from each of the realms to their world, to see whether or not a creature of Order could become consumed by Chaos. How they each individually chose to do this is lost to our knowledge. We only know of Lembin's choice. She snuck back through a distant wormhole and conspired with some of her old companions. She took thirty-seven volunteers back into the Void with her. One thing every translator has attempted to bring across is the shock at how quickly Lembin received her volunteers. She had expected to be hard pressed to fill the slots at all, let alone as quickly as she did. Time grinds on." Clerin smiled warmly to her audience. Partly because she was having such a warm time on stage, and partly to align herself opposite of where she was headed. To gain momentum and follow through during her speech, she had practiced appearing calm just before explaining a harrowing account, rushing into a period of respite, and smiling right before discussing atrocity. She felt that dichotomy provided the emotional energy she needed to press her point.

"The changes that the Yavens were put through are very difficult to translate. The first couple of translators died during this point of the History. The emotional distress that Lembin conveyed during this section was too much for us to handle. The deadly guilt. The filtered version that eventually came through is still horrific. Though the third translator went insane, between his ramblings and the fourth translator's efforts, we have gained an intimate knowledge of what the Yavens went through as they morphed. Physically the change was massive. The Yavens lost all the elasticity that they had. They became formed, and stuck, into the derlian shape, our shape. They could no longer sift through the shifting elements that once cradled them. They gained the five *solid* senses, and lost all their ethereal senses. Their bodies, now ruled by Chaos, deteriorated and aged. No longer eternal, the Yaven-derlians gained a much faster reproduction rate. They could no longer control the element surrounding them. They were no longer merely of one element. They had Chaos inside of them. Much like the Belegs." She had decided to tone down some of the description here. When she had first heard the histories, publicly, the speaker had spent quite some time on the agony that the first derlians endured. Afterwards she had experienced horrific dreams. Strange twisting shapes being severed and mashed back into another form, all punctuated by terrible screams. Their change from eternal element to ephemeral chaos was unimaginable to Clerin. She had never endured such a suffering and she truly wished to never have to.

"The first one hundred and forty eight Yavens brought to our world were an experiment. They were placed directly on our world by the Belegs and did not cushion themselves with the Void. We know now that Yavens may be summoned here, but that they must go through the Void, and bring some of that emptiness with them. Shielding themselves on their way here and appearing only in their full element. Then they may walk this world. Only with those precautions can they survive unchanged. The originals did not have such luxury or knowledge. They were affected by the Chaos that comes from the mixing of elements. They became the derlians. They became us. The Belegs watched them closely, guiding their morph, and helped them as much as they could. Each Beleg around their original element of derlian. Assisting in capturing food, procuring water, and finding procreation. The Belegs, somewhat to atone for their callus experiments, spent most of their time separated from each other, assisting their own derlians. Each spent many cycles watching and invisibly coaching the actions of their younger sisters and brothers. Or maybe 'children' is a better term. At last there came a day when the catastrophe was averted. Each group of derlians had become self-sufficient. Each could stand to be separated from their unknown benefactor for a while. The Belegs began to meet again, as peers this time. The camaraderie that stemmed from their earlier feeling of kinship was being replaced. The feelings of belonging that they mutually needed and took from each other were shifting to the maternal instincts of a new parent. There was no animosity towards each other, but there was no longer the level of understanding that there once was. Each Beleg began to associate themselves with their original element again. Their new meetings more closely resembled the first times that they saw each other, when they were unsure of each other, rather than the close supportive ring that they so recently were.

"The first meetings were to discuss the changes to the world. Chaos caused more problems than was at first noticed. Amongst age and decay there was magic. With the mixing of the elements came chaos, with chaos came possibility, with possibility came magic. The Yavens may control any element that is a part of them. They have greater and lesser degrees of control, individually speaking. Since the Belegs are of each element, they could manipulate their environment at will. They had difficulty in understanding the derlian's helplessness at first. Until they realized how powerless they were in the face of all of the constant chaos. The first derlians could not manipulate anything. They were caught up in the catastrophic change, the task of surviving, the building of shelter. They built houses and culture, to shelter from the storms of the land and the storms of themselves. It was not until the second generation began to pass through adolescence that magic was found. With magic, the derlians began to gain some ground, to prosper. Though, since magic is born of chaos, it is ephemeral. But this advantage was enough to turn the tide." Clerin was not as naturally gifted in magic as she would have wished. She supposed she knew enough about it to speak of it in a story. Her family was related to the monarchy, and she had received a full and excellent education. She, however, did not know enough about it to explain the intricacies of it to an audience. To a knowledgeable audience, at that. Sometimes it seemed as if Clerin was the only non-practitioner that she knew. This, unfortunately, made her quicken the pace of this section of her story a bit.

"The discovery of magic led to many more discoveries. The more we learned of it, the more we learned about our world, and the more we learned of ourselves and our surroundings, the more we learned of magic. The growth was, and still is, exponential. Each previous discovery leading to the next. It was not long before the derlians made the most shocking discovery that they could imagine. They discovered the Yavens. First there was some communication.

Then it was found that under the correct circumstances and willpower, a Yaven could be summoned to this realm. At first they could only be summoned into a 'solid' portion of their own element. Protected from every other element by being surrounded by their own. This made the Belegs nervous, more nervous than magic alone had made them. And rightly so." Clerin flashed a sinister smile to the audience. A quiet, maniacal grin, showing her fine white teeth. Then gone, as quickly as it had come.

"They began to meet more frequently. They helped the Yavens to make themselves *sticky* enough to bring some of the Void with them, to protect them from the constantly warring elements that we have here. For it was found that service on our world could reap rewards in their own home realm. Each time a Yaven is summoned here, they could take a small piece of a different element back with them to their realm. They make Menels with their collected elements. The Menel acts as a sort of declaration of experience. Understanding not only of their own element, but of the foreign ones as well." Clerin strode to the front of the stage, hunching her back to make it appear as if she was stalking something. "So if you see a Yaven wandering our fair land, remember that it is not just on an errand for the one who summoned it. But that it is on an errand for itself as well. Becoming more and more like a Beleg, gaining in experience and imagination through their servitude." Clerin flashed another sinister smile to the young ones at the front of the audience, just for dramatic effect.

"There was one last meeting before the Belegs were never to see each other again. They met in the Northern Desert, that which separates our lands and the lands of the Pyrans. Which separates the Gaens from the Luftens. They met in the middle of our world." Clerin felt the end of the story coming. She could see the end coming near. She felt elated, ecstatic. All the worry, all of the preparation, everything that had led her up to this point, was now falling behind. She was about to complete her first Telling. She could not really compare the feeling to anything that she had felt before. This was something foreign to Clerin, and she wished to savor it. Whether the audience would cheer or boo, praise or slander, did not mean as much to Clerin as she first had thought it would. Just the feeling of completion, that of accomplishment, was enough for her right now. Her grin beamed into the audience as she began the last part of her story.

"The Belegs were not really there, not physically. For though they could be anywhere in our world because they are of all elements, they were not real. They were ethereal." Clerin felt herself blush briefly. She had worked over this part in her mind, over and over, and even though she had felt uncomfortable with her description, it had seemed more correct than what she found herself saying. She silently chastised herself for relaxing her rigor this close to the end. She found herself skipping parts of her rehearsed speech to keep the continuity in line. "The meeting had been called by Lembin and she addressed them all when the last of them arrived. 'I have come to a decision,' her voice flowed clearly through the dry thin air. 'I have decided to work with, and help, the Fluen derlians exclusively. I think I have figured a way to communicate with them directly, without the use of dreams. I feel there is more that I may accomplish here, in this world. I have decided to take up permanent solid residence amongst my derlians. I wish my derlians to not only gain an expertise of the world and the realms, but to cultivate them into a society. Into a collective that works together, with each of its individual parts working towards a common good, a common goal. I intend to give that to them by being in constant communication with them.' 'Then you are a fool!' " Clerin spat the sentence out, pinching her face and gesticulating wildly at the crowd. She tried to convey the instant argument that erupted physically, as well as verbally. She, however, did not truly know what the argument consisted of, only its outcome.

"The other three Belegs united against Lembin in their shock and disdain of her plan. They did not understand her reasoning and felt it was an unnecessary risk. They left her, alone in the desert, with only her foolishness to keep her company. She had done her best to persuade them, at least one of them, that she was not crazy, but to no avail. So she returned to us. She opened up communications with many of the most skilled Fluen mages in existence, through their dreams. They envisioned a mighty Temple, under the ocean, that should be built. They convinced others to help. Soon the massive structure was built, half under water, half above it. In the deepest depths of the Temple, the mages gathered. There were thirteen of our most powerful mages that we had at that time. They entered the water to their necks, wading above the great Chamber of Lembin, and cast the greatest magic of their lives. Lembin was willing, almost desperate, to have this accomplished. She helped them build the energy in themselves and in the Temple. No Beleg can be captured against their will, but even with the greatest desire emanating from them, it was still next to impossible. The thirteen were slain, one by one, by the force of the magic that they were invoking. No one knows exactly what killed them. When the great mages' acolytes entered the antechamber, they found the thirteen bodies floating in the salt water. They scoured the area for a sign of their masters' success, but found no immediate signs. It was several days before the custodians of the Temple began to feel *impressions*. It took several more to figure out that it was Lembin, attempting to communicate with us. It took cycles to glean our society, the advances in farming, herding, architecture, magic, and, of course, our History, from Lembin. It was only after our advances that the other Belegs realized the benefits of Temples." Clerin felt as though she would collapse, but made sure that even her smile did not slip in the slightest.

"The tale I have told is old. The span of it is the span of time itself. No tale may be told before this. All other tales are merely an extension of it, continuing along time. Only when you know and understand the beginning can you continue until the end. It is with this gift that I end." Clerin's grin seemed to be bursting through her entire face. It consumed her cheeks and threatened her eyes. She felt thin and weary, but she felt larger and greater than she had ever felt before. It was not until the crowd erupted into applause that tears began to stream down her face, into her grin, leaving the taste of salt water in her mouth. She had done it, she had made it. She could not conceive of a more ecstatic moment. She raised her hands over her head and bowed deeply, running her hands past her legs to rest parallel to her body. She held herself for a count of three, straightened, turned, raised her hands and bowed again. She bowed in the four directions, turned towards the door that she had entered by, and began her slow procession off of the stage. The noise was deafening. The echoes swirled around her chaotically, immersing her in sound. She felt as if she would drown. Her lungs heaved gasps of breath into them. The air itself seemed to be shaking so much with the vibrating sound that she was having problems breathing it in. She kept her face towards the door out, her exit, and made herself put one leg in front of another. She had always wondered why derlians walked offstage slowly, while they walked onstage quickly. She had assumed that it was to bask in the frenzy of the audience. There was nothing in the world that she wanted more than to stand there on an island amidst cheering waters all around, nothing in the world. That was not what slowed her down, however. She knew now what it was, though she could not name it. There was a certain deliciousness to her lack of energy, to the thickness of the air, to the difficulty she was having in walking a straight line. She had spent herself, truly spent herself. There were just no more reserves of energy in her at all. She could not run if there were a hundred Pyrans behind her with swords. She could honestly say that she had never felt better in all of her life.

She finally passed through the door, the applause thundering across her back. She walked over to where her father was waiting, hands outstretched, and collapsed into him. She felt completely beat.

"That was wonderful, derling, better than I, if you can believe that." Her father's smile could be felt through the top of her head. As a child, she had always hated when he had said that— "derling." He was always making the worst jokes. She felt oddly comforted by it now, though, almost nostalgic. He stood there and hugged her, until she had her fill. When she felt like she could walk again, Clerin pulled away from her father and smiled, the tears not quite leaving her eyes. He beamed back at her. "You've always made me so proud. You'll have to retell it to your mother, you know." He was still holding her shoulders, gripping her lightly with his large hands.

"She's already heard me tell it, dozens of times. She still has to see me perform." Clerin knew that she would act it out again for her mother. She would try to recreate all of the nuances of her performance and probably take twice as long doing it here, for real. Clerin's thoughts drifted for a brief moment to her mother's face. She seemed to be saying something.

"I won't say that you told the Histories better than I did, but you did amazingly well." Clerin's sister slid past her father's arms and gave Clerin a large hug. "You did great, I mean it." She ruffled Clerin's hair, and stepped back turning smiles from Clerin to their father. Clerin could barely keep her own grin from splitting her face. She thought that she must look like a crazed lunatic with oversized eyes, hair all akimbo and a ghoulish mouth grinning from ear to ear. Her sister looked at the roof, to the sky beyond, and said, "We should begin our trek back through the rain before it gets much worse."

"Actually. Actually, I was thinking that I could walk home alone. You know, to ground out a little." It was not their main house they were heading to, here this close to the sea, but a stately townhouse they used during their city excursions. Clerin smiled up at them and waved her hand ever so slightly in front of her. "I'll meet you at the house, in a little while."

"Please, do not take too long, Clerin. We have a special dinner waiting for you. We will have a celebration of your Telling with our closest friends and relatives. And, as the guest of honor, you will have to be charming and elegant. So, if you end up in the rain too long, you should come in through the back and dry up before your appearance." Her father kissed her on the forehead, stood back, and nodded to her. Her sister gave her another squeeze and a whispered good-bye. Clerin smiled at them as they opened the door to leave. She let them get a distance ahead of her before she left through the same door.

Chapter 3

There were two types of Luftens in the city of Ariellyna, as there were two cities. One living and working aloft in the giant Helioarc trees, the other stuck fast to the ground. As aware as Vrric was of this, he was even more aware of which category he belonged to. Mudfoot. That was the word that most often rung in Vrric's ears as he trod along the forest floor, head down, watching the ground so that he wouldn't stub a toe. But not this day. Well, not this moment at least. He was sitting at the base of an alder, avoiding the giant Helioarc trees that the Airborn Luftens built their cities in. He was sitting at one of the rare ones that did not directly abut the stream, thus keeping the mud to a minimum. Vrric liked the feeling of the bark through his thin shirt. Most of the Groundborn avoided trees all together. Some even made their houses out of a special mud mixed with ash, fired in a giant kiln to make bricks. They would even use grasses for their roofs so that they could avoid wood. Vrric, however, enjoyed the feeling of the trees. He would often in his youth climb the smaller trees and pretend he could fly. In truth he could still be called a youth, since he had yet to take his Trivaste tests. But he would soon, very soon. Vrric was a skinny Luften, which are known for their willowy stature already. His length was lanky where others were lithe. His muscles were taught ropes keeping his bones from knocking around in his skin. He stumbled often and talked too fast. His green eyes held the shimmer of an emerald when he spoke. His short black hair had so many cowlicks in the back that he always looked as if he had just gotten up from bed. His long hands were heavily callused with the last few sun cycles of working as a blacksmith's apprentice and he often wondered when he would bulk up into the mass of muscles that his mentor was. It had certainly not happened yet.

As he leaned against the alder, he let his mind wander through the wishes of childhood for a while more. He was on an errand for Kaihlu, his mentor. He was to take a message to the ironworkers for some more stock. Twenty-two strips to be made into swords, fifteen rounds for plates, ten pegs for shoeing the horses, six short strips for making daggers, and one giant ingot. Vrric was not really sure what the ingot was for, but he memorized the list before setting out to the workers' shop. Kaihlu would always write the list down and insist that Vrric take the workers the list. Many of the ironworkers were illiterate though, and Vrric hated to read in front of them like some pompous Airborn. So he took to memorizing the list and burning it in the forge fires before leaving. This had, unfortunately, caused one or two errors in the past, but he felt that he memorized it better if he burned the list. Vrric thought the list to himself once more then let his mind wander back into the past for a while longer.

He was thinking back to his parents, back to when he could remember them. To the one real memory he had of them. It seemed odd to Vrric that his memories seemed to fade into a dark fog about his childhood, especially since he took such pride in his recall nowadays. He would sometimes spend hours fishing for old memories. Casting back his mind to the oldest things that he could think of, which weren't really things, but more like impressions. Maybe even just impressions of feelings, with a small portrait to flit past his brain with the impression attached. There is one that he usually started with. Bushes. Something about bushes that he just could not fully recall. It was a good feeling, a safe feeling. He wasn't really sure if the portrait changed over the years, or if he saw the same split second scene every time. He was sitting with his back to something smooth. He was looking straight ahead. He could not feel the dirt around his bottom, but he could around his legs. There were certain things that he knew about the impression, and he felt that it was the oldest one that he had been able to call up. So this was his embankment, where he would stand and fish. Attempting to cast farther and farther each time. Unfortunately, he seemed to habitually cast upstream. Not about his parents, though. None of his earliest impressions contained anybody. It seemed to Vrric that he had always been alone, even when surrounded by other Luftens. No, there was only one memory that Vrric could faithfully call up about his parents. They are smiling. They are definitely happy, enjoying themselves. They are waving goodbye. They are in a carriage, on the ground, and they are waving. Vrric cannot remember them entering the carriage, cannot remember anything leading up to that moment. Nor can he remember who is holding him. He remembers feeling tall, feeling like he was floating, and he is sure that he is being held. Held up to see his parents riding away. Yes, they still look happy.

Vrric opened his eyes again, letting his self-pity ride into the distance, waving. Looking at the sun askance through the trees, he realized just how much time he had spent fishing. He leapt up and began his run. His eyes were on the ground, watching. His mind, however, was chanting. "Quick feet, swift feet, fast feet, fly. Let time stand still and watch me go by." Vrric always felt that the drone of his mind could keep him from being tired, from slowing at all. In no time at all, Vrric had reached the ironworkers and placed Kaihlu's order with them. He then ran back as fast as he could, so Kaihlu would not think him a shirker. Truly, if it wasn't for Kaihlu, Vrric would probably still be stealing food, beating up smaller boys and dodging the larger ones. Kaihlu had definitely changed Vrric's course in life. Learning how to beat a shapeless lump into something useful was priceless, but what Vrric really loved was liquid metal. Something inside of Vrric got called to whenever he watched molten metal pouring into a mold. And as it got called it came, pushing against his chest, crawling and squirming, seeking escape from him. However, it, along with Vrric, was trapped.

As Vrric reached the edge of the town, and the scattered huts started to line up in rows, he made sure he could recall the trade that the iron workers had insisted upon. It had seemed a little high for the items that Kaihlu had ordered. Vrric slowed down to a jog, then a walk, as he neared the smithy. Making sure that his breath was inaudible and even, he opened the large wooden front doors. Held to the carved stone building with giant, filigreed steel bands, they were the only wooden part of the structure besides the roof. After closing the doors he glanced quickly at the forge before heading into the back, jumping over the small stream that flowed through a small sluiceway in the floor of the building. There was a stone slab crossing the water just a few feet away but Vrric always liked to leap over it if he could. He walked to the opposite wall and through the archway to Kaihlu's office area. A large oaken desk rested itself in the far corner, with Kaihlu's back receiving all guests. Vrric politely coughed to make sure that Kaihlu was just finishing up his paperwork.

"Ah, Vrric. You seem to get faster every day." Though Vrric was unable to see his mentor's face, he could see the smile in his mind. Big and toothy. Vrric paused a moment to reflect on how apt of a description that was for Kaihlu, big and toothy.

"Maybe I'm practicing for the messenger Trivaste tests." Vrric smiled into Kaihlu's back. He could not imagine testing for anything besides smithing. Pounding metal seemed to be the only real skill that he had. It was certainly the only guild branch that he had any training in.

"That you may, Vrric. You never know what you will be gifted in. I would not mind, however, continuing to teach you, you know." Kaihlu tilted his head back, glancing a smile off of him. "You have a lust for knowledge. An unashamed lust." Vrric's cheeks pulled up in response to his mentor's brashness. They grew a little pink at his gratuitous flattery as well. Kaihlu lived a very gratuitous life. He was kind, loving, and full of life.

"The iron workers seemed a bit stingy today. I could not get them to drop below a hundred and twenty heads." Since the last few kings had died so quickly, Luftens had begun to call their money "heads" instead of by the ruling king's proper name. Poor King Hulgert inherited the throne at the ripe age of one-hundred and forty-seven. His father had held the throne for too long, but his older brothers for too short. One could only hope that Hulgert could reign longer than Islen, the middle child.

"Fine, fine. They have been giving me the finest of their ware of late, I shan't begrudge them a little profit every once in a while." Kaihlu finally rested his quill, turned from his books, and looked at Vrric. "You did get everything on the list, yes?"

"Of course, they were very quick about it." Vrric glanced at the shadows on the barren west wall. He was not gone for too long, he surmised. He wondered what Kaihlu was getting at, briefly. "They said they would have the wagon here by tomorrow evening, to drop it all off."

"Good. You did well. Will you be needing your study week off?" Kaihlu turned back to his books, blowing down upon the ink.

"Yes, if it is not too much trouble." Vrric doubted he would study much, but it was an excellent excuse for a week off.

It was the day of the Trivaste tests. Vrric awoke refreshed and invigorated on this, his first cycle that he was allowed to take them. There were five sun cycles that a Luften could choose to take tests. You could even take the same test cycle after cycle until you performed so well that you received the offer you wanted. Vrric, however, did not need to concern himself with offers. He knew that Kaihlu would offer him a job and knew that the wages would be competitive. He surely doubted that another smith was vying to steal him away from Kaihlu with the promise of higher wages. Even if that happened, Vrric doubted he would accept a higher offer that would take him away from the forge that he had apprenticed at. Kaihlu took him in when no one else would.

Vrric had decided to try to take his test as early as possible. There were three rounds of smithy tests during the morning, and he wanted to get into the first round. Then he could have plenty of time to find a good spot to watch the parades. The mornings of the Trivaste tests were always taken up with seriousness. You could only take the one test that you have apprenticed for, the one you have a sponsor for, to gain entry into a Guild Branch. And the morning tests were much longer than any of the afternoon tests, those tests that anyone can take without sponsorship or expertise. The streets were sparse of Luftens and quiet with concentration in the mornings. Afterwards, however, the parades began and you could take whatever test you desired. There were a few afternoon tests that Vrric had been thinking about taking as a lark, but so far he had been just planning on watching the parades.

Vrric had always enjoyed the parades ever since he could remember. Every guild that had a presence near Ariellyna would put on a demonstration of their particular craftwork and parade through the town with it. Though much of Ariellyna was built high up in the helioarc trees, the vast majority of the parades were walked low along the ground. The best viewing was usually the low balconies that encircled the helioarc's giant trunks. The stairs for each tree were always filled with late-comers, doing what they could to gain a little height. To look down upon the second city from the low branches of the first. Last cycle, Vrric was on Kaihlu's wagon as it rumbled through the parade. They had small braziers and foot-pedaled bellows to get the iron hot enough to strike it. Though they had melted everything down that they had banged out that day, due to the shoddy quality that was induced from the swaying platform of a wagon, Kaihlu stated that the advertising value alone was worth it. And, indeed, the shop was full of orders for a full moon after the tests. For Vrric, however, the worth of the parade was just that he had been in it. He could not forget the feeling of looking up at all of the faces beaming down at him, all the waving and the cheering. It felt as if the parade was for him, not that he was just a small part of it, a tiny cog in a wheel. It had made him feel special, like he belonged to a Royal Branch. He planned on making the other participants feel special by cheering and waving for them this cycle, rather than just smiling silently upon the passing participants as he had done in the past.

Kaihlu had already left by the time that Vrric was ready. Not only was he going to help oversee the morning smithy tests, but he had even forgone his post in the parade to help with the less formal afternoon tests. It was definitely going to be a busy day for the both of them. There was a certain quietness about not having Kaihlu take him to the test and almost a little sadness. Vrric had decided to get as much rest as possible, however, in lieu of traveling with a companion. The preparations to oversee a test were involved enough that Kaihlu had already been gone for almost two hours.

The road to Ariellyna proper and the smithy tests was mercifully short. Kaihlu's forge was at the river's edge for many various reasons, but it was also close enough to the city to quickly carry heavy loads overland. Vrric arrived for his test invigorated, not tired out, by his walk. He arrived such that there were enough apprentices in front of him that he did not feel desperate, but he was still easily in the first group test and would not have to wait. It was perfect.

It continued to be perfect. All his tests went smoothly and without error. He was not nervous or high-strung, nor was he sloppy or lackadaisical. Each individual task segued into the next so smoothly that each test seemed to flow into one another like water being poured from cup to cup. Even at rest Vrric's mind hammered away at what he knew would come up next: how to best overcome the following challenge. Then, almost suddenly, it was over.

Kaihlu was busy with other apprentices, but paused long enough to give Vrric a huge grin and large wave. That was what seemed most odd about the experience. He had, he felt, given an extraordinary performance during the tests. Vrric could feel it through any Luften who glanced at him. His peers emanated envy, while his betters emanated admiration. More than any external source, however, Vrric knew that he had done wonderfully. Every hammer strike had felt fluid and natural. Nothing jarred or skittered the entire time he worked the anvil. Each time he pulled a piece of steel from the forge, it had a vibrant white glow on the section to be shaped, the bright red on either side framing the striking point. He did not even think that he breathed heavily throughout the tests. But no other mentor was going to give him an offer. No other smith so much as approached him. Kaihlu smiled brightly, but did not need to rush over and give congratulations either. If Vrric had thrown the hammer into the audience or burned another apprentice, Kaihlu would have still, most probably, given him a job offer. Probably at the same rate even. The tests were a foregone conclusion and no matter that he performed exceptionally. Nothing would have been different if he had performed poorly. It was in this odd mood, one of pride mixed with a baseless mediocrity, that he decided to wander.

After quite some time of wandering aimlessly, Vrric glanced upwards and slowed. He was in an unknown portion of Ariellyna, and a platform placed low to the ground with a wide stairway up to it caught his eye. Truly, Vrric thought, *it is only during the Trivaste festival that I get to make my feet leave the ground.* He began to smile unconsciously, almost trotting to the wide first stair. He stopped briefly upon reaching that bottom step. Resting a hand on the wooden rail he began a measured ascent to the platform. The huge branches stretched out over the crowd walking on the forest floor. They were like arms radiating outwards from the trunk where the platform encircled. Branching continually towards the air. Vrric smiled at the beautiful giant and was thankful for being able to walk up into the magnificent tree. He turned to the edge of the platform, near the next stairway up away from the landing, and looked out over the other Luftens walking on the ground. It was a beautiful rainless day and the street was hard packed and solid. The Luftens were making good time since they did not have to battle the mud, and Vrric thought about the timing of the tests. The parade would be next to impossible to perform during the rainy season. Looking out at the derlians bustling to the first of the afternoon tests made Vrric want to raise up to the next platform. *Maybe from up there*, Vrric thought, *I can see if the parade is starting to come through soon.* Turning from his vantage point, Vrric jogged up the next circling flight of steps.

When he reached the top of the second platform, he immediately noticed the group of young Luftens milling about. Vrric skirted the edge of the group, to rest his elbows upon the railing overlooking the street. He overheard several comments about the upcoming test and passively eavesdropped the constant chatter around him. It was the pointless chatter of the nervous, more of the letting off of some pressure than any real conversation. Vrric was beginning to become at ease with the buzzing atmosphere when he noticed a coalescing of adults at the doorway into a small guild testing hall. He smiled lazily at them and glanced again towards the ground as they fanned out amongst the young Luftens. Soon the call to begin the testing was ushered through the crowd and the adolescents began to shuffle inside. Vrric watched from the rail as the crowd began to disperse.

"Hey you. Yes, you." Vrric was surprised to find one of the adults speaking directly at him. "Are you coming in or staying out?" The question took Vrric off guard. He did not think that he looked like he belonged there, but the voice seemed insistent.

"Well, I was just…" Vrric's voice trailed into a quiet uneasy whisper.

"We don't have all day. Are you coming in or staying out?" The older Luften's voice began to take on an edge of irritation, and before Vrric really realized, he was answering.

"Of course. I'm sorry to waste your time…" It began to fade into a whisper again as Vrric shuffled towards the open door. He almost voiced another "I was just…" but it was just his lips moving. Just before his bowed head entered the darkened cool interior, he noticed what guild this test was for. It was the Mage's Branch.

Vrric headed towards the back of the room, where there was an empty desk beckoning from the corner. Vrric had always liked being next to walls in an unfamiliar place. There were several mages standing along the walls, ringing the room, but all eyes were on the five mages standing at the head of the room near the door. These were the mages who administered the tests, stern faces with sour looks on them, and as they glared at Vrric and the others he wondered why he had come into this room. He did not even know what their tests entailed. He had meant to watch the parade.

"During the various tests a mage will tap you on the shoulder for your outside testing. Since this can only be done one at a time, the rest of you will continue uninterrupted. Now for the first skill assessment." The small mage in the middle spoke first. After her announcement, the two mages on her left went over to the young derlian closest to the door that they had all entered through and tapped him on the shoulder. All three went outside. The three remaining mages began to pass out candlesticks to each of the prospective students.

When it came to Vrric's turn to receive a candlestick, the female mage spoke again. "When you receive your lit candle you shall concentrate upon the flame growing larger. When you feel that you have raised it as high as you can, raise your hand and a mage will check your flame." There were already Derlians with their hand in the air by the time she had finished her short speech.

"Lodepiarc!" The word was so soft that Vrric was not quite sure that he had heard it. The candle in front of him, however, must have for it immediately sprang forth a flame. Vrric tried to get out a "thank you" before the mage left, but they were already wandering towards a raised hand. Vrric, instead, decided to concentrate upon the flame.

He waited until it had spent its first incendiary fuel and began to burn off of the wax. Vrric then placed his hands, palms down, on the table to either side of the candle. He stared into the flame as he exhaled slowly through his nose. He felt a warm tingle begin in his abdomen. In his excitement he almost stopped concentrating. With each exhale, he tried to bring the tingle up farther. It crept up his chest and expanded through his lungs. With each inhale he could feel his abdomen more, as if he were more aware of it. The tingle began grow larger, to feel more insistent. Much like that of a leg fallen numb because it has been crossed over the other for too long. When the numbness slips away like night at dawn, then the tingles begin. The pins and needles get so powerful that most will stamp their feet to bring the hapless limb back under control. This is what the tingles began to feel like to Vrric. On the verge of pain. He kept bringing them further up with each exhale. The tingle in his lips grew so powerful that his head began to shake slightly. The flame turned into a blur of yellow, smeared through sweat or tears, Vrric was unsure of which. Or maybe it was his eyes themselves which were failing to work properly. The yellow overtook his sight while he was concentrating on moving the tingle. With each breath Vrric could feel his body vibrate more. With each breath he could feel the pins and needles making their way through his body. With each breath he became less and less aware of his surroundings, the other derlians, the rustling of mages' robes, the fact that he was even taking a test. Until a robe stepped directly into his peripheral vision.

"Do you wish a measurement? We are ready to pair up for the next challenge. Do not worry, that is a nice long flame you have there." The mage's robes rustled quietly as he held a stick next to the flame and marked the height. The voice was soft yet insistent. It pierced through Vrric's meditative trance quickly, but comfortably.

"Yes, yes, of course, the next challenge." Vrric smiled up weakly, but the mage had already turned away. By the time the mage returned, carefully carrying a shallow pan filled with water, a young Luften had sat down across from Vrric. The Luften was almost as large as Vrric, which was remarkable because so many in the room were much smaller. He was young, with blonde hair feathered to one side of his face. The face seemed soft, almost plush, but the dark brown eyes stared unflinchingly into Vrric.

"So. Who is your mentor?" The voice was deep and sharp. Each word in the small sentence was clipped, as if for emphasis. The result was that each word had the same clipped respect built into it, as if each word were equal, emphasizing nothing.

"I don't have a mentor. I'm really not sure what I am doing here." The small laugh that Vrric let out at the end of his retort was because the stranger's face lit into a huge smile.

"Then I have picked the correct seat. My name is Lushgoe. My lineage is through the Ineare Branch." Lushgoe's voice stopped dead at the word "branch." He stared at Vrric with impassive dark eyes, waiting. The mage that had brought the pan returned with two corks.

"I am Vrric. I, ah, don't have any lineage…" Vrric had trailed his voice off with shame, like a hair curling away from the heat of the fire. The mage placed the corks in the water at each end of the pan.

"Each of you must, using only your will, push your cork to the opponents side of the pan while deflecting the oncoming cork. Whoever reaches the other side first gains credit for this round." The mage looked at Lushgoe, who nodded, then turned to Vrric. "Are you ready?" Vrric did not know what to do, so he nodded. "Then begin."

Vrric tried to bring his mind back to the state it was in during the candle challenge. He slowed his breathing, tried to become conscious of it, and blew air out of his mouth slowly and forcefully. He kept conscious of not actually just blowing on the cork, however. He did not want to be accused of cheating. Vrric imagined his breath as a gust of wind pressing upon a tiny cork ship. He imagined a full sail raising out of the cork and popping taught against his breath. To his amazement the cork began to move. Attempting to stay calm through his excitement, Vrric tried to take larger and quicker inhales so that he could push all of the air out as forcefully and continually as he could.

To his utter surprise it seemed as if his cork was going to reach the halfway point before Lushgoe's. As the corks slowly raced across the pan Vrric noticed that Lushgoe's cork was heading straight for Vrric's. Vrric tried to make the imaginary sail on the cork tack against the wind slightly, so as to alter its course. He was thinking that a collision would slow his cork down, and he was trying to dash for the other side. The cork was extremely slow to respond, however, and the corks barely tapped together.

Vrric immediately got the worst headache that he had ever had in his life. It seared into his forehead, between his eyes, with a thumping clanging feeling. He watched in horror as his cork ricocheted almost all the way back to his side of the pan. Lushgoe's seemed to hardly move backwards at all and was immediately pushing for Vrric's side of the pan again. Vrric tried to regain his concentration, to regain his focus. He closed his eyes and tried to bring his breathing back under control. The headache was dimming slightly and he could almost get his abdomen starting to tingle again when Lushgoe's cork reached his side of the pan.

"That was an excellent attempt. You had an impressive amount of momentum built up very quickly." Lushgoe was extending his hand out towards Vrric. As Vrric shook hands his headache began to clear.

"What was it that you did to me?" Vrric had meant to say something else, but his head was still cloudy.

"Don't worry, it won't effect you for the rest of the challenges. Sorry I had to resort to that, but I can't lose, you understand. Listen, to make the cork sink, don't just throw raw energy at it, though you seem to be good at that. Build it up in it. Contain it all in that tiny cork. That will sink it faster than trying to push it down." With that Lushgoe stood and placed his hand over his cork and closed his eyes. The cork made a small popping noise as it sunk under the surface of the water. The dark eyes smiled briefly at Vrric before they turned and left. The mage then turned expectantly towards Vrric.

Vrric placed his hand over the cork and closed his eyes as Lushgoe had done. He began his breathing slowly. This time he tried to bring the tingle through his shoulder and found that it flowed easily towards his hand. Vrric imagined the tiny cork as a ship again, it seemed easiest since he had been thinking of it like that already. He built up the energy in his hand and imagined it as water pouring into the ship. He imagined the bottom hull as tight and secure, the walls as solid and impenetrable, and he imagined it filling with water from his hand. The popping noise came as unexpected as the tap on his shoulder.

The mage that had brought the pan and corks over smiled at Vrric and nodded towards another mage to Vrric's right. It was the second mage that had his hand on Vrric. The mage's voice was light and springy.

"Good job. Good job. Now if you will just step away with me we can cover air real quick." The mage tugged Vrric towards the door that he had come in. They walked out of the room into the blinding sun. Vrric squinted briefly and tried to take in his surroundings.

"You may sit or kneel, or even stand if you wish. Whatever is more comfortable for you. Then you must call forth the wind and we will judge its speed and the distance from whence it traveled." The mage tossed one arm casually upon the railing and stood watching and waiting on Vrric.

Vrric decided to sit more to give his mind some time to rest and take everything in rather than it being any more comfortable. Everything had been happening so fast that he had had no time at all to ponder what he was even doing here.

Sitting, with the weight of the mage's stare upon him, Vrric closed his eyes and tried to calm his breathing. He had no clue as to what he was really doing. He was merely trying to repeat the serendipitous feeling he had found while staring at the candle flame. This was the third… no, the fourth different challenge so far, and he had only one trick. One that he had learned just recently.

At first he was inhaling quickly and exhaling with much force. In his mind, however, he began to wonder if he was not pushing the wind in the wrong way. He tried to ignore it but this worry began to eke into his consciousness. Vrric's eyes began to flutter, letting in shards of daylight. How was he supposed to know what to do? Why was he even here? Vrric's mind began to shift and race randomly. He was losing his concentration. A sudden thought stopped him though. What if he would flare his energy when inhaling? Could he draw a wind from far away towards him by sucking energy in? Vrric re-closed his eyes and concentrated on breathing inwards. The tingling feeling began again in his abdomen. Vrric kept his outer self calm and kept repeating images of trees bending towards him with the wind. The leaves shaking with energy, branches bending towards him, small branches snapping off into the vortex. Vrric's mind was a maelstrom of wind as he drew in as much energy as he could. Finally, exhausted, Vrric opened his eyes again.

"Excellent. Quick work." The mage muttered something under his breath and the wind died completely. "Come, I must switch you out with another hopeful." Vrric followed the mage inside and sat at a different table than before. There was a strange looking plant next to him. "Good luck." And with those words and a conspiratorial pat on the back, the mage was gone.

Vrric turned his attention on the plant in front of him. It was a seedling, with four small leaves peeling open from the top. It was green with a whitish stem. The pot it was held in was brimming with soil and much too large for the scrawny plant. Vrric had no clue as to what to do with the plant so he started to look around at the other Luftens in the room. Several had huge plants in front of them, some had smaller ones. As Vrric continued to look around he watched as one Luften's plant grew right before his eyes. At last he understood what he was supposed to do during this challenge.

As Vrric closed his eyes and raised energy he imagined sunny, well-irrigated fields. He felt the dichotomy of hot and cold, dry and wet, the dichotomy that life must feed upon. He peeked open with one eye and saw that his plant was slowly growing. He resolved not to look again until he could feel the plant under his chin.

It seemed to take hours. Vrric sat there with his eyes closed, concentrating. Waiting, in the back of his mind, for a touch. Breathing, tingling, and imagining. Over and over. Finally, when Vrric could no longer take the wait, he opened his eyes again.

The plant had grown at least seven times its original size. Unfortunately, when Vrric looked around, there where many taller plants sitting in front of different Luftens. He was feeling frustrated when he raised his hand for a mage to measure and take away the plant. He could not seem to get it to grow any more than he already had. His newly awakening confidence began to shrivel under the thought that he was no match for all of these Luftens. After all, they had had training and mentors while Vrric had learned the art of shaping metal. And not with his mind either, but with his hands.

The mage that had wandered off with his plant came back with a rod of metal and three crucibles. One crucible was three times the size of the other two. As the mage placed them down and he started to turn and walk away, Vrric lightly tugged upon his sleeve.

"Please, what am I supposed to be doing here?" Vrric had meant to phrase the question differently. To ask what this particular challenge was or maybe ask for a hint of how to accomplish the challenge. Vrric's mind betrayed his growing nervousness.

"Melt the metal into the crucible. Then separate it into the heavy metal and the light metal." As he spoke he pointed to the various crucibles in front of Vrric. Though Vrric did not think that it mattered, he made a mental note of which crucible the mage had motioned to for the heavy metal and which the mage had indicated for light.

"Thank you. Very much." Vrric stared at the small metal rod with consternation. All of the other challenges seemed to be at least doable to him. This one seemed to reek of nonsense. There was no way that he could just melt a chunk of iron, not without a good forge. Vrric reached out a tentative hand to the rod. With an unconscious gasp he lifted the rod up to his face for inspection. This was certainly not iron. It felt as light as a feather. He had never before seen a metal this incredibly light. He tapped it lightly upon the edge of the table to listen to the ring. It was very high pitched but was such a soft and quick sound that Vrric almost did not notice it. He scored it with a fingernail and marked it. As he studied the tiny rod he noticed that he could see the two different metals. There was a cast line. It was faint but obvious to someone used to looking for it, straight down the middle of the rod. Vrric then took his fingernail and scribed the surface of the rod along its cast line. After he had gone around three times he felt that he had enough of a demarcation line.

Vrric pulled the two small crucibles in front of him. Placing them side-by-side, he placed the rod over them with his fingers prying at the cast line. He began his breathing and concentration. He let the tingle build up in his palms for some time. It took all of his concentration to keep it from slipping into his fingers, but he controlled it. He built it up until he could no longer stand the pins and needles in his palms and then he let it go. With his mind, as he let the energy go, he imagined the rod splitting into two halves. In his mind it made a sharp snap and he could feel his hands lose resistance as they pulled apart. However, when he opened his eyes, he saw that the rod had melted and fallen into both of the small crucibles. There was even some metal cooling on the top of each of the crucibles, welding them together. Vrric, without thinking, brushed the liquid metal into the crucible on the right and let out a howl of pain. Everybody turned to look at him with his finger in his mouth.

Vrric was trying to think of why it had hurt him just now, but not earlier when he had melted the metal. He had been trying to pull them apart in the first place, not melt them. Now he would be unable to compare the weights of the two halves. Vrric decided to wait a moment before picking up the crucibles to check their relative weights. As he waited, another nameless mage walked over to his table, obviously waiting to take away the crucibles and bring the next unfathomable challenge. Vrric then picked up both crucibles, gave them a quick mental weighing, and handed the heavier one to the mage first.

"This one is the heavier one." Vrric smiled up at the mage in the hopes of a hint as to whether that was enough information. The mage, however, was very stoic and did not reply. Instead the mage pulled a small knife from his belt and placed it on the table before Vrric.

"I must see the cut before I let you heal it." The mage's voice seemed almost a whisper to Vrric, which did not make him feel any better. His stomach dropped slightly at the thought of what the mage was implying.

"You want me to cut myself?" The question popped out before Vrric could rein it in. The answer was obvious and would just make him look foolish in front of the mage. It took all of his strength to not ask how many more challenges were left. He could not even recall how many he had been through already, but he was getting ready to see the end of them.

"Do you need me to do it?" The way that the mage whispered made the question seem conspiratorial to Vrric. The last thing that Vrric wanted was for another Luften to cut him.

"No, no, I'm fine. Sorry to keep you." Vrric kept an ingratiating smile upon his lips as he reached for the small knife. He took the unsheathed blade and pressed it against his skin. The metal seemed cold enough to pull heat from his body. Vrric drew in a deep breath and slid the blade across his forearm.

"There! There you go." Vrric clumsily wiped the blade upon his shirt before handing the knife back to the mage.

"Very good. Once you show the scar to one of us, you may take a seat over there." The mage waved behind Vrric's right shoulder.

When Vrric briefly glanced over he saw most of the young Luftens already sitting facing the front of the room, waiting. The next series of challenges must occur to all of them simultaneously. Vrric turned his vision back to his arm and the small red line that was beading droplets of blood. He closed his eyes to concentrate. He felt that he knew what to do here, just bring the energy to the wound and concentrate on its healing. This is what he had been doing since his accidental beginning of these tests, it should have been easy. The burning pulse in his arm, however, kept his mind from keeping to the task. Every time that he would build up the energy, the throbbing in his arm made him lose the shape he was making it in his head. It would then slowly dissipate as he struggled to regain control.

When his frustration seemed to be getting the better of him Vrric decided to open his eyes and look at the wound. To his amazement it looked several days old. It was no longer weeping, and before his very eyes it turned into a thin red line. Now that he knew it was healing, the pain did not seem as incapacitating as it had before. Vrric again closed his eyes and began his breathing. In no time at all his arm started to feel better. He stole a moment with his eyes closed to wonder at these new skills. He knew that, in theory, anybody could *use* magic, but he had never dreamed that he would be able to make such a remarkable difference in so short a time. He had been cut many times before, why had he not healed them? He began to wonder if it was really him doing these things. As he did so, his arm began to throb again.

Vrric showed his arm to the mage that was wandering by and went to the tables facing the front of the room. Everyone seemed so quiet and calm. He turned his neck around to glance at some of the other Luftens' arms, but could not see much. After what seemed a silent eternity, a mage walked to the front of the room.

"You will be shown a series of objects. If you believe that the object was created with magic, raise your left hand. If you believe that the object is an illusion, raise your right hand. If you believe that the object is a natural one, then raise neither hand. The mages behind you will tally the results. This is the last challenge, and I wish all of you the very best." The mage's voice was that of a young luften, but the cowl had fallen to hide most of her face, making it impossible to visually verify her age. She seemed to quickly scan down the row of prospective students before walking towards a group of mages to Vrric's right.

"This is your first object." The same young mage walked back from the group of mages holding a sword. She held it high with both hands so that everyone could get a good look at it. She lightly tapped it upon the table. She swung it around with a flourish.

"You have five seconds to decide." She placed the sword's tip against the wooden floor with a small thunk. Vrric glanced around. Some had their right hands up, some their left, but most seemed to think that it was a real sword. Vrric kept his hands down but wondered how he would be able to tell something real from something illusionary. The young mage took the sword back to the group of mages and grabbed another item.

"This is your second object." She walked to the middle of the room with a lit lantern. The way it swung made the shadows dance crazily around the corners of the room. Vrric wondered if you could even make light come from something not real. He had decided that he would leave his hands down once more when he noticed something. It did not make a sound, which made the lantern seem somewhat eerie. The lantern swung from its handle back and forth. Vrric was sure that the hinge was metal rubbing against metal. He tried with all of his might to hear a squeak, but he could hear nothing.

"You have five seconds to decide." The mage held the lantern up high so that all could see. Vrric made his mind race to make a decision. Many others had hands up, but he could not really tell if they were left hands or right hands. In the last moment, Vrric let the eerie silence that he had felt be his guide and raised his right hand. The young mage brought the lantern back to the group and came forth with a piece of rope.

"This is your third object." She swung the rope around briefly before she came to rest in front of the room. She began tying knots in the rope. She would pull the ends tight and hold the rope up so all could see, and then she would begin tying another knot.

"You have five seconds to decide." As she repeated her tricks Vrric strained his eyes to see something, anything, out of the ordinary. Vrric could find nothing wrong with the rope, so he abstained from raising his hands. The mage returned her piece of rope and came back to the front of the room with a glowing stick.

"This is your fourth object." She held the stick aloft for a brief moment and then began to swing the stick back and forth. The glow seemed to follow the stick a little so that it seemed that there was a long glowing line in the air. Vrric knew that he must raise one of his hands but he was unsure as to which one.

"You have five seconds to decide." The mage stopped moving the stick and held it in front of her for all to see. There was a large rustle as each participant raised one of their hands. Vrric's mind raced but he could not come to a solid conclusion. Since he had yet to do so he decided to raise his left hand. The mage raised the stick and said, "The test is done. I hope that each one of you is chosen."

It was only after the final test that Vrric began to breath comfortably again. He did not think that he had ever concentrated so hard in his life. His head hurt, he felt fatigued, and his hands were incredibly shaky. He had to hold his hands together in front of him so that they would not give him away. But through it all, and especially now that the ordeal was over, he could not stop grinning. His cheeks hurt with the constant tension, but he could not relax his face. He noticed the other young Luftens filing out the door opposite of where they came in. He was in no hurry at all, so he let many of them slide their way in front of him. The others seemed to be in a rush to get through the door first, some of them getting physical with each other to claim the first spots in line. Vrric vaguely wondered if it was the order that you went through the door that denoted your ranking in the tests. He was shuffling forward at a snail's pace, trying to see into the unknown doorway, when he felt a hand on his back pushing on him.

"Hey, I can only go forward as fast as those in front of me." Vrric's angry voice snapped backwards across the line like a whip.

"Well hurry, the wizards are making their picks as we waste time in the testing room." A small and plaintive voice sounded from behind Vrric.

"Don't the judges need to confer, to score and rank all of the testers?" Vrric didn't understand how they could be making choices already. He technically had to wait until evening to find out how well he did in the smithy tests.

"Judges? The only judges here are the wizards. And most of them have already decided whom to pick. Nieces and nephews, old debts paid off, that sort of thing. We'll be lucky if we are even looked at. I tried to sit next to the exit door, I did. But I'm so small…" The non-corporeal voice behind him ranted. Vrric felt the urge to turn and look upon the dejected Luften, to see who seemed to know so much about the tests, but obviously did not have a sponsor awaiting him in the next room. Instead Vrric stopped, whipped around, and grabbed the little boy, though assuredly of testing age, and pushed the boy in front of him.

"There, you are ahead one more derlian at least." Vrric was not trying to be kind so much as quiet the pestering voice. While he had spun around he noticed that there was still a quarter of the Luftens left in line. Vrric had the sudden urge to stop and get in the back of the line. After all, what was he really doing here? Did he truly think that he could just change his mind as to what guild he wished to enter? And even if he did, if he were remotely that bold, what made him think that he had any talent? He had no skill, that was for sure. He had never even met a wizard, or a mage for that matter. He knew none of the tricks, none of the meditations, nothing about casting spells whatsoever. Therefore his only hope lay in talent. "Talent," what a conceitful word. How arrogant, how proud must you be to assume talent. Even the voice of shame in Vrric's head that resounded out loud, reverberating like a bell, even that voice did not stop Vrric. He did not step out of line, did not take the last position, as he should have if there were any fairness in the world. No, Vrric decided he was where he was. That was enough.

There was no thank you from in front. There was no voice at all from the front, not directed backwards at least. The boy that Vrric had let in front of him was now cajoling the poor Luften in front of him, and so on. To make matters worse, the boy behind Vrric began to cajole him. If he had known that his action would have brought an avalanche of voices behind him alive and clamoring, he would have left the first thankless youth behind him. But, "The future is never known until it is the past." Kaihlu's remembered voice wafted fondly amongst the cacophony behind Vrric. Grinning and exhausted, Vrric finally shuffled into the wizard's room.

It made Vrric think of the word "gauntlet." A gauntlet was invented to stop crime amongst the Luftens. A convicted criminal is run through a mob of citizens. These can be anyone, non-convicted criminals of course, who has the fiery volcanic urge to cause pain to a stranger. These Luftens line up along the Murderer's Way, a series of streets used in the gauntlet. They could carry with them any stick of their choice, maybe a small willow switch that will leave a red streak upon the offender's back, maybe a large stick meant to brain the criminal to the ground, as long as it was smaller around than the wielder's thumb. They then wait until the criminal makes it far enough down Murderer's Way that they can get a good whack at them. That is when the real societal healing begins. The frustration pours down the gutters with the blood, urine and accumulated garbage. One could argue that walking down any hall with Luftens on both sides of the walls would feel like a gauntlet, and maybe so. However, the haunting similarity for Vrric was the noise. It was deafening. Luftens were pointing, shouting, grabbing. The ones at the other end, unlike convicted criminals, were loathe to leave. They milled about, hoping that their mentor, whomever that would turn out to be, was merely having difficulty tapping them. Not that they simply were not chosen, that they should leave so that more Trivaste takers could enter the disorganized room. Vrric had never really seen a room that could be described as completely chaotic as this one. Now, in the very bowels of the most prestigious guild's Trivaste ceremony, Vrric truly understood chaos. He wanted nothing more than to make it out. To escape. He had no illusions that one of these dignified, wizened, yelling, old, wrinkled Luftens was waiting for him. He knew that this was pure folly. He had entered on accident, the whole test was an accident. He pushed forward as some in front were tapped by the writhing mass of derlians on either side of him. Forward he went with only one thought. To escape into the fresh air. He should watch a parade, he should get some wonderful food, and he should enjoy the rest of the festival while it lasted. All thoughts of talent and its vanity had fled his mind as he neared the exit.

Vrric wondered vaguely what had happened to the obnoxious boy that he had let in front of him earlier, but the Luften was no where to be found. *He must have been tapped*, thought Vrric. He was just steps from the exit, from where the sun shone delightfully through. *I hope that he enjoys the guild as much as he thinks he will.* Vrric's mind began to wander away from the boy when he felt a light tapping on his shoulder. Just before the exit, Vrric could have leapt the distance, Vrric was tapped. He stopped, not really conscious of what that meant, and looked off to his right, for it was the right shoulder that had felt the tapping.

There was a wrinkled old face haloed by flowing gray robes. A cropped, well-groomed beard, as silvered as his hair, surrounded a small smile. Brown unassuming eyes peeped from under large brows. He was smaller and thicker in stature than what Vrric typically thought of as a mage, more like Kaihlu. "Didn't think it would happen, eh? Certainly not to you. Well, I saw what you did in there, my boy. I saw *talent!* You haven't trained have you?" The voice was large and deep like a canyon. It had to be loud to be heard above the din, but there was also a gentle softness to it. The incompatibility of the Luften's voice would have shocked Vrric into silence had he not already been tongue tied. It had the paradoxical effect of shaking Vrric out of his reverie.

"Talent? I don't think you understand… I… I don't know anything." It was all Vrric could work out. He did not know anything. That was what was wrong here. He could pinpoint it and name it. He did not know anything about magic at all.

"Will you promise not to align yourself? Do you swear that your fealty will not waver to a faction that may offer you more than I? Do you promise?" At the "Do you promise?" the old Luften had grabbed both of Vrric's shoulders in his hands and turned Vrric to face him. He could smell alcohol on the old Luften's breath, he could feel the shaking hands on his shoulders, he could see the yellowed teeth of neglect. "Do you promise to remain a grey mage forever?" The intensity of the voice was palpable. It penetrated him to his core. It was as if a geas was being laid over him, that if he swore and broke his word he could die. Die just from the intensity of the oath. Vrric did not know what to do, he did not know what he could do. He knew that he must speak. He must say *something* to remove this lunatic from him. The words came unbidden to his mind, almost as if he had heard them before.

"I swear upon all my powers, both real and imagined. I swear upon all of my family, both living and dead. I swear upon all of my life, both here and otherwhere." As Vrric said the words, he felt a sudden drain of energy. He wished he could just sleep, just lie down there in the middle of a contorting arena of life, and lay his head in slumber. He blinked several times as if to remind himself that he was awake, that he was aware. He saw the too-huge face of the old wizard grin. The yellow teeth seemed to blacken slightly near the gums. The details of an important moment, even before the realization that the moment is important, can be burned into the mind. The unconscious mind often knows what is important before its thoughtful counterpart. And for some unknown reason, Vrric's mind decided that this old crazy derlian with yellowed teeth was important.

"Come with me then, come with me." The old Luften started to drag Vrric towards the exit door. Vrric's body was so overjoyed at the thought of escape, and all that it entailed, that he followed the old Luften willingly. "What were you before today?" The voice seemed less forceful as they pushed past the last of the bodies to gain the fresh outside air. "You seem rather strapping… Hmm, you must have had work down below. Yes, must be. You are a mudfoot, are you not?" The old Luften's voice seemed kind and friendly. *The perfect voice to send you on a long impossible journey*, Vrric unconsciously thought.

"Yes, that name has been thrown in my face before." The unbidden ire that flowed forth into Vrric's own voice surprised him. He took a slow breath. "I am," Vrric stated to let the old Luften know of his intentions, "I am a blacksmith. I have taken the morning test and I feel that I have pleased my mentor well." Vrric felt good saying that, felt like he was exercising some control. "I seemed to have taken the Mage's Guild tests by accident."

"Accident? Oh no, you can't simply write me, my guild, or your promise off by saying the word 'accident.' In fact, I don't believe in accidents." The old Luften was steering Vrric up some more stairs, circling the great Helioarc tree that they had started upon.

"Well, coincidence then, surely. It just happened, you see. I was standing outside and they just started to herd us in. I was just kind of included in the 'us.' " Vrric's fatigue was beginning to plague him. It seemed that he could not think straight. *Wait*, he thought, *what promise?* "I… I certainly didn't promise not to become a smith?" It was a statement in his head, but it became a question when voiced. "I mean, well… I have a mentor that I am completely comfortable with. We get along great, Kaihlu and I, and, no offence to you or your guild, but I am to be his apprentice. You see, I am orphaned and he took me in when no one…" Vrric was not sure what he was doing, let alone what he was saying. The old Luften merely let him talk, leading him farther and farther away from the mud. *No, not the mud*, a small voice in Vrric's mind tried to explain, *just the ground. He is leading me farther from the ground.* The word "mud" stuck in Vrric's mind, though. Stuck just like the hateful mixture stuck to his boots. Mud! Why did the word bring bile in Vrric's throat? How could one simple three-letter, one-syllable word make Vrric's blood rush into his face with rage.

"I am sorry. Listen, wait, I am sorry." Vrric stopped himself on a landing. He used both arms to try to push at the old Luften. "I do not mean to seem what I am not." The words would not even make sense in Vrric's own mind, even as he tried to voice them. "I… I am not a mage. There, I have said it finally. I am not a mage. I know nothing of magic. I know nothing of spells. I… I know nothing." He repeated himself from earlier, but here Vrric's voice began to trail off. He had much more to say, yes, much more. But his voice betrayed him by becoming quiet at the integral moment. His mind thought briefly, so quickly that a hummingbird might have been stunned, of living in the clouds. Living above and beyond the mud, into the outstretched arms of the Helioarcs. Living in a world where a mere thought may become reality. Oh, how his mind betrayed him.

"Nothing. Hmm… One should wonder why one wishes oblivion. Do you really want nothing? Do you wish, in the cold nights with the rain whipping down towards the sodden ground, nothing? Emptiness, hollowness, not even the echo of your own screams? Oblivion? Do you think that I do not know fear when I smell it?" The last question stopped Vrric. It stopped him so completely that he began to climb the stairs again, almost leading the old Luften with his haste.

"Fear? I have no fear, good sir. None. It is something else. Wait." Here Vrric stopped again, on the stairs this time, not on a landing, "It is more of the unspoken promise to my mentor, to Kaihlu, that I hesitate. I cannot go with you. Believe me, I wish I could. I would love to create things with my mind. I would be overjoyed to live above the mud, yes, the mud. I would kill, even kill, to be able to see the lives of those who change the world. Let alone become someone who could affect history as it happens. I could talk a thousand cycles and not explain all of the things that I could, no would, do to become better than I am. I… I…" Here Vrric could go no further. Maybe it was the fatigue. Maybe it was his thoughts of his past. Maybe it was the idea of betraying his only real relation, Kaihlu. Whatever it was, it left him a drained, empty husk. Nothing rational would come forth. Nothing intelligible could be uttered.

Sweet darkness kissed Vrric's forehead and then faded. Faded quickly back into light. The feeling that he was betraying something larger than Kaihlu wavered, but did not fully extinguish amongst the light.

"Ah, my son, do you not think that I understand you?" The Luften's backwards way of speaking was oddly soothing. "Why do you think that I chose you? Why do you think that I made you swear, yes swear, an oath of fealty to me? It will be hard, harder than anything that you have ever done, but it will reap rewards beyond your currently limited imagination. I do not offer, I compel, that you become the great Luften that you are destined for. I did not speak of skill earlier, no. Your mentor that you speak of, your Kaihlu, will be crushed in his spirit. I do not deny this. He has obviously given you great skill without asking for anything in return, and for that you should, no you must, be grateful for. But no matter your skill, your talent wishes to lead you into another direction. Your talent, your destiny, lies with me, a complete stranger, not with the familiar loves of your youth. Why did you swear the Mage's Oath?"

"The Mage's Oath? I merely spoke. I mean, I merely said what was in my head…" Vrric was taken aback by the old Luften's talk of oaths.

"Yes, the Mage's Oath. You spoke an oath that is older than this world, brought to us, in thought-form, by the Yavens. Why do you think that you should know such an oath? And if you do not believe me, I will show you in my books the exact oath that you spoke." The old Luften's voice seemed to start to become more gruff.

"Well, I… I did not realize, I mean I did not know the oath. I do not know that oath! I was just trying… It was so loud, you see… There were just so many Luftens, all motioning and yelling. It was just there in my head, it appeared there so that I could appease you… So that I could escape back into the world of air, so that I could breathe. My subconscious was just regurgitating something that I heard as a child perhaps, certainly long ago. I just wanted to be able to escape." Vrric was feeling like a stranger. Like somebody he had never known had leapt into his body. And before the stranger could learn anything about their surroundings, it was forced to defend an unknown position. No matter whether or not it made sense, it must defend its position, the position handed to it upon arrival. Vrric could not make his mind make sense to itself. That, more than anything, made him wish for the old Luften's home, a place of solace and rest.

Vrric knew, in the back of his mind at best, but he knew that the world had just changed. Right under his nose, the world had become a completely different, unknown, place. He was ready to give in if it would mean some rest, some respite. He could not possibly understand what he was going through.

"Like it or not, the oath was spoken. The oath was spoken to my request. Whatever unvoiced promise you may have made, whatever quiet agreement you had with your anvil and fire, you have spoken your oath to me." The voice from the old Luften became harder and harder until it sounded like the exact anvil that he spoke of. "Come, I am not unreasonable. Whatever your promises, both to me and to Kaihlu, you must see where you will begin your training. I will take you to my home. I will feed you my food. I will even explain to you your lot in life in learning the ways of the Magi. I will tell you all before the setting of the sun." Here the old Luften pointed upwards to the waning sun. "If, at the end of it all, you decide to leave me, to learn your smithing, then I may let you leave. However, you must be attentive to me and what I have to say in the meantime. Do we have a deal?" The old Luften smiled at Vrric. It appeared to be a sincere smile.

"Well, I guess I have already agreed to much deeper commitments. How can I refuse this?" Vrric smiled sickly towards the old Luften.

With that the old Luften guided Vrric up through the Helioarcs, into their vast foliage, into the deep green that hid the houses from view from the ground. *From the mud*, thought Vrric. He had never seen what lay between the leaves of the great trees this high up. He had imagined much of what was there, cubic wooden houses cradled in between the branches. But he had never actually seen it before, nor would he ever forget.

A vast panoramic vista lay before Vrric. He saw, for the first time in his life, the true city of Ariellyna. Not the clustered shacks that he had grown up with, with their rotting wooden walls touching the sodden soil, streaking black lines up towards the trees, their living brothers. The first image that burned itself into his memory was that of the floating walkways. *Luftens climbing along a giant spider's web.* Vrric's mind reeled briefly with vertigo. Only after he could regain his balance did the rest of the city reveal itself to him. Around each trunk, directly above the largest lowest branches, sat a huge round building. These were the terminal points for the walkways. The roofs were heavily slanted with healthy eaves. On each roof designs that seemed almost foreign to Vrric were painted with vibrant colors. The windows and to some extent the doors were oval, or even circular. This, contrasting with the stark linear roofs, made Vrric seem as if he had stepped into a Pyran or Fluen city.

"Is it like this… all the way up?" Vrric paused in breath and in motion after the word "this." He had seen the large platforms from the bottom, had even, on days such as today, stood on the bottom platforms watching life parade below him. Never had he been allowed to see the top of the first level. He had never walked above the dense leaves that shroud the lowest buildings. Now, higher than he had ever ascended before, he could see how infinite the city really seemed. It branched off into the giant leaves above and below, cutting across his vision, but he could sense that it kept branching off and kept branching off. He felt that if he could climb high enough the city would spread as far as his eye could see, until the curvature of the land swallowed his very sight.

"There are over forty stories in some trees, I hear. In fact, the Mage's Helioarc might have more than that. I know that the tallest Helioarc belongs to the Nijorn family branch, but of course you know that. Unfortunately I am not sure how tall that one is. It is said to be the oldest of the Helioarcs. My home is a mere eight stories up and, unfortunately, is quite a bit south from here." The old Luften's words seemed kindly enough. Vrric was trying his hardest to keep up his guard. *This derlian wants to steal you from your future!* The thought was forced, though. It did not appear naturally in Vrric's mind. Vrric tried to think of Kaihlu, tried to think of the hot forge fires upon his skin, tried to imagine the screaming hiss of hot metal in water. He tried his hardest, but something in Vrric seemed to be enraptured by the sights before him, by the sheer idea that he could be a part of *this* world. Vrric shook his head slightly to regain control.

"Listen, maybe I should just go home… I… I don't even know your name." Vrric had certainly not intended his sentence to end like that. He did not need any more attachment to this wizened old wizard. He felt his muscles weaken in response to his resolve. He wondered if the old Luften was using magic upon him at this very moment.

"My name is Revkin! Perhaps you have heard of me?" Revkin paused, searching Vrric's face for some sign of recognition. "Then again maybe you live too far down to hear of one such as I.

Well, is it the time involved in our prospect that brings you down?" The old Luften chuckled at his own little joke. "Then let me show you a small token of what you may one day accomplish. Lumkinderclo!" The last word seemed to reach into Vrric's gut and shake his intestines around. Vrric felt vaguely ill. Maybe uneasy was a better word.

"What's going on? What did you do to me?" Vrric finally realized that he was no longer touching the ground at the end of his exclamations. He was floating above the stairs. He stared down in disbelief, stared hard. He tried, with just his sheer will to be on the ground, to put his feet back upon the stairs. They floated higher.

"Hey now, are you trying to jinx us?" Revkin smiled widely at Vrric. "It would be best if you did not test your will against mine. At least not in this point of our training." With that Revkin looked away from Vrric, towards the direction they were traveling. Not that Vrric had noticed that they had started traveling, but he noticed the trees moving away. The sick feeling stayed in his gut, and he could feel some wind on his face, hands, all of his exposed skin really; but the flight still seemed motionless to him somehow. It was as if the world were moving underneath him, rather than him moving over the world.

"How do I know..." Vrric trailed off because he did not truly know what he was going to say. Probably something about trust.

"You do not know. That should be your first lesson, apprentice, 'you do not know.' Realize, however, how different that is from 'you know nothing.'" Revkin's voice had regained some of its ferocity. "Tonight I will tell you of what you finally will know." Revkin let his enigmatic response float in the air as they did. It stayed with Vrric during the entire trip, for he decided to look at the city rather than argue with the mage. His mind was aflutter with questions about the flight, about magic, about the word Revkin spoke, about jinxing, even about the city. Vrric's mind would not slow down even for a split second. Every time he made a mental note to ask a question later, another would pop up. *What is a grey mage? Why must I swear to stay one if I become a mage?* It took all of Vrric's willpower to use the word "if", even in his own mind.

The flight was short and mesmerizing. Vrric's mental maelstrom slowed down to a comfortable eddy as he watched the city pass by. He enjoyed watching all of the Luftens floating on the walkways of the city beneath him. *It must be fairly common to see Luftens lilting through the air like sparrows*, thought Vrric. No one glanced twice at them as they floated by. Most did not notice enough to even glance once. The trees seemed to flow around the buildings like water. It was so difficult to see what was moving and what was stationary that Vrric's mind seemed to be playing tricks upon him.

They slid in a complete circle around the Helioarc's trunk. They suddenly moved away from the trunk into the open air. Across the way, but close by, was another gigantic trunk. For some reason Vrric felt less uneasy near a trunk than he did out in the open air, even though the drop was the same distance. Up and up they went. A tier appeared from above and slowed to a stop at foot height. Vrric had completely lost count as to how many stories they had flown past. The walkway ringed the trunk with space enough for two large Luftens to walk side-by-side alongside the building. Vrric was lifted up and over the railing. The landing was so soft that Vrric did not realize that he was under his own control for several moments.

"This is my humble abode. I own this entire tier. My laboratory occupies the back half of the structure. My office is in the front left lobe, and my personal sleeping quarters are in the front right lobe. There used to be three separate buildings, you know." The last sentence was spoken as a statement, not a question. The last word that Vrric would have used for this abode was humble, especially with Revkin's grand gestures and descriptions.

"What do you think of the profession so far? Not bad for a mudfoot. You should be proud, not wary and ungrateful." Revkin was patting Vrric's back in the direction he wanted him to go. It seemed that he wanted Vrric to enter through the office door. Vrric opened the door and entered without the courtesy of a reply.

The door was wooden, as was all else: walls, floors, ceilings, and the like. It opened easily inward. *So that an occupant could not be trapped inside*, thought Vrric. The rug seemed like a tapestry, with the depiction of a battle upon it. It swept throughout the rectangular room leaving a small swath on each side to see the wooden floor. Vrric's eyes rolled up from the chaotic carpet into the room proper. There were three doors in the room: the one they had entered through, one along the opposite wall, and one on the side of the room behind a massive desk. This desk was the obvious focal point of the room. It carried all manner of children's story objects upon it. Such as a skull, colored liquids in bottles (presumably potions), large iron-bound tomes (with the obligatory quill pen and inkwell), scrying ball, and, of course, a huge throne-backed chair in which the impressive Revkin should be seated. The two leather chairs facing the desk were most humble compared to Revkin's. Vrric glanced at the writing on the walls, which he assumed were covered with glyphs and wards. The writing was quite unfamiliar to him. Along the walls and framing much of the room were vast shelves filled with aged texts. The cracked and worn covers stood like badges of valor rather than signs of age. There stood about various censers and candelabras cluttering the walking space. The image was clear. It was supposed to make one think of magic. Vrric wondered briefly what Revkin's living quarters looked like, if they would have the same ambiance that his office did.

"I will make that meal I told you of. All that I ask is that you eat, drink, and listen to me prattle on. If, by the time that your belly is full, you decide that you wish to return to the ground, then so be it. Now if you will excuse me, you may peruse through my office." Revkin's smile seemed incredibly benign to Vrric. Much like a doddering old grandfather. Revkin left through the door opposite the one that they came in.

Vrric's eyes flowed naturally down the long room to rest past the desk at the third door. He was trying to imagine where the kitchen would be. Revkin was moving towards what had seemed from the outside to be the laboratory, not his private chambers. Vrric decided to look around the office rather than try to snoop through Revkin's sleeping quarters and risk getting caught.

Vrric went straight to the massive desk. Standing on Revkin's side of the desk, just to the left of the throne-backed chair, he placed his hand on the crispy brittle pages of a large volume that sat propped up facing the chair. The paper felt thick and fibrous compared to Kaihlu's dictionary that he kept on his bedroom desk. Thinking of the dictionary, the Maiden of Creativity and Knowledge, made him think of Kaihlu. Vrric used to mark words that he had memorized. It was a favorite game of theirs that Kaihlu would use words that he noticed had been marked in everyday conversation, to see if Vrric actually knew them.

The sudden thought of Kaihlu slowed Vrric's finger upon the tome's aged thick pages. He unconsciously stopped it at a picture while his mind went wistful. Thinking upon the past kept his mind from thinking about the future, and he indulged himself for several moments. Re-focusing his eyes into the present, he noticed an odd shape depicted in the book. It looked like a five pointed star with a circle surrounding it. Vrric squinted unconsciously at it as he read the caption beside it. The words and the picture seemed to blur slightly and shift over one another. It was as if he had stared too long at one spot and now his eyes were crossing with weakness.

"Tec: Sphere of protection. This Syllable brings your Mind to the Path of Protection. This Sphere is Polymorphic, so most Mages use lower ranking Elements in the Word. This Syllable may be used with any Effect of the Caster's choosing. Protection is defined as the stopping of physical harm/damage from immediately happening. This Syllable may not be used to Ameliorate or Heal."

Vrric blinked again at the text to bring the words into sharper focus and reread them. He then brought his eyes back upon the walls of the room. He began to scan along the wall for the strange symbol he had seen. Sure enough, after walking back along to the entrance, he found the symbol inked in several spots. It was on the door that he found them, the door to the outside. He could not make any sense of the other symbols around them but he did notice some similarities. It was always the second symbol in the group that it was in. And it seemed that each group had four different symbols in it. In fact, now that Vrric had noticed it and looked around, every group of symbols in the room came in bunches of four.

Vrric began to wonder what it would be like to be able to change things. To be able to think something and then make it so. Not just to do it, but to be able to do it. How different would other derlians treat him if he had that ability? Nobody would sneer at him anymore, that was for sure. Power breeds respect because power could force respect if it wished. His mind had wandered to the simple abasement of tormentors with his future powers when the back door flew open and Revkin entered smiling with two glasses of an golden-amber liquid. Vrric thought it must be mead.

"That was incredibly fast." Vrric did not know what to say, but his burning cheeks told him that he should say something. He had done nothing wrong and so was unsure of where his guilt stemmed from.

"The meat is cooking and so we must be patient. Please sit, I wish to talk." Revkin motioned to one of the humble chairs in the front of his desk while he took the other. Vrric had a small moment of shock when Revkin did not take the large chair behind the desk. "What do you think magic is?"

The question took Vrric by surprise. He was expecting a lecture. More to the point, he was hoping for a lecture. Unfortunately this unpreparedness left Vrric without a response. "Changing reality for my imposed fantasy." Vrric thought about his words after he said them. He felt that he had answered well for not having a ready response. He was rewarded with Revkin's quick smile.

"Close enough. Close enough. How do you think that is accomplished?" Revkin's voice seemed completely innocent, almost vibrant.

"Through my ability to do magic?" Vrric made it a question because he knew that it was not an answer. Revkin was not to be deterred though.

"What skill, what secret is behind magic?" Revkin took a large draught of his drink after this sentence. Giving Vrric the gift of time.

"Willpower?" Vrric made this statement into a question as well. Revkin's face immediately lit into a wide grin.

"I knew that I picked you out for a reason. Now the tricky one. The one that stumped all derlians for many many cycles. How does a mage focus their willpower finely enough to affect reality?" Revkin took another drink from his glass. To gain a small fraction of time Vrric did the same with his. It struck Vrric as being very sweet, but also very, very, potent. When Vrric pulled that viscous liquid into his throat, it seemed to burn sweetly the entire way down. His thick, sticky tongue seemed to hang in his mouth as he tried to think of what Revkin wished for an answer.

"I… I don't know." The sentence was one of defeat. Vrric started wondering why he was even there. Why should he be chosen to rise above his given station? He started to gaze down at the floorboards beneath them, instead of at Revkin.

"Come on, how would you communicate with reality?" Revkin seemed not to notice Vrric's defeat.

"Maybe a special language?" It was the book that Vrric had glanced at briefly that influenced his answer. His connection with that book to Kaihlu's beloved dictionary made him think of language.

"Perfect, my son. I could not have wished for a more salient answer." Revkin smiled and put his now empty cup on the edge of his desk. Vrric felt encouraged enough to attempt another drink of his. It was not unpleasant. "Another language indeed. This language has special words that allow a trained mind to define a precise fantasy with which to usurp reality." With that Revkin gave a sharp laugh and leaned forward to pat Vrric's left arm.

"The words of this language are made up of syllables, four of them usually. Each syllable in each word is a pillar. The pillars are Power, Sphere, Element, and Effect. There are eight syllables in each pillar, each defining a different aspect of the pillar. These syllables are the mental definition of reality at its simplest. When one syllable from each pillar are combined, you have a word. This word explains every aspect of your desired reality morph. Thereby focusing your will upon your desired morph in the most exact and simplest process." Revkin's voice took on a distant ring to it. He was no longer looking directly at Vrric. Vrric took the opportunity to drink the rest of his shallow glass while Revkin was preoccupied.

"All life is probability. What are the odds that you would take a test that you haven't prepared for? Not very good. But it happened, yes? I wouldn't have believed it had you told it to me. But here you are. Things that are not very probable happen all of the time. The dice are rolled. Some path, out of a thousand different things that could happen to you, some path must be chosen. The main difference between a mage and any other Luften is that the mage has more say in choosing the path that they walk upon." Revkin stood and smiled at Vrric. His head was bobbing up and down constantly. Without another word he went through the back door, leaving Vrric alone with his thoughts. Mere seconds passed before Revkin returned with a bottle of mead that was only one-half full. He quickly poured a splash in both of their glasses, the larger splash landing in his own.

"Where was I? Oh, yes. That is where willpower becomes an ingredient. Probability is waiting for the dice to be thrown. A mage's focused will then slips probability to possibility. Everything has a chance of happening at some time, but most possibilities have such a low probability as to be considered zero. These trends are the laws of nature. A magician is able to sift through infinity to find the desired possibility, as defined by their imagination, then bring it into reality with a focused willpower. Every being does this, from weak old Luftens lifting fallen trees off of children, to not falling when you slip on an icy path. A mage, however, strives to do this consciously." Here Revkin leaned forward in his chair, his face pushing uncomfortably close towards Vrric's. His voice seemed an urgent whisper.

"The trick is to do *it*. Realize that you are doing *it*. Accept *it*, continue *it*, and understand enough about *it* to repeat *it*. Then you may begin to attempt the arduous task of convincing others that what you just did was real." Revkin smiled, leaned back, and drank his entire glass of mead with one large quaff. He placed his glass back on his desk while watching Vrric. Seeming to judge his every movement, or non-movement as the case may be.

"Any derlian may use magic. And any derlian can attempt to counter magic around them. Usually by disbelief or jinxing. Then there is the will of the world to contend with." Vrric had thought, at first, that he was completely following Revkin's line of thought. He wanted to bring Revkin back to the word. The pillars and elements that had filled Revkin's earlier speech. Why magic worked did not interest Vrric very much at all. No, it was *how* magic worked that enthralled Vrric.

"About the pillars. How do you, or how does one decide what word defines what reality?" Vrric had been holding back on his drink until he could remember and execute how he wanted the conversation turned. He almost took too big of a swig and coughed into his glass. With his lungs on fire, he found it difficult to concentrate on what Revkin was saying.

"Ah yes, pillars. The first is Power. This is the first syllable of any magic word. It defines how long a spell lasts, how fast you can fly, how deep of a wound you can heal, how many Derlians you can mesmerize with an illusion, by how far from current reality the spell can deviate. It also dictates how difficult the spell is to cast. It is, in essence, the amount of personal energy that you are willing to commit to the spell. If you bite off more than you can chew, however, you can pass out, become a mindless automaton, or even die. The headaches will seem to come non-stop at first." Revkin seemed to be motioning for Vrric to finish off his drink, to which Vrric complied.

"The next syllable is the Sphere. There are eight different Spheres as well. Each one corresponds with a different effect you may wish to have. Here…" Revkin grabbed a piece of parchment and began dabbing his quill pen in the ink. His lips moved silently as he scratched fervently on the parchment.

Power	Sphere	Element	Effect
Lo	Kin	Luf	Pri
Nu	Fin	Ge	Arc
Mek	De	Pi	Del
Nar	Tra	Flu	Sfe
Eqe	Tec	Der	Clo
Lum	Li	Hep	To
Sur	Sid	Pan	Kha
Tor	Morf	Tot	Ref

"These are all of the Majora syllables. They are placed into four groups, the pillars: Power, Sphere, Element, and Effect. These syllables make up the language of magic. Kin is the sphere of movement. When I cast the spell to fly us here I said, Lumkinderclo. I used Lum for the amount of Power, much much more than I needed, but I wanted to be ready in case you wished to fly around Ariellyna for a bit. Then, since I wanted us to fly I used Kin as the next Syllable. The third Syllable is the Element that you wish to be dealing with. We are derlians, are we not?" Revkin paused here, waiting for Vrric's reply.

"Yes, of course." Vrric did not like the stammering way in which he replied, but he was too enraptured by the conversation to be deterred. "So you used Der for the third Syllable." Vrric spoke the sentence as a statement, not a question.

"Very astute. Yes, I used Der to inflict movement upon derlians. The last one is a little tricky. The Effect Syllable stands for whom you want to effect. If I just wanted myself to fly, I would say Lumkinderpri. Using the Pri ending to denote only myself. If I wanted to make somebody I touched fly under my control, I would use the To ending. Since I wanted several derlians to fly together, I used the Clo ending." Revkin smiled into Vrric's face, tasting his eager curiosity. "The food should be ready, let us retire to the kitchen." Revkin rose and carried his empty glass and the diminishing bottle through the back door.

Vrric quickly snatched up his own glass and the parchment and then followed Revkin through the door. The hallway that he entered was long and narrow. The entire building had seemed so wide and spacious from the outside that Vrric had imagined large rectangular rooms sharing walls and connected by thin doors. This hallway seemed to split the house into more than just three sections. At the end of the hallway stood another door. Revkin opened this and showed Vrric into the kitchen. The room was surprisingly bright because of the glass roof that let the waning sun beam down heavily into the room. Revkin ushered Vrric towards the long table at one end of the room. This was obviously the dining table even though it was not thoroughly separated from the kitchen. Vrric sat down at the place setting near the head of the table. He placed his empty glass next to his plate.

Revkin busied himself with the oven for quite some time before returning with a plate heaping with steak and potatoes. He added another splash to each of their glasses before sitting himself down. Vrric was amazed by the hefty portion that filled his plate. Revkin certainly did not have to worry about where his meals were coming from.

"Do you think that there's enough on your plate? You can always have more if you have room. Now where was I?" The last sentence was muttered to himself, but Vrric was not about to let an opportunity go by.

"I think you were explaining each of the Spheres." Vrric let slip the prod before realizing that he had not thanked Revkin for the hospitality. He quickly took a bite so that he could compliment his host. "Wow. This tastes amazing. I'll probably be full for a week." Vrric patted his belly lightly.

"Ah, yes, the Spheres. I've mentioned Kin. Then there is Fin which deals with all illusions or hypnosis or anything to do with intelligence. After that is De. This Sphere rules over damage and destruction. Next is Tra, which allows you to change an object's Element. Like changing rock into wood. It can make the only five Syllable words. The fifth Sphere is Tec, that of protection. You would use a Tec spell to counter a De spell." Here Revkin chuckled heartily. Vrric only understood about every third word. He was having difficulty eating and comprehending at the same time.

"Li refers to healing, to life. Sid influences spirits and communication, basically information, but also summoning. Last of the Spheres of influences is Morf. This Syllable allows you to change the shape of the object, though it leaves it the same element. Each Sphere that you wish to influence has to be made real through an Element. That is what ties the mage's willpower to the world. The first four are easy to guess..." Revkin's voice trailed off as his gaze bore down on Vrric. Vrric swallowed his half chewed meat before looking at the parchment.

"Hmmm. Well they appear to be the four races. Luf, Ge, Pi, Flu. They refer to Air, Stone, Fire, and Water." Vrric felt warm and happy at this moment.

"Great. Can you guess what the other four are?" Revkin stared at Vrric.

"Well, we have already covered Der. As for the others..." Vrric hoped that answering the first one off the cuff like that would earn him a reprieve. He was not disappointed.

"Yes, yes. Hep refers to metals, salts or crystals, including glass. After that is Pan, which refers to nature. That includes plants, animals and anything wooden. The last magical Element is Tot, the Mind. From here, after choosing how powerful it will be, what it will influence, which element it will take form in, we decide what to affect. You can easily affect yourself, Pri. You may direct your will at a visible target with Arc. If you wish to set a spell to happen at a particular place at a later time, you end it with Del. That type of spell discharges in a shape that the ending Sfe also takes." The way Revkin's voice lilted upwards at the end of the last sentence made Vrric realize that he was supposed to respond. Vrric's mind raced as to what shape could be so represented and then he knew it.

"A sphere! The spell effects everything in a ball around the mage, right? But how big of a ball would it be?" Vrric had forgotten about his food, if not his mead.

"The size of the sphere is determined by its difficulty. By the first syllable, Power. Power also determines the length of time that a spell lasts. Magic is ephemeral and must always come to an end. You are doing excellent so far Vrric, you really are." Vrric felt warmed by the old Luften's words. "Sfe does not affect the caster, but Del would. To get around that, such as to make the two of us fly, I used Clo. Clo is a rectangle of area placed where the caster wills it. I placed the area around the both of us for the flying spell. Clo is also great for affecting a group of derlians away from you. Then, as I mentioned before, To affects the next thing that I touch. Kha affects random 'beings' around the mage. This does not affect the mage but will affect nearby friends, trees, animals…" Revkin's voice trailed slightly at this explanation.

"Well, that doesn't sound very useful. If you can't control what the spell targets, then why would you want to cast it?" Vrric was puzzled by this Effect. It did not seem very practical.

"No, it is not. I have used it less than five times in my entire life. Sometimes you are only surrounded by friends, or enemies. The longer the spell lasts, the more its Power, the more 'beings' it eventually strikes. But no, it is not a terribly useful Effect. It is easier to cast than, say, Clo, which has a higher ranking. Which brings us to Ref. Ref is a special syllable that allows you to add another Syllable to your spell. The only times I use it are with Tra. That way you say which Element you are changing into what other Element. To change an iron lock into a water lock, one that will just splash away, you would say Nartraheprefflu. So you see it is quite simply another language. One that has very few words actually." Revkin finished off his meal smiling to Vrric and to himself.

"It doesn't sound that simple at all. Am I to memorize every Syllable in every Pillar? To know how long a spell that starts with Nar lasts? And what of ranking? You haven't even told me of that." Vrric was feeling flushed and hurried now that the meal was ending. His curiosity was piqued, truly whetted. He had often thought about mages and their powers when he was a young mudfoot… It was actually the thought of this word that solidified in Vrric's mind what he wanted. Not only what he would do, but what he wanted. "But I want to learn it. More than anything I had ever thought of, I want to learn it. I will pay you back someday, somehow, for I cannot afford to pay you at all now. But I just don't want to go back. Anything but going back." Vrric's voice struck him as odd, and so did his words. The only thing more sobering to Vrric was the truth that they resounded within him.

"Great. Perfect. I have a spare room set up for this very purpose. We shall start on your training tomorrow. As for tonight?" Revkin raised his thick eyebrows at Vrric asking the question.

"I should tell Kaihlu. I don't know what I can say, but… If you give me directions, I will come back here tomorrow midday." Vrric felt his stomach begin to descend the giant Helioarc without him. And his mind started to feel a little clammy at the thought of talking to Kaihlu.

"I will meet you at the bottom platform at midday. We will fly again so that you might appreciate it more. Come, I will take you down in the dark." Revkin began to bustle out of the kitchen into the long hallway. Vrric had the sinking feeling that his entire life had just changed. For better or worse he could not tell. Certainly more intriguing. Possibly more dangerous. Through it all, though, he mostly felt right about his decision. It was only what he would have to do to Kaihlu that felt wrong. It seemed like it was all out of his hands now. It was all decided for him. There was nothing left but for him to try his best.

Chapter 4

"This is where you get off, little girl. Just place her against that wall. Don't worry, we won't be long." Greshcly's voice seemed kind, but Trela could not believe he would be so uncaring as to dump her at the side of a walkway, stuck along the wall like some kind of bug.

"But, but, what if something happens?" Trela knew she was stammering, not really being persuasive, but she did not know what to say. Her pride would not let her yell her fears at them even though she wanted to beg them not to leave her alone underground, with so much weight of stone held above her. So she did the only thing she could. She smiled up at them and nodded, knowing that her voice would betray her.

They all smiled back at her, which maybe reassured her, she couldn't remember, and then they left. About three rods down the walkway it split in half, one half going down, one half chopped into stairs going up. They went up the stairs, past three sconces holding torches in the wall, to a landing at the top. There were several guards there, all nodding, as they went through a door and out of Trela's vision. It was then that Trela realized the noise. The constant chiseling, the constant chatting, the constant clanging. Her head was suddenly pounding, and all she wanted was to sleep.

She had her eyes closed to help her sensory overload, not napping really, or not meaning to. But when she jerked around at a voice, it was hard to tell if she had actually reached sleep or not. "Well, hello there. And who might you be?" The voice was quiet above the din, but she knew it was for her. She took a moment to ignore it. "I've not seen you around here before." The voice seemed insistent at bothering her.

Trela opened her eyes and looked up, and there off to her right was a young Gaen. He looked so tiny that Trela mistook him for a child at first. His brown eyes looked oddly like a deer's. His mouth was too small and his brows were too large. He was beaming at her, holding out his hand. It was looking at his hand that she first thought that he might be her age or even slightly older. His hand was more wrinkled than her grandmother's. "I'm Knill, and you are so breathtaking that I had to come and talk to you. Are you wounded?"

"No, I'm not. Well, not really. What's your last name?" Trela was embarrassed at his outburst. Who was he anyway?

Certainly not important in this world. Anyway, Trela was feeling like being alone more than anything at that moment.

"I'm not that old! I won't get a last name for several sun cycles yet." Knill's voice was a slight comfort to Trela. "And you are hurt. My father's a physician, I could look at your wound."

"If your father is the physician, then why would I have *you* look at my wound? I was resting peacefully until you came along, and that is the best medicine for me." Trela wasn't trying to look fierce, but he backed away quickly. She closed her eyes and hoped that when she opened them he would be gone.

Trela had fallen asleep by the time that Croy and Nolt were done. She woke up as they were carrying her towards Croy's cave. The slow sway of the litter was comforting and since neither of the Gaens seemed inclined to pick up conversation Trela closed her eyes again and waited until they had reached their destination.

"Still asleep?" Croy's soft voice peeled back Trela's fog for a moment. She tried to move slightly, but the pain held her rigid.

"She has been sleeping since Nolt and I brought her here yesterday." Croy's voice tugged again at Trela's consciousness. Who could he be talking to?

"Good, that is excellent. She needs rest more than anything else. Come Croy, we must not be late for your interview. Nolt will be by soon. He may watch her sleep." The voice sounded aged and rough. Trela was sure that she had not heard the voice before, but its style had a familiarity to it. As she began to wake up, to regain her consciousness, she kept her eyes closed. As a young girl she used to listen to her parents while pretending to be asleep. Nobody will tell a child anything, but if they think the child is asleep, they will spill secrets throughout the night.

"Of course. Uhm… I was wondering if you could do something for her. For her wound. I didn't know how to ask, but since you are here…" Croy was standing as he was talking so that his voice appeared to float away from Trela.

"Your concern is touching Croy. Lumliderto!" The word was said softly, under the speaker's breath, but as soon as it was spoken, a hand touched her shoulder where the bandages started. There was an incredible tingle and then a wash of cool played over her torso. Trela was still trying to appear asleep but was unable to stop herself from gasping aloud.

"That was probably more than necessary, but you have an odd effect upon me Croy." The voice was turning away from Trela, ignoring her gasp. "Come. I abhor being late."

The door swished open, then swished quietly closed. Trela waited for as long as she could stand it, which was a few quick heartbeats, then opened her eyes and sat up. She immediately felt her chest where her wound was. There was no more pain. She pushed into her chest with her fingers and still no pain. *That Gaen must have been a mage*, Trela thought. She tried not to think of what Croy was in the midst of and instead thought of Nolt.

Trela sat and waited for Nolt to show up. She waited for a while before the great adolescent boredom entered her. In truth, it did not even take a few minutes. She began to look around in the living room for something of interest. She decided that if she did not go into Croy's bedroom, it wouldn't really be snooping. The living room was a large and rounded room. The floor and ceiling were slightly curved to meet each other in the middle of the wall. The furniture was sparse, consisting of two ornately carved wooden chairs, a small table, and four pillows heaped up near a wall to sit upon. What bothered Trela most about the room was that there weren't any paintings or windows or anything on the walls. Only the curtains separating the rooms. It gave the room an empty and sterile feeling. In fact, Trela had yet to see a painting in Serif during her short time here. She was slightly surprised at the amount of wood that the Gaens had taken underground, however. They seemed to have most of their furniture made out of it, or at least Croy did. She was thinking about what might be in the bedroom while staring at the carving on the arms of the chairs—there just wasn't enough to inspect in the living room—when a quiet knock startled her.

She immediately jumped, thinking that it must be Nolt, and ran to the door. Maybe a little too quickly, but just a little. When she flung open the door, however, it wasn't Nolt's benevolent face staring down at her. It was the little annoying Gaen from yesterday. *How did he find out where I was staying?* was Trela's first thought. Her second thought was that if she just stared holes into his head, maybe he would go away.

"Well, hello. It's a fancy meeting you again. I never did get your name." He was beaming a huge grin from under his wide, wide eyes. His voice was quiet and quick, which had an insistent calm under it. Trela couldn't figure how he could combine insistence and calm into one voice, but she thought that the insistent part was the part that really annoyed her.

"Why are you here?" Trela didn't mean to make her voice sound quite so sharp—well, she did a little—but she couldn't believe he was standing in front of her, smiling.

"My father is Aren Mur'rem, and he needs to set up an appointment time with Croy Sie'tin. The 'jin council has requested a physical on Croy. Don't worry, it's very routine." He made a short little bow that took Trela quite by surprise. Was this a custom? She hadn't seen anyone else do it. Of course, she hadn't been down here for very long. She would have to pay more attention to her surroundings, she decided.

"Croy is out right now. As a matter of fact, he is out with the leaders of the 'jin council." She had meant it as an expedient lie, with no knowledge of the truth. "So if they want his physical done, they should have done it earlier." She almost tried that little bow back to him, but she just couldn't make herself go through with it. "It's been very pleasant talking to you Knill, but as you can see, I'm very busy. So if you'll excuse me, I shall be going." She almost had to shut his face in the door before he hopped back out of the way. For such a quick little voice, he was awfully slow to react.

"I'll, ah, just come back tomorrow then?" His muffled voice sounded somewhat comical. Almost as if he was in on the joke and enjoying it. She stood there with her back to the door for a few minutes. Listening to his footsteps pad down the hallway outside. Despite herself she was smiling. Before she could muster up enough boredom to enter the bedroom, another knock sounded on the door.

Opening the door, she peeked outside, and was relieved to find Nolt standing there. His quick and easy smile comforted her confusion of Knill. His smile reached his hazel eyes and showed just a little of his white teeth, a small white line behind his lips. She just stood there and smiled back while he thought of a way to invite himself in. She stayed quiet, her sweetly innocent face turned up towards the older Gaen.

"I, uh, was told to come and keep you company until Croy returns from his interview. He probably won't be back for a while. So you may want to let me in so I can wait while sitting down." Nolt's decisive pauses between each sentence, while at first seeming charmingly simple, must have been waiting for her to react, Trela decided. Somehow turning up the exuberance of the smile, Trela gave a quick nod. Cheeks now warm with a fleeting embarrassment, she stepped back to allow his entrance.

Nolt walked towards the cluster of pillows, grabbed the whole pile, and made two little seats with a shared footrest. Trela tried to be nonchalant, but all she could think about was that Pyrans weren't half as stolid as Gaens. A faint flush began to seethe underneath her skin. This bothered her a little bit, as she had never felt this clumsy or forgetful in front of another derlian before. So instead of saying anything embarrassing, or regretful, she sat down in his homemade chair.

"So, how do you like it in Serif so far, Trela?" His voice seemed nervous and uneasy. *Maybe he is lightheaded as well*, thought Trela. She definitely did not want to carry the burden of conversation, so she interrupted his halting start.

"It has only been a day, and I'm too weary to talk about me. Why don't you tell another good story? Like the one you told in the forest. Hmm. How about when you and Croy went cave exploring for the first time." She knew that he enjoyed telling those types of stories, for she had studied his face while he spoke. When derlians speak fondly of something they love, they tend to get a subtle glow. Not just of a light shining out of transparent skin. More like the skin is splitting apart and you can see the luminescence from between the cracks. Sharply glowing in one section, softer in another. Anybody who glows for too long *has* to forget their fears and shyness, she reasoned. So she folded her feet into the crooks of her legs and smiled warmly.

"Aha, now that is a long one." His face immediately lost its confused frailty. The lost-child look shifted into a comfortably lined face. The eyes scrunching up with tendrils of fine wrinkles flaring from their corners. The wrinkles didn't age his face—they were not deep and he was not old—but made it seem wizened and mature. While the way he seemed to grin while talking so rapidly gave him the appearance of boyish youth. Trela sat there and half-listened, half-watched Nolt explain who he was. Which was, seemingly to Trela, who he most wished he could be. Trela wondered if age had made him forget that's who he still was, or if newer events had brought him full circle back to himself. Either way, Trela could forget time existed for a while and just listen.

The week passed in comfort. Trela had nothing to do except heal and talk with Croy. She felt that he was actually very insightful, especially for being a farmer. She had told him all about her homeland and Qizern and her destiny. She had begun to feel impatient deep down, underground, but tried not to let on.

Some sort of sound had awoken her. She was unsure of quite what it was, but it sounded like metal banging against metal. She glanced around to see where the clanging came from. She knew that the noise must have been coming from the tiny kitchen. She waited a brief moment before Croy came walking into the room with two plates full of food.

"I see that you're up, good. We have some different matters to discuss. Here, have some sautéed mushrooms." Croy's good spirits rubbed off on Trela and she ate gladly. It was amazing to Trela how often Croy woke up in a good mood. They ate in silence for a while, nodding to themselves and smiling.

"Do you know what a school is?" The question, though timed towards the end of the meal, annoyed Trela.

"No, what is it?" Trela tried to concentrate on finishing her food before getting too involved in conversation.

"Well, where do you learn the knowledge and skills you'll need for life in the Pyran lands?" Croy seemed to think that talking during a meal was not rude at all. Trela wondered how such an ordered society seemed to have no idea of basic manners.

"You learn from your elders. Mostly your family teaches you, but if you have a specific desire you may search for a master to teach you." Trela finally finished her mushrooms, which tasted a little like dirt to her, and pushed the plate away, signaling that she was ready to converse.

"Well, here in Serif, we have schools to teach skills. Such as our history and the rules of language and certain trades. You get a nice overview, a general education, before you attempt to learn a vocation." Croy's voice was muffled slightly as he chewed the last of his repast.

"What does that have to do with me? Those don't sound like skills. What do I need to know the history of the Gaens for? It seems pretty simple to me. You came here from the Yavens by the Belegs. You decided you really wanted to never see the sun or rain so you built the most amazing hole in the ground I've ever even heard of. Since then you have been chiseling away." Trela was wondering when she could ask Croy about the future, her future. A sudden thought of Synde interrupted her, which seemed for the best because she was just showing Croy her frustration. When would she learn *real* skills? Things that she could do, not just talk about. In the Pyran realm she was barely too young to learn anything really dangerous, and here it seemed as if Croy was saying that no one was taught anything she would need to know, no matter how old they were.

"It is not that bad! Really, the teachers can be very engaging. And if you need any help you can always discuss it with me." Croy's smile seemed a bit too stretched.

"Well, when does it begin? How long will it take? When do I learn how to fight?" Trela felt as if she would never get back to Synde. "And anyway, when does Synde come back? You haven't mentioned him once since we have reached this… here. Since we have reached Serif." Trela's voice softened at the end for she felt a sudden rush of sadness at thinking of Synde. He was always so proud of her. It always amazed her that someone so competent, so perfect with so many different skills, could look up to her. She must accomplish her destiny, she must!

"Slow down, Trela. Uhm, first of all, you won't be able to learn how to fight for quite some time. School takes many cycles to complete before beginning to learn a trade, even the 'jin trade. Most Gaens have already been going to school before they reach your age, so I don't know where that will place you. I do know that for a while it will just be in the mornings. And, I know I should have told you sooner, but it begins today." Croy was smiling at Trela. He had obviously never thought of a life without school.

"Today? Hey, wait, you can't dodge me. What of Synde?" Trela wanted to argue as to whether she should go to this school or not, but she felt urgent about Synde.

"Synde? Yes, of course. I was getting to him. He will be coming to speak with you in a couple of moons. I know I should have told you this sooner, but you may be staying here for several cycles. Listen, I have something for you from him." Croy spoke too quickly for Trela to interrupt with her myriad questions. He jumped up and disappeared behind his bedroom curtain. When he reappeared he was carrying a small leather pouch. He placed it in the palm of her hand very gently. "He wanted you to have this. He gave it to me just before we parted ways. He told me to teach you peace because you were born with war. You see, Trela, Synde wanted you to stay here in Serif and be safe for a little while. He will be coming to talk to you about it soon, I promise."

Croy's voice faded into the background as she studied the pouch. It was an incredibly supple leather, brown in color with some splashes of dark stain. The first thought that entered her mind was bloodstains, so she attempted to banish it by upending the pouch over her other hand. The necklace that flowed out of the pouch like water was made up of blinding white orbs. As she looked closer at it, she could almost see little rainbows playing across the white surface. She had never seen a stone like that before. The necklace itself was a plain strand of these stones, and as she held it she noticed that it seemed too light.

"Croy, what are these stones?" Trela held the necklace out for Croy to see.

"I don't know. We could take it to the 'tul guild hall, they should know." Croy was smiling softly to Trela. "I'm sorry to have to go so soon, but I must go back to the battlefield with a mage to verify a few things. If you want I can walk you to the school." Croy patted Trela's shoulder and stood. She could not take her eyes off of the necklace. It was so smooth, she had never felt a rock so well polished and perfectly spherical.

"Yes, I would like that." Things seemed distant to Trela all of a sudden. The world seemed farther away and much quieter. She would surely be unable to learn anything today. Trela placed the necklace back in its pouch and the pouch into one of her breeches pockets and stood. She was not quite used to using pockets instead of pouches, but she thought that she was beginning to like them.

Most of what they taught in school she already knew, like a league is a thousand paces, or it was stuff she did not care about, like the other large Gaen city near the Fluen realm was called Hifrim. In fact, her first day she really only learned one useful thing. Since it was something that had bothered her since she arrived underground, she was very grateful to have learned it. It was the bizarre way they named themselves:

Sie – Peasant	Tin – Farmer
Beo – Apprentice	Lak – Merchant

Ona – Member

Mur – Overseer

Fyr – Teacher

Cru – Guild Leader

Dea – Assembly Member

Ata – Assembly Leader

Cha – Blacksmith

Wir – Carpenter

Tul – Stoneworker

Sol – Artist

Rem – Physician

Jin – Warrior

Vyx – the Guild Lord

The teacher—she could not remember his name—was astounded when he realized that she did not understand the caste system. He immediately took her aside and wrote out the castes and vocations. The first syllable of a Gaen's last name immediately spelled out where they stood in their vocation. How many other Gaens worked under them, how respected they were, and how much money they were allotted. The second syllable explained where their skills lay. Each vocation was technically equal, though it was common knowledge, the teacher said, that they were not. He then went on to explain how each guild tried to push their own as the most important one, thereby making two caste lines. The first one was dictated by law, while the second one depended upon the opinions of the derlian hearing it. A Gaen named Ona'rem might still try to look down upon one called Mur'tin. There could be any number of peasants, or any number of foremen, but there were only one hundred and thirteen teachers for each vocation. Then fifty-five guild leaders within each guild, each with their own specialties. The Assembly was made up of thirty-three members and five leaders from each guild, with any tie votes going to the Guild Lord to break. The current Lord was named Devar Vyx. The Lord did not have a guild, the teacher explained, so his name did not have a second syllable. Leave it to the Gaens, thought Trela, to make something complicated out of something as simple as a name.

Trela had been underground for what seemed like a long, long while. She tried to think of where the moon was in its cycle, but could not. She did not even know which moon of the sun cycle they were in. Time flowed differently under the ground. It flowed by Gaen time, not by real time. The days themselves were counted the same, however. Even though the vast majority of Gaens never went above the ground to see the passage of the sun, at least not daily, they had Gaens whose job it was to tell them the time. At discrete times of the day—when to wake up, when to take lunch, when to stop working—they would ring bells throughout the cave system. For five minutes, the ringing would echo through all of the caverns and tunnels, bouncing from one end of the city to the other. So each day was split evenly for the Gaens, and they followed the unknown circles of the sun.

Trela had been underground long enough for her to begin to understand the simple rhythm of the Gaens. But she understood what their daily lives were comprised of much sooner than she had understood their way of life. Croy had been trying for the last several days to make Trela understand the Gaens' incomprehensible government. Trela couldn't really say that she had tried too terribly hard to understand the ways of the underground, which must have been a small source of frustration for him. Finally, today at school, she grasped it. The way each guild chose its members, the way the members chose the guild leaders, how the guild leaders were a Council, how each guild's Council convened in the Assembly. She just couldn't imagine that derlians could get freely elected. To become the ruler, a member of the Assembly must be voted by that very same Assembly. If that were tried in the Pyran lands, each member would vote for themselves and nobody would be Lord. Some things seemed so very different and alien underground. But she couldn't really think of why she hadn't understood before, it surely wasn't as difficult as she had complained to Croy. Even though the teacher did not say anything of particular genius, nothing new or jarring, Trela had finally felt herself wanting to know. Wanting to bring their way of life into her life. At last, all of the different little societies, all of the different levels of caste, they fell into place into her mind. She felt elated, more than elated, ecstatic! She was walking with the rhythm of her feet instead of the other way around, instilling rhythm into them. She felt as if she understood the entire universe at this one moment. She felt in control of her destiny. If understanding things made you feel like this, she thought, this was what was worth pursuing.

Trela no longer knew how long she had been in Serif. Looking around at her surroundings, she thought of what it must be like to have grown up underground, to live here all of her life. To have your surroundings never change. That was one thing she still could not understand. Trela doubted she would ever get used to living under the immense weight of stone. There was just something missing. Out of the corner of her eye was something that shouldn't be there. Or maybe she was waiting for something to pop back into place, as if the world was askew. Then, while she was walking back to Croy's cave from her morning classes, carefully dodging all of the tiny rocks and pebbles along the trail, she saw the dark opening of a tunnel, branching off in an unknown direction. She realized that what was missing from her vision was space—or choice. Each path that she may take in this underground realm was distinct, discrete. Separately carved out of the surrounding space, her destination pre-determined. From the beginning of the tunnel to the end, she was sure of where the tunnel would eventually leave her. With barely a pause in her rhythm, she decided to take the beckoningly empty tunnel.

Her mind raced along her thoughts, and she felt in control of her feelings of life. SHE could decide how she felt at any given moment. Everything seemed to fall together. What to do, how she would fulfill her destiny of Kriishan, how she would train herself for her coming fight, even the brilliant images of her victory. Especially the brilliant images of her victory. The one thing she needed was choice. Her own ability to overcome all obstacles that might stand in the way of herself and her prophetic destiny was undeniable, unthinkable. It was a fact, cold and unmoving. She had to do that, it was how to go about it that was up in the air. That was how she finally knew what she had to do. She could not just wander the narrow and distinct images of space here. She wanted wide-open fields to run in any direction she chose. She wanted to feel the rain. She had to escape from the caves. And she had to do it alone. Synde wasn't coming back, not on schedule at least. He was probably held prisoner somewhere and needed her help. Anyway, she couldn't just sit back and let the world roll over on her. She needed to take control.

Her feet increased their rhythm, her head was down now, filled with images of her triumph over the overlord Qizern. His face cracking open, the lines of fissure etched in blood. She saw herself holding aloft a great sword, the crowd around the coliseum shouting indecipherably. Those shouts of hatred from Qizern's faction mingling with the cheers of praise from her own faction. The falling rain of sound pounded into her head with a deafening rhythm. The rhythm of her feet. Yes, she must escape from this rocky prison, must set her mind and body to the rigors of battle. That was the one key to overcoming the overlord Qizern, the only true thing that mattered. She could not see herself learning more of consequence here, underground. She just had to figure a way past the guards and out into wilderness again.

She looked up for a brief moment to see what new corridor she was heading towards. The torch at the next crosspaths was flickering wildly, casting crazed shadows on her face. Making her triumphant and giddy smile into one of a lunatic's. The first time she had seen a torch flicker with such life in the caves she had assumed that the crosspath had to lead to the surface. To the wind. She had soon found out that there were countless air-shafts criss-crossing the ever-present ceilings. After deciding she would go straight at the crosspath, she tilted her head down to the lightening pathway. She had to think! Who would know of a tunnel leading out that guards wouldn't be stationed at? She didn't really know anyone who would tell her such information, even if they knew it. It would come to her, it had to. Her mind was tossing itself from her eventual triumph to whom she knew down here. The light at her feet was dimming as she escaped from the torchs' light. She decided that at the next crosspath she connected with she would turn right.

As she turned, she realized that she was going into a more occupied section of the caves. Gaens could be heard in the distance. Her mind was wandering lazily now, her feet had slowed their rhythm, she was thinking of whether or not she should ask somebody how to get back into the corridors where she could find her way to Croy's dwelling. Nolt! She could ask Nolt for a way out. Smiling to herself, she sped up her pace. She was going to get directions and head straight for Croy's. She would find a way to talk to Nolt alone—at that thought she unconsciously smiled even wider—and get him to help her escape. She looked up at the commotion up ahead, and saw that the crosspath coming up was the one that Croy lived on. She almost laughed aloud at that. She knew now that her destiny was beginning to take form. Nothing would be able to resist her now!

Trela walked down the tunnel for a few minutes before she found herself in front of Croy's dwelling. As she had been walking, her mind was bent on one immediate problem. How to get Croy to tell her where she could find Nolt? No, not only that, but how to speak to him without Croy being around. Her mind had been racing too fast, sliding side to side rather than moving forward and achieving any new thoughts. Nothing useful had come to her. Now, standing in front of her door, she couldn't open it. Usually when she felt this charged, this close to destiny, her mind would just happen upon the solution she needed. It almost shook her confidence that she had nothing in mind now. Maybe she wasn't supposed to escape yet? Maybe there was something more for her to learn here, or at least to acquire before she left? She was stuck, frozen. She almost turned away at that point, almost walked away to rethink her future, to recapture the rhythm of her feet. She would never be able to count the times in her life that she thought back upon this moment and wondered. A life is comprised of so many divergent paths, what distant future would change from a small sidestep now? Truthfully, she never had the chance to walk away, even if she had decided to.

The grainy wooden door flew open in front of her hand, as if it opened for her mind. "Trela! There you are, we've been waiting for you. Must have taken the long way home, huh? Or are you making some friends I don't know about?" Croy's softly comforting voice seemed somewhat strangled and distant. "I've invited Nolt over to keep you company. I have to... well, I have a meeting I have to keep. Wish me luck!" Croy's lined face looked a touch more aged at that moment.

"I'm sure you will do wonderfully, Croy, you always do. That, if anything, is your gift." Trela's optimistic voice seemed to just pour out of her. She certainly hadn't meant to sound that joyful. Maybe it was the fact that she could talk to Nolt in private now.

Croy's face lightened a little, and he turned from girl and home. Trela watched his retreating back for a brief moment. She didn't know why she stared at his back so. It seemed to her as if she were trying to see his future by watching his back but, of course, she didn't have that skill. So she turned towards her own future.

"Nolt, it's nice to see you. It sure has been a while, hasn't it." She was talking while she was walking, with the door swinging slowly shut behind her. "One would think you were avoiding me." She sat down on a pillow facing him. She was attempting to act sweet so she could get the information she wanted easier. She was pouring all of her energy into this conversation, for this was the conversation that would gain her freedom. It was only because so much of her energy was being placed into perception that she noticed the softer her voice, the nicer her words, no matter her intent, the more nervous and cold Nolt seemed towards her.

"You are pretty late from your school, Trela. Didn't Croy tell you how important this day was to him?" Nolt sat there and stared into Trela. Not much moving on his face at all. Maybe a slight twitch or an odd blink, but that was all.

"No, actually he didn't. I had no idea that this day was different than any other, or that you would be here, or that Croy would leave. I was merely walking through the tunnels, thinking." Trela's mind was racing. She tried very hard to keep that urgency from her voice. Her mind kept bobbing back and forth again, not accomplishing anything while Nolt just sat there. In silence. She could almost hear the blood in her ears, thrumming away.

"Well, I guess he didn't want you to worry." Nolt's voice lowered, like he was talking about the dead. His stony countenance melted quickly back into life. "His entire way of life depends on decisions he makes on his way to meet the Blind 'jin. I wish Ilanna was here, she would knock some sense in him. Oh well, I don't suppose you want to hear about such things." The more he talked, the more energy seeped into him. Nolt became more alive with each utterance.

"Listen, Nolt, I know how to help him." Trela couldn't believe what she was saying. The instant the thought had formed in her head, she found herself spouting it out. "If we could get past the guards. If we could sneak outside for just a moment, I could make a sign to leave outside. Something that only a Pyran would leave. It would pique their curiosity, it would make them stop and wonder. It would buy Croy the time he needs to make the true decision that he needs." Trela rushed through the last sentences. She could not help herself. She wanted this so badly that all thoughts of caution were promptly forgotten.

"Well, there is that hole north of the lake… No, it's no use." Nolt guffawed and harrumphed. He groaned inwardly and outwardly. "Croy has probably already made his decision, and anyways, he is already under the scrutiny of the 'jin. They wouldn't find the sign soon enough. There just isn't enough time." Nolt's voice had started strongly, but ended like a newborn sheep. Very shaky upon stick legs, quivering with non-committance. Through his list of excuses to not help his friend, Trela could do nothing but marvel in stunned amazement. The hole north of the lake.

"Listen, Nolt, I have to leave here. I'm needed in the Pyran lands, not here. You don't understand what it is to be the Kriishan. I have a future to live far away from here. I know you probably don't want to and you surely do not have to, but I would really appreciate it if you would at least show me the way out. I'm not asking you to help me after that. Well, I might be asking, but I certainly don't entertain any…" Trela would have trailed off into nothingness from the mere look on Nolt's face if she would have been given the chance. She had been caught up in the moment and let everything fall apart for want of caution. Maybe it was a small lingering infatuation that had done it, maybe it was something more.

"What!? What are you talking about? We were talking about helping Croy." Nolt's voice began to gain in strength and volume. His pitch wasn't high enough to make Trela think of hysterics, but it was as close to hysteria as she ever wanted to see from a Gaen. She couldn't understand why he was reacting this strongly. "Listen, I've always liked you, Trela, and it seemed that you had always liked me. So I hope that you trust what I'm going to tell you. If you leave Serif, Croy will be in a world of hurt. He is accountable for you, don't you see. This is a very structured place, and you are lucky that you can even walk around freely. There have been many special concessions made for you, mainly because of your age. But you cannot just leave here, not now. Not while they have Croy." Nolt had stood up by now and was slowly reaching for Trela.

"Listen, Nolt, this is all wrong, I…" Trela couldn't believe this was happening. Not just her grave mistake of blurting out her plans to Nolt, but his reaction to them. It wasn't enough that she should realize her mistake and attempt to not repeat it. Now she had to deal with someone who was determined to stop her. She couldn't think of anything to say that would even slow him down. So she didn't. She turned and ran headlong out the door, pausing for the fraction of a second it took to open it, and then sling it closed behind her.

She hated running down these tunnels. The Gaens always stared as she rushed past. She wished with all of her might that there were more turn-offs and less straight-aways in this cursed cave system. She could faintly hear Nolt re-slamming the door behind him, rubbing his flattened nose, at least metaphorically. She could hear his cries slowly changing from the "Trela come back" style towards the "Somebody grab her" type. She just ran even faster, taking a turn at every crosspath, never the same two in a row. Right turn, straight, right turn, left turn, straight. Her legs churning as if her freedom depended on them. Finally, while glancing backwards to check on her invisible pursuit, she tripped over her own feet and came crashing down upon the stone. She gained another body length of distance or so skidding to a halt. Sitting up quickly, she again glanced behind herself making sure that Nolt was still out of sight. Her chest went up and down with her breath, her throat was on fire from her running, so she sat and calmed herself for a moment. What to do, what to do?

She got up and ignored the stares of the three small Gaens kicking rocks at each other. Lightly dusting herself off, more from habit and something to do with her hands than anything else, she decided that she should walk for the rest of her escape. Passing the children, she smiled upon them briefly, with lots of teeth.

She turned randomly for the next three crosspaths and then considered herself out of harm's way. Not that she could not just turn the next corner into the frowning visage of Nolt, but at least she did not imagine the sound of footsteps behind her anymore. She wandered aimlessly for a while before she realized that she didn't know where the lake was. She might be able to get there through the main hall, but she wanted to avoid the large crush of Gaens. The problem of living underground, she was thinking, was that you couldn't just turn the direction you were headed and walk. Many of the streets towards the edge of Serif were dead-ends. She hated to admit it, but what she needed was Knill. She knew that Nolt would not think of Knill, and he was the one Gaen who might help her. She asked the nearest Gaen where the physicians were located. Everything was grouped together underground.

Trela walked for the next hour twisting and turning, going up and down, until she finally came upon the physician guild's section. It opened off the main path she had been walking along into a large cavern, with physicians lining the walls. Not just on the bottom floor where all of the traffic was, but stacked up on top of each other, higher and higher up the walls. They had yet to fill the uppermost wall space with little cave entrances, but it was high enough to make her take a step back so as to not fall over staring up at all of the openings. Little ramps and ramparts climbed the walls. Criss-cross stairways hatching their way up the side of the cave. The question of how many different physicians were actually needed in a city the size of Serif entered her mind, and stayed. There seemed to be more physicians than patients! Trela tried to walk down the wide aisle that was the roadway towards a destination, towards the physician she wanted to see, but she ended up huddling along a wall, thinking. There was no conceivable way to find Knill's father. She could not seem to remember his name. She felt she might be able to reason the last name out, but it seemed no use. Without his first name, she was lost. Trela felt true despair encroach upon her for the first time since she had been in Serif. She had ruined her chance of help from Nolt, she had left Croy, and now she was lost. How was she to find Knill without being able to find his father, here, amongst hundreds of other physicians? It seemed so hopeless that she felt the urge to cry. Her eyes filled, her mucus loosened in her nose, her face began to burn its soft glow. She even sniffled a few times before her anger seared through her self-pity.

She knew what she needed. She needed Knill's help, not his father's. She could cut to the chase and look for him directly. She scanned the milling crowd for a younger Gaen, someone who looked like they were on a mission. Someone who ran errands for the adults. As she looked deeper into the crowd, it was easy to spot the two or three boys running amongst the older Gaens. Trela took a deep breath and started her way through the throng. At first it wasn't too bad. She was headed in a straight line through the derlians. The closer she got to the middle, however, it seemed the harder it was to guide herself. Trela found herself drifting amongst the other flotsam and jetsam of this underground derlian river. It took her two times to finally pin a boy outside of the raging torrent.

"Hey, HEY! Little boy. C'mere," Trela had caught the youth's sleeve as he was striding purposefully past. "Listen, do you know Knill? Kind of short, a little skinny." She couldn't even remember what color of hair was on his head, to be honest.

"Yeah, yeah, his father works up there." The youth was sweaty and his left hand was rubbing his neck. His right, however, was pointing up towards the uppermost entrances. The farthest on the left as far as she could reckon. She would have asked for more detailed directions but the kid had snuck out of her grasp as she was looking where he was pointing. He was already heading out of this hall into another tunnel. She followed the stairs down with her eyes to see where she would have to start her ascent and walked stolidly over there. She had to push her way through the crowd, but she arrived there shortly.

Staring straight up the wall was worse than she thought it was going to be. She had been around cliffs most of her life, but putting a roof over the cliff seemed to magnify the distance. Each landing was tiered a little farther back. There were stairs to climb with a nice width. *All in all it shouldn't be that bad*, she thought to herself.

Trela was grateful that the stairs weren't nearly as crowded as the hall. After about the third tier, she felt comfortable enough to let her mind wander off her path. She began thinking of her escape. Her escape from Nolt, her escape from Serif. It felt completely right to be leaving this underground prison, to be able to breathe fresh air again, to eat something that you had killed yourself. She was thinking of all the different things she would do when she escaped, the smell of wildflowers, the glow of the moon, when a small figure almost darted past her unnoticed. All she saw was the brown flashing of skinny pants. If he had been moving at the same speed as the crowd, she would have missed him entirely. She looked up at his passing and saw his profile as he jumped down the last two stairs onto the tier that she had just left.

"Knill! Wait, Knill, it's Trela!" She spun around and attempted to grab a hold of his fleeting figure. She passingly cursed herself for yelling her own name out loud like that. Her attention was held before her though, on the little Gaen who stood in place staring into one of the physician nooks, squinting and bobbing his head. Trela caught up to him easily while he peered around.

"Knill, we have to talk. I was kind of hoping for some help from you. To leave here." She flashed him a large, out-of-breath smile, exhaling heavily. He immediately broke into a grin of his own. "Is there somewhere we can talk, away from all these derlians? Towards the lake maybe? I might be being followed."

"Sure thing. I know of a tunnel that hardly anyone takes anymore. I just have to run this message to the bleeding chambers. Then we can go to the lake." His head kind of ducked before he started off down the stairs. Trela lengthened her stride a little but let him get ahead. A Pyran girl dashing down the stairs appeared a little suspicious to Trela, she had already escaped from enough desperate traps for one day in her opinion. She glanced at the open physician nooks as she passed them, easing her stride somewhat. Most them had just one Gaen sitting at the far end of the chamber. They were either scribbling something on a funny little table that you sat on the ground in front of or staring at the derlians walking by, mainly her. There was a cot or small bed along one side wall, while a bushy rug usually occupied the rest of the floor space. The last opening before the stair was occupied by two Gaens, one lying on the little bed, the other was rubbing his back. Trela stopped for a second, thinking on what a massage usually meant in the Pyran realm, but then kept walking. Surely the Gaens seemed too proper for that.

Reaching the bottom floor, she patiently waited for Knill to come back to the stairway. She watched all the Gaens wandering the hallway and was slightly awed by all the derlians. Pyrans were very nomadic, and she had never been to any of the large townships. It seemed doubly strange that there was no violence associated with such cramped quarters. Maybe she just missed all of that. After all, there were an awful lot of physicians here.

"There you are. I wasn't sure how far out you had followed me. Are they looking for you already?" Knill's excited voice popped her reverie. "You're lucky, my father will be closing up in a couple of hours or so. So I have some time before I have to get back then, you see."

"Good, good. It is urgent that I'm able to talk with you. I've been meaning to talk to you for a while, but..." Trela was going to continue to, in her mind, placate Knill on her past behavior as well as soften him up for the favors she was about to ask of him. Knill, however interrupted quickly and assuredly. His left hand flowing out towards the direction they should head, while simultaneously his right hand was lying gently on the small of her back, a slight pressure encouraging her that they would talk while walking briskly.

"No, no, that's all right, Trela. You don't have to tell me stories. I do like you and will help you no matter what the task. I've always liked to think of you as honest to a fault. To a cruel fault at times, but honest still." His smiling eyes and quick laugh were the only reason Trela continued to walk with him. Her shame was fighting with the glint in his eyes. They seemed wet, though without tears. And what was her shame anyway? Only to exist if she was caught openly? She felt much better by just leaving her anxious thoughts on the subject with the crowd as they mingled through it towards an unseen exit. It was a nice feeling to let her guilt fall off of her like old mud. Big chunks, little specks, each step was lighter.

"What are the bleeding chambers anyway?" Her mind had begun to find a little reverie, and already she was picking up on inconsistencies in the knowledge of her recent past. "We certainly don't have special rooms for derlians to bleed in. In fact, I would say that most of our need for doctors is for blood. Oh, we have a few burns now and then, but really even the majority of our peaceful accidents involve blood somehow." Trela was using the collective to refer to Pyrans in general. It was an unconscious habit of hers and she hoped it was not confusing to Knill. He did not appear to be phased at all. They were starting to pull away from the crowd and Trela was beginning to feel better already. Her stride shortened slightly and her breath unconsciously slowed its rhythm.

"Well, actually, they're not just for bleeding derlians. It's just the term we use for the ground floor. All of the emergency physicians are on the ground floor. Whether for poisons or very bad fevers or for bleeders. We just call them the bleeding chambers because they are for deadly ailments only. My father was giving some antidote to a child who had eaten some poisonous berries, nightshade I think, because the physicians at the bleeding chambers didn't have any. My father knows all about plants and their poisons. I'm still learning, of course, but one day I will have my own practice. I'll be an important physician." Knill was starting to gesture more and more openly. By the end of his little speech he had almost swiped Trela with his balled up little fist, on the word "important," no less.

Trela must have been a little too comfortable and relaxed. Her mouth would sometimes say the strangest things if she did not have complete conscious control over it at all times. "Did you see how many physicians there were in that canyon, crevice, chamber, whatever? It is completely impossible to think of yourself as important surrounded by hundreds of others doing your exact job. As far as the eye can see. As far as the eye can't see." Trela's mind involuntarily flitted over her destiny as fast as a hummingbird, and then her mind was back to where she was.

"Well, I happen to think it is a very difficult and honorable trade. In fact, I can't think of any trade, here, that you wouldn't have hundreds of other Gaens doing your exact job." This was the first time that Trela ever heard a bit of touchiness in Knill's voice.

" 'Here' is exactly the problem. Listen, Knill, what I really need is a way out of here. I know of an unguarded exit to the north of the lake. I, well, I got in a fight with Nolt and I'm really running out of options here. I just want to make it back to my own derlians, back to the Pyran realm. I'm sure that if you could just help me find the lake I'll be fine." She kept her voice low but insistent. The last thing she needed was to have to fight Knill into her way of thinking.

It was here in their conversation that they came around the last bend in the passage to Serif Lake. Trela had yet to visit the lake and she was stunned. Her legs fought the twin dichotomous responses of stopping so she could stare wide eyed, or rushing forward to the actual beach to see with wider breadth. There were some tiny boats upon the water, with lanterns dangling from their prows. She came closer to the exit of the tunnel and the lake just kept extending into the distance. The far side was impossible to see, even with the moonlight pouring through the giant hole in the roof of the cavern. The ceiling still seemed slightly rounded, like the Great Hall, but its slope was so slight that she could barely detect it. Trela had not realized that there was a place to see the sky from the underground. If she had known she would have spent all of her time down here at the lake. She had almost talked herself out of her amazement with her indignation over the fact that nobody ever told her about this.

"I would be willing to bargain with you. If you will show me your Pyran lands with all of its unknown wonders, then I will take you past our greatest wonder. You might be able to find the waterfall from here, and truly it only takes a few minutes to reach it, but you won't be able to find the actual exit. Even the forgotten exits from this city are well hidden." Knill was smiling too widely. Trela wasn't sure if it was habit or some bizarre way of persuading her that he was sincere, but she wished he would stop doing it.

At the mention of waterfall, she had involuntarily turned towards the roaring thunder off to her right. It took several seconds to let Knill's words sink in as she was staring at the gigantic fury of the fall. She felt her fists clench and unclench involuntarily in rapid succession. She even felt her breath get deeper, as if preparing her for the cardiovascular assault of battle. She had to consciously think to keep her voice low in pitch, slow in rhythm, and firm, as firm as she could make it. "Listen, Knill. You don't know anything about me. You don't know what I'm doing. I'm not just going back home to see the different sights, nor to settle down with, with a family or something." The last part shouldn't have been necessary, and if it wasn't it would sound weird to him, but she couldn't help putting it into her speech anyway.

"I have no illusions of what you wish to do with your freedom, or that the world is a safe place. I wish to see what is beyond these caves, these walls. I wish to breathe the thick and hot air of the desert. To smell flowers that don't grow outside of my front door. My father went on a pilgrimage when he was younger, many Gaens do. Almost all of the stories that relate to his happiness are from that time. To be truthful, almost *all* of his stories come from that time. You can't tell a good story without the unknown, without a mystery. I've spent a long time trying to find out why I feel like I am dying. At night sometimes I'm afraid to sleep for fear of slipping from this world. My grasp feels so tenuous some days. What I've decided is wrong with me is that I don't feel as if I've lived. Not even a day, really. Oh, I do well in our schools, with my chores, and even helping my father. I put all of my energy into everything I do. Folks are annoyed with my ceaselessness more than anything. But I still feel like a ghost living in a phantom world. One of my own design, too. That's the scariest part, I think. I want to see something completely foreign, something that warps my mind because I cannot swallow it whole. Anyway, I'm not arguing, I'm making a deal. If you accept, I will show you the tunnel out of here. If not, we'll both be lost." Knill's passion flared up at once, but then seemed to boil down, thicken in his eyes and his eyes alone. His body had ceased its quiver by the end, and all of the tenseness in Trela's neck finally relaxed.

Trela didn't know what to say, she hadn't expected such a barrage. Knill had seemed smart, poignant even, but she wouldn't have ever suspected these thoughts. He had always seemed so chipper. In those few seconds it took to find her voice, her mind had madly raced through all that had been done today. It had made itself up. She could not afford to lose any more time. "Show me the way out and I'll take you with me for a while. For a while only. I'm not dragging you all the way across the Pyran realm and back." Her heart was thumping in her chest, she kept expecting Nolt to burst around the corner at any second. She would turn her head from one side to the other, not even really looking, thinking that she should have explained that Nolt had told her of this exit just a little while ago. Every possibility seemed poised just above the ground. There was nothing that she could grip to change what was going to happen. She just wished that they would get on with it.

Knill merely smiled a toothy grin, one that seemed too large for his face. He started to jog down towards the beach, towards the waterfall. Trela immediately followed him, grateful for a moment of silence. She had been trying to collect herself for what seemed like hours now. When she had been running alone she had just been concentrating on escaping. Each face had seemed to be conspiringly watching her. While she was with Knill, though, her mind and energy had been focused on bending him to her will. Whether or not that was truly necessary, it was what had kept her occupied. Now, with Knill on her side and leading the way out, the way of escape, she had a few moments to think about what she was really doing. And unfortunately she was thinking of Croy. When she had thought about escape before, she had thought that she would miss the petty things, the little things about Serif in general. Maybe some odd musty odor would hit her cycles into the future and she would find herself reminiscing about her moons under the ground. Her mind, however, kept telling her horrible secrets about Croy's future. What would they do to him with her escape? Surely they could not really blame him for her actions. He was even forced to be with them, the 'jin, while the deed was done. Somehow, in her treacherous mind, she was realizing that derlians, whether Pyran or Gaen or Luften or Fluen, didn't really care about truth. No. What they really cared about was responsibility. Just who is to blame for all that goes wrong in the world? Give enough time and a derlian will find someone, other than themselves, who is responsible for the blame. And while Trela was trotting along the greatest beach of the greatest underground lake in all the world, she realized that it would not take the 'jin long to find someone to blame for her escape. And that somebody had to be Croy, or maybe Nolt. Probably Croy, considering the 'jin's interest in him. These thoughts, these traitorous thoughts, almost made Trela turn back and wait the cycles that it would take for her to be considered an adult here, to leave of her own volition. Almost.

Knill had stopped and was staring up into the curving floor towards where it would be called wall. Trela had never really enjoyed the way that floors and walls were conjoined here—she always liked the nice distinct line of separation that characterized walls above ground.

They were a lot closer to the waterfall than Trela had consciously gotten. In her reverie she had missed much of the tedious traveling. In her paranoia, the boats that had at first seemed placed haphazardly along the lake, seemed to be slowly coming in now. Like a giant net encircling and growing tighter. "Knill, why have we stopped? The waterfall is still a hundred feet away at least. The boats kind of look like they want to land along this stretch of beach to me, don't they to you?"

"You know, you kind of ramble when you get nervous. Now, don't look at me like that. I do it as well. I even do it if I'm remotely excited." Knill was smiling easily now, and had turned to face her instead of the rock wall that he had been studying.

Trela shifted from annoyed to angry, though for time's sake she stifled it as best she could. "Weren't you looking for something up there? Or are you just admiring the scenery?" She had tried to sound natural, but found that it was difficult to do with clenched teeth.

"Don't worry, don't worry. I've found the marker I'm looking for. You know if you had told me that you wanted to leave Serif earlier, I could have been better prepared. You will have to learn to trust me if we are going to work together." While he was talking he had started a quick scramble through the strewn rocks towards where the wall was ambiguously beginning. Trela was wondering how it seemed that his breathless voice never seemed out of breath from physical exertion. She assumed he must have practiced a lot while he was younger. She climbed back into the rocks with him, leaving the thunder of the waterfall with the pale moonlight behind her.

"Did you ever have a younger brother that you drug around behind you while clambering around in these caves? Making him listen to a bunch of made up stories of yours, when all he wanted is to be back with his mother helping cook or something?" She watched him kicking at something behind a boulder. The lake seemed to chill the already cool air in the cave. All of the boulders were slimy slick with the humid air. A small shiver went through her spine while he kicked and stomped. Right before she was about to lose patience with whatever it was that he was doing, he finally knocked loose what he was attacking.

"There was a kid who got caught in this hole earlier in the year. It happens about once a year I guess, has since I've been clambering through these caves. I figure someone decided they should block it off before anyone else could hurt themselves." Knill seemed especially pleased at having destroyed the safety catch. "You know, I think that whenever you seal something off, it just makes it more appealing to the young and stupidly curious. It's not like anybody who tries can't get around it. Soon they are going to have to have a group of Gaens whose job it is to go around and make sure that nobody has kicked holes in any of the seals. What a waste." Knill was already halfway down the hole he had kicked into the floor. His arms and head the only things above the ground, he was smiling up at her looking incredibly ridiculous. "There is about a two rod drop once you let go. I'll make sure there isn't anything sharp or dangerous down there." He dropped immediately after that. Long before she could refute his idiotic remarks about the holes in society.

She glanced back at the beach quickly, and stopped. Three of the five boats on the lake were now on the beach. The third one being helped onto the beach by several Gaens from the first boats, assumedly. Trela gulped down her anxiety and sat at the hole in the floor, dangling her legs into the pitch black opening. "It's OK. You can drop, I've moved out of the way." It was Knill's voice that made her leap into the void as assuredly and adroitly as she did. Not because it was comforting to know that the way was safe, nor because she was finally close to escaping from here. It was because he was making so much noise, yelling and echoing down there, that she knew she had to get down there immediately to shut him up.

Once on the ground, she quickly put her finger up to her lips in the universal shush command. She pointed up through the hole with her other arm hoping beyond all hope that he would realize that the boats had landed and were ejecting Gaens. The almost complete blackness of this tunnel made Trela want to retreat and scramble back to the moonlit lake. But way off into the distance there was a small bluish circle that Trela realized must be the exit. Knill nodded and started walking uphill towards the pale light. Trela glanced, briefly, backwards and could see only darkness. As Trela followed Knill towards escape, she realized just how steep this tunnel was. And not only was there the small blue glow of moonlight but a slight breeze found its way down into the tunnel.

The farther from the hole they got, the faster they went. Making noise seemed a small price to pay to gain the freedom of the mountainside. Once there, Trela felt sure that she would be free. They were almost jogging when they heard the unmistakable crash of rocks striking the floor behind them. They must be making the hole big enough to accommodate a large muscular adult Gaen, thought Trela. She cursed herself for not realizing the boats had been coming for her. But how could she have known? For that matter, how could they have known that she would be here? It was at that thought that Trela realized there was something against the side of the tunnel wall. Knill had ran right past it, head down, and now it waited for her. She was sure.

With the tunnel exit so tantalizingly close, and with Knill up ahead, limbs pumping like mad, she decided to speed up and try to pass the dark mass in the darkened tunnel. A hand shot out and grabbed her arm faster than a desert snake and had a stronger grip than she could ever hope to break free from.

"What in the name of Gunzgak are you doing? Don't you know that Croy's freedom depends upon you? He is risking everything, right now, and you're just… just… Argh! I'm not even sure what you're doing. Do you? Why do you have to leave, what is it out there? Do you think that we're going to keep you as a slave or as an exhibit? Answer me, girl! Talk to me. Haven't you thought this through? We are treating you as an equal, as one of us. You can leave after a while, but first you must learn. What is so terrifying about that?" Trela had known it was Nolt as soon as she had seen the blackened lump against the wall. She should have known from the beginning that he would immediately go to the 'jin class. Of course, she couldn't blame him, his friend was in their grasp. And how could she blame him anyway, truly? His mind was so completely foreign to hers, how could he understand her need to leave? This was the reason she had decided to sneak away to begin with. Everyone seemed so content to live their lives in this cave that they could never understand her claustrophobia, nor her urgency. She opened her mouth the try to explain these things. Knill was on his way back to do who knew what to Nolt, and she was getting desperate with the sound of dropping Gaens in the background. She didn't want Knill interfering, but she couldn't think of what to say to Nolt. Her mind raced and raced but she couldn't think of one thing, one way, to deter him from dragging her back to Serif.

"I have to leave, Nolt. It's not my past, but my future that drags me. You don't know what it's like being who I am. I have to think of greater things than this. I must. I will lose myself in anonymity in here. I will grow comfortable, then I'll grow old. And I will have done nothing with myself but walk in a circle. I know I can't explain… I must find Synde. He will teach me what I truly need to know." Trela couldn't slow herself down. It no longer seemed as if just her mind were racing, but that everything about her had sped up. Her body, her spirit, everything. Her mouth had sped up so much that she didn't think she could speak anymore. Her hands had sped up so much that they were shaking uselessly against Nolt's iron grip on her arm. She could feel panic beginning to tighten her throat and make it almost impossible to breathe. She felt as if she would scream at any second.

"Synde is dead, Trela. Dead. Croy didn't want you to know. He was trying to protect you. It is safe here. Now come with me before I have to drag you back." Nolt raised himself to his full height in front of Trela.

"No! You're lying! He has to be alive…" Trela didn't know what to do. She couldn't think straight this was all happening so fast. She kept thinking of the bloodstains on the pouch that held her necklace. Maybe she should go back.

She heard a twang!, a thrumming of air, a vibrating echo. A mere second passed before she understood the consequences of that noise. A dull thunk. A heaving of air from Nolt. His arms went rigid against her shoulders. His face stopped, frozen. His expression was of pure surprise. Nothing more. Not a thing more, and certainly nothing less. His eyes were wide open, as if seeing the world for the first time. Trela remembered, when she looked upon this instance with the vision of retrospect, wondering if a newborn looks this way, eyes flaring impossibly open like Nolt's did. His mouth hung open as well, though Trela certainly wasn't transfixed upon it like she was on his eyes. His grip loosened and he turned her, very gently as a matter of fact, so that he was in the center of the tunnel between her and the 'jin. She would never know if he had done this on purpose or not. Either with the realization of his own death and his need to not add another death to the moment, or with actual concern for her safety, from enjoying her company in the past, or some other such connection. She would never truly forgive herself for this, but the theory that stuck out most in her mind as the truth was that he was merely spun by the impact of the arrow. For the air was definitely thrumming now, and Nolt's poor surprised face flinched two more times before Knill's voice broke through her trance.

"Trela! Run, Trela! They have bows. Our only chance is to escape the tunnel. They can't miss shooting down this tunnel. Trela!" Knill's hectic voice seemed to be coming from far away, as if he were outside of the tunnel completely. As he grabbed her arm, she made one last glance at Nolt before running with Knill up the tunnel. That last glance would be the glance that would haunt her for the rest of her life. She had known before derlians who had died, and she was resilient enough to get over it. But it was more that she had ignored it, suppressed it, rather than had a full comprehension of it. Glancing back at Nolt that one last time gave her the understanding of horror. Not merely of terror, that feeling that something is going to shred you into pieces as painfully as possible. But of horror. Her stomach churned with the stench of it. Her heart beat to fly away from it. It was the first time that she had felt true horror in her life. It was what Nolt was looking at right then. He stared at something in the face, and was ultimately despaired by it. It seemed more than the proclamation of what happens to derlians who don't live. It was more than the statement of death, destruction, or even oblivion. It was an unreasonable fear of leaving all dreams unfulfilled while living day to day. That life should be meaningless, that one's small ripples, no matter their thrashings, could not move the boat of the derlian world in the slightest. Nolt died for no reason. None whatsoever. And he died before he even lived. Trela knew that her interpretation of what he saw at that moment was a reflection of her own fears. He was unable to speak his despair to her. But when she would feel so tired that mediocrity told her, with its comforting voice, to just lay down and rest, it was the horrible image of Nolt's vacant despairing face, with wide eyes and blood pouring from his open mouth, that spurred her forwards. That haunting image was never to be forgotten by Trela.

Turn. Run. Flee. She heard several more arrows, several more thunks. She did not know how long Nolt stood there taking arrows, like an overused pincushion, but it was long enough. She heard his carcass finally smack into the stone floor. By the time arrows were skittering along the stone floor amongst their feet, Trela and Knill had reached the opening of the tunnel's exit. And from there the real chase started.

Trela followed Knill blindly, not knowing where to go. She was not sure if he knew where to go either, but he was going fast. The full moon shown down upon them, giving everything around them an eerie blue glow. Trela knew that she should revel in the fresh air and moonlight, but the thought of the chase kept her mind on her feet. In the distance, a mere eighth of a league or so, stood a black line of trees. It was towards this blackness that Knill bounded. Trela followed on his heels. She fought the urge to glance backwards as that would only slow her down. She merely kept her head down, watching the blue rocks flash beneath her feet. Her heart hurt and it felt like she was breathing flames. She knew that she could only concentrate on one thing—not tripping. She stumbled slightly as her mind briefly betrayed her, but she was able to stay upright and keep on running.

Finally the night-blackened trees loomed before them. Knill ran straight between two trunks and into the darkness. Trela could not tell if there was a trail or not—it seemed like not—but she followed at the same breakneck speed that they had built up. The trees scratched at her like a desert cat. The noise they made was deafening. The snapping of branches and deadfall was sure to give them away. She could not make herself slow down, however, until Knill ran straight into an old willow tree.

"Agh! I can't see. Go on without me." He had landed on his back, but rolled over while clutching his head. He kept making low grunting and raspy breathing sounds, like an animal. His body would clench up and then straighten back out. Trela knew that he must be in incredible pain.

"Shhhsh. There, there. I'm not going to leave you. Shhshh." Trela was trying to be comforting but had no real clue as to what she should say. She knelt next to his slowly thrashing body and placed her hands on his forehead. They came away with a sticky wetness that could only mean blood. Trela began to panic.

"There, there. It's going to be all right. They've stopped chasing us. Shhsh. We'll just wait here for a little while. We'll wait until you can walk again." Trela wanted nothing more than to flee, to keep running. Instead, she kept touching his face with her bloody fingers and crooned to him.

Chapter 5

There was darkness, but no feelings of isolation. Croy felt the wind on his face. He knew it represented movement, but he was unsure if he was flying sideways or falling face down. The light began softly, surrounding him. It had no pinpoint of existence, no source, but soon all the nothingness around him glowed brightly. The wind rushed about him, faster but not more turbulent. It was comfortable.

There was a wall ahead in the distance and Croy wondered if this dream was to be the same as his first dream, but filled with confidence and comfort. If it was, he promised himself to solve the puzzle before the figure arrived. To not stand in stunned silence as the puzzle ball fell apart. He even thought about trying to grab it and keep it together before it was able to shatter into pieces. But this was not the same dream. There was a large, open, gate in the wall. The wall itself engulfed Croy's vision. There was no top or bottom, no sides. It spread eternally in each direction. The gate was round. The only sense of direction given to Croy was that there were black iron spikes barely visible at the top and bottom of the entrance. The portcullis was open. Though he still felt confidant and comfortable, the spikes peeking through the stone wall made the gate look like a giant mouth. Gaping open for the moment, but with the possibility of crashing shut at any time. A small nervous twinge echoed through his being.

Then he was through the gate. It was a large, roundish hallway with a small flat spot at the bottom. To walk upon, if walking was what Croy did during his dreams. There, up ahead in the distance, was a cloaked figure, gliding along. There was little color to the figure, an odd and muted mixture of gray and brown. The cowl was up, muted breeches and boots stuck out from under the cloak, and the figure's back was to Croy. They were both floating slowly along the corridor, but Croy must have been traveling slightly faster, for he was slowly catching up. There was still wind associated with the movement, and there was still no sound.

Doors started to appear on either side of the corridor. They were roundish with a small flat spot on the bottom, just like the hallway was. Croy watched them as he floated past. They were of some dark wood, wide vertical slats, with black iron banding confining the planks back to the hinges. There was a black door handle, a long swooping tail with a thumb latch at the top and large keyhole above that, on each door. The doors to his right had the handle on their left side, the doors on his left had a handle on their right side, such that they were a mirror image of themselves.

Quickly, the doors started having bronze-looking plaques centered in their width, about three-fourths up their height. As he passed them, he tried as hard as he could to read the black writing on the plaques, but could not make them mean anything. The writing appeared to be letters of some sort, a somewhat flowing cursive script, but they were in a language that he had never seen before. Maybe they were not letters at all, maybe they were not words, but only filigree.

Every once in a while, the figure would stop, half turn, and open a door. The doors opened inwards, towards the figure and hallway, and the cowl would stare towards the open doorway for a brief moment, then turn back down the corridor and continue floating forwards. It did this on the right side and the left, with no discernible pattern, but fairly infrequently, leaving the vast majority of the doors closed. As Croy floated past he peered into the open doorways expectantly. But there was always just another hallway. Some might have had doors to the sides like the one he traveled in, way off in the distance, but it was difficult to see since he could not slow himself as he floated past them. The wind would flow into the open doorways enticingly, seductively, but Croy could do nothing to change his trajectory no matter how hard he tried.

Eventually there appeared a door at the end of the corridor. It happened so slowly, the end was so far away. Croy was getting close to the figure since he did not stop periodically to open a door as the figure did, so it was difficult to see around the looming cloak to see what the end of the corridor was. Eventually, he made out that it was just another door. As they neared, as the figure stopped to examine the door, Croy could just see the plaque beyond the figure's cowl. It was like a figure-eight on its side. Croy slowed and stopped before he could reach out to touch the cloak in front of him. As he reached for the cloak, the figure's arm reached to open the last door.

There was a mirror behind the door. Croy could see part of the figure and himself, tilted to one side for a better vantage point, and the many doors behind them vanishing slowly in the past distance, but he could not catch a glimpse of the figure's face. It was too close to the mirror and the cowl was too deep.

The figure immediately entered into the mirror, as if the corridor continued. It flowed through Croy's own reflected image and floated back down the hallway. Croy watched in a slow stunned silence as the figure passed through him. As it passed each pair of doors, they swung open. There was a loud click as they opened, as if there was a hidden latch that engaged each time. The sound, however, appeared to come from in front of him, through the mirror. There was only silence behind. It made Croy want to turn around, to see if the real doors were opening or if they were only opening in the reflection, but he could not move himself in that direction. So, instead, he reached and struggled to touch the mirror. Finally his hand touched solid cold glass. He pushed as hard as he could against the mirror. The mirror exploded into blinding light, slicing through Croy's essence, eviscerating it...

Before Trela's recovery, before her schooling, before she left, before Ilana returned, Croy needed to show the 'jin the site of the burnt-out Pyran caravan. He walked alone to the southern gate. He was incredibly nervous about meeting with the Blind One. He hoped everything would happen without a hitch. He could show the mage the site, they would examine Synde's body, and they could all leave.

The gate was a massive iron structure. It had outlaying doors, a portcullis, a blood room above, and a second portcullis just in case. Croy smiled at the wondrous Gaen engineering as he neared the sunlight. As he exited the gate, he noticed Greshcly standing there.

"Well, hello there, Croy. You look like you haven't slept at all." Greshcly's voice was so pleasant that Croy couldn't figure out if he was making fun of him, or just in a good mood. *Maybe he is trying to cheer me up*, thought Croy briefly. "We are waiting for Crydlak to get back before we set out. You can get in the carriage if you don't want to stand here in the sun."

"Is, well, is the carriage empty?" Croy was trying to sound solid. It didn't work.

Greshcly just smiled and said, "No. *He's* in there. The Blind One." His little head jerk towards the carriage made Croy's eyes stick to it. And instead of continuing to talk to Greshcly, he just stood and studied the carriage. Like a Cru'jin studying a potential battleground.

His eyes started at the horses in the front of the carriage. They were short for Pyran horses, but quite average for Gaen ones. There were four of them, the two lead ones both black. One was glossy while the other was more of a flat black. Croy didn't know that you could contrast a color like that on animals. He wondered briefly if it was a conscious choice of the carriage drivers to make the horses so similar to the quick eye, and so different to the aware eye. The next two horses, however, were the most random horses Croy had ever seen. They were white, mainly, with brown splotches scattered over them like islands in a white ocean. He wondered if the drivers recently found out that the carriage needed four horses instead of two, and so they had to borrow the second two horses after so carefully cultivating the first two for dramatic affect. Off to one side were two saddled horses, unconnected from the carriage. Croy figured that they were for their escort.

Croy's eyes started to look at the carriage itself but stopped. Instead he looked back at Greshcly and asked, "Will you be in the escort?" He wanted a friend near, desperately, or at least someone friendly. He didn't know what to think of these 'jin, and certainly didn't know what to do around them. He knew that every time he opened his mouth they were calculating his words. He just wasn't used to thinking everything through before he said something. It was probably a bad habit, he was sure of that, but he liked talking from the front of his mind.

"No, I have to stick to guard duty until the moon empties. I still have some time before my shift's end." He was still smiling. It was very relaxing, that smile. It made Croy that much more unhappy about the fact that Greshcly couldn't be coming. "Crydlak and Verin will be escorting the carriage. She is who Crydlak went to go fetch. She wasn't planning on coming, but *he* decided that another guard would be a good idea. Just in case some Pyrans are out there investigating as well."

Croy didn't want to get into the carriage. As a matter of fact, he didn't really want to leave the caves again for a while. His earlier meeting with the 'jin had shaken him up somewhat. The light of the sun was blaring into his mind. He squinted his eyes, hoping to filter some of the brilliance, but it didn't work. He wished he was on the other side of the mountain. Not just to be away from this carriage, this journey, being trapped with the Blind One and the other 'jin, but also to be in the shadow of the rock, the peaceful soft shadows.

Instead he could see every distinct and jagged outcrop on the ground in the brilliant sun. He breathed in deeply and let it out very, very slowly. By the time he had exhaled, he opened his eyes fully. He almost wanted this to begin, but instead he wanted to be home.

There was a soft rustling to his right and slightly behind him. At the same time Croy heard voices bouncing and echoing down the cave hallway, towards the sun. Croy turned towards the cave entrance, to watch as the last of their party were coming out of the tunnel. Crydlak was dark red and hairy, broad and thick. The other warrior, Verin he supposed, was a slight figure, like an aspen in a grove of oaks. She moved with her whole body. It was a beautiful and almost mesmerizing walk. Every section of her was shifting at every second. She looked like she was ready to fling her body in any and every direction at once. Her eyes never rested on one item for too long, though they always came back. It was like watching a paranoid hummingbird. Well, maybe not paranoid. Too much grace, thought Croy. Definitely a hummingbird, though.

Crydlak grinned down at Croy, a big laugh coming out of his huge body. "Well, well, well. What are we all standing around for, huh? Climb on in, Croy, and we'll get this started, finally." He laughed again at Croy's hesitation. He then walked over to the carriage with three big strides of his thick legs and opened the door.

Croy turned towards the carriage and heard the rustling again. At the risk of looking shaken, he glanced down at the noise. It was his fear, scratching at the back of his mind, it had finally come out full force. It was purple and black, and it was shaped as limbs. Just limbs. No body to control all of the moving limbs. Croy's fear scrambled up into the carriage before him, leading him into the darkness contained in the carriage. There was one small window in the front, blocked by the driver, and another window in the back. Certainly not enough light for any Gaen to be comfortable in the carriage. Well, maybe one.

When Croy clambered into the carriage, he glanced at Crydlak's face. It was too close, laughing, big beard jouncing with his reverberations. And Croy had the sudden impression that Crydlak was bleeding out of his mouth and ears. With that quick glance, Croy leapt into the carriage. With a loud click, the door on Croy's life closed.

Underneath the only light in the carriage, under the only connection with the outside world, sat the Blind One. He had a heavily carved and gnarled staff leaning against the carriage wall farthest from the door, looking more like a weapon than a walking aid. The Blind One was scowling, looking unhappily at Croy's nervous face. His filmy white eyes were very unnerving to Croy. *Not that he can see.* Croy's inner voice was trying to be assuring. It didn't work.

"I hope that you will find yourself more cooperative today, Croy. This is very important, you must realize. I am sure that you do not comprehend the repercussions of what has transpired." The Blind One's unapproving blind stare was unsettling. Croy wanted to say something, to at least help with the heavy silence, but everything that came into his mind either sounded stupid or like an automatic retort from the Blind One came in to his mind right after his thought. The retorts were always sharp and cut deeply into Croy's psyche. So he stayed quiet.

As the carriage shuddered into life and the world began to rock back and forth with its movement, the Blind One's face softened a little. Croy's heart beat quickly, suddenly, and he couldn't explain why. There was a thick feeling in his throat for that brief second as well. The Blind One smiled to himself. And was quiet. The quiet was deafening. It wouldn't end; it seemed infinite.

"Croy, have you noticed anything different about yourself?" The Blind One's voice took him by surprise. It had been a while since he had spoken, and Croy had almost regained his comfort. While he was thinking on the sound of the voice, there was something familiar about it which tugged at the edge of Croy's mind, and while he was thinking about how the atmosphere of the carriage shifted whenever the older Gaen spoke, how the air became thicker and heavier like a perfectly clear fog, the words of the statement took a while to seep into his skull. By now the Blind One had blinked twice, not quickly or impatiently, yet Croy could almost feel the time passing. As if he were a mountain with an aquifer straining out of him, the water of time pouring through his stolid rock body, taking eons to dry up. Croy's first real thought was the dreams. He had just started having vivid and vibrant dreams. About what, he would probably never know. Yet, there was something peculiar about them. The thought, however, was as fleeting as a lightening flash. What almost immediately replaced it was: Why? Why would the Blind One ask him such a question? Croy knew that he was in over his head. He did not truly understand what was going on. The only thing he knew for certain was the urgency of Greshcly's warning, and the immediate paranoia of his life being on the line after the warning. This thought, as well, was a lightening flash in Croy's brain. But since he had opened his mouth to say that the dreams he had been having lately were a little strange, he said, "W-Why do you ask?" He hoped that he did not sound as nervous as he felt when he uttered that.

Instead of answering Croy's question, however, the Blind One smiled slightly and said, "Do you know why there are so few mages in Serif, Croy?" His voice was light and energetic, the first light thing to come out of his mouth as far as Croy was concerned. Despite the tone, though, Croy still felt that gentle nudge of fear that had been sitting beside him the entire ride in the carriage.

"No. Actually, I don't think that I had thought about that before." Croy was feeling a little better now that the conversation was no longer directly pointed at him.

"You naturally flinch when something flies at your head, to save your eyes. Gaens do much of the same with magic. Whenever it happens, they close their perception to it. To save their 'sight' that they never seem to use. Do you know what magic is, Croy?" The Blind One was actually smiling now. His gaze had a faraway look, even through the cataracts. His head was held slightly to the side and tilted upwards. The move almost went unnoticed by Croy. Which made Croy mad at himself, for if fear would not make him pay complete attention to his surroundings, he didn't know what it was good for.

"Magic is… Magic is the ability to do things with your mind?" Croy meant it as a statement, but it came out as a question.

"Something is not defined by what it does, but by what it consists of, my friend." The Blind One's voice could have been considered condescending, but his smile was like that of an old grandfather telling a child about his younger days. "You know that there are four elements, and that each element has a realm that the Yavens come from, yes?"

"Yes, yes, of course." Every Gaen was taught the histories when they went through school, and Croy had enjoyed that subject much more than many of the others. As a consequence, he actually remembered some of the histories, while most of his schooling memories were of him and his friends climbing through the caves.

"When the world, our world, was created, all of the elements were blended together. One realm was made out of pieces of the other four realms. And from this mixture was born chaos. You see, it is like when water and fire meet. You have boiling water, chaotic in its rumbling shape. You have steam flowing every which way upon the wind. You have the fire flaring and ebbing as it is being squelched. You have turbulence, my friend. Chaos. It is this chaos that is magic." The Blind One's head tilted back down, to pierce Croy with unseeing eyes.

Croy smiled, trying to show the Blind One that he understood. It wasn't until Croy was berating himself for having such an uncomfortable smile and that anyone would know how uncomfortable he was just by looking at it, that Croy remembered that the Blind One couldn't see his uncomfortable smile. And yet, either he could read minds or he could taste the atmosphere like a snake.

For the Blind One continued on, as if the pause was just him collecting his thoughts. "This chaos opens up what most derlians would name possibility. Possibility is the odds that the water will bubble up over here, or the steam will flow in this direction or that direction. It is what keeps life interesting, don't you think?" This time the Blind One was truly trying to get Croy to open up, relax, and just enter the conversation. His smile was soft and large, and his voice kept up the energy that he had started the conversation with.

"Yes, it certainly would be boring if you always knew which way the steam drifted." Croy grimaced after he spoke the sentence. He was glad that he grimaced after he had finished talking, so that maybe the grimace wouldn't be conveyed through his traitorous voice, but he hated saying something as lame as that. *Why did I just restate the exact sentence he just said? Why can't I look semi-intelligent for once?* The thought slid right through his grimace.

"What different possibilities does this carriage have right now?" The Blind One seemed almost to be slouching. He seemed to be so relaxed in casual conversation that he was no longer really paying attention to Croy. Croy, while hating himself for it, began to relax and enjoy the ride. Thinking up random possibilities was easy for Croy, he was a daydreamer by nature.

"Well, let's see, the carriage wheel could fall off." Croy was smiling as he said it, because he was thinking that if the wheel fell off, they could get out of the dark little carriage and sit next to the wildflowers on the roadside. Breathe the clean air and maybe chat with one of the carriage drivers.

"Yes, that would be a possibility, now wouldn't it. It is of my opinion that most Gaens would answer that exact possibility. Which means two things. One, that chaos tends to dissolve everything; all objects in this world, our world, are in some stage of breaking down, of rotting and decay. Even you and I, yes. So that would be one of, if not the most probable possibility. Two, that Gaens tend to be pessimistic and unimaginative. It is this second point that I had wished to make. Now, if I asked you why the very extensive Gaen caste system does not have a Mages Guild, what would you say?" The Blind One was pressing on even though Croy was tripped up at the pessimistic and unimaginative part. He wanted to tell the Blind One that he was actually being very optimistic when he said the wheel could fall off. That he wanted an excuse, any excuse, to not have to be inside this carriage with the Blind One and his questions.

Since he couldn't make himself say that, he instead stammered out, "Because there aren't that many Gaen mages. Because Gaens are pessimistic and unimaginative." Croy's voice sounded a little dead, with no energy in it.

"You disagree, do you? Good, tell me why." The Blind One was beaming, his smile covering his entire face.

The sheer relaxed happiness that exuded from the Blind Gaen was almost too intense to believe. It was an oddly dichotomous feeling. "Well, I just don't think that most Gaens are unimaginative. I also think that there is more to being a mage than just imagination. There has to be, otherwise there would be more mages, don't you think. I, myself, daydream quite often. And my dreams, if you could see some of my dreams…" Croy trailed off almost wistfully. He felt better even just saying that. As if the Blind One's statements about the majority of Gaens were an attack on him personally. He didn't want to back down. After all he *was* imaginative.

"They are really fascinating, are they? Please. Tell me about them." The Blind One's cataracts were staring into him, boring holes into Croy's chest. His voice was no longer light, it had become taught and serious. His smile had slipped a little, although Croy thought that the Blind One was still enjoying himself. That is what got Croy's fear up and moving again more than anything. The fear was jumping up and down, climbing over his lap by the time he was able to find his voice.

"Well, I, uhm, I guess I had the first dream while I was a child, but I never finished it, you see. It always ended with me failing to put this puzzle ball together... And, well, I had the dream again, recently. And I seemed to have finished it this time. I ended up putting the pieces together this time. After that my sleep has been a bit queer." Croy could not help but try to leave out as much information as possible. He knew the outcome of this carriage ride. He knew that there was no detail that this blind Gaen would not know by the end. Yet, there was something stubborn in Croy that made him try to resist. In the end, however, none of Croy's tenacious persistence would survive. In the end, Croy almost begged to explain everything. Everything in his life, his whole story. Croy would eventually curse that shredded piece of pride that had told him to resist. For, in the end, all it did for him was to make him ashamed of his complete failure.

After Croy had emptied his soul, after he had explained every detail of any dream he had ever had, the carriage finally stopped. The timing was perfect. They had sat in hollow silence only for about two minutes. Croy's own admissions still reverberated in his head. The Blind One sat perfectly still, brow held taught in deliberate thought. Actually, not truly still; his head swayed side to side with the sway of the carriage, his countenance swishing across the back window. In the carriage his head moved side to side, but Croy knew that to the outside world his head was held perfectly still. It was this, quietly and certainly unobtrusively, that Croy was contemplating when the carriage was reigned up. The driver's voice could be distantly heard whoaing the horses. With a slow and silent flourish, the Blind One motioned to Croy's exit.

Croy popped the door open and felt a gentle cool breeze wipe his troubled brow. He almost jumped out of the hot and stuffy carriage. He had almost forgotten how confining the carriage was until he had opened the door. A large, sincere smile placed itself on Croy's face, and he was truly elated. Had he not already told the Blind One everything? Could he not rest his mind about further interrogations? He swung his arms widely, back and forth, over and under each other. Enjoying the breeze over his body. He felt, more than anything, relieved to be done with the carriage ride. The Blind One stepped gingerly out of the carriage, his large knobby staff almost piercing the soft soil with his first step onto the ground. Croy glanced at the drivers briefly, then upon Crydlak and Verin, dismounting from their own horses. Then he consciously surveyed the plain. It was vastly different from the last time he had seen it.

The scorch marks still lined the grass, and there were still some items of small debris, pieces of charred wood and metal that was starting to rust. Everything large was missing, however. All of the burnt-out husks of wagons. All of the bodies. The plain looked naked under the sun. All in all, it seemed as if the carnage had never happened. Croy was stunned, though pleasantly, that the Gaens would have this area cleared so quickly. He couldn't imagine what it took to remove everything. While he was thinking on this, Crydlak had sidled up to him.

"Pretty impressive, huh? I was on clean-up duty last night." He was grinning brightly, proud of his achievements during the night.

"How many derlians did this take? I mean, there were so many bodies and wagons and everything. How did you manage?" Croy's voice, unnoticed by him, was small and distant to Crydlak. Crydlak stopped for a brief second, wrinkled his nose and brow, and squinted at Croy. And Croy never did figure out why Crydlak had stared at him that way.

"Only about twenty of us, actually." Crydlak's unease lasted but a moment. His deep voice sounded somewhat wicked to Croy, but his smile never left his face. "We salvaged what wagons we could and brought in any debris that we thought would help our investigation. Any weapons or books or identifying uniforms. Unfortunately, we had to burn most of the wagons, you see. The metal we piled up, to the left of that rise over there"—Crydlak's arm pointed back towards Serif —"so that we could run teams of wagons to take it back to Serif. Whereas the bodies... well, let's just say that half of us were digging the entire time the plain was being cleared. There was already a kind of sinkhole, but it took quite a lot of work to make it large enough to accommodate everyone. I think that's where we're headed now." Crydlak's smile stretched quickly and then settled back into its usual place.

Verin had wandered ahead a little. Croy could still see her lithe frame outlined against the distant trees, and Crydlak and Croy had begun to walk towards her shrinking silhouette. Croy craned his head briefly to see if the Blind One was following but did not see him.

His quick glance flitted over the two drivers sitting upon the carriage and over the six hobbled horses, but could not find the aged wizard.

"Where is the Blind One? Doesn't somebody need to help him find the way?" Croy was not so much worried about the Blind One. He was more worried that the ancient Gaen would swoop down upon him like a giant bird of prey than the thought that the mage would be unable to find his way. Croy was often very aware of the absurdity of his fears, but still seemed unable to quell them.

"Don't worry about him. He has faster and more reliable ways of travel. In fact I was fairly stunned that he wanted a carriage ride at all. Very rarely does he waste his time on something as mundane as travel. He must like you." Crydlak seemed to be studying Croy out of the corner of his eye. Croy stifled his innate sense of panic with the thought that his imagination was playing with his natural fear. Croy's emotions, however, knew better than to mistrust his intuition. Unfortunately for Croy, his recurring sense of panic and the sweat, the butterflies and the roaring in his ears that typically accompanied it, kept him from hearing Crydlak's words of comfort that followed.

Croy's whirring mind, instead, went over Crydlak's first few sentences, especially the "He must like you" part. "What do you mean by more reliable?" Croy's mind had finally latched upon a safe subject with which to converse.

"Well, as I understand it, and I don't understand it very well, the Blind One knows where he wants to be and can go immediately there. He doesn't necessarily have to know the geographic location of 'where,' just enough of the details to differentiate that place from other places. Or, at least, that's how it was described to me. You must realize, of course, that I am as far from being knowledgeable about this kind of thing as you are." Crydlak's gruff voice seemed to be softening up a little more as he talked to Croy.

Croy looked up to see where Verin was, and noticed that she and the Blind One were talking at the edge of what looked to be a crater. As Croy closed upon the edge of the crater he realized that it was a vast pit in which the bodies from the carnage had been piled.

Croy's feet had stumbled slightly during his realization, but they had found themselves by the time he reached the others at the edge of the hole. He did his utmost to avoid actually seeing into the pit itself. His mind understood what was there, he could almost visualize the various pained visages of the violently dead, but he let his mind bring back images from the past rather than replace them with the current truth. In the back of his mind he was sure that time, no matter how little, had not been kind to these corpses. He kept his eyes straight, either at his companions or the distant hills.

"Well, here is the moment of truth, is it not?" The fact that the Blind One was facing Croy was lost on him. Croy neither answered nor acknowledged the fact that the Blind One's statement was directed at him. For his part the Blind One let it slide. Instead, he took a deep breath, faced the pit, and spoke deeply and clearly, moreso than anything Croy had heard him say before. "Eqesidtotclo!"

At that word, Croy's heart skipped a beat. His hair felt as if it were standing straight out, as stiff as pine needles. His breath came, after a pause, quick and hard, almost gasping. Followed by another, longer pause, and another gasp. His vision flashed a pulse of color through his eyes and a dull glow seemed to outline the whole pit. At the least it seemed to outline all of the bodies of the pit. A sickly yellowish-green color enveloped the bodies, which was difficult to see through the afterimage left from the first flash of color.

"Great Gunzgak!" The soft, yet insistent, curse left Croy's lips a moment before he gained control of his own faculties. The only thing more disturbing than the Blind One's quick smile and almost imperceptible nod were the exclamations of bewilderment from both Verin and Crydlak. They had either seen what he had seen and were inured to such things or they had seen nothing; but they seemed to be only reacting to his emphatic curse. A small, pessimistic, nagging voice at the top of his spine told him it was more the latter of the two.

Croy noticed a great stirring in the pit, as if all of the bodies were shifting to a more comfortable position. A small part of Croy's mind morbidly wished to participate in this vision, but it was outvoted and he refused to lower his gaze into the pit.

"I wish to ask of your purpose. I wish to ask of Synde, a Pyran of your group. I wish to ask of Trela, a Pyran of your group. Finally, I wish to ask of your chase and destruction. All those that are ignorant may rest." The Blind One had his arms spread open and his staff was held perpendicular to the ground in his right hand. His face was eerily lit up by the glow of the pit, while his gaze was focused into the pit itself. Croy wondered if the Blind One could *see* magic, or if it was otherwise presented to him. Croy involuntarily followed the Blind One's gaze towards the pit and saw four glowing images approach the edge. To his astonishment both Verin and Crydlak turned and walked to opposite sides of the pit. Both seemed unaware of what was happening, if not completely bored by what was going on.

Of the four apparitions at the edge of the pit, one stepped forward an extra step. "I may answer your questions most rightly of all, mage." The apparition's voice seemed hollow and stoic. It looked wiry and lithe, like a male version of Verin, but much taller. There were no visible wounds on the apparition, or on any of its fellows. It was clothed in a formal looking uniform and stood with its back perfectly straight. Croy was unable to distinguish specific colors, for the apparitions glowed all the same, but the crest on the tabard that the apparition "wore" was outlined in the yellowish-green that the apparition itself was outlined in. Croy was not only deeply puzzled by how a difference in the color of a tabard could be outlined, but also by the apparition's use of the word "may" in its sentence.

"Speak, then, and be as thorough as you may." The Blind One no longer had his staff raised so dramatically, but carriage and stance suggested he was still *intent* upon the apparitions. Rather than just being filmy white, his eyes seemed more opaque and milky, almost reflective.

"Our purpose was escape. We have different political and philosophical views than Qizern, our ruler. We believed that he was not the Kriishan but an antoshan. His personal greed was destroying us. We set out to do everything in our power to dethrone him. Unfortunately we were not comprised from warriors, but rather artisans and farmers and children. So we did what we could, we attached ourselves to the Kriishan." The apparition did not have to breathe, and yet took a decided pause before continuing.

"Synde was our leader. He gathered us and organized us. He was a prominent member of the Guard, the elite personal warpack of Qizern. He taught those of us without martial skills the basics of fighting. He financed our wagons and horses. He was the reason that Qizern's name began to be whispered as antoshan. He was the harbinger of our destiny, we thought. We now know that he is the blame of our destruction." The last sentence was said with actual emotion, with not a little angst.

"Trela was the child Synde told us was the Kriishan. She was amazingly self-confident in this fact, and not one of us ever saw her hesitate or fumble in anything she did. This coupled with Synde's assurances convinced us of it. We put our faith and energy behind her. We entwined our very lives with hers." The apparition's voice had retreated again to its dull echo.

"Our escape started while Qizern and the Guard were overseeing a skirmish near Virkan, for the town had attempted to revolt against him. Synde had snuck away from the rest of the Guard and met up with us at the edge of a desert. We gathered our water and crossed not only that desert, but part of the wasteland, the Northern Desert, as well. Qizern sent word to a nearby warpack somehow and they followed us. We doubled back and cut into the Gaen lands, crossing the Yagoi river, to try to circle around and re-enter the Pyran realm farther south. They sent a Pyran Yaven from the south to head us off. There were no mages amongst us. We fled right into the warpack's hands and were crushed between the warriors and the Yaven."

"I give you many thanks for your information freely given, Pyran. May your rest be peaceful." The ritualistic quality of the Blind One's voice was not lost on Croy. The Blind One then made a curious circular wave towards the apparition, and it slowly fell back towards the pit full of its glowing fellows.

The other three stood there, at the edge of the pit. Staring sightlessly back at the Blind One. "You others may rest as well. I may come back." The Blind One actually looked tired there for a brief moment. Then the glow faded, as does the darkness at dawn.

"Well, Croy, it seems that we will have much to talk about on our ride back to Serif. But first I wish you to show Verin where Synde's body is. Then bring it back to me." The Blind One's face turned away from Croy, sure in his obedience. "Crydlak! I want a second set of graves dug! Come here while I'm talking to you!" The Blind One's voice grew more distant as he wandered the edge of the pit towards Crydlak and as Croy walked south, towards where Verin had set herself on top of a small rise.

Croy tried not to let his mind wander over his first real experience with magic too much, but it was no use. He was sure that this was the most fantastic thing that would ever happen to him, and he couldn't get the moment out of his mind. The implications of his seeing the magic alone were enough to crush his brain. *I am a simple Gaen.* That one thought kept repeating itself over and over. He put more and more of his personal energy into the sentence every time he repeated it. The sheer will behind it should have been enough to make it true. But, if that was true, then it was his magic that would make it true. And if that was true, then Croy's life was no longer simple.

"Are you to show me the Pyran leader's body now?" Though her voice was lilting, its entire effect was overcome by the steely look in her eye. Croy decided that he liked the overbearing joking of Crydlak better than the pure efficient grace that came from Verin.

"Yes, the Blind One told me to show you where I last saw it." Croy had stopped at the rise and surveyed the Blind One and Crydlak at the edge of the pit, conversing.

"You will have to lead the way then." Verin's voice seemed braced with impatience. "Whenever you're ready."

"Oh, of course. I think I started in the treeline over here..." Croy's voice rambled quietly into the wind. When he finally realized that it had faded to nothing he was on his way to the forest.

"You don't sound so sure that we will find the body. Why is that?" Verin's long stride had quickly caught up with Croy. "You don't happen to know something that we don't, do you?" The flash of teeth at the end of her question didn't seem much like a smile to Croy.

"What do you mean? I..." Croy's mind went over what he remembered of his last few sentences to find his mistake, but could not. He had just been trying to retrace his steps. He decided to stay silent for the rest of his life. Except around Ilana, maybe.

"Don't worry, Sie'tin. I am only teasing." Her eyes, however, explained that she would prefer it if they could quickly find the body.

Croy entered the forest where he had remembered exiting the day before and quickly found the tree that Trela had been sheltered by.

"This is where I first saw him... From here I went to the stream for water, and by the time I got back he had wandered off. I followed his trail... Ah! Here it is." Croy didn't really know why he had kept talking except that explaining his movements aloud sometimes kept him on track.

Croy's feet followed the path that he had taken, while his mind wandered, just the day or two before. Just two days? Time seemed to be flowing along a different stream. He wondered what it must be like being a 'jin. This type of thing just seemed to wear him down. He felt thin and drawn. Maybe a little punch drunk as well. Definitely not at the top of his form, and only a few days! Verin, however, seemed to be riding the crest of the excitement. It was as if she somehow gained energy through exertion, rather than losing energy by expending a limited resource like a normal Gaen. Croy was glad that he had tromped down the path earlier, it sure made following it a lot easier.

While trying to find the blood stains that he had followed the last time, he kept his head turned down towards the ground. With such a straining eye for details he almost tripped over the dead Pyran lying in the middle of the path. Croy ran into a young ash tree while stumbling. With a quick glance at the bloodstains on the ash he hopped sideways out of the way. Verin strode up past Croy and inspected the body.

"I take it this isn't the Pyran we're looking for." Her dry voice, accompanied with the casualness that she flipped the body over to inspect it, gave Croy a slight case of the shivers. Her hands, quickly and deftly, touched each bloody spot on the Pyran's body. Fingers sliding callously into the entrance of the dead derlian's wounds. To watch made Croy incredibly queasy.

"He was killed by a sword, nothing else. He didn't take too many strikes to fell, either." She made a small "tsk" after her words, as if judging his fighting skills to be negligent. "I suppose he was felled by this Synde? I wish his fellows hadn't taken his weapon…" This last sentence was accompanied by a quick, almost furtive, glance around the body. Croy was relaxing slightly at the realization that she wasn't talking for his benefit, maybe not even meaning to speak. He felt a little better thinking that another Gaen had a problem with talking to themselves. "I can't tell how many blows he had fended off…" Her mind was obviously distant from Croy.

She stood suddenly and soundlessly. "Lead on, Sie'tin. How many did this Synde kill before death?" Her eyes were lit but seemed distant.

Croy started back upon the path towards Synde's body, his head slightly bowed to the tracks on the ground, but with an eye out for more bodies. It seemed slightly out of place to be tracking himself. "How can you admire battle so much? I mean, well, that there are so many beautiful things in this world. Not just things either, but I guess I mean happenings. Experiences, yes. There is so much wonder in the world, I don't see how fighting enters it. I would even say that violence is the opposite of wonder, the defiance of beauty." Croy kept his head bowed. Even had he wished it, and truly he did not, he could not look into her face as she pondered him. He was nervous and uneasy merely talking about fighting, and he was too frightened to glimpse a real warrior during such a conversation. For then he might receive the thing that he was dancing around: understanding the warrior's mind. There were so many times in his life that he could feel understanding creeping upon him, and his best defense against it was to not look it in the eye.

"You wish to have this conversation? Very well, you are a child and a fool, Sie'tin. Do you not see the world, nor understand it? There is no end to the violence, Croy. That is what makes up the world. If you were to have no 'jin, do you know what would happen? Gaens would walk up to your house, whether you are there or not, and take whatever they felt like taking. If you were there, then all the worse. They would walk straight up to you and push you, to start. To judge you. Then would come a wary glance, a circling walk. Hands upraised, with their gnarled knuckles facing you. And all the while you would be talking, babbling like a brook. Half-formed ideas of placation. Half sentences of pleading, to reasoning, back to pleading. Nothing completed, no. Not for you. Then do you know what would happen? Yes, you do, don't you? You've been there and seen what a monster true violence is, looked into its face. They would smile at you. Without a touch of warmth leaving those eyes. Just the preparation for joy, for excitement. Because by this time, Sie'tin, those eyes would know that you are weak." Verin's voice floated from behind Croy, cruel and non-corporeal. It reminded Croy of what he imagined a grinning, savage ghost would sound like. Without looking at her, any part of her, he could tell that she was smiling.

"I don't believe that, though. I think that if it were left to derlians like me and like my friends, there wouldn't even be fear in the world. Why would I wish to walk into someone's home, someone else's home, and destroy them? Destroy all those thoughts and memories. I bet you, and I'll bet whatever sum you could wish, as long as I can pay it, that I could talk to that person. Invite them into my home, to truly talk with them. Not only while I fed them, not only while we conversed and I learned from them, learned things I could never have even dreamed of, but while we traded compassions. Not just the passions of our lives, but the compassions. Not just the reasons with which we've sought life, but the magnitude of our willingness to embrace it. That which gives us our senses through which we understand our truth. The filter that our experience is sifted with, that which decides how our memories stay with us. Agh! I know it, but cannot seem to explain it. There is no real reality, you see. There is just memory, and everybody remembers differently." Croy's frustration was beginning overtake him, and he bowed out of the conversation, as his head bowed away from Verin.

"That was nice, Sie'tin, truly, a good effort. In fact I am pleased to say that was one of the better efforts I've ever come across. Unfortunately, that is just a dream and you can never convince me of the opposite. Because I am the type of derlian that can kill, Sie'tin. In fact, as you had pointed out so fervently before, I am the type of derlian that can enjoy it. Don't get me wrong, I would never kill without a reason. Without something that I believed in more than I believe in life. I can, however, understand a lust for blood. There is no other true competition in life. None. There are games, of course, but they are not real. Have you ever lost a game on purpose? To make someone feel better, or to not hurt their feelings, or to make them laugh or cry out in joy? Of course you have, you probably enjoy that form of manipulation." Croy almost turned and confronted her on that sentence. He could listen to her deranged view of life objectively, he could listen to her say he was weak, and he could even listen to her do her best to destroy his basic premise of Gaens and derlians in general. Her remark against his personality, however, attempting to suggest that he consciously, no, viciously and with contrivance, tried to bend another's will. Well, that was almost too much. Oddly enough, however, he did not turn around, he did not yell at her, and he did not correct her. And the slight laughter in her voice whispered something to him. It was one little word: weakness. "Nobody, ever or wherever, has lost a battle on purpose. You don't even know what reserves of strength you may have, you don't even understand the things you are capable of, you could never dream of the sheer power you posses, until you *must* win something. Must win!" A small chuckle escaped her, its reverberations twisting deeper in pitch with her mirth. "What am I saying! You do understand, don't you? Tell me then, farmer. What did it feel like when you crushed that Pyran's skull?"

"I would never have done that if it wasn't necessary! I would never... That is not the same as the violence you speak of." Croy almost said "It can't be!" but stopped himself.

"You're right, farmer, it isn't. But you do understand, don't you? There will always be derlians in the world who live by violence. So you must become violent to stand up to them. You must gather all your skills and strengths and fight against them with all the might you can bear." For the briefest of seconds Croy thought she had said "bare." He kept focused on the task at hand, however, and held his mind steady, focused. He knew he would be able to explain himself if he just kept his will pushing full force on the idea, like rolling a boulder uphill. If he could just put enough time and energy into his words. "You should be thankful that, as a Gaen, you have the 'jin to protect you from experiencing the full brunt of the world. The Pyrans have no such luxury."

"The reason the world will appear like the way you infer is solely in your own mind. You are your own reason, don't you see. Your own excuse. If there wasn't so much defense, there wouldn't be so much attack. You breathe in fear and exhale hate. Paranoia has a way of spiraling like vultures on..." Croy's voice faded as they came upon the sight of the carnage. There was no clean-up crew here, nothing had been disturbed by Gaen hands. The impressions of the fight returned to Croy, entering his body like a ghost, its chill touch seeping from his shell, to his core. The echoes of his own screams. He was afraid, and he almost agreed with Verin. Mouth slack, attempting to find words of defeat. That not only is the world violent, but that it has to be violent. Then he saw what was missing. "Where is Synde's body?" Croy's own voice sounded hollow and incredulous to him, which made him worry about what it sounded like to Verin.

Croy ran to where he recalled Synde's body had found its peace. There was only a black-red, with much more black than red, stain on the forest floor. Even half soaked into the wood and leaves that littered the hungry dirt, the stain was roughly derlian shaped. If the shape wasn't bipedal, then it was very strangely splayed out. Croy could not understand why the body wasn't here. His only explanation was that the other Pyrans had found it and carried it away. He had seen Synde die. He had seen it!

Verin's head slowly surveyed the entire seen. She had stood in the center, or the closest proximity to center that she could muster under the circumstances, and slowly turned. Her eyes were taking in the history of that place. Her arc was slow and deliberate, and when she finished she began back at the Pyran that Croy had killed. Croy stood and momentarily forgot the mystery of Synde, staring at her examinations. She seemed more methodical than any other Gaen that he had ever seen. This being a dominant Gaen trait was saying a lot about her. Not only did he not really expect one of the 'jin to be this completely thorough, but from their conversation of a few moments ago it seemed unlikely that she would be this, well, patient. Croy's attention was short-lived, however. And when he began to look back at the forest floor, he noticed a small trail of splattered blood. It was small enough to make Croy wonder at it. Surely Synde was bleeding enough to leave a larger trail than that.

Croy started to follow the blood trail, letting Verin take in the battle zone. He heard a loud snap from her direction and looked quickly. She was pointing at him and frowning. Her hand made a second, quieter snap. Her front forefinger was pointed at him and she made a slight, though emphatic, downwards motion with her arm. Croy recognized this universal motion of sitting down as readily as the first time he had ever seen it, with his mother's angry face behind the arm. His body had actually recognized it first and was in the motion of sitting down next to the bloodstain when his mind was beginning to wonder about the gesture. Croy wondered if there was some prior knowledge given before birth, one that encapsulated all those strange emphatic motions his parents used to always make, to allow him to understand them immediately without ever experiencing them before. It was either that or telepathy was real, and derlians did it so readily that they didn't even have to really try. They just had to put enough energy behind it to reach through to the recipient.

Croy was caught between the options of watching Verin do her investigation, or angering her with his own investigation. It was odd, but their very conversation earlier made him want to chase after the trail without her. He felt an odd mixture of feelings swirling together in him. He couldn't really separate them enough to find out what they were individually, though he tried. All in all he merely had one generalized feeling, as if his emotions had been canceling each other out and there was just one overall mood left behind. He wanted to be rebellious. That was the vague itching at the back of his mind. He did not really care about what, or why, he just wanted to act perpendicularly from orders. To obviously disobey. However, it did not take too much willpower to keep himself from doing so.

Verin had passed the first Pyran that Croy had killed and had quickly looked over the thoughtful Pyran's body, with its large entrance and exit wounds. She was now crouched over Brycca's body. She seemed to be taking more time with his body than the others, and Croy's curiosity and his vague impatience got him up. He walked carefully over to Verin and the body, as if breaking a twig would break her concentration. When he reached the body, he crouched down opposite of Verin. She had the corpse flipped over on its back. And, for the first time, Croy examined his own violence. The smiling Pyran didn't affect Croy like Brycca did. When he looked at the Pyran's body, he recalled his savageness. His overkill, you could say. Something that he would have never thought that he was capable of. He still knew he was right about peace, though. He knew he was right.

"If it makes you feel any better, he was probably dead before you got to him. Not that he could have been alive after you had finished with him." Her smile was lost on Croy, who was watching her examine the body. She had her knife in a ragged opening in the Pyran's neck, prying it open so she could peer into it. "It looks like Synde got to this one as well. Not bad at all." She turned and stared at Croy, having him bend his head up from Brycca's shattered skull to look at her face because she was smiling so intently at him. "Do you know what this cloak is, Croy?"

Croy glanced down at the bloodied, muddied, and tattered cloak. "No, I don't know anything about Pyran military matters." Croy tried to put a little heat in his words, but his heart wasn't really in it.

"No, you wouldn't, would you? This is a Guard's cloak. They are the tiny elite warpack that protects their King, you know. Didn't you say that this Brycca, right?, called Synde one of the Guard as well? Hmmm, smells like a revolution to me." Verin's dagger was absentmindedly tapping Brycca on the chest while she was thinking. The motion made Croy somewhat nervous.

"Brycca also mentioned a ring and a sword of Synde's. They were yelling about rank and stuff." Croy was having problems recalling the recent battle. It was as if his mind were in a haze. He couldn't find his bearings.

Verin's dagger stopped tapping. "Well, the sword is no big deal. They have what you would call swordmasters, I can't remember exactly what they call themselves. But they have these specific smiths who make amazingly well balanced and weighted swords, and a warrior will train with this one sword until he becomes a master with it. Once he loses it, he must begin again with a different sword. They even name the swords and everything. Synde's must have been very well made, and that is probably why Brycca wanted it. As for the ring, I'm not sure. I know there is something about proving that you killed someone, if you are trying to raise yourself in their caste system, but I don't ever remember hearing anything special about a ring. Maybe it was just something that would prove Synde's death to the King." With the last sentence Verin's eyes began to turn inward slightly, unfocusing in thought. She stood while still looking past Croy and tapped the tip of her dagger against her chin. Luckily none of the blood was liquid anymore, and she had not soiled her blade.

"You should go back. Tell Crydlak and the Blind One that I'm going to follow that trail of blood. If the Blind One wishes to know more, he can *whisper* to me. I'll head back in one hour if I don't hear anything from them. We'll talk more later, farmer." Verin turned and walked back to the stain that was left by Synde. From there she began to crouch forward and follow the minute blood splatterings.

Croy watched her disappear into the woods, then turned and walked back the way he came. His mind mulled over a way to explain peace. As it was meant by him. He knew in his gut, in his soul, what he meant. Every time he tried to explain it, however, it never sounded the same as it was in his head. He was so involved with his internal discussion that he didn't realize he was out of the forest until he was almost upon Crydlak.

"Where is Verin, Croy? What are you doing coming back alone?" Crydlak's tone was deep and serious.

"We didn't find Synde's body. It's as if he just laid there for a while, then got up and wandered off. Verin went to follow his trail of blood. And she said the Blind One could 'whisper' to her if he wanted. Or something like that." Croy had attempted to remember everything in that burst of speech. "Oh, and she'll head back in an hour if she doesn't hear from you."

Crydlak merely growled and strode towards where the Blind One was talking with one of the carriage drivers. Croy decided to walk slowly over there, so as not to catch any ill temper from either of them. He was not that worried about the driver's opinion.

As he neared the carriage, Crydlak strode back past him towards the forest. He smiled at Croy and waved, so Croy smiled and nodded back to him. Then Croy was before the Blind One.

"You have been very valuable to us here, Croy, but I think that it is time that we left for Serif." The Blind One motioned Croy up into the carriage. He felt much more secure this time in entering the carriage, his fear staying at the battleground behind him. He clambered up into the carriage and then waited for the Blind One's entrance. It seemed to take a very long time for the Blind One to climb aboard. Once he entered, however, the carriage almost immediately started to ramble in a slow half circle as they turned back towards home.

"Listen, Croy. There are a few matters that we must have understood between us. Mainly there is the issue of Trela. You must keep her under close observation. I will expect you to answer any questions I put to you about her. She is central to why the Pyrans have come into our realm, and I will have the whole story of this. Most important is the fact that we have her. I do not want to scare her or make her uncomfortable, for she is still a child, so I will leave her in your care. She is, however, not allowed to ever leave Serif, even to accompany you on herding expeditions, and she will participate in our schools. If she ever attempts escape, or you overhear her planning anything of the sort, you will immediately come to me. Then we will come and keep her under our supervision. Do you understand, Croy? The 'jin do not always have the most comfortable accommodations, you know. I wish to be perfectly clear on this. This is not just a little girl. She has much to do with our peace." The Blind One's voice seemed flat and quick like an automaton of myth. It was as if he were reciting from rote memory.

"Yes. Of course, I understand. I, uh, thank you for letting me keep Trela under my care." That last part seemed to jump into Croy's head from nowhere. He supposed he was just being polite.

"And Croy, there is much to talk about with your training. Nobody can be forced into something as tenuous as magic, Croy, and I am not about to try to force you. But, please, you should think about it. I will give you three moons of no pressure at all. At the end of these three moons I expect you will give me a satisfactory answer. There are few anymore who have the gift you have," the Blind One said while smiling, and his voice was beginning to loose some of its sudden edge. This was comforting to Croy because he was more used to the Blind One appearing deliberate than eager. And the familiar, no matter how awful, is always more comfortable than the strange.

While the carriage was rattling and shaking, Croy attempted to think of a question he could ask the Blind One. One about magic. Not that he was necessarily interested, but more to relax the Blind One. Let him know that they could work together in this business. Croy had decided to never investigate anything again. No matter if the entire forest was burning down.

"How come I could see the ghost? Both Verin and Crydlak seemed oblivious of it. No, wait. I know what you will say, I can think of a better question… How come I could see the outline of the ghost's crest?" Croy knew that his mind would finally remember something that had bothered him about the encounter, other than the encounter itself.

"Ah, that is a good question. Most Gaens would have skipped that in their minds, or at least in their memories. The crest was visible because it was a large part of that Pyran's identity. You see the ghosts as they would see themselves." The Blind One was nodding to the sway of the carriage.

"If you had the apparition under your control, then why couldn't you just ask it if Trela was the Kriishan?" Croy could feel questions welling up inside of him, one after another. They moved so swiftly and seamlessly that he had problems remembering the first ones. He shut the entire process off with a quick thought that while he wasn't quite interested, he was becoming curious.

"I could have, but all I would have gotten was the apparition's opinion. At best. The ghosts are the same as they would be when they were alive. The same loyalties and mischiefs. The ghost could have been a habitual liar when it was alive. It could have been told false information. It could have sworn against telling anyone the answer to your query. That is why the 'may' is so important in the apparition's reply. It is attention to detail that gains you success. If the ghost would have replied, 'I will answer your question to the best of my abilities,' or some such sentence, then you know to steer clear of that one and ask the next apparition. Did you feel my teleportation? Or did you just feel my spirit-talk?" The Blind One shifted the topic so quickly that Croy was left silent for several moments. But the regaining of his verbal balance happened so suddenly and assuredly, like a quick dive into icy water, that he was almost knocked off of balance again.

"I only noticed you missing, not the fact that you left." Croy slipped back into blushing silence.

"Then you can see the effects of magic, not the magic itself. Sometimes it comes about naturally, but it can be learned as well. I myself had to learn that skill, and it was a difficult one at that. In a situation such as combat, however, there really is nothing better than being able to sense when magic is being done." The Blind One was still nodding slowly with the motion of the carriage, smiling slightly.

The silence that surrounded them was that of a morning frost, nothing too dense or uncomfortable, and held for quite some time. The swaying of the carriage was as gentle as a lullaby. Croy's contented face swayed back and forth with the carriage.

"Croy, how many dreams did you have? Was it just three?" The Blind One's voice low and hushed, as if he had been resting along with Croy.

"Yes, it was just three. You had labeled them after the elements. The first was Gaen, the second was Fire, or Pyran, and the last one was Air, Luften." Croy's soft voice filled the carriage.

"I wonder where the Fluens are? In you, of course, I wonder where they are in you?" The Blind One's voice faded back into the walls of the carriage. Croy could not have hoped for a more peaceful carriage ride. Both Gaens sat at their own sides of the carriage and rested. All Croy could think about on the way home was Ilana. Even when she was absent, she balanced his unsure mind.

Chapter 6

Clerin awoke with adrenalin pumping through her. It was akin to the panic she felt trying to let go of a rope swing over a river. Her forehead was drenched with sweat, making her hair stick to her face. For a moment she struggled to hear something in the dark, assuming that a noise had awoken her. As the fog from her dream began to lift from her mind, she realized why she had startled. It was a dream that had made her heart pound, not an intruder. Quickly, before the last wisps of her sleeping life evaporated like the morning dew, she cast her mind back to find what had so rudely roused her.

Stairs. There was something to do with stairs. Was she running up them or down them? There were pillars, cut ionic pillars, as well. They flanked the open side of the stairwell. The surrounding walls seemed green, with slime maybe. Lots of cracks between the stones, and through the stones for that matter. The cracks almost looked like writing to Clerin. She wondered, briefly, if in her actual dream she could read them. Or, maybe, they had just looked like cracks and in her wakened state she associated words with them. She had the image, almost an emotion rather than an image, of looking down through the center of the stairwell. Deep inky blackness. It was like looking at the infinite. Or maybe looking into nothingness itself. The vertigo made Clerin feel sick to her stomach. The walls around her began a slow spin. Even with her eyes open, even sitting in bed, she again saw the blackness. It seemed to consume her vision, it seemed to reach out with empty tentacles. The blackness snaked around her and seemed to grab at the edges of her mind. The tentacles began to envelop her, to choke her.

A terrible scream tore the air around Clerin. The scream she heard was her own. It was this noise that jarred Clerin back into wakefulness. Was she asleep earlier? Did she have two dreams? Clerin's heart would not stop crashing itself against her chest wall. Her skinny limbs shook, knocking her bones against themselves. With her blankets pulled up around her, so that no flesh other than her head was uncovered, she stared out at the burgeoning light filling the hallway connected to her room. She had not meant to cry out like that, but now she felt more at ease with another Fluen coming to check on her. She smiled slightly as she realized it was her father walking briskly down the hall.

"Clerin. Clerin! Are you all right?" Her father's voice, usually very deep and measured, seemed shaken.

"Yes, of course, Father. I'm sorry that I woke you. It was a very vivid nightmare. Like the ones I used to get as a child." Clerin's voice seemed too soft to herself, almost weak.

"Strange. I wonder… Well, anyway, you are safe and that is what matters. I was already awake, though. Your mother contacted me while I was sleeping. She is on her way home for a respite. She should be here by the morning. Now then, do you think you can fall asleep again?" As her father asked the question, Clerin knew what he was hoping she would say.

"Of course. There is no need to worry about me. Go ahead and get the house ready for mother." Clerin managed a lopsided smile for him.

"Good. I, ah… She will want to talk with you for a while when she gets in. It has something to do with the translating she is doing. It is nothing to worry about." Clerin's father smiled a tender, warm smile. Clerin returned the favor even though her mind was awhirl.

"I can hardly wait. It has been several moons since she has been home." Clerin wondered silently what this could mean. His last sentence did not make a lick of sense. If there was nothing to worry about, then why say it. In fact, Clerin had not been worried at all until her father had said that. She beamed one more smile at him and turned her shoulder, signaling that she was ready to sleep.

"Rest soundly, my dearest." As he stood to walk away, she thought he muttered, "You will need it," but it might have been her overactive imagination. The light slowly dimmed until he turned a corner and shut her into darkness.

Her mother was not supposed to return for almost another two moons. It seemed, though it was hard to tell from her brief conversation with her father, that her mother was returning to talk to her. Though she had to be careful about what she assumed. Jylohan, her poetry teacher, always commented that Clerin thought she was the center of the world. He was always teasing her that if a hurricane struck the coast, she would think it was her fault. All of these thoughts kept Clerin up most of the rest of the night, so that she was indeed ragged by the time the sun burst through her windows.

****

At dawn Clerin chose her clothing carefully. There was usually a lot of fanfare for someone returning from translating. Clerin thought her dress should indicate that she knew her mother was returning, even though that was not conventional. Sooner or later her mother would realize that Clerin knew, and what would her mother think of her if she had met her wearing her normal morning robes? Not much. Clerin's mother was a stickler for formality. "If you do not know the proper way to conduct yourself, then go home and lock the door for no one will wish to be around you." Clerin doubted she could count the times she had heard that from her mother.

The cobalt blue dress with the white trim. That should do nicely. The blue signified the special occasion while the trim along the edges was to indicate receiving a wonderful present. That of her returning mother, of course. While she was laying the dress out, she mentally went through her various shoes while brushing her hair. Her hair should be braided because even though she has already made her first performance, her mother had yet to commend her upon it. Therefore, in her mothers eyes, she was still a child. After brushing her hair, Clerin chose the necklace that her mother had given her right before she had left for the translation. She held it up to her neck and watched it scintillate in the mirror. The giant sapphire in the middle of the necklace looked stunning coupled with her dress. While she braided her hair, she stood at her open closet staring at her shoe collection. It was morning, so they should be soft sided. It was a special occasion, so they should be gilded. With her ambiguous childhood status, they should be flat footed. Frantically her eyes scanned the bottom of the closet until they fell upon the perfect pair. Clerin shod her feet, patted her hair and dress one last time, and walked down the hall towards the breakfast dining room. She tried to keep her hands from fidgeting with the front of the dress too much while she walked, but she had always had difficulty controlling her hands.

Clerin almost fainted when she entered the breakfast dining room. There was her father, looking regal in white though not very festive, and talking to him was her mother. It was a way that she had never seen her mother before: disheveled. Her mother's hair was a mess, almost a bird's nest of snarls. The dress that she wore was tattered along the hemline and caked with mud. She still had on her riding boots, and she looked as if she had been in the sun and wind for too long. Her mother was usually so adamant about protecting herself from the ravages of the weather.

"Mother, I…" was all Clerin could get out of her mouth before her mother whirled to face her.

"We are leaving as soon as you change, Clerin. I hope, for both of our sakes, that this will not take long. Wear your riding clothes, the sturdiest you have. Well, come on now, we are pressed for time." Her mother's sharp chin, drawn cheeks, and pale blue eyes made her look feral in the state she was in. With one mighty clap from her long-fingered hands she roused Clerin from her shock.

"Of course, mother." Clerin hopped in place in her eagerness to please. She turned and trotted as fast as she felt decorum would let her. A hundred questions swirled into Clerin's frantic mind. There were too many to really recognize any of them. She had never needed to head anywhere in a hurry with her mother. She had never been summoned anywhere. For that was the only thing that Clerin could think of that would make her mother behave such. Which led her mind to the next question. Why would they ride? Oh, most of Clerin's traveling had been on horse or in a carriage. It was simple and less strenuous than magical modes of transportation. But if they were in a hurry, as was made obvious by her mother, why would they not just fly? While Clerin changed her clothes, her mind teased at the knot of questions that assailed her. Twisting and pulling, she followed one thread to another, but she could not figure out why they should ride.

As she pulled on her boots, she noticed the small hunting dagger that was sheathed on the outside of the right boot. She thought about removing it as it was a gift and she thought it might chafe on the ride, but remembering the disheveled look on her mother's face made her leave it in her boot. Clerin quickly tucked her thick breeches into the top of her boots and strode through her bedroom doorway. She hurried almost to the point of running towards the breakfast dining room. She was grateful that she had followed protocol so closely as to already have braided her hair. Her mother had never been known for her patience, especially not with Clerin.

When she entered the room she slowed and stopped for there was no one waiting for her. She waited for one long breath hoping that a servant would burst in to show her where her parents were waiting for her. As she slowly exhaled she tried to let her tension out with her breath as her magic teacher, Olwinn, had taught her. She did not feel that much better, but she was able to think more clearly.

Clerin left the breakfast dining room for the stables. She walked as quickly as she could without making herself sweat. Her mother often told her how unladylike it was to be noticed sweating.

As she reached the ambulatory along the wall of the courtyard, she could see her parents at the far end with two saddled horses. Clerin could tell that the horses were agitated by the way they shuffled sideways. Horses were very good at sensing nervousness, and her mother was obviously exuding it. Clerin left the catwalk-roofed ambulatory for the courtyard proper and approached the horses. She could make out Gymnie's voice as she got closer. The stable-hand's voice was slow and concentrated.

"Of course you are the Lady of the house, I had meant no offense. I was merely suggesting that the young mistress would like to take an older mare. Ranger here is barely broken." Gymnie showed his own nervousness by bobbing his head up and down. Clerin felt sorry for the old stable-hand and decided to yell across the courtyard to detract attention.

"I am ready! Good, you've got the horses ready." Clerin trotted the last bit of courtyard to stand next to Ranger. She smiled up at him and patted his rust colored flank.

"Finally. Gymnie, help Clerin up." Clerin's mother swung herself onto her own gray mare with finesse. "We have no more time to waste. Goodbye Aillel, goodbye Gymnie." She tapped her heals against the horse's flank and it began walking towards the open back gate.

Clerin swung her leg over the pommel with Gymnie pushing on her other foot. He smiled up at her and patted her thigh. "You be careful with Ranger, remember to only mount on his right side, he can't abide by the left."

"Thank you, Gymnie, and farewell. And farewell to you, Father. I will miss you." Clerin wanted to ask him if he knew how long she would be gone, where she was headed, and why the need for such urgency. Instead she smiled large enough to keep her eyes dry.

"Take care, my little derling. Think twice before you tell anybody that you will do something. Scratch that, think three times." He patted her leg affectionately and turned his head away.

"Are you following or not?" Her mother's crisp voice pierced Clerin's emotional cloud. Clerin bounced her heels into Ranger's ribs and he trotted past Gymnie towards the open gate.

"Of course, Mother. I was just saying my goodbyes. Where are we headed?" Clerin tried to keep her voice light during the question. She had learned long ago to be very conscious of the inflections in her voice around her mother.

"That is none of your concern. We have time to make up for. I will tell you more when we stop for lunch. Now you must keep your head down and ride." With the last word, her mother stuck her boots into her mare, and the horse flew forward. Ranger needed no more encouragement than that and started galloping after her. Clerin bent her back forward and watched her fleeting mother while Ranger's head bobbed up and down in her peripheral vision. His dark walnut brown mane caressed her face. She squinted her eyes to keep the wind from blurring her vision too much.

It had been a while since Clerin had taken a pleasure ride around the grounds let alone a full gallop. Luckily for her, Ranger seemed to know what was expected of him—to chase the mare—and Clerin could just hold on. Her thighs felt good right now, but she figured that her mother would not stop for lunch before noon, so she kept her bouncing to a minimum and tried to flow with Ranger's motions below her.

The sky turned gray during their ride. The clouds seemed poised to empty themselves at any moment, but held back. The air became thick as they rode across the plain and then up along the switchbacks of Scout mountain. The morning dragged on in a dreary haze. Clerin was no longer sure of which direction they where headed. The droning horses' hooves and the heavy air started to weigh on her. Her thighs began to burn, and her mother seemed as if she would ride all day and all night before slowing in the slightest.

Even though the clouds were high up, they made it seem as if a fog encompassed the land. Clerin was squinting so much that she almost had her eyes closed. She caught herself several times wishing to just shut them tight and trust her mount. She had been tossed off of enough horses in her lifetime to know that was foolish, however. A horse's mind was an enigma to Clerin, and she could never tell when a horse would decide to try to brush her off with a tree branch let alone make a sudden turn. So she kept her energy focused outward to the horse and the land rather than resting her mind with some daydreaming. Still the horses galloped on. She was unsure of how long her thighs could take the constant abuse but knew better than to try to yell up to her mother. The odds of her mother even hearing her were not good, and she knew that her mother would not react well to her pleading for a quick rest. So she kept on in silence. Watching the horse ahead of her and the horse under her and wondering. Wondering what this was all about.

Clerin looked out over the bleak landscape. They were getting closer to the river, she noticed, which meant that they were heading a little east as well as south. They had crested the small foothills to Scout mountain some time ago. Since then Clerin had been watching the trees become more dense. Now that they were closer to the river though, the trees were getting thicker in small bunches. There was one copse in particular that caught Clerin's eye. It was near a bend in the river, and her mother seemed to be heading towards it.

Without the sun to guide her, Clerin was unsure of what time it was. She thought that it felt like noon, but her thighs thought it was coming on to evening. That may have just been how out of shape she was, however. Clerin was seriously considering risking her mother's wrath for a break in the torrential riding when her mother started to slow down. She veered towards the small copse in the distance and slowed to a canter. Clerin took the opportunity to catch up with her and ask some questions.

"Are we headed for the copse, mother? Just for a quick lunch in the shelter of the trees?" Clerin was hoping that her mother would tell her that they were stopping for an hour or two but knew better than to ask.

"Yes, we are heading towards the copse, Clerin. And no, we are not stopping for lunch. We are meeting someone. Now stay alert, my little one. We do not want any surprises." With that she slowed her horse to a walk. They were still far enough from the trees that she could not make out the leaves on their branches. Rather than ask any more questions, however, she decided to study the landscape. Her mother had not called her "little one" for some time. Clerin knew that she should be annoyed that her mother had referred to her as a child, but her heart was warmed at the use of the term of endearment instead. If her mother wished her to keep a look out for danger, then Clerin could surely oblige her.

When they were a quick sprint away from the copse, her mother stopped her horse and called out. "I have returned. Come forth so that I may continue my journey in good speed." Clerin's mother kept a keen eye in several directions at once. Her horse had started shifting sideways, probably sensing her unease, but she controlled it with a tight rein. The more her mother showed her agitation, the more nervous Clerin became.

The gray day seemed to suck any natural noise down to the ground. It was so quiet that Clerin should have been able to hear grass seeds dropping in the field. The silence made her wonder if there were any animals nearby at all. Or maybe she had been struck deaf. She began to wonder if she should pull her dagger from her boot.

Clerin started as her horse snorted and began to dance sideways away from the river. As she was reining in Ranger, she looked over to the river just in time to see it boil. The sound of the roiling water gained in volume until it roared like a waterfall. There was a small eddy in the center of the bubbling river. While Clerin watched, it turned into large whirlpool dipping to the rocky river bottom. With a sudden burst of noise a geyser shot forth from the whirlpool. She was completely transfixed by the image. In her mind she knew that she should be watching in all directions, making sure that no one was sneaking up on them. But she felt like she was made of stone, that she could not move a muscle to save her life. The geyser arced into the air and landed a stone's throw away in a great column of water. The water was constantly flowing over a stable inner shape. The column split along the bottom into legs and along its sides into arms and it grew smaller at the top for a head. Clerin waited for the Fluen Yaven to devour her and her mother in one great gesture, but it merely stood there looking at them.

"Midinarre! Even though you had promised to be back before noon, I did not believe it possible. You amaze me. As you can see, I brought Wilthenharkenopnorang here for the transport you desired. Ah, Clerin, are you going to ignore me all day?" Olwinn's voice was unmistakable. He had always seemed in a good mood even if he was being reprimanded on her behalf. Which, unfortunately, had happened more than once. Even though Clerin had seen several Yavens before, all Fluen of course, she could not stop staring at the creature. She finally tore her gaze from the Yaven and looked over at her old magic teacher. He was fairly young for a Court Mage, and had been incredibly young when he first began tutoring her sister and herself. His soft brown eyes under thin eyebrows had always glimmered with a slightly mischievous happiness. He had a smooth, clean-shaven chin, with a small dimple in the middle of it. He was rather muscular for a mage, which gave his jaw a strong profile. It was his smile that Clerin remembered most, though. It was always warm and sincere.

"Good day, Olwinn. Why did you not fly us to this meeting point?" Clerin knew that she was overstepping her bounds by asking such a question, but since she directed it at a servant of the household she felt she could get away with it.

"Haha, I see more of your mother in you every cycle you age. The gist is this, magic can be sensed fairly easily, even a couple of days gone by. While the passage of a horse, and especially a Yaven, is undetectable in a mere hour or two. Your mother and I..." Olwinn was happily prattling on when Clerin's mother interrupted.

"Enough! You should not ask questions, Clerin. Everything I do, I do with a reason, that should satisfy you. As for you, Olwinn, you talk too much, you always have. Need I remind you of why you are in our service?" Clerin's mother arched her eyebrows at the mage, her blue eyes piercing into him as a spear would.

"I am forgetful of my place, Lady, and I beg your pardon most humbly." Even though his words were quiet, his eyes still danced and a smile was still perceptible on his lips. "Wil, get into position."

The Yaven, which Clerin had somehow momentarily forgotten about, flowed down to the ground. It took the shape of a large box. Clerin's mother dismounted her mare and walked over to Olwinn. Lowering her voice, she whispered to him while Clerin dismounted and walked over to the Yaven.

"Hello, my name is Clerin. I am very pleased to meet with you, Wil." Clerin used the shortened form of its name. It was considered impolite to directly use a Yaven's full name unless you were summoning. "I understand that you will be taking us from here, yes?"

"Hello, Clerin. I am also very pleased to meet with you. If you will lie down on top of me, I will encapsulate you for our voyage." The Yaven's voice rumbled underneath itself like boiling water, but sounded a bit higher pitched, like steam.

"Will I get wet?" Clerin was mainly waiting for her mother to be done with Olwinn but she was also curious.

"Yes, a little. I will make myself a hard solid, so you will not be too wet, but some of me still seeps out." The Yaven spoke so matter-of-factly that Clerin could not help but wonder what its voice would sound like if it were emotional. She even wondered briefly if it could be emotional. She knew that derlians came from Yavens but they just seemed so incredibly different that it appeared that they were completely unrelated.

"How long have you been in this world?" Clerin was unsure of how to phrase her question correctly.

"I was summoned a moon ago by your reckoning of time. I have been here many times before, however. Have you ever seen a Menel?" The Yaven's voice changed a bit at the last sentence. Clerin thought she could imagine a tone of emotion in its voice, something akin to pride. She had certainly never heard a Yaven offer up something so personal. In fact, Clerin was unsure of whether or not she had ever heard a Yaven say something besides answering a direct question.

"No, I have not. I am awful curious, though, and would truly like to see yours." Clerin kept her voice low just in case her mother could hear her talking to the Yaven. She was unsure as to the protocols of dealing with a Yaven, but she was sure that her mother knew them. Clerin glanced over to where her mother and Olwinn were standing. Their backs were to her, probably so that she would not be tempted to try to read their lips, so she assumed she had a small window of opportunity.

"Watch here, young derlian." At the word "here" Wil made a small whirlpool in the center of itself. Clerin knelt on one edge of Wil and stared into the center if its being. The whirlpool dipped into Wil until it almost reached the other side. The bottom of the whirlpool shifted slowly around the back of Wil as if searching for something. The bottom of the funneled water alighted upon something dark and stayed in one place for a moment. Then the whirlpool centered itself and grew milder and milder until the bottom reached the surface that Clerin was staring at. Up popped a small amulet that floated upon the surface of Wil.

"May I touch it? Or is that asking too great a liberty?" Clerin wanted to study the object. To feel it and taste it and stare at it with a magnifying glass. She had heard of these all of her life and she would probably never see one again. Especially since magic was one of her weaker suits.

"I apologize, but no derlian may touch a Menel. It is for your protection that this law has been made. Each section is a pure element and could sap you of life." Wil seemed so nonchalant about letting Clerin see its Menel that she wondered briefly if it showed its Menel to every derlian it had some spare time with.

Clerin placed her hands down upon Wil and crouched over the Menel to study it closer. It seemed to be made of a dark gray metal. It had carvings all along its face. It could have been writing in a secret Yaven language or just heavily filigreed, she was not sure. Its face was clearly split into three sections. Each section had the rudimentary symbol for an Element embossed upon it, all except for water. One for each element that Wil has procured, thought Clerin. Each group of three made an incredibly thin plate that was sandwiched by other plates to make a thick medallion. Looking at just how thick the Menel was suddenly made Clerin realize why Wil was showing it to her. Pride! Wil must have an impressive Menel compared to most Yavens, she thought to herself.

"How do you make a Menel?" Clerin knew the question, which sounded simple, was impossible to answer, but she did not know the right question to ask.

"The first plate is the most difficult. After that you add each elemental gel to the plate below it and it solidifies into its proper place." Wil dropped the Menel from view, which made Clerin stop in the middle of her next sentence.

"Elemental gel…?" Clerin quickly glanced up to see her mother and Olwinn heading towards her. She rolled from her hands and knees to her back and smiled sheepishly up at her mother.

"If you insist upon smiling like that, you will make me think you are up to no good. Now lie back and get comfortable so that I may board." Clerin's mother glared at her for one long second then turned to Olwinn. "Be quick, then meet us at the Temple. I wish that I did not need you elsewhere at the moment, but there is no going back now. Remember to wait until you are past Scout mountain before speeding up the process. Farewell, Olwinn, until we meet again." Clerin was no longer looking at the two, but staring at the clouds above. She wished that she had been paying more attention to the exchange because her mother sounded soft and wistful at the end there.

"Farewell, Midinarre. Try and be somewhat cautious with the little one." His voice was muted as well, lacking its usual vigor. "Farewell, Clerin. Farewell, Wil. I will meet with you in a few days. Obey Midinarre as if she were I." Olwinn waved and walked out of Clerin's sight towards the horses.

"We are going to have to make up for lost time, Wil. I want you to move as fast as possible without being too visible or leaving too much spore." Clerin's mother laid down onto Wil and pressed her hand into Clerin's. It was this small act of kindness, or maybe weakness, that made Clerin really worry. The day was getting more and more stressful by the moment, and they still had not eaten yet.

"Prepare yourselves for the encapsulation." Wil's voice had become more monotone again. Without another word, waves rushed up from all sides and hovered, waiting to crash down onto them. Clerin squinted her eyes against the impact. The crash never came. She opened her eyes back up when she felt movement and noticed that the water had made a sort of lid that enveloped both her and her mother. There was a small tube sticking up out of the lid, and Clerin wondered if that was an air tube for breathing. Wil flowed over the land to the river and slid right into the water. They sank into the river until Clerin was sure that the lid was covered with river water, the hollow tube their only link to the world outside of Wil.

They started to slowly float downstream with the current. Clerin stopped herself from unconsciously holding her breath and inhaled slowly and evenly. It was disconcerting to be underwater, surrounded by water, and the only thing that stood between her and drowning was water with consciousness: Wil. They flowed downstream, northwards towards the sea, very quickly. Though Clerin could feel the motion in her stomach, there were none of the other indicators of movement that Clerin was used to: the wind in her face, the pull of friction, or the small sounds of hooves or water sloshing on the sides of a boat. The blurry sight of the clouds racing by and the riverbank trees sliding past her vision made her stomach queasy even more than just the feeling of movement.

Though Clerin knew in her mind that she was in no danger, she began to feel trapped. She could feel her chest constricting with panic. She felt her own heartbeat in her neck. Her breathing became labored and shallow. She used to have panic attacks as a child, so she knew what was happening. She closed her eyes to shut off the cloudy sky scrolling by. She began breathing nice, long, slow breaths in through her nose and out through her mouth. She tried blanking her mind in meditation, but that seemed to make things worse. Instead she kept her breathing under control and tried her best to daydream. Throughout her whole ordeal, she kept her hands perfectly motionless. She did not want her mother to know she was panicking. Her mother had never really understood what Clerin went through. The advice of "Stop panicking!" never seemed to calm Clerin down much.

"Clerin, I suppose now is a good time to tell you why we are here. As you know, I have been translating with Lembin quite often in the last few cycles. Lembin thinks that I have an affinity for understanding the Beleg's telepathic speech, and I do. We have finally finished all that Lembin wishes to communicate about the Histories, Yavens, and derlians. It has taken many generations of Fluens to work all of this out, and Lembin has grown tired. Before Lembin rests, however, it needs some errands begun. I volunteered, of course, to run the errands, but it refused my offer. Lembin thinks that I am too valuable a translator to be sent out of the Fluen realm. Do you understand so far?" Clerin's mother squeezed her hand lightly. Clerin's mind raced. As far as she could tell, her mother had yet to really say anything. She already knew that her mother was one of Lembin's favorite translators. She also knew that the great work was coming to a close. So what was there to understand? Suddenly Clerin's heart began pumping ice instead of blood.

"Are you suggesting that I run Lembin's errands for you? I have barely had my first public Telling. I have never even been near the borders of our realm, let alone stepped beyond them." Clerin began to feel claustrophobic again. Her breathing came more rapidly. She suddenly had an ugly thought. "Is this why you have refused to tell me what we are doing? Is this why you waited until I was trapped inside a Yaven with you to tell me?" Clerin knew that her voice was sounding crazy. It was high pitched and began to crack at the last sentence. She felt like she needed to fight, to hit something at least.

"Stop panicking, Clerin! It is unbecoming of a lady of your stature. You are jumping to conclusions, dear. I have offered nothing to Lembin besides my own willingness to help, I swear. I did not even mention you." Clerin's mother's voice sounded calm and even. She took Clerin by the hand again and gave a comfortable squeeze.

"So what are you saying? Are we headed for the Temple?" Clerin knew that there was something being left out of the conversation. Knowing her mother as she did, however, she knew that there was no way to push her mother into telling her what it was. She would have to wait for her mother to tell her when she had finally decided the time was right.

"Yes, we are going to the Temple. And yes, Lembin wants to communicate with you, but it was Lembin who mentioned you to me and not the other way around. No one will force you to do anything that you do not wish to. Except, of course, to communicate with Lembin. That you must do as any Fluen who is called must do. The law of the land lays with the one who created us, none can refuse a summons from Lembin." Clerin's mother was not necessarily making her feel any better. In fact, it was only the knowledge that she had no escape that kept her from trying.

"How…how did Lembin mention me?" There were so many thoughts swimming in her head it was difficult not to just shout them all out. Clerin attempted to keep them queued up in her mind to be able to ask them one at a time.

"Lembin asked for my daughter that was making her first public Telling. The ways of communication with Belegs are tricky, Clerin. It is hard to pin down the exact meaning of the pictures you are made to imagine. I do know that Lembin wished to see you, however, because it was the night of your Telling that it communicated to me about you. I kept seeing you on the main stage bathed in white light. The images were clear that I should bring you with me to the Temple. They were also clear about the need for secrecy." Clerin's mother seemed to be warming up to the conversation. Her voice held what Clerin thought might be pride. For Clerin it was a difficult dichotomy to come to grips with. She did not want to run off on adventures. She wished to continue studying with Jylohan. She would soon be allowed to create her own poetry instead of just memorizing the great classics. She had many visions of herself in the future. All of them had her speaking publicly and living in the wondrous castle of her father's. None of them were about leaving her home and having to run errands in foreign realms. The pride in her mother's voice seemed to calm Clerin somewhat, however. She had always longed to hear that in her mother. It seemed as if her mother had always loved her sister more and gave Clerin the "love scraps" that were left on the plate after everyone else was full.

"What is the errand, anyway? You can stop being cryptic any time you want." Clerin found herself snapping at her mother, even while her mother was reaching out to her. She often felt herself feeling snappy when she felt vulnerable or uneasy.

"I do not know. The images were very choppy. It has something to do with the Luften realm, that I do know. I am not positive that what Lembin wants from you is the same errand that it communicated for me. I am not even sure if Lembin wants you for any errand. Maybe Lembin wishes to see how well you communicate and then it would send me on the errand." Her mother paused in her speech for a moment to collect her thoughts. It was here that Clerin decided to interject.

"Well, then why have you refused to tell me what this is about until now? You could have mentioned all of this in front of Father earlier." Clerin was doing her best to stay calm, but the effort was straining her.

"There are several reasons why I waited until now to tell you where we are headed. If something is spoken aloud, then it can be heard. If you had known we were going to the Temple, you might have been more worried on the ride. And finally, and this is the real reason, I have no clue as to why we are doing what we are doing. All I know is that this is what Lembin wants. I have been working so close with Lembin for so long that sometimes I feel as if I am a mere extension of it, like a fingernail. Connected but without being able to feel. I... I am sorry, this is probably not what you wish to hear." Clerin's mother trailed off and became still.

"No, I appreciate you talking to me. I am just scared and confused. This is just so unexpected. Last night ended so normally, and suddenly I am floating down a river in a Yaven." Clerin suddenly thought of her dream, but decided not to mention it. The feeling of motion without anything else was disconcerting. She still had her eyes closed and was racking her brain for the other hundred questions that she was supposed to ask.

"Your father has no idea of what we are doing or where we are going." The words hung in the air of their small chamber, trapped by Wil as much as they were. Her mother had spoken softly enough that Clerin understood there was some contention with that decision. She wondered if it was not her mother's choice that had kept her silent. This thought led to the image of her mother and Olwinn whispering to each other, though Clerin was unsure of why.

"Why would you keep secrets from Father? He is the council representative for our entire region. If not for personal reasons, then he should at least be notified for official reasons. I..." Clerin felt herself winding back up again. Her mother interrupted her speech before she could say anything more, however.

"Clerin, your father is a great Fluen. And he is an even greater advisor, especially concerning politics. He has an incredible mind for changing what words mean, without derlians noticing. But this is something different, something larger. Sometimes I think that we lead completely separate lives, your father and I. We remind me of old friends who stop by to check up on each other at times. Sit down and chat a little in front a nice fire, warming our hearts from without. I agree with you on some levels, Clerin. He is a good Fluen and should know what happens to his own daughter. It is just so much easier to leave him out of affairs of the Temple. But I digress. Hopefully you will understand when you are older and begin to forgive me." Clerin's mother had spoken quietly and left her hand flaccid in Clerin's. She thought hard but could not think of another time that her mother had spoken so plainly about her own problems, as if she were an older friend to confide in. The words stung her of lackluster love and stale marriage, but Clerin was glad that her mother thought enough of her to speak so honestly.

"You do not need my forgiveness, mother. You are a translator, one of Lembin's favorites. No one may look down upon you. Your whole life has been in service to the Temple." Clerin was unused to the role of consoler, except for consoling herself. She was unsure of what to say, but her anger was leaking from her as water leaves a sieve.

"You are too kind. I used to think that doing great things would validate me, justify my existence, and would make me forget anything unsavory that I have done in the past. As I get older, I am not so sure that I had the right idea. You know that I have never been one to dote on compliments, but I do not think I have ever heard you utter an unkind word about anyone. That is an admirable trait." Her mother trailed off here leaving Clerin alone with her thoughts. The one thought that kept prancing luridly in Clerin's mind was that the only reason her mother had never heard her say an unkind word was because she only spoke ill of her mother, and never face to face.

They flowed downstream quite some time in silence. Each engaged in their own private struggle to feel good about themselves. Clerin had the disturbing insight that she was more like her mother than her father. This poured more fear into her than the idea of meeting and maybe communicating with Lembin which, though an honored position, had struck many derlians greater than her with paralyzing dread. It outpaced even the thought of leaving the safe confines of the realm she was raised in. Though it was greater than these other fears, even collectively, it was quieter than them. It did not make her panic or cause her stomach to go queasy. It did, however, chill her bones. As youth flies in the face of experience and age, you follow the path that lies straight in front of you, that which you have grown accustomed to by watching it and loathing it as a child. Clerin made a silent vow to herself inside of Wil that day. No matter how much she admired her mother, she would never become like her. In doing so she completed one of the oldest rituals of the world. And she did so knowing that most before her had broken those same internal promises.

"We are here." The simple statement from Wil sounded bizarre from in the midst of it. Clerin had not noticed their slowdown at all. She had been lost in her own thoughts, oblivious to Wil and even her mother. Maybe it should be said, "especially her mother." The long silence had given Clerin time to run an entire gamut of emotions, leaving only a vague emptiness behind. She had chosen not to converse with her mother, even though this opportunity would probably never arise again. Her thoughts had centered on her mother's relationship with Olwinn, but she knew that she had only the slightest inkling of truth in this area. In youth it is often easy to lose yourself in the mock plays in your head. Rehearsing things that never happened and never would be.

"You are sure there is no one near?" Clerin's mother sounded hoarse, almost as if she had been sleeping. Her hand gripped Clerin's in the grasp of clandestine friends. Clerin supposed they were that now, sharing small secrets between each other. She gave her mother's hand a comforting squeeze before taking her own away.

"As far as I can sense, there are no derlians or Yavens. If you would like to sense with magic…" Wil started to float to the surface of the river. Clerin watched as the waves became opaque and choppy, then dissolved into the unmoving sky. Her stomach gave a small cheer for the cessation of motion.

"No, no magic. I thank you for your assistance, Wil. I will tell Olwinn of your exceptional service, maybe secure you an early release." Clerin's mother sat up and clambered off of Wil. She held out an assisting hand to Clerin.

"You have not only my admiration but also my gratitude, Wil. Remember me as I will remember you." Clerin wished she could more eloquently speak to the Yaven, but her mother's scowl kept her comments to a minimum. She knew that it was considered beneath her to speak kindly to a "servant," but she wished more than anything to have some more time alone with Wil. There was very little of Yavens that Clerin actually knew. Most of her knowledge came from the Histories or other tales and poems she had memorized. Little of the knowledge came from first-hand experience. Which, although she felt she had little of it in her young life, she felt in her heart that experience was the one true way to understanding. She just needed the time to gather it.

"Come, Clerin. We must let Wil get back to Olwinn. We have dawdled enough on this journey already. There should be some horses in a nearby copse." Clerin's mother seemed to be getting her old self back in order now that they were on land, and Clerin was already beginning to forget the brief closeness that they had experienced together.

She began to look around for a stand of trees large enough to hide some horses in. There is nothing like concentrating on the task at hand to relieve your mind from thinking. Looking around her she noticed that they were close to the sea. Not so much from the sights as the smells. The cry of a gull could be heard over the river. The smell of salt and fish lightly wafted up towards them. The river snaked out of their vision around a large section of trees in the distance. Clerin attempted to remember which forest near the sea would be close to a river delta. Though she was not sure of which river they had traveled down, there were only a couple of possibilities. Considering the forest, it could only be the Yamhill or the Wyfrond. She wished briefly that she had paid more attention to geography when she had been tutored.

"Come this way. The horses should be on the east side of the river." Clerin's mother walked stiffly away from the hydrophilic trees along the river and towards their more coniferous cousins facing the foothills.

"Should we have dismissed Wil so soon? What if the horses are on the other side of the river?" Clerin felt bad for walking away without even watching Wil leave.

"Clerin, please. We need to concentrate on the task at hand. You make one wonder as to your motives with the Yaven." Clerin's mother walked into the trees fast enough that Clerin had to trot to keep up. Her mother had long legs and was used to striding in both palaces and the countryside.

"Who left our horses here? Surely it wasn't Owlinn or else he could have been detected. Did you leave them here before you came home?" Clerin felt oddly exposed next to the river. Either it was leaving the fairly safe confines of Wil to the open riverside or, maybe, she was getting the feeling that they were being watched. She tried not to think too much about being watched because she knew that would just make her more nervous. And the more nervous she got, the more she felt like she was being watched. Clerin vowed to herself to get a better handle on her intuition. Both Olwinn and Jylohan had chided her that she thought too much in retrospect, changing her mind and back again, to be able to distinguish between intuition and paranoia.

"Clerin, you are as easy to read as a child. Next time you are feeling nervous, do not start babbling about the first thing that jumps into your head. Only when you have mastered that will you be able to cloud your true feelings from me." Though her mother's voice was sharp, Clerin had noticed that her mother had slowed down a little, showing her own nervousness.

"Why do I need to hide my feelings from you? You are my mother." With a great effort of will, Clerin decided to not feel nervous anymore. Whether she would be killed in the next few moments should not deter her current actions whatsoever. There was no use in worrying about the inevitable. Try as she might, though, she could not shake the feeling that they were being watched. She did, however, stop herself from continually talking to her mother about it.

"Yes, your mother... If you will not even try, then..." Clerin's mother stopped talking in mid-sentence. They were just at the outside edge of a circle of trees. Midinarre placed her palm parallel to the ground to stay Clerin from advancing further. Slowing to a crawl Midinarre stepped carefully towards the wood. Her foot turned inwards to avoid a stick. Her hands were still outstretched, for balance or to make sure that Clerin was not right behind her, Clerin did not know. She stopped and watched into the trees for a sign of movement. Try as she might she could detect nothing. Her mother continued to stealthily creep into the small copse. Clerin watched until she could no longer see her mother, just the movements of the nearby trees being pushed out of the way. Soon even the treetops had stopped swaying. She thought about all of the worst moments in her life and decided that they somehow always involved waiting. She hated waiting.

Clerin pricked her ears and attempted to focus on hearing something from the copse. She could not even hear her mother. She gripped her hands into fists and closed her eyes. She could remember Olwinn trying to get her to understand perception. "Perception is a skill, not an ability. Though it has its limits in place from birth like an ability, it can atrophy as quickly as a skill. You must practice a skill to keep it sharp. You must use your perception constantly to increase it. Listen for the cats stalking in the night. Peer deep into the fog and find the shadows that are substance. Close your eyes and your ears while eating and tasting wine. Always seek to increase your perception, for you will find one day that you need it, and you will attempt to draw it forth like an ability, and there will be nothing there." Clerin was never clear as to the distinction between a skill or an ability, but she knew that she never practiced. She could hear nothing, see nothing, smell nothing. She concentrated so hard that she felt as if she would give herself a headache, but still she could sense nothing. She felt a small urge to cast a spell but stopped herself short. She knew how fanatical her mother had been about magic earlier and did not suppose that had changed at all.

"Aahh! Clerin!" The cries pierced Clerin's psyche. As she had stood still and poured all of her energy into her admittedly small perception skills, her body had relaxed. With the sudden rush of panic that flowed into her veins at the scream, her body convulsed forward into the trees. Her feet were moving before she had really noticed. She suddenly thought of her boot knife and regretted not pulling it out while waiting. She felt as if she could not slow down until she could see her mother, so she would face whatever awaited her with her bare hands until she could take the time to arm herself.

As Clerin rushed into the trees, her face and forearms became scratched by the grasping tree limbs. The panic stole her breath and clawed at her throat as the trees clawed at her face.

"Mother! I'm coming, Mother!" Clerin was already misplacing the scream. When she had first heard it, it had seemed to come from somewhere near the center of the copse. Now the circle of trees seemed much larger, and she was not sure that she was headed into the center. What she needed was another yell from her mother to gain her bearings.

"Mother, where are you!" Clerin knew that her mother would disapprove of Clerin giving herself away by yelling, but she did not know how else to find her. As she jumped over a small log, her foot caught an errant branch and she fell. The ground came up hard against her chest. She started gasping for breath and tried to crawl onto her hands and knees. As she was gasping, she remembered her knife and gripped it in her right hand. Slowly she straightened out her trunk and tried to catch her breath. Gripping the knife with white knuckles, she moved more cautiously forward in a crouch.

As she peered through the leaves in front of her she thought she noticed movement in a small clearing. There were a couple of large dark blobs. The bush in front of her continued to sway from her crashing about which made it difficult to see clearly. She knew that she should wait to be able to see into the clearing before she made her move. She also knew that whomever had her mother would surely have heard her approach, even if they did not notice the bushes moving. Clerin decided that time was of the essence. She made sure of her footing and leapt forwards through the bush.

"Yeaah!" The wordless cry was all that Clerin could yell out as she moved into the clearing of hawthorn trees. Flashing her knife around wildly, she slashed the air in front of her. As her cry faded from the heavy air she took in her surroundings. The two dark blobs were large horses, saddled and ready to ride. Her mother, who began laughing most heartily, was sitting on a stump near the far edge of the clearing. As Clerin whipped her head back and forth she realized that her mother had just made a fool of her. As her mother wiped tears of mirth from her eyes, she walked over to Clerin.

"You are not planning on sticking me with that knife. are you?" Clerin's mother's eyes flashed a cruel sapphire blue.

"That is not funny whatsoever! I cannot believe that you would scare me like that... What if something had happened to you?" Clerin knew she should not be so worked up, that she was really angry with herself for looking like a fool in front of her mother.

"I apologize for misleading you, Clerin, but what will you do when it is not a joke? You should never panic, Clerin, never. When you panic, you release yourself from your mind. This could be advantageous running from a charging bull, but not when dealing with a conscious enemy. You must keep your head at all times, no matter what you think may be going on, okay? Promise me." Clerin's mother had walked over to her and grasped her shoulders with both hands. Though her eyes were still smiling with humor, her face looked serious.

"I promise not to panic, Mother." Clerin knew in her heart that she was lying, but it seemed the easiest way to get out of the situation. Clerin hugged her mother briefly and then bent over to place her knife back in her boot. Her mind was awhirl with thoughts, but she could not slow them enough to grasp what they were.

"Come, let us finally have lunch while the horses graze a moment. From here we will need to ride a little past dark before we reach Tureyn. We will sleep in Tureyn before going to the Temple and meeting with Lembin. You will want to be fresh before communicating, so I will allow you to sleep in a little. We do not have to meet with Lembin until the afternoon, how does that sound?" Midinarre smiled once more at Clerin, then turned and walked back to the stump she had been resting on.

"Sleep sounds great, but food sounds even better." Clerin felt that her time with her mother was limited, and she may as well try to be in a good mood for it. She tried to put the prank behind her, to pass it off as a lesson learned. It seemed to epitomize their relationship, however. Clerin had always felt that her mother unfairly tested her, and that she truly enjoyed it if Clerin failed. Though her mouth was smiling, her cheeks were hot with annoyance.

After she had seated herself and ate enough to satisfy her immediate hunger pains, her mind began to wander. She wanted to talk, but did not know what to talk about. She knew she should not mention Lembin or the mission if she did not want a lecture. She thought that her mother would not mind talking about Clerin's embarrassing moment with the knife, at least if Clerin seemed properly admonished. Between bites of bread and cheese she tried to think of something neutral to speak about.

"Do you think perception is a skill or an ability?" The problem with her own mind, thought Clerin, was that it did not have to travel far between thought and speech. She would try to lengthen the traveling distance between the two in the future. Jylohan had always tried to get her to think about a thing three times before she spoke it. "If, after the third time it has fully traveled your mind, the words still sound good to you, then speak them, but not until they have made three complete revolutions in your mind." He had always held up three stubby fingers to emphasize himself. Clerin thought that Jylohan really must have liked the number three, he was always saying something had to come in threes and would hold up his squatty fingers.

Her mother had taken a moment to think of an answer which is why Clerin's mind had so much time to wander. "Hmm, I would have to say an ability. It cannot drop to zero, like a skill can. You don't have to know how to swim to survive in the world, but it is impossible not to be able to perceive, now is it? Why do you ask?" Clerin's mother had stopped eating briefly and was looking at her. Clerin often wondered why she felt that she had to break the silence, as if she would be crushed by its oppressive nothingness.

"Well, when I was waiting for you to check the copse for enemies, I was thinking of something that Olwinn had said about perception. He had said it was a skill because..." At the mention of Olwinn's name her mother's eyes flashed out at Clerin.

"There is your problem right there, Clerin. Whether it is a skill or an ability does not matter. What matters is your own inner silence. Perception is outward based, and you, child, have never been able to create enough inner silence to understand anything outward based. Besides, listening to Olwinn will just get you into trouble." Her mother brushed her hands free of crumbs and stood.

"I suggest you eat quickly. We will be leaving shortly." With that, her mother walked, stiff backed, into the surrounding hawthorns. Clerin assumed that her mother was going to relieve herself and decided that she should probably go do that as well. She folded the bread and cheese back up into the napkin and tied it off before wandering into her own section of trees. She decided there that unless her mother spoke to her first she would rather die than utter another word. The anger was mixed with hurt and that was mixed with the sure shock of it all. She had just been trying to engage in a little conversation, after all. Certainly nothing to warrant an outburst like that, and her mother was usually so calm. She felt as if she would never understand her mother.

When Clerin returned to the horses she found them packed with her mother astride the mare. Without a word Clerin mounted her own steed. Her body protested greatly, having ridden all morning, but she chose not to voice it. She grabbed the reins and waited for her mother's instructions.

"I apologize for being short with you, Clerin. I have been running at top speed for several days now. I know that is no excuse but it is all I can offer you." With that, and without waiting for Clerin's own reply, her mother walked her horse out the small path in the back of the copse.

Clerin could not believe her ears. She wanted to say something snide at first. Then, after they had left the trees and started upon their road she wanted to say something consoling. Nothing that sounded good came to her mind in either case, and besides, her mother was starting to ride far enough ahead of her that she would had to have shouted at that point.

The ride, much to Clerin's relief, was uneventful and fairly short. They rode, at most, for three hours and it felt like only one. She began to feel good that she had not spoken a word to her mother, especially not an unkind one. Evening turned swiftly into night, and just before the blue sky turned to black Clerin could make out the fires being lit along the towers of Tureyn. They looked magnificent. As much for their promise of warmth and protection as for their promise of derlian companionship. Clerin could not think of a time when she felt so excited about a bath before and she was one that enjoyed bathing immensely. As they approached the gates her mother slowed to a trot so that Clerin could catch up.

"Keep close, Clerin. We will be staying at the Liar's Lyre. If we get separated, meet me there. Keep your eyes sharp and your perception outward for it is late enough for the thieves to be starting their day." Her mother spurred her horse towards the town and Clerin followed, wondering if thieves ever stopped their days. The strong smell of the ocean made Clerin smile briefly. Tureyn was at the edge of the world, sitting atop a massive cliff overlooking the sea. She breathed in deep before urging her horse forward. She had only been to Tureyn a few times before and the ocean only a dozen, but once experienced the distinctive smell was etched into her memory. It was the pungent mixture of salt, fish, and water that permeated everything.

She briefly wondered why they were not to stay in the townhouse. The answer was obvious, that they were travelling incognito, but it was another item that her mother had not bothered to explain. She knew instinctively that to ask her mother was to invite ridicule, so she kept her lips shut and her eyes open.

The massive gates of Tureyn were open, as they always were except in rare times of war, and their gold gilding flashed wildly in the firelight. Clerin deliberately slowed her horse to stare at the massive golden gates. They were each shaped like an arch, rising smoothly towards their centers. The tops of the gates were shaped to look like waves, poised to crash down upon the onlooker. Their massive bodies were filigreed so densely that an arrow would be hard pressed to filter through them. Though Clerin knew that there was iron underneath the gold, the gates looked exceptionally delicate with all of the opalescent seashells and golden starfish decorating them. Even though she had slowed her horse, the gates flowed past much too quickly for her—and she was still forced to catch up with her mother. She lightly bounced her heels against her Ranger's flanks and steered towards her mother's fading back.

After what seemed like an eternity, though in reality it took very little time, they finally reached the inn. Her mind, rather than piercing the darkness for thieves, stayed fixated upon the glorious bath that was surely awaiting them at the inn. The dirt and sweat was so encrusted upon her body that she felt as if she was wearing a suit of armor. Heavy, thick, cumbersome armor that made her sweat even in the cooler night air. The pungent tang of, well not quite of rotting meat but of something close to it, hovered around Clerin's nostrils like a thick cloud. Finally, though, the inn's stablehand was taking her reins and letting her slip back to the ground. The comfort of the inn would soon envelop her. She almost shook with excitement.

Clerin's mother grasped her hand tightly to lead her into the inn. Somehow her mother always had an iron, bone-crushing grip, no matter how tired or worn out she should be. Her mother's long bony fingers had always reminded Clerin of a bird's talons. These thoughts melted like butter on warm toast as they entered the Liar's Lyre.

Though the noise was a loud cacophony of various sounds, they were all jovial sounds. Derlians laughing, conversing and even squealing in delight all mixed together into an indecipherable mix of emotions. There were two giant fireplaces against the wall to Clerin's right, though they were difficult to glimpse through the crush of patrons. Long oaken tables lined the drinking hall splitting it into ribbons of bodies. There were at least five barmaids that Clerin could count while her mother almost dragged her to the innkeeper's desk off to their left. There were various flags and banners hanging from the ceiling, while colorful tapestries danced in the firelight against the walls. There was a small stage opposite the front doors that held a Fluen with a lyre and another sitting with a harp in front of her. Clerin strained her ears to catch the tune that surely emanated from them, but she was unable to glean even one note from the two.

"Midinarre! What a pleasure, I was beginning to wonder if you were going to make your reservations. Come along. No, no need to pay now. I am sure that you would like a good meal and a good bath before business. Oh, yes, he was here a while ago, but you know his kind. He said he had some errands to run, said maybe he would be back before we stopped selling drinks. Of course, of course, right after I get you two settled. That is a mighty fine one you have brought here, if I may say so." Though Clerin could not hear her mother's voice at all, she could hear the innkeeper's quite readily. His voice was deep and almost as large as he was. His smiling face was shiny in the firelight, almost pulled too tight. There were red lines shooting haphazardly from the bridge of his nose to his cheeks, and his breath smelled of too much wine, but Clerin took an immediate liking to him. He led them along the wall to a set of stairs leading up to the second floor. Her mother was whispering to him too quietly for Clerin to hear a word she said no matter how hard she tried to listen. Even the last sentence when her mother hissed a violent retort to the innkeeper's unwary words.

"Daughter! Why, I should have known such a comely creature could only come from a Fluen of legendary beauty such as you, Midinarre. Please forgive my wagging tongue, it quite has a mind of its own, it does. I meant no offense I assure you, only an appreciative word. Ah, here we are. The baths will be drawn shortly, just peek through the oval doors to see if the water is warm enough for you. Ah, yes, of course. Forgive me." Clerin's mother had hissed something else to the innkeeper who, it seemed, had a wide jocular smile even in the face of an angry Midinarre. Clerin was amazed at the endurance of his demeanor. The innkeeper walked back several steps and, with a flourish of his short arms, let them both enter without him.

"I have some business to attend to briefly, Clerin. So make yourself comfortable and start the bath whenever the water is ready. I shall be back up as soon as I possibly can." Her mother was frowning with fierce eyes and a stern jaw, so Clerin just nodded in acquiescence and let her mother leave without a word. Clerin even controlled her desire to press her ear to the door just as it closed. She was sure her mother would still be whispering fiercely anyway and be inaudible over the noise of the common room. So, instead, Clerin decided to relax a moment before checking on the bath.

The room was a simple wooden cube with two beds occupying most of the room. There was a communal dresser between the beds and a small table with three chairs placed around it at the foot of the far bed. The table had a loaf of bread, some cheese, and several apples making a small pyramid. Across from the foot of the other bed was a small oval door that she had to exert her willpower not to immediately go through. She went to the table, sat, and began sampling the cheeses. The cheese was all made from a pungent milk, maybe goat. It seemed to go particularly well with the crusty bread that lay next to it. She had not realized how hungry she was until she noticed over half the bread was gone and most of the cheese as well. Grabbing an apple, she decided to check on the bath.

The oval door was small enough that Clerin had to stoop slightly to fit through it. She doubted that the innkeeper would be able to fit through his own doors. The steam rushed past her into the cool sleeping quarters. The room was almost spherical but with a flat floor. There was a tub in the middle of the floor, full of hot water. There was a chair near the door with several towels laid out neatly on it. Clerin could barely make out another oval door where she assumed the servants entered and left through. The tub itself was huge, with a small trough at the top disappearing into the wall. As Clerin looked into the tub, she noticed a tight, flat-slatted grate in the bottom of the tub, against the floor. With a squeal of delight, she began to toss her clothes at the chair. She had heard about these tubs before, had even pestered her father for one. The hot water should seep up through the grate in the tub which also allowed all of the dirt to float up or fall away. The surface water would seep out through the trough, keeping the tub at a somewhat constant temperature.

As Clerin slowly lowered herself into the hot water, she watched a small river form in the trough, displaced by her encrusted body. As she cleaned herself, she wondered how the dirt was collected from wherever the water came from. As she soaked, however, her mind began to blank in a blissful, non-meditative state of pure enjoyment. She decided that she would stay in the tub until her mother arrived to use it. She had not felt this good for quite some time. She wondered briefly about why it takes a difficult time to truly appreciate an easy time, but then let her mind go blank again.

Clerin awoke with a start, her head flying up from the edge of the tub. She was not sure when she had fallen asleep or what had woken her, but she figured she should leave the tub before she accidentally drowned herself.

She dried off, left her clothes in the tub room in case they would be washed by the servants through the night, and stooped back into the main room. Her mother was nowhere to be found. She thought about getting dressed and going down to the common room to look for her mother but decided against it. It was not her mother's wrath that kept her from going. Nor was it the thought of all those strangers. She really would have liked to have joined the festivities and maybe even heard a poem or some songs. In fact, that thought alone almost made her leave for the common room. She was just dead tired. That and the repulsive thought of putting her dirty clothes back on made her slip into the far bed and sleep.

When Clerin awoke, her mother was sitting at the tiny table eating the last apple. She looked cleaned and refreshed. Clerin turned towards the door, holding her mouth open in a fake yawn. The other bed looked like it had not been slept in. This might not mean much because her mother was the type of Fluen to make a bed neat and tight after waking, but it made Clerin wonder.

"I trust you had a restful sleep, my little one. That is good as today will be taxing. Interpreting can be stressful, especially your first time. I have ordered food to be brought up, the stale bread will not do. I have also readied the tub with the appropriate herbs and oils so that you will be properly cleansed before entering the Temple. All of the proper rituals must be observed." Clerin's mother seemed happy and light. The mood struck Clerin as odd, but she could spot no insincerity amongst it. Besides, she was getting tired of trying to second guess everything.

"I had a wonderful sleep, Mother. I do not think I have rested that well since I was a babe. Do we have a brush?" Clerin had washed her hair out in the tub the night before, but had been unable to brush it before sleeping. She stifled another yawn, a real one this time, while her mother rummaged through a small bag to produce a brush. "Where did you get that?" Clerin's voice sounded drowsy even to her.

"From my saddle bags, of course. You should braid your hair to keep it dry for your bath, but then you can take it back down. I know I was not there, but your father told me how wonderful your Telling was. Let me take this time to tell you that I commend you. You have a great talent and you will be a wonderful poet, Clerin. Your creative mind and veracious curiosity will make you a force to be reckoned with. I know that I do not tell you often enough, but you make me proud." Her mother had stepped across the small distance and held Clerin's face with both of her hands. Clerin, herself, was struck dumb by the shear weight of emotion that came crashing into her. She had never expected this, especially from her mother. "You are a beautiful girl and you are blossoming into a beautiful lady. Now go and steep yourself in the bath. I will get you when we are ready to eat."

Clerin felt elated, but could think of no way to explain her feelings to her mother. It was as if she had a bevy of woodworking tools and was told to make a marble sculpture. She was deathly afraid of cracking the stone in twain with a clumsy blow. So, instead, she beamed at her mother with unshielded emotion. "Thank you." The words were brief and could not convey the depth of her feelings, but they would have to do. Clerin ducked through the small oval door without another word.

The tub room was thick with smoke as well as steam. The smell was too complicated to be greatly appreciated, at least by Clerin. There were some wonderful scents like sandalwood, cedar, rose, benzoin, and lavender, Clerin's personal favorite. There were other scents as well that made the room heavy, such as sage, yarrow, and valerian. Then there was a hint of acrid wormwood that mixed the scents and made an unruly cacophony of smells that clamored for attention. Clerin sank herself into the bath and waited. She was not sure how long she had to soak before she was considered cleansed. She was sure that her mother would keep track of all of the formalities. Indeed, even though the water was a tad oily for her taste, she found herself truly enjoying the experience. Even the overpowering smell of the room began to mellow as she relaxed. She decided that some rituals and traditions were worth observing.

After some time, Clerin was unable to decipher how long, nor did she have much of a desire to quantify her time in the bath like that, her mother rapped on the small oval door. "Come in, Mother. I am steeping as you wanted." Clerin could not help the languid smile that crept across her lips.

"Good, it is time to get ready. I have brought your robes and a special towel to dry yourself with. Remember to use these slippers. Your bare feet are not to touch the ground until after you have entered the Temple proper. There is food in our room, but you should hurry." Her mother smiled warmly at her, pulled the stout chair close to the tub, and placed the puffy white bundle that she was carrying on the chair.

Clerin moved to touch her mother's hand as she was placing the towel and robes, but her mother moved swiftly away. "Remember that you cannot touch another derlian until after the communication either, Clerin. Now, hurry, we must not be late." Her mother backed away until she came to the door. She then turned and ducked through the fog out of Clerin's vision.

Clerin, for her part, could not remember anything about the communication ritual. She was not even sure if she had ever heard what the specific dos and don'ts were. The thought came into her mind that she should probably not touch food, but her mother did not seem fazed by it, so neither would she. Clerin stood and let the water bead off of her body before she dried with the stiff white towel indicated by her mother. She placed her feet in the slippers and donned the robes before she left the bath room.

There, on a wheeled cart, was a feast of fresh fruit and salads. Clerin tried to think back and wondered if there was something about not eating meat before a communication, but cast the thought from her mind. She had decided that no one had explained the ritual to her and she would stick with that. Besides, how long ago had she even had lessons to memorize? How was one to know which lessons would have to be recalled with her mother's fanatical attention to detail and which ones would never be used? Clerin remembered clearly which forks to use while dining in front of the royal family but had yet to ever be invited to such a dinner.

"After you eat, come down through the common room. There is a carriage waiting to take us to the citadel. After you communicate with Lembin, we will come back here to get your things, so do not worry about them. I have left the brush on your bed so you can let down your hair." Midinarre smiled warmly at Clerin and slid out the door.

Clerin ate with her hands as there were no utensils on the cart. She wondered briefly if there was something about not touching metal. She ate until she was beginning to feel sated and then stopped. She did not want to feel sluggish or bloated for the day ahead of her.

As she walked down the stairs she breathed in how empty the place felt. How her soft footsteps quietly echoed hollowly down the staircase. Maybe it was because it was so full of life and noise last night, the warm firelight and boisterous laughing coming from a hundred mouths, but the common room seemed almost dead. Not just lifeless, as an inanimate object should be, but dead, because it had been alive last night. The only comforting thought for Clerin as she left the Liar's Lyre was that it would be resurrected once more by the time she came back.

The carriage awaiting her was magnificent. If she had known how resplendent it was while she was in her room, she would have skipped eating and come straight down. It was gold and filigreed with a team of four white horses pawing impatiently at the ground. The wheels were large, reaching half of the carriage height easily. They were not shod with gold but something darker, maybe brass. There were scenes in the filigree of hunting and the like, but Clerin could not take a closer look as her mother was motioning wildly for her to enter. The windows were covered with a thin black cloth, making the carriage look empty except for the open door and her mother's hand. There was a young, thin Fluen holding the door open, and he somehow bowed his head lower than her waist. Clerin recalled such treatment before at some of the small villages that her father lorded over, but this was Tureyn, the heart of the Fluen royalty. She smiled warmly at the porter and walked stately up the steps into the carriage. She sat opposite her mother so that she would be facing where the carriage was heading. She did not like the feeling of moving backwards for it made her stomach upset sometimes.

"It feels good to be on the last leg of the journey. Sometimes in the middle of things I get a little flustered. I just like being able to see the finish line I guess." Clerin let out a small nervous laugh.

"Life is one long journey, sometimes it is easy and simple, like last night in the bath. You might not be as close to the finish line as you think, Clerin. No matter, things are coming to a head and that does feel wonderful." Her mother was glancing through the curtain as she spoke, as if speaking of trivial things. "This journey may just be starting for you."

The carriage ride was incredibly short. The inn was fairly deep into the city already, and the horses moved quickly through the morning streets. The cobblestones had seemed a little uneven, but it was an enjoyable trip for Clerin. Not knowing how to make small talk with her mother, she decided to watch the city flow by through the curtains. As the carriage lurched to a halt, she felt her heart begin to thump. She consciously quieted it as her mother stepped out of the carriage. She would not show her nervousness in front of her mother today. Her mother had been inordinately kind to her lately, and Clerin did not want to give her any reason to regret that. She took a large breath and let it out slowly and evenly as she stepped out of the carriage.

The citadel was incredibly massive. A huge circular turret that seemed to kiss the clouded sky. It made her stomach queasy to stare up at its colossal height, so she focused on the entrance instead. Her mother walked towards it without a word, so Clerin followed. The portcullis looked like huge teeth, waiting to fall down and masticate her into the stone floor. As they walked beneath it, she noticed that the small tunnel they were in had a closed iron grate for a ceiling. Clerin thought back to her siege defense lectures and realized that they must be walking through a blood room. She had never seen one before. After she realized that, she noticed the large cauldrons in the room above her, filled with hot oil, she presumed. The room above was lined with sharp pikes to stick down through the grating. She had troubles seeing in the dimly lit tunnel, but she did notice the small holes at the edges to let the gore drain out. As they passed the second portcullis, the one that would trap the attackers in the blood room, Clerin thanked the fates that she had been born into a life of poetry, not of violence. The world lit back up as they passed the second set of teeth into a great courtyard. Midinarre was stopped as they stepped into the cloudy day, and Clerin felt grateful that they were not detained in the darkened tunnel. Though she could not make out what was said, indeed she did not even try, she could tell that they were expected and respected by the swift change in the guard's demeanor. He walked briskly in front of them as they crossed the courtyard towards another grand turret.

This turret within the outer turret was at the cliff's edge overlooking the sea. Though Clerin could not see through to the ocean, she could sense it. It was more than just the smell or the distant sound of crashing waves. There was also a feeling of expectancy, or maybe of anticipation, coming from the ocean. The gulls circled above like buzzards, screaming endlessly for food.

The guard walked them straight towards a smaller double-door on the side of the turret. This door could only handle three warriors walking abreast, unlike the giant mouth gaping open in the center of the turret. The guard opened the door and bowed low to both Midinarre and Clerin. There was another guard at the door who blocked their entrance. Even though he could plainly see the other guard's humble posture, he held a large halberd across the entrance.

"State your name and business with the citadel." The guard was much older than the bowed guard that had walked them across the courtyard. Clerin smiled to herself as she thought of the word "grizzled." That would describe him nicely. Like a tough and charred piece of steak. One that you had to chew upon for an hour or so before it would go down.

"I am Midinarre Toswin, this is my daughter Clerin. We have come at Lembin's request to communicate about matters of state." Though her voice was polite, Clerin could imagine her mother's fierce eyes flashing angrily at the old guard even though his impassive face did not show it.

"Of course. You are expected." The guard snapped the halberd upright, turned sideways, and stepped back two paces for them to enter. After they had walked through, Clerin could hear him snapping back into position. She wondered how long he stood in front of a closed door as impassive as a statue. A different guard motioned for them to follow him, and Clerin had to leave her thoughts behind with the veteran.

They followed this guard for quite some time, around corners and bends, along long hallways and down various flights of stairs. Clerin had not been paying attention when she had first entered and so had not glimpsed his face. His back was broad and well armored. He walked quickly without a glance backwards to make sure his charges were still following him. Finally, after she had thought that this turret must be the size of her father's entire castle, they came to another guarded door. There were three guards standing in the room. They had no armor or weapons that Clerin could see, so she figured they were mages. Their robes were dark with gold glyphs crawling up sleeves and along hemlines. Clerin had always wanted to have a stronger affinity to magic, to be able to sense the skill in others. Olwinn had certainly attempted to teach her the trick. At the thought of Olwinn, she wondered where he was. She had a vague memory that he was supposed to meet them here, but he was certainly not amongst the mages in the room. One of the mages stepped forward and gave a quick bow to Midinarre and then to Clerin.

"We welcome you to the Temple. Lembin has been stirring for some time now. I believe that it is excited to communicate today, almost eager. Will you be breathing for yourself?" The question was directed at Clerin, but she was not sure how to answer it.

"Well, I would rather not depend upon my own…" Clerin started to say that she would rather have one of the mages cast the breathing spell upon her, but her mother interrupted her.

"No, please instill enough time in her to communicate effectively. She is not sure how long Lembin wishes to meet with her." Midinarre's voice had its usual cold, distant tone, but there was something warm underneath. Clerin doubted that the mages would be able to tell, but she could.

"Surtecfluarc!" The mage pressed his thumbs towards Clerin's throat with his fingers fanning out to encompass her neck. His hands were so close she could almost feel them. They were very businesslike, but the rush of energy was intense. Clerin felt her throat open up until it seemed as if she no longer needed to breathe at all. She could not feel her chest moving, yet knew that she was breathing. She could not feel the air enter her nose or lungs. She was slightly stunned as she had not thought she would be able to feel anything until she entered the water.

"Please accept our gratitude." Midinarre placed a coin into the mage's hand. "We will be waiting your return here, Clerin. Remember to not try to hide anything in your mind, that only piques its curiosity. Try to be open, Clerin. Flow downstream, not up." Her mother bowed briefly to her and then stepped back.

The mage that had cast her breathing spell for her opened a wooden door opposite the one that she and her mother had entered. Clerin followed, resisting the urge to glance back once more at her mother. The room they entered was small, round, and almost barren. There was a spiral staircase in the center of the room that led down into a pool of water. A small bench sat near the circular hole to the Temple. The smell of salt was strong in the air.

Clerin disrobed and placed her clothing on the bench. She waded into the water up to her knees and then took off her slippers and tossed them below the bench. She could not remember if her feet could touch the stone in this room, but figured as long as she was in the water before she took them off it would be good enough. Even though she knew that she did not have to, she unconsciously held her breath as she descended the stone staircase. Her lungs kept trying to cough even though she could breathe just fine.

Usually when Clerin would hold her breath while swimming, she would feel lighter, more buoyant. This time, however, she felt like a stone, completely solid. She did not have to swim downwards or fight against floating upwards. She walked down towards her destiny as if she were on dry land, though a bit slower.

When she reached the bottom of the landing, she paused to look around. The entire room was lit by an eerie greenish glow. The walls loomed upwards towards the yellow glow of her entrance. They somehow seemed taller now that she was on the bottom looking up. At first Clerin had thought that the walls were cracked with age. But she realized that the walls were actually just covered in glyphs and ancient writing. The eerie green glow came from the moss stuck to the walls in crazy patterns. There was only one doorway leaving this room, opposite the stairway she had come down, so she headed towards it.

The door arch was at least three times Clerin's height. As she passed under it, her hand strayed to lightly caress the rough stone. Her mind, however, was not perceiving what she was feeling with her hand. She was stunned by the massive scale that the Temple proper was made at. The room simply went on until it faded from her vision in all directions. There were four gigantic pillars in the distance, so she walked towards them. The floor was made of flagstone, huge blocks pulled from the bedrock to be sunk into the sea.

The pillars became more focused as she approached them. She could tell that they were covered with the same archaic writing that the walls were. As she passed the two front pillars she noticed that there was what looked like a well centered between the four pillars. She could not think of anything more bizarre than an underwater well, so Clerin decided that that must be where Lembin was. She walked towards the upper wall of the well with trepidation.

There was a gigantic rumbling noise like an underwater seismic tremor. Clerin slowed slightly, but then pushed on towards the well. The rumbling built up in intensity, changing from something that she faintly heard to something she felt course through her. The rumbling became more rhythmic the closer that Clerin got to the well. It reminded her of the drum circles that would congregate outside her father's castle on the solstices and equinoxes. They would start almost randomly, one drummer then two, arrhythmic with the sounds coming from different areas of the crowd. Then they would begin to crescendo, building a leading voice out of the many tiny rhythms. This is what the rumbling sounded like to Clerin. The cohesive pulling together of one giant beat from the chaos of sound. The sound beat through the water, sending waves of pressure against her, almost as if they were trying to push her back. As the pressure against her grew, her ears felt as if someone had boxed them. When she had decided that maybe Lembin did not wish to communicate with her, the rumbling suddenly stopped. She glanced around, surprised to notice that she stood at the edge of the underwater well.

Color burst into Clerin's eyes so ferociously that she immediately closed them, but to no avail. The color was in her mind, at the point where her eyes met her brain. She could not stop the image forming by merely clenching the palms of her hands to her eyelids. A swirling kaleidoscope of color shimmered in front of her, the pressure of her hands merely made the colors shift more intensely. As she dropped her hands and tried to see the well that she was standing in front of, her stomach started to feel vertigo. A burst of panic flashed through her as she thought, briefly, that maybe she had fallen down the well. The vertigo, however, was much too strong to just be falling underwater. Clerin flailed about until her hand struck the edge of the well. The sudden feeling of cold, rough stone brought her back to where she was and what she was doing. Drawing in a deep breath of water she tried to scream out a name: Lembin!

The pulse of colors slowed, along with the rumbling rhythm, and Clerin began to see images in the kaleidoscope of her mind. First she could clearly see waves crashing down upon each other. She could feel the water around her, pressing against her movements, she even thought she could taste the salt in her mouth. Then, just when she had the image in her mind, it changed again. Suddenly there was a rush of air against her face and she felt light enough to float out of the Temple. This sensation changed into heat and she could feel the water around her boil away from her. She could even feel bubbles of air on her arms. As quickly as the last changes, she began to get heavy. Heavy enough to drop back down next to the well with an almost audible clicking sound. While Clerin was frozen in motion, a new panorama began to unfold amongst the swirling colors of her vision. She could distinctly see four different shapes, each prominently displaying itself as a different element. They started circling a central point, spinning faster and faster. Slowly they began to sink to the epicenter, spiraling inward. Right as they touched, there was a blinding flash of light accompanied with searing pain. Each shape recoiled slightly, leaving a space of nothing between them as they spun. Slowly a small cylinder of white light grew out of each shape towards another. Soon all four shapes were linked by the white cylinders, and Clerin felt a cool sensation of peace. The shapes seemed to shrink in her vision or maybe float away from her. Next Clerin saw four crude derlians. She could not see faces or features, just enough to know that each was of a different element. They began, like the amorphic shapes before, to circle a central point. As they grew close enough to touch, however, they began to strike out at each other. Slowly they began to separate and leave a small space of nothing between them. Now the four shapes grew larger, or closer, each to be behind a different derlian. The water and air shapes grew a cylinder between them, which allowed them to get closer together and even touch without striking at each other. Soon a cylinder grew between the water and stone shapes as well as the air and fire shapes. A last cylinder grew between the fire and stone shapes, which made each of the derlians shrink inward until all four touched. The images of the derlians and shapes began to shrink away until there was just the kaleidoscope of colors swirling in her mind once more.

The four shapes grew into Clerin's vision again. The one shaped as a water drop appeared close enough for her to touch. It stayed in front of Clerin for some time, while the other three were circling her. The water shape shrank back slightly while the other shapes slowed down. As the flame shape was circling round her, it suddenly ducked in and ran into the water shape. The shape was absorbed, only the water shape remained with the other two shapes still circling. When the fire shape was absorbed, the kaleidoscope colors flashed and whirled wildly. The feeling of vertigo, which had almost gone away completely, increased by almost tenfold from the earlier sensation. Then, in the center of her being, Clerin felt a burning sensation. Swiftly the sensation increased. It felt as if she had eaten coals and they were searing through her insides. Her blood began to boil, pushing bubbles deep into her and giving her the sick feeling of someone who has to burp but cannot quite release the air. She could feel her stomach split open under the heat, exposing her guts to the surrounding water. Soon the heat reached her arms and legs, the water next to her began to boil away again, taking all of the water from her body with it. Her limbs felt like crispy charcoal, all encrusted upon the outside of them so they could not bend or twist. The heat reached her throat, swallowing her scream before she could voice it. As the heat reached her brain her thoughts increased in speed and veracity. They grew so fast that she could no longer think, just watch all of the different images fly past her burning mind. Clerin could feel her mind lose its ability to think coherently until even that thought could not make sense since it flew through her brain so rapidly redundant. Just as she was reduced to gibbering insanity, the stone shape slammed into her like a boulder. The encrusted feeling on her limbs increased dramatically, making it impossible to move any part of herself. Her thoughts, which had been streaming by in a constant rush, slowed and stopped upon one thought. Clerin was going to die, she felt it, she knew it. Nothing could survive this, no one should survive it. The magma from the fire and molten rock felt almost comfortingly liquid, and if she could have smiled from this reprieve she would have. Finally the air shape hurtled into Clerin, dispelling the icy grip on her mind that the stone had set in. The fire was fanned into a ferocious whirlwind, turning her mind into a race once again. Instead of a stream of rushing thoughts, however, they seemed disjointed and chaotic. One thought having nothing to do with the next. Haphazard. The physical pain she was in kept wanting to become a numb throb but instead just switched from one form of pain to another. Clerin was at war with herself, each part of her trying to destroy the other parts. The feeling of self-mutilation and suicide began to grow in her mind, becoming all encompassing. Her stomach, what was left of it, began to heave with the vertigo. She wished there was something she could do to curtail the pain, anything at all. Her mind, grasping desperately at everything that flew by it, grasped on the idea of drowning. She breathed in sharply, forgetting that she could not drown, and tried her best to quench the pain. As simply as it started, the pain ebbed. The different shapes shot out of Clerin and faded into the distance.

Clerin, for one brief moment, felt whole again. More than whole—normal. The way she used to feel before she entered the Temple. An overwhelming feeling of gratitude, of relief, made salty tears seep from her eyes to the sea. Before she could get comfortable with herself again, however, the colors began to swirl around her once more. The colors coalesced into a flat plain. It seemed to shoot off in every direction from Clerin, dwarfing her with its flat straight symmetry. The plain scrolled underneath her as if she were flying above it. The color fluctuation was slowing but nothing seemed to be happening. She waited with her breath held uselessly. A small dot in the distance began to grow closer. She inspected it as it neared. It seemed a glowing ball with rainbow colors playing upon its outside surface. The sphere came up to Clerin and then stopped. It was slightly larger than her own head and spun slowly while the colors rippled over it. She smiled to herself at its beauty. There was a small dark spot at one point on the ball. She wondered what it signified as the spot rolled over the surface of the ball. The spot leveled itself in her vision, floating in front of her. As she was staring at it, the sphere exploded into hundreds of glass-like shards. She tried to raise her hands to protect her face, but was too slow. The shards tore through her body, some of them embedding in her flesh while some of them pierced her right through. The pain was excruciating. While most of the blast had hit her stomach, chest and arms, a few of the shards had struck her face, though luckily none had pierced her eyes. Clerin could feel her blood leak into the sea. The violence took less than a second, and she peered through her fingers with gritted teeth to see what was going to happen next. There was a misshapen glob of black ooze floating where the rainbow ball had been. As she watched it, it slowly dissolved into the water and disappeared. While the salt water was playing with her open wounds, another dot appeared in the distance. As it grew closer, Clerin noticed that it was a glob of black ooze. She tried to swim backwards, to escape the glob, but it readjusted and swiftly came before her. While this sphere slowly spun, she noticed that there was a spot of rainbow color shifting over its surface. She watched the rainbow spot level itself in her vision, and she immediately raised her arms to cover her face, bracing herself for another attack. This sphere exploded as well, but its shards entered into Clerin's flesh and soothed her wounds. As the black ooze stabbed into her, it healed the cuts that the earlier sphere had left. Clerin tried to make sense out of what was happening to her and suddenly she felt like she started moving again. The flat plain had a small outcropping in the distance. It was towards this that she was headed. She slowed as she neared it until she was right next to it. It appeared to be a well, just like the one in the center of this Temple. As she watched, the four elemental shapes burst out from the well, circled her once, and then rushed back into the well. Clerin stood there, not knowing what to do, when they popped out and circled her again. The same thing happened a total of five times while she struggled to make sense of the vision. Then the colors swirled in her vision again, drowning out the well completely.

When the kaleidoscope ebbed, there were just two shapes in front of Clerin. The water drop and the air cloud floating there, facing each other. A white cylinder slowly peeked from the water shape towards the air shape, but disintegrated when it reached about halfway there. The cylinder tried two more times to reach the air shape, but disappeared each time before reaching its target. Then a white cylinder slowly came out of the water shape towards Clerin. She braced for the impact, but when it touched her, she felt no pain whatsoever. The cylinder slowly sank into her head, feeling slightly cool. She could feel the diameter of the cylinder resting inside her skull. Then the cylinder left, floating to the air shape. This time the cylinder did not disintegrate, but slowly penetrated the cloud. For once Clerin felt like she understood the communication. She nodded to no one in acceptance.

"I will take your message to Linchon, Lembin. I will keep it safe and secret until I am able to deliver it." Clerin spoke aloud not knowing if Lembin could hear at all or if it just read minds. Either way, Clerin felt a wondrous relief. The colors faded and the well came back into focus. She squinted into the distance and could make out the giant pillars. Everything was the same. Clerin bent over the edge of the well to take a quick look at the resting place of one of the Belegs. At that moment, a white cylinder was flying up the well. While Clerin knew that it would have to enter her, she still flung her body back to avoid it out of reflexes. The will of a Beleg, however, is not so easily avoided, and the cylinder buried itself, painlessly, into Clerin's skull. It caused Clerin to cough, even though she could breathe underwater. Her body curled into a fetal position with her racking her lungs. Her eyes watered and her lungs burned for quite some time. The cylinder seemed to be shifting inside of her, moving slowly downwards towards the center of her being. It was unnerving to feel it travel through her. Slowly her lungs and diaphragm stopped spasming. Slowly she felt like she had more control over her body and could straighten out. Clerin did not know what to do, but felt as if she had been dismissed, so she headed back to whence she came from.

As Clerin walked up and out of the water, her body felt like it had doubled in weight. She lay at the top of the landing for some time before she felt like she had the strength to stand. At last she picked up her discarded robes from the bench and clothed herself. She walked over to the only door in the room and opened it. There were the mages smiling and nodding amongst themselves off to one side, and Midinarre was sitting on a stool staring at the now-open door. She immediately leapt off the stool and crossed the room to Clerin.

"How was it? Are you hurt or scared? I was worried that the communication would be too much for you. But what was I worried for? You did great, I am proud of you." Midinarre was hugging and smiling at Clerin.

"I have to deliver a message, Mother. I need to go to the Luften lands... I am scared, but more than that, I am tired." Clerin wanted to collapse. If she had felt the least bit worn out after her travels to reach Tureyn, she was drained a hundred times that now. It was as if all of her liquids had been sucked from her and left her body as an empty shell to try to continue coping with life without her. She shivered uncontrollably.

"Do not worry in the least, we have planned for this contingency. I have a message and a gift that you will deliver to the Luften king to make your journey less suspicious. Come now, let us get you rested so that you can journey tomorrow. You have another difficult road ahead of you, one that you must take alone." Her mother's words were soft and distant, and Clerin realized that she was passing out. Her vision shrank to a tunnel, and she could distantly see the ceiling and someone's head peaking over the rim of the tunnel. It may have been her mother. It may have been a mage.

Chapter 7

It was closing in on midday and Vrric was standing at the bottom platform of the helioarc that Revkin lived in. He was staring down onto the road he had walked along to get here. There was trash mounded on both sides of the road, leftovers from the Trivaste festival. His hands gripped the railing with white knuckles as he watched some leaves spiral around in the wind. *Those leaves have more autonomy than I,* thought Vrric. *Was it destiny that brought me here, or am I spitting in her face? How could I ever know?* He could still see the tears of frustration upon Kaihlu's face, in fact he would probably remember that image for the rest of his life.

"What?! No warning. None whatsoever. I believed you when you said you wished to be my apprentice. I took you in when no one else would spend the time and money on an orphan that you required. You could have warned me that you were thinking of another guild branch to enter. Maybe then I would not have spent so much money on the iron ingot for the head of your forge hammer. Maybe then I would have trained several apprentices and chosen to teach the best. Maybe I would have saved myself the grief. I put too much effort and joy into your upbringing, I see that now. No, don't talk. I do not want to hear your excuses, your condolences. Just leave. You may go, do not think twice about me. Did you hear me? Go!" Kaihlu's wide leathery face had clean tracks down the soot on his face. Etched by tears, they looked like veins to Vrric. The anger had been palpable. Kaihlu's huge hands beat upon his own thighs. *To keep them from throttling me,* Vrric had thought. Since there was no talking to Kaihlu, certainly nothing that could justify his betrayal, he had turned and walked away. He could still hear the large Luften's sobs until the huge wooden doors had swung shut behind him.

Vrric hated himself for wanting more than just smithing. That had been his destiny ever since he could remember. Now, after just one incredibly long day, all that had changed. He used to be sure of his future. There was a clear straight road in front of him, even if it had been a little muddy. Now, there was just open sky. More opportunities surely, but he was much less certain of direction or altitude. Vrric knew that he could bend metal to his will with heat and force. He had been doing it for years. Magic, however, he knew nothing about. It frightened him that he knew nothing about his own skills or capabilities. He knew nothing about Revkin's skills or abilities. He had even heard rumors of villages out in the desert where mages lived after they went insane. He closed his eyes and breathed out slowly trying to keep his body from shaking. Since he had been taken in by Kaihlu, he had not risked the unknown, not even been challenged really. The whole prospect seemed suddenly overwhelming to him, and he had the sudden urge to descend back to the mud and hide.

Vrric cast his mind back and tried to remember. How did Revkin fly? Which syllables did he speak? Slowly he teased the answer from his reluctant brain. Though he thought he had not drunk too much mead, his memory of the night before seemed cloudy. Maybe the haze was brought on by the morning's fiasco with Kaihlu, he was not sure. Finally his reluctant mind brought forth the information he sought. "Lumkinderclo!" Vrric tried to say it with the same grand fanfare that Revkin had. Nothing seemed to happen, however. There was no sinking feeling in his stomach, no tingling whatsoever. His feet were stuck to the wooden platform as if they were glued there.

Vrric was not sure what he was expecting, but he had been expecting something. "Lumkinderclo!" He almost yelled the word and shook his fists upwards. He had his eyes squinted tight so he could not see that he was still on the platform, but he could feel his weight pressing his feet down onto the wood. The sudden thought of failure entered into him. Earlier he had only focused on the pros and cons of switching his guild. He had not thought that he might not be able to do anything. That he could wind up crawling back to Kaihlu, begging to let him be an apprentice again. With nothing gained at all, only everything lost. Vrric felt his blood slamming through his veins. His head grew light with fear, and he felt a small tingle in his lips and fingertips. He tried to breathe slowly to calm himself, but it was no use. The beating of his heart began to drown out his hearing. He stood for some time with his head bowed and his hands gripping the platform's rail, just breathing and trying to clear his mind.

"Good, you are early. I like enthusiasm in an apprentice." Revkin's voice seemed to come out of nowhere, startling him out of his reverie. Revkin had floated down behind Vrric, unbeknownst to him.

"How do you do it?" Vrric did not realize there was an edge of anger in his voice until he heard it with his own ears. Maybe not anger, maybe just frustration. "I mean *do* it. I can memorize the syllables, I can speak the words, but… How do you make what you want happen? I tried to make myself fly, but nothing happened at all." Vrric's words came crashing out too quickly. He knew he was sounding like a child, with the words tripping over themselves in his emotion, but he could not stop himself.

"Interesting. Which word did you use?" Revkin seemed unruffled to Vrric. In fact, he thought he detected a hint of amusement in Revkin's voice. He was smiling down at Vrric, floating just above the platform.

"Lumkinderclo. It is the word you used earlier to fly us to your house, I remember it distinctly." Vrric was beginning to calm down. He was not sure if that was because he was starting to feel embarrassed at getting himself worked up, or if he could feel the embarrassment creeping into him because he was calming down.

"Good, this is good. There are several things wrong here, and I think you will learn much from each of them. First of all, the word is partially incorrect. Let me explain each syllable. Lum is much too powerful for you to even attempt right now. You will start out only using Lo until you have proven yourself to me. Kin and Der are correct. You have movement and flesh, fine. Lastly, the spell you intoned is intended to lift quite a few objects at once. The ending Clo refers to a large area, though using Lo will make it almost like Arc. If you would like to try to fly you should start with Lokinderpri. That has the lowest complexity involved with it. But that is not what you were talking about was it? I think you were referring to *it*. How to do *it*. I am glad you have brought this up, Vrric, because *it* is what we will be focusing on for the next moon or so. The *it* is exactly what the Trivaste tests attempt to uncover. Whether or not you believe it, I think that you have a great potential for grasping and taming *it*." Revkin was grinning ear to ear by the end of his little speech. The grin was so genuine that all of the frustration and even the embarrassment seeped out of Vrric.

"Come, I will fly us back to my home where we will continue this conversation. Lumkinderclo!" This time when Vrric heard the word spoken, it was accompanied by a tingling sensation in the pit of his stomach, rather than the nothingness after he had tried the same word. Vrric stared straight into Revkin's eyes as he spoke the spell, trying to see if there was something different. Something visible that would show him Revkin's intent. Revkin's eyes were slightly glassy and seemed to be staring into the distance, but he could not tell from watching Revkin how the mage summoned his magic. Vrric's stomach fell away from him as they took to the sky, flying around the great helioarc's branches until they came to Revkin's home. Instead of watching the panoramic scenery, this time Vrric closed his eyes and tried to get the flavor of what was happening magically. They flew around for quite some time before finally alighting at Revkin's abode.

They had a long, quiet meal before Revkin stood and headed back into the front room. Vrric looked at the soon-to-be familiar mess of papers, glyphs, tomes and, of course, the stained table. Revkin motioned his hand towards one of the wooden chairs at the table and sat himself into a large cushioned chair. The chair was placed in the far corner of the room at one end of the table. The dark upholstery made the pattern difficult to make out in the dim light. Vrric had not really paid much attention to the chair before. He scraped his chair closer to Revkin. Grasping a glass, Revkin took a long, silent look at him.

"Vrric, what do you want from life?" Revkin suddenly smiled warmly and sipped his mead.

"Everything! I want to see it all, to do it all." He burst into a grin. Most of all, Vrric did not wish to be known as a Mudfoot. He wanted to live high in the trees and fly from canopy to canopy like a bird. Though he missed the repetition of the hammer and anvil, for some reason it just felt *good* to make a dagger from a strap of metal, the pound-pound-pound of his muscles, he did not, however, miss the heat. The burning forge was unlike any other fire. Though Vrric grew up around it, and so it was somewhat normal to him, the forge was unique. The roar of the blowers came to him suddenly. How many times had he turned those handles to keep the fire hot enough to melt metal? The heat was unreal. It was as if he had traveled to the Pyran realm, the Yaven Pyran realm, to be surrounded and immersed in flame.

"Vrric! You continually amaze me. You gave me a spectacularly enthusiastic response, which is what I was looking for, and then your mind wandered away. How can you live from one extreme to another like that? Please! Pay attention. So you want a great life, then?" Revkin sat back into his chair and sipped his glass. Vrric tried not to think about Kaihlu.

"Yes, of course. Who would want any other kind of life?" Vrric was unsure as to whether Revkin had been asking a rhetorical question or not, so he answered just to be safe.

"Oh, you would be stunned by what some derlians wish for, but I digress. How do you think you will accomplish this great life then?"

"Well, I… by being great." Vrric smiled at Revkin and leaned back into the stiff back of his chair.

"Perfect answer, Vrric. I was hoping you would say something like that. So the next question is, of course, how does one become great? Are you familiar with the tapestry analogy of life?" Revkin's voice was soft and yet Vrric knew there was more to the question than just the words. Revkin smiled big into the silence, awaiting his response.

"Um, yes." Vrric was going to say more, but everything he thought of was either too rudimentary or too vague. He felt somewhat unsure of where Revkin was going with this.

"Good, then I won't bore you with the details. Do you know why we use that analogy for life?" Revkin leaned back in his chair, smiling smugly. Vrric thought wildly of what Revkin was getting at but could come up with nothing. As the silence grew, Revkin broke his gaze and took a sip. For some reason this eased Vrric's mind some and he decided to take a chance.

"Well, each derlian is like a thread and all of us together make a tapestry. So I think it is mainly the interconnectedness of everything. How each being or even thing in this world is somehow connected to each other." Vrric spoke with confidence even though he knew he was regurgitating common knowledge. He waited happily for Revkin's correction.

"Good, that is the general thought. Seems a bit simple, though, doesn't it? I mean, everything is connected, so what? How does that model help you make specific decisions in your everyday life?" Revkin leaned back again, swirling his drink slightly.

"Well, maybe you could see a simple pattern and figure out what will happen later down the tapestry?" Vrric was grasping at straws, he knew, but he felt good about it because the answer was his own.

"Excellent! That is very close to the point I am trying to make. You see the language of a tapestry being woven, or at least the semantics of that language, means that once it is woven it can not be unwoven. It may be unraveled, by extraordinary forces to be sure, but it can not be unwoven. This, of course, is time. Now you have a specific idea of what you want your section of the tapestry to look like at the end of its weaving, correct?" Revkin's voice had sped up enough that Vrric had assumed he would lecture for a while, so he was a little unprepared for the pause.

"Well, I know some things. But I don't think I have a specific idea or anything." Vrric kind of trailed off. He was trying to think up a better answer, but Revkin took that as his answer and retorted before he could think of anything less insipid.

"Would you like to be a mage?" Revkin took another drought.

"Yes, of course. That is why I am here." Vrric wondered if he should counter with other things he would like for himself in the future but kept silent.

"How do you think you become a mage?"

"Training."

"What is training?"

"Practice…"

"What is practice?"

"Practice is when you do something that is simple enough times that you can eventually do a more complicated version of it." Vrric smiled, feeling he might have gotten an upper hand in the lesson.

"Good definition, Vrric. No, what I mean is how do you think you start that first iota of skill? What brought you to me? What strange coincidence placed you in my path?" Revkin stood and walked over to the table. Holding his cup in one hand and a sizable jug the in the other, he skillfully poured a refill.

"Oh, well then, destiny?" Vrric said questioningly.

"What did I tell you about speaking a statement as a question? What good does appearing to falter do you? Who cares if you are right? In fact, what if there is no right answer at all? Or if all answers are correct? Say it like you mean it, even if you don't, Vrric. You will never get anywhere playing the mouse, at least not in magic. Maybe I am jumping ahead of myself. What do you think the threads, the connections, are?" Revkin's facial muscles relaxed back into their normal shape.

"Magic?" Vrric was slightly taken aback by his mentor's flash of temper and became even more unsure of where the entire conversation was headed. Luckily, Revkin ignored the fact that he posed his answer as a question.

"Close. I'll even say close enough. It is energy. The difference between magic and energy is that magic is under a derlian's mind's control while energy is the mere form, the substance, of magic. It is magic in its pure unadulterated state, and that is under the control of the unconscious. This is why dreams are so important. They are our simplest way to interpret the multitudes of energy that surrounds us. What you performed in the Trivaste tests, what you had accomplished there, was all done through energy. That is why those tests are so unstructured, to be able to assess natural ability and not training. You know how magic works, in general, and you will know the specifics soon. You know, in general, how to change your destiny, right? You find what you are aiming for, way off in the distance of the tapestry, and you note its general direction and distance. You then, simply, tug on the threads that will lead you there, or more specifically, lead there to you. So the big question is how does one tug on the threads? How does one use their unconscious to positively affect their destiny?" After the last sentence Revkin sat back down and sipped from his glass. This was an obvious signal to Vrric that he was to find a good answer to the question, or questions. Revkin was allowing him enough time, without pressure, to figure something out.

Vrric did not know what to say. He could not sound out a theory in his head, so he started speaking aloud. "Well, if it involves my unconscious then I suppose it would involve changing myself, the way I am. Maybe my personal make-up is connected to the threads and I can move them by changing myself..."

"Great, that is even more clear than what I was going to say." Revkin had leaned forward in his chair and his smile seemed too large to Vrric, making him uneasy.

"Well... what were you going to say?"

"Don't worry about that, I'm sorry I interrupted. Quickly now, before you forget what were you going to say. Epiphanies are ephemeral." Revkin leaned back to give Vrric more headspace.

"Just that... if you have something you want to tug to you, well then you have to find how that thread, however far into the future, is attached to you and then change that part of you to be more receptive to that thread. But what about the tapestry? It is not just a tug-of-war between various derlians' wills, is it? I mean, what led me to be standing on the platform before the Mage's Trivaste, was it just me? What if another derlian wanted to be there in my stead?" Vrric went from feeling he was on the verge of a great understanding of life, one that would make his successive years easier to live through, to being even more confused in one small moment. No longer sure of what he was saying, he sat back heavily against his chair.

"Don't fret Vrric, you are on the verge of a wondrous journey. Did you know what you felt? Did you *feel* it, Vrric? You were discovering a *truth* for you. I saw it in your eyes, heard it in your voice. Whenever you cross a mystery, and it interests you, delve into it and find your own interpretation, find your truth. This is the only way that derlians truly learn something, from themselves. I can talk to you for hours on a subject, but unless you can think of it in your own terms you won't remember anything for long. Just remember that feeling, that physical response, so that you can recognize it later. When you feel like that you are close to learning something. Remember to spend the time trying to find your whole truth about a mystery, it really will save you time in the long run. Now, what did it feel like?"

Actually Vrric was feeling that he never had a chance to feel much of anything with Revkin constantly interrupting his thoughts with questions. But they were just beginning the process. He had agreed to be studious and did want to learn magic. Besides, it had felt very good actually. Like he could be somebody of note, someone great, someday.

"Like jagged tiny icicles zig-zagging very fast under my skin, in my head and face. I felt light, like being in water. I felt just, well…happy, I guess." Vrric half smiled to Revkin.

"Perfect. It is best if you enjoy the sensation. As for Destiny being a tug-of-war, do not worry, she is very powerful in her own right and often has different ideas about the final weave than we do, no matter the intensity of our squabbles. Though it is early, you should get plenty of rest tonight. Tomorrow your training starts in earnest. Now that I have your commitment not only to me, but to yourself as well. You will learn to be great, I promise. This is a long and arduous process. Now you will see why you will never read about how a mage is trained. You forgot to ask what it means to be great. It means to be able to overcome any obstacle. And, with a Mage's fascination with and small control over Chaos, the obstacles are varied and unpredictable. This makes the training, necessarily, particularly difficult. You may think I have changed in the morning, but remember that I am still me and that I believe in you until the end. Good night." Revkin rose gracefully for his full frame and, downing the last of his mead, walked to his bedroom and closed the door. As a light flickered from underneath the door Vrric realized that even through Revkin's veiled threats his first thought had been: *I cannot wait until I can call fire from nothing, just to put on a nightgown for sleep.*

Vrric awoke feeling cold. Before he even opened his eyes he knew something was different. Since it was cold, he would assume that the room would feel larger, more airy. He distinctly felt closed in, however, and when he opened his eyes his feelings were shown to be true. He was in a tiny room, barely longer than himself in either direction. The bed he was laying on, a hard flat piece of wood with a mattress poorly stuffed with hay, took one entire wall. The other space was cramped with a small table and a chair with his breeches draped across it. Both were austere wooden structures, devoid of any decoration. On the table stood an ink well, dauber, sand jar, quill and a small book. Vrric assumed the book would be full of blank pages. Looking up he noticed a small shelf stuck out of the wall adjacent to the foot of his uncomfortable bed. Upon this shelf were about seven or eight different books of various thicknesses. Under the shelf was a line of hooks, several of which had brown robes hanging from them. Above Vrric, high up in the wall, was a heavily grated window that let the morning sunlight through. Finally, opposite where he lay, there was a stout-looking door, with iron strapping covering almost a third of its form. There was a small "window" cut into the door covered with iron bars and a little wooden door for its shutter. A little door within the door. An unconscious groan escaped from his lips.

Vrric got out of bed and grabbed a robe to clothe himself with. Since it was chilly he pulled his breeches on under his robe. His mind wondered how, exactly, had Revkin placed him here. The short answer was easy: he used magic. Vrric wondered where this place was. Maybe a hollowed out branch near Revkin's home? Dressed, he pondered his situation. He assumed this might take a while and so decided to collect some basic information. He pushed his mattress to one corner of the bed. He then carefully clambered his staunch chair onto his bed frame and stood on it. With a small hop he was able to grasp the metal bars of his tiny window. Hoisting himself up with arms roped with too-skinny blacksmith muscles, he peered out of the window. He could see tree branches above him and around his field of view. The window was obviously hidden from passersby's eyes. It seemed that Vrric's earlier guess about being in the trunk of a large branch was correct, as far as he could tell. Straining to see where the sun was, he pressed his face to the bars. He could make out the sun straining above a mountain top. Then, as long as it was morning, that way should be south. His arms, though accustomed to much work, got tired in the odd position he was holding himself in so he dropped back down. He made a small scratch in his table top with his fingernail to indicate the direction the sun was hanging. He then took down his chair and made his bed, as much of a bed as it was. Underneath his bed was a small unmarked ewer, though he worried that he knew what its purpose was. It was surely his chamber pot.

Vrric then began to examine his room in earnest. He quickly made sure that the bed, table and chair were as boring as he had initially assumed. That left the door and the bookshelf. Figuring the books would take a while to survey, he chose to examine the door. The door was excessive by anybody's standards. It was made of a thick solid wood, probably oak. He had never learned the various species of wood as much as he did metals. The hinges were iron, forged, not simply cast pig-iron, so they would not be brittle enough to crack with anything Vrric had on hand. The bolts had large, easy-to-grasp heads, and if he was desperate he figured that would be the simplest way to get around the door. He was sure, however, that they would be held fairly tight on the other side. The odds of him attempting an escape without the use of magic seemed fairly slim. Finally, he examined the bars covering the tiny door within the door. They were thin but also of forged iron. The tiny door looked to be made of oak as well and seemed just as dense and tough as the rest of the door. Though he could not detect the hinges on the other side of the tiny door, he was sure they were of iron as well. He then placed his ear to the ground and peered under the door. There was a curved wall opposite, so he was along a hallway, and he could see another curve, veering right, in the hall off to his left. So, if his directions were correct, after leaving this door he could at least go immediately to the south, his right, or turn the other corner and go east. He sneezed suddenly.

Vrric got up and dusted himself off. He walked over to the bookshelf and took the first book against the bookend. He grasped the bookend to push it against the remaining books and paused. The bookend was a large rock and the exposed portion, a hemisphere that was flattened on the bottom, was like any rock. It was an ugly gray-brown color that had many small, sharp protuberances on its surface. But when Vrric moved the book he saw the flat side. It was a hollowed-out, tiny cave. The interior surface was covered with spiky quartz. It was a vivid purple in the center and lightened towards its crusted edge. Vrric had never seen anything like it. He smiled to himself as he gently placed the bookend back to its duty. Even in this tiny dirty cell there was something new and beautiful.

Vrric sat down in the chair, pulling it over to the table. The book he had grabbed was bound in black leather with the words *Principles of Grey Magic* embossed upon it. There was no author listed. Vrric let the book fall open near the beginning.

The first principles:

The eight syllables of the four pillars, the parameter definers, the will and the word.

The pillars are: Power, Sphere, Element and Effect. There are eight syllables in each pillar, each defining a different aspect of the pillar. These syllables are the mental definition of reality at its simplest. When one syllable from each pillar is combined, you have your word. This word explains every aspect of your desired reality morph. Thereby focusing your will upon your desired morph in the most exact and simplest process.

Your focused will then slips from probability to possibility. Because of the mixing of elemental realms there is a constant "turbulence" drifting immeasurable throughout the world, our reality. This is the chaos of eternal change. With the addition of chaos comes infinite possibilities. Everything has a chance of happening, but most possibilities have such a low probability as to be considered zero. A magician is able to sift through infinity to find the desired possibility (imagination) then bring it into reality (willpower) using their focus.

Every being does this, from grandmothers lifting trees off children to not falling when you slip, but a magician strives to do it consciously. The trick is to do it, realize you're doing it, accept it, continue it, and understand enough about it to repeat it. Then you may begin to convince others that what you just did was real.

The book gave almost the exact same spiel as Revkin had given earlier. It was uncanny.

"Good! You are reading." Revkin's voice sounded cheery, but it was difficult to make out his face with enough resolution through the iron bars to truly tell his mood. "If you can answer my question, I will give you your breakfast. What are the four pillars?"

Vrric smiled to himself. Not only was that an easy question, but he had just read it in the book in front of him. Resisting the temptation to glance down at the book, he said, "Power, sphere, element and effect." His voice sounded crisp and clear to him.

"Excellent. Keep that up and you will be out of here in no time." There was a clickety-clank sound of the iron key in the lock. Vrric folded the book closed and placed it upon the bed. As the massive door swung outward, Vrric noticed its silence. The hinges were obviously well oiled and the door was finely balanced. The noise came from Revkin lumbering in with a metal tray piled with various containers. He let out a small exhale as he lowered the tray to fill Vrric's small table. Glancing quickly at the tray Vrric noticed bread, a crock of butter, one of jam, a bowl of warm gruel, a glass of juice, and one of milk. He wondered what percentage of the tray's weight was made up of food. A small one, to be sure.

"To become great, you must become more than you are. To start with this, we must begin a new foundation, which means we must remove the old foundation. I will no longer refer to you as Vrric, but only Mudfoot. Once you have demonstrated your capabilities and, finally, your proficiencies in your new life, I will allow you to choose your new identity. Until then, Mudfoot, eat well. I shall be back quickly to pick up the dishes." Revkin smiled into Vrric's face and then turned away and out the door. Vrric thought the whole "prisoner" idea was being played at bit overdramatically. He smiled to himself at the thought of Revkin leaving so quickly so that Vrric would not realize what a softy he really was. That was the one idea that kept Vrric from panicking, that he knew Revkin liked him and was putting on a show of being stern to motivate him. He thought of Revkin like a doddering old derlian. The absent-minded grandfather, the grocer that let children "steal" fruit, or the weepy drunk, quick to commiserate on a life-long friendship. These thoughts warmed the small cramped cell that had quickly become Vrric's world. In fact, the only thing to stick in his gall, including the cell, austere surroundings, lack of control, feelings of inadequacies, and even the forced betrayal of Kaihlu, the one thing to really stick was that horrible name, Mudfoot. Vrric knew that Revkin had consciously chosen that word to spur him to greater learning, but what a crude and cruel tactic. Had he not already proved his dedication and enthusiasm for learning? Had he somehow shown that he could not accomplish without goading? Or maybe Revkin's own training comprised of humiliation as a motivational factor and he knew of no other way to teach? No matter the reason, Vrric was committed to putting this section of his training behind him as quickly as possible, and not just because of the hated label. Right as he began to break his fast he suddenly wondered what Revkin's "real" name was.

The food was delicious and filling. It was a testament to how extravagant Revkin's usual meals were that the breakfast felt lacking in any way. His cooking always seemed as gregarious and friendly as he was.

Vrric was not long finished with his meal before the tiny door in the door opened. "Good, you have finished." The sound of the key and lock meeting rasped into the room. Revkin bustled in, gathered up the tray and its denizens, and bustled back out. Vrric pondered the open door for half a moment before Revkin reentered. With the petulant waving of both his large hands, he shooed Vrric over to the bed. He then grasped the chair from behind the table and placed it in the center of the room.

"Mudfoot, if I asked you what one thing there is that is more chaotic than this world, what would you say?" Revkin's voice was light and airy. Vrric pondered briefly whether or not Revkin had started drinking yet. His own mind immediately admonished itself for such an errant and offhandedly mean thought.

Vrric tried to think up a good answer. One thing… He then tried to think up an incorrect and yet intelligent sounding answer. More chaotic… Finally he cast his mind to find something, anything that sounded like it could work. When he found his mind pondering the way the question was posed instead of the question itself, as if looking for a loophole in the semantics, he finally blurted the only thing that his mind had mocked him with: itself.

"The derlian mind. There can be nothing more chaotic than that." Vrric had almost said "mine" rather than "that," but had decided to keep up the charade of a real answer.

"Perfect! You are a quick whip for the heart of the matter, though it is a hard riddle to figure which one is more chaotic, the world or the mind. So, in essence, you must prove to the world that you can control the chaos of your mind before your mind can prove to yourself that it can control the chaos of the world. We will begin with something easy: visualization. You will close your mind and center yourself, then I will tell you what to bring forth in your mind and you will attempt to bring that object, and only that object, to the forefront of your mind. Do you think this will be an easy task?" Revkin smiled smugly at Vrric.

"I doubt any task you give me will be easy. I will welcome every challenge from you whole-heartedly as a learning opportunity." Vrric wondered if he was pouring it on a little too thick.

"We shall see, my apprentice. To begin with, I will have to see what you visualize so I can see where to shape you. I am going to cast a spell on you, and I want you to do whatever you can to stop it. Well, nothing physical. I want you to try to stop the spell with your mind as I cast it. Ready?" Revkin was still smiling, which reassured Vrric somewhat. Vrric closed his eyes drew in a deep breath and nodded.

"Nufintotarc!" Vrric was thinking of being a tiny ant amidst huge thorny brambles. He tried to be small, insignificant, at the same time surrounding himself with steely protection. As for the spell, he had been so inwardly focused that he barely heard it spoken aloud, though the word echoed lightly in his mind.

"Hmmm, we will have to work on that. Keep your eyes closed, good. Now for the hard part. Clear your mind. Make it a black emptiness. Envision the Void. Think of nothing. Hmmm. Think of a blank piece of paper. Notice its torn edges, the tiny grain of the pulp. No, no writing on it. Make it blank. Make it larger, make it fill your inner vision. Hmmm. Think of an orange. See it in every detail. Notice how the pockmarked rind puckers near the stem. See the color as well as the shape. Move the orange from side to side. Good. Now move it back and forth. Not up and down! Make it grow and shrink on your horizon. Now let the orange fall away, shrink to nothing. Good, now one last thing. Imagine an anvil. See the smooth polished metal, notice its weight with your mind. This weight is its reality. Excellent! Nice touch with the firelight flickering its edges with life." At this last sentence Vrric's eyes popped open. The vividness of the anvil had taken him by surprise.

"You have a sustainability problem, Mudfoot. Next time try thinking of the object over and over rather than just one long stream of object. Have it move from the back of your inner vision to the front, quickly. Push it forward until it becomes too big for you to grasp it anymore and then let it go, just let it vanish, and place it to the back of you inner vision again. I think this style of 'permanence' will be easier for you to accomplish at first than trying to hold the object still in the Void for any length of time. Sometimes something is easier to hold if it is moving rather than if it is still. Your mind's focus seems to be one of these things." Revkin had cut the lesson off the second Vrric's eyes betrayed him with their popping open. He had not even seen firelight in his vision. Or had he? Could Revkin have seen something that Vrric did not, if he was seeing into his mind? He decided to use more familiar tools while visualizing alone, and the anvil had seemed simple enough to bring into his mind. Just heavy enough to achieve permanence. Revkin stood and brushed his belly with his hands.

"We cannot be finished yet, surely? I was just beginning. I need to implement your advice, to try your moving permanence trick. And I have plenty of questions. I am not sure why you used Fin instead of Sid in your spell." Vrric had felt certain that Revkin would spend more time than this with him. Maybe he will come back with each meal, Vrric thought.

"Why did I use Fin instead of Sid? Because Fin is me seeking outward and Sid is me receiving inward. As for your visualizing, you need a lot of time alone working on it. Only when you understand and can will your mind to visualize can you move to meditation. Then, finally, we will try trance work. Trance should not be done alone, so you must be well practiced at the former two before we even begin the latter." Revkin smiled so quickly that Vrric was unsure of whether or not it was a smile. His mind raced to find something that would stop Revkin, but could think of nothing. So he let Revkin leave in silence.

Vrric decided not to read another word until he could hold an anvil in his mind. He practiced the entire day, until the sun was setting outside his small room. He found that if he consciously thought about what was helping and what was impeding, he could improve more quickly. He found that sitting with his back straight helped immensely, though, for some reason, he did not like his back against something, like the chair back or a wall. He spent some time trying to find the most relaxing position for his legs. He found two positions that worked with a rigid spine. One was to be at the edge of his bed and have his legs hang over the edge. The bed seemed an ideal height for his feet to lay flat against the floor without an excessive bend in his knees. The other way was to sit on the bed with his feet crossed in front of him. He tried this position on the wooden floor but it seemed to pull at his joints more than on the bed. He realized that he would have to start stretching to be able to feel comfortable in any position. It seemed that the trick to visualization, besides the practice needed to exert his willpower, was to have his body feel so comfortable that he only had to think about his mind. For that was what the real focus of the exercise was—his mind.

For the mental part, it was a completely new experience. Vrric was well acquainted with training his body. He could watch Kaihlu pound metal and replicate the exact same motion. If it felt uncomfortable he could repeat the blow until his muscles worked properly. Making tiny musculature adjustments was simple—you just paid attention to how it felt and slightly shifted how you swung and tried again. Once he had a good-feeling rhythm, he could replicate it ad infinitum. A fact that always astounded Kaihlu, who had said that Vrric was the fastest learner he had ever taught. It seemed, however, that Vrric's innate physical self-awareness did not enter into the mental realm. His main gift for physical awareness was that he could isolate a small group of muscles and work them until he had control over them. For some reason, Vrric thought of when he first figured out how to wiggle his ears. Vrric had seen another child do it for the laughter of her friends. At first Vrric could not get anything to move. Then it was a simple twitch, something felt but not seen. After some time he could move his right ear independent of his left, and finally he could move either ear that he wished. To achieve this, Vrric would stare at his reflection in a shallow calm pool and *will* his ears to move. He cast his mind back to try to find his trick. How did he become aware of those tiny, and usually worthless, muscles at the base of his skull? How did he first feel those muscles, only used unconsciously up until then, and make their control conscious? This was *the* trick, Vrric thought. He thought that if he figured out how he had created conscious control of something unconscious, he would be well on his way to figuring out how to exert his willpower over his own thoughts. Throughout so much of Vrric's life his mind had been under unconscious control. While trying to learn something or maybe when a difficult question came up he would, of course, consciously reach with his mind towards some unseen answer. But by and large his mind had just sort of followed along his daily activities with him, like a faithful dog. Willing to help in any way, happy and sometimes assertively courageous, but certainly not under complete conscious control.

Vrric curled his legs into his body a little more and straightened his spine fully. With eyes closed, he slowly wiggled his ears, trying to hone in on the sensation. He breathed slow, deep breaths and began to clear his mind. He was better at imagining something blank than nothing, so he tried to visualize a blank piece of paper like Revkin had suggested. Right before he began to try and visualize an anvil in his mind's eye, he shined his awareness upon his own mind, searching. Searching for the taste of a new sensation or of a new type of awareness that he could identify and cultivate, grow into a powerful conscious control. Vrric slid an anvil past his mind's eye. He wanted to do it slow enough to stop it in the middle of his vision, but was unable to control it. The deep breathing seemed to help him from becoming frustrated too quickly. He slid another anvil into his vision and this one slipped away as well, being overrun by images of Kaihlu's face, images of the room that was now his home, and a hundred other unwanted images. During the failure, however, Vrric noticed something. It was an odd feeling in his mind, like something was pushing his vision away. He knew that there was no such thing, that it was his mind that was unable to keep a hold on the vision rather than something pushing it away. However, what he had been seeking was the sensation itself, and this he found. All he had to do from here was to find a way to counter that sensation to be able to hold the image for longer. From there it was all practice and practice was what he was good at.

"Good, you are still working on your visualization. Please, I hope I am not interrupting, but I am sure you have worked up an appetite. I came by a little earlier and you were in the same serene position. It warms my heart." More than his mentor's voice, the clanking of the lock shook Vrric back to the solid world, like a splash of cold water on his face, though much more soothing.

Revkin walked in with a tray of dishes and food. The food was still simple: bread, beans, lentils, and a thin slab of meat. The difference was that there was a glass with a splash of mead on the tray as well.

"My mentor used to reward me for a hard day's training with some mead, so I thought I would let you have a little bit. You have impressed me with your diligence today, Mudfoot. I believe that you will be casting spells before long if you can keep up the intensity. I suggest that you read some more on the syllable of each pillar tonight. We will discuss each syllable tomorrow, depending on how much studying you get done. You will need to spend two to three hours a day on visualization. This is the exercise of your mind, what will make your willpower strong and healthy, like swinging a hammer at your forge. Hopefully you will be ready to move to meditation soon. I will let you eat in peace. When I come for the tray, I will bring you a candle to study by." Revkin smiled widely at the end of the last sentence and made a small nod towards Vrric. He smoothly turned and exited the small cell without another word. Vrric was unsure of what to say so he had simply stayed quiet. He had not realized how hungry he was until he started eating. It was as if exercising his mind took just as much energy as exercising his body.

By the time Revkin returned, the drink was gone as well as the food. Vrric was enjoying the excuse to rest that the meal had afforded him. The honeyed spirits had made his body feel heavy. He had found a small scrap of paper in his breeches pocket and was inspecting it as Revkin noisily unlocked the door. It was the list of syllables that Revkin had made the other night.

"Ah, what do we have here? You kept that? Hmmm, let me make it a little more useful." Revkin grabbed up paper and dipped the quill into the inkwell and quickly added a rank column beside each pillar. In the end it looked like this:

Power	Multiplier	Sphere	Rank	Element	Rank	Effect	Rank
Lo	3	Kin	2	Luf	2	Pri	1
Nu	5	Fin	2	Ge	1	Arc	2
Mek	8	De	3	Pi	3	Del	2
Nar	11	Tra	1	Flu	2	Sfe	3

Eqe	15	Tec	2	Der	3	Clo	3
Lum	19	Li	3	Hep	1	To	1
Sur	23	Sid	1	Pan	1	Kha	1
Tor	27	Morf	1	Tot	2	Ref	0

"To get an idea of the difficulty of a spell, you add all of the ranks and multiply them by the power. So the lowest is 9 and the highest is 243, just so you can see the range in difficulty, numerically speaking. These numbers are not real, mind you. There is no actual benchmark. They are a learning aid to help you realize how quickly difficulty can increase. The tendency is to overcast your spells, especially in combat. However, you need to be able to pace yourself and gauge difficulty and know your limits. A mage can go mad with the strain and can even kill themselves, depending on the circumstances. This simple ranking system will help you somewhat with that. Get some good rest tonight, Mudfoot. I want to see you refreshed in the morning." Revkin slipped out the door with the tray of dishes before the ink dried.

Vrric stared at the paper after Revkin had left. He felt fine with the power pillar. It was a simple hierarchical scheme, the smaller leading to the greater. The multiplier and rank columns seemed easy as well. It is what made one type of spell more difficult than the others. Now *why* or *how* some elements or spheres were more difficult than the others, he had not a clue. Of course, he did not have a clue how any of it really worked. He felt he had to keep his head down and learn what he could now and worry about the exact knowledge later.

It was the sphere pillar that confused him the most, he thought. How could you encompass every type of *influence* that exists? There had to be more, though Vrric could not think of them immediately. Kin equaled movement and Fin equaled the mind or illusions, Vrric thought as he looked at the list. De was used for combat while Li was used for healing and Tec was used for protection. Those all seemed simple, if incomplete. Sid seemed difficult. What had Revkin said? Communication, but something about spirits as well. That did not seem to make complete sense. Tra was used to change something into different elements, but Revkin mentioned it used a fifth element, with Ref as the effect, but Morf changed shapes but did not need another syllable? What defines the shape if the definition is not a syllable of the word? All these thoughts whirled through Vrric's head haphazardly. So he began to write his questions down in the blank book in front of him.

Vrric then scanned the Element pillar. They seemed fairly easy, if not complete. He had to think a moment to remember that Hep corresponded with metals *and* crystals/glass. The next one, Pan, had too large of an auspice, it seemed. Wood, plants and animals— that was practically the entire world. Finally, Tot went with the mind, which probably went with Fin, Vrric thought.

The last pillar, that of Effect, was easy except for Kha. Maybe since Kha had a smaller rank it was easier to cast and you could lessen your spell difficulty with it. Pri was for himself, simple to remember. Arc went to one other target, and Vrric wondered if the distance it could travel was governed by the Power of the spell. Del made the spell happen at a later time, and he wondered how you chose where the spell took place. He thought it was probably by touch, like To. Sfe affected all around the caster, but not the caster themselves, while Clo was a cube or some large volume. Easy. Vrric did not know how long he had been sitting there but the candle was the only light in his small room. After snuffing the candle, he gratefully lay down in his uncomfortable bed and slept.

The first thing Vrric did upon wakening was visit the chamber pot, which, unfortunately for him, was the last thing he had done last night. He wondered if he was supposed to throw it out the window somehow, or if Revkin actually took care of that for him. He decided to take the chance that he would forget about it and pushed the chamber pot back under the bed. He then got dressed in his breeches and a robe. He figured as it got warmer he would have to just wear the robe, but for now he felt more comfortable in both. This got him thinking about how long he would have to live there, use an old ewer for a bathroom, wear only scratchy robes, and be called Mudfoot. Vrric sat himself on the edge of the bed and slumped. His spine collapsed into a soft arc and he sighed as his chest caved in slightly. He felt a slow heat in build his cheeks. He went so far as lowering his face to his hands before he stopped himself. He slapped his face lightly, then harder. Then again. The sting felt good, if a little angry, and made him stand up.

"No. I will not submit." The words were soft and spoken to the floor. In fact, Vrric was not even sure what he meant, besides no. He refused. What exactly was he not submitting to? He had no idea, but he was certainly not submitting. He had to flail his arms around briefly and even had to do some push-ups to burn away the feeling of self-pity.

Many days passed and flowed. Vrric had difficulty keeping track of time trapped in the tiny cell. He had taken to waking, exercising, eating, visualizing, reading short passages from his books, eating, exercising, visualizing and speaking with Revkin. He grabbed a book from the shelf, the *Principles of Grey Magic*, and sat at his small table. He sat stiffly in his uncomfortable chair and opened the book at random.

The nine sacred points: learning the points. There is no order or hierarchy really, though it seems so because there is an order for you to conquer that is easiest. Once one point is mastered it helps you master other points. Points are described as sharp, and this is their potency. Their ability to hurt you while you learn them is coupled with their power given once understood. What does not affect you will not be remembered by you. They are mainstays of learning life, not just magic. Each point has its counterpoint (of course).

> *Patience – Inertial sloth*
> *Tradition – Ruts*
> *Deviousness – Cruelty*
> *Meticulous detail – Tunnel vision*
> *Virtue – Foolishness*
> *Self knowledge – Circular knowledge*
> *Persistence – Stubborn sloth*
> *Remember – Automaton*

*Patience – Many a magician has mastered every other point but been ultimately consumed for the lack of patience. Each individual learns at different speeds. This is a mental and spiritual safety net. To learn too fast can cause insanity. For if you do not learn the how and the why of a mystery, but you see the full mystery anyway, your understanding warps your view of your reality, which *if not checked will drive you insane, basically unable to cope with the "real" reality anymore.*

Traditions – You are not alone. Many before you have attempted to understand the mysteries. Sometimes the path they have taken is the same shape as your path. If so, you can learn much from their experience. Always keep a look out for some way you can learn from them. Never let anyone else steer your ship, however, for that numbs you and you forget to think for yourself. You must not allow someone's mental hand-me-downs to cloud your own learning.

Deviousness – Your mind must always attack with deviousness. To not do so is lazy and weak. Think on your life. Do you wish? Do you wonder? Do you dream? Then lazy and weak should obviously be ruled out as an option. With the word "attack" I mean consume, not kill. You attack yourself for betterment, a mystery for learning, the world for enjoyment. Attack is a mountain to be climbed, not a deer to kill. Attack should always be constructive, which needs some destruction. Deviousness does not mean aggressive—there is the fine line to cruelty—but intelligent, cunning, ferocious, persistent, intuitive and inventive.

Meticulous detail – Everything has parameters to be understood. The amount of intelligence you have about something is the amount of power you have over it. This should not be confused with control, however. Notice how siblings, with much detailed knowledge over each other, do not always control one another, though this may also be the case. This is because each has a large amount of power over the other, negating each other's individual power. To conquer you need detail, but you also need to not give away detail. To gain intelligence on something takes time, and because many find it entertaining, you may not notice the time go by. In this way the counterpoint could be inertial sloth like Patience. Instead, I have listed the lack of perception because all of your energy then goes into minutiae. You must also be able to see the entire scene. You must be able to notice all the characters of the play at once and their motions and their words and how they interact. This is the raw ability of perception.

Virtue – Every time you lie, a piece of you goes numb. Every time you break your word, a part of you falls into slumber. Every time you hurt another for your trivial gain, a section of you dies. Listen to what feels bad in you. Refuse to do things that you hate in others. Each derlian is different. Find what is virtuous to you and be that. Under no circumstances, however, should you assume that others shall, or even should, follow the same rules that you have set for yourself.

Self knowledge – What is the first thing you must do to build a house? Build an axe. The tools that make your job easier are the first you should create. The first thing you should know to become a mage is yourself. This is a never-ending quest, to be sure, but if you do not know how you learn, what motivates you, what your virtues are, what you actually want, what you need, what drives your curiosity, what enables you to begin each day, then you will learn very slowly. It has been suggested that this is the best point to learn first.

Persistence – Notice this is not perseverance. Perseverance is likened to being held captive. There is only one thing you can do: persevere. While persistence is like being outside of the jail, trying to break a friend out. If you have failed the first three times, and the last time you were wounded, how many more times will you try? Once more? Are you already done? There is no true need to try again. All of your friends will agree you gave it your best shot. No one will shame or guilt you if you stop at three tries. Perseverance, while it is bad because you have no choice, it also good because of that. The tremendous amount of energy needed to try something after a failure or several failures is many times insurmountable. To be a mage, you must surmount the insurmountable.

Remember, always remember – Though it might not seem possible to forget something as mind shattering as a beautiful deepening of truth, an insightful realization, a secular epiphany, it happens. And when it does, you won't feel it go. You won't even feel that it's gone. You will only realize when you re-learn the deepening (which is easier than the first time, thankfully) that it was gone. This life takes energy. How much you put in is how much you get out, and if you start slipping, things will slip from you. I hear keeping up energy gets easier, but sometimes I think they are just trying to make me feel better.

Though Vrric did not hear Revkin come in, he somehow knew he was there. "This book is written oddly, like a conversation. An informal, close conversation." Vrric wrinkled his brow at the book before looking up. "Who wrote it?"

"My mentor, Elange, wrote it. He was a great mage and a great derlian. He was respected by many. He was one of the first grey mages. He even made the Primary Law, the Law of Respect, for all grey mages. Hmmm, let me think. I used to have to have so much memorized. Now that I don't *have* to, it is hard to remember sometimes. The Primary Law begins with how you gain knowledge and power. The way you gain power defines your shade. There are several different ways to gain in magical power: Dark—gain power first, with promised payback to the entities gained from. However, if you think you can outmaneuver an entity that has been bargaining for millennia, then you are a fool. Light—pay constantly, through meditations, sacrifices, chants, and prayer to a more powerful entity in hopes that you will become recognized and given power, which, to me, is still very stifling and risky. Grey—to find power within yourself, practice until it grows, sort of like paying unto yourself, which is slower but much more rewarding, no masters but yourself, which, of course, means NO excuses. This type depends upon respect completely, hence the law. The Law of Respect states that the only way to gain respect from the elements and other entities is to first show respect, always and constantly, to the forces around you. To gain in knowledge and power without some higher entity slipping you clues and answers, you must learn from friends, allies, even enemies if possible. A friendship is based upon mutual respect. A friendly element or entity will only teach to one they think will comprehend the lesson, so you must always expand and learn. In this way, being grey is the most difficult. This is a law of grey, and all other laws are linked into this law if you choose grey. Incidentally, both dark and light use grey, though they would both probably deny it if asked." Revkin slowly opened his eyes and smiled at Vrric. "I almost sounded like Elange. It seems a long time since I have thought of him. Thank you, Vrric. Taking on an apprentice has made me remember why I wanted to learn magic in the first place and those who taught it to me."

"Why haven't you started me out with these points, then? It seems almost a completely different way of learning." Vrric was unsure of whether or not he wanted things to be explained or represented differently, but he thought it was odd that his mentor taught differently than he had learned.

"To be honest, they never seemed to help me much. I guess the reason I have some problem being clear on these points is because I gained their understanding too easily. I was not hurt by their cut, so I have a blurrier image of their sharpness."

"Why did you understand so easily?"

"They were just so quick, a little paragraph. How was that supposed to provide learning?"

"So you felt that you didn't gain any power over them because you lacked the meticulous detail about them?"

"Maybe, Vrric, maybe. Learning from Elange was very difficult for me. He was always being intentionally vague. Dance *around* the mystery, let the knowledge come upon you rather than you to it, learn from your dreams and the whisperings upon the wind. Only I couldn't remember my dreams, and I never had a ground-shattering breakthrough that increased my powers tenfold or some such ridiculous notion. I had to work incredibly hard for each grain of progress. He said it was because he wanted me to figure it out for myself. But I always wondered why I would need a mentor if I could figure it out myself. I don't know, he just never seemed to answer anything for me. With you, I will try to answer everything. I felt like I was not learning fast enough, like there was no way to measure my progress. So I will try to make your lessons build. Master visualization, move on to meditation, then trance and so forth. So you can have a sense of progress. I do realize that many derlians learn differently, however, so I have included my mentor's teaching materials along with my own instruction. Vrric, you are my first apprentice. I am currently trying to make a manual of instruction myself, but since I am just now trying to teach, it may take me a while to write it. Elange did not have his book written until his third apprentice." Revkin's voice sounded oddly old. Vrric wondered why it had taken this long for Revkin to accept an apprentice. He also thought, unbidden and unwanted, about being taught by Elange instead of Revkin. The thought, ephemeral as it was, left him feeling warmly pleased. He wondered if the feeling was because he could never truly experience a different tutelage, and therefore it had to be easier because he did not experience it, or if it was recognition of a tendency in himself to learn by leaps and stalls rather than incrementally.

"So, where was I? I believe you are doing very well at visualization already, so I wanted to discuss meditation. What do you think meditation is?" Revkin smiled warmly. Vrric's mind raced. Had he read something last night from Elange's book?

"Hmm. Meditation is the thinking of something impossible until your mind has no choice but to give out and realize that nothing is truly understandable?"

"No, absolutely not. Well, maybe for a different type of learning like out at one of the eshrams. But while you are under my tutelage, meditation is used to give a deeper understanding of something. It is a way to clear the clutter of the mind. It is an exercise of willpower over the body and even over the mind itself. For me it is like an exercise regime, meant to make your mind strong. For you will need a strong mind to even begin to cast spells under your conscious control. We will try a guided meditation at first." Revkin looked serious, so Vrric did not ask him what an eshram was.

"Pull your feet under your seat. Yes, cross-legged. Close your eyes. Sit straight, always straight. Feel your spine. This is a conduit of energy, you must respect it. Pull your head up. Don't open your eyes, Mudfoot. Move your arms so they are resting comfortably. You want to minimize distractions. Yes, perfect. Now, with your back straight, breathe in through your nose, hold briefly, then let it out slowly out through your mouth. Good. Notice your breathing. Notice your spine. Be aware of yourself. Breathe from deep within you, from your belly. Relax and breathe, breathe and relax. You want to build a slow and steady cadence. If you have to make a little noise while you are breathing, that is all right. As you breath in, notice a tingle of energy. This happens naturally. Cultivate this feeling. Each time you inhale, bring more energy up into your chest. Bring it from further down, further away. With each breath feel the energy moving up into you. You are sending roots down, tapping the energy all around you. Feel the roots. Feel the energy. Good. Now, when you exhale, let the energy leave you through your breath. Inhale, bring the energy into you. Exhale, let it slip from you. Notice branches of energy leaving you. They flow out from your head and arms in a myriad of tendrils. Don't speed up your breathing. Keep it steady. Feel the energy come up through you and then out of you, with each breath. Let it fall as it leaves. Let the energy have weight. Pull the energy, then push the energy. Nice and slow. Your spine is your tree of energy, make it grow straight and tall. Keep doing this until you feel comfortable. Inhale. Exhale. Feel the energy move with each breath." Revkin's low monotone voice was almost a chant, an incantation. "With each breath." It was a comforting sound, it lulled Vrric. He slowed down his breathing and almost pursed his lips during the exhale to feel it going. To put more power behind it, like a nozzle. "With each breath." While he inhaled, he could feel his nostrils flare unconsciously. Just slightly, just enough to allow more air in, but not enough to consciously move a muscle. "Keep the flow until you feel at balance. Is the amount of energy within you still changing?" At first Vrric felt light headed but that eventually faded. "Once you can pull and push and feel it flow through you, once it no longer changes how much energy is stored in you, you may open your eyes. Inhale. Exhale. Good. Very well done! Now your energy should be balanced. Your tree is grounded." Revkin was smiling at Vrric as he opened his eyes. He had wondered if he was quitting the exercise too quickly, but that smile reassured him. "Excellent. That was your first grounding meditation. I want you to do that at least once a day, Mudfoot. Whenever you have too much energy or too little, that meditation will even you out to your natural level. How do you feel?"

"Good. Tingly. Maybe I have a little more energy than my natural level." Vrric grinned. He *did* feel good. "Do I need you to lead me through the meditation every time?"

"No, no, of course not. I will tomorrow and the next day, but you should be able to do that in your sleep soon. I have many other meditations as well, and we still have trancework to cover, but you are advancing very quickly. You make me proud." Revkin stood and walked over to the door. "I will be back for your meal. Once you feel comfortable again you should work on some more visualization." He turned, left, and locked the door while Vrric was still sitting cross-legged. Right after Revkin was gone, Vrric remembered the questions he was going to ask.

A couple of weeks from the first meditation came Vrric's first attempt at a true spell. The day had been a typical one until his after meditation conversation with Revkin turned to Elange.

"Why did Elange choose you as an apprentice?" The question was unthought of before Vrric spoke it.

"Well, I guess I do not know. I come from traders. My family spent a fair amount of their time and energy in several guild trades for me, but not for magic. It was very expensive to hire a magic tutor for one who did not have a quick knack for it. I was not blessed like you are, Mudfoot. I had to sweat over every miniscule gain in skill. I think Elange admired my determination to become a mage. He had several apt pupils under his tutelage. His first student, Nuada, had just won a panel on the High Mage's Council, a first for a Grey Mage, and Elange was probably feeling generous." Revkin had soft distant eyes, peering over Vrric's head.

"I remember walking out of that room, you know, the one during the Trivaste festival. The room had seemed so dim, maybe because I had my eyes closed during most of it. Keeps my concentration up. But I remember the sun burning into me. I was walking in a thick column of derlians. Others to the left and right getting chosen. The line seemed like a herd of lemmings, walking unto their doom, unable to turn or stop. As the line thinned, I realized I wasn't going to be chosen. The sun became huge in my vision. I knew that I had to walk straight, straight down those stairs if a mentor did not tap my shoulder. It was so bright that I didn't notice Elange coming towards me. I had sped up, you see. The pressure seemed too great. I could *feel* the rejection. It was like stones being piled upon my chest. Rats digging through my eyes. It was like walking over hot coals and being told you have to stop. Just stop and stand there. But then it happened. Elange steered me from the doomed column stretching towards the spiraling downward stairs. No, maybe I am unable to tell you why Elange chose me as an apprentice. But I can tell you, in any way that you like, how he captured me." Revkin breathed in the past. He held it tight in his lungs. His eyes narrowed and focused upon the wide-eyed Vrric. Out came the future.

"I want you to levitate. Do it. Lokinderpri. Lo for the ease. Kin for the levitation. Der for what you came into this world being. Pri for yourself. For yourself, Vrric! Now!" Revkin was staring into Vrric. His eyes burrowed spirals into Vrric's skull, mind, essence. There was no denying him. There just, was, no, denial.

"Lokinderpri!" It was a yelp, a puppy's cry. It was wrenched from him. The squeal was the shock of it all. The stunning command. The control. It was too much. It was beautiful. It was truth. It was madness. There was no way to describe it, for it was *all*. The secret whisper to a lover. The heart skip of death. The Mystery. The natural chaos. The gulp of breath that awakens from nightmare. The scintillating light that reflects from virgin crystallized snow. The ache for the love of a father. The shadow. The Shadow? The torn asunder and the made whole. It was the mixture, the amalgamation, even the amelioration, yes, of *all*. It was Cleelok, and it did two things to Vrric. The first was wonderful, as was the second. It was the understanding of magic. The understanding of spells. The understanding of syllables, words, Will, chaos, the thing that you do when you do what you shouldn't be able to do but you know it, you feel it, you breathe it, you are it, and it is you. It all suddenly made sense. He knew the gut feeling. He could wiggle his ears. He understood what cannot be understood so that it must be danced around as the mystery should not be spoken until after the understanding or maybe... maybe the bubble could pop. So it was best not to pop the bubble, as it was his original goal to make it. The second thing was Nothing. It was black and it consumed. Floating? Maybe. Falling? Definitely. There is no rest like that of the unconscious. Truly unconscious.

"Vrric! Come on, answer!" Revkin's face loomed large in Vrric's vision. His hand was pulled back to slap, and Vrric managed a cry.

"Ay! I am okay. Why? What... what happened?" Vrric had meant the why towards the raised hand, but the what was what he really wanted answered. His hand that unconsciously wiped his face came away with blood on it. It would have stunned him if Revkin had not immediately started gushing.

"You did it! You did it! That was amazing, you are amazing. Remember being amazing, Mudfoot. For you will have to do it on a regular basis, ha!" Revkin's joviality was infectious. Plus, he had done it. It had happened. Nothing anyone could say or do could change this one fundamental fact about Vrric. He had levitated. Only for a split second, but it had happened. He had made it happen. The joy sprouted through him, bouncing from his middle to his outer and back. Reverberating through him.

"You called me Vrric." Vrric did not know if he could smile more widely. Both his bones and muscles ached. It was a good ache, though, and he didn't mind.

"And, after you have a vision quest and choose your magical name, I will call you something else. Something of your choosing. But for now, I will still call you Mudfoot. Realize, however, that I am more proud of you now than I have ever been before. You accomplished much today. I will grab something to drink and maybe a game hen. You haven't had a nicely cooked meal for some time, have you?" Revkin grinned and prattled off, absentmindedly locking the door behind him.

However, even in the torture of learning, when each second must be analyzed and interpreted and memorized for future gain, even then time pasts swiftly. For Vrric it seemed an eternity, but when he was older and slower, the pace amazed him. So much in so little time. If life is given in certain amounts, and to burn the candle at both ends is to encourage an early grave, then Vrric ate heartily at this time in his life. His voracious appetite knocked many a year of comfortable old age off the far side of his life span. The next few moons, the next few sun cycles, would etch themselves into his mind. It was strange how the nostalgia for the past can affect one's future, and how the nostalgia from the future can affect one's present. There are times in your life that you can tell, at that very moment, that you are going to remember them forever, and this is exactly what Vrric was feeling. Moons passed from the future into the past.

Vrric awoke with a start, the darkness complete. He was drenched with sweat, not a hot type of sweat, but more from a massive exertion of physical endurance. His tongue unconsciously licked the salty tears of his body off his lips. Vrric wondered why he was awake. What was his dream? He had a vague impression of figures draped in black robes crawling all over a giant stone laying on the ground. In a daze, Vrric stretched up to his barred window and peered out. The pitch black night sky lit up. It was as if it was noon in his room, he could even make out the books on his shelf for at least a full second. A gigantic sound, one of rumbling anger, tore through the sky. The thunder seemed incredibly near. Rain splashed softly in between the bars down onto his already soaked face. For the rain to get to his sheltered window through the foliage meant that it was coming down incredibly hard. Vrric smiled to himself. It had been some time since he had seen a good lightning storm. Certainly nothing this powerful had emptied upon Ariellyna since he had moved in with Revkin.

The lightning flashed for quite a while, Vrric was not sure for how long. The deafening thunder following each strike. He was yawning and about to head back towards his hard bed when a particularly close strike happened. He had still been watching the window, and he was able to see its shape for what seemed like a long time. More than anything he noticed that it was blue. In his mind he tried to think of the different colors of fire. He knew there was some blue, and knew that was really hot, but it seemed different somehow. The blue of the lightning was more white, with almost a cold after feeling. Though that could be attributed to the rain that accompanied the lightning... Vrric shook his head, rubbed his eyes, and stared out again. One question kept creeping through him, one riddle that would not leave his mind, *what element was lightning?* His mind listed the eight elements that were defined by magic syllables. It was surely not Water, even in the midst of the rain. Certainly not metal or wood or derlian. Maybe Fire, maybe Air or, probably not, but conceivably it could be made up of mind. Something in the middle of Vrric knew, but he could not get his mind to think of it.

He stopped and watched strike after strike, even watching the fading bursts of light as the storm passed over Revkin's helioarc. Vrric closed his eyes and concentrated, pressing the palm of his hands against his lids. Nothing. It could not be any of them, it just did not fit together. He had wondered, when first confronted with the list of syllables, if they could encompass all of magic. He had not thought about it correctly, though. It was not just all of magic that they were supposed to encompass. No, the thought had not properly formed earlier. What was magic if not chaos? Was that not the central point that Revkin had been trying to make these last moons? How, even in the most imaginative of minds, could twenty-four total syllables and only eight elemental syllables encompass all of chaos? All of Chaos. There was no way that was right. There was a zero percent chance that Chaos could be contained in so small a categorization system. There had to be more... More what Vrric was unsure of. More syllables? How many would be needed to encompass all of anything? More adroit minds or imaginations? More powerful magic systems? Maybe another way of defining the Will? Or just another way of defining what the Will can imagine? Vrric's head hurt. He wanted to just sleep, but the thought kept haunting him. The magic he was learning was incomplete. But not only that. The magic he was learning could not, even after eternity, be complete. No matter how clever the system.

Through the night Vrric thought of many absurdities. He tried to argue with himself about infinity. If chaos meets eternity does that mean that all things exist? Phrases fell amongst the echoing cavern of his mind, things that he had thought he had heard before. If you have numbers to infinity, then you could have just odd numbers to infinity. Meaning the world would have an infinite amount, but only half of them would remain, the others would not exist. Certainly not all possibilities would be required to fill all of infinity. He felt like he was lost in a maze. He felt like he was at a great height. He wondered if there was a third set of numbers, unknown to him and his kind, but that they completed the unseen world somehow. Odds, evens, and triends. The smile on his face as he slept was one of a lunatic. If Vrric could have seen his twitchy grin, he would have wondered what he was dreaming about.

***

Revkin came in quietly, like he somehow sensed that Vrric had slept poorly last night. He placed the tray of food on the small table and sat in the uncomfortable chair. He looked slightly nervous.

"Before we begin today, I need to ask you a question." Vrric's voice almost startled himself. It sounded raspy, like he had been smoking. Revkin nodded in silence, a small grin on his face, like he was glad for the distraction.

"What element is lightning?" Vrric could not think of another way of asking it. It struck him as funny how the most difficult questions could be asked so directly or succinctly. But instead of a fatherly lecture, or a quick blithe answer, or even an attack on the appropriateness of the question, Revkin looked surprised and a bit sheepish.

"I actually thought about that myself when I was younger." Revkin's laugh was small. "But there is a difficulty in truly understanding something. To be able to 'tell' chaos what you mean in a syllable, you must have a complete understanding of that something. This is why there is an accepted learning base of magic for every Luften. The broad use of it makes it easier to understand. So many before have built upon the same building blocks, the Majora syllables. The exact same elemental framework that you are attempting to grasp now. Of course there is more to magic. There are a huge amount of Minora syllables. But there are great difficulties in such a thorough understanding, such an individual deepening. Tell me, Mudfoot, do you know what a mindtrap is?" Revkin was staring hard into Vrric. To Vrric it had been a simple question. Revkin could have said, "No, actually, I do not know what element lightning is." But he chose this instead.

"No. Actually, I don't know what a mindtrap is." Vrric attempted to make his voice deep and cold, like a well.

"A mindtrap is when one thought automatically cascades upon another. Which is a way of learning, actually. So it is more that you cannot control the cascade. Like a crazed, unrequited lover who hears the scorn in her voice but still thinks the words represent a secret love. Or, more accurately, it is when something nags at the back of your mind so much and so vigorously that you are unable to think of aught else. Or—and this should accompany a more in-depth story of Elange—most specifically, for a mage, a mindtrap is just that, a trap that you cannot remove your mind from. The reason the syllables are taught as they are is that they are easy to understand. To completely understand. To be able to wrap your mind around. When you look into chaos, Mudfoot, chaos looks back into you. To be able to understand something, such as lightning, you must have a cathartic revelation after years of hard study. To be able to understand it so deeply that you can encompass the element with the whole of one thought, one syllable, takes an incredible amount of effort. Effort wrought with difficulty and pain. Once or twice is usually fine. But there are mages who have spent their youths trying to reach the stars, only to end up as husks of old derlians before their time. Do you want to live so much so young that you become old so quickly?" Vrric had not a clue as to what Revkin was talking about, but that did not slow him down in the least. "Worse! Worse, however, is to get caught in that final mindtrap. Everyone has a limit of what their mind can endure. Everything has a breaking point, where the tool loses its effectiveness and can not be repaired. Like a mother holding her newly dead baby. She knows the child is dead. She has to. But her mind refuses reality. She coos to it, nuzzles it, talks incessantly to… to the empty air. Afraid that silence will bring the revelation that cannot be drowned out. Elange was obsessed with learning new syllables. He eventually had to move to an eshram on the edge of the desert. He was no good to anybody anymore, Mudfoot, not even to himself. His mind is not only trapped, but it is lost. Completely. It is good that you are curious and have the drive that you have. It will serve you greatly in your life. While you are with me, however, we will concentrate upon the given Majora syllables. Leave exploring the frontiers for later." Revkin took a deep breath. "This is all smoke in the wind, however. I have a task for you." Vrric couldn't help notice that Revkin was starting to use the word "however" more frequently in his conversation. "I know I shouldn't be doing this, but I need you to take a message to King Hulgert. Now, now, don't ask me about it. The message is sealed, and not by me, so I am unsure of the actual message myself. I do, however, have a letter written by me to get you in to see Hulgert. You must take this letter and give it to the guard at the southern pinnacle tower, third up. He is the only one you can give this to, understand?" Revkin looked stern and a little nervous at the same time.

"I am not even sure what you are talking about. I mean, who is the original message sealed by? Why would I have to take the message rather than you? What do you mean by 'third up'? What if the guard you want me to give that to isn't there when I arrive, like what if he is sick or something? I haven't left this room for moons, maybe a full cycle." Vrric knew that he was talking back to Revkin but could not seem to help it. The world seemed to be shifting under his feet. All he could think was that another derlian had made Revkin deliver a message and that he was going to make his apprentice take it instead. What was the use of being a grey mage if you were still beholden to other powers?

"You need not concern yourself with the message, I have already said that, Mudfoot. The same goes for your second question. Third up means you go to the southern tower and then get to the third tier before alighting and speaking with the guard. As for the guard, his name is Salien and I spoke with him this morning at that location. Has that answered all of your questions?" Revkin's voice added the thought, *if not, then too bad.* Vrric merely nodded in assent. Revkin handed Vrric a letter, folded upon itself and sealed.

"This other letter that I have written, you will have to give it to Queen Vanelia herself. The first will arrange your meeting with her, and the second is for her eyes only. Do you think you can remember that?" Revkin was already holding out the second letter.

"So, it is the third letter that I will give to King Hulgert?"

"Maybe, you might have to give it to Queen Vanelia, that is her decision, not mine. Of course, most decisions are hers now anyway…" Revkin trailed off slightly. He started tapping the second letter against his other hand, then held it out for Vrric to take. "I know this is unprecedented and that you are unprepared for such an errand. Think of it as your first test, Vrric. If you accomplish this task well, then we may begin to talk of when to start your vision quest, when you may choose your name. You have progressed quickly, Mudfoot. This will show me where your training is lacking and what you excel at." Revkin looked smug. Vrric was beginning to get annoyed. It seemed as if he was doing a favor for Revkin and accordingly Revkin should be grateful, or at least ask. Instead, he was making it sound like he was doing Vrric a favor. Vrric breathed in slowly. Of course it was a test, everything in life was a test. There was no way that he would not do this for Revkin, so to complain would only make the situation more awkward. He mentally willed himself to remember humility and deference to his teacher. He breathed out slowly through his nostrils.

"Excellent, leave the third letter and I will get changed. Then I am off to the third tier of the southern tower to speak with Salien and eventually Vanelia. I cannot fail you." Vrric exhaled as Revkin nodded in approval.

"Perfect, Mudfoot. You will be a great mage. Sooner rather than later if my guess is correct." Revkin smiled and turned to leave the room. Out of everything odd that had happened to Vrric that day and the night before, Revkin not pushing the door closed and locking it behind him was the strangest.

After changing, Vrric found Revkin outside of his room. "I am going to need directions on how to get to the royal helioarc." Vrric felt he only had to keep up his enthusiasm for another couple of moments.

"Here is the last letter, the letter of import. Here is, also, a rudimentary map of Ariellyna. See, here, it has my helioarc, the royal one of course, the main guild helioarcs, and some others of note. I was going to give you this when you had finished your training and had named yourself, but this will only be a slight bit early." Revkin was actually beaming at Vrric.

"Nukinderpri!" The feeling still astonished Vrric. Almost enough to make his mind slip, which would bring him tumbling to the ground. This was Vrric's first long distance solo flight, and he wished he could spend more time inhaling the heady scent of success. He felt amazing. He almost forgot Revkin, almost forgot about his betrayal of Kaihlu. But he did not have the luxury of time. Casting anything at the Nu level meant precious little time for the spell to be in effect. Vrric might even have to stop along the way to recast. Going up to Mek may have gotten him there in one swoop, but he had rarely cast anything that difficult.

Vrric flew due west, with the sun beating down on him, in a large curve away from Revkin's helioarc branch. He needed to get high enough to see the royal helioarc. Revkin had said it was the largest tree in Ariellyna, probably the largest anywhere. Vrric finally spotted the gigantic helioarc after cresting a nearby tree's canopy. He shot towards it, folding the crude map while trying to make a straight line to the third level of towers. He kept to the southern section of the Royal Branch (the official name of the family line and the tree that housed them), its various sections strewn through the ancient helioarc that had been the center of Luften life since the beginning. Each section of the Branch was connected by rope bridges, hanging heavy with moss and lichen, in an intricate spiderweb, wafting in the breeze. Vrric began to feel heavy and dizzy, so he furtively cast his eye about for a quick landing spot. He alighted on a large branch in a random helioarc, still a ways from his destination. He crouched for some minutes gathering his breath and strength with his face pressed against the rough bark.

"Nukinderpri!" With this last launch towards the royal helioarc he thought about taking a quick side trip. Just as quickly he banished the thought from his mind, instead heading toward the southern towers. As he spiraled in towards the towers, he noticed a small figure on the third platform. He swooped in with a minor flourish.

"Are you Salien?" Vrric was unsure how to approach the Luften.

"Yes, and shush. We need not exchange greetings here. Follow me quickly to the second throne room's antechamber, I have much other business to attend to." Salien was curt and staccato in his speech and mannerisms. He walked towards a large, solid-looking door that seemed to lead further into the tower. He turned at the entrance door suddenly and held his hand out, looking at Vrric with cold eyes. Vrric automatically handed over the first letter. The odd thing was that he had never read the letter, even though he had been allowed to. He had, in fact, been planning to.

The antechamber that Salien took Vrric to was small and covered with aging tapestries. Small hunting scenes, large war scenes and, of course, woven images of Hulgert in his finery and the trappings of state. Vrric looked in upon the room from the small barred window in the door as Salien fumbled around with his keys. He could make out the image of another heavy door at the opposite end of the room.

As Vrric was lead into Vanelia's, and Hulgert's, antechamber he couldn't help but notice that there was another petitioner waiting, sitting casually on an ornately carved bench that was sidled up against a side wall. The Luften was young and somewhat waifishly thin. Thick black hair lay flattened down upon his skull. He had oddly imposing eyes, dark but bright. His clothing was incredibly formal with the lace spilling forth at his throat and cuffs. His long hands seemed like delicate flowers pushing out from a wide clunky vase. He had the blue heraldic lion above a green field of savannah grass sown upon the shoulder of his shirtsleeves. A representative of a noble branch rather than a guild, the Branch of Largon if Vrric's memory of insignias served him. He smiled and nodded to Salien, but seemed to ignore Vrric completely.

"Chiavel," Salien's whispered voice echoed softly through the chamber, "I am in a bit of a pinch. Is there any way that you could show Revkin's apprentice to Vanelia before you convene with Hulgert?" The speaking only made the chamber seem smaller. The echoes pressed in rather than conveying vastness.

"Well, if it is a favor that you seek, then you have only to ask. Of course I agree, Salien, you can run to where you are needed." Chiavel's voice was silky smooth, like that of a horsetrader, relaxed and friendly while having a strong undertow. The voice of someone who will laugh off all of their own promises or admonitions, but hold you to every word spoken from your lips. Vrric wondered as to the capabilities of the Luften's memory. Throughout the quickly spoken sentences there was also the haughty overtones of someone who had never known poverty.

"Well, I do not think it would be an inconvenience or anything…" Salien trailed off while staring wide-eyed into Chiavel's narrowing gleeful eyes.

"I said that I would do this favor for you, Salien. Do not worry yourself about anything more." Chiavel seemed to be almost smiling.

"Uhm, thank you." Salien nodded to Chiavel and, without another glance towards Vrric, left the room they way he came in. Vrric could hear the cling-clang of distant keys rattling together as the door was secured behind him. A small silence began to grow in the small room.

"Please, settle yourself here. What the bench lacks for in comfort it makes up for in frivolous decoration." Chiavel had on an easy smile. His bird-like hand fluttered in a small dive over the empty portion of the bench.

As Vrric rested himself on the bench he felt how austere its planks really felt. "This must be an incredible piece of art then, because it has almost no comfort whatsoever." Vrric laughed easily at himself. Chiavel seemed to enjoy the cheap humor as well, for he laughed earnestly. Vrric decided that he had been kept in captivity for too long. He had not even spoken to anyone besides Revkin for what seemed like forever. And also to Salien, he supposed, but that was pure business. The sense of any derlian camaraderie brought an unbidden swell into Vrric's chest.

"Revkin, huh? I did not even know the old gray mare had an apprentice. How is he anyway? Still enjoying the drink?" Chiavel's smile had a little too much intelligence in it. He thought just a little too highly of himself, Vrric's mind warned itself.

"He is a very competent mage. He is passing his mastery of chaos onto me with the individual attention that few apprentices enjoy. He always tells me that he was waiting for the perfect apprentice before he wanted to begin teaching." Vrric felt suddenly defensive over Revkin. As soon as the words were out, however, the defensiveness vaporized and he was left feeling sheepish.

"Yes, I am sure that he was. But it all hinges on the definition of perfect apprentice doesn't it? You are not from a noble branch, are you? Your parents didn't put you through guild training, did they? Yes, I bet you were the perfect little mudf…" Chiavel's eyes were narrowing for the kill. His verbal fangs were scratching the surface of Vrric's tender neck, and he reacted out of pure dumb reflex.

"The name is Vrric! I am Vrric, not Mudfoot!" *No reason,* thought Vrric. No reason at all. There was no way that Chiavel could know what Revkin called him. He felt flustered and hot, he knew his cheeks would be burning. He could not recall ever losing that much control over that small of an issue. He vowed to think more before speaking. Who was this Luften that could unnerve him so? Chiavel had leaned backwards with both of his hands up in front of his chest, fingers splayed in a wide pacifistic display. His eyes were wide with shock at Vrric's vehemence, but there was still, way in the back, hidden, guarded, distant, that bit of too much intelligence.

"Please forgive my hasty words. I meant no offense, Vrric." Chiavel smiled disarmingly. His words were quiet and respectful, making Vrric's anger only seem more out of place.

"So what does Revkin wish with Vanelia anyway, if you do not mind my asking?" Chiavel had waited into the silence just until it had almost become uncomfortable. Vrric knew that the question was meant to soothe and distract, but he also knew that what Revkin wished with Vanelia was none of Chiavel's business.

"I wish I was able to tell you. Revkin is always slipping notes here and there. Questions, orders, decisions. These things are not spoken amongst apprentices." Vrric felt a little better about himself after witnessing the quick double-take that Chiavel's eyes betrayed. He promised himself to keep his wits about him more continually.

They spoke of oddities and curiosities. They spoke of the weather and the state of the farmer's crops. They spoke of the helioarcs and various guild branches. They spoke, in essence, of nothing. Only the neutral territory of the mundane and banal. Yet, and maybe it had something to do with his thirst for another voice besides Revkin's, Vrric thoroughly enjoyed the time he spent with Chiavel. Once you got past the prying and sparring, he was incredibly easy to get along with. Funny, observant and quick-witted, their conversation of vapors blew back and forth between them. So in tune was their conversation that it seemed to Vrric that he had known Chiavel for a long time. Of course, he hadn't. And it seemed odd that he had to keep reminding himself of that so that none of smithing, Kaihlu, Mudfoot, his missing parents or anything not already in common knowledge about Revkin slipped from his lips.

"Do you know what a mindtrap is?" The question stemmed from Vrric's sense of ease with Chiavel more than what insight he might lend to it.

"Loops. Circles. Distance traveled with no ground gained. Really, though, I know nothing of mindtraps or eshrams. I have higher aspirations than just manipulating reality with controlled chaos." Chiavel's smile invited the question. *What could be a higher aspiration?* thought Vrric.

The door at the end of the antechamber opened with a soft creak, slicing through the unspoken words. The air in the room stirred in a sigh. One soft white slipper peeked from behind the door, then Vanelia entered the room. It could be none other than the Queen.

She was dressed head to toe in white. She had a small tiara of lilies upon her brow. Her curly chestnut hair bounced down her head and shoulders as a waterfall splits itself upon the rocks below. Her robes were painfully white. An embroidered undergarment with a heavier outer robe with heavy lace trim outlined her figure. Vrric realized that the bawdy barroom ditties and the slow playful sonnets had all tried to capture one thing about Vanelia: her striking beauty. Though Vrric could see the effects of age upon her radiant face, the small lines that cracked out from her smiling hazel eyes seemed only to add to her beauty by giving it a solidity that only wisdom, and therefore age, could lend.

"Chiavel, you may visit with Hulgert in the second throne room. And who is this?" Her eyes startled a little wider.

"This is Vrric, apprentice to Revkin, whom Salien brought here to quietly meet none other than yourself, handsome lady." Chiavel's entire demeanor melted and fluttered along like his bird hands. With a sweeping bow that took in all of Vanelia and even a bit of Vrric, Chiavel theatrically left through the door that Vanelia had just entered through.

Vrric handed the second letter to Vanelia. She smiled politely to Vrric but read in silence. Vrric studied her face as she studied the letter. Her eyes darted purposefully over the words, but her face remained a serene calm. Before he realized how long they had been there, she was speaking again.

"Horrible. This is horrible." She sighed the words, almost inaudibly. Her eyes suddenly snapped into focus and her back straightened. "Well, you had better come with me." She turned and walked regally through the door to the second throne room.

As Vrric walked in he noticed how small it was. He had assumed throne rooms to be huge, stately, cavernous and full of echoes. This, however, was a small, cozy, richly tapestried room. Vrric glanced at the dais in the near corner of the room. Chiavel had been kneeling and handing something to an aged, decrepit-looking derlian. He nodded twice, rose, and left with only one quick glance in Vrric's direction. The old Luften seemed sunken to Vrric. As they walked closer and he could more completely see the bearded apparition before him, he realized it must be Hulgert.

Vrric wondered what had happened. Hulgert should be the same age as Vanelia, but there was a marked difference in their energy. Hulgert had white wispy hair, thinned to frays on top, floating, dancing in the air like a strange sea creature. The white continued down his chest in a long elaborate braided beard. He was covered in cloth. Robes, capes, stockings, pantaloons, shirt, tunic, mantle. He seemed to be the most expensive pile of clothing that Vrric had ever seen. What struck him most, however, was Hulgert's face.

The eyes were sunken, but not too terribly dark. They were lined with worry. They seemed flat and distant. His nose was a red-veined, bulbous one. The oddest feature, the one that explained the most about Hulgert and what a predicament Vanelia was in, was his mouth. Through the beard and the parched lips, the mouth hung open uselessly. Drool spilled from one corner of his mouth to the expensive pile of laundry on his shoulder. It hung there in a thick string defying both Vrric and gravity. As Vrric watched, the lower jaw began to twitch up and down. A small "ahayahayha" noise came from him. Vanelia walked over and handed him the letter.

"Where is the last letter?" Vanelia's voice rang through the small room. Her eyes pierced into Vrric.

"Can he read?" Vrric had not meant to say anything. He had just wanted to hand over the last correspondence. His hand was dutifully moving to hand her the letter. His mouth, however, had betrayed him. Similar, in a way, that Hulgert's mouth betrayed him.

"Yes. The rot has left some things to him. He can hear as well." Vanelia smiled courteously. It was a smile of patience. Hulgert stared briefly at Vrric with wide, wrinkled eyes and open mouth before going back to the letter. The mouth seemed like it was poised in a silent scream. It unnerved Vrric immensely. He hastily handed over the last letter.

"I meant no offense." Vrric's face felt hot and flushed.

"It is fine. Soon all of Ariellyna will know. Then the true difficulties will begin." Vanelia was reading the letter while talking to Vrric. "I don't suppose that Revkin explained why he only used one Yaven for the…" There was a large commotion at the front doorway. The double doors seemed to shake from the verbal force of what was going on outside.

"Thank you for the letters, Vrric. You should leave the way you came in. We will be in touch with Revkin soon." Vrric could hear snatches of words as they tumbled through the double doors as he was exited through the single one.

"We demand entrance! We demand to see the king! If he is unfit to rule, we must know!" There were at least five different voices, with five different questions bombarding the poor guards on the other side of the doorway. Vrric did not look back. He stepped into the antechamber and closed the door.

Chapter 8

It had taken most of the night to make it to middle of the forest, after Knill had recovered enough to walk again. They slept in a wide circle of large holly. Trela had wrapped torn cloth around Knill's head before they rested behind the scratchy leaves which made a dense cover. He said he had known of the place from his childhood.

"My father had gotten lost as a child, and the Gaen search party was unable to find him because the spot was on a crossing of ley lines."

"What are ley lines?" Trela was drowsy but interested in Knill's explanation of why they had come here to hide. She had wanted to make it to the Pyran border by daybreak, but Knill was still shaken up by the tree incident, so they were going to be traveling slowly.

"They are where the concentrations of chaos are strongest. Kind of like streams of water, they allow greater magic to be performed near them. They also wreak havoc with detecting derlians with magic. My father said it was like, magically, staring into the sun. So he slept through the night and was found the next evening after walking back towards Serif. He said he got hungry and figured they must not have sent out a search party since he had yet to be found." Knill laughed to himself. Trela thought that he laughed to himself a lot. She also thought that maybe he was making this up. That the 'jin would be upon them soon and she would be dragged back under the ground. She would not put it past him, lying to make her feel better. She, of course, would much rather know what the inevitable is, to prepare for it. She was too tired, though. Too tired to care.

The daylight brought the soft sounds of the forest. Trela opened her eyes slowly to the image of Knill smiling in her face. She wanted to be happy about it, but his breath smelled. Either he was telling the truth about the ley lines last night, or she was not as important to them as she had thought. She sat up to move her face away from Knill's.

"We have to get into the Pyran realm as quickly as possible. I will not feel safe here, not on the hill, not in the mountain." Trela suddenly became silent, realizing she had panic in her voice. "Never speak with panic in you. Try to never think with panic in you. Panic is insidious and serves no one but himself." Synde's voice filled Trela's mind. She knew why she had to reach the Pyran lands, and it was not just her fear. She had to find Synde. The one thing that she'd realized in Serif was that she needed help to become the Kriishan. And not just any help, but the help of experts. She needed a tactician for her army. She needed a personal trainer to make her deadly with all manner of weapons. She needed a personal advisor who would tell her what it was to be the Kriishan when she was up against an incarnation of an antoshan. The one Pyran that could teach her these, and other things, was Synde. He could not be dead. She needed him too much for him to be dead.

"Well then, we should run along the old stream bed, I think that is the fastest way." Knill had jumped up and proceeded to brush himself off. He made a move to brush her off as well, but Trela stared him down. Brushing herself off, she walked towards where he indicated the streambed should start.

"Here we are." Knill had somehow gotten in front of her. "The journey to the Pyran border, the Yagoi river, should only take a day or so. Though, if you do not know where to go from there, I am not sure what we will do." Knill was speaking over his shoulder, his small legs pumping down the streambed. Trela wanted to yell at him, but thought better of it. She walked behind him quickly. Keeping up with him should not have been difficult with her longer legs. He seemed to have no end of energy, however.

"When did your father show you this area? You seem to be fairly confident of where we are going." Trela spoke to Knill's back. She did so more from boredom than any actual desire for the knowledge.

"Well, he showed me the circle of holly quite a while ago. That is how I knew where to go after the incident in the tunnel." Here Knill paused. If Trela had not been paying attention, she probably would not have noticed. But for as long as she was to know Knill, he would never refer to what happened that night except as "the incident." "The streambed I did not know about until I woke up. I dreamed it, you see." She could hear Knill's smile in his voice.

"So, you are saying that you have no idea of where we are actually going?" Trela was trying to keep her voice light.

"No, I know exactly where we are going. It is just that the way I know is from a dream. I never dream, Trela. Well, I never remember my dreams, at least. So when I had the one last night I knew it was something special. We are being helped, Trela. We are of concern to the powers that be. Besides, if you are thinking that a dream is not enough to plan an escape route off of, we are heading northeast, which is where you want to be." Knill kept trotting along, his legs relentless in their motion. Truth be told, Trela was not as concerned as she wanted to be. She thought she should be furious with Knill. For all she knew, or all he knew for that matter, they were heading back to Serif. In the pit of her, though, she felt calm.

"Fine, fine. Just let me know when we have reached the river." She felt that she should just trust Knill right now. She felt she would have a better idea of where to go once they were back in the Pyran realm.

It was barely dusk before Knill admitted that he did not know where they were. The sky still had a little light and the emerging colors were blushing orange, threatening to turn red. They had walked, jogged, and sporadically ran down the streambed for most of the day until she made them walk up a hill to see where they were going. Trela's stomach was a mass of angry knots. Her legs burned even after their rest stops. They walked up another hilltop; the land just kept rising. Everytime you felt like you had reached the peak, another rise became visible in the distance. There were scattered trees and rocks along the hill making the animal path they were following wind back and forth. Finally they reached the top.

There, well below them, ran a large river. It had to be the Yagoi. Just the sight of the river gave her another burst of energy. It seemed to have the same effect on Knill, though she was not sure if he ever ran out of energy.

"If we can get down to the river before nightfall, I can show you a fishing trick my father taught me." He turned and struggled down the hill back towards the dry streambed. She let him struggle while she followed. It offered her a little rest. Once they hit the streambed they made much better time. She wished she had not made them climb the hill to find out where they were, but it had not taken too much time out of their day.

They reached the river just before nightfall. Trela was sick of berries, so she was excited to hear about Knill's fishing trick. He stood staring at the huge amount of water flowing past with a slightly crestfallen look, however.

"This... this is much too large of a river for my trick." Knill blushed and sighed.

"So we find a stream that feeds this river?" Trela knew that he was beating himself up over the ordeal, so she did not want to unduly add to his burden.

"Yes, but... I might be a little tired." He sort of started wandering downstream along the bank.

Trela was also tired, but she was quite hungry as well. They walked until it got dark. They had no fish. They did not even have any more berries. Eventually, much to Trela's surprise, they got more tired than hungry and curled up on some moss that was only sort of damp.

The next morning Trela awoke to her stomach attempting to eat itself. It was making oddly aggressive noises and, once she had peeked open her eyes, would not let her fall back asleep. Luckily Knill was waking up as well.

They found some berries and walked downstream some more. Finally, they came across a large log near the water's edge. Trela could not take the walking and hoping to find a smaller stream any longer.

"Let's float down the river." She smiled widely at Knill. She had a whole speech planned to convince him that it was a safe way to travel. She needn't have bothered for Knill was immediately enthusiastic about the plan.

Soon they were partly laying on, partly clinging to, and partly swimming along with the log as it floated downstream. She was still starving, and now she was soggy wet, but the effortless motion made it bearable. More than bearable, it was almost entertaining. They stayed in the river until late afternoon, when Knill spotted a tributary stream. They struggled but were unable to change the course of the log. So they let go and swam for the opposite shoreline.

Knill's fishing trick consisted of them driving sticks into the streambed like a picket fence. The stick-fence made a funnel shape, like a "V" with a small opening at the bottom. There they crouched, with Knill's shirt made into a weird net, waiting for almost an hour before they were able to catch an actual fish. Trela had begun to doubt him but it had finally worked. Knill was able to start a fire, and they dried themselves out and ate fish. They stayed the entire afternoon and into the evening, eventually catching five fish. It was fantastic. That night they slept next to their cooking coals. Trela felt in complete bliss. She had escaped, she was on her way to the Pyran realm, she was no longer hungry, and she had a companion. She really was happy.

The next day they mostly walked. The day after that they found another log to float with. It was the day after that, while they were walking again, that Trela felt that they should start to meander further across the border. Further into the Pyran lands. Towards the interior, towards her destiny. She did not know what the impetus was for her to change directions, but she felt it clearly. She had honed a way of listening to herself, a way of feeling the rhythm of her feet, that made her feel like an agent of destiny. It was scary to leave the food-providing river, and it took another full day of travel, but she was rewarded for her constant inner awareness.

"Knill. Wait, we have to rest again." Trela was feeling ashamed that she could not walk as long as Knill. She could easily beat him in a sprint, but in the long journey he was indefatigable. "We have to figure out where we are going. We need to find some more food. I think the sour berries we had earlier are disagreeing with me." Trela sat on a fallen tree. She heard Knill speaking in part of her brain. He was rambling about whether to try to find a stream again or to look for more berries. Trela was sure that he talked for some length while she was staring at a spot in the distance. Staring at nothing, really. She was just so tired. As Knill's voice continued in the background of her distracted mind, she realized what she was looking at. There was a plume of smoke rising from the valley floor. The valley floor looked dusty and sandy, with scrub-brush, sage, and lonely cypress. She smiled at the familiarity of it all. She traced the smoke down to the ground.

"Knill! A warpack! We've found a warpack at the edge of the Pyran lands. This is where I will start." Trela jumped up from her wooden perch and started to trot down the hill. "I cannot believe our luck. They must be smoking meat or something at this time of day." Trela charged towards the smoke. Her last sentence spoken to the wind rather than to Knill.

"Trela, wait. What is a warpack?" She could hear Knill's short legs pounding the hillside as he tried to keep up with her. She ran until she could run no more. She was still slightly elevated on the hill and the sky was turning red. She came to a stop with her heart still pounding heavily in her chest. Knill finally caught up with her as she gasped for air. She had her hands on her knees, half bent over. Knill kept waving his hands in front of him like he wanted to speak.

"How… how do we know that they are friendly?" Knill finally wheezed out his question. Trela straightened herself out and smiled at Knill. They began to walk leisurely down the rest of the hill. Once Trela felt she could speak without panting, she finally answered Knill's question.

"We do not. Hopefully it is not one of Qizern's warpacks. If so, we will have to be circumspect about who we are. If not, then we can ask for sanctuary. After we have traveled for a little while with the warpack, I can find those I trust to leak my true identity to. If we are very lucky, then someone here will have heard from Synde. We just have to get close enough to make out the war banners to see who leads this pack." Trela was walking abreast with Knill and she had been looking at him and not where they were going.

"Iventorn leads this pack." The voice was neutral and gray, without any animosity in it. Trela spun her head around attempting to see who was speaking. She quickly cursed herself for talking so freely this close to what might be an enemy. There, resting in the shade off the path, was a Pyran. He looked young and suspicious. He had a large spear leaning against his shoulder, which he grasped and held like a staff when he met Trela's eyes. His armor was simple leather, without any studding. Trela assumed he must be low ranking considering his appearance. This made her think that the pack had been here a while, for if it was a recent encampment there would be more trusted guards at the sentry. "And what makes you think that one such as Iventorn would give sanctuary to one such as you. Not to speak of a Gaen." He made a small spitting motion when he said "Gaen." His smile was weak, but his eyes hungrily took both of them in.

"That is for Iventorn to decide, not one such as you. The information I have for him, concerning the Gaen 'jin, must not be passed through a lowly sentry such as yourself. Look, you cannot even afford real armaments. Scuffed leather and only a spear. If this is what Iventorn has made of his warpack, then we are surely doomed." Trela was unsure if this tactic would work. It all depended on how strict Iventorn was as a leader. The more used to taking direct orders the sentry was, the better. Trela tried to look at Knill askance and nod slightly towards him—she was unsure of whether she was projecting that he was a trusted ally or someone that she could not speak in front of—but it was all she could think of. The silence was beginning to thicken as the young Pyran thought.

"The situation is dire! We need to speak to Iventorn immediately. You do not understand what is about to happen, and it will happen so quickly that you do not have time to question me. Do you want the overrun of this encampment to be because you failed in your sentry duties? I do not know this Iventorn, but if he is anything like Synde, leader of my warpack, you will rue the day you failed to take action. How can you just stand and stare like a deaf-mute? Move boy, your life and our future depends upon your decisive action." Every time she paused, he just stared at her. She was unsure of whether to press on, or if that was working against her. Suddenly he sprang to life.

"Hah! You show your ignorance of Iventorn by your fumbling use of passionate persuasion. But do not worry, I will take you to Iventorn anyway. He will be mightily amused at your attempts to coerce him." The young Pyran just stood there and grinned. Trela could tell that he was pleased with himself.

"Then lead on! We do not have all day to stand and chat with such an underling." Trela knew that she should stop the mental pushing she had been attempting upon him. Somehow, however, she felt she could not let up, or else he would know that it was all a ruse. Which he might already.

"Follow me." The grin had slipped a little. Trela hoped that was a good sign.

She followed, not looking back at Knill. Her face was hot with the feeling of blush. She consciously tried to walk fast behind the sentry so the wind would cool her face as she neared the encampment. She knew that she could not show any sign of embarrassment, or at least that was what she thought she knew.

The encampment was broad. There were many little tents, each with its own firepit. Trela knew they were next to a forest, but it seemed odd to have so many small fires. The amount of wood they consumed must be huge. There did not seem to be that many Pyrans at the encampment, however. Trela wondered if the rest of the warpack was out campaigning, but assumed not because she doubted a general would stay behind and let the pack campaign without a leader. All these things wandered through Trela's mind as she walked behind the young sentry, which helped because by the time they stopped in front of a large, white, marquis-style tent her blush had faded.

One of the large tent flaps flew open at their arrival. The young sentry shifted to the side so the guard could look at Trela and Knill. This was what Trela had expected to find in a warpack, not the young sentry. A large foot soldier with breastplate and greaves on stared quietly at them. His body was rippled with muscle and his shaven face was serious. There was a slight sheen of sweat on him, probably from being inside the tent with full battle armor on, but it had the effect of making his huge arms glisten in the dying sun.

"These two wish to speak to Iventorn." The sentry made a small bow and took another step backwards to the side of the tent.

"Are they armed?" The large Pyran had a deep voice that seemed to rumble through his chest up into his thick neck before being spoken. Much like a reverse echo, Trela thought.

"No, of course not, I checked them myself." The young sentry looked nervous in his lie. Trela thought briefly of harassing him further by calling him out, but she suddenly felt empathetic towards his predicament. Besides, they *were* unarmed.

"We are unarmed, sir. We merely wish to parley with the great Iventorn." Trela gave a small bow to the guard, showing she was of warrior class and not a domestic female.

"Hmph. Well, I suppose it could not hurt to ask. Wait here with Jingen." He stood there for one more second, drinking in both Trela and Knill with his stern eyes. Then, as quickly as the flap had opened, it shut.

"Don't worry about Cavish, he is like that with everyone." Jingen did not say it, but his eyes were saying "thank you" as his head bobbed slightly towards the two. The silence lingered for a little while. Trela kept wondering if she should look back at Knill, to give him a smile. She had kept her face turned forwards since they were interrupted by Jingen. Then the flap flew back open.

"He will see you both." With a large gesture of his arm, he welcomed them into the dim heat of the tent. It was not very large, but it seemed to be because of the lack of furnishings. There was a curtained-off section that cut off maybe a quarter of the tent to their right, presumably where Iventorn slept. And there was a curtain in front of them that shielded their view of the reception room. Trela thought back to Synde's tent, with its colorful carpets and small chairs and tables. He had even taken to leaving the reception area uncurtained so that he could see everyone as they walked in. This tent had no signs of domestic life at all. When they got to the reception curtain, Trela waited to be called in. Instead Cavish returned from the front of the tent and opened the curtain for her.

"The great leader Iventorn!" Cavish almost yelled in her ear. Trela immediately bowed before she could see what Iventorn looked like. She hoped that Knill would follow her lead. Some warpack leaders were incredibly unforgiving of cultural slights, and you never knew what could send one off. She was unsure if Knill even had enough knowledge of Pyran custom for him to realize that Iventorn could have them killed for just about anything he wanted until he had given them sanctuary.

"Rise, rise." The voice was cold and slow. Trela would have even said bored if she had to describe it. As she raised her head, the first thing she noticed was the lack of anything in the room. Iventorn sat in a large chair, but other than that there was nothing. No carpet, no tables, no chairs, just the canvas tent bottom glaring white at her. Then she noticed Iventorn. He was muscular, yes, but not bulky like Cavish. Lean. Lean and tall, she would guess—sitting there it was difficult to tell—but his torso seemed to rise out of the chair forever, his knees bent upwards because the chair was too small. He was not wearing armor, nor did it look like he had a weapon, but he did have the crimson cloak of a warpack leader on. His clean-shaven face seemed long and gaunt, his bald head shimmering slightly with the sweat born from the hot tent. His eyes, however, were what held Trela. They seemed cold and emotionless, almost dead. She could swear that there was no iris at all, just black pupil.

"Cavish has told me you wish to speak with me. So speak." His long skinny hand waved impatiently in the air. Trela had to take in a deep breath to even find her voice. The air tasted stale.

"I am Trela, and this is my traveling companion, Knill, who is a Gaen. We have just left Serif, and originally I am of Synde's warpack." Trela would have continued, but Iventorn suddenly smiled brightly at her and leaned forward.

"Terrific, how great it is to meet the both of you. I had no idea this small creature was a Gaen." His long hands clapped in front of his face, and it faded back to its sullen gauntness. "Now, tell me, Trela from Synde's warpack, why are you here? I mean, why are you talking with me? What do you want, girl?" Iventorn's long fingers tented in front of him as he rested his back against the chair again.

"I… I am the Kriishan. I need sanctuary until I can meet up with Synde again. I cannot travel through Qizern's lands unguarded. He has already attempted to take my life." Trela did not know what to say. She hated herself for bursting out like that. It sounded childish when she heard it.

"Ha! There is no such thing as a Kriishan. There is no such thing as an antoshan either, for that matter. There are only Pyrans, some good and some bad. How do you know that I am not from Qizern's hunting pack? I could be looking for you right now, and you have just given yourself to me…" Iventorn stared hard into Trela. His black eyes glaring over his tented fingers. "Besides, Synde has no warpack. Synde, if I remember correctly, was one of Qizern's Guards. He showed the ultimate betrayal of any servant to any master. Synde, in my opinion, is part of the walking dead and probably should be a ghulzan. What do you think of that, girl?" He just sat there, staring his black stare. Trela wanted to kill him. She could feel her muscles tensing, almost twitching. She felt a rage beyond rage boil up in her being. As her fists clenched, she realized that there was no way that she could combat Iventorn, let alone Cavish. She closed her eyes for a split second to gain some inspiration.

"I notice that you have spent a lot of time and energy trying to make your warpack look large. You know that will not work for long. All your little fires may make an impressive statement at night, but you will not fool anyone during the day. Who are you running from? We should be working together, you and me, not at odds with each other. Give me a task to prove my worthiness." Trela lowered her head slightly, not just in subjugation, which is what she hoped to convey, but also because she could not look into his eyes as he made his decision. She realized she had to make him commit to something. If she could not be useful to him, he would turn her away at best. And at worst? She did everything she could to not think of that.

"Maybe you are not as foolish as I first thought." Iventorn's voice was quiet. The silence lingered. Trela realized that she had heard nothing from either Cavish or Knill for quite some time. Even though she did not want to, was loathe to even, she raised her eyes to stare at Iventorn's black voids.

"You know that I actually knew Synde briefly? We campaigned together at the coast of Hidaltha. He was incredible with a sword and a consummate Pyran, until he turned traitor." His right eyebrow arched sharply. Trela knew that he was again attempting to bait her, though a bit half-heartedly now. She merely stared back at him, hoping that her silence symbolized strength and not immobility. "You are correct, however. I do have a task for you or else I would have refused our parley completely. I am having trouble convincing one of my Seconds of the necessity of teaching the town of Parthia a lesson in obedience. He is from there and apparently thinks they should be allowed a grave amount of latitude. Normally I would not worry about a Second, but he is an older derlian and some here think he has the gift of prophecy. He has threatened me that he will prophesize our doom if I go ahead with the attack. He needs to be won over. If you do this for me, I will offer you sanctuary." Iventorn had leaned forward for his little speech. He almost seemed lively to Trela. The difference was shocking.

"Why do you need to attack Parthia? What was their transgression?" Trela stared boldly at Iventorn, but he had leaned back against his chair and tented his fingers at her question.

"That is my business, not yours. Will you accomplish or will you just converse?" Iventorn's eyes seemed even more black than before, as if they were drawing light into them. The use of the old Pyran saying of "accomplish or converse" seemed excessive to Trela. Of course, she would accept the task, she had no other choice. It was obviously Iventorn's way of ending their parley.

"Accomplish, of course." Trela felt embarrassed to have pushed the issue with Iventorn. Fighting with that, however, was her pride in extracting a promise of sanctuary from him. Before she entered the camp she knew the price of failure, but now she knew the reward for success.

"Cavish will have all of the details." Iventorn was no longer even looking at her, his long right hand sliced the air briefly as a dismissive gesture. As she turned to leave, Knill led while Cavish fell behind. Leaving the tent was like a jump in a lake. The breeze felt incredibly good after being in the stifling air of the tent.

"Well, I think he likes you." The way that Cavish was smiling at her made her think he might be serious. He started walking away from the tent, and Trela and Knill naturally followed. They wound for a while in silence through the scattered encampment.

"The Second's name is Lishean. He is inseparable from his ghulzan. Not that it matters, but the ghulzan's name is Tumu. We are not sure where Lishean retrieved the ghulzan, but he has been around for many moons, almost a full cycle. As Iventorn mentioned, Lishean is from Parthia, which we believe to be his major reason for resisting the attack. As you well know, Pyrans are relieved of their town patronage once they swear an oath of fealty to the warpack. So there is no real reason that Lishean should suddenly attempt to renege on his fealty. Lishean is ancient, almost two hundred cycles old. He had a small gift for foreseeing the future before, but his abilities have increased as he has aged. This is why the younger Pyrans have taken to his words so much of late. This is the only reason that he has been able to pressure Iventorn to change a strategy. Tactics are one thing with Iventorn. If you have a suggestion for how the warpack could work better together within the eight principles of war, then fine, suggest it. He will listen intently, I swear. But change a strategy? Never. Or at least not as long as I have known him. Which is most of his adult life." Cavish seemed to walk and talk effortlessly. It was up to Trela and Knill to not only keep up, but to be close enough to hear the conversation. Trela was on Cavish's heels and therefore had no clue where Knill was. She strained to hear every word. Most was gossip, she assumed. In a warpack there was a constant flutter of meaningless details. It grew from living in such close quarters with others. However, she knew that through this gossip Cavish, who was probably worse than most Pyrans about menial details, was attempting to communicate all that he knew of the current situation. The problem with gossip, thought Trela, was that you never knew if what you were hearing was useful. Therefore she struggled to hear it all, so that she could maybe sort it out afterwards.

"Lishean was horrible with swords. Was... Listen to me. He most definitely is horrible with swords. And staves, maces, flails, spears..." Cavish was slowing down slightly. Both in movement and in speech. They were approaching small rope bridge crossing a muddy creek. As Trela looked up she noticed a line of Pyrans crossing towards them. She realized Cavish had slowed to let them pass.

"How come he is in a warpack, if he can not fight?" Trela was not really interested in his answer, she was merely attempting to start Cavish talking again. Cavish turned from the bridge towards her, smiling.

"Oh, I didn't say that he could not fight. He is actually quite proficient with his bare hands and feet. Mainly, though, he is a knife expert. You must not get close to him in combat, not that you should be in combat against him. He is also very good at tossing his knives, so you probably shouldn't be very far from him either." Cavish laughed at himself heartily. She thought that Cavish probably laughed at his own jokes a lot. She wondered if it was because no one else laughed at them or that he was used to others laughing with him. She thought of Iventorn's black eyes and thought she knew the answer. She was wrong, however.

"What weapon is his... his ghulzan proficient in?" Trela turned as she heard Knill speaking to Cavish. The passing line of Pyrans barely glanced at them.

"Ha! You really don't know anything about Pyrans do you? A ghulzan *is* a weapon." Cavish smiled at Trela, looking for camaraderie.

"Well, I... everyone seemed to be talking like a ghulzan is a Pyran..." Knill looked pleadingly at Trela. "I mean, Iventorn said that Synde should be one." His face turned back and forth between Cavish and Trela looking for an answer. Trela was about to answer when the slow shock of Iventorn's insult sunk back into her, making her clench her jaw instead of speak.

"A ghulzan *is* a Pyran." With that Cavish laughed again and began to cross the rickety bridge.

"Don't worry. I'll explain tonight, when we are alone." She knew that he would not understand. She smiled at Knill. She hoped it was a warm comforting smile, but he just stared at her. She turned and caught up with Cavish over the bridge. She had information to glean.

"Why Parthia? I know that Iventorn would not want to lose face publicly, but is Parthia that important?" She had planted herself in front of him as he watched Knill cross the swaying bridge. She watched Cavish's ample chest slowly rise and fall. She wished, more than anything at that moment, that she knew what he was thinking. Really thinking. The truth of the matter. It would make so many things simpler.

"Why not Parthia? It should be a simple siege. There really is no reason to thwart it." Cavish almost grimaced. Trela's only consolation was that Cavish felt uncomfortable with his own answer.

"What about Lishean, then? Has he ever married? How long did he live in Parthia and when did he leave? Does he drink or gamble? How am I supposed to gain his confidence?" Trela decided that she should concentrate on the task at hand. But she had no edges, nothing to grip.

"Ha. I suppose I have not been very helpful. Unfortunately I do not have the information you seek. If I, or Iventorn, knew that much about Lishean, then we would not have to enlist your aid." Cavish had stopped again. He stood staring at her, his face suddenly serious.

"Then why is he a Second?" Knill's voice broke the quick silence. "I mean, if you don't know him, how can you trust him with combat decisions?" The smile crept back into Cavish's face as he turned towards Knill.

"Lishean produces results, good ones. Iventorn is not a Pyran that is interested in others' life stories, he is interested in results. Questions are not asked or sought... Listen, there are many hundreds of fighters in this warpack. Iventorn has over thirteen Seconds, though only one First. Many Pyrans leave the life of the village, or town, or even farm, for reasons that they will never tell another. Where do you go when your skills haunt you with their results?" Cavish paused here and turned, smiling softly, towards Trela. "You join a warpack, yes?"

Knill looked away when Cavish turned back to him. Cavish stared hard into the side of Knill's face. Then the smile came back, full and vibrant. "That is a great question, though. That is what we hope you two will find out for us. How can we trust Lishean? What can be done to restore the old balance between the Second and the leader? Please, we are almost there." Cavish turned and began walking again. "Iventorn is willing to hear Lishean's argument. He respects Lishean's opinion. But Lishean keeps his own counsel and will only say that he refuses to enjoin the siege. Unfortunately for Iventorn, there are over three score of warriors directly under Lishean, and they are very loyal. Not only that, but because of his 'gift' of prophecy, well, let us just say that more warriors might be left behind than would move forward. So you must gain his confidence, figure out why he refuses to fight, and convince him that his reasons are misguided." Cavish stopped again. He turned towards a group of tents through the trees and down a small hill. They had many smoldering fires about them, and with a flourish of his hand he gestured towards them. "We are here. Lishean is there. Your destiny awaits, my Kriishan." He made a small bow towards her, and Trela tried with all of her might to see if he was mocking her, but she could not be sure either way. Cavish turned to leave and began striding back the way they had come.

"Wait! What about supplies? Where shall we sleep and what shall we eat?" Trela suddenly realized that he was just going to leave them to their own devices.

Cavish waved them over to where he was standing. "Tell Lishean that you are from Tanguzo, that is the last town that we traveled through. It was a week or so ago and it is very close to the Gaen border. Tell him that you were thought to be a scullery maid, but have proved yourself worthy to call warrior. Tell him that Iventorn wishes peace with him and he is increasing Lishean's ranks to prove that there is no bad blood between them. And... hmmm..." Cavish stared at Knill for some time, like he had not thought of how to explain the Gaen. "Well, you are going to be difficult to make a believable story for. I would suggest that you two are lovers, somehow, or that he is your ghulzan. Yes, I would tell Lishean that you saved his life somehow and he has entered your service. Really, I must be going though. If Lishean sees me with you, it will not matter what you say to him, he will distrust you immediately." Cavish smiled at them both and ducked away.

"I will not pretend to be something if I don't know what it is." Knill narrowed his eyes at her, his arms crossed and his lips pursed. Trela had finally grown to like the chipper, hyper Knill that she had met in Serif. She had never thought she could, but it was definitely better than the petulant, annoyed derlian in front of her now.

"I think Cavish is right. It would be easiest if you just went along with the idea and let me say that you were my ghulzan. It would not raise suspicion, you see? You would not have to lie to anyone, because you would not be allowed to speak openly in public." Trela realized that she had said the wrong thing a moment too late.

"Now hold on!" Knill actually looked angry. She had been unsure that he was capable of that emotion, and she knew that she had never seen that look on his face before. She decided to interrupt before he could continue.

"Please wait. Let me explain. There are two different types of ghulzans." Trela realized that they could not continue towards

Lishean's encampment until they had decided upon a story together. She gently took Knill's hand and led him into some trees as she talked. She kept her voice low and gentle, not only so that they would not be overheard, but to soothe and calm Knill. She realized that now, more than ever, she needed his complete and unwavering cooperation.

"There is a ghulzan that has their life saved called an honorable ghulzan. Say you were about to be gored by a wild boar and I killed it at the last moment. Or you had fallen down a cliff and broken so many bones that you would have starved, and I mended you. Or any accident—it just can't be combat related. You can become a normal Pyran again once your debt is paid. You can break your geas. Do you understand?" Trela had stopped in a small clearing but was still holding Knill's hand in hers. She thought it felt incredibly soft.

"I guess. What is the other type of ghulzan?" Knill began to sit down upon a fallen log and Trela followed, trying not to break their eye contact.

"The other type is the unhonorable ghulzan. Which, to be truthful, is the vast majority of ghulzans. They are just referred to as ghulzans. The accidental nature of the honorable ghulzan makes it difficult to prove through both parties. The unhonorable ghulzan, however, usually has only one decision maker. The ghulzan themselves. There is very little escaping this. Once you have become an unhonorable ghulzan, you must follow your geas until your death. Only if you somehow break your geas, only if there is even a way to break your geas, can you become a normal Pyran again." Trela was staring into Knill's eyes. It was as if he had no iris, just limitless black. It made her think briefly of Iventorn. "What if something horrible happened because you failed? There are some things that are more precious than life. When you choose life over them, then it is as if you have died. You become the living dead." Trela understood that her words had no meaning for him.

"Who would not choose survival? I mean, if I had to die or feel bad about my choices... What is the real decision?" Knill's voice sounded solid and sure to Trela. She took a deep breath.

"You cannot understand that kind of self-hatred. That is… that is… that is why I enjoy your company." Trela stared at Knill for longer than was appropriate. "You see… You cannot choose against yourself. You cannot be other than who you are." It was so simple in her mind and yet it was impossible to impart unto words. She thought back to the first ghulzan she had known of. "What if you were hiding from a violent enemy? What if a farmer, a civilian, gave you sanctuary? You would owe them something, yes? What if those looking for you broke into that farmer's home while you were hiding in the attic? What if they tortured the farmer, pushed her hand against a hot iron cooking pot until the skin melted and peeled away? What if you stayed there hidden and chose to survive? Would her screams not haunt your life, haunt your dreams? Your every waking moment, every time you tried to rest? Would not your death be your only release?" Trela realized that she had drifted off course a little in her struggle with her explanation. She took another deep breath. "Listen, if you would just agree to be an honorable ghulzan it would go so much smoother. You would not have to make small talk or invent tales about yourself. You would not have to blend in. It would explain why a Gaen is in the Pyran realm. It would even give me an edge over some of the other new soldiers. I would really, really appreciate it, Knill." The torrent poured out of her in a sweaty rush.

Knill stared at her quietly. She wondered what he was thinking. His two eyes flashed in synch to each of her eyes individually a couple of times, back and forth. They narrowed quickly on her right eye. Trela took a deep breath, expecting the worst. Then they crinkled into a smile.

"You are right, I am here to help. So what shall it be? I guess I could have fallen off a cliff or something. That sounds like something I would do. I'd rather not be attacked by an animal. I... think they're innocent." Trela broke into a grin as well. The foolish smile on Knill, the way he never made any sense, it made her feel invincible again. Everything would fall into place. She was the Kriishan.

"Excellent. So, why were you near Tanguzoa? Hunting? Were you running from something, something Gaen?"

"No, not running. Searching. I was looking for nightshade root. Looking for a poison to make an antidote. There I was, perusing the dusty dark berries, searching for the largest, juiciest ones, not paying attention to where I was going, when BAM! I tumble down a cliff, making sure I strike every stone larger than my head on the way down." Knill was laughing as he made up his story. His eyes getting brighter by the moment. "And what were you doing by that fateful cliff? Were you running or searching?"

"Running, of course. But not away from something, no. Towards something." Trela giggled at him.

"Running towards what? My pitiful screams for help?" He giggled with her.

"Later, yes. But first... I was chasing a vision. Traveling on foot all day to get to Tanguzoa, where I was supposed to meet my brother, who was coming from Parthia to meet me. I decided to rest, so I slept in the shade of the largest holly bushes I had ever seen. My sleep, however, was fitful. Visions entered my dreams and would not let me rest. I saw things that don't exist, and when I realized what they were, they chased me. I hid in a large sand castle. There, etched in its walls, was my name. My trembling hand reached up towards the crude engraving. As I traced it, a chill overcame me. I knew then that I was going to trap myself in my own obsession. In a futile bid to stop myself, I punched through the sandy walls. I looked out of the window I made and saw a lush glade. Widening the window, I climbed through it. There, in the clearing of my mind, was a hart. It blinked slowly, as if telling me that all would be as it should. Then it laughed. I awoke to the laughter, the image of its perfect teeth stuck in my mind. Right then a deer ran by. I jumped up and gave it chase. I would not let myself be pushed from behind, but I gave chase without a second thought. As the deer slid from my view, for no matter how fast I ran I could not keep up with her, I heard a horrible scream. That was when I found you." Trela was no longer laughing. Her story had broken their entertainment, had been drug too seriously from her own dreams, but she still felt closer to Knill at that moment than she had ever felt to anyone else before then. They were lost at sea and had only each other to cling to.

"Wow. If you tell the story like that, they'll have to believe you. I even believe you, and I know it's a lie." Knill was still smiling brightly. "So what do ghulzans do, unhonorable ghulzans? Why are they necessary?"

"Hmmm. Your first part is easy to answer, but I am not sure they are really necessary. I mean, they just *are*." Trela thought hard for a moment. "They are a product of our culture, not a requirement." She lapsed silent for another moment, trying to think of why ghulzans existed. Unable to find something that would satisfy someone as innocent as Knill, she decided to answer the first question. "As for what they do, they do all sorts of necessary things. Mostly, the are used as assassins for high risk targets. You know, suicide missions." Trela chuckled slightly at Knill's aghast look. "Sometimes, if there are enough in a warpack, they are used as shock troops. Sometimes they are used as berserkers, wearing only bear pelts in battle to ensure their ferocity. Rarely, they are used as commandos. They are mostly fighters, but also servants. The vast majority of ghulzans are personal, meaning they follow a specific warrior rather than a warpack as a whole."

"So they are just meant to die? Not that I know what a shock troop is, but none of those 'uses' seemed like they have a large survival rate..." Knill's smile lost a little of its brightness.

"But that's what they are. They are already dead, don't you see?" Trela tried to think of another way to put it. "They die when their failure happens, but they are given a second chance at life if they can somehow can break their geas. In the interim, they are ghulzans." Trela sighed. "This is just something that our cultures differ on." Knill stayed silent for too long. "I will promise you this, however. I will not use groups of ghulzans in my warpack, once I get a warpack. I cannot change the use of personal ghulzans, even for myself, and I cannot guarantee that I will not use shock troops. Only that they will be volunteers."

"Well... as long as honorable ghulzans are not involved in any of that." Knill was still smiling, but not very brightly and his voice had toned down. Trela suddenly felt older.

"We should head into the camp. We'll talk to this Lishean. We'll get our tent and some provisions. Then, maybe, we'll rest well tonight." Trela wanted to touch Knill's face, but she could not understand what compelled her. So she didn't and instead stood and stretched. It was odd, and maybe a little sad, that Trela followed every compulsion, no matter how small or seemingly insignificant, that brought her closer to embodying the Kriishan, while she hesitated and faltered at other compulsions. Especially at those harmless things that might comfort others.

They stepped out of the little patch of trees and walked down the hill towards the small encampment. As they approached, a short Pyran walked towards them. His gait was unhurried, so when he shouted at them to stop with a raised hand they were taken a little aback. They waited for the Pyran to approach them.

"Who are you?" The sentry seemed young. It seemed that Iventorn used all of his younger warriors as sentries.

"I am Trela and this is my honorable ghulzan. I was told to come and join Lishean's unit of the warpack. If you will lead on." Trela kept her voice taught and deep. She attempted to flourish her hand and scowl at the young Pyran at the same time. As the sentry built himself up to rebuke her, Trela noticed that there was another Pyran approaching them from the encampment.

"You expect me to just let you walk into Lishean's encampment? Who do you think you are?" Unexpectedly the sentry pulled his short sword out and slashed the air in front of them. His eyes narrowed into slits. Trela kept expecting the approaching Pyran to yell out. Knill had backed away several steps. She knew she should move back, but she could not make herself do it.

She waited as calmly as she could as the young Pyran laughed at her, swinging his sword slowly back and forth. Unbidden, the image of Synde came to her. "If you do what your enemy expects, you will lose. Every time. Surprise is the ultimate advantage. It is the only real advantage." He had then stared over her shoulder until, finally, she had glanced sideways. Then he knocked her on the ground. She had never really known why she took her eyes off of him. She had even known that he was up to something. He had told her so himself.

She stopped watching the young Pyran's sword tip waving hypnotically back and forth. She squinted over his shoulder at the approaching Pyran. Slowly, to seem as if she had just noticed them, she tilted her head slightly. Quietly she whispered, "What could that be?" The sword tip lowered slightly as the young Pyran tilted his head. At that moment, right when the young Pyran realized that she really was looking at something, she reached out and grasped his wrist with her right hand, shifted quickly on her feet while pulling his arm straight, and then struck his outturned elbow with her left palm. She did not mean to break it, but there was a horrific sound as the young Pyran dropped his sword and fell to his knees. She immediately let go, but it was too late. He knelt there clutching his right arm to his chest at an odd angle and howled. The sound made her cringe, but the feeling of his elbow hyper-extending under her palm had made her feel ill. She had not meant to follow through that fully. At that same moment, the approaching Pyran sped up.

"Wait, Nylse, they are expected!" He stopped in his tracks, as if to take in the scene. "You two stay where you are. Nylse. Nylse! Come here, warrior! Now!" Trela watched in amazement as Nylse stood and hobbled over to the older Pyran. She doubted that she would be able to stand if that had happened to her, let alone walk. The older Pyran whispered in Nylse's ear and touched his arm briefly. Nylse's face relaxed and then he trotted down the hill towards the encampment. The older Pyran must be a mage, thought Trela.

But as he approached, she thought to herself that it must be Lishean. The image that Iventorn and Cavish had placed in her head was that of an aged invalid. A crusty angry Pyran who was unable to change or accept another's opinions. Yes, his hair was white and his beard was wispy, but she could see his chiseled muscles under his lightly flowing shirt. Mostly, however, she noticed his piercing blue eyes. They were as light as the clear sky just after a summer's rain and seemed to have a bright, bright light behind them.

"You must be Trela. Dartsyle told me of you. He mentioned that he had misjudged you, but he certainly didn't mention anything like what I have just seen. I am Lishean, and I am always looking for skilled warriors." He smiled largely and held out his right hand. Trela noticed his ropy forearms as she tried to grip his hand as hard as possible. For an old Pyran, he had an iron grip, and she could only hope that he even noticed hers. While their hands pumped she tried to recall the name that he had spoken. Cavish must have had another Second talk to Lishean. She wondered how it could have happened so quickly. He let go of her hand, and she immediately knelt before him.

"I place my skills under your leadership. I look forward to serving with you and learning from your unit. I only hope that my meager capabilities will bring honor and glory to your unit and to yourself. You are my liege." Trela hoped that her immediate oath of fealty would allay any seeds of doubt in Lishean. That he would not question her sudden appearance or her placement in his unit.

He laughed. "Stand. Come with me to my tent and we will get you outfitted. I assume you will keep your ghulzan with you?" Lishean turned slowly and started to walk down the hill towards the encampment. Trela was unsure if his statement was a question, but she figured it was good timing to explain Knill.

"Yes, of course. My honorable ghulzan must stay close to me, until he fulfills his geas." Trela motioned for Knill to follow them as she trotted slightly to stay abreast of Lishean. She had wanted Knill to hear her use the word "honorable."

"Of course." His long legs moved quite quickly down the hill. "Each morning, after breaking our fast, there is mandatory group calisthenics. Afterwards there will be some optional drilling and sparring. You will, of course, be required to participate for a while at first, so that I can gauge your skills. Once I feel comfortable with what you can accomplish, I will place you into an appropriate position. I like to keep a close eye on my unit. Each Pyran has a perfect position, and it is my job to find it." They walked straight to a large white marquis tent, though not quite as large as Iventorn's.

Lishean held back the flap to the tent and let both Trela and Knill into the tent first. The darkness and heat of the tent was very much like Iventorn's. As her eyes adjusted, Trela looked around. Lishean walked past her, still talking. More than noticing much herself, she realized that Knill was staring at something in the corner. As she was trying to see what he was seeing, she realized that Lishean was asking her a direct question.

"Sorry, must be the heat. What were you asking?" Trela realized that it was better to be slightly embarrassed at first than to try to lie about what she did not know.

"Your skills. What are your skills? Swords, knives, staves, maces, flails, halberds, pikes, spears? Or do you just excel in hand-to-hand combat?" He had wandered over to a chair and sat down. He waved her over to him.

"My specialty is hand-to-hand, but I have had training in swords and bows. I was hoping, more than anything, to learn how to use knives." She was going to continue, but he interrupted her.

"Bows are for cowards. You will get no more training in a coward's weapon. But, as for knives, you have come to the right place. And we will, of course, continue your sword and hand-to-hand training. I have a strong belief that all my warriors should know how to fight weaponless. In many conflicts, such is the chaos of combat, a certain percentage of warriors will become disarmed. The faster you can re-arm yourself, the larger your chances of survival." Lishean's hands twitched while he talked. His fingers would stretch and spread, then fall back on his palms like a spider pretending to be wounded. Slowly the spider would harden into a fist, then the fingers would spread again as his voice picked up in the conversation. His ropy forearms kept twisting around as if they had a mind of their own. The patterns of movement were obviously Lishean's, but the actions themselves... Trela was not sure if Lishean could stop himself if he wanted to, or if he even noticed.

"Have you ever seen large scale combat? I am sure you have trained against more than one Pyran at a time, but have you seen the chaos of melee?" Lishean suddenly stopped and stared his eyes into hers. They had turned a shade of steel in the darkness of the tent.

"Only once. I was in Synde's splinter warpack. We were chased by Qizern's Guard into the Gaen lands. There, while we were already outnumbered, a Yaven appeared. Our caravan was burned to char. It was a complete rout. Brycca and several other Guard finally caught up with Synde and I. I was wounded, but I believe that Synde escaped. I was taken into Serif and lived amongst the Gaen for some time. That is where I acquired my ghulzan as I escaped." Trela felt as if she was in a trance. She was not supposed to tell him this. She was not supposed to tell him anything.

"You are either very trusting, very stupid, or... or the rumors are true. I knew Synde from the Hidaltha coast. He has never commanded a proper warpack, did you know? He was a consummate warrior and one of the deadliest with a sword I have ever seen. And he was skilled with any sword, not just one." His praise of Synde reminded Trela of Iventorn's. "He did rise to lead the elite unit of the Guard, but I don't think that he worked well with large groups. He was very comfortable with a loyal few, those he felt he knew. I have met few Pyrans that I admired as much as I did Synde. He never let fickle emotions direct his actions. It was certainly a shock to hear that he, after cycles of loyal service to Qizern, claimed to find the Kriishan and turned traitor towards his liege. Yes, quite a shock. However, I also know Brycca, or should I say knew Brycca?" He paused, and Trela nodded into the silence. "If Qizern had wanted vengeance and not prisoners, then he picked the right Guard." Lishean's hands were animated at first, but now lay serene in his sides. He just stared at her. Waiting.

"I am the Kriishan. And I have come..." Trela was unsure of what she was going to say, she was just speaking what entered her mind. Lishean's hand flew upwards in the universal gesture of stop.

"I have never been convinced of something through words. Never. Only actions impress me. If you are, then maybe I will see it proved one day. If not, then maybe I will see that proved instead. What you say to me today will not change what I see." Lishean slowly lowered his hand. His blue eyes drifted from steel back to the clear blue she had seen in the sun.

"Of course, you are a Pyran of reason. I was merely expressing my conviction." Trela was screaming at herself in her head. How could she have told her most hidden secret just after meeting Lishean?

"How do you know? I mean, did you always know? Did you wake up one day and think, 'I am the Kriishan. I will wreak havoc on a previously honorable Pyran's life. Making him and many others leave their safe world to be massacred in a foreign land by a vengeful and unforgiving ruler.' Does that haunt you?" His eyes turned back to steel.

"No. I feel horrible about it. I wish, daily, that it did not happen. What it does, however, is prove to me just what Qizern is. It shows me how ruthless and cruel he is, and how much I have to learn before I destroy him. It solidifies my anger and resentment of his regime that I have harbored as long as I have lived. It makes me realize that ruling power over another must be done with conscious humility. That is the only way to see the greater truth that justice is based upon. If an eye is kept glancing towards personal gain, then that eye becomes clouded with cataracts. No, as horrible as that brief rout was, it does not haunt me. What haunts me is the look on the Gaen's face who tried to save me as he was pierced by a dozen bolts. He was completely innocent, never a warrior. He didn't join a warpack, he didn't swear an oath of fealty, he didn't even have a clue as to what a Kriishan was. All he was doing was trying to warn me, and they shot him down for it. I will never know if he was trying to stop their arrows from reaching me, or if he was just in the way. What I do know is that I will never forget his face. That is what haunts me. The Pyrans that followed Synde and I into the Gaen lands knew their risks. They hated Qizern as much as I do. They loved Synde as much as I do. They believed in changing their world and chose to fight to do so. They chose their life, even if they did not choose their death." Trela found that she was glaring at Lishean and she was unsure of why. She stopped and took a step back, watching him. He seemed to have no reaction to her at all.

"Never speak of this to anyone outside of this tent. I will not compromise Iventorn's warpack with your foolishness. As long as you are loyal to me, I will keep your secret safe and teach you all I know of combat. Tumu, come here." Trela had forgotten about

Knill. As she turned towards the shuffling noise, she saw Knill and a small Pyran in a corner. The Pyran approached. And Knill followed him towards Trela and Lishean. The Pyran looked lumpy in a brown robe as he came closer. A mass of unkempt hair hid his face from Trela. The Pyran stopped to the side of Trela and bowed briefly to her before kneeling in front of Lishean.

"Tumu is my ghulzan. Unlike your ghulzan, there is nothing honorable about him. He is, however, incredibly important to me. I do not normally do this, but I need to ask you a favor." Tumu had stood up, but was looking at the floor. Trela was unable to see any of his face, let alone his expression. Lishean also stood up and began walking around the tent as he was talking. It seemed that he did not want Trela looking at his face while he asked her of something. She pondered the shy similarities between master and servant. Everyone is shy when they are not in control.

"Of course, my liege. What is the favor?" Trela knew that she should ask what the favor was first, but she wished to impart her loyalty and willingness to help. She only had so much time to convince Lishean to agree to the siege of Parthia. And in that brief span of time, she felt she needed to convince him that she was the Kriishan as well. As he walked around he rooted through sundry items.

"I need your ghulzan to watch mine while I am away at training. I like to see everyone as they practice so that I have a good idea of what my warriors' strengths and weaknesses are. I have heard wind of someone attempting to hurt, or even kill, my ghulzan. There is always a lot of political maneuvering going on around here. Nothing incredibly dangerous I think, or I would keep him next to me. I think that even the deterrent of a witness would be enough to stave off any attempt to 'teach me a lesson.' It should not be dangerous for your ghulzan, but I figure that if you are away at training the same time that I am, I could leave your ghulzan in charge of mine's safety. Would that be agreeable?" Lishean had made a small pile of stuff in the center of his tent while he was talking. There seemed to be a tent and some sleeping rolls, as well as some cooking utensils and some other random items. Trela realized that he must be outfitting them. She glanced at Knill to make him feel better about the decision, as if she would have not agreed to help Lishean out. He was smiling and nodded briefly as she glanced over. Good, thought Trela. That would make everything that much easier.

"Of course. I would be happy to help you." Trela then gave a deep bow. She knew that it had a little too much flourish, but she was worried that he would be looking away when she did it and wanted him to witness her gesture.

"Excellent. Then I will see you after revelry in the morning. You will have to pick out a site for your camp behind the tent here and downhill towards the creek. Keep your distance from the other tents and build a small fire. I look forward to helping to train you." Lishean smiled and sat down. Knill immediately began scooping up the tent and other items. Trela walked over and picked up her share.

As they left, she glanced back to nod at Lishean again. Lishean and Tumu had their heads down together, discussing something quietly. Trela would had given much to know what they were discussing. The tent flap fell back in place after Knill let her through. She started walking to the back of the tent where Lishean had waved. Towards the creek. Knill naturally followed. She stopped in her tracks, trying to think of what he must be thinking.

"Go ahead, Knill. Pick out a good spot for us." She knew that he was going to have a lot of time alone here. That she would be involved with the other Pyrans while he would be sitting in their tent. She realized that the last thing in the world that she wanted was for him to feel unimportant. To hide his face in his hair and stare at the floor.

"But, I don't know what a good spot is." He smiled at her. They were both stopped, heaped with stuff, and he just stood there waiting.

"Me neither. Go ahead." She prodded him with her sleeping roll.

"All right. But no complaining if you don't like it." His smile was real and looked relaxed.

"I promise." Trela smiled back at him.

They walked for quite a while. Her arms started to ache holding all of the various gear. She couldn't imagine what Knill's arms must have felt like. He was carrying all of their cooking pots.

"Here. This looks great. The shade is in the afternoon, so we can wake easily in the morning and have comfortable evenings. It is close enough to the creek, but not too close. We can see the other Pyrans, but are far enough away that we could hear them coming. Yes, this is a good spot." Knill dropped his items unceremoniously on the ground. Trela followed his lead. They began clearing a spot for the tent. They took their time, since who knew how long their tent would be there. Afterwards there was a fire pit to dig and food to start cooking. Trela enjoyed working alongside Knill.

"I always thought that the Pyran lands were just sandy desert. It's so lush here." Knill waved his hand in a vague half-circle.

"And I thought that all the Gaen lands were just filled with rocks. The snow melt from your mountains makes a lot of streams and creeks through here. We also get some large rivers from the Luftens. Further south it does get a lot dryer, though." Suddenly, Trela felt oddly that if she had to go to a Gaen school then Knill should go to a Pyran school. But, of course, he would be watching Tumu while she was training.

The camp was finished quickly. No one came to visit their camp, which was fine with Trela, because they had already had long day. While she collected firewood, Knill filled a medium sized pot with water from the nearby creek. They had a simple but delicious stew.

"Do you know why I believe the warpack will accept that you are being led by destiny?" The question came out of nowhere.

"No." It was a simple answer, but the only one she could give.

"Lishean does not believe in you. In your destiny. I am not even sure that he likes you, though he may. Yet, you are going to do your best to befriend him, are you not? You are going to do your best to convince him of your destiny." Knill raised an eyebrow.

"Of course, though I do not completely know why I have this compulsion. I guess there is the mission from Iventorn..." He interrupted her.

"You don't have to understand your compulsion, your destiny does. And this has nothing to do with Iventorn, no. An older derlian, maybe even one who is passed by or washed up, is a million times better to have on your side right now than any other younger, more charismatic or politically connected derlian." Knill leaned back. "Young Pyran leaders merely preside over what a warpack does, not what it thinks. The more venerable father figures are considered wise and bend others more easily to legends and prophecies. And if you can convince a skeptic to your side... But that is not it either, no." He leaned back forward. "I feel that I know the best way to go about convincing others about you, but because of my analysis, my premeditation, others would get a sense that I was being fake, whether or not I was actually fake. Too much forethought makes other derlians nervous. This is why society, or Gaen society at least, pushes manners and right versus wrong upon every child, as soon as they are born. That is the civilized way to have a bunch of derlians be polite to each other without any forethought." He smiled widely at her. "You come to the same conclusions as I do, but by way of compulsion, not forethought. That is why the warpack will accept your claim.   You exude a genuine earnestness even while unconsciously performing the most logical, cold, and calculable actions to assist your rise."

Trela wanted to continue their talk, but it had been one of the longest days she could recall. They crawled into their separate sleeping rolls and fell asleep with nothing more than a "Good night."

The days flew by. They stretched into weeks and moons. Trela was learning more about combat than she could have hoped for. Cavish was right, Lishean was amazing with a knife. The daily workouts were getting her in the best shape of her life. She knew the clock was ticking with Iventorn's siege, but she was enjoying just living. No, not just living. Bettering. Gaining skills in almost every aspect in her life. Everything was going great. Well, almost everything. Her only problem was Knill. He hated it in the warpack. She could understand, if not commiserate. He was not allowed to talk to any of the Pyrans and only to her when they were alone. He didn't complain aloud. But she could see that it was getting to him. She was unsure exactly what it was about him that was different. He looked down a lot. He stopped arguing with her. He seemed quieter even when they were alone. Except that he had always watched his feet while walking and he had rarely argued with her. She finally decided that she would ask him. After all, if he said that everything was fine, then she could stop worrying.

Except that when she got back to camp from the morning training, he was already there waiting, fit to burst. He was smiling and waved her into the back of the tent as she threw back the flap. She sat down on her bedroll, smiling back up at him.

"I found it out. I finally figured out why Lishean won't join the siege. I've been talking to Tumu for the last…" Trela knew that she shouldn't interrupt. She had to let him tell her the news—it was what they were sent here for—but she couldn't stop herself.

"Knill! You are not supposed to converse with a ghulzan."

"Ha! I am a ghulzan. What do you think ghulzans do when no one else is around? Anyway, I'm not even a Pyran, so these rules don't really apply to me." Knill's eyes narrowed, but he was still smiling.

"Knill! Never mind…" Trela decided to try to explain what he was doing wrong later.

"Lishean is not the seer, he cannot foresee the future any more than you or I. No, the seer is Tumu." Knill grinned at her. "But, and here I think this is where the problem lies, he blanks whenever something big happens to him. He can't see much about himself. So… he is blank about Parthia. He has not mentioned anything in particular, but I think that Lishean is worried that something bad will happen to Tumu and therefore he will lose his edge with the warpack." Knill paused, waiting for her response.

"You mean… you mean that if we find a way to protect Tumu, Lishean might go along with the attack? Hmm… I wonder if we could leave him behind, or something." Trela was so stunned that she forgot Knill had broken the most basic tenets of dealing with ghulzans. She was just thinking aloud, rather than filtering herself. "Yes, what if you stayed behind, with Tumu, and protected him during the siege. We could hide you both away, maybe. I should have been teaching you combat skills, been getting you into shape. Lishean will take a lot of convincing." Trela trailed off, her thoughts roiling inside her head. She hoped that she had not damaged the opportunity by not recognizing it sooner. She would have to think of how to convince Lishean that Knill was enough of a protective force. Currently Lishean was allowing Knill to be Tumu's bodyguard but obviously because he believed there was little direct threat.

"Well, I can tell you that Tumu also wants the siege to occur, so he will try to convince Lishean as well. But he cannot broach the subject, of course, so you must be persuasive enough that Lishean will ask Tumu what he wishes. Can you do that?" Knill was smiling at her, waiting.

"Whether or not I can, I must. There has got to be a way to convince Lishean that Tumu will be safe in his absence. I would stay myself, but I know I have to be at the siege, to show Iventorn that I am the Kriishan."

"I wonder if Iventorn would loan us some trusted warriors to help guard Tumu? If Iventorn didn't know why we needed them, maybe…" Knill was sharply interrupted.

"No! Never. Lishean would sooner kill Tumu himself than let Iventorn help save him. I have to convince him that you are enough protection, I just don't know how." Trela furrowed her brow in concentration.

"Maybe we could say that I've had previous training, you know, before I became a ghulzan. I could be the youngest Fyr'jin ever. Knill Fyr'jin, that sounds great, doesn't it." Knill laughed heartily at himself.

"No, no. Lishean would want to spar with you. How about magic? You could be a skilled mage." Trela was enjoying the frivolous nature of their suggestions. It took some of the weight off her.

"Ha! I don't know if you have noticed, but Gaens are not known for being skilled mages. No, it has to be something that can't be proven. I wonder what protective skills I could have that I would not have to show Lishean?" Knill's face was pinched in concentration. She hoped that he was making a caricature of himself, because he looked ridiculous.

"Well. What *can* you do?" Trela joked.

"All I know are poisons and antidotes. Hey, I could make Tumu appear dead and revive him when the siege is over. No one would want to assassinate a corpse, would they?" Knill was still joking. Trela thought briefly about that one, though. Unfortunately she did not think that Lishean would trust Knill to not kill Tumu, accidentally or not. Did they have the necessary plants in the Pyran realm? She was also a little worried that Knill might get the dosage wrong. It was such a great suggestion that she really did want to use it, but she could not quite bring herself around.

"I don't think we can protect Tumu with poisons. I'll have to think about this through the night. You have given me great hope, however, and a lot to think about. Thank you." Trela looked softly at Knill. She felt herself growing warm inside.

"Wait. I have it. We just have to create the illusion of safety, right? Since Tumu is away from the siege, he won't really be in danger, right? So what you do is say that you found out who is trying to hurt Tumu and you've killed them. Or you will trap them at the siege. Or that it is someone from Parthia that wants to hurt him. As long as Lishean thinks that whoever he thinks is planning to attack Tumu is gone, then he will let someone useless like me protect him." Knill laughed a little uneasily.

"Knill, you are far from useless. That is a perfect idea, we'll work out the details. Together." Trela stood up quickly, the tent was becoming too warm. "Make a fire, I'll get some water for the soup." She left into the fresh cool air.

It took until nightfall to figure a good story. Trela was not sure if it would be better to talk to Lishean now or in the morning. Knill had finally suggested that she see Lishean now, in case he drank. That way, Knill had said, he would be easier to convince. That was how she found herself walking towards Lishean's tent by the soft light of the moon.

As she approached his tent, she could see shadows dancing along the tent's walls. The front flap, however, was closed to her. She was unsure of how to get Lishean's attention without raising alarm.

As she got close to the entrance to the tent, the flap suddenly opened. The light flickered across the darkened sky. Out came Elzie. Trela had seen her a couple of times at training, but not very often. That was one of the odd things about a warpack, a small community. You not only heard all of the gossip quickly, spreading like a virus, but you knew who was supposed to know whom. You could tell when Pyrans were socializing out of the accepted norm. Immediately. Trela had never talked to Elzie, and felt she probably would have liked her, but she knew, without ever being told explicitly, that Elzie was not supposed to be at Lishean's tent at this hour.

Elzie had a wild mane of curly hair. Too long to be practical in combat. Though Trela could not see very well with the back lighting, she knew her eyes to be lushly lashed. She had a delicate nose with a slight upturn at its end, and her lips were full and red. Her body, while not necessarily a warrior's, was athletic and lean. Trela thought that male Pyrans must find her very attractive. Trela wished briefly that she had realized sooner, so that she could have studied Elzie's mannerisms. Now, though, it was too late for any of that. Elzie stopped in her tracks with a quiet squeal. If Trela was unsure of this being a secretive tryst, Elzie's reaction would have put that to rest.

"Oh, you startled me. You… ah, you're Trela, correct? You are here to see Lishean? At this hour?" Elzie narrowed her doe eyes at Trela. The tent flap was still open. Whoever had opened it realized that something was going on outside and was watching. Trela could suddenly smell alcohol on Elzie's breath.

"I have an urgent message, for Lishean alone. I am not here to entertain." Trela wanted to say more, but felt a sudden urge of restraint. She should just parry, not counter-attack.

"Trela? Is that you? What are you doing here? Come in at once." Lishean sounded more anxious than angry. Trela bowed her head briefly in supplication as a peace offering to Elzie. Then she turned and trotted into Lishean's open tent. The bright light dazzled her eyes, leaving her temporarily blind. As Trela passed Lisehean, he closed the flap behind him. Trela noticed, briefly, that she could not see Tumu anywhere. For which she was very grateful.

"Well, Trela. Do you fancy yourself a gossip?" Lishean's eyes were shining brightly in the candlelight. Not with mirth, but with some other unspoken emotion.

"No, never. I do not care about such things. I am only here for one reason." Trela watched his face relax. A little.

"And what is that?" Lishean sat down in his chair and motioned Trela to sit as well. But she couldn't sit. Her mind was spinning too fast and she needed to stand to be able to concentrate.

"It is about the task at hand, of course. I have figured out who wishes to harm Tumu. And I have figured out a way to keep him safe during the siege." Trela paused for a moment to catch her breath. She hoped that Lishean would stay silent until she had said all that she had to say and, tonight, luck was with her. "The aggressor is in Parthia. I did not overhear his name, but I know that he is another Second, like you. He knew Tumu before you did, he knows the extent of Tumu's powers. He wants to take them for himself. To force Tumu to be *his* ghulzan. Part of his plan is to lure Tumu into Parthia itself and try to take him there. You are right to be worried about that. But he has a contingency plan. Since Iventorn's warpack has been sitting here for so long, he is worried that the attack will not happen. That he cannot lure Tumu into Parthia. So the other plan is to take him here, while you are out on a hunt. The hunting party will be attacked at the same time that he, personally, will attempt to steal Tumu from the encampment. So, here is my plan." Trela had hoped to just be able to keep talking. To talk all night if that is what it took.

To talk until Lishean was convinced. But, just then, the tent flap opened and in came Tumu. Trela's heart almost stopped. She had hoped that she could convince Lishean before Tumu returned. She had not even had the opportunity. Tumu hesitated for a moment, then walked over to Lishean.

"Tumu, you will not believe your ears. Trela has figured out who is attempting to kill you. Wait, not kill you, but to steal you away from me. And, even more amazing, it is someone that you knew before. A Second from Parthia." Lishean was staring at Tumu, his face emotionless. Trela, try as she might, could not figure out what Lishean was thinking.

"If I might speak?" Tumu was barely audible. Trela turned towards him. It was rare that she was able to hear him at all. His voice was quiet but insistent.

"Yes, please." Lishean sat back in his chair. Trela was sure that he had wanted to keep talking. However, there was enough... respect?... in Lishean to defer to his own ghulzan.

"I think I know who Trela is speaking of. It is Feinsley. He is not a Second, at least not when I knew him, but he is a warrior. I foresaw that he would lose a Fight of Right. He had somehow blamed me for his loss and had harassed me. Luckily others were more level headed, and he was forced to leave for Parthia. He must have come to the realization that I was right, that I merely foresaw his failure and had not caused it." Tumu lowered his head demurely after his short speech.

"Well, I... I have to say that I had not believed Trela. You are sure about this Feinsley?" Lishean was not looking at Trela; he only saw Tumu.

"I do not know of his plans, and he is not in my visions. But he is a warrior in Parthia, he does know about my abilities, and I am sure he does not like me." Tumu kept his head lowered.

"Trela. How did you come by this knowledge?" Lishean turned towards Trela and gazed intently at her. His eyes were bright with a different emotion this time.

"I was near Iventorn's tent when I saw Cavish run into the tent with great urgency. My curiosity got the better of me, and I skulked near the back of the tent to listen. They were quite loud with emotion so they were not difficult to hear. It is through Cavish that I heard about the aggressor from Parthia. I was just unable to catch his name. Both he and Iventorn were quite worried about him, though. I could tell from the strain in their voices." Trela did not know how much further to go on. She wanted to say as little as necessary so that she would not catch herself up in a lie later. Luckily, Lishean broke in.

"Well, I guess I had better hear your plan, Trela. I hope it is a good one." Lishean leaned back and smiled.

"Mainly we, meaning you and I, must go into Parthia and find this Feinsley. Once we find him, we will make sure that he has told no one of Tumu. Then we will destroy him. It will be easier to do in the confusion of combat. I think I can convince Iventorn to slip us into Parthia the evening before the attack. That way we can find Feinsley before the heat of battle consumes the town. In the meantime, Tumu can be safely hidden here with Knill to protect him. That way he will be nowhere near the combat and nowhere near Feinsley. What do you think?" Trela knew it was not much of a plan. It had seemed so much more complete when she and Knill were talking about it earlier. She could only hope for the best.

"It is not much a plan, but it will have to do. I have been paralyzed by fear for too long. If the problem is a warrior in Parthia, then we will have to fix the problem. I will think about it tonight and maybe come up with some more details. You should talk to Iventorn tomorrow, convince him that we will need a couple of my warriors with us when we enter Parthia. We will need disguises also. Tell him we will need some coin as well. We may have to bribe our way into the town." Lishean was smiling, but it seemed to be reflected inward. He abruptly focused his eyes and stood. "I will see you out." He strode towards the tent's entrance and tossed the flap open. As Trela walked towards him, he seemed to remember something. "We shall be working together. We must have confidence in each other. Can you keep a secret? Can I trust you?" Lishean seemed suddenly serious.

"I told you I do not care what you do with your spare time. Besides, you are my teacher. You took me under your tutelage, I could not betray you. Even more than any of that, you are the only one here that I have told of my destiny. If you keep my secrets, I will keep yours." Trela bowed deeply. She certainly did not mention spilling her secret to Iventorn and Cavish.

"Excellent. Meet me after you give Iventorn our demands." Lishean waved briefly and then dropped the tent back closed. The darkness that enveloped her was almost complete. She walked slowly while her eyes adjusted back to the moon. Trela thought about his last word on her way back, "demands." That must have been why he was smiling earlier. Knill was still awake when she reached their humble tent, and they talked excitedly well into the night.

Iventorn and Cavish were ecstatic to hear of the plan. They listened patiently to her story and did not begrudge her any lies. To Lishean, to them, to anyone. She was told that they would give her everything she needed. Warriors, weapons, coins, whatever she asked for. And got them, she did. Lishean's plan was pure self-serving vengeance and included coin and honor to be handed over for the privilege. Iventorn did not seem to mind, however. Whatever it was that he wanted in Parthia, he was willing to pay for it.

Three days after Trela first proposed the plan to Lishean, they were ready to leave. Knill had set up an extra tent, hidden in a copse of trees, for Tumu and him to stay in until the siege was over. Trela, Lishean, and two of his best warriors were outfitted and prepared to leave in the evening. They wanted to arrive in the dark, but not too late to be let into the town. They were also bringing Dartsyle with them. Iventorn and Cavish had insisted upon it, and Lishean seemed to trust him. Trela was just not sure if she did. She could not, however, voice her concerns. Of course, she did not know at that time the depths of Dartsyle's relationships.

She had spent the day with Knill. A nice lazy day watching clouds. The previous days had flown in such a rush, it seemed like the dusk would never come. But, of course, it did. She liked Knill because, with him, she could enjoy just *being*. She was never rushed or pushed, and they always laughed a lot. But there was something about the anticipation of espionage and the thrill of battle, her first real battle, that she could not escape. It gripped her and would not let go. She could have laid in the sun with Knill forever and been happy. This feeling, however, filled her with sheer excitement. She felt like she could take Parthia all by herself. This is what she lived for, what she was meant to do. She could not wait for her future to start. She was the Kriishan.

Knill and Tumu were already in their hidden tent. They did not want to call attention to themselves. Soon Trela found herself walking with Lishean, Dartsyle, Yarsurle, and Estfale. She had yet to meet Dartsyle, only knew of him through others, but she had met both Yarsurle and Estfale during training hours. They were both excellent warriors, and she felt they could be trusted. They seemed loyal to Lishean first, the warpack second. And, though she was trying not to be paranoid about Iventorn's loyalties and plans, she at least knew Lishean's agenda. What, she thought, about her own agenda? It was her lies that had brought them all here. That would start the attack of a city. Did she really know what she was doing? She drew in a deep breath. She thought that destiny was not so much a choice but like trying to steer a log down a raging river. She had to accept that she was where she was supposed to be. She let out her breath and shifted her backpack and her short sword. The hike was short, but she did not want to start any blisters.

Just as the sun was beginning to disappear they crested a hill above Parthia, and Trela was able to see it for the first time. The wall around the city was small, it seemed only about twice the height of Trela. The last of the sun's rays glared off the white rock wall, making the city glow like a beacon. There were three large buildings rising well above the wall. Trela knew one was the fortress and that one was a library. She was unsure as to what the other building was, but did not want to bother Lishean about something trivial. They hesitated for only a moment at the sight of the city before them and then walked down the hill towards it.

The plan, as Trela understood it, was to find the Dew Drop Inn and secure three rooms. After that, they would split up to try to find Feinsley, checking the city's various military haunts and taverns. Once found, he would be quietly assassinated, and then they would set the roof of the inn on fire. The smoke would signal Iventorn, who should be prepared, and the siege could begin. If one or more of them could get into the fortress, that would be even better. Trela had promised herself that she would be the one to infiltrate the fortress, thereby securing Iventorn's admiration. She felt that if she was just able to make a name for herself in this warpack, she would be able to have one of her own soon. It was the only way to get to Qizern. She had to work quickly, though. She did not want to be trapped as a Second for cycles on end. No, this was her chance. Her one chance.

Before she knew it, the five of them were at the city gates. The wooden doors slowly opened to them. Lishean talked briefly to the porter and slipped him some coins. They were quickly ushered inside, and the guards did not even glance at their weapons. Estfale had been to Parthia several times before and knew the way to the inn. They went straight there in the flickering light of the street torches. As they approached, Trela realized that the inn was the other tall building she had seen in the city. It was a wide stone building that reached four stories into the night sky. Various windows shown with firelight, winking like eyes in the dark. There were two sets of stairs leading into the inn, one from each side. Above the large open alcove that led into the lobby was a large green leaf with drops of dew like magnifying glasses showing the enlarged veins of the of the leaf. They entered the lobby and Lishean walked up to the front desk. Trela was amazed by the opulence of the place. There were several little statues placed around with lots of plants scattered amongst them. There was one huge statue in the center of the room with a small pool at its feet. The statue was of a large muscular warrior aiming a bow at the ceiling. There was a mounted deer head high up on the wall that he might have been aiming at. It made her smile, thinking that whoever placed the head there was making a joke. Trela wandered over to the pool and saw small colorful fish flitting around in the water. There were all different sizes, and Trela wondered how they fed them all. Do the big fish eat the small fish, she thought, and if they did, what did the small fish eat?

Lishean walked over to her and produced a key. "Yours is the smallest room, but at least you don't have to share. Tonight is free for us. Spend some time getting to know the city, but be back here by midnight at the latest to get your rest. We will be meeting tomorrow morning just after dawn in the dining room." Lishean waved a hand vaguely. Trela tried to hold the image in her mind long enough that she could bring it back in the groggy hours of the morning. "Dartsyle and I are going to be checking the nearby taverns. If you stop by, I'll buy you a drink." Lishean patted her shoulder and wandered down the hall. She glanced down at her key and stared at the number three stamped on it. She always had liked the number three. She waited for a while so that she didn't seem to be following the others down the hall, though they had all come in together. Once she started to get bored watching the fish she went and found her room.

Lishean was right, the room was small. She tossed her backpack onto the small bed. The pack sunk slightly as it hit the mattress. She was hoping it would bounce. She dropped to her knees and checked the ropes holding up the mattress. They sagged depressingly low under the small weight of her pack. She sighed as she stood up. She tossed her sword onto the bed next to her pack. Rather than stay in her cramped quarters, she decided to walk about the town. Get to know Parthia, as it were. She left her room without another glance at her pack. She locked the door and then wandered the ground floor of the inn. She marked where the entrances and exits were in her mind, and she checked where the dining room was. Which was good since Lishean had waved his hand towards the wrong door.

She had not realized that it was warm inside the inn until she left it and the cool night air invigorated her. The moon shone through some scattered clouds making them black underneath, but cast with the orange glow of the torches below. She walked aimlessly for a while, watching the faces. Nobody seemed worried. There were no frowns, no furrowed brows. They did not have a clue. They did not realize what waited in the forested hill, overlooking them. She thought again, briefly, on why Iventorn wanted the siege. She put that from her mind quickly, though. She would follow orders until she could start making them.

As she walked and marveled at the city's lack of preparation, she began to gravitate towards the fortress. It towered over the rest of the city. Even the library was three stories shorter. The main thoroughfare led straight to the fortress and split around both sides of it like a river skirmishing an island. Trela stopped in front of the portcullis. She stood with her hands on her hips and tilted her head straight back until her hair fell from her face and she felt the pinch of her knife in her belt against her back. The middle tower seemed to rise into the dark clouds. She counted over twenty arrow slits on this face of the tower alone. The wall surrounding the tower was in the shape of a triangle and had three smaller towers, one in each apex. The parapet was crenellated, and the guards walking the wall would flash into vision and then back out as they walked behind the stone defense. As Trela began to move again, she stared through the portcullis at the other side of the wall. Smiling to herself she noted that the catwalks along the wall were made of wood. The other two apex towers were like the first. A story higher than the wall, with a crenellated parapet around the top of the tower, they were a quarter of the height of the central tower. She walked all the way around the fortress three times, staring hungrily at it. She looked for any chink in the armor and when she found none, she memorized all that she could about it. She knew that the second story of the apex towers held the gate mechanism that would lift the portcullis and give the courtyard to Iventorn's warpack. She knew the tops of those towers would have arrows and cobbles to defend with at best, and boiling oil or small ballista hiding up there at worst. She timed the guards walking the wall. She thought she should return before midnight to see how many guards were still walking the walls. There were two spots that someone quick might be able to scale the wall. One spot was at a small group of vendors hugging the exterior of the wall. One of the more enterprising merchants had built a small wooden booth against the wall. Provided that the roof was sturdy enough, and the booth was unoccupied at the time, she thought she could leap high enough to breach the wall. The other was a gigantic crack in the wall. Not a hole, but a diagonal fissure. The shifting of the wall left a lightning strike of stone creeping up it. She put her hand on the edge of the crack as she walked by the second time and was delighted when the entire length of her fingers could lay on the exposed rock. This meant the shelf was wide enough for decent footholds as well. That part of the wall seemed quieter than the vendors and their customers. She had a lot of choices and strategies to ponder. The small apex towers seemed simple. She felt that she could sneak over the wall somewhere and kill enough guards quietly that she could open one of the portcullises. She knew that she was stretching her own competence in her mind, but she did not feel by too much. She felt confident.

The courtyard looked like a killing field. At each portcullis she would scan between the iron bars to find some cover, somewhere to regroup before the main siege. She never found any. It was just flat grassland with nowhere to hide. You had two choices on terrain like that, thought Trela: charge forward to take the tower or fall back behind the wall. Using their own wall for your respite. More importantly, how do you know when to do which? She would have to watch Iventorn's tactics closely.

The real problem, Trela felt, was definitely the inner tower. There did not seem to be a door at ground level. There was one for the second story, just opening out into nothing. She wondered if they only used removable ladders, or if the door was hidden or if maybe there was a tunnel that popped up from underneath. If worse came to worse she figured they could smoke them out, but they would have to clear the rest of the town before that. Plus, if the defenders did have a tunnel, they might even be able to escape. She had to figure out how to get into the inner tower. She would let the others find Feinsley. She would find a way to take the tower.

"What are you lurking around for!" Trela stiffened when she heard the gruff voice. She turned slowly and tried not to show her hand twitching towards her knife. She could not believe that she left her sword at the inn. Her narrowed eyes widened in surprise. Estfale had a large, warm smile for her. "I should have guessed that you would be here. You seem like a skulker."

Trela watched him as they laughed. He had short, curly, dark hair. Muscular shoulders and large hands, his waist tapered down nicely and he had knee length tight black boots. "And what are you doing? Following me?" Trela smiled at him, but started walking.

"No. Of course not. I came to check out the fortress. The same as you, I suppose." He seemed suddenly a little more shy.

"You've been here before. Do you know how they get into the central tower?" She started to walk around the fortress in the opposite direction than her previous circles. Estfale easily kept up with his long legs.

"Well, I have seen them use a ladder sometimes to get to the second story door, but I know that some of the local council members are fairly infirm and they still get in. I suspect there is another entrance, but to answer your question, no I don't know how they get in. How about the outer towers? Do you have a plan for those?" Estfale was staring up at the parapet to see if there were any guards near. Trela thought it was a little late for that, but chastised herself for not checking either. She told him of the two ways she had seen that might allow the wall to be breached. They strolled and huddled and talked conspiratorially to each other. He listened to her ideas intently, sometimes offering advice and sometimes giving praise. They talked for a while before she realized they were headed back to the inn. As she began to recognize the neighborhood, she decided to duck into a tavern. She did not feel up to going back to her tiny room yet.

"Let's stop in here real quick. We shouldn't be in a rush to return to the inn yet, the night is still young." Trela blushed slightly.

"Of course, sounds great. I'll buy." He laughed and jingled his coin purse at her. They had all been given the same ample stipend, of course.

As they shouldered their way to the bar, Trela heard someone yelling at her. Finally, squinting and on tiptoe, Trela could make out Lishean through the smoke. It looked like Dartsyle and Yarsurle were with him. Trela waved and poked Estfale in the back so he could wave at them as well. She had not meant to find them, but it seemed incredibly odd that they were all there. Was it coincidence? Was it something more? At the least, she thought, they might be able to do some preliminary planning.

"What type of grog would you like?" Estfale's voice was distant as he pushed his way to the bar.

"What? I don't know, I've never had grog before." Trela was talking into his back as she followed closely in his wake.

"Do you like citrus or nutmeg spices or just fruit?" Estfale had made it to the bar and was apparently ordering something. She was just going to get some water, but his question had put her off.

"They are not in the same category. I mean, how would I even rank those things, compare them? If you are going to ask something, you should just ask it." Trela was kind of rambling. The tavern was so loud with private conversation that she really did not expect Estfale to be listening. She was just talking to make herself feel less crowded.

Estfale turned towards her with a large clear mug almost full of brownish liquid. "Here. I'll keep that in mind." After handing her the grog, he reached back and got his own mug from the barkeep. He must have paid when he ordered because he started ushering her forward towards where Lishean and Dartsyle were waiting. She hoped they had some room at their table. "I hope you like limes."

There were two empty chairs next to the small, round, dirty wooden table that Lishean and the others were guarding. As she and Estfale sat, the three immediately raised their mugs in a toast. "To quick friends and slow enemies!" They shouted it out into the general cacophony. Everyone was clinking their glasses and drinking and laughing.

Trela did not realize it at first, mainly because she had not paying attention, but eventually she noticed the way Dartsyle and Yarsurle looked at each other. Yarsurle had always laughed a bit too loud, always moved his hands a little too animatedly during conversation, so it was Dartsyle's mischevious and slightly crooked smile that made Trela realize what was happening. It was the beginning of a long and beautiful relationship.

Trela felt alive, truly and fully alive. She could never really remember the entire conversation. They laughed and joked, got suddenly serious and then laughed some more. She had only two glasses of grog, but everything seemed out of focus in memory. It was as if she remembered the feeling of it, but not the details. The whole night seemed more like a mood than any specific actions. It was that night that she learned camaraderie. The warm fuzzy confusion that makes strangers with a mission feel as old friends.

It took three days for them to find Feinsley. Yarsurle had found him at a tavern near the river dock. It was just before the day turned into night. He had lured Feinsley outside, somehow, down by the dock. There, with the help of Estfale, Feinsley was knocked unconscious. They had swiftly carried him to a nearby abandoned warehouse and hid him until Estfale gathered everybody else up. There, in a group, over the bound, gagged, and bleeding form of Feinsley, they decided what to do.

Iventorn's plan was that they could move at least a score of warriors in through the small side gate before any commotion was noticed. They would then be able to hold the gates while the Parthian guards attempted to route them. Unsuccessfully, of course. With the rest of the warpack in the city, they would march straight to the tower and try to take that. Iventorn wanted a quick and decisive victory. No citizens hurt, only other warriors. He was not there to punish Parthia, but to get something.

First things first. Lishean and Dartsyle were to go to the inn to start the fire. They would take care of everyone's belongings. Then they would come back to the warehouse to take care of Feinsley, pick up Trela and head to the side gate that they had all entered the city through on their first day of arrival.

Yarsurle and Estfale were to head straight for the gate and wait until the fire from the inn's roof brought Iventorn's warpack sneaking up. Then they would attack. They were hoping that Lishean, Dartsyle and Trela would be back by then. Their plan was simple. The last two nights they had stopped by on their way from a tavern and given the guards a little drink. They said it was their civic duty to help such hard working warriors. Today the two would show up much earlier, but they all agreed the guards could be talked into imbibing a little grog.

As for Trela, she was just supposed to protect the warehouse and Feinsley until Lishean and Dartsyle came back. It was a very good plan, but it left out one very important factor. She needed to be able to access the tower. It had to be her, she could feel it.

The warehouse was quite small. It was more of a large barn. There was a vast open space with a mezzanine ringing the perimeter, almost making a second floor with a large central hole. The aged wood was grey with the weather and the rust from the nails flowed groundward like tears. Or like blood.

"Admit it! You should at least own up to what you have been planning. It will make things go easier for you. We can put an end to this nonsense if you would just admit it." Lishean savagely punched Feinsley in the face. His teeth were gritted in anger. His shoulder dove into the punch with his arm. Feinsley was a stationary target, tied heavily to a straight backed chair. The third punch knocked the chair, with Feinsley in it, over backwards.

"We should go. It's getting dark." Dartsyle's hand gently tugged on Lishean's left shoulder. Estfale righted Feinsley and the chair.

"Yes, we all need to hurry. Yarsurle and I still have to purchase a jug of grog." With that, Estfale and Yarsurle ducked out of a creaking side door. Lishean looked deeply into Dartsyle's eyes.

"Of course. We must leave and fulfill our duties." He nodded to himself as he let Dartsyle usher him out the same side door. "I'll be back, though. We'll talk then. You'll admit to it then."

When the door creaked to a stop, the lighting stopped shifting. Even with every door closed, there was a lot of light streaming through the cracks between the warped ashen boards. Trela watched the crazy pattern on the floor for a moment and then walked over to Feinsley.

He was a small Pyran. He had a thin mustache and sparse beard. It made Trela think of dog mange. He was dressed in rags and smelled slightly of urine. She pulled his gag out of his mouth, being careful not to have her fingers too near his teeth. His wild eyes stared at her.

"They're going to kill you, you know? You have precious few moments left." Trela slowly circled him, so he could only see her in part of her orbit. Like the moon.

"Please. Please! I didn't do it. I didn't do anything. I don't know what he's talking about. I don't know what you think I've done." Feinsley looked truly pitiful. His eyes bulged out at her with fear.

"It's not what you have done, but what you are planning. It would be easier on you if you would just admit it." Trela said this as she was behind him. She knew he was innocent, but was unsure of how to appease all parties.

"I'm not planning anything! All I have done for the past two moons is drink. I swear to you that nothing has entered my mind except my next meal and my next glass. I swear! Don't let him kill me. Please. I don't want to die. I'm innocent!" Trela was staring at the back of his head. He kept swiveling around trying to see her. The tears, snot, blood, and spittle that seemed to cover the lower half of his face flung about like a dog's drool. Long strings flowing ungracefully in the wind.

"I need something from you." Trela said it quietly when Feinsley had stopped babbling. She almost whispered it, as if the thought alone was too loud. That someone might hear.

"What? Anything. I'll give you anything. I don't have many coins, but I... I..." His eyes were shoved all the way to the corner of his head in his attempt to see her.

"I need in the tower. The central tower of the keep. You know the way in. You have to show me how to enter and help me get in, and then I will set you free." Trela knew she would not be able to kill Feinsley herself. Nor did she think that she could watch, or even hear, Lishean doing it. No, she had made up her mind on that. She would have to set Feinsley free. There was only one way that she could be forgiven for leaving the warehouse before Lishean and Dartsyle returned. And that was to get into the tower. Feinsley had to know a way in. He just had to.

"I... I can't." His voice was tiny. A resigned little bird, realizing its wings had been clipped. But he did not quite say that he was unable to, thought Trela.

"Then it will be a short and painful trip. Well, I hope it will be short. The last Pyran I saw him kill took two whole days. He made them eat their own toes. He cut off their eyelids. His arms never get tired. It is amazing how long he can beat someone for. Personally, I get tired just watching it. And the blood, don't get me started on how much Pyrans can bleed when they are punched in the face repeatedly. Of course, he'll have to put your chair against a wall or pillar or something. He can't have you falling over every time his fist crushes into you…" Trela wondered how much longer she could go on, making stuff up. She wondered how far his eyes could bug out before they became detached. Luckily for her, she did not have to wait too long before Feinsley broke.

"Okay, okay. I'll help you sneak in through the tunnel. Please, you can't let him beat me any more." There was a wild plea in his face. She would have to handle this delicately, she thought, because the main thought in his mind was escape. She had to think up a way to keep him safely under her control until she could let him loose.

She pulled her dagger out and slid the broad side of the knife blade along his neck. She gripped the hair on top of his head and cruelly pulled his head back. She then turned the knife and let the blade lightly touch his neck.

"If you betray me, your death may be quicker and less tortuous, but it will still be assured. We are laying siege to this city tonight, and there is only one way for you to survive. That is to get me into that tower." Trela stood over him staring into his frightened, buggy eyes. She turned the tip of the blade into the notch above his breastplate, just where his neck began. She pressed ever so slightly, just enough to let some blood drip down onto his chest. Just then an alarm went up. She could hear derlians yelling and running. The roof of the inn must be blazing.

"I can do it. I can get you into the tower. Only me. I'm your only hope. Please, just let me live." He had a hard time swallowing with his head jerked back that far. She watched his throat contort up and down while he tried. Trela wasn't sure if it was an oath of fealty, but she knew that Lishean would be back soon now that the inn was on fire. If he came back, there was no saving Feinsley.

She cut the rope from his legs away from the chair, always careful to keep her dagger in easy striking distance. She let him stand for a moment while she was behind him. She was trying to judge if he was a runner. Some derlians freeze when frightened, some run. She made a noise as if to sheathe her dagger and scuffle her feet as if she was turned around. He did not twitch. He did not even try to look back to see if she was paying attention to him. *Good,* she thought, *maybe he is not as foolish as he looks.*

"You just might make it through the night." Since her short sword was tied to her left thigh, she placed him on her right side. She had her arm around his waist, as if they were confidants, with the dagger still clutched in her fist. The blade lay flat against her forearm, its tip sticking slightly past her elbow. The hold was a little awkward, but she mainly wanted to be able to steer him. She felt as long as he could feel the knife on him, he would be docile. Besides, she figured she was quick enough to get a good stab in before he would be able to run. That should slow him down.

As they walked abreast out the main door of the warehouse, she quickly looked around. Nobody seemed to be paying attention to her. They were all running towards the inn, or away from it. She stopped for a moment and looked at the roof. Flames were shooting into the night sky casting an orange glow around the town. Trela thought she could almost make out shapes amongst the flames. As if Lishean and Dartsyle were still on the roof. They would be at the edge looking down at her from across the town. Lishean would be frowning, scowling at her. She knew that he would not approve of what she was doing. She shook her head to clear it of useless visions. He might not approve of her letting Feinsley go, but he would approve of her infiltrating the tower. Besides, she was one of the few that knew Feinsley was innocent, at least where Tumu was concerned.

They quickly walked towards the tower. Trela wondered what information Feinsley might have. She wished they had gotten information about Parthia's siege capabilities out of him earlier, but Lishean had had only one thing on his mind. They decided it was too close to nightfall to try to keep Feinsley hidden for a full night and the next day. So they had decided to start the siege.

"How defensive is Parthia? Will they suspect an attack and draw the guards, or will they just think that the inn caught fire?" Trela kept pushing him forwards. He swayed slightly while he walked, and she was wondering if it was his hands tied so tightly behind his back or if he had a small limp.

"They have not yet sounded the horn. They sound a huge horn when they want the guards to converge at the tower." His voice was quiet and despondent. She did not want him to be without hope. He might do something stupid if resigned to die.

"That is good news, Feinsley. The longer they don't know about us, the better your chances of surviving. Once I am in the tunnels and feel I know enough to get around, I will set you free, how about that?" Trela was trying to smile, not only for Feinsley, but for all the running Pyrans. She did not want anyone too close or too suspicious. The ropes crossing Feinsley's chest would be very difficult to explain.

The night grew darker the farther they were from the inn. As they were getting closer to the tower, Feinsley suddenly tossed his head to the left, towards her. It was such an awkward move that, at first, Trela thought that he was trying to head-butt her. She tightened her grip on him, pulling him towards her with her dagger.

"Down that alley. Turn left." Feinsley's eyes were starting to bug out again. She was not sure if she could trust him, but she knew that hesitation might destroy her. They turned and walked down a dark and narrow alley.

"Where are we going? If this is a trick, you will be the first to die, trust me." Trela had a hard time staying abreast because of the narrowness of the alley. He started speeding up a little. Not knowing what to do, Trela grabbed the back of his gag that was still hanging around his neck to choke him to a halt.

"I asked you a question. Where are we going?" Trela would not let him turn around to face her.

"Look behind you. Out on the main thoroughfare is half of the warpack in this town." He sounded frightened. How, thought Trela, could she have missed them coming? She watched in fascination as row upon row of warriors walked past them, their torches throwing flickering shadows all along the alley walls. Had she been looking down at her feet? Surely she should have noticed them marching.

"Where did they come from?" Trela half spoke it aloud and half to herself. She had let Feinsley continue walking down the alleyway.

"There are old barns and shops that don't have any businesses in them. They just hide the entrances to the tunnels. Some of the tunnels can hold four Pyrans abreast." Trela thought she sensed a trace of pride in Feinsley's voice.

"So, are we headed towards one of these hidden entrances?" Trela was trying to calm herself down about Feinsley. Surely if he had wanted to ruin her plan, he would have alerted the guards out there to her presence.

"Yes. There is only one that leads straight into the tower. That is the entrance that I am taking you to." Feinsley was starting to sound less frightened.

They left the alleyway and turned right. Trela sped up to walk beside him, keeping her dagger flat on his back. After walking past the first apex tower they turned left into another alley. They walked a little down the alley for a while, approaching a cross street when Trela realized that Feinsley was speeding up a little.

Her left hand reached up for the back of Feinsley's gag. He suddenly burst into a sprint. Her right hand reflexively pushed out towards him, but he was moving so fast that she couldn't push the dagger into him. She jumped forwards and luckily her left hand was still flinging out towards the gag. She stretched her left arm with every fiber of her being. Her fingers barely wrapped about the knot at the back of his neck. As she pulled back he began to slow down. She was finally able to pull back against his throat in earnest as her feet regained the alley. She thrust with her right hand as she pulled back with her left, but since she was still hesitant to kill him, she struck with the hilt of her dagger.

He dropped to the ground at the cross street in front of them. She bent down to grab his gag again when she realized that there were two Pyrans staring at her. They were flanking a gated stone arch. The shock of seeing them here, all of a sudden, made her freeze in the crucial moment. As Feinsley staggered up and took off running with his tied arms swishing back and forth, she slashed with her dagger bringing an arc of blood to stain the air. Her entire being wanted to chase him. Each muscle was poised to run him down and punish him for his betrayal. There was a small part of her mind, that which understood what was happening, that made her twirl in a half circle and fling her knife at one of the guards instead. That small part of her realized that he *had* actually taken her to the tunnel in some instinct for self-preservation. She could not waste precious time on him.

She had thrown the dagger underhand, point first, instead of overhand twirling in the air. Lishean had made her practice both styles over and over. Overhand could be thrown much harder and therefore was usually preferred. However, you must judge the distance with that type of throw so that the point of the dagger struck your target, not the hilt. She had no idea of how close they were, so she threw it the less powerful way. It bounced off the guard's armor as he and his partner ran towards her, slowing him slightly through the shock of it.

They held aloft their brandished swords as they ran screaming. Trela unsheathed her short sword and swung it in a wide arc with one fluid motion. Her sword made a loud clang against the guard on the left. She quickly hopped forward and side-kicked him in the soft flesh under his ribs, into his liver. Pulling her sword back after the first guard's parry, she stabbed forward at the guard on the right. Her arm jolted with the shock of the sword striking bone. She was used to sparing, where you pull back before striking hard, and the shock of it almost made her lose her grip. She had to kick at him as well to free her sword. He dropped to one knee with a groan.

She jumped backwards as the first guard regained his balance and slashed at her midsection. She cut at his forearm as he was trying to pull back after missing her. With an ear-splitting cry, he dropped his sword and clutched his arm with his other hand. Trela did not hesitate to bring her sword down with both hands. His body jerked as it crumpled. She made sure they were both dead before she picked up her knife and searched them. She pulled a ring of keys from the first guard and ran over to the closed gate. The gate was unlocked, however, and she was able to just push it open without resorting to sifting through the keys. The gate moved without a sound, and she closed it quietly behind her. She crept as quietly as she could down the hall cursing Feinsley in her head. How was she supposed to find the way into the tower from here and, for that matter, did she even know that the tunnel led there? What if Feinsley had led her to the wrong gate? At least, she thought, there were torches on the wall.

She trotted down the hallway on the balls of her feet. The archway sloped downwards as she ran forwards. She had been exercising daily for what seemed like forever, but her breath rasped in and out too quickly. She could feel her heart pounding in her chest. It was the intensity of the moment as much as it was the exertion.

She heard an insanely loud noise through the gate, a huge metallic clash along with a roar from a hundred throats. Along with the adrenalin rush from the brief combat came the elation from the realization that Iventorn's warpack had reached the wall. She figured she had a small head start before Feinsley ran into some guards. She could hope that he would try to escape, to just leave Parthia. But she knew that she could not count on that.

She ran until she came to a "T" in the tunnel. There was one torch in the middle of the wall in front of her, but there was darkness both to her right and her left. She tried to figure out which direction would lead under the tower. She had walked around it enough that she knew the only way into the tower, except by ladder, had to be from underneath. She suddenly got an idea and took the torch from the sconce on the wall. Staring at the sconce she wondered why the only torch was here, at the split of the tunnel. She held the torch with her left hand and reached up with her right to pull at the sconce. She tugged and twisted, but it would not budge. She was hoping there was a secret passage here, but there did not seem to be. She stepped back and held the torch aloft. The motion of the air, shown by the flickering flame, came from the entrance and flowed to the left hand passageway. She thought for a moment, then decided to go down the right hand passage. She figured that the air under the tower would be trapped, would be immobile. She carried the torch with her as she started to run again.

As she flowed down the passageway towards what she hoped was the tunnel to the tower, she started to worry about the light from the torch. If there were more guards down here, she was alerting them to her presence. She felt torn between the need for speed, in case Feinsley was alerting the guards to her, and the need for caution. If Feinsley was only thinking of his own survival, she might have plenty of time to sneak up on the denizens of the tower. She slowed down slightly, looking for another sconce to place her only source of light. As she was walking, however, she thought of something else. Iventorn and his warpack were at the gates. There was no way that the guards in the tower would be caught unawares. They would be expecting an attack. Hopefully they were expecting it from the outside and not from underneath them. She thought briefly about waiting down there, underground, until the warpack was closer to the keep, then trying to surprise them while they were looking outwards. She discarded this idea quickly, though, because she was worried that other guards might swarm the tunnels attempting to reach the tower before the warpack. She felt like her mind was useless. Every time she thought of something, another thought would immediately counter it. She gritted her teeth at the frustration she felt at herself. Pausing to breathe for a moment, she thought she heard something from behind her. She turned quickly, but nothing was there. Finally she decided that there was nothing to do but continue. She pulled her dagger and did her best to hide it along her forearm. If she ran into any guards she would try to lie first so that she could get close enough to make the first strike. As she turned another corner she found an empty wall sconce. She tried to move this one as well, to trigger some other passageway, but to no avail. She left her light behind her and began to move faster, if not more assuredly. The tunnel was getting darker, but she felt she could no longer bring attention to herself with the torch.

As she trotted along she realized that there was a dim glow in the distance in front of her. There was another torch around a corner or something. She sped up as she noticed it, passing other empty sconces as she ran. She turned the corner and there it was. There were two torches flanking a wooden staircase. The stairs had to go to the tower, she thought. If they just led out, maybe into an empty alleyway or abandoned warehouse, she felt like she would scream. Against her better judgment she kept running, intending to take the stairs three at a time. Suddenly, but too late to change her course of action, she noticed boots on the stairs. There was someone waiting, she thought. She could only hope that there was only one.

"Help! Help, they are coming. They're chasing me." She bounded onto the first stair as the large Pyran in front of her noticed that he was being charged. He was huge. Not just tall but in girth as well. It did not look like it was all muscle, but it was amazing just how wide he was. A long fluffy beard trailed to his waist, next to a huge, heavy, double-bitted axe. She stalled on the step and pointed with her left hand behind her. "How? How could they have found the tunnel so quickly? There must be a traitor in our midst. Hurry!" She had sidled up next to him as she was speaking. She placed her left hand on his chest as she stared into his dark eyes. She hoped he wouldn't realize that he didn't know her. "I would try stop them myself, but one look at you will freeze them in their tracks. We have to secure the tower. I'll let the others know." She took another step up the stairs, her hand sliding from his chest to his shoulder.

"I think I would remember a bright candle like you." He was reaching for his axe, but he was still smiling at her. She swallowed hard, smiled at him, and opened her mouth to speak. Instead she thrust her dagger into his neck with every ounce of strength in her right arm. She didn't even see his arm move but was tossed against the far wall so hard that all of the air was crushed from her lungs. She fought with all of her strength to not pass out. Her chest tried to move, but her stomach would not let her take a breath. It was as if someone had kicked her in the stomach. Hard. Repeatedly. Her vision dimmed, and an image of Knill came unbidden before her. She shook her head to try to revive herself. She slowly began to breathe shallowly, trying to drag air into her burning lungs. She watched the bearded Pyran slump to the ground. His eyes were glassy and lifeless, but his body kept trying to jerk the axe from his side. The blood had sprayed the wall, the stairs, and now pumped slowly out of his neck.

Trela was unsure of how long she lay at the bottom of the stairs. It seemed to take forever for her body to remember how to do the simplest of things, like breathe. She finally staggered to her feet. She thought about taking his axe with her, but was unsure if she could heft it with any skill. She got her knife and sheathed it. As she stood there leaning against the wall, catching her breath, she looked around the stairwell.

The stairs led up to a wide trapdoor. The wooden slats were pushed tight against each other, keeping any light that might be above from filtering down. The large black iron hinges and straps made the door look impenetrable from below. She stared for quite a while before she realized that there was a keyhole at the opposite side from the hinges. Though she did not want to, she searched the dead guard looking for his keys. He did not seem to have any. She stood back up and looked at the door, wondering if it was even locked, when she remembered the key ring that she got from the first set of guards she encountered. Before pulling them out, she pushed tentatively on the trapdoor. It was definitely locked. She stepped back down the bottom of the stairwell and pulled out the other keys. She was terrified of making too much noise, though she could not hear anything from above.

She shifted the keys in her hand until she had several pointed out and could try them without jingling the ring. She crept up the stairs trying to hear anything from beyond the door, but she strained to no avail. It took her three tries before she found a key that began to turn. She slowed herself down, held her breath, and turned the key until a loud click pierced the stairwell.

Trela removed the key as quietly as she could and crept back down the stairs. The click had seemed to reverberate through the passageway, so she pulled her short sword out and waited for the guards to come pouring down through trapdoor at her. She waited until the sword began to get heavy. She sheathed it and pulled her knife back out. She waited until her heart regained a calm cadence and then she slowly walked back up the stairs. She placed her hand on the door and tried to feel for vibrations. There was nothing. She could not see through door, could not hear through the door nor feel through the door. She was torn between two truths. Knowing that if a guard was on the other side of the door she would not stand a chance in combat. And knowing that she was running out of time. Iventorn's warpack would soon be at the interior gates, unable to reach the tower. Her mind felt foggy and she had trouble making decisions. That was what finally sealed it for her. She sheathed her knife, pulled her sword and rushed up the stairs pushing on the door with her shoulder. She did not yell, but slashed wildly as she reached the landing.

And connected. The small Pyran's yell alerted all of the guards in the room. Then the trapdoor slammed open onto the stone floor with a deafening boom. She pulled back her sword with a grunt, and the Pyran fell to the floor. There were maybe eight other guards in the room. She did not have a chance to count. Trela jumped forward and stabbed another guard, sinking her blade deep into his stomach, then turned and ran. She could hear swords being drawn and orders being yelled.

She leapt down the stairs four at a time and jumped over the bearded guard. She was unsure of where she was headed, but she knew that there was no way that she could fight that many trained guards at once. As she skidded around the first corner, she glanced backwards and saw that three Pyrans had already made it down the stairs. She ran full force around the darkened corner. Then she stopped and walked quickly back to the corner, gripping her sword hilt with both hands. She waited until the shadow was as large as life, then swung with all of her might. She yanked her sword back and began running into the darkness without checking to see how badly she wounded the guard.

Trela heard curses behind her, but the sound of footsteps eased. She thought she might have slowed them down. She turned back to see and realized that the guards had stopped at the bright corner. She stopped and pulled her dagger from its sheath. She crouched in the dark and waited while her eyes started to adjust.

She could hear them regrouping, muttering amongst themselves. She watched the shadows dance and shift. She tried to get her heart under control. She held the sword in her left hand and the dagger in her right. She seemed to wait for a long time for them to come around the corner, but she knew that hardly any time passed at all. Four of them came in a group, two in front and two behind.

They were knotted together, crouching and wary. She waited for them to get closer. She knew they were composed to conquer, trained and in their own tower, but they did not seem to see her. She waited until she could hear their rasping breath. She threw her dagger and made a wide slashing stroke with her sword. The sword crashed into the guard with such force that it bounced out of her left hand. Her hand stung with the reverberations. As the sword clanged around, heading for the ground, as she was turning to flee yet again, she realized she no longer had a weapon. As she turned the other corner into the hallway where she had left her torch, she made a promise to herself. She swore to herself, then and there, that she would always carry an extra knife. She would always have something hidden, something dangerous, to fall back on. Maybe something small hidden in her boot. For the first time in the last three days, she felt fear. Pure, excruciating, horrifying fear. She could hear the echo of slapping feet on the stone floor behind her.

She slowed for a brief moment and grabbed the torch from the sconce. She swung around behind her in a wild arc. There was a great clash, and she was showered in sparks. She was unable to see through the fireball that erupted, but she knew there was a guard behind the flash somewhere. She thrust with her torch at the guard and felt something connect. She grabbed the shaft of her torch with her other hand and pushed forward with all her might. The guard fell backwards, and she swung the torch in another arc. As the torch passed her face and then away from her face, she saw what she did to the guard who was chasing her. He lay on his back with arms and legs flying around like a beetle dying in the sun. His beard had caught fire. The screams were ear shattering. She stood there stunned for half a moment, not long at all. Then she got stabbed.

The other guard had been rushing behind them both. He must have side-stepped the burning guard and struck while she hesitated. She fell backwards and dropped the torch. It stayed lit, but the passageway suddenly became very dark. The anger at herself for hesitating almost overpowered her fear that her destiny was ending with her life.

She looked up at the guard standing over her. He was nodding to himself, his sword waving slightly back and forth. Just then a loud deep horn sounded in the distance. It cascaded down the stairs and flowed through the tunnel like a rushing river. The guard turned his head towards the noise, towards the tower, briefly. Her booted foot flung upwards, almost of its own accord, at the hollow sound of the horn, straight between the warrior's legs. The impact jarred her entire leg. The guard fell to his knees with a grimace on his face. He slashed down with his sword at her. She rolled out of the way. Barely. The sword sparked as it hit the stone floor. As Trela rolled, she almost put her hair into the torch lying on the ground. She kicked out with her heel, striking the guard in his nose. She tried to stand but slipped back to her knees. She grabbed the torch and smashed it down at the guard, but since he had fallen backwards, she only managed to hit the floor. More sparks cascaded onto the stone floor. She staggered into a half-crouch and swung again with her torch, managing to strike the guard in his knee. He rolled over and tried to crawl away. She dropped her torch and took up the sword he had dropped. She had to stab him several times before he lay completely still. She staggered along the wall, past the sickeningly sweet smell of the burning guard, keeping herself upright by the power of her will alone. The wound in her side burned like fire.

The horn blasted again through the tunnel. She suddenly thought of Parthia's warpack flooding through the tunnels towards the tower. She did not know what to do, so she sped up. She moved past the bodies of her victims as she stumbled towards the trap door. She did not know if they were alive or dead, but none of them moved as she shuffled past. Her rasping breath and shuffling feet were the only sounds she could hear. She knew that some of them must still be alive. One only has a knife in him, she thought. But she could spare no time to even retrieve her weapons, let alone do something as unsavory as finish off the wounded. It was one thing to fight with something that is fighting you, or at least has the capability of such. She was unsure if she had the stomach for massacre. They, for their part, were doing their best to not attract attention. It was nice to see both sides of the fight agree on something so basic. She hoped that the courtesy would be returned to her someday.

She finally turned the corner and moved to the bottom of the stairs. It seemed quiet and the trapdoor was still open. Trela took a deep breath and squeezed her arm to her side tighter. She slowly ascended the stairs, trying to make as little noise as possible. She crouched under the door opening and then popped her head up as quickly as possible. As impossible as it seemed, there did not seem to be anyone in that section of tower. She went up the last of the stairs as quickly as she could. She was struggling with flipping the trapdoor closed when she began to hear a noise. There seemed to be shouting from far below. Trela was able to lift the corner of the door finally. She jammed her knee under it so that she could get more leverage on the door. She got her shoulder under it and heaved. It made a horrible crash when it fell. She quickly shoved an iron bar through the hoops in the stone floor, locking it. She spun around with her heart hammering in her chest.

The room was circular, with stairs hugging the outside wall in a spiral up to the next level. There were a lot of windows ringing the perimeter, and there was an odd assortment of weapons on various racks placed about the room. She could see torches ringing the triangular wall outside the tower like the stars in the night sky. There were no side doors into this level of the tower, so she concluded that the parapet must enter into the level above. There were rope ladders with wooden slats rolled up next to the windows that they must use during times of peace. There was one dead guard, but she did not know where the wounded one had gotten to. She glanced up at the trapdoor above her. First things first, she thought.

She picked up a broad, heavy sword and lugged it up the spiral stairs along with the sword she took from the Pyran who stabbed her. She could hear the banging start on the lower trapdoor. She did not know how many were down there, but it sounded like a lot. The hinges on the trapdoor above her were on the side, so she crept up until she could jam the sword between the wood and the stone, acting as a wedge. She shoved the other one up there as well. It would not hold them for long. Eventually they would crush the wood enough to get it open, but she thought it would buy her a little more time. She scuttled back down the stairs on her butt, one at a time. The lower trap door was bucking like a horse, but with all of the iron strapping and the bar holding it shut, Trela thought it would hold for quite a while. Luckily those above her did not even seem to know she was there. She got herself over by a window and peered out into the distance. She kept her head low for fear of being seen. One of the apex towers was on fire. That was a good sign. The ruckus coming from the tunnel was getting louder. She went over to a weapons rack and began hiding knives all about her, making sure to stash one in her boot. She also found a well balanced sword and took a few practice swings before her side bade her to stop. She was stripping bandages from the dead guard's tunic when she heard the top trapdoor begin to creak. Just then a great cry erupted from the courtyard.

To her relief, there were torches flooding into the courtyard. She began to fling the rope and wooden ladders out the windows. Circumnavigating the tower she pushed every ladder there was over the window sill. They were tied to iron rings jutting out from the tower wall. She waved down at the warriors fighting in the courtyard with an urgent hand. Though the lower trapdoor was being attacked with much more vigor, it was holding nicely. The upper one, however, was prying open enough on occasion to see light filter through.

Though there were some Parthian guards in the courtyard and the ones left on the parapet were harassing Iventorn's warpack to the best of their ability. His warriors, as a whole, were not slowed in the slightest. The first to reach the ladders tossed their torches on the ground in their haste to gain entrance into the tower. Then the boiling water splashed from higher in the tower. Stones rained on the warriors in the courtyard. They had the ladders though, and were beginning to climb from all around. Trela grinned widely as she sat with her back against a wall. She had done it.

Suddenly there was a large crack. The heavy trapdoor above Trela began to heave open. They were rocking it with what looked like a heavy iron pry bar. She staggered back up to her feet and held her sword feebly in front of her. The first of Iventorn's warpack began to swing into the tower level. When the trapdoor finally opened, there was a loud commotion. Realizing they had already lost the lower level, the guards were stunned that they had destroyed their own defense. As more and more warriors poured in through the windows, the guards above realized their defeat. They tossed their weapons down in front of them. Suddenly Cavish was yelling next to her and Iventorn was climbing through a window. Trela could not have felt more relieved. She slid back down the wall and began to black out, dropping her new sword.

"You? I dare not believe it." Cavish was grinning in her face and trying to get her to stand. "Ah, you are wounded. Mekliderto! There that should hold you for a little while. Magic will not heal permanently, but it will heal you for long enough that you can savor the victory." When Cavish's hand touched her side, it was as if a flow of icy water poured into her, soothing and numbing at the same time. "We will get you to an ameliorator or at least a real mage later in the night. Now, though. Now it is time to be a hero!" Cavish picked her up with one huge sweep of his arms and put her on his wide shoulder. "To the hero of Parthia!" His shout was deafening, and Trela doubted whether or not many of the warriors there knew what he was talking about, that it was her who dropped the ladders. They were all cheering though.

Not all eyes were on her, of course. Iventorn was upstairs with many of his warriors accepting Parthia's surrender. Some were opening the trapdoor in the floor, and some were still climbing in, stunned at the quick victory. She looked for Lishean, Estfale, Dartsyle, and Yarsurle but was unable to see them if they were there. Knill and Tumu were a world away, safe back at the camp. It was just her and Cavish and the crowd.

The round room was packed with Pyran warriors, shaking weapons and shouting. Their eyes were huge and wild. And they were all staring at her. She could feel her heart beat along to the rhythm of their cheers. This was what she wanted more than anything. This. She knew she should feel ashamed. That, more than anything, she should want to be the Kriishan to make others' lives better. Right now, however, she basked in the glory. And she greedily enjoyed it.

Chapter 9

It was one little sentence, two to three words only. That little sentence played over and over in Croy's mind, however. It had changed his life. It had sentenced him to chains. "She's escaped."

They had gone out again, Croy and the Blind One. They had been traveling together often, but to what end Croy was never sure. There was no real agenda, no known purpose. They would ride out to some distant grove or ley line. They would discuss magic and chaos, Gaens and 'jin and 'tin. Like many of those in the past, the return carriage ride that replayed so often in Croy's mind was made in silence. He remembered feeling this incredible compulsion to tell the Blind One that he would be his apprentice. It would well up in him and build energy. It took all of his will not to blurt out his fealty. He had figured that he would, one day, someday. But he wanted to speak to Ilana first. So he used all his strength to keep the fateful ride in silence. The Blind One, for his part, merely looked bored and kept quiet the entire ride. As if he were waiting for Croy to speak first.

When the carriage arrived back at Serif, it was dark. *The inside of the carriage was as dark as the Blind One's world,* thought Croy. The idea of being trapped in this carriage forever made Croy feel sorry, briefly, for the Blind One. As the door to the carriage opened, moonlight relit Croy's world. He waited while the Blind One gingerly stepped out and onto the ground. He was stooped over near the door, awaiting his turn, when he had heard Greshcly's hurried voice say, "She's escaped."

"What? No. It is too soon." The Blind One's voice had not been filled with anger, nor vitriol, but only sadness. He had moved forward enough to let Croy out. As Croy stepped down he realized how many 'jin were standing around. There had to have been a score of them and they had looked ready to fight. "Of course, you know what this means, Croy? It may be some time before you can see the sky again." The Blind One began to walk away. The crowd had parted in front of him and had resealed itself behind him. The hard faces stared into Croy, as if their master's displeasure was somehow his own fault. The only Gaen smiling had been Greshcly. And Croy had thought he was smiling more out of habit than any actual enjoyment.

"Well. I know it will not be necessary, but we have to bind your hands before we take you to Rycher." Greshcly moved slowly towards Croy, still smiling. Croy knew there was nothing he could do. There would have been nothing he could have done if it was just Greshcly. Being surrounded just made him more nervous. He turned around and put his hands behind his back. He closed his eyes as Greshcly wrapped cord around his wrists.

Croy had tried to remember all he knew of Rycher. The stories he was told in school. How the cells were hewn from solid basalt. How the steel was tempered to withstand any blow. How the air itself was restricted so that the prisoners were never at full strength. No one outside of the 'jin class knew the way there, not even the prisoners. Croy had no illusions that he would escape from there. He only wished that he had offered to be the Blind One's apprentice in the carriage, before all this happened. He would certainly make that offer as soon as he was allowed.

A hood was placed on his head and he was seated in a chair. The chair had wheels so that he would not actually walk to the entrance, nor have to be carried. They spun him in a circle a couple of times before wheeling him quickly uphill for a while. His hands hurt bound up behind him, but he felt it was wiser if he did not complain. After some time he began to be pushed downhill. There were a lot of random turns, and he even thought that they would spin him in a circle every once in a while. Even had he been trying, Croy doubted that he would be able to retrace his steps. Of course, he had not been trying. He was only thinking of what he could say to the Blind One. He knew that would be his only way out. He would have to convince the Blind One that he had nothing to do with Trela's escape. That he wanted nothing more in this world than to help the Blind One find her again. That he would do anything and everything that he was asked, to the best of his ability. Croy, for one fleeting moment, was suddenly glad that they had both been out of Serif when she escaped. At least his own incompetence could not be used against him.

At that thought, Croy suddenly wondered about Nolt. He had asked Nolt to keep Trela company while he was gone. Not to watch her or guard her, but just to keep her from getting too bored. He had not realized that she was planning on leaving Serif. He had known that she was unhappy, but he thought he had her convinced that Synde was coming back for her, that she should wait for him.

The chair had finally squeaked to a halt. He was told roughly to stand up, which he promptly did. His hands were unbound and the hood was removed from his sweaty head. The flickering light was dim; the torch was out in the hall. They wheeled the chair out of the cell and slammed the door shut. The light grew even more dim as Croy listened to the metal clanging sound of his life being locked away. He heard the footsteps recede. He went over to the only furniture in the room, a ratty looking cot, and sat heavily upon it. Luckily they did not remove the torch in the hall, so he was able to see a little in the darkness. It was the last thing he wanted to do, and he hated himself for it, but he began to cry. It was just so incomprehensible to him. He had not done anything wrong. He had been summoned to accompany the Blind One again and he went. That was the extent of his crime. He found it difficult to stop crying and sleep. After a long while he became more exhausted than scared, and that was when blissful sleep overcame him.

When he awoke, it was with a start. He was drenched in sweat. Though he could not remember his dream, he knew it was alarming. He had a vague image of boiling water. He tried to wipe the sweat off his cheek, but it was sticky. He tossed aside the scratchy wool blanket and stood on the cold stone. He felt the heat rising off of him and flowing into the rocky walls. It felt good. The half light cast by a torch far down the hallway cast wild, dim shadows about the cell, continuing the sense of unease still lingering from his forgotten dream. He took up his shirt from the end of the bed and dabbed the sweat off his brow. As his body finally cooled to a tolerable temperature, he wiped the rest of his face off. As he looked down at his shirt, he realized that the sticky sweat on his cheek was really blood. He tried to trace it with his fingers in the near dark, feeling a crusted line to his ear. He scraped off a bit of derlian rust and stared at it on his fingers. It looked pure black in the half light. Not knowing what else to do, Croy spit on his shirt and wiped crusted blood from his cheek. He stood naked in the cell for a while, trying to tell if his ear was still bleeding. He did not think so, but his ear was sore when he fished around it with his finger. He stood there until he began to shiver, then crawled back onto his uncomfortable cot, pulled the wool up to his eyes and did his best not to dream.

Croy lost track of day or night. The gong that told of the passage of time in Serif could not be heard here in Rycher. Meals came regularly, but they always consisted of the same gruel, so it was hard to figure out which meal it was supposed to be. There was never conversation between the guards and Croy. Not for his lack of trying, but they were a quiet, stoic lot. He got to the point that he could hear the food cart coming down the hallway and perk up. He would stand next to the bars, straining for the first glimpse of the guards coming down the hall. He never yelled at the guards from a distance, for he learned quickly that they hated that. The cells were staggered, so that he could not see across the hall into another cell, but he could tell that they were there. The one across from him and to the right held a prisoner that used to yelled a lot. One of the first meals that Croy had was interrupted by the yeller, until the guards went over to the cell and yelled back. Finally, they entered the cell and he could hear violence erupting from it. The prisoner's angry yells soon turned into terrified screams. Croy was unsure of what they did to him, but he never wanted to find out for himself. He found that it was easier to accept your food and attempt a little light-hearted small talk than to argue with the guards. He kept asking them when someone would come talk to him, but they only said that they knew nothing about prosecution, just incarceration. Sometimes a prisoner would try to yell to another prisoner, just for a little derlian contact. As often as not a guard would come down the hallway and threaten the loud prisoner, so after a while Croy was resigned to only speak to the guards. He just wished they talked back a little more. Or, even better, that they would give him some information. Once he tried to convince a guard to take a message to the Blind One, or Greshcly, or to any of the 'jin. The guard laughed Croy off, however, stating that when one of the 'jin were ready to talk with him, they would.

The routine dragged on. Croy was always a little surprised when he spoke to a guard and his voice worked. It was raspy and he croaked a lot, but he enjoyed being able to speak. For a while he would try to speak to himself at night, or what he thought might be night, but eventually he ran out of things to say. After that first night, he did not dream any more. He was grateful for not waking up sweaty and shaken, terrified of the dark. He was also grateful because when he had shown the guards his blood-stained shirt, they told him that he was not allowed any more clothing, so he had better keep what he had in good condition.

Croy finally got up the nerve to ask for a book, or something to help him pass the time. The guards gave a resounding no. They did not do it threateningly, but forcefully enough that he did not ask again. He had wanted to ask if he could see Ilana and was glad that he chose not to since their reaction was so quick and heated about the simple book. He wondered how much time had passed and whether or not Ilana was back from Larelt yet. He kept thinking that she should be in Serif by now, that she was alone in their home, wondering where he was. Or maybe the Blind One had told her lies about him being a traitor. Or maybe, and this was worse yet, she was also being held in Rycher somewhere. Alone and trapped in a cell like his, wondering what had happened. Wondering what had gone wrong. He hoped, more than anything, that she was not being punished as well.

Croy wondered what the Blind One was doing. Why had he not come down here to talk with him? Why was it that Croy had to guess at what he did wrong, at what his punishment might be, or how long it might last? He began to think that the wondering, the not knowing, was worse than actually being trapped. He came to the realization that only one Gaen could help him. He would have to convince the Blind One to let him go, somehow. He would have to convince him that he had nothing to do with Trela, that he wanted to help the 'jin, not to hinder them. That he wanted an apprenticeship. Needed it, not for his freedom, but just because it was a strong desire. He had wanted to keep farming, to love Ilana and lead a simple life. However, he realized that the only way out of rotting in Rycher for the rest of his life was to learn magic from the Blind One.

The routine continued. Croy finally had a way to pass his time, however. He mulled over what little conversations they had had over magic. He tried to recall every word and each nuance that the Blind One may have given, purposely and accidentally. He realized that they had not spoken much about the actual mechanics of magic, merely broad ideas. He was hoping that he would be able to spend his time in practice, but all he could do was spend it attempting to recapture something to practice. Anything, really.

He thought about chaos, about possibility and probability. He tried to recall the tingle that he felt while watching the Blind One talk to the apparition. He tried to recall the way his hair felt, the color that pulsed through his mind. In the quiet of his cell, he attempted to recreate the scene in its entirety. He would close his eyes and breathe slowly and replay the scene. Each time he did it, he would try to remember an extra detail, something that he had forgotten that might help him understand magic.

Like so much in Croy's life, by the time he became almost comfortable with the routine, it ended. When he heard the commotion of guards walking down the hall, he thought it was too early for the next meal, but he had been having problems keeping time. Then he realized that there was no sound of the food cart. It was merely the sound of footsteps and occasional muttered words. He wondered what was going on. Finally the guards came into view, and he fully realized what was happening. In the midst of the guards stood the Blind One.

Their keys clanged on the iron bars, echoing in the confined space. The guards filed quietly in and the Blind One followed. He made a small gesture with his hands and the guards filed back out. "We'll be at the guard station. Let us know when you're ready." Croy thought it odd that someone who was blind would use non-verbal cues, but Croy was unsure of when the Blind One went blind, or anything at all about him for that matter.

"We lost her. She somehow removed herself from this world. I had a young apprentice watching her. Well, not watching, but feeling for her. He was able to track her until the exit near the lake. Then, she just vanished. Did she, in your opinion, know magic?" The Blind One was standing before him, so he stayed standing as well. He was briefly amused by the thought of the Blind One trying to look impressive sitting on a prison cot.

"No. She knew nothing of magic. Her only concern, from what I could tell, was to learn combat. Honest weaponry, no tricks. I almost think she had a disdain for magic." Croy was unsure about his last sentence, but since he had already broken inside and would be begging to be an apprentice later, he had a little bile to work out first.

"That is what I had thought. The Gaen who helped her escape is by no means a mage either. That only leaves one thing left then. A Yaven." The Blind One was smiling to himself. "That theory, however, leaves more questions than it does answers."

"I know that Synde's caravan was attacked by a Yaven. If they had a Yaven working with them, there would have been more evidence of that. Even if the second Yaven had lain low during the attack on the caravan, it would have surfaced when Synde was getting killed. At least it would have shown up to protect Trela. No, I don't think there is any way there was a Yaven working with Synde. There must be another answer." Croy did not want to disagree with the Blind One, but the introduction of a Yaven working for Synde or Trela just did not make sense.

"Then what? A mage that we can not detect? There is not much here that makes sense, Croy." It was the first time that Croy heard anger in the Blind One's voice.

"Maybe a Beleg? Maybe she really is the Kriishan and Gorbanax is taking an interest." Croy said it quietly, almost to himself. Another first then happened. Croy heard the Blind One laugh. Truly and heartily, without malice.

"Well that is certainly an imaginative answer. Croy, what I am saying is that we do not know where she is and we need to find her." The Blind One was smiling towards Croy.

"Why is she so important? What do Gaens care what happens to Pyrans? Where do your orders come from?" Croy knew what the Blind One wanted. He also knew that he was going to comply. What he did not know was why. Why him, why Trela, why must everything suddenly seem crazy? All Croy really wanted was to wander the hills with his sheep. "Most importantly, why have you left me down here for so long and let her trail get cold? This must have happened moons ago." Maybe it had not been that long, but he had no real idea of how much time had passed.

"There are forces coalescing that we mere derlians can not comprehend. I cannot tell you why she is important, all I can tell you is that she is. As for where my orders come from… You know what I will tell you, and you know that it is not quite the truth. I am part of the 'jin and my orders stem from their council. Listen, Croy, I have bad news. I was unsure of how to tell you, but I suppose I will just say it." The Blind One took a deep breath. "Nolt was killed while Trela was trying to escape. He was shot full of arrows at the exit that she left through. I, ah, didn't want anything like that to happen, Croy."

It was if Croy was being shot full of arrows, as the Blind One had put it. Each moment that passed another hit would strike him. Each time he thought he comprehended what was told to him, he felt the pain anew. He was not sure of how long he was quiet. In his shock he did not realize that the Blind One did not answer his last question.

"I know it must be hard for you to hear of it like this, but I wanted to tell you before you found out once you were released. You see, Croy, I was going to come here with an ultimatum. Instead I will ask you. I want you to be my apprentice, Croy. I need your help in finding Trela and bringing her back. Join us, Croy." The Blind One reached towards Croy with his hand. He seemed suddenly old. His hand looked wrinkled and papery. Croy took it in both of his hands out of compassion as much as any other reason. It was odd that when he should be receiving the comforting, he was asked to give it. He almost felt better about that, actually. He wanted to be alone to fully take in the news of Nolt, and he knew there was no way that he was going to be alone unless he acquiesced to the Blind One.

"I have been thinking about little else since I have been trapped here. I do want to be your apprentice, but I need to speak with Ilana. I have not seen her for over a cycle and must speak with her before I make any decisions." Croy had not thought about making any ultimatums of his own until just that moment. He had not realized that he might have the upper hand in anything, and when the idea came to him, he did not hesitate. He had to make a stand for something. He had to take at least a modicum of control about something. He chose that to be Ilana. Surely the Blind One could not complain about Ilana.

"Of course, of course. I will have you removed from Rycher immediately, and you can go home. I believe Ilana is there. She arrived home from Larelt a couple of days ago. I will let her know of your return personally." The Blind One began to shuffle towards the iron gates. "Guards!" He turned and again outstretched his hand towards Croy. It did not seem as feeble as it had before. "You will not regret this decision, Croy." As he shook the Blind One's hand, Croy's only thought was that he already did regret his decision. He regretted it before he made it. He could take comfort, as small as it was, that he did not really have a choice. The Blind One was correct about one thing at least: forces larger than Croy were in charge of him. He could not believe that one of his oldest friends had died in the middle of this. There was no reason for it, he was sure. Nolt never wanted anything more than to work hard and enjoy his simple pleasures of life. He had spent his entire life being kind to those who were weaker than him and deferring to those stronger. There was surely no justice in his death. Nothing made sense anymore.

The ride back from the depths of Rycher was much more pleasant than the ride there. Croy was still blindfolded, still had a hood on, and still had to sit in a rickety wheeled chair. But he knew where he was going. And he knew that Ilana was there waiting for him at his home. His own home.

They dropped him back off where they had picked him up. He stood there, in his blood stained shirt, for some time before deciding to get back underground. The smell of the fresh air was invigorating. He stared at the moon for a while, watching the stars peeking from the dusk. He was glad that they had left him alone. He was not sure what he would do if he had to talk to Greshcly or someone. It just felt refreshing to be by himself and outside. He would have stayed for a while, but he knew Ilana would be waiting for him, hopefully with some real food.

He walked into Serif and began to wind the familiar pathways toward his home. It felt good to be able to walk and wander. He did not waste time, however, and soon rounded the corner to his home. He stood in front of the wooden door for a few brief moments before knocking. The door sounded hollow as his knuckles rapped lightly on it.

The door flew open, and there stood Ilana. He stared at her for what seemed like an eternity. She had blond curls that cascaded down her shoulders. Light freckles dusting her nose. But most of all he missed her bright green eyes. She leapt from the doorway into his arms. As he kissed her, he realized that he had a hunger for more than just food.

After being fully satisfied, Croy and Ilana lay together amongst their pillows. His stomach was full and his arms were full. They lay there quietly enjoying being together for quite some time before he asked her about Larelt. He knew it was a school that taught something about healing the mind. And he knew that the progenitors of the school were trying to make it into a guild. So far they had not made any headway.

"So, can you finally tell me what you left to go learn? Or are there still secrets that you have to keep?" Croy kept his voice light because there had been some arguments about Larelt in the past. Luckily she laughed. He had always loved hearing her laugh.

"No. No more secrets. You have to understand, though, that the time of birth is the most vulnerable time in the life of anything. The need for secrecy is still great, so you can't tell anyone what we speak of." She laughed again, but Croy knew she was serious.

"Of course, you have my word. I will not even tell my sheep." She raised herself up onto an elbow. Her hair cascaded across her long, thin neck. She looked down upon Croy as she began speaking again. Not haughtily, but still above him.

"First of all is health. The whole of health. We know from our study of magic how powerful the mind is. Through our minds, we can heal or kill. Through our magic, we can do this to others, through our will. But how does magic begin? Do we start off with words of power? No. We start with little things. We push reality in a tiny way, in a direction it was close to going anyway. We do this without meaning to—consciously, at least." She seemed to be glowing slightly as she spoke. Croy wondered if she was casting a spell on him. He tried to remember if the Blind One seemed to brighten when he used magic. "This is one of the main tenets of Larelt. We push energy unconsciously. Many Gaens can *only* use magic unconsciously. The easiest thing to control with unconscious magic is, of course, yourself. You don't have to fight another will to control yourself. But, of course, the problem arises when your conscious and your unconscious are in conflict."

"What? I was with you for most of that, but why would I use my energy against myself?" Croy thought he might be able to answer that if he thought about it long enough, but he wanted to see what the masters of Larelt would say.

"Well, that is the issue, isn't it? That is exactly why the school of Larelt was created. We have several images of ourselves. Some of them we consciously project and try to cultivate. Some of them are more hidden and difficult to control. That is why we learn to DreamWatch. Only a derlian's dreams allow a view of the purely unconscious image that we hold of ourselves. And that image is often the most important, because it is the most difficult to change or control." Ilana was speeding up in her speech. Croy knew that she was enjoying talking about what she believed in, what she had learned. He did not want to interrupt her.

"DreamWatch?" It just popped out of his mouth.

"Yes. I am not a great mage, but at Larelt we learned several spells that allow me to see what another derlian is dreaming. Then I can interpret what they think about the world, those around them, and—most importantly—themselves." She smiled down upon him with large pupils.

"Could you influence them? Could you make someone dream what you wanted?" Croy had a harried thought about his own dreams.

"No. Well, it is hard to say no. Larelt herself said that she was still unable to achieve that. But she tried and tried. If there is any Gaen who will figure that out, it will be her. Oh, it was so exciting there." Croy stretched his neck up and kissed her lightly on the lips.

"I did not even know that there was a Larelt. I thought that was just the name of the school." He laughed briefly, but happily, at his own myopic assumptions. He realized, too late, that Ilana might mistake his laughter.

"Of course it is named after someone, what else are things named after? Can you imagine being around when Serif found the main entrance of our great city? Can you imagine knowing him? That is exactly why I had to go to Larelt. Soon there will be a guild, and I can say that I was at its pregenesis. I can say that I watched its birth. This is almost as exciting to me as learning the knowledge of Larelt. The secrets that I am privy to will be passed to others eventually. Some of those who follow will find and learn even more amazing secrets. But I… I have experiences that few will ever even hear of, but many will dream of. All of those who follow will wonder what happened at the first convocation of Larelt, before the guild was recognized. They will wonder what Larelt was like, how she taught, what *her* dreams were like. You cannot imagine some of the things that other Gaens dream of, it is completely amazing." Croy was happy that she was not paranoid about his laughter. That is one of the many things that made Ilana great, thought Croy. They talked long into the night.

When Croy awoke, Ilana was already moving around. As he rolled over, she came over to sit next to him on their bed. "You won't believe the dream I had, I wish you could have seen it." Ilana spoke quickly with her excitement.

"It was in the Northern Desert between us and the Luften lands. There in the burning center was a deep, placid lake. I was flying over in… it was like being encased in feathers, but they were leaves. When I looked down at the lake, I could see a Derlian floating in the center of it. He started to spin in a circle faster and faster until he turned into a black dot, like a pupil. I fell back towards the ground and landed in a tree. The leaves molted off of me and melted back onto the branches. I fell down and started to run. I couldn't tell what type of run it was. I don't think I was scared or that I was trying to escape something, but it was more that I just had somewhere to go." Ilana paused for a moment, her eyes lifting upwards in thought. "I don't recall where I was headed, but as I was running, I noticed a vulture circling overhead. I sort of jogged along, looking upwards at the carrion eater while my feet blurred underneath, when another swooped into view. Then another. I think I was beginning to get worried. The sky began to dim with the silent soaring vultures. I arced my run back towards where I had started—the lake. The vultures started to get bolder, swooping down at me. My heart was racing with my growing fear. I pushed myself harder and harder, going faster and faster. The vultures swerved and dove. The lake looked black, the sky was so thick with them. Finally I was able to throw myself into the lake. I crashed through the darkness and swam through ink. And there, on the other side, was a bright sky through clear water. As I surfaced and filled my lungs with fresh air, I realized I could not get back. But when I awoke... I felt so refreshed and energized... It was amazing. I had to get up and move around so as not to wake you." Ilana laughed infectiously.

The next three days passed in a blur. Croy did not realize that the Blind One was giving him a gift until it was taken away. It was after breakfast, but before lunch, when the knock came. It was loud and insistent but had a measured, almost slow, cadence. Croy had warned Ilana, explained as much as he could about all of the different things that had happened to him while she was at Larelt, but he felt that they were woefully unprepared when the knock came.

It was not the Blind One and an entourage of 'jin to haul him away, as Croy had imagined, but just Greshcly. "Croy, may I speak with you?" Greshcly eyed Ilana briefly and made a nod to the side with his head.

"Anything you want to say to me you can say in front of Ilana." Croy was slightly annoyed that they would attempt to take him away without Ilana around. He, at least, wanted to be able to say his goodbyes. Apparently Ilana was not thinking along the same lines.

"Of course. I will return shortly, Croy." She kissed Croy longingly, but much too quickly, before she left. The door sounded hollow when it shut behind her. Croy's eyes drifted from the solid closed door, so slowly, to Greshcly's face. Greshcly broke into a large, sincere grin.

"Do not worry Croy. The Blind One is privy to your situation, and the last thing he wants to do is to make things more difficult for you. Therefore, we will be moving you, and Ilana, to the 'jin section of Serif. There, instead of herding sheep, you will be learning magic under him. Each night will be yours to spend at home. How does that sound?" Greshcly patted Croy lightly on the shoulder.

"That sounds amazing. Thank you." Coy did not know what to say. His mind was too pessimistic to let him fully enjoy the news. Even though the offer was better than he had thought it was going to be, in fact it was amazing that there was even an offer, a part of him resented anybody telling him where he and Ilana had to live, what they could do. He was, in effect, stunned between two thoughts. Greshcly, for his part, continued with gusto.

"Not immediately, of course. I will come by in three more days with some Beo'jin to move your things for you. And then you will be given a few more days to get settled. So, in about a week, your apprenticeship will truly begin. Oh, I almost forgot. Your stipend." Greshcly's hand flipped over in a blur. Luckily, Croy's hands automatically flopped over to catch the coin purse. "Three days' time." Greshcly waved three fingers and let himself out.

Time, as is want to do, passed quickly. Soon many moons had passed. Croy was unsure of what he had learned about magic in that time. He could still not cast any spells. He did, however, learn a lot more about Ilana and Larelt. It was on a night with a full moon that he finally put them together.

The Blind One had spent all day speaking about what he called the Guardian. "There is something blocking you, Croy. You won't let yourself believe in you. To be able to control magic, you have to know that you are capable of it. That trick, of pulling yourself up with no leverage, is very difficult to learn in the best of conditions. It is impossible to do if you cannot trust yourself. You have created an obstacle within yourself. Fear will keep you paralyzed. Self-loathing will poison you. There is an infinite amount of ways to stymie yourself, but they all point to one thing. Unhappiness with your own internal make-up, with who you are. When did your destiny diverge from your dreams? Or is it your dreams that have diverged from your destiny?"

"I… I don't think I know what you mean." The question had caught Croy off guard. He was truly not sure what the Blind One was hinting at.

"A derlian's happiness and self-respect hinge on one thing. That is how close the path of their life is to the path of their dreams. Unfortunately for us, there is very little we can do to change our dreams. It is also, paradoxically so, very difficult to change the course of our lives. That is why we make up ideas such as destiny to be able to verbalize the chaotic frustration that stems from not being in control of our own happiness. Do you see where I am getting at?" Croy could remember the Blind One's face clearly as he finished his little speech. There was a smugness that almost irked Croy pasted on his face.

"No. Not really." Croy could not understand why the Blind One did not just say what he meant. Why was he supposed to guess?

"When the path of divergence becomes too great, we create something inside of us. Maybe it was always there and the divergence gives it strength and substance. Anyway, Gaens call this creation the Guardian. The Guardian protects your inner self, where your power is seated, from the outside world. But as the divergence increases, the Guardian ends up blocking ourselves from this same self. For some Gaens, conquering the Guardian is easy. It is mainly naming it and understanding its composition. Then overcoming it follows naturally. But for you, Croy, I have a sneaking suspicion it will be a difficult uphill climb. I believe you know all of the words, Croy. You know as much of magic as I can teach you. I can do nothing for you until you defeat your Guardian. Our apprenticeship is in a state of remission." The Blind One's face shifted from smug to morose in the blink of an eye.

"I don't know how, though. How can I identify my Guardian? I don't even know what my dreams are or what my destiny is. Are you saying that you refuse to teach me any more? That I have to figure something out that I don't even know what it is before you will teach me how to figure anything out?!" Croy had suddenly become emotional.

"Yes. I am saying that there is nothing I can do for you, Croy. Not about this. Believe me when I say that I wish I could do more to help you. I would not have put all of this time and energy into you if I had thought I could not teach you. But the truth of the matter, Croy, is that I do not know what is holding you back. I have tried to find it over the last couple of moons you have been learning from me. It is not that I won't be available for advice, but just that we can no longer have our daily sessions. Once you have cleared this blockage, we will pick up where we have left off. But until then, I am worried that any more time put into learning things beyond what you are capable of will be unproductive. Magic is something that must be learned in two parallel and equal paths. One is that of knowledge. You are doing wonderful on this path. The other is the internal change necessary to accomplish. This is where you are stuck. The knowledge will flow off of you like water from a duck's back if you cannot put it into practice." The Blind One had trailed off to nothing.

"But how do I do it? What if I can't? Do you just want me to go back to herding sheep?" Croy felt resigned. He felt defeated. Was all of his effort wasted?

"No, Croy, I want you to succeed. It is just that this is a personal issue, and I cannot help you with it. You need to look into your past, back to when you did the worst thing you can think of. Or maybe it was that you did nothing when you needed to do something great. Examine what you find there, why did you do what you did? Name your Guardian. Then, when you understand why you have fed your Guardian while starving yourself, you can figure out how to kill it. Send a message through Greshcly when you feel you have defeated your Guardian, and I will see if that has done the trick. Hopefully we will be meeting regularly again soon." The Blind One stood and waved his hand. Croy figured that was his signal to go. He had so many more questions, but apparently the Blind One was no longer willing to listen. He turned and walked away.

Thankfully Ilana had been home. He was embarrassed to weep in front of her. He was just so frustrated. He was angry. Just the thought of the Blind One made his blood boil. He was angry at Synde for forcing Trela on him. He was furious at Trela for running away and getting Nolt killed. He felt like he had no control over anything. He felt impotent. The spells just would not come. He had tried as hard as he could. He kept expecting to pass out, get a nosebleed, or give himself a hernia. Something was just missing, though. Truth be told, he was angry with himself for not being able to make any ground. He could not improve if he could not even start. He felt nothing while trying to cast a spell. Not a thing. That was what bothered him the most. The desire to succeed, to not let anyone down, had made him forget that he had not wanted any of this in the first place.

Ilana waited patiently until he had explained all he could. She let him talk himself out. Then, while he lay sad and spent on some cushions, she made her suggestion. "Maybe the Blind One is right. I… I would like to watch you trance. I think I can help, if you let me." Ilana's eyes were bright.

"Trance?" Croy knew she had mentioned it before, but he could not think of what it was. Not in definition definitely, and not much by impression either. He was hoping she would explain rather than lecture him on paying attention. Of course she did, she was wonderful in that way.

"Trance is like a controlled dream you have while half awake. At Larelt I learned how to watch them as well as dreams. It is much the same on the observing side. You can control your own trance after you have some experience, but at first I can guide the trance. I can nudge you towards what you need to learn. At Larelt we would guide each other, learning both how to trance and how to watch, puzzling out old pains, pitfalls and snares. I bet I could help you find this 'Guardian' that the Blind One speaks of." Ilana sounded excited and earnest, and it began to infect Croy.

"How do you do it? Is it difficult?" Croy paused slightly for dramatic effect. "Is it painful?"

"Well, we get you relaxed first. There are herbs that will help, and incense is beneficial. I talk you from the clouds down into the ground. By the end you will be in your cave. Every time you trance, you should begin in your cave. It's nice to start somewhere safe and peaceful. You see, trance is like a different world. Every time you visit, you make a larger impression, like footprints packing dirt into a trail. So each time you reiterate a haven for your beginning, the safer that haven becomes. Then, if something bad happens during the trance, you can always retreat to your cave and enjoy the peaceful solitude. Wouldn't it be great if the real world had a place of solace you could always escape to?" Ilana smiled warmly at Croy. "But you have to remember not to talk. The communication is only one way. If you try, at all, to communicate with me, or even remember my existence, you will be yanked out of your trance and back here. There is only you in trance, nothing else. To acknowledge the outside world at all pulls you out. Believe me, it is not that comfortable to be jolted out of trance."

"What is in trance, then? I thought I would see other things. Other than myself, I mean." Croy was not sure if he was confusing himself.

"Oh, you will see things other than yourself. But even they are your ideas of other things. They are how you see the world. Like a representation of something, a symbol. Hmm… you think you know me pretty well, don't you?" Ilana had her brow furrowed. Croy had always liked that, how she would concentrate really hard in conversation. As if she were picking the perfect words to express her thoughts.

"Yes, pretty well. Of course, I don't know everything about you."

"Right, exactly. So what you have of me is a symbol. That symbol represents what you know and think about me. You have that in you. It is not actually me. Therefore, you see, you can experience much of the outside world in trance. It is just that it will only be your own symbols that you see." Ilana's face relaxed, and she smiled when she finished talking. Croy assumed that she felt she'd explained what she needed to. He was not so sure, but he did not want to make her explain it all again.

"Well, there is no time like the present. I think some tea and relaxation would be great." Croy laughed a little, but he knew he was going to have an incredibly difficult time relaxing.

"You are weightless. Floating. Lose all sensation in the tips of your fingers and in your toes. No, keep your eyes closed. Listen to me, Croy. Let yourself feel your exhale. Forget the inhale, just concentrate on breathing out. Every time you let out your breath, feel your body less and less. You want constant, even breathing. Feel yourself getting lighter. Rise… Rise…" Ilana's voice was soft; quiet but insistent. At first Croy felt tingly and excited. He thought he would never be able to relax. But listening to Ilana's smooth voice, he felt a warmth creep into his veins. He was afraid numbness would feel cold, but it was not that at all. He warmed up until he could no longer feel the air. His breathing slowed until he could not feel himself breathe. All there was, was Ilana's soft voice. It enveloped Croy in a soft, fluffy cloud.

"Let the dark behind your eyes lighten and turn white. Blank white. You are floating high in the air, surrounded by white. You are weightless. You have left your body. Now feel the white disperse into smoke cut with purple. You start floating back towards the ground. Slowly. Safely. You can feel the pull of the soil. Feel the wind coming up from underneath you as you descend. The vapors wafting past you are shifting slightly, getting lighter. Turning a light blue. Breathe in the vapors as you descend. Let them filter through you. Feel them travel in and out through your lungs. Focus on breathing smoothly, becoming lighter with your descent. The vapors are getting lighter along with you. They are turning a brilliant green. You can no longer feel your body. The only way you can tell you are still falling is the wind coming from underneath. Keep your breathing smooth. You need to forget you are breathing. The vapors are getting lighter as you descend further. They are yellow now, and bright. Your temperature matches the air. You feel no heat nor cool. The air passing you as you descend does not change you in any way, does not affect you in any way. It only lets you know that you are slowly falling. Breathe shallowly, forget your body. The vapors are getting dimmer, shifting to a low orange. The air passing you becomes lighter, you are slowing. You feel nothing. You have no body. You can no longer feel yourself breathe. All you are is a mind, a color, and the sensation of descending. Which slows. The vapors are torpid now, a low red that is almost imperceptible. Your descent is slowing to a crawl. The vapors are pitch black. You are floating in the void. There is no sensation other than my voice. There is nothing but your essence floating in nothing. There is only your essence. The descent stops. The emptiness stops. You feel a cold firmness under your back. You have reached your cave. Take some time to familiarize yourself with your surroundings. Once you feel safe, you may leave your cave to find your Guardian. There will be a path that will lead you there." Ilana's voice faded into the distance. Croy no longer felt that he was moving, but Ilana seemed to be getting further away. He suddenly seemed completely alone. He thought he could hear a whisper off in the distance. Nufintotto! He wanted to see but did not want to open his eyes. He should have asked Ilana what to do once the trance had started, but he had not thought of it in time.

When he opened what he thought were his eyes, he saw that he was in a dimly lit cave.

He wandered the perimeter. There was a stout door at one side of the large circular room. It looked much like the one he owned now. Much like most of the doors in Serif. There seemed to be writing in the stone walls. Croy wandered over to where he noticed some and squinted hard to see the words. He wished that there was more light, so he could read them easier. Just then the room grew brighter. Stunned, he forgot the writing on the wall for a while, and shifted the room from complete darkness to blinding white light, back and forth. When he had exhausted his interest in that, he refocused on the cave walls.

Croy could now see the writing easily, but it was incomprehensible. The symbols looked vaguely familiar. Some appeared to be Gaen letters, others were magical glyphs, some were a mixture, and they all seemed to be in a random order. It also appeared that there were no vowels, but Croy quickly became weary with attempting to tease meaning into them. Instead he felt an irresistible urge to explore. He opened the door with his hand, though he felt he could have done it with his mind. As he walked outside, he noticed the sky first. The clouds were a low orange, framing his view closely, making it seem like he had a roof over his head. It was strangely comforting. There was a lot of sagebrush near the cave's door. A small grove of trees were in the distance and, almost comically, a small path led towards it. The path was a dusty wandering trail, but he could not feel any rocks under his feet. Though the path had seemed long, Croy was soon approaching the trees. He was not sure if time sped up or the distance got shorter. He stopped at the first tree, outside of the main bunch, and stared at the rest of them. He suddenly felt fear. It was like a dagger. It pierced quickly and stymied him. He paused for a moment with a parade of possible horrors flashing through his mind. He stopped to take a quick breath and clear his mind. The trees were crammed against each other tightly making it difficult to see into them even along the open path. They were incredibly large hazel trees, with limbs intertwined like the threads of a woven fabric, larger than should have been possible. Steeling himself against the unknown, he walked amongst the hazels.

The orange light was filtered through so many leaves that the path was getting dark. The tree limbs were high above him, though, and the path was wide enough to hold both of his arms out and not touch a branch. To either side, however, the trees were so closely locked together that they were almost a solid wall of wood. He walked further and further into the heart of the wood. Croy got to the point that he could barely see, so much of the sky was blocked out, and had to walk with his arms held out in front of him. He had finally decided to stop when it happened. The air burst into light.

He gasped inwards as a black figure emerged from the light. The paralyzing fear from the edge of the wood came unbidden back to him, but he was able to peek through his fingers at the blinding image. It had the horns of a ram and a great mane of hair merging with its beard. Great, green, glowing eyes. Wide shoulders and rippling biceps, there he stood. But not on derlian legs. The bottom half of him was a great chestnut horse. It reared its front hooves and stretched his arms towards the dark sky.

"I am the swarming maelstrom of life. The pulsating energy of the natural world that chaos thrusts upon you daily. The overwhelming force that is unseen but felt. This is what you use as an excuse for failure. Your incessant need to be alone. But this does not have to be so!" The apparition's front hooves struck the ground with a thunderous crash. "I am what keeps life surging forward. Tap into to me, Croy. Feed from the purest source. Shun me no more!" The beast rushed quickly forward with its four feet quick like a spider. He picked Croy up with both of his powerful hands. He held Croy aloft like a babe in an obscure ritual. "You must learn to live, Croy. At the most basic level, in the most amorphic and primordial sense. Beyond me are the riches that dreams begin at, but failure could be catastrophic. In my own way, I hate you for your cowardice. You force me to be strong, to be aggressive. I will do my best to destroy you." At that, however, the great, hairy, grimacing face shook its curled horns and let him down gently onto the forest floor. "My only aid to you I give because I must. I give you my name only, merely my identity." The horns thrashed the air above Croy. They moved so quickly they seemed to make a whistling noise. The great mane tossed in rough paroxysms around a leathery face that pinched together, whether in pain or anger, Croy was unsure of. "I am apathetic cynicism. I am myopic introversion. I am the chaos of indecision. I am petrification. I am cessation of action for terror of error. I am happy to not be counted on. I am the suffocation from so many options. The fear that uses Mediocrity as a salve. The unattainable and, therefore, unassailable peak of perfection. I am Inertia of Opportunity, Croy. That is what I am. The hunt has begun, it is time you gave chase." With that, the being leapt back into the brush, deeper and darker into the trees. Croy was unsure of whether he should leave the trance to talk to Ilana about his encounter. Maybe to plan his next move. Or maybe the beast meant to chase him now. Through the impenetrable undergrowth, scrambling and scratching. He stood there for a moment trying to figure out what the best option would be.

It was then that he realized what the Guardian really was. He flung himself forward into the clawing brush. Thrashing wildly, Croy ran the mercifully quick gauntlet of trees before bursting onto another path. He could see the sky again as the path widened. From behind, the Guardian did not look derlian in the slightest. Hooves pounding the hard packed dirt, great muscled flanks stretching out in stride, and the wild mane flashing in the orange light. It was pure beast. Croy realized it was much faster than he was. As the horse beast sped away, Croy started to slow down. It was almost as if the two speeds were diametrically opposed. He knew that he could not catch it. It had four legs and a hearty disposition, while he had two legs and was feeling more defeated by the moment. He paused in his running to catch his breath, his hands resting on his knees, panting. He realized again that he was in a trance. It was bizarre how he could be chasing a beast that he had never even thought of before, but felt he could not be fast enough to catch up. It was his trance, was it not?

His feet churned underneath him. The trees on either side of him began to blur. He could feel the wind whip by him. As he came sprinting over a small rise, he noticed the Guardian in a leisurely paced canter. The trees spread wider as he rushed after the Guardian. As he was gaining on the beast, it turned its head and noticed Croy. With that, it began to speed up. They thundered across an open plain. Croy was slowly gaining, but he kept trying to go faster. He was moving faster than he ever had while awake, even on horseback, so he seemed able to do anything he could think of while in trance. Yet he seemed unable to go any faster. He was getting close, but he was just not gaining as much ground as he had been. As his mind focused on his speed, he seemed to slow down.

Then he suddenly realized he could fly. He jumped from the ground into the air. Somewhere in his mind he knew that he should theoretically be able to run as fast on the ground as he could in the air. After all, he was already going faster than any bird he had seen in the sky. Somehow, however, it did make a difference in his mind. He caught up to the galloping beast while running in the air and leapt down upon it. His legs gripped the beast's flanks while his hands grappled with its horns. He felt alive and excited. So much energy coursed through Croy that he glowed. He felt the curved ram's horns in his grip, and they were cold and rough like stone.

Croy pulled so hard on the horns that it felt like he was going to tear his arms out of their sockets. The beast let out a horrible roar and its whole body shook. It began to buck and bellow. Croy had one foot planted on the beast's equine back and another braced against the beast's derlian back. Legs spanning two spines, he yanked with all of his might. The beast gave a deafening scream of terror and pain while Croy screamed with the exertion of it all. There was a noise that rose above the din, a horrible crack that sounded like a felling tree. Croy was flung end over end into the air and impacted hard onto the rough ground. The wind was knocked out of him, and he lay there for a little while. Just breathing. Finally he felt that he had the strength to stand.

He walked over to where his Guardian lay. The beast did not twitch as Croy approached, and he was suddenly afraid that he was not supposed to actually destroy it. Was he not going to get information from it? Was he only to get its name? Or did the simple fact of vanquishing it set him free in some way? He wanted to jolt awake and attempt some spell. Something simple and easy, just to prove that he had accomplished something. Then the beast stirred. He rushed closer and knelt by its head.

"Tell me what to do." Croy stroked some of the wild hair from its sweaty face.

"You must never say that again, Croy. That is what you must do. You must rise above your insecurities and fears to do what you want to do. Follow your heart, Croy. Even if it takes you through the tallest of mountains or the driest of deserts. Trust that you will find the sustenance you need." As the creature died, it faded. Soon there was nothing left, and Croy was just staring at the ground. There were no wildflowers there, nothing spectacular, just grass. With that thought, he wandered back to his cave. He did not know where he was going, or how he arrived so quickly after being so far away, but soon the cave loomed before him and he entered.

Croy was not sure how he was to leave, so he walked in and laid down in the center of the cave. He closed his eyes and relaxed. Soon he felt himself rising slowly, and quickly thereafter he heard Ilana's soft, smooth voice speaking to him of clouds and colors. He simply let the words wash over him and he awoke from trance.

"That was amazing! You did great, Croy. I can't believe that you accomplished what you set out to on your first try. Most neophytes spend their first couple of times in trance exploring the world, learning the basic rules and mores. I took three vacations before I even tried a work trance." Ilana was glowing above Croy.

"Did you see the whole thing?" Croy felt drained. Slowed.

"Yes. And I think I know what we should do. We need to go to the desert, Croy, the Northern Desert. It is there we shall find our destiny." Ilana kept smiling at him. He remembered the last words of the Guardian. It seemed strange to him that much of the trance was already slipping from his mind. That last part, the last words, however, was seared into his brain. He wondered why Ilana focused on the desert rather than further up the mountains. Taking her advice, though, would literally be following my heart, thought Croy.

Amazingly enough, the Blind One was incredibly enthusiastic about the idea. Croy felt as if his luck had turned a corner. There would soon be a group of Gaens heading towards the Northern Desert. It was through the 'sol guild that the expedition, if it could be called that, had originally been put together. Croy never did understand why the 'sol guild was the expedition's sponsor. There would be a total of six of them traveling together. Aedon Dea'sol was in charge of the tiny band for she had petitioned the expedition. The other civilian was Nyhan Cru'wir. Verin Mur'jin, whom Croy already knew, and another warrior called Tesjuk Fyr'jin came to provide protection. Tesjuk was already planning on going with Nyhan and Aedon, but the Blind One added Verin after Croy and Ilana were added. Croy was unsure if it was because he wanted someone of solid trust with the group—Verin was certainly in the Blind One's inner circle—or maybe he just thought that they should keep the ratio of one 'jin per two civilians. Either way, Croy and Ilana had barely packed before they were on their way. The expedition used donkeys rather than horses for the difficult terrain. Croy thought that they would lengthen the journey by some bit, but he was fond of the donkey's reputation for reliability.

The first night was awkward and quiet. It was not until the second night, after a long hot ride through the foothills, that the group tried to get to know each other. The fire was low, but still glowed nicely. The food was fantastic. It had been prepared by Tesjuk, and it turned out he was quite a cook. Croy would never have imagined it. Tesjuk was one of the largest Gaens Croy had ever seen. Both in height and in girth. It seemed he had muscles over his entire body, bulging and rippling across his thick frame. Croy had felt sorry for him in the heat of the day, but he appeared quite comfortable after the sun had set. He collected the dishes and wandered off to wash them after the meal.

Nyhan was almost the opposite of Tesjuk. He was short and wiry, with curly reddish hair and a slightly freckled face. There seemed like there was no fat on him whatsoever. But they both somehow moved with a quiet grace. Croy knew that Nyhan was on the expedition because he was an expert on different trees, but Croy was unsure of what the actual expedition was for. The few small conversations he had with Verin only proved his intuition. That Aedon had planned the entire thing, and she alone truly knew where they were going, what they would be doing, and why.

Aedon herself was taller than Nyhan and Ilana but shorter than Croy or Tesjuk. She had jet black hair. It flowed straight down her back like a frozen waterfall. She was lithe and had long expressive fingers. Not that Croy had known any, but she looked like she should be a short Fluen, not a Gaen. Croy decided that tonight he was going to find out why the expedition existed.

"So, I guess we are heading due north. Will we continue that course until we get... to where we are going?" Croy stared pointedly at Aedon. She gave him a sardonic smile and stood.

"The trail was long today and the trek tomorrow will also be so. I bid all of you a good night." She nodded towards Nyhan and left to her tent. It was incredibly quiet until Tesjuk came back to the glowing coals.

"Did Aedon turn in already?" Tesjuk started to quietly put the cleaned dishes back into the camp box.

"Yes. The farmer was pressing her for details." Nyhan pointed towards Croy. Croy felt the hot burn of embarrassment reach his cheeks. He felt like he should stammer something in his defense. Then Nyhan smiled widely and nodded towards Tesjuk. Tesjuk leaned towards Croy conspiratorially.

"I tried to get her to explain this whole thing when we first met. She won't tell anybody what is going on. She won't even tell Nyhan why she needs him. Or at least, that is what he says." With the last sentence Tesjuk elbowed Croy gently in the ribs.

"So why did Aedon hire you?" Croy was looking at Nyhan, watching his shoulders as they started to rise, and a smile crept into his lips. Before he could protest, Croy continued. "What is your specialty? What area of expertise brought you to your surname of Cru'wir?" Croy flashed a wide smile back at Nyhan. Verin stood and wandered over to her horse. Slyly pulled a tiny cask from her saddle bags and handed it to Nyhan. He laughed and pulled the small bung from the end. But he glanced at Aedon's tent a little too worriedly as he did so. Croy realized that he should carefully filter anything that Nyhan said about Aedon or this mission.

"I specialize in wood. Well, in trees. I specialize in the different species of trees that produce different types of wood. The various ways to dry the wood for different applications. The densities and strengths of different types. You know..." Nyhan waved his hand towards Croy vaguely. He took a large drink and then passed it off to Tesjuk. "Apparently we are searching for a specific tree. In the desert. You know..." He waved again slightly. It seemed weird to see someone as naturally controlled as Nyhan seem to talk nervously. Either he was nervous because he was embarrassed not to know what Aedon was up to or he did know something and was trying not to say anything. Croy figured that if Nyhan was uncomfortable admitting what the expedition was about, then he should let him off the hook.

"And what is your specialty, Tesjuk?" Croy turned towards Tesjuk and realized that he was holding the tiny cask out to take from him. He took it and imbibed mightily. There was a pleasant sensation in his throat as the warm and flat beer slid down.

"Well, since you asked, I specialize in fighting groups. Since we have a small expedition, it was decided that we should be protected by the best." He made an obvious wink and nodded towards Verin. She was taking the tiny cask from Ilana. She smiled slightly and held it aloft before taking a drink. "And just what is your specialty, farmer? How come you are in this expedition?" Croy's mind raced trying to think of something. Truth be told, he was unsure of why he was in the expedition.

"Actually, I am here to further my apprenticeship with the Blind One. It is in the desert that all of our destinies await us." Croy was looking at Ilana.

"And you, Ilana? Why are you with us?" Verin was looking intently at Ilana.

"I have just come back from Larelt, where I had visions. All of them ended in the center of the Northern Desert. I have felt a compulsion to find that spot ever since. When Croy's Guardian told him to head to the desert, I got this amazing tingling sensation. Like I was about to pass out but without my sight blurring. It was a delicious feeling." Ilana leaned towards Verin as she was talking.

"Oh, when Croy told you about his trance. I have heard of mages trancing before. Seeing their own dreams. Sometimes I wish I had any skill in that area." The cask had come around again, and Verin took a last mighty draught. She looked comically into the open bunghole. "Libations," she said dryly, and tossed the cask into the fire.

At that Tesjuk laughed, stood, and produced another tiny cask from his own saddlebags. He tossed it over the coals to Verin. "I would appreciate it if you would start that."

"I'll bet you would." Verin laughed back at him. It was suddenly quiet, then Ilana spoke up.

"No, when I saw his trance. In fact, I am trained to see dreams. I could even help you trance." Ilana smiled a little too wide. Her cheeks were high and tight with her smile. Verin laughed nervously and passed Tesjuk's cask to Nyhan.

"You should sneak a peak at Aedon's dreams." Nyhan had a devious look on his face. Through the gathering haze in Croy's brain came the thought that Nyhan might have been telling the truth about not knowing what the true purpose of the expedition was.

"No, I could never do that. I can only work with willing participants." Ilana suddenly looked flushed.

"Can't... or won't?" Nyhan looked boldly at Ilana.

"Both. You would have to be highly skilled to accomplish such a task, and I am just a neophyte. More importantly, however, the mere idea of working without consent is repugnant to the ethos of my school." The speech seemed to straighten Ilana's spine.

"No offense intended. I was just curious what you meant." Nyhan took a large drink and passed the tiny cask to its owner.

"You know what I hope is in our destiny? A good fight so that I can see you at work." Tesjuk was staring intently at Verin. He watched her hungrily beyond the cask as he drank.

"You should be careful what you wish for." Verin let out a throaty laugh. Croy took the cask and swore to himself that it would be the last drink of the night.

The night stretched out a little too long but it was enjoyed by all. They did not learn anything specific about each other. There were no heart-to-hearts or long soliloquies. But afterwards they all felt more comfortable with each other. They immersed themselves in camaraderie. They would look upon this night, many sun cycles later, as the moment when their friendship began. The morning came early but relatively painlessly.

It took four days to reach the edge of the Northern Desert. They had followed a stream through the last of the foothills and planned to follow it as far as they could. The crew set up a semi-permanent camp. They were going to wait there until one of them had hunted down a big game animal. Aedon figured that at least one large elk would almost add a full moon to the amount of time the expedition could be wandering the desert.

Croy was not as optimistic as she was, but maybe that was because he was still unsure as to what their mission was. He did know how hard and stony the ground ahead looked. And he had heard about the sand dunes, shifting and shapeless, without a thimble of shade across its entire expanse. It separated each of the derlian's realms. No Gaen had been known to make it all the way across it. One could go from the Gaen lands to the Pyran's or the Fluen's lands, but never straight to the Luften's. Croy could not think of a Gaen alive who had even seen a Luften. Most of the few descriptions of Luftens were verbal tales from Fluen or Pyran traders at the borderlands. He made the unsettling realization that he had not really thought about what they were up against. He had never dreamed that he would be at the edge of the Northern Desert, let alone contemplating finding its center. He was suddenly afraid of not being able to endure the coming hardships. The whole journey began to seem alien and surreal. He was unsure of why he was there. His

Guardian had mentioned a mountain as well. Maybe he was supposed to be traveling further into the Gaen lands, ascending the tall peaks of the Uryol mountain range instead of wandering in a deadly hot desert. He wondered what he was supposed to find in the desert. What lesson learned? What breakthrough could possibly enable him to become a mage? To be able to call upon chaos at will. To shape the very reality around him. So he was in a pensive, not panicked, state when the sound of a horn blasted through the last scraggly trees amongst the foothills. The horn signified that the hunt was over. That just as they were getting settled they would be getting up and going on again. Croy shook himself from his reverie and reached down to help Ilana to her feet. They should be following the sound of the horn to help haul the kill back to camp.

"There goes our peace and quiet." Ilana bounded up the hill. Croy followed with the paced gait that he used while herding. For a while Ilana grew farther and farther away. Eventually, though, he began to catch up to her. Finally she stopped, just barely out of breath, and waited while he caught up. They walked together up into the hills for a while before another horn blast shook the air.

It was Nyhan who had killed the elk, and he had already quartered the gigantic beast by the time of their arrival. Croy and Ilana were the first to show up and were each quickly outfitted with a packboard and a humungous piece of elk. Nyhan promised to catch up with them as soon as another member of the expedition showed up. He made good on his promise after about a half-hour. Tesjuk and Nyhan could be heard crashing through the brush behind Ilana and Croy. They finally reached the camp after another hour of walking together. They all took time salting and drying what meat they could, preparing for the journey. They packed up their camp and loaded the donkeys. They headed out into the unknown.

It was another week into the desert that the stream finally dried up. It traveled down into a gully, and then just sank into the ground in a muddy pool. They took their fill of water before it got too murky. Aedon decided to head a little west. She felt they had followed the river too far east. That night they knew they would no longer be following a natural landmark. They all sat around her and begged her to explain their mission. Or at least let them know more of the short-term goals. She hemmed and hawed for some time before she broke down and told them what her research was.

She made it clear that the only reason she was telling them anything was that there was no turning back at this point. They were about to embark deep into the dunes, the true desert. The Northern Desert. She made them all swear to solidarity. To the mission. Croy thought it odd that she would want them to swear to something before they knew what it was, but no one protested. It seemed inconceivable to quit now, so what was the point in protesting the promise of cooperation?

"We are in search of Vijen. An elusive tree. It walks when you are not looking and stands still under observation. It is said to have the gifts of prophecy, though often speaks in such riddles as to be incomprehensible. There are rumors that they have showed up uncalled for, sometimes to aid a Gaen. There are even some Gaens who have been a magnet to them, almost to the point of being harassed by them. Unfortunately, they have not been seen for some time. Some amongst the Dea' had even begun to think that they were the stuff of legend. Recently, however, there have been reports flooding in of contact with the Vijen." Here she paused briefly. "Recently as in the last two moons before we left Serif. At first we assumed that there were some pranksters who had learned of the legend of the talking trees. Then we debated about whether the heat wave that had been assaulting the desert as of late had been 'cooking' the brains of its trekkers. Many of the witnesses spoke of other hallucinations brought upon by the heat of the desert. It was difficult to believe some who freely admitted to being delusional at times, even if they would swear they were lucid for certain experiences with the most vehement of oaths. The Assembly was eventually convinced that the phenomenon was real. That is why this expedition was made so hastily." Aedon spoke slowly and with purpose. It gave her words an air of fiction to be spoken so deliberately. But she always seemed to speak like that, so it was hard for Croy to be completely prejudiced against her speech even though he was naturally paranoid.

"So, what do the trees say to the Gaens?" Croy wondered aloud.

"I am not at liberty to say, Croy, but your point is well taken. I will try to include more information in my directives. I, too, am dedicated to the expedition's success and will answer any questions that I can." Aedon took a deep breath and looked around the circle.

"Why do we not have a member of the expedition that has recently seen a Vijen?" Verin nodded towards Aedon. Her eyes were narrow. Croy was unsure if they were playfully so. Aedon cleared her throat quietly.

"Many of those who came back are still under observation. Plus, not all of the encounters were… shall we say… pleasant? To be sure, this will end up a dangerous mission. You should all keep aware at all times. Just because this leg of the journey is vast and empty does not mean we should let our guard down. Tomorrow will come quickly and the day will be long. I suggest we all get some good rest." Aedon instigated her nightly disappearing act. This time, however, everyone else seemed ready to turn in as well. They had begun to ration themselves from the luxury items that they had previously shared so gluttonously. A brief amount of time passed as they stared at the fire before heading to their individual tents.

Another week passed and Croy was certain they were completely lost. Aedon would periodically check her compass, the needle always pointing north, but it seemed like they kept going different directions. They would head west for a while, then they would wander east. Their path would switch like that, seemingly at random. Or the needle on the compass would switch like that, at random. They had not even seen a single tree yet, let alone a Vijen. Croy was still unsure of how to tell between a normal tree and a Vijen. "Shimmering leaves," was all Aedon would say. Or all she could say.

Ilana and Croy were whispering sweet nothings at each other when they heard the call. It was not the horn, but an excited yell, that got their attention. They had taken to loading up one donkey with all of their stuff and both riding on the other donkey. They quickly spurred their donkey on towards the noise and pulled the other behind. Silhouetted over the next rise was Tesjuk. He seemed to be pointing off in the distance, towards the west if Croy's intuition was correct. They half slid down the dune they were on and then hurried up the other side. By the time they got there, almost everyone else had already gathered. Verin was coming quickly from where she had been scouting on the opposite ridge.

"There it is. We need to keep it in constant sight, understood? At least one of us has to have an eye on it at all times. Tesjuk, secure the extra pack animals." Aedon was pointing and giving orders when Croy and Ilana showed up. Their second donkey, the one with all of their stuff, got tied up with the other pack animals. Not wanting to slow the pursuit by shifting gear around, Croy and Ilana sat dutifully on their shared donkey. "The Vijen can escape in a less than a second if we lose our direct sight line. We will take turns in twos watching it. Then we can leap frog our way over to it. Croy and Ilana will watch first. We will try to keep an eye on it as well, but… Try to coordinate your blinking." Aedon spurred her donkey forwards, with Tesjuk following quickly behind. Nyhan and Verin were the next group. There were four camp-laden donkeys staked to the ground with long ropes around them, but Croy dared not glance at them. They had gotten off the donkey so that it would not betray them by meandering. Eventually they agreed upon a system where they would give each other warning before blinking, rather than blinking on specific intervals.

"How do you think the other Gaens snuck up on the Vijen?" Croy asked as they stared fixedly in front of them. "Blink."

"Ok." Croy gratefully blinked while Ilana talked. "I think that the Vijen must sneak up on them. In fact, I wonder if some could be sneaking up behind us right now. We would not know until it was too late. Blink."

"Ok." Croy tried to answer as quickly as possible, so that Ilana would not have to wait to blink. "Do you think the donkeys would stir? Maybe bleat out at something?" It was hard to talk of something else while trying stare intently into the distance. It was like a game to them. "Blink."

"OK." Ilana blurted it out. "It is amazing at how often you have to blink when cannot do it naturally. Especially in a hot desert with a dry wind. Hey, when I blink I think I am just going to keep one eye closed for a couple seconds and then the other one, all right?" She waited for him to reply, "Sure," before saying, "Blink." They decided to still warn each whenever they had an eye closed, but they felt much better for leaving one eye open.

So they went, passing the time until the other four from the expedition were yelling at them. It seemed that they had Nyhan and Verin looking at the magnificent tree while Aedon and Tesjuk moved even closer still. Croy helped Ilana onto the donkey before slinging himself up. The donkey was spurred to action but never did achieve great speed.

They kept their eyes forward as much as possible. It seemed more difficult to talk together on the swaying donkey than while they were standing and staring at the Vijen. It was not long until they overtook the first set of stony faced watchers. They said quiet goodbyes as they passed, not wanting to distract Nyhan and Verin from their duty.

The dunes seemed close together, but they were so tall that it still took a while to reach the next peak. As they got close to the peak with Aedon and Tesjuk perched atop, they could count the dunes to the increasingly large tree. There were two empty hilltops before the third, and tallest, dune supporting the grand tree sprouted from the desert floor. It seemed taller than any of the other dunes nearby. They said quiet goodbyes as they passed Aedon and Tesjuk. Aedon called out to them as they tried to hurry down the next hill, "Quickly, we are close. The weeks that we have been out here will come to fruition soon." She sounded out of breath. Like she was excited and exhausted at the same time, and they were still only within sight of the creature. Croy wondered how she would fare when they were within speaking distance. But, then again, he was unsure of how he was going to fare if he got to talk with the Vijen himself.

They moved up the next rise much slower than they had descended. It seemed to take forever before they reached the apex. Finally they were able to dismount and get situated. Croy made sure Ilana was ready, then turned and yelled back to Aedon and Tesjuk. He then turned back to the tree and really gazed at it. The words "shimmering leaves" did not give justice to the vision before him. Reflections of golden light burned into his brain through his eyes. They seemed delicate and thin, spinning in the desert sun, the color of burnished gold. The vision was so stunning that he imagined hearing music to its accompaniment. The overall shape of the tree was large, but not ill-proportioned. The top half was tall and round, covered in golden leaves. Truly, the canopy appeared solid, it was so thick with foliage. A massive sturdy trunk descended to the ground from the golden dome. It was the light brown of a hart's hide. The Vijen had strong, ropy roots snaking their way into the sand, making them seem like tentacles. It was a breathtaking sight to behold. And Croy was still barely within sight of the creature.

"Blink." Ilana's voice cut into his stunned appreciation of the Vijen.

"Ok." Croy tried to be quick but it seemed like he had taken forever to answer her. He had not been paying attention at all. "Wouldn't that be horrible. What if we blinked, instinctively, not on purpose, and the Vijen disappeared on our watch. I bet you Aedon would skin us alive. Blink."

"Ok." Ilana chimed in immediately. "I think you underestimate her reaction. She seems like she would be very passionate about her vengeance. She might end with skinning us, but I bet she starts with disemboweling. Blink."

They prattled on for quite a while before Nyhan and Verin came up behind them. Nyhan stared forwards while Verin had her donkey walk over to them.

"Keep watching. Aedon and Tesjuk are traveling currently. When Nyhan and I get to the top of the next rise, we will signal for you to follow. Come as quickly as you can, we want to have as many of us around it as close as we possibly can when we make contact." Verin nodded towards them and then hustled back to Nyhan. They descended quickly out of sight.

Ilana and Croy blinked and talked. Oddly enough, keeping a steady eye on the tree and not on Nyhan and Verin's progress was incredibly difficult. Finally Aedon and Tesjuk caught up to them. They trotted by, intensely staring ahead. The more time that passed waiting for Nyhan and Verin to reach their peak, the slower time seemed to pass. It took an excruciatingly long time to get called ahead. As soon as they heard Verin's voice, they mounted the donkey with excitement. He closed his eyes for half of the ride down the dune in an effort to remoisten them. It felt like he had sand scratching at his eyes, trapped under his lids. They pulled up next to Nyhan and Verin, and Croy glanced down briefly into the small valley below. Aedon and Tesjuk were just beginning the ascent of the hill that the Vijen occupied. Croy was unsure of when Aedon and Tesjuk would take over the observation, thereby freeing Nyhan and Verin of their post, or what type of signal they would use. He urged the donkey down the slope, chasing after Aedon and Tesjuk. As they were about halfway down, they heard Aedon yell to Nyhan.

"You are free to catch up!" She yelled towards the tree, not even twisting her head. Croy and Ilana's donkey was soon climbing the last dune, forcing them to look up. The tall round foliage of the giant tree loomed over them. When a slight breeze flowed by, the golden leaves rattled and rustled while the branches slowly swayed.

They were soon traveling in its flickering shade. As they reached the summit, they could see the magnificent tree in all of its glory. The sunlight, blinding in the open desert, was shattered into a soft golden glow. Croy estimated that the trunk was so massive, that even if every member of their expedition held hands and stretched out their arms, they would only make it half way around it. He could feel his heart pounding in his chest. He hopped off the donkey and helped Ilana dismount. It felt good to have four pairs of eyes on the Vijen. Croy was wondering if Aedon had thought of how to begin a conversation with the tree or if they were just waiting for Nyhan and Verin before starting.

"Derlians! Ha! Gaens! Ha! You who come searching for me think I do not wish to be found. I find you. You do not find me. Time is wasted by holding me still." The voice seemed to emanate from the air round them, with very little tone or inflection other than the periodic Ha! Croy's vision vibrated with the bass of the voice.

"We offer apologies, Great One. We merely meant to impress upon you the intensity of our intent. That we wish to be found by you." Aedon bowed her head at the end of her speech.

"Since time does not exist for me, I suppose I can forgive you. We move from time to time. That is how we move. Or should I say 'how I move'? No, it is more interesting to say how we move. You wish to converse? Your wish is granted. Look back upon this moment, after time has ravaged you, and regard it with awe. The opportunity is limitless. Ask your question. Speak!" The tree shook with a golden laughter. Or maybe a golden rage.

"Why are the Tlana increasing in numbers? What change is happening? What storm is brewing?" Aedon spoke up into the branches. Her black hair flowed away from her face in a sudden wind.

"Names! A thousand times. Names! Some birds fly so fast and so quiet and so high and so small and so hidden and so perceptive. We do not speak their names. As for the storm, like attracts like, and this counts doubly so for evil. The increase in the desert does not lead. It follows. The increase is with you and your kind. That makes more birds, the unspeakable ones. They fly, you know. The birds cause their own evil, that is true, which may increase the evil from derlians—Ha! —which may increase the birds, and so on. Armed, however, as you are now, with the knowledge of which is cause and which is effect, you can directly influence a decrease in birds. Stop the evil in your house. The evil will then leave the neighborhood. We all have a vested interest in inducing a shortage of birds. We all agree to be sure friends. You must do your part. You must begin." The tree shimmered and shivered.

"I do not wish to be redundant, but I need you to be clear in your explainings. What is the root evil? What derlian practice creates more of these birds?" Aedon looked beseechingly at the tree

"I have the roots, you do not. Evil is evil. Evil instigates only. It has no feel of its own. It is a hollow tool of convenience. The expedient, but incorrect, answer to a difficult and trying riddle. Why your kind revels in it, or which evil it is, I do not know." The voice echoed in the shimmering sunlight. Croy found it unsettling to not have a face or anything to look at while talking. No reading unspoken emotion through hand gestures or the tiny muscles around the eye, the shape of the lips in speech. It made the voice seem more like a Yaven's. Un-derlian. Croy could not get a good idea of the thing's mind. It was not just non-verbal communication cues either, but its basic speech and logic. For one thing, it kept saying "birds" instead of Tlana, but if anything was eavesdropping they would know exactly what the Vijen meant when it said birds. The other thing was that Croy doubted the Vijen was really saying anything at all. It spoke around subjects not about them.

"Is the recent increase in Yavencide causing the creation of more birds?" Aedon narrowed her eyes at the Vijen.

"You do not let me be me. I do not get involved in the affairs of Yavens. I cannot speak on that matter even if I had a wish to. I will, however, suggest that Yavencide is steeped in evil. Now, no more questions about that." The tree shook with rage, or maybe with laughter. With that, Aedon turned her donkey around and started back towards their pack animals. Everyone was staring at each other when Nyhan spoke up.

"How do you nourish yourself, here in the Northern Desert? How come you are never found outside of the desert? Is there a food source that keeps you tied to the desert?" Nyhan blinked up into the branches of the tree.

"Nourish implies malnourish which implies decay. Time has no meaning to me. Not for the physical manifestation of me. You are right about the desert, though. My kind does not venture out of it. Rules are rules, and different realms have different rules. We are comfortable here, to be sure." Before the tree had stopped shaking, Ilana spoke up.

"What is at the center of the desert?" Ilana's voice rang clearly in the hot golden air.

"Ha! Would you dare? There is a well that heals all wounds and satiates all hunger. One drink and you will never need regular water again. It is deeper than the sky is tall. It is older than time. Which means older than chaos. For what is time except for the cadence of decay? We would not need time if it were not for chaos. Ask the Yavens, they will tell you. That is all. I am no oracle." Ilana looked nervous but nodded. Whether it was to the Vijen or to herself, Croy was not sure. The tree had stopped shaking. Croy had hoped that there would be some leaves scattered on the shady dune, but he could not spy a one. He helped Ilana onto the donkey and then swung himself up. He looked over and saw the rest of the expedition quietly mounting up as well. It seemed better to walk away when the Vijen was finished talking than to try press it for more information.

They finally caught up with Aedon as she was ascending the last dune to where their other donkeys had been tethered. There was an eerie hush over the expedition. They all dismounted and shuffled around for a few brief moments. They were staring at sand when Aedon finally spoke.

"We may as well camp here tonight. Do we have any firewood left?" Aedon was staring away from the sun, towards the east, while she was talking.

"Yes. That sounds great. We can light a nice fire, have some more elk steaks, relax a little before we head back to Serif." Tesjuk laughed nervously. No one was sure if the expedition was over. Croy did not think they had accomplished anything to speak of, but they only had so many more days of provisions left. Croy got distracted during the awkward silence by trying to size up the expedition's provisions.

"The Vijen did not wish to cooperate at all." Aedon said that to no one in particular, and then turned back towards the group.

"It seemed about as forthright as they have ever been known to be. I believe you have enough to make your case to the Assembly." Nyhan spoke his words quietly to the ground, but every ear was listening.

"Did you get any wood?" Aedon walked over to Nyhan. Everyone else began to gather around in response.

"No. Just one small leaf. It is not much, but I think the 'wir will be pleased. I thought about going back to where it was to try to find anything that might have dropped from it. But I am not sure what kind of creature it really is. It seemed to be pretty sensitive on the issue of decay." Croy knew that he should not laugh, and it wasn't really a joke, let alone a funny one, but he found himself suddenly giggling. Even though it was only mid-afternoon, the day had seemed incredibly long. It felt good to release a little, and soon everyone else was joining in. Suddenly Verin was handing him the leaf. He took it with shaky hands. It looked and felt exactly like gold, but stiff for its thinness. It had the shape of an elongated and slightly spikier oak leaf with many extra veins. The lines kept criss-crossing and getting tinier towards the edges. It looked intricate, but somehow not quite natural. Croy smelled it, and it even smelled like metal. He passed it to Ilana without being the wiser as to what it was.

"I looked all around for a leaf lying on the ground but couldn't find anything. Where did you find it?" Croy looked over at Nyhan. Nyhan's face burst into a large smile.

"I asked for it. I was the last to leave the Vijen, and I thought I might as well take a chance. The Vijen just laughed out Ha! and then a leaf wafted down towards the ground. It then said that I, well derlians in general, were easier to deal with than the birds. So I just picked up the leaf and left." Nyhan had finally ended up with the leaf again, and he carefully wrapped it in a swaddling of cloth before he made it disappear back into his jerkin.

Tesjuk started a fire and everyone separated to put up their tents. They all took a long time doing everything. They took a while setting up the tents, and Verin took a while cooking dinner.

"I did not want to seem obnoxious, but it seems like you had a pretty good idea of what you were going to talk to the Vijen about. I was just hoping that you would share some of your knowledge. Like, if we are headed back now, or what Yavencide is?" Verin spoke what most of them were thinking but were afraid to ask.

"I suppose I owe you all that." Aedon sighed a little but did not appear to be crestfallen. "The Tlana, or birds I guess I should say, have been attacking some outpost settlers with more frequency. Since we knew that the Vijen and birds are linked somehow, we thought the Vijen would be able to offer some help. Of course, that did not happen. There has also been a new cult of Gaen magicians that practice Yavencide. My theory was that the new increase in the birds was in direct proportion to, and even a direct cause of, the cult." Aedon paused with almost another sigh, but her mouth curved into a small, wry smile instead. "Magic is transitory, you know, ephemeral. To make a sword that cuts through armor you could cast Mekdehepto, but that would only last a certain amount of time, right? There is no way to make it last for very long. Until the Cabal of Lochom found a diabolical way to trap a Yaven into an item, such as a Pyran into a sword, to make the enhanced properties permanent. So far it seems that they have succeeded, the enhancements do not appear to fade. The issue is that the Yavens then lose consciousness, if you will. They become unable to communicate or to show signs of life or even to recover. We have not been able to remove a Yaven from an item and have it survive. I have been trying to get the Assembly to ban the process and directly outlaw the Cabal. I was hoping that coming out here, braving the desert, and talking to a Vijen would help me get closer to my goal. I don't know what to do now. I am going to have to rest before I make a decision on whether or not we are headed back to Serif. I wish you all a restful night." Aedon stood and half bowed to everyone before heading back to her tent.

"Don't worry about anything. I am sure she has enough to convince the Assembly. We will probably head out early in the morning." Nyhan laughed quietly and got up and headed towards his own tent. Verin started collecting the dishes from everyone. Croy and Ilana got up to head to their tent and heard Tesjuk speaking quietly to Verin. "Here, let me help you with those dishes." The sun had barely set, and Croy and Ilana were already asleep.

The next day, Aedon decided that they should take the long way back to Serif. She said that way if they ran into a different Vijen, they could talk to it as well and maybe glean some more information, but if not then they were at least headed towards home. The group broke camp and began to follow Aedon with their donkeys at a slow walk. It was not until that evening that Aedon realized that the compass was no longer working. It would just spin in a slow circle rather than point in any particular direction.

They wandered for three days before they realized they were truly lost. They did not have a map so there was not much navigation besides the compass. Not that a map would have helped amongst the shifting dunes anyway. Plus, the sun seemed to hover directly above them for the vast majority of the day, giving no indication of its direction of travel. It was obvious that no one knew where they were headed. Aedon began to wish aloud that she would have been able to request a Gaen Yaven for added protection. Apparently no Yaven had ever seen a Vijen. Croy was unsure if the reverse was true as well.

The next day started badly and steadily declined from there. Ilana began to have a dry hacking cough in the morning. Her lips had been getting chapped over the last couple of days, but she had seemed to be feeling fine. At least she had said she was feeling fine. This morning, however, she admitted to feeling ill. The hoarse cough that had begun lightly the night before was almost constant now. They had agreed to try to travel the rest of the day, to get as far as they could before deciding what to do next.

Ilana wavered on the donkey while Croy walked beside. She had a flimsy parasol that they had rigged to the donkey's pommel. Croy had to trick her into drinking his share of the water, but she was becoming mildly delusional, so it was not that difficult. They finally stopped when dusk began to show. Croy and the others set up the tent as quickly as possible. They all helped until Ilana was comfortably set up in the tent. Then they all quietly disappeared. He looked down upon Ilana. Her face looked terribly unhealthy, wet with a sheen of sweat. It looked stretched and waxy. Her chest rose and fell raggedly. Croy was not positive, but he thought he saw black smoke drifting from her mouth. It would fade almost immediately, but it seemed quite thick when she coughed heavily. He did not know what it was, had never even heard of it, but he knew instinctively that it was a bad omen.

Croy sat hunched over her, sweating almost as much as she was. He knew what he had to do, but he was not sure if he could. He had to try to heal her. He was almost petrified with fear, but there was nothing else to be done. He knew it could not be permanent. But he hoped to heal her for long enough that they could get back to Serif.

He knew the word to use, Loliderto, but was not sure if it would last more than a few minutes even if it did work. And he was deathly afraid of not even being able cast it. He was afraid that he would try and try, only to watch Ilana die in front of him. He dared not try a higher power than Lo, though. He had never cast a successful spell yet, so he could not aspire to anything but the weakest power. He wiped his wet hands on his trousers to dry them. His thoughts circled wildly in his head.

Croy took a deep breath and held it. He placed one hand on Ilana's clammy head and his other on her belly. He wanted to be able to push energy from his right hand into her forehead, let the energy heal everything on its way through her, and pull the energy back up through his left hand. He took another deep breath. He knew that he could not think about it too much. He knew that delay and inertia were his mortal enemies. He tried to pull energy into him. He took it from all around him. The ground beneath him was full of it. He drank like a drunkard who was three days sober and had finally found a mug of beer. He pulled with all of his might until he thought he would make himself pass out.

"Loliderto!" Croy shouted it out. He could see a turquoise blue light flow from his hands and into her body. He felt the energy pour out of him. It was exquisite. Her spine straightened in a convulsive snap. She breathed out a puff of dark smoke and fell back against the pillows under her. He suddenly had a terrific headache. He ended up curled next to Ilana and he closed his eyes, waking an indeterminate time afterwards when Ilana bolted upright.

"We must go. We must find that well or I will die; I feel it deep within me. You must come with me and heal me along the way. Help me, quick, help me pack." Ilana was staggering about the tent, her shift stuck to her in spots where the cold sweat had yet to evaporate. "Just worry about getting yourself dressed. I will pack up our things." Croy attacked the bedroll while she put her traveling clothes on. They packed up their donkeys and mounted to leave. It was in the middle of the night and everyone else was asleep. Croy knew it was a bad idea. To not tell anyone where they were going. But Ilana needed to move, to head somewhere. He was not sure if she had a dream, or if she was just feeling panicked. Either way they had to leave. He wrote a quick note for the expedition and mounted behind Ilana. They trotted off into the night. Croy held on to the donkey with their meager provisions while Ilana steered the donkey they rode upon.

They rode all night like that. Ilana was as quiet as a stone, and Croy followed her lead. She would make the donkey zig off into a random direction and she would follow that line through the dark until some other impulse struck her. Then she would zag off into a completely new direction. Then they would race off straight for a while. When the sky began to lighten in the pre-dawn they were trotting with great speed, at least great speed for a pair of donkeys.

The lighter the sky got, the more it looked like they were heading for something. It looked like a low wall in the distance. They were getting closer when the sun crested the dunes. He could see the outline of a well amongst some larger shapes. How she had found it, he would never know. He supposed that it was her destiny.

They arrived at the well just as Ilana was beginning to start coughing again. They looked around. There were several small shacks nearby, but they looked dilapidated and empty. Croy even yelled out a hello to draw some derlians out. They seemed to be completely alone, however. Ilana was pulling up a bucket before Croy knew it. She poured a huge drink into her mouth and swallowed mightily. She then dropped the bucket back down into the well. She sat there panting on the stones. "Do you need a drink?" She smiled at Croy.

Then she dropped to the ground. She cried out in pain and hugged the side of the well. Croy ran over to her. He silently cursed himself as he held on to her. He had not even checked the water. It could have been black with slime and he would not have known. He should have tried it first. Tested out its toxic effects before he let her drink from it. She screamed again and shivered. She retched in the mud. All Croy could do was hold on to her. She had tears streaking her mud-caked face. She retched again. Croy felt so helpless. Then, out of nowhere, he shouted "Nuliderto!" and retched right next to her.

The sun was high in the sky when Croy awoke. There was an old derlian peering over him, dressed in simple rags. The derlian had thick leathery skin, with a patch of white wispy hair wafting in the breeze, and had a high forehead with dark spots peppered about. He still had all his teeth and looked to be in good health, though.

"You're alive. That is fantastic. I believe your lady friend is alive as well. Ahem. I was wondering if either of you drank from the well." He had an intense, crazy-looking smile on his face. He was too interested in the answer, thought Croy. He seemed too eager.

"My wife took a drink. She was sick, and our expedition got lost in the desert. A Vijen had mentioned a well that had healing powers, and we just happened upon this one. Is this your well? Are we trespassing?" Croy seemed suddenly confused. He felt weak.

"My well? Well, yes, I guess it is my well." The old derlian stood and took a step back. Croy made sure that Ilana was not lying in anything, and then he returned his attention back to the old derlian who had continued to talk unabated. "I should have been here. I am usually guarding the well. She is poisoned now, you see." The old derlian's words pierced into Croy.

"What?! What did you say? No, I've healed her. I healed her myself." Croy was not sure if he understood what the old derlian was saying.

"The Vijen was correct with half of what it spoke. Which is the whole problem with talking to Vijens. The half that they do not say is often more important than the half that they do. Wake her, I must speak with you both." The derlian looked so serious that Croy did as he was told without thinking of how much Ilana needed the rest. He roused her as gently as he could.

"Ilana. Ilana, we have been found out." Croy had to shake her shoulder repeatedly. She finally awoke and looked blearily from Croy to the stranger.

"I do not mean to be rude, but who are you?" Her voice sounded cracked.

"I am Lemniscate. I am the oldest Fluen derlian that there ever was." He smiled broadly, showing his perfect teeth.

"Where are we?" Ilana kept her gaze upon the stranger.

"You have drunk from the well, yes?" Lemniscate smiled as Ilana nodded. "And you have not?" At this, he looked directly at Croy. Croy started to shake his head and then realized that the derlian might think he was answering "no" to the question.

"No, I have not drunk from the well." Croy did not normally like ambiguity and felt it was best to be completely clear in this instance.

"Then I have two speeches to give. One for you, and one for you." He pointed at each of them in turn. He then turned to face Croy directly.

"This well does cure all ills. It even, if taken for long enough, enables a derlian to live as long as a Yaven. The problem is that they are poisonous waters. They kill someone within three days of tasting them. Of course, since the well cures all ills, it cures its own poison. Meaning, in essence, that once every three days you must drink from this very well. Since you look well traveled, I will not waste the time explaining how there is no way to escape the desert in three days.

Once you have tasted the eternal waters, you will die without them." The old derlian suddenly looked very serious.

"But... what about canteens?" Croy got caught up in arguing the details because his mind could not absorb the truth.

"No good. Oddly enough, the water loses its potency in direct proportion to how much you have. Meaning a small vial will stay potent a hundred times longer than a canteen. Magic has also failed to prove effective for long. We have tried every spell we can think of. There are other questions as well. Such as, why are we not able to stay in contact with our derlian brothers outside of the desert, even using magic? How come there is not a trade route through our little village? Because nobody ever finds the center of the desert. Few who do not drink from the well, that is. The well changes position daily. At the least. And it pulls the little shanty town with it. Even if you have found the well this time, if you leave, you might never find it again. This is why I have been stationed here. To warn the next traveler about the well water, so that they can make their choice in full consciousness. You have been warned that the water is poison." The ancient derlian shifted his gaze over to Ilana.

"As I have spoken, you may live here. Forever. The little shanty town is a difficult life. We are unable to grow crops in the dusty ground. Even if we could, we would probably move away from them the next day. We do make a version of soil with pieces of ourselves mixed in with the sand. Blood, fertilizer, sand and hair. With this we each grow some small vegetables in clay pots that we will take out to show the sun during the day, but they must be moved into a shack before nightfall, or else they will stay as we move. You may make your own shack, and clay pots, as we move near some resources. Usually, when a newcomer has tasted of the well, we will move to an area that had some dried weathered wood or a bit of clay or loam. Then we may all gather what we can to make our shacks sturdier and our potted soil more... well, more soil-like. It is a great celebration for a newcomer to drink from the well as it typically means more provisions for us old-timers." He paused to smile at his own joke. When no one interrupted, he continued with his speech. "When I say that the well is poisoned, I do mean poison. However, it could also be thought of slightly differently. It is addicting. You may have vomited when you first took it, and you will probably do so for the first couple of times that you partake. Soon, however, the feeling will shift from nausea to euphoria. Conversely, the pain caused by not drinking of the well on a daily basis can get to be excruciating. It begins with clammy skin and cold sweats. It progresses through a nausea that makes what you just felt seem pleasant. It shifts into delirium tremens that the most sordid drunk would wish themselves dead to be rid of, and finally, you begin to sweat blood. Then, of course, after a few days, death does come. Though I cannot say whether or not it is welcome for those who go through it, it is certainly welcome for everyone else in the town. The screaming is difficult to sleep through, you see." He smiled at Ilana. It was not a friendly smile, but it was not cold either. It was a smile in recognition of an ugly truth. "Now, before I can speak more of the well, I must ask your companion a question. Do you wish to drink from the well?"

"If you can live forever by drinking from the well, how come there are not more derlians here?" Croy tried to peer into the shanty town to see anyone, any movement, but he could detect nothing.

"Well, you do not know how many are here, do you? Also, it is incredibly difficult to find the well, you see." Lemniscate's smile was somewhat fatherly.

"Let me ask you plainly then. How many derlians choose death after choosing eternity?" Croy stared hard back into Lemniscate's large pupils.

"I am not able to speak of suicides until you choose. It is a paradox of wills, you see." Croy did not see, but he knew he could not drink without knowing.

"No, I will not drink from the well." He felt Ilana squeeze his hand in hers.

"Are you sure? We could be together. Forever." It was Ilana making the plea.

"Maybe. Maybe later. If you had known then what you do now, would you have chosen to drink?" He did want to stay with her forever, but not in this town. Not in this way.

"No later. If you leave this well, you may never find your way back, understand? This may be your only time to choose." Lemniscate's eyes were piercing.

"I can't... I can't drink from the well right now. You should have given us both the same choice. You should have given us the same chance. She drank unwittingly, but I cannot." Croy could not look at Ilana.

"To which I have failed. I must ask for your forgiveness, Gaen. I relaxed in my vigilance." The old derlian stared down at Ilana. Croy's gaze fell on her cheek mere moments before his tears did. He did not want to leave her, but he did not want to stay here forever either.

Chapter 10

Clerin and Wil were traveling through rivers again. They had mercifully let Clerin rest for three days before beginning her next journey. Midinarre had convinced Olwinn, with her usual charm, to lend Wil to Clerin. Clerin and her mother rode for about half a day outside of Tureyn, beginning at midnight, before stopping by the river. They had a leisurely breakfast picnic, just enjoying each other's company. Olwinn and Wil arrived as it was getting towards evening. Everyone made their farewells and Clerin found herself inside a Yaven inside a river again.

They stopped well after dark and made a quick camp. Clerin just ate hard jerky with cheese and a little bread. She slept without a fire but with the promise to be able to sleep for as long as she could the next morning. She had a deep and dreamless sleep.

Clerin ate cold food again and headed out quickly after awakening. After a couple hours on the river, the noon sun began to pierce through the tree cover. She had been fairly quiet on their travels so far, but the glaring sun motivated her to be more gregarious.

"Ahem, could you... Is there any way you could make yourself darker, or denser, or something. Then sun is too bright on my eyes." She was unsure of how to bring it up, so she decided just to say it.

"Of course. I do not always think of things like how sensitive derlian eyes are to light. It is sometimes difficult for me to think of how to serve my job better. Which is whatever I may do to make your travel easier. Let me know if you think of anything else I can do for you." Wil somehow shaded Clerin's face, but still let the sun warm her body. She had a sudden urge to shift her head around really quick to see if Wil could keep the shadowed portion of himself above her face, but she stopped herself from being obnoxious. She realized she was thinking of Wil as a male. There was so much that she did not know about Yavens. Realizing that they planned to travel together for another week, Clerin decided to get to know Wil.

"Let me know if you do not want to answer any of my questions, or if they make you shy. I was incredibly curious, if you don't mind, as to why someone as powerful as a Yaven would serve a derlian?" Clerin bit her lip while waiting for the answer.

"Serve? I think you misunderstand my motives. Did you not see my Menel?" Wil sounded slightly peevish.

"Well, yes. I understand that you are rewarded for your service. But aren't you told what to do?" Clerin felt that her words were not conveying very well what her mind wanted to communicate.

"If someone tells you to take a drink of water or to sleep, do you begrudge them that? Does that weigh on your mind? I am capable of doing anything I want to here. In this realm, in relation to my home, my comparable strength is magnified manifold. These tasks that are requested of me do not tax me. Some of the tasks can even be entertaining. It is so unpredictable here, and there are always so many different things happening. It is exciting and I enjoy it." Wil ended speaking quicker than it had started, almost sounding like a derlian.

"So if the mage who called you ordered you to do something against your basic nature, would you have to do it? Like, say, Olwinn told you to kill me. Would you do it?" Clerin was back to biting her lip.

"Ah. Where do loyalties lie? You are asking about compulsion? You do not cast much magic, do you?" Wil was a little terse.

"No, unfortunately not. So, you see, I have no reference as to the conditions on which you arrived at this realm." Clerin was wondering where Wil was headed.

"I am called by a derlian. I can fight the call if I do not wish to come to your realm. I might be compelled to appear before the mage if they are stronger than I. This derlian proposes a task, or series of tasks, or a general genre of tasks. Then they propose how they will cater to my needs while here. They offer up the element I use to add to my Menel. I can fight the deal if I do not wish to do the tasks, or I might negotiate with the mage. I might be compelled to agree to the deal if the mage is very much stronger than I. The more repugnant the task, the stronger the mage must be to compel me. After a deal is struck, the mage's ability to compel, especially in regards to the task, increases. The mage may cast a spell to briefly gain much more control, but that will incite nemesis. If a mage compels me to do something especially repugnant, it may incite nemesis. I do not want to mislead you. I cannot choose nemesis. For a Yaven there is no control in nemesis and only vengeance fills its mind. If I die while in this realm, I am merely thrown back into my own. I will not die like a derlian mage will, forever faded from both realms. So, the mage may make their choice, but I make mine, and the world makes its own. What happens during, and especially after, this struggle of wills is what is called reality." Wil had slowed its speech back down.

"I wonder… Have you ever had this, this nemesis, incited in you?" Clerin wanted her voice to sound natural, but she was getting a sudden rush. Her blood raced as if she were afraid but she felt very protected. It was an interesting juxtaposition.

"Yes, even though it is a fairly rare occurrence, unfortunately I have. There was a Pyran mage named Shafile who had summoned me. We were outside of a castle under siege. You may not know any Pyrans, but believe me, these little sieges happen quite often. There was a stream that flowed underground through the side of a mountain. Where the river exited the rock was a giant grate, and that is where the castle was built. The stream left the exterior wall of the castle through another gate and, from there, meandered down the hillside. It had been a drawn-out struggle for some time in derlian reckoning. The castle and the invaders both had a Pyran Yaven to throw fire at each other. They had tried to dam the river on the other side of the mountain, but could not find the birth of the effluence. So, instead, they wanted to flood them out. I drizzled into the mountain and found the stream. I then called all of the water with me. We went charging down through the tunnel as fast as able. By the time I crashed through the first gate I had almost half of all the water from the underground stream involved in the surge. I flowed ahead, faster than any of the other water, and blocked the exit. We easily breached the banks of the canal. We soaked their panicked Pyran feet. We rose to extinguish their cooking fires and drowned their granaries. The water pooled at the lowest edge of the wall, since the exit was blocked by me. The water eventually saturated the ground underneath the wall, percolating up on the other side, undermining the wall. Both of the Pyran Yavens fought fiercely at the small breach, but soon it was a large breach. The siege ended soon after, and the castle's Yaven was sent back to its realm. The victorious were taking prisoners from the ranks of the castle's warriors when Shafile approached me. " There was a small pause as they floated along.

"He took me to a sataurine, a small, dry ravine or disconnected canal. It was filled with civilians. I would estimate there were about fifteen females and about a hundred children down there. He thought it would be easier to drown them. He did not want to offend his troops but wanted to be rid of the derlians. He thought it could have been an accident. I explained that it was common protocol to avoid hurting civilians, especially if it was unnecessary. He insisted, and I refused. He threatened, and I gave rebuttal. He attempted to put me under a geas and force my action. I remember calling the water over to me. Bringing a deluge up and out of the shortly placid canal, I made it rush towards us by instilling in it a longing for me. That is how I control much of water, which makes it a more personal request, adding insult to injury to me. Then the water came rushing towards the sataurine, and I was filled with a whirlpool of rage. The closer the river that I created came, the more I boiled. Before the wall of water arrived, I had lost control. I am forever grateful that the water never reached the civilians. But I was not expecting the nemesis to come over me either, I was merely trying to reverse Shafile's geas. I remember reaching into his chest, but it was as if I was watching myself. I pulled every drop of liquid from his body through his navel. His scream was impressive but short, collapsing with his body. I had never personally killed a derlian before. I have drowned many random derlians, but this time it seemed more personal. I knew what I was doing, but I was unable to deter myself from doing it. I was not able to decide what I was willing to experience. I had finished the task that Shafile and I had agreed upon, to breach the castle walls and to help secure their victory. Since he was dead and therefore unable to ask for more tasks, I returned to my realm. After that experience I have learned to filter the derlians that I will work with and refuse service to those tasks that impose a higher probability of experiencing a nemesis again." Clerin wished she could hear more nuance in Wil's voice. She knew that he was recounting a traumatic experience to her, but it was impossible for her to get clues through his voice.

"How do you filter derlians? I mean, isn't it a struggle to not be summoned?" Clerin was really enjoying listening to Wil. She asked more to keep it going on their current topic than for any particular or specific curiosity. She watched the clouds roll by the tinted ceiling.

"Do you know my name?" Wil asked quietly.

"You mean the part that comes after Wil?" Clerin replied coyly. She tried vainly to remember his name. She thought she had briefly heard it once. She felt obliged to try, however poorly.

"Wilthanikanong?" Wil actually gave a start. Clerin found it reminiscent of laughter.

"Oh. No, no. That would not work at all. You would never be able to summon me." Clerin was a little embarrassed at guessing so wildly.

"Well, I would not be able to summon you even if I knew your name. In fact, I hesitate to add, that may be why I do not remember your name. I think if I could cast summoning spells, I would be better trained to remember the complexities of the Yaven language." Clerin knew she was rambling a little.

"I must say that manner of speech makes me think of Midinarre." Wil spoke quietly. It was exactly the last thing in the world that Clerin thought Wil would say. She was stunned into silence for a brief moment.

"That sounded like you were a derlian. Ha, I did not realize that you were paying attention to familial similarities, especially emotional ones." Clerin blushed reflexively.

"Thank you, Clerin. There are some Yavens who would become annoyed at your compliments, but not I. I have been studying derlians, and especially Fluens, for epochs. You are incredibly difficult to study because you are so hard to pattern. All I was trying to say, before you were complementing my derlian observational skills, was that it is very hard to guess Yaven names. The way most wizards gain names is through another wizard or through another Yaven or through the Yaven themselves if they happen to meet and recognize compatibility. I can filter by letting incompatible derlians know that I will not work well or hard for them. They will find other Yavens that they like to work with. It is better for everyone that a smooth working relationship be maintained between all parties. If need be, if other options are not working, I can put up quite a struggle if I need to." Clerin imagined that Wil's voice swelled with pride.

"Then why would you ever go back to your own realm? If you are so powerful here. In the derlian realms." Clerin watched the trees go by above her.

"Would you not get homesick? Would you not wish to be surrounded by old friends?" Wil paused for a moment, and Clerin thought about what it said. "You are correct, though. There is another reason. Yavens are of Law, not Chaos. We are immutable and intransigent. To be here, to be amongst derlians, slowly kills me.

Your realm picks pieces off of me and runs away and hides them. In essence, I shed myself, like steam escaping from the kettle." Wil paused again, and Clerin interjected to keep it explaining.

"Is it permanent damage, like a cumulative poison?" Clerin wondered if a Yaven, who was not harmed by poisons, would know much about them.

"I replenish myself of my constituent parts while in my own realm, if that is what you mean. It does take some time, though, and it is not an equal ratio. It is a difficult experience to describe, slowly dying. I do not know if a derlian could understand it. The pain of it. The terror of it. Death to a derlian is inevitable. A cold, uncaring, unmoving, fact. There is no more sure of a thing. Death for us is more steeped in mystery, being such a rare occurrence. For this reason Yavens have an intense fear of death and will go to great lengths to avoid it. And it is because of this phobia that many Yavens have never even been to the derlian realms once." Wil dove a little deeper into the river as they talked.

The rest of the first day passed quickly for Clerin. They stopped a couple of times for her throughout the day to eat, dry out, and stretch her legs a little. She felt like she was holding up their mission, but did not know what else to do. She had to air out every once in a while. As solid as Wil made itself and as little water that wicked into her clothing, it was still humid all around her. When dusk arrived she was ready to take a rapid walk and lie in a dry tent on solid ground. There was a small group of apple trees that she steered clear of setting up her tent. Many of their fruits were lying about their roots and had the sweet smell of rot already upon them.

The second day started quietly. Clerin arose with the sun having to relieve herself and then she decided to get a fire going before returning to her tent. She set up the kindling in the rock ring, leaned over and spoke softly to it, "Lodepirarc!" The whisper shot a flame from her lips into the dry wood. She piled a couple of larger sticks left over from dinner onto the fire and headed back to her still warm bedding. She waited until the flames had died back down a little before dressing and taking down her tent. She cooked the eggs her mother had insisted she take with her. Her mother had said that Clerin would never again have the chance to have fresh eggs on a cross-realm journey, that having Wil to carry her provisions for her was a once-in-a-lifetime opportunity. She tried one of the apples, straight from the tree, but it did not taste like the apples in the market. It made her realize how far away from home she already was. Just the morning before her mother was giving her advice in their rooms at the Liar's Lyre. Now she was in the middle nowhere traveling with an unknown message to some Luften King in a faraway city in a faraway land. It seemed surreal.

Wil rose from the river while she was rinsing her pan and took its general form. "We shall travel when you are ready." Clerin was feeling unmotivated but she knew that they should start soon. There were only a couple of more days before they were deep enough into the Luften lands, which made Clerin wish to drag her feet. She knew once they had gotten that far, once they had gotten close to populations of Luftens, she would be on her own. Wil was only allowed to travel with her until it might become detected. A Fluen in the Luften lands would be cause enough for curiosity. But two Fluens, and one a Yaven at that, would not go unnoticed. Clerin was worried about a lot of unknowns in her future, but what worried her the most was to face them alone.

"Let me finish packing, it should not take too long." Clerin walked the pan back to her rolled-up tent and bedding and finished putting everything away. She hauled everything to the riverside and waited for Wil to get itself ready.

As she settled down for another long day of being a passenger, she had a sudden thought about all the equipment she was hauling around. As they started to slide down the river she began to wonder about how she was going to carry everything when Wil left.

"Wil, how long will you be able to travel with me?" Clerin was not sure what she was hoping for. She knew that it could only carry her so far.

"You know the plan. We will travel in rivers as far as we can into the Vaupicke range. Eventually we will need to walk through the lowest saddle of the ridge to reach the Luften side. From there we should be able to find the headwaters of the Ariel river, which flows directly to Ariellyna. I will take you as far as is appropriate." Wil repeated Olwinn's words almost verbatim, with the proper pronouns thrown in.

"What, do you think, does the word 'appropriate' mean? Here and now, for us." She wanted to ask what signs she should look for that would indicate Wil was going to leave. She knew deep down that there would be no real sign, that Wil would just tell her that it was time for her to begin traveling on her own.

"I do not know what answer you are looking for. The word 'appropriate' is ambiguous on purpose. It means that we do not know what will happen that will trigger the need for me to head back. If I was leaving before we reached the Luften lands, then we would know when I was heading back. However, since I will be assisting you for as long as possible, we must be comfortable with not knowing when the actual appropriate time is." Wil found several ways to say the same thing, but it was not its fault. Clerin knew that she was asking questions with no real answers. If she was honest with herself, it was because she was afraid to be alone. Not just at the other end of the house, or out for a long ride with only her horse, but alone amongst strangers. Amongst foreigners. Clerin did not know anything about Luftens. She had never even met one. And now she was headed to converse with their leaders, and not as a representative of Fluen royalty, but as an ambassador of Lembin, a Beleg, one of the four most powerful beings ever known to exist.

"I know, I know. Sorry. I am being intentionally vague and difficult. I am just ruing the time when you must take your leave." Clerin was suddenly desperate to change the subject but could think of nothing to say. They traveled for quite some time in silence.

"I was incredibly curious, if you don't mind, about your conversation with Lembin." Wil paused for a moment after speaking, and in the interim Clerin laughed heartily.

"Did you memorize that?" Clerin was still chuckling under her breath at Wil's use of her earlier verbiage.

"I know that you cannot tell me of what Lembin asked from you, or ask you to allude to the content of the message, but I *am* curious as to what the communication was like. I have a confession to make." Wil's voice quickened slightly. "Though I have always wished to, I have never before spoken to a Beleg."

"Well, at first you have to understand how strange the entire setting was to me. I was trapped under water, breathing because of another's spell. The enormity of the task bore down on me. The lighting was bizarre, and I could not see much. I was incredibly nervous. But, when I finally found the underwater well, I think most of my fear was overcome by the intensity of my surroundings. Then there came a low vibrating bass that rumbled through my entire body. That was the only sound, though. We did not speak to each other as you and I do. We did not use language. Actually, I am not sure what I did or how Lembin interpreted my part of the communication. I did speak aloud, underwater and unintelligible to my own ears. For my understanding of Lembin's communication, it was mainly visual. Though I also felt a lot physically, like shards piercing into me. Or my skin would get hot while I was seeing fire, those kinds of feelings. The images were sometimes rudimentary but at other times they were mosaics of glimmering beauty. They told a story, the story of the communication which I cannot relay to you. To be honest, I am not sure if I understand the images myself. Which makes it difficult to say anything because I am unsure as to which parts of the images were important to the mission and which parts were not. I do know, however, that even if I could explain everything that was communicated, it would not be easily decipherable. It is through no fault of Lembin's, of course. I am an imperfect vessel…" Clerin began to trail off. She was trying, with all of her mental might, to bring to her mind exactly what visions she had had. It seemed that she had decided upon an interpretation and was already forgetting the specifics. She especially did not want to forget the little anomalies, those faded details that would make the flash of remembered images make more sense. These were fading fast, though. She was already questioning herself as to their true sensations.

"You might be describing a thought amalgamation. An ancient way of communicating that allows participants to exchange experiences as a way to explain things to each other. It lost vogue when the common language was created, which was so long ago that there are few now who remember how to do it. Language had been around long before the first wormholes were exploited, but the Belegs had been around long before that. I wonder if the Belegs could be so ancient that they would be more comfortable with thought amalgamations than language? But that cannot be correct because they had to use language through the wormholes, didn't they?" Wil trailed off, lost in its own thought. Clerin waited awhile in silence before prodding it again.

"How ancient are you, then? Are you older than language, like the Belegs?" Clerin was completely relaxed and enjoying her ride. She wished that she could always keep the company of Yavens. Some derlians, thought Clerin, enjoy being in the company of inferiors, so that they seem superior by contrast. She always thought that was backwards logic. You should surround yourself with superiors, so that you might be pulled up to their level. Like how a siphon through a hose lifts water up because of the surrounding pressure pushing down on the reservoir.

"I am not nearly as ancient as the Belegs may claim to be, for I came after language. Though it was close enough to the dawn of that time that I did learn the arts of thought amalgamation. I am ancient enough to remember the Choosing. The available positions were filled before I had even heard about the Choice, but I remember the celebration that was put together for those who began your race. This may sound odd, but I may have known the Fluen that began your line. Your family can be traced back to one of the original derlians, can it not?" Wil seemed to be slightly more engaged than when it was speaking of distant pasts.

"We never lost our lineage, and we were from a prominent enough Yaven pairing that we have a small estate. We are from the Toswin family. That does not, however, sound at all like your name." Clerin tried to recall the full name of her ancestors. She knew it was written somewhere... She did not know much about Yaven names, but she had known that they were much more complicated than the family names she was used to. "Of course, none of the original families sound like your name. I can't even recall if the name Toswin was a combination of two names, or if it was a shortening of the more prominent name. I wonder why the Yavens would have changed their names when they changed into derlians?" Clerin realized she was trailing off. It was more like thinking aloud than communicating.

"Derlians have a way of shortening everything. Everything changes so quickly here. But in answer to the question, I do not believe I knew your ancestor." They talked for most of the day's journey, though there were many times that she was able to relax and just watch the scenery go by. When it got dark, they still had a ways to go to reach the shallow part of the river, so Clerin tried to rest while Wil sped further up the mountain slope. Finally they reached a point where Wil did not think it could carry Clerin immersed anymore. They stopped and, against better judgment, Clerin built a fire. She felt like she needed a hot meal, and she felt damp. She kept the fire small and made a small light shade with some evergreen branches. The night air seemed to be getting chillier each night that they were on their journey. After the meal she slept without the benefit of her tent. Luckily for her the night was clear, but it meant that she awoke with the early dawn.

✳✳✳

After breaking her fast she cleaned up the rudimentary camp. She sat down on a large boulder and waited for Wil to appear. The rock was cool underneath her. There were small patches of sun, but they had yet to warm up the stone. She clambered up the boulder a bit more to situate herself more comfortably. Then she half closed her eyes and watched how the low sun cast hazy light beams diagonally through the trees. The misty morning air felt heavy in her lungs, the weather seemed close and thick. She breathed in and out, slowly and consciously. Time lost meaning and she just rested; it was delicious. Her mind was wandering lazily by the time Wil showed back up.

Wil took up her things and they began to walk towards a saddle in the mountains. It was the first time she fully noticed that Wil did not use legs to walk. Wil's bottom half looked more like a long skirt, just a solid, non-shifting form. She wondered briefly what really made Wil move. At first they kept up quite a spirited pace, and she walked for a while in silence, concentrating on making good time. She soon forgot her curiosity. Clerin wanted to see how far she could make it before asking to be carried. She was unsure as to why she felt more guilty being carried over land than through water. Maybe it was because Wil was made of water or that it seemed to take less energy to float than to walk. She knew that they would want to cover a lot of ground today, though, so she did expect to have to be carried at some point in the day.

"Where do you go at night? I mean, you don't have to sleep, do you?" Clerin thought she could walk further if she was distracted. She followed behind Wil, in its muddy footprints. Wil had its face looking back at her to talk more easily, but still seemed to be able to see where it was going. Clerin wondered briefly if there was another face staring out in front of Wil.

"I do shut down periodically, but I do not need as much time as you derlians. You do everything else with such haste, it seems odd that you derlians sleep for as long as you do." Wil's arms moved forwards while his head looked backwards; it was eerie.

"But, where do you go?" Clerin felt bad about setting such a slow pace. She realized that she, and she alone, was the only reason they were not to Ariellyna already.

"I will scout ahead, so that the trail is less uncertain." It seemed that Wil was slowing a little, and Clerin figured it was slowing for her benefit.

"I do not wish to be the burden of this mission. I am not even sure why this message was entrusted to me. Ha, I am not even sure what the message is." Clerin suddenly felt very tired.

"You are not a burden. You set the pace. Derlians have an affinity to the opportunity buried in chaos. I have found, through much experimentation, that my time in your realm runs smoother if I follow your lead. The major reason we are traveling so slowly is to leave as little trace as possible. We must, above all, stay hidden, both for now and for in the future." Wil had shifted so that they were walking side-by-side. She felt better about being so slow, but now she felt like she was pressing Wil into saying nice things to her. Fishing for compliments, her mother always used to say. Clerin wondered why she always felt so guilty. The reasons always shifted, but the malaise stayed the same. She realized it must stem from her. So she decided to put more energy into walking and less into thinking.

She made it until an early lunch before she asked to be carried. Wil kind of morphed around her so that she was almost sitting on its shoulder, held high above the stream bed. Wil also carried their belongings. Luckily for Clerin, they were beginning to thin out a little. She hoped, however, that she would never have to carry them all by herself. There was a small trickle of water still weakly finding its way down the mountainside. Wil kept its head off to one side and a little higher, making it easier for Clerin to talk to Wil, but the image was a little unnerving. The hill increased in steepness quite rapidly, and she felt a little guilty to be riding. They moved quickly up slope, more quickly than Clerin could walk on flat terrain. It might have been the height at which she was being carried at, but Clerin thought they might even be moving as quick as she could run. Downhill. It seemed to take no time at all to get to the last section of their uphill journey. It got steep and rocky enough that Clerin eventually got down to clamber her own way up. She had not been sure if Wil was having difficulties carrying her, but when she asked if she could walk, it did not hesitate to let her down. The going was fairly steep and, though they did not have to climb too much, there were a couple of small cliffs. Clerin was completely worn out by the time they neared the top.

When they finally crested the saddle, Clerin was only looking down at her feet. She almost did not notice that the scenery was changing except that Wil had stopped. She glanced up, her fog clearing without the rhythmic trance of placing one foot in front of the other. She glanced over the valley that lay before them and gasped.

It was a verdant tapestry in front of her. There were wisps of cloud misting the vision before her eyes, like pulled cotton scattered through the myriad branches. They appeared stuck down in some places and fluttering in the breeze like a vanquished flag in others. There was the snow-capped mountain ridges framing the view, piercing the sky in three directions. The valley below funneled up towards them, eventually being cut off by the mountain they were standing on. They were in the lowest spot of the funnel, the saddle of the ridge, and they were still high enough to give Clerin a touch of vertigo as she stared into the valley. The most awe inspiring sight, however, were the trees. The entire forest floor was covered with swaying trees, looking like fuzzy moss on a felled tree trunk. Occasionally peppered lightly amongst their shorter cousins, jutting up from the forest floor with sweeping majesty, were the largest trees Clerin had ever seen before. They thrust high into the air, towering above the surrounding greenery. She was stunned for a long moment, unaware that Wil was wandering ahead of her. It was a joyous shock, one she would remember for the rest of her life. The thought that she was given this gift, this vision, humbled her. She finally understood why Yavens like Wil come to her realm. It was not just the glory of Menels or the gain in strength or prestige. But the privilege of experiencing something wonderful. What else was life, thought Clerin, but a series of wonderful experiences? She waited, letting the image before her sink in, memorizing it. She stared at it like a glutton stares at their last meal. Wil finally returned to see why she was no longer close by. Wil was quiet for some time, looking at her. Or maybe it was looking at the valley at the same time as looking at her, she could not be sure.

"Beautiful, is it not?" The words broke through to Clerin, reawakening her.

"It is so, Wil." Her voice sounded quiet to her own ears. Her chest tightened slightly, like a wide belt being cinched to high. She suddenly felt like crying but she did not know why. She was overwrought with emotion. Verklempt. She took a deep breath and looked around, blinking. She started down the slope letting the cool air waft against her skin. It made her feel better, more derlian. The mountainside was less steep on this side than the other, but it dropped off fast enough to keep her mind off of herself, and by the time they arrived at the first trees, she was completely collected.

It did not take them too long before the path was comfortable enough for Wil to carry her again. Wil took her up and headed down the mountainside at an angle. Wil shifted back and forth through the trees, eventually finding a spring. They stopped and had an early dinner. More properly, Clerin had an early dinner. Wil just dipped its foot in the spring, making them link in Clerin's mind. It looked like Wil just flowed straight into the stream, disappearing away down the mountainside, but without diminishing.

"Are you willing to try something a little dangerous if it would speed up our journey?" Wil's voice sounded serious.

"Sure. What?" Clerin was not sure what a Yaven would consider dangerous.

"I was considering that there are not many prying eyes around here. Therefore we could travel more above the surface of the water as it is too shallow to stay hidden in it for a while. If you do not mind standing." Clerin was unsure of how that would quite work. When it did, however, it was incredibly exciting. Wil made a small platform of itself and she stood on top. Most of Wil was in the water, before and after Clerin, but a small, immobile, rudder-like handle shot up that she could hold on to and steady herself. She would bend her knees to lower herself and do her best to keep balance. They were moving fast enough down the small stream that the wind fluttered her hair. And it was exhilarating. She had never before had an experience like it. Clerin was disappointed when the stream turned large enough for them to descend into its depth. They had passed no one out fishing or picnicking, so they should still be hard to trace, Clerin thought.

Even though it had been well into the afternoon when they found the stream, they made such good time that when they found a spot to camp, they were getting close to some sparse Luften farmsteads. Just the fringe members of the outer villages. Clerin was incredibly nervous. She thought that the next day's journey would be her last one with Wil. Soon she would be on her own way with just her messages and her meager camping equipment. She wanted to make the night last a while, reminiscing in the drug of nostalgia. But she knew that they should not make a fire, which made the night seem less comfortable. This was the last night that she could do something to get caught with a Yaven. She knew she should go to sleep early and wake up at the first rays of the dawn sun. Wil and she had a lot of ground to cover tomorrow and they were getting close to civilization. Tomorrow was important. The most efficient and correct choice was not nearly as fun, thought Clerin. In the end she closed her eyes with the setting sun, in the hopes of opening them with its rising.

Clerin did wake up early, but it was not because of the rising sun. There was a loud commotion outside her tent. She could hear several voices but had a hard time telling them apart enough to discern the definite number of derlians nearby, most assuredly Luftens to boot. She pushed down hard on the rising panic that boiled within her. She knew that if anything too dangerous were happening, Wil would have already taken care of it. She hoped. If, however, it was just some snoopers, Wil would probably hide to keep their mission safe. Clerin hoped that it was just the latter scenario, because in the back of her mind was the possibility that Wil was nowhere around and out of range of her screams. Luckily she was partially dressed already. She finished the job as quickly as possible and began to arm herself. She had two knives hidden and a small sword in her hand as she burst from her tent.

There was no one in the immediate vicinity, much to Clerin's relief. The voices that sounded so near inside a cloth tent sounded more distant now that she was not enclosed. She strode to the edge of her little encampment and peered through the trees. The ground between the copious rough tree trunks was white with a soft cotton of mist from the evaporating morning dew. Clerin thought, briefly, back to yesterday when she was able to see the whole valley. Realizing that she could only hear others yelling orders or something to each other and that there was no attack imminent, she went back and tidied up the site as best she could. She felt it took about twice as long as she had originally thought necessary because she kept looking over her shoulder into the persistent mist. It had seemed mysterious and beautiful at first but was starting to seem a bit sinister. When she was finally finished compressing her camp, she squatted next to the stream and whispered to it.

"Wil? Are you there? Hello?" She waited for some time, trying to figure out what the voices were yelling while hoping Wil would appear. They seemed to be trying to coordinate something, something that took a lot of individuals. There was an overriding voice that was apparently giving orders. But there were a myriad of others talking to and fro, some high pitched and some more subdued. She could not hear them very well, except when one would periodically yelp. She waited for a while longer then began packing her belongings around her. She did not know what to do with the extra supplies. She only called them extra because she could not carry them. Eventually she hid them by sinking them in the stream, somewhat tangled in a dangling bush. She hoped that Wil would be able to pick them up before heading back into Fluen territory. One last time she appealed to the burbling stream, and after waiting in complete silence for a reply, she shifted her pack on her back and began to walk along the stream. She hoped that Wil would suddenly pop out of the water at any moment, keeping her company and making her feel safe. She could not imagine feeling more safe than having a Yaven for a protector. Walking seemed to take so incredibly long. She felt spoiled by the travel she had experienced so far on her journey. Plodding along she realized that it could take her a fortnight to get to Ariellyna on her feet. After resigning herself to not having Wil with her, she then resigned herself to finding a horse to purchase.

Quickly she found that she could not walk next to the stream. The hydrophilic plants crowding the banks kept her from being too near. She was soon pushed towards a path that loosely followed the river. As she was leisurely strolling along the path, she could hear the voices getting nearer. The path had started out fairly wide but now seemed to be closed in by trees. She could still not see the source of the noise, but she could tell she was getting closer. She thought about turning back, finding the stream, and waiting for Wil. She knew that was not an option, however, just a vague and unattainable wish. Doggedly she pushed herself off the path, towards the voices.

It was only when she reached the edge of trees that she realized she was about to jeopardize the safety of her mission. She quickly faded back and took in the scene before continuing. She kept the trees about five deep and crouched down behind a boulder that looked half eaten by the humus and leaves. She set her pack down next to herself and peered around.

There were about eight or nine different derlians in a small clearing. They did not all look the same, but they somehow all looked a little different than Fluens. They were all a little taller and swarthier than Fluens, but still slight. Not stocky like the images of Gaens that Clerin had seen before. Most of them seemed to have straight hair, though there were a couple with waves, while their hair coloring seemed mostly dark, mostly black, but there were some darker browns and a chestnut or two. They were gathered around a large wooden cart, and several of them were trying to push on the spokes of one of its oversized wheels. There were four horses tethered to the front of the cart, with a Luften driver loosely holding their reins. The horses seemed restless, with their nostrils flaring. The cart rocked back and forth but did not seem capable of getting going. Clerin could not tell what they were stuck on, but watched in fascination. She kept trying to get a view of the cart's contents, but she had a poor vantage point to see around its wooden sides, and the top of it was covered in lumpy burlap and half-frayed hemp ropes. There was a larger, muscular Luften with a whip staring at the side of the cart. His biceps glistened with the sweat of his efforts in wringing more effort from the others.

"What are you doing? Keep the horses moving! Everyone now! Together!" The one with the whip was yelling at the ones doing the work. The Luftens straining at the wheel spokes were grunting as the whip slashed near them. "Move, move!" The whip lashed out again but this time struck the flank of one of the rear team horses. With a great yell, the horse tried to rear up and flail its front legs, but was partially held down by the team's collective harness. It looked like the cart was going to falter backwards, but the Luftens grunting at the spokes were able to hold it from turning. Suddenly, all four of the horses screamed and surged forwards with the panic of the rear horse. A shudder seemed to pass through each of them in rapid succession, and then they all moved at once. With a great bounce the cart finally heaved up and over whatever it was stuck on, and then the wheels came crashing back down on the soft forest floor. The Luftens grappling with the spokes, luckily, all fell away from the bone-crushing wheels as they turned forwards following the cart's momentum. The driver leaped out of the way just in the nick of time.

The horses, however, did not stop once the cart was free but raced away from the cracking whip. Snorting and whinnying, they crashed down the path they were on and dragged the cart behind them at a dizzying speed. They disappeared from view almost instantly, but Clerin could still hear the cart groaning and bouncing. The dazed Luftens on the ground just stared at the retreating cart, while the one with the whip stared stupidly at them. He suddenly got a cruel sneer upon his face.

"What were you doing? You imbeciles! Now how are we going to get the crystal colony to Vanelia?" He was going to continue screaming, Clerin was sure of that, but for a thundering crash. It sounded like the cart had been blown apart. There was the sound of rupturing and splintering wood followed by the frantic sounds of the horses neighing. She was incredibly curious as to what was happening, but was afraid of being seen, so she just stayed crouched behind her boulder.

The Luftens began walking and cursing towards the site of the crash while Clerin listened to their voices fade a bit. After a while she realized that she should be doing something. She wondered about attempting to further spy on the Luftens, to see what they truly had in the cart. She was still a little worried about being seen, but they seemed to be incredibly preoccupied. Deciding that satisfying her curiosity was the best course of action, she turned to hide her pack before following them and heard a loud crack. It had sounded like someone stepping on a large dry twig. She hoped it was an animal, but she was unsure of what animal would make that much noise. Besides a derlian, that is. Clerin peered into the trees behind her trying to see anything at all that could have made the noise. She was about to start hiding her pack again when she saw some movement in the distance from amidst the trees. Deciding to solve the closer mystery before solving the more interesting one, she donned her pack and began to walk towards where she had heard the sound emanate from.

She looked around for some time, but could not find anything. Finally, Clerin decided that she had heard a branch falling from one of the trees and not something being stepped on. She turned to head back but was unsure of the exact direction. She wandered for a little while before hearing another large crack. She ran towards the noise without a thought for her own safety, just her animal need to find the source of the disturbance. She crashed through the underbrush for a reckless moment before she saw the horse. The sight of the majestic beast eased her concerns of ambush but did little to slow her racing heart. She stopped herself, spreading her arms to steady herself. She then turned her palms outwards, towards the horse in the universal gesture of peace.

"Shhh. There, boy. It's all right, I won't hurt you. Pretty eventful day, huh? Are you from the caravan? Are you supposed to be working?" Clerin walked slowly towards the horse, her arms still held aloft. She tried to keep her voice soft and steady. The horse, for its part, eyed her suspiciously with its head turned sideways. Nostrils flared wide as she approached, but the horse seemed calm enough for her to slowly continue. It was a proud chestnut with a long blond mane. The horse had a saddle, so Clerin did not think it was one of the team horses, but it was obviously someone's. She figured that the owner must be close by, and she could hopefully purchase the animal with all of the tack and accoutrements included. She eventually closed the distance to the horse, still talking quietly.

"That's a good boy. No one is going to hurt you. I just want you to take me to your owner. Can you do that for me? Can you show me which way is home?" Clerin gently took the drooping reins with her left hand while she held her right palm open under the horse's nose. An unexpected snort made her hop unconsciously, but she had enough self-control to keep herself from yanking on the reins.

"See? There is nothing to worry about. I told you that you could trust me. Didn't I?" Clerin patted the horse gently on the side of his face, and he started nodding at her. She continued to pat his neck. "There, there. We are just going to try your saddle now. Don't worry." Clerin slipped her boot into a stirrup and hauled herself up into the saddle. It was effortless. As if it was meant to be. The horse turned and began to trot down the hill. She kept a lookout for the owner, fully intent on giving a fair price.

The horse seemed to know where he was going, seemed to trot along with purpose and direction. They seemed to be on a faint trail, and the horse trotted along the skinny, winding way with a businesslike air. The trail started as beaten brown soil, a snake of dead undergrowth. Soon the horse could travel, more or less, in a straight line. The path before them began to open up, becoming more defined. The horse began to pick up speed as they headed downhill. Clerin began to pull back on the reins, but the horse did not seem to notice.

It was just then, as Clerin began to question her wisdom of mounting a strange horse, that she first heard the scream. She tried vainly to keep the horse from reaching a full gallop.

"Stop! Thief! Someone stop her!" A Luften was waving his arms in the distance. Clerin raised her arm to wave at the small figure, but the horse leapt forward with gaining speed. Her hand clutched the pommel in desperation, while the other still pulled ineffectually on the reins.

"Thief!" The yells gained in strength and volume as the figure began running to intercept Clerin and the horse. She bent over the horse's neck as he reached full gallop. She hung on for her life. The Luften yelling at her was running in a long arc, intent upon intercepting her. She tried to yell back, but the frantic rocking of the horse made it difficult for her to get her breath. "I'll pay you! I have money!" Her voice was loud in her own ears, but it was hard to hear much over the hooves. The Luften certainly did not acknowledge that he had heard. Her eyes were glued to the ground, watching the brown legs flying underneath her, churning the soil. She was mesmerized by the motion. Time slowed.

When she looked up, the Luften was right in front of her, swinging his arm and screaming. His face was dirty and grizzled. There was a scar running down the left side of his face, a deep cleft. Clerin thought he was ugly. This was not because he was attacking her, though that could have a serious effect on how one thinks of beauty. His left eye was milky white with something dense and dark underneath. Like a black pebble wrapped in white gauze, stretched taught and thoroughly wet. There were more holes than teeth in the gaping mouth, and a scream of hatred was being torn from his throat. Clerin screamed as well but hers was torn out by fear, not anger. Time sped back up as the knife slashed into her thigh. She had not even realized that the Luften was holding anything. Pain now clawed at her throat. The horse, luckily or not, kept running. Clerin hugged the horse's neck with one hand and clamped down on her bleeding leg with the other. The pain seared through her, making her want to pass out, but she knew that she could not slow down, let alone stop, or the Luften would catch up and finish what he had started.

"Lolid..." Clerin whispered. She felt a small tingle in her arm, but then all of the blood drained from her head suddenly. She felt faint with the effort which, when mixed with the moving horse and her wound, threatened to force her to fall. She had no illusions as to her fate if she happened to fall. She wished that she was proficient enough at magic to cast it from a galloping horse while bleeding, but was resigned to the fact that she would have to wait to heal herself until after she had dismounted. Unfortunately, she was not sure if the horse would ever slow down enough for her to get off. It took all of her strength to just stay on the horse as he streamed down the hillside. Amazingly enough, though, the horse's back glided smoothly along. She was thankful that he was not attempting to trot.

Finally the horse began to slow its outright flight. He raised his head taller, but still kept his feet blurry—at least to Clerin's mind. She let herself lean over the pommel to rest her head on the horse's neck. Her cold sweat mingled with the sweat of the horse, along with her tears and, unfortunately, some watery snot. The pain did not seem to ebb, but she was still coping with it, so she figured she must be getting numb. Finally the horse began to walk, and luckily for Clerin, the transition between running and walking was quick. They had come upon some more trees during the flight, and it was there that Clerin was able to dismount. She could not swing her cut leg over the horse, but she could not land on it either. As she tried to swing her good leg over the pommel while keeping herself seated on the slick saddle, she realized her right hand was stuck on her thigh. Not literally, but each time she let up slightly with her hand, the pain would shoot back through her. No extra blood seemed to seep out, however.

She had hoped to find a stream, but that would have to wait until she had more time. Clerin realized that the horse was standing perfectly still, not doing the little sideways dance they often do while nervous. Instead of getting off the horse, Clerin decided to risk falling if she happened to pass out.

"Mekliderpri!" Clerin said as forcefully as she dared. The magic flowed through her arm and into her leg. She felt a little woozy but did not feel faint, even though she was casting a more powerful spell than she had tried earlier. She sat on top of the horse for some time, just listening to the quiet woods. She could not hear the ugly Luften yelling at her in the distance anymore, but she assumed he was still chasing her. She was at a loss of what to do about the horse. It was not hers, she knew that. She knew the Luften would always think of her as a thief, and her interest in self-preservation made her nervous about meeting him again. She decided to leave the horse here. She knew she could take the horse no farther. The closer the horse was to the ugly Luften, the higher the likelihood of them being reunited. However, she would rather have been much further from danger before having to walk again. She finally convinced herself that this was the best location to leave the horse, considering all of the circumstances. Having finally made a decision she felt comfortable with, she dismounted. Her leg was tender, but did not buckle or cause her much discomfort.

"Thank you for running away from him, and thank you for running so smoothly. You really should not have started to run away though, you know. You probably gave your master quite a scare that he was going to lose you." Clerin was feeling a little emotional and unconsciously patted the horse's rear flank. The horse moved sideways quickly, away from her hand and bared its teeth. It was then that she realized his flank was covered in scars. Some looked ancient, old, faded, and stretched. Others, however, had a freshness to them. Not quite pink, but obviously tender. Clerin reached her hand out to touch them lightly in compassionate commiseration, then realized what she was doing. Instead she reached for the horse's neck, stroking it lightly.

"There, there. I won't make you go back. You don't have to go back." Clerin did not know what to do. She felt out of sorts. She finally decided to leave three gold crowns for the horse, figuring that it would easily cover the cost of getting another horse. She found a small bag she had, made of a supple leather, and transferred the hair accoutrements that had filled it into the large pouch she kept hanging from her belt. She found a low branch that swooped into the clearing she was in. Since the horse had seemed to know where it was going, she figured that he traveled through here often enough. Its master was probably still on the chase, so she hung the pouch as obviously as possible from the hanging branch. She stepped back to look at it from the path and it seemed to be unmistakably visible. Now that she had settled on a choice of action, she wanted to continue to add distance between her and the horse's owner. She gingerly mounted the horse, and they left the bag behind as fast as seemed prudent.

She rode through the entire day. The horse would walk for a while and then gallop for a while. She did stop several times, but each one was very brief. Whenever they would get to a cross-roads, Clerin would take the larger road, hoping it would lead to Ariellyna. She felt she could no longer follow the river as long as she had planned. She now placed her hope in speed rather than stealth.

As the sun set and darkness rolled in, Clerin finally stopped and made camp. Instead of starting a fire, she ate bread and cheese. She rubbed the horse down with some clumps of grass, being especially careful near his scars. She decided to let him wander instead of hobbling him or tying his reins to a tree. She felt that if the horse wanted to head back home or wander to another rider, it was his prerogative. It was still early evening, when the sky transferred from dark blue to black, that she set up her bedding. Using the saddle as a pillow, she fell asleep almost instantly. The day had been long and harrowing, and she felt like she had aged a whole cycle that day. She hoped that a long night's sleep would erase the weariness in her.

She awoke with the lightening sky. The horse, thankfully, was waiting for her as she slowly got herself moving. A quick, cold breakfast started her morning. She tried to get the horse saddled and ready as fast as possible, but it seemed to take forever. Time seemed thick and viscous, like honey. Finally she was remounted and back in motion. She talked to the horse the entire day. "Shall I call you Arrowfoot? No, that doesn't sound good at all. Maybe Riverlightning. Do you like that? How about Moonshadow? Or Landstrider?" Clerin listed names, hoping the horse would snort or some such thing, while she was speaking. That way he could choose his own name. Unfortunately, he did nothing of the kind.

The day flowed blurrily by, much like the scenery. She forced herself to ride mercilessly throughout the day. Of course, this meant more to the horse than it did to her, though she suffered greatly as well. She was astounded and grateful at the little horse's stamina. They ended the day close to town. If Clerin had really wanted to, she might have entered the grand city of Ariellyna by midnight. But the small benefit of gaining the finish line was highly outweighed by the cost of getting there, let alone attempting to find an inn lost in a strange city in the middle of the night. She did not want to be too close to the main road into Ariellyna for fear of thieves, but she also did not want to back track a lot of distance.

She finally decided to shift over to a small grove of trees as the sun was turning red. One last night, she thought, without a fire to warm her would not be too bad. Clerin let the horse wander during the night so he could eat his fill. If he decided to leave for home, she told herself she would not hold it against him. After removing his saddle and accoutrements, she made her own bed. She spent the time between lying down and sleeping by thinking of a nice room with a large bed and, most lovely of all, a private bath. She realized that she would have to count her money before entering Ariellyna. She was unsure of how long it would take to get an audience with the King, and she had no idea what would happen after that. Luckily she fell asleep before she could work her worry up.

Clerin awoke the next morning feeling giddy. She had made it, she had arrived. She never would have dreamt that she would see the capital of the Luften lands. She dressed in riding clothes that would portray some status but were not incredibly clean. As she mounted her horse and headed back to the road, she looked for signs of Ariellyna. It was not very visible from where she was. Not that the helioarcs that the city was famous for were not visible. But the giant trees were filled with so much foliage that the buildings, which were built closer to the trunk where the branches began, were completely camouflaged to her.

She was still a little sore from her previous rides but excited enough not to notice. The closer she got to the city, the wider the road got. Eventually she began to pass more and more Luftens heading out of the city into the rural countryside. Though she received a few stares, no one tried to speak with her. For her part, she only nodded towards them and kept her eyes fixed on the road ahead while they seemed to be looking. When it seemed that they were not fixating on her or when they were still in the distance, she tried to glean information from them. She had seen paintings and read books about foreign lands, but she had never been able to see them for herself. She knew that the Fluen dress had many different subtleties that showed rank and status, but they were sometimes difficult to tell. A poorer Fluen, for example, might wear many little pieces of jewelry to hide the fact that none of the pieces were worth very much. That happened so often, however, that the sight had become a caricature of what it originally intended. Every Fluen of wealth knew that look immediately and would see through its illusion. But would a Luften know what that meant? What little things, thought Clerin, would tell her about who she was talking to in a completely foreign land, in the Luften realm?

As the road widened, it became more defined. The trees— the small ones, not the incredible helioarcs which were still further in the distance—thickened along the edge of the road, making the image of an aisle to ride down. Clerin's good mood followed her down the road and into the town. It was difficult to tell when the town actually started. The sides of the road began to open back up from the trees but were still defined by the more frequent buildings built along the road. The buildings started out as shacks, gray and dilapidated. The further she went along the road towards the start of the helioarcs, the better the buildings looked and the closer together they got. When she passed the gigantic trunk of the first helioarc along the road, she finally realized how dim it was underneath the heavy canopy. The change had been gradual enough, the shadows thickening as she moved in space as slowly as when dusk moves through time. She looked straight up in amazement, the rocking view moving in time with the horse. There were leaves after leaves, dense into the distance, with a light green glow backlighting the entire shifting scene. The first layer of leaves was so high up into the air that Clerin had difficulty making individual ones out. They seemed to be a moving mass, rather than singular pieces. She was stunned by a form of reverence. The horse strode quickly along, passing more and more helioarcs. She passed an inn but was too mesmerized by the forest to stop. Maybe it would be better to find the palace first, she thought.

Clerin did not really know where to go, but she knew she had to speak to the King. So she let the road lead her to the largest helioarc in the forest, or what she assumed was the largest. She could not see the top of the helioarc, just like all of the other ones. It was wider than any of the others she had seen so far. She would have bet that it was as wide as a castle tower was high. The more important sign that she had found her destination, however, was the large contingent of guards surrounding the staircase that spiraled from the ground up into the branches. She found herself steering straight towards the magnificent tree despite the desire for a bath.

Before Clerin got too close, she decided to dismount and approach on foot. In the Fluen realm guards were always extra wary of mounted strangers, and she assumed it would be no different here. She walked up to the center guard, letting a peripheral one take the reins of her horse. She had tried to mentally prepare for this moment while riding here, but she still ended up pulling the rolled scroll out of her jacket with a little more flourish than she wanted.

"I am on official business from Tureyn, and I need to submit for an audience with King Hulgert." Clerin stared at the guard with her chin held high as he read her note. She knew that the impression of importance was vital to a guard. The quickest way to get past a guard was to make them feel important. And the only way they would feel important was for you, yourself, to be important.

"Unfortunately, the King is not receiving today. Or, well, to be honest with you, not for the last three moons." The guard was reading with wide eyes. Clerin thought that if he could help her, he would. She had to make sure though.

"That is unacceptable. I have an important message that he alone must hear." Clerin spoke with as much authority as she could muster.

"You don't understand. I would like to help you, but…" The guard was suddenly interrupted.

"Do not worry, Klonfyl. She may come with me to see Vanelia. Unless, of course, you think she is a secret assassin." A young-looking Luften was suddenly beside Clerin. "I am Chiavel, and it would truly be a pleasure to assist you. I, myself, am just on my way up to visit with the Queen." While beaming a smile at her, he deftly took the scroll from Klonfyl's inert hands. He was thin and tall, close to gaunt but not unattractive. His hair was like a raven's—black, slick, and shiny. His ruffles stood out pompously from his blue jacket; they shook and swayed while he spoke. "And, if I may be so bold, what are you called, besides beautiful?" The compliment took her aback, and for a moment she was unable to think, let alone speak.

"Herance. I would be delighted for you to assist me." She did not want to seem coy, but allowed herself a split second of fluttering eyelash. The name had been one of her family's servants, a maid. She had worked for them a long time ago when Clerin was quite young.

"Funny. You do not look like a Herance." He had piercingly light blue eyes. They were squinted at her with an odd intensity. She was not sure if he was squinting inquisitively or accusingly.

"It is a very common Fluen name, Chiavel. I am not one to question my mother's motives in naming her daughter after such an ordeal as giving birth." Clerin was unsure of what to make of Chiavel. She could not figure out his motivation for helping her. It did not seem to be centered in an altruistic mood. Since she could not put her finger on what was off-putting about him, she gave him a large warm smile. She briefly wished that she had visited an inn before seeking audience, if for no other reason than to feel more in control of the current situation. She felt much more confident when she was cleaned up.

"I would be honored if you would accompany me." He quickly rolled up her scroll, handed it to her, and began to walk past Klonfyl. Rather than risking more questioning, Clerin kept her eyes glued on Chiavel's back and sauntered past Klonfyl and all of the other guards gathered around without a glance.

Chiavel led the way past the guards and up the stairs. It was not until the first landing that he paused so that they could ascend side by side. "Would you believe that I have never known a Fluen, let alone one of royalty?" Clerin, for the life of her, could not remember exactly what the scroll claimed her to be, though she did recall that it did not specifically name her. It had used the ominous sounding title, "The Bearer of This Note". She silently cursed herself for not re-reading it on the ride into town. Or at least stopped at an inn where she would have most certainly read it again in preparation. Of course, then she might have been stymied for days waiting for an audience with the Queen, so it was difficult to assign bad luck to her current situation.

"Actually, I *would* believe that you do not know any Fluens. I, myself, do not know any Luftens. Well, I guess I should say that I *did* not know any Luftens." Clerin smiled at Chiavel and lightly touched his arm, watching his face while she let her link sink in. He did not seem to notice her lapse in continuing his royalty line of thought, so she charged ahead with her misdirection. "You must tell me. Why does King Hulgert not receive audience anymore? I must confess that I know next to nothing about the Queen. Queen Vanelia, did you say?" She figured if she peppered him with questions, he could choose his own misdirection.

"You do like to strike at the heart of the matter don't you?" Chiavel gave the most honest smile she had seen from him so far.

"Well, you have the advantage of knowing our time constraints. Since I do not know how long it will take to walk to the reception area or whether or not we will have to wait for her after we arrive, I assume I must glean the information I need in the shortest time possible." Clerin suddenly realized how verbose she had been in speaking about the necessity of brevity. She giggled at herself.

"No, by all means. It is refreshing." He made a vague gesture with his hand as they continued up the stairs. "More to the point, however, our realm is in the midst of upheaval." He paused for a moment, watching her from the corner of his eye. Before she could respond, however, he continued. "Luckily, no one seems to know." Here he laughed quite heartily. Clerin even paused briefly, her feet on different steps, while he collected himself. "No, I should probably let Vanelia decide what you know about that. You see, she is what is keeping us on our current arc. Extending the stasis, if you will. The remission. Not that she seems to know." The last sentence was spoken quietly, but was obviously meant to be heard. She wondered if he was trying to emphasize a rare insight of his own, or if it was his vanity at making a semi-witty comment that would not let it go unheard. She realized that the key to getting useful information from Chiavel was figuring out exactly that distinction. Was what he was saying important?

"How much power does the Queen normally wield? When things are not in such a state of upheaval." Clerin wondered what would happen if she was unable to give her message to the King. He might even be dead right now, she thought. Who should receive Lembin's message if not King Hulgert?

"It was the King who had claims to lineage, so the Queen is nothing without his presence. Luckily, there is a child, so the Queen may stay on as regent, but maybe not. The scramble for that responsibility, if history has taught us anything, will be quick and brutal. I do not know about your Fluen society, but here in Ariellyna we only use the illusion of civilization to subdue the masses, not the real thing. There have only been four regent family branches in our history, and each one began and ended in a glut of bloody violence. I would only suggest staying in Ariellyna for more than a few moons if you have some perverse need to see the worst of the Luften race." Chiavel's face softened into a pensive expression.

"How old is the child now?" Clerin wondered if the Luftens still had a direct line to the original King, the first Yaven changed. The story she had always been told was that the Fluens were the only derlians to have kept their lineage intact. The rumor that often accompanied the story, in hushed tones of course, was that even the Fluen line had been broken several times. She would have to remember to ask Chiavel what he thought about that later.

"The child is still with the Queen. Or, better put, the Queen is still with child. You see how delicate the situation is?" Chiavel smiled at her. They stopped on the landing that they had just ascended to.

"And, are you sure… I mean, is everyone positive of the lineage of the child?" Clerin was unsure of what Luften protocol dictated in this situation. In some Fluen circles infidelity was a taboo subject. But in other circles, those considered less cultured by those who think themselves polite, that was all that they seemed to talk about.

"That is the delicate part of the situation, yes. I have yet to be able to figure all of that out to my satisfaction, and that is one of the reasons I am here today." Chiavel slowly turned Clerin towards a dark archway that led from the landing to the innards of the tree. "Listen, Clerin, I think we could help each other. How about this? We go in to speak with the various forms of power that we are granted access to. We glean from them every last interesting tidbit. Then, later on tonight, we meet at the Cloak and Stagger tavern and trade our intelligence with each other. What do you wish to know about us; Luftens as a society, the King and Queen in specific, or something more mysterious? What secrets may I help you uncover?" He was standing in front of the dark entrance, both arms outstretched to her shoulders. Clerin was not sure if it was a trick of the sun behind her, glancing off of him, but his face seemed to glow with an intense light. It was oddly unnerving, and Clerin had to consciously think of not just answering. She almost felt compelled to not think before speaking. She was not sure if she just felt comfortable with him, for it felt like they were old friends, or if it was something else.

"I have enough secrets of my own that could be hinted at if I told you what knowledge I was looking for. I am unable to compromise myself in such an unconscious manner. For myself, you may assume that I wish to know everything about Luftens. I may actually show up at the Cloak and Stagger to discuss what I need to know. For you… Well, to be honest, I can promise you nothing about my own reconnaissance. I would assume that you have already used whatever skills you have at your disposal? I would assume you could glean more information than I would ever be able to acquire. You do have impressive skills, yes?" As Clerin talked, he lowered his arms and straightened. He was still smiling and, oddly enough, still had a slight glow.

"That, unfortunately, is where you have strayed. There are some comfort zones that are only surpassed by being with one's own gender. And this, I have to say, is one of those topics." He held out his hands, palms upraised, and bounced them lightly. Clerin knew he did that to imply the origins of the unborn. She knew it, but was unsure of why she knew it. Her first impulse was to wonder why he would not just say it. Why did he have to imply obtusely? That was followed quickly with the realization that he completely assumed she knew what he meant. And, actually, she felt she did know what he meant. She kind of liked that. Her hand unconsciously moved up towards her mouth to hide a tightening smile.

"I do not believe you have any idea of what females talk about when we are alone. Just because you are never there when it happens, does not mean anything special happens. We are not all gossips." Clerin was confused about her own words. They sounded aggressive when she listened to them, even though they did not seem so in her mind. She raised her right hand up, palm towards Chiavel, and nodded her head lightly. She gave him a small smile and said, "We will have to meet after sundown, after I have had a chance to remove the stains and drains of travel from me."

"You are in luck, then. The Cloak and Stagger is also an inn. The owner is a friend of mine, and I would be happy arrange a good price for your lodgings for as long as you are in town." He bowed his head to her. "But, come. We shall soon be amongst royalty." He flourished his arm towards the dark arch, wanting her to walk first. Since she did not want him to study her face while she tried to remember again the exact wording on the scroll, she ducked her head in what she hoped was a nod and strode quickly past him.

The change from the bright sunlight to the inky blackness that was the interior of the tree was instantaneous. At one moment Clerin could see and was heading into darkness, and at the other she was blind. She took two steps into the black and then stopped. Her footsteps seemed to echo back to her. She decided let her eyes adjust before going any further. As she stopped, she could feel Chiavel's hand touch her arm lightly as he strode in past her. Her eyes quickly improved enough to see the outline of his back. They walked through what seemed like a hallway bored into the wood. Soon she could see that the very center of the tree had been hollowed out somehow. It seemed like the open vault was about a fifth of the diameter of the tree. There was a platform circumventing the interior. Clerin was happy to note that the platform had a firm-looking guardrail around it, except for one section right in front of them that looked a little dangerous. She looked up into the center of the tree and saw that it was ringed with platforms, as far as she could see. Shafts of light pierced the ancient wood at each level. The light shot at random angles, in a loose spiral, as each platform had an entrance from the exterior stairs at different points along its circumference.

Chiavel turned and began to talk to someone sitting cross-legged on the floor of the platform. It looked like he placed something into the Luften's hand. That Luften nodded at Chiavel and then went back to staring straight ahead.

Chiavel walked out to the part of the platform that had no guardrail. He motioned for her to join him while he stood there. She walked out onto the wooden planks and felt a small shudder of fear. The section they were standing on was bobbing up and down slightly, as if it were floating in water, and was large enough for four or five derlians to stand on it comfortably. Clerin looked down over the edge and realized she could see another wooden platform section rising up towards them. As it dawned on her what this was, they started to rise up into the air. She naturally gravitated towards the middle while she restrained the urge to clutch at Chiavel's arm.

"So, what are these called?" Clerin felt less nervous if she was talking.

"Sleds." He smiled shyly. "I have never investigated why, though."

"And the Luften you paid? He just sits there and levitates these sleds all day long?" Clerin wondered what kind of derlian would want to do that.

"She, actually. And I paid her one gold head for less than a minute of work. Trust me, these jobs are coveted. What do Fluens do? Pay a carriage driver to torture a horse into doing his work for him? Plus, having a small amount of Luftens responsible for all of the sled traffic makes for a safer trunkway. They used to allow anyone to levitate their own sleds. That worked when only the aristocracy were allowed to enter the King's helioarc. When we realized that power sharing reduced the abuses by the aristocracy and their appointed cronies, the traffic that was allowed audience with the King increased greatly. So, really, this system of sleds in the trunkway came about because the other Branches, quite rudely, imposed their will upon the ruling class. Of course, this mainly just spread the corruption around, but it did thin it out a little as well." The sled they were on seemed to be moving awfully fast for Clerin.

"Well, that certainly is civilized. Unfortunately, we Fluens opted to keep the corruption heaped up at the top. So what branch are you with?" She laughed nervously. Not because of the talking so much, but more because the sled seemed to be rising at an incredible rate. She wondered what Chiavel thought was the source of her nervousness.

"I am from the branch of Largon. We are, as much bad lip as I have given the aristocracy, not part of a guild, but of a family. My branch is very much a part of the aristocracy. Much like yours, yes?" He smiled warmly while Clerin racked her brain. She smiled back at him for a moment when, luckily for her, the sled came softly to a stop. She disembarked with a small leap onto the adjacent platform. Her heart was pounding in her chest as she landed. After her feet found solid purchase she looked up. Though there were still some splashes of light further up in the trunk, there did not seem to be anymore platforms. She assumed they were finally at the main royal platform. Clerin took a deep breath and let it out slowly.

"Please. Lead the way." Clerin swept her arm vaguely towards the giant shaft of light that she assumed led back out. Chiavel merely nodded towards her and began walking. As Clerin left the trunkway's exit hall, her eyes unconsciously looked out over the horizon. The left side of the branch was open to the sky. There was a sea of green treetops as far as her eye could see with a scattering of helioarcs punching up towards the sky. Even though the branch they stepped out on was wide and sturdy, she felt a dizzying vertigo.

Clerin could not tell how far the building that engulfed the right side of the branch stretched up into the tree because she was unable to force her head to tilt back. She could only strain her eyes upwards. Her right hand unconsciously reached out to steady herself at the edge of the archway.

Chiavel walked out onto the branch completely nonchalantly and turned towards two giant doors. He looked back at Clerin as he lifted the large knocker. "It is an amazing view, is it not? They used to have the entrance to the palace here, at the trunkway, but they decided to make waiting for an audience with the King a little more impressive. You know, no one is allowed to build a permanent structure higher up than the palace. If you look up, you can see how far up it spirals around the trunk." He dropped the knocker three times on the door while staring up to where he wanted her to look. She gripped the bark hard with her right hand as she tilted her head back. She looked up briefly just to appease Chiavel. The glance was quick enough for her to see plenty more of the building above the leaves, spiraling upwards at a soft incline.

The door opened swiftly to a vast interior. Clerin moved into the building on Chiavel's heels. Once safely inside, she took a long look around the room. Chiavel was speaking with the half dozen guards who had come to the door at his knock. The ceiling was high and coffered, checkered with large gilded squares. Tall skinny doors led into various depths of the building. Or the helioarc. Clerin was unsure of where one structure ended and the other, made by nature, began. She knew from standing outside that part of this room must be within the giant tree. Paintings of old Luftens were hung all around the room. In fact, it reminded Clerin of the time she got to see the palace in Tureyn. Candles in sconces ringed the room, but none were lit, for there was a bank of windows along the exterior of the room. The sun shone brightly through them, leaving golden checks on the floor to contrast the ceiling. Clerin wandered over to the windows as Chiavel kept chatting with the guards.

She was stunned by the beauty that lay before her. It was strange being so high up, looking out over the vast forest, and not feeling the least bit of vertigo. It was comforting to be inside. She could have watched that sea of green until nightfall. Unfortunately Chiavel was cleared by the guards and ready to have audience with the Queen.

Clerin followed him and two guards through a rabbit warren of hallways and chambers. By the time they reached the antechamber, she was completely lost. She waited outside the room with a silent guard for what seemed an eternity. The guard, for his part, stared straight down the hallway they had just come from, with his back against the tall narrow door that Chiavel had entered. She waited in silence.

Finally, the door opened and Chiavel came walking back out. He nodded and smiled at her. She even thought she detected a quick wink. The guard held the door open for her. She had assumed that he would enter in front of her, but then she figured there had to be several guards already in the chamber with the Queen. Clerin walked through the door with a minimum of trepidation.

To her surprise, the room was much smaller than what she had anticipated. It was certainly opulent, though. There were tapestries covering each wall and a sea of candles peaked out from between them. There were crisscrossing burgundy rugs covering the floor. There was even some light filtering in from some small clerestory windows high up on one of the walls. There were two large chairs against the far wall up on a small dais. She was not sure if they were actual thrones because they did not seem to have enough filigree. Or not enough to be a Fluen throne, at least. The leftmost chair was conspicuously empty. Out of everything in the room, however, it was the Queen that Clerin focused upon.

Her lush brown tresses offset the fact that she was dressed entirely in white. Her hair had some silver streaking, but she looked younger than Clerin had supposed. The Queen sat regally with her back flat against the chair, her hands resting lightly on the lion heads that sprouted off the ends of the chair's arms. Clerin walked down one of the burgundy carpets and dipped low in a curtsey with her head bowed.

"You must be Herance." The Queen's voice was low and husky.

Clerin raised her head and looked the Queen in the eye. "I apologize for any subterfuge I may have used with those whom I did not know. My name is Clerin Toswin, daughter of Midinarre." Clerin rose from her curtsey and reached into her jacket and brought out the second scroll. "I have been in contact with Lembin, through the underwater Temple, and was told that I must speak to Hulgert. Here are my credentials." She walked forward to hand the scroll to Vanelia. The Queen held out a hand and slowly took the scroll. "And here is a gift from the royal line of Tureyn. For your assistance..." Clerin plopped the rather bulky uncut ruby into the Queen's other hand. It was foggy and scruffy, but her mother had assured her it would clean up quite handsomely and, even more important, the rarity of the gemstone in the Luften realm would make it much more valuable than in the Fluen.

"We accept your gift most graciously, but cannot promise any assistance." The Queen slid the ruby into her robes with barely a glance at it. Clerin wondered why she had even handed it over. The rich, who could most afford extravagant purchases, were always getting free things. This seemed to taint their capability of appreciation, thought Clerin. "The King is unable to see anyone for a while. He is, we shall say, indisposed." She dropped her eyes down towards the rolled up parchment. "As for giving Chiavel another name, do not worry. If he did not already know mine, I would have given him something else as well." Without lifting her eyes she slowly began to unroll the scroll. Clerin laughed quietly to herself.

"He left the impression that you two were close. Or maybe that he was close to Hulgert." Clerin was suddenly unsure of what actual impression she had gotten from him.

"Yes, well, Chiavel works entirely on impressions. Do not think twice about it." She did not look up from the scroll, so Clerin decided to let her read in silence. The Queen took quite a while before rolling the scroll back up. Clerin had to struggle inwardly just to keep her back straight and not yawn. Once again she wished she had gone to an inn before finding the Queen.

"This is… interesting. Let me say that I understand the seriousness of this message. I would, if I were able, let you speak to Hulgert immediately. However, that is not possible. You will have to come back in three days' time. Is that acceptable?" Vanelia's hazel eyes pierced into Clerin.

"Of course. I will… I will just come back in three days." Clerin was unsure what would have happened if she tried to tell Vanelia that coming back later was not acceptable.

"Fantastic. I will have the guards watching for you. Please come later in the afternoon, towards evening." Vanelia kept the scroll and waved Clerin away. Clerin went through a wave of emotions before deciding it was easiest to just leave. She wanted the scroll back, but it *was* intended for the King. She wanted to find out more about Vanelia, Hulgert and even the Luften lands. She wanted to be given a plush room with its very own bath. She would have even tried to find out about Vanelia's burgeoning progeny for Chiavel. But she was just too tired to try to argue for more time. She made another deep curtsey, turned, and walked out.

The guard stayed mute as he led her back out of the maze. She, for her part, followed in silence. The group of guards in the entrance room all bowed when she entered. One opened the door for her and waved his hand towards the exit. Clerin was unsure of why, but somehow all of them bowing made her feel a lot better.

She immediately turned into the helioarc and walked through the wooden tunnel. She soon popped out into the trunkway. As her eyes attempted to adjust to the dim light, she peered around for the seated figure. She handed the figure a gold coin. It was a Fluen crown, not a Luften head, but the figure took it without question. "Take me as close to the ground as you can. And take your time, I'm in no hurry." The figure nodded and gestured vaguely towards the sled. Clerin could not tell if the figure was male or female. As Clerin embarked on the sled, she wondered if the mages in charge of the sleds were supposed to wear dark folds of cloth that made them disappear into the background or if they did that on their own. She figured it had to be a uniform of some sort.

The sled floated slowly downwards. Clerin wondered briefly how much they were supposed to be paid. The way down seemed much better than the way up. As the sled came to a halt, she hopped off and headed around the platform as quickly as she could. Back into the blinding light and the external stairs. She took her time walking down outside, watching for her horse as she spiraled around.

As she touched the ground again a guard walked her horse over to her. He bowed at her as he handed her the reins. She smiled briefly. "Thanks for keeping an eye on him. Say, could you tell me how to get to the Cloak and Stagger inn?" She knew that it was bad manners to check her saddle bags, but she could not help herself. As she was making sure everything was where she had left it, the young guard began giving her minor directions.

"Take the main road until you reach the next helioarc, then turn left. It should be about three or four intersections after that. They have a large sign, you should be unable to miss it." He smiled at her even though she was rooting through her bags.

"Thank you." Clerin nodded briefly at him before stepping back so she could mount her horse. The guard bowed low to her and backed up as she swung herself onto the saddle. She tapped her horse's ribs lightly with her heels and he trotted sprightly down the road.

She quickly reached the next helioarc and turned down the road indicated by the guard. She passed rows of wooden buildings, many of them with large wooden signs stuck out into the road from above their front doors. It seemed as if the buildings constructed on the ground were more shoddily made than what she could glimpse in the helioarcs. They seemed grayer, more weathered. As the intersections passed, she kept a sharp eye up at the sign level of the passing buildings. Finally, as the weariness pulled at her spine, she saw the sign she was looking for.

Clerin tied her horse outside the inn and began the onerous task of removing her saddlebags. A young-looking Luften came trotting out of the inn as she was unbuckling some of her straps.

"Are you the Fluen?" His eyes were wide in his dirty face.

"Yes. I suppose I am the Fluen." Clerin smiled to herself.

"Then may I take your horse around to the stable?" He had already begun untying the reins that she had so recently knotted. Clerin sped up removing her saddlebags and slung them over her right shoulder.

"Of course." She waved her hand for him to lead the horse away.

"Just ask for Thyramin at the bar." He almost ran off with the horse. She took a deep breath before entering the inn. Apparently Chiavel had already stopped by and spoken to the owner. If she had been less tired she might have been annoyed.

She walked into the inn and had to squint through the haze to get to the bar. The air was thick with a sweet-smelling smoke, so much so that Clerin's lungs began to burn almost instantly. She spoke to the large Luften behind the bar.

"Are you Thyramin?" She waved the thick air in front of her.

"Why yes, I am. You must be Herance." He smiled broadly at her. "I have a room ready for you. And do not worry, it has a private bath. Let me show you the way. Retalle!" He cupped his hands around his mouth as he yelled. A short, pudgy Luften walked over to the bar. "Watch the bar for a moment." He slapped the bar with his palm. He then walked around the bar and held a key up for Clerin to see. "Do not worry. A friend of Chiavel's is a friend of mine."

He reached out and plucked her saddlebags from off of her shoulder. Then he walked over to some stairs hidden in the haze at the back of the common room. They walked up two flights of stairs before turning down a hallway. At last they stopped at a door at the end of the hall. Thyramin unlocked the door and swung it open with a flourish. He walked in and tossed the saddlebags on the bed and swept his left arm in a wide arc and ended pointing at a door in the far wall.

"There is your private bath. There is some water on the fire, but it has probably not started to boil yet. Do you need anything?" His hands were lightly wringing each other as he smiled at her. She thought about just saying no, to see if he would leave. Instead, though, she pulled a silver crown from her pouch and handed it over.

"Thank you for the bath." She gave him a quick smile before pulling away.

"Of course, of course. Thank you." Clerin counted three deep bows as Thyramin finally backed out and closed the door.

Clerin let out a large sigh. It seemed like one of the longest days she had ever lived through. She wanted to sit down on the edge of the bed for a moment, but she knew she would be unable to get back up. She forced herself to turn and open up the door to the bath.

The steam billowed weakly out of the room over her, trying unsuccessfully to push away the stench of smoke. The room was tiny, with a large circular wooden tub in one corner while a cauldron was barely steaming away under a chimney in the other corner. The cauldron was on a wheeled contraption with chains and gears. She thought briefly that Thyramin should have shown her how to use it, but at the thought of his bulk and his large gestures filling the tiny room, she discarded the idea. Rather than let the water heat to a roiling boil, she decided to begin the bath right there and then. The copper-ringed tub already had some cold water in it, so she grabbed a towel to push the metal contraption over to it. There was a long lever on the side to tip the cauldron. She poured about half of the cauldron water into the tub and then wrestled it back over the fire.

As she undressed fully for the first time in days, she looked down at her right thigh. There, previously unbeknownst to her, was a large white scar. She stared at it for a while, pushing on it. There was no pain, but it was the longest scar she had ever seen. As she sunk herself into the warm water she pondered why she ended up with the scar. It was not as if it had healed naturally. Not really. It certainly did not take days to close up. As the water pulled the tension from her body, she remembered her first failed attempt to heal it, flying away on her horse. She laughed lightly to herself. *Now I match my horse,* she thought.

Clerin ended up using all of the cauldron water. She waited until it was uncomfortably tepid before she even thought of leaving. Finally, after she dried off, she remembered Chiavel. All she wanted was to go to bed. It was not Chiavel, he seemed nice, but she just did not want to go back downstairs. Back into that smoky common room full of strange Luftens. She tried to think of a congenial way out of meeting with him but nothing came to mind. So she got dressed as quickly as she could, intending to cut the evening as short as possible.

She was halfway down the main stairs before she noticed Chiavel. He was sitting alone at a small table towards the back door. She trotted down the remaining stairs and over to the seat he had kept empty. She tried to smile widely as she spoke to him. "Sorry it took me so long to get down here. I got a little held up in the bath."

There were two glasses of mead on the table, and he scooted one of them over to her. He looked at her intently for a brief moment. "It is I who should apologize, Herance. You have, no doubt, had an incredibly long day. In my haste to offer hospitality, I did not realize that I put a weight of obligation on you to lengthen your day. Allow me to switch my offer to a later time. Tomorrow around noon, perhaps?" He smiled his question at her. Clerin smiled back at him and took a small sip from her glass. The flavor was thick and sweet. Much too sweet. Clerin wished she had brought some wine with her. She had tried mead before, a dignitary had presented her father with several bottles, but had never gotten the knack for drinking it.

"Thank you for noticing, it *has* been a trying day. Besides, my meeting with the Queen did not culminate in any information for you. It was a pretty quick meeting. I have to go back in a couple days." She took another drink. The weariness was catching up with her, but the mead was making it more bearable.

"Oh. Are you… If you do not mind me asking, are you meeting with the King?" He smiled at her again and took another drink of his own. There was an odd look in his eyes, though. An intensity that was not there a mere moment ago.

"No, not that I know of. I had just given her a request for some information. I think she needs some time to gather everything." Clerin realized she was being clumsy. And, if she was honest with herself, she was not quite sure why she did not just tell Chiavel the truth. Instead of thinking about it, she took another sip.

"Of course. The King is a very difficult Luften to meet with." He laughed quickly. Clerin decided that she was just tired.

"Well, thank you again for having the room set up. I am looking forward to meeting with you tomorrow, but I am pretty tired." Clerin pushed the rest of her drink back over to Chiavel.

"Actually, you never th... That sounds wonderful. I will be here at high noon." He smiled warmly at her.

She smiled at him in return and stood to leave. It seemed smokier as she was standing, though she had not thought that possible. Clerin walked back upstairs to her room without looking back at Chiavel.

She closed her door behind her and locked it. For some reason she felt a little nervous still, so she took the wooden high-backed chair, spun it around, and wedged it under the door handle. She kicked the back legs a little closer to the door to stick it in place. She got undressed, put on a semi-clean shift, and tucked herself into bed. She had wanted to read the last scroll, the one for Hulgert himself, but could not keep her eyes open for much longer. So, instead, she blew out the candle on the nightstand and fell immediately to sleep.

The days flew by. Against her better judgment, she completely enjoyed her time with Chiavel. He showed her the sights of Ariellyna, or at least as many of them as they could fit within the short time allotted to them. He even walked her back to the royal helioarc on the evening she was to meet with Hulgert. He had said goodbye at the base of the tree but she figured she would see him again at the inn later. She did not know what would happen after her meeting, but she figured she would have another couple of days before anything else was required of her. She had truly enjoyed her relaxed time in Ariellyna and did not want to leave anytime soon. She had never spent time in another realm, and it was incredibly refreshing. So many little idiosyncrasies were the same as in the Fluen lands, but so many things were different as well. She thought about that while soaring upwards in the trunkway, her comfortable robes wafting in the moving air. Magic was pervasive here. It was not just for the upper classes or the gifted. It was almost… menial. Though not in a degrading way. There was not much music, however. Oh, there were the occasional minstrels in some of the taverns, but in the Fluen lands they were on every corner. She did not see one single play or opera while with Chiavel. The modes of entertainment seemed so different. Clerin's thoughts stopped with the sled. She dismounted and walked quickly to the huge front doors, trying not to look over the edge of the giant branch.

She dropped the large knocker once and it gave a loud hollow sound. The door opened swiftly to a gaggle of guards. "State your business." It was spoken in a dull monotone from the guard who opened the door.

"I am Herance, here to see Queen Vanelia. She should be expecting me." Clerin's tone was a little more sharp than she intended, but at least it brought the guard to a semblance of attention.

"Of course. Follow me." He turned on his heel and led her back into the bowels of the helioarc.

She followed through all of the twists and turns without paying attention. That was what was great about having a guide—she could let her mind wander. They finally stopped at a door that she recognized.

The guard made a knock, paused, then made two more. Clerin was listening for a response but could hear nothing from the other room. He waited for a moment before he opened the door, and she walked straight in.

Clerin noticed that both chairs, or thrones, were occupied. She recognized the Queen immediately and, therefore, assumed that the white-haired Luften next to the Queen must be Hulgert. He had burgundy robes flowing over him and many large rings on his fingers. What struck Clerin most, however, was his face. It was deeply wrinkled, with a well-trimmed white beard. His eyes were a striking light brown. They were oddly glazed, though. Not cataracts, but they looked unfocussed and distant. She stopped right in front of them both and curtseyed. Before she tore her eyes from the King, she thought she noticed something wet at the edge of his mouth, glistening into his groomed beard. She realized it must be drool.

"Well, Clerin, here is the Luften King, Hulgert." It seemed to Clerin that Vanelia was glaring at her but she was not sure. Just in case, Clerin curtseyed again to the King.

"Very pleased to make your acquaintance." She did not really know what to do.

"Do not worry about speaking to him." Vanelia waved her hand vaguely. "I was hoping he would be more... coherent by today. But as you can see... he is not." Vanelia's eyes looked moist to Clerin.

"Well, I am very sorry to hear that." Clerin almost laughed nervously but luckily did not.

"Why? Did you do this to him?" Vanelia's eyes flashed briefly.

"Of course not. I just meant that I feel bad for your loss. It must be very difficult." Clerin did not know what to say.

"Yes, it is. I do not know what to do. The assembly has been more and more aggressive about pressing to see him. They know something is wrong, and I can only stall for so long. I… well, I should be the one to apologize to you." The Queen looked down for a moment. Clerin assumed that Vanelia was composing herself and did not feel she should interrupt her.

The pause widened to an uncomfortable silence. Eventually it got to the point that Clerin knew she must say something, anything, to break the deafening quiet. But there was nothing to say. She could not think of anything at all. Finally, the dearth of conversation lasted long enough that Clerin's emotions came full circle back to the banality of boredom. Hulgert, for his part, did not move or even twitch. Clerin thought about staring at him to see if he blinked but felt that she should keep her eyes on the Queen. She could not look at Vanelia's face, however, so she stared at her white dress.

"Then I suppose you will have to give your message to me. As you can see, the King will be unable to communicate with you." Vanelia looked up at Clerin, and she could tell that Vanelia had been crying. The entire situation had grown so uncomfortable that Clerin would have much rather been choking in the haze that was the Cloak and Stagger's common room.

Clerin handed Vanelia the last of the scrolls. "Actually, it is more of a request. From one Kingdom to another. I was hoping to be able to see your Temple. Where do Luftens commune with their Beleg?" Clerin spoke a little too quickly. As if the silence was what was normal and her speaking was more like a barking dog. Making noise just to exclaim its existence.

Vanelia would not be deterred, however. She read the scroll completely, then began at the top and re-read it. After what seemed like forever, she laid the scroll down on her lap.

"The only one who communed with Linchon was Hulgert. It is a privilege of royalty, you know. Direct royalty. So no one really knows where the Temple is. There is a cliff near the desert where he would camp alone for fortnight or so, but I am not positive of the exact spot. However, I do think we can help each other." Vanelia was looking down at the scroll, not at Clerin. When she finally looked up at Clerin, her eyes were wet and bright, and they stared at Clerin with a strange intensity. "You see, I need a favor from you as well. Magic is having a fading effect on Hulgert. He no longer responds to the daily treatments he has been getting, not like he was even just a moon ago. He needs something permanent, Clerin. And that is the one thing, as we all know, that is impossible for derlians. There is, however, a legend of a well in the desert. It is said that the water from this well can cure anything." The Queen looked down silently for a moment. Clerin was stunned into speaking but could think of nothing to say.

"Can you fly him over to the well? You have a bunch of levitators just working in your trunkway. You could just..." Clerin trailed off. She was having a difficult time looking at Vanelia's eyes. At first they had just seemed distraught, but now there was something deeper in them, and they seemed to strain slightly against their sockets.

"No, no. It is never in the same place twice. And even if it were, you must walk there. No one has ever reported seeing the well from the air. The real problem is that those who have seen the well have not always tasted from it. Most never even arrive there." Vanelia laughed briefly. "But the legend speaks of a Fluen being able to bring enough drops back to cure one derlian. You see? If Hulgert is healed, he can take you to commune with Linchon himself."

"But surely that has been tried before. I am certainly not the first Fluen visitor to Ariellyna." Clerin did not know why she felt shy about agreeing to help.

"You are the first I felt I could trust. You are the first who asked me for a favor. And you are the first who appeared after he took a turn for the worse. Some would say it was merely auspicious timing. I, however, like to think of it as fate. Fate brought you here to me. Implacable fate." Vanelia started to trail off.

"Well, what I had meant was that surely this has been tried for someone else, earlier in history. A Fluen has come back from this well with the healing elixir, yes? Many times? What is the success rate, do you think, on average? And does this elixir always work, each and every time?" Clerin felt oddly claustrophobic.

"Yes, of course. In the legend it works great." Vanelia's cheeks turned a shade more rouge.

"So you are implying that no Luften in living memory has seen the elixir." Now it was Clerin's turn to laugh nervously.

"A need like this does not come by often. This is a convergence of fate like none that has been witnessed in living memory. The Kingdom needs your help, Clerin, and... we would be prepared to compensate you." Vanelia nodded at Clerin during the last sentence.

"Are you with child? Is it Hulgert's?" Clerin asked the questions in such quick succession that Vanelia would have been unable to answer the first one before the second was spoken, even with each answer consisting of only one word. As it was, however, Vanelia sat back in her opulent chair and stared down at Clerin. The silence began to grow between them again. Clerin understood Vanelia's desperation, but did not share it. Everyone believes their crisis is a convergence of fate. Everyone inherently knows that they are at the center of life. That is all they have ever known. The rich in general, and royalty in specific, thought Clerin, believe in this mantra even more strongly than the common citizen. She knew that she was asking a dangerous question. And if she were honest, she did not even really need to know the answers. More than anything she needed to see that Vanelia needed her help badly enough to make personal sacrifices. Clerin thought that forcing the Queen to confide in her would bring about an honesty that she could trust. The only way she could agree to help the Queen was if she trusted her, and the only way she could gain that trust was to be given it.

"Yes, I am with child. But no, I am not sure who the father is. To be honest, if you must know, the odds are low that it is Hulgert's. It is in the realm of possibility, though. I do not know what to do, Clerin. I cannot speak any of this to another Luften, and, now, neither can you. They can smell weakness, you know. I sometimes think of the Branches as a pack of howling wolves with the scent of blood in their muzzles. No, not even wolves, but coyotes, yipping nonsense at each other in the red dusk." Vanelia sank back heavily.

"If I try and fail. If I come back empty handed or the elixir does not work. Then you will do your utmost to show me where the Temple is, yes? I can only divert a limited amount of time for this quest, for I am on one of my own." Clerin was in mild disbelief of herself.

"I will send my mage with you. Of course, you may have as many warriors as you feel wise, but be warned that the desert is a harsh environment, and more mouths to feed can make travel difficult." Vanelia began to speak in a more businesslike manner. That made Clerin suddenly realize what she had done.

Chapter 11

Vrric had poured himself into his study. He spent moons enwrapped in magic and meditation, maybe even a full cycle. It was hard to tell in the beginning how much time had passed. He read every night and spent his days exercising his mind. At first it was incredibly difficult and filled with frustrations and headaches. Vrric struggled with comprehending chaos. Training himself to see possibility was hard. He remembered one particularly trying evening when he broke down crying because he could not *see*. He yelled at Revkin, striking out randomly, and threw his books against a wall. It was embarrassing for him to recall, even now. But even worse than *seeing* possibility, was sifting through it to find the desired outcome. Once he was able to do that, once he could figure out what path his mind had to take, where to turn in the blind chasms that enshrouded the future, came the most difficult trick of all. Part of it was just the knowledge of how to go about casting spells. Part of it was that his mind started out relatively weak, and it took a while to strengthen that. Part of it was that chaos is limitless, if not infinite; no, not quite infinite, just eternal. The worst, however, what caused Vrric to sweat during the sleepless nights that he cursed his own ineffectiveness, was once he had found his particular possibility, pushing his willpower through the destiny of the future. Surpassing the natural order of things by imposing his own mind upon reality. He could not explain how he finally gained that skill. He certainly did not understand it enough to be able to teach it. Finally, after all of the constant pressure, the effort and work had paid off. Vrric was able to cast spells consistently, without passing out or getting nosebleeds. He still got headaches occasionally, but overall he felt like he was making progress.

It had taken so long for him to feel like he was making progress that he had honestly wondered whether or not he had made the right choice. There were times when his mind felt like gelatinous pudding, when Revkin kept yelling at him, that he missed the simple repetition of bending steel to his will with his arms. His apprenticeship was so intensive that he had almost forgotten his name. If someone had called out "Vrric" within his earshot, he would not have even turned towards them. It was only "Mudfoot, get up, you have failed again. Mudfoot, why can't you even light a tiny candle with your mind? Mudfoot, you are a disgrace!" over and over and over. Vrric almost went mad with the pressure. He hated the fact that it took so long to get anywhere, he hated himself, but most of all he hated Revkin.

Not anymore, though. There was a point, the tipping point Revkin called it, where Vrric could do small things whenever he wanted. He could cast Mek spells regularly, Nar spells most of the time, and had even cast one or two spells at the Eqe power level. He felt that each day brought him greater power. After meditating, he would feel like he gained a little, learned a little. Once he had passed the tipping point, it seemed that he could improve. Some days it was imperceptible, but it was there. Each day he felt he was traveling along a path. Heading towards self-betterment. He felt like he was gaining ground on becoming a mage.

After meeting Chiavel and Vanelia, so long ago, Vrric had felt even more empowered. He could leave the helioarc occasionally. He could be around other Luftens besides Revkin. Chiavel made Vrric feel more… Luften. He would say the oddest things while they were standing on the platform waiting for audience with Vanelia.

"It's all in the voice inflection, not the nomenclature. You know how you can yell horrible things to a dog in a nice tone of voice and they will never know? The same rule applies to derlians. With the proper tone and intonation, maybe some well-timed hand gestures, you can explain how the Luften in front of you has the mind of an insect, with only the most basest of instincts, and they will thank you for the information. You know? You know, politics only work because the vast majority of Luftens are utter idiots. Why would one give power to another for nothing in return? We are all idiots." It was simple, almost childish, but it made Vrric laugh.

Vanelia was something more complicated. There was an air of desperation around her. Like she was hunted. Vrric was not sure why, but it made him a little nervous. Surely Hulgert's health condition was part of it, but there was something more, something deeper. To keep himself out of the prison that Revkin had made for him, though, he gladly put up with his unease. He had been trying to heal Hulgert for at least a moon, visiting almost every third day.

Vrric had been going there so often that the guards stopped looking at him. In fact, his arrivals had become so frequent that they had become rote, almost redundant. Though the research itself was definitely interesting, healing as an act of chaos was a flimsy thing. Attempting permanence with the temporary. As a whole, Hulgert was maintaining, which was better than the alternative. But no matter how hard he tried, Vrric could not actually heal Hulgert. He just tried to keep a status of remission, to avoid losing ground, and he hoped that Hulgert thought the same. To be honest with himself, though, Vrric had not the foggiest clue as to what Hulgert thought. He hoped, more than anything, that he was not merely prolonging Hulgert's pain.

It was on a random day that the queen asked for an audience with Vrric. He had been meeting with Vanelia every third day, like clockwork. She had one of her messengers *whisper* to Revkin that Vrric was needed at sundown. Vrric hoped, against his better judgment, that Hulgert was showing signs of improvement.

Vrric arrived early, so he dallied at the tower. He leaned against a baluster and stared out over the guardrail towards a dying sun. The red stain had soaked the entire horizon in a deep velvet slash. It was like a beautiful murder scene: breathtaking. Vrric waited until the sun slowly faded behind the distant trees. Then, before he could get too bucolic, he entered the maze of hallways, walkways and doorways. His mind wandered as his body made the twists and turns automatically. Finally he wound his way to the second throne room.

The guard let him in immediately, and he strode towards the King and Queen at the back of the room. He walked halfway across the room before he noticed there was another derlian standing in front of them. He faltered a brief moment before continuing his walk. He stopped and bowed deeply to the Queen and then to Hulgert. He turned towards the stranger and immediately bowed deeply to her, just in case. When he rose he took his first look of her. She had to have been the most beautiful derlian he had ever set his eyes upon.

She had pale blue eyes, the color of a lightning strike. They seemed to glow from underneath. They dominated her face with their large wet depths. She had shoulder length pale hair, floating behind her. She had a lithe body that even the amorphous robe she was wearing could not hide. She had a quick dimpled smile that filled Vrric's vision.

"Vanelia is sending you? Well, I guess it could be worse." She grinned at Vrric. There was something devious in that grin. Vrric couldn't think at all. He felt his blood hammer in his neck. "My name is Herance. You must be my guide?" She was definitely not a Luften, thought Vrric. She couldn't have been a Pyran, and Vrric did not even know what Gaens looked like. She must be a Fluen. Yes, Vrric's mind said the word quietly in his mind, *Fluen*. "Does my guide have a name?" The eyes were still giggling even as her voice became serious.

"Vrric. My name is Vrric." There was no way he was going to introduce himself as Mudfoot. He was quietly stunned for a moment before the words she spoke sunk into his foggy head. "I am not sure what you mean by guide, though." He laughed nervously before the Queen spoke up.

"I have a task for you, Vrric. Do not worry about Revkin, he has already agreed to let you leave the nest for a moon. I need you. No, Hulgert needs you. No, our entire realm needs you to guide Herance through the Northern Desert. We need you to find the healing waters of the well, to help Herance bring enough water back to heal Hulgert. And we will be incredibly grateful for your service, Vrric. Both to you and to Revkin." Vrric was listening to Vanelia. However, he was also watching Herance out of the corner of his eye. This made his face turn towards Hulgert. The glazed eyes and drool glistened at Vrric. When Vanelia said the word "grateful," Vrric could not be sure, but he thought he saw the edge of Herance's mouth twitch slightly into a smile. This is how quickly life can change, thought Vrric. "We, the Throne, are thinking of recognizing grey mages." He would have acquiesced anyway, but now he knew why Revkin had agreed to let him go.

"Of course, my Queen, I am at your service." Vrric bowed again to Vanelia.

"Fantastic. It will be a day or two before the entire team can be assembled and provisioned. I will contact Revkin when we are prepared." Vanelia waved at him somewhat dismissively. Instead of annoying Vrric, like it usually did, he was easily able to ignore it. He bowed to Hulgert and yet again to Herance, turned and walked back the way he came. He did not look back even though he wanted to.

He flew straight back to Revkin, feeling somewhat giddy. It was well into his flight that he realized he had not cast any healing on Hulgert while he was there. Which made him wonder, briefly, if he should show up for the regular appointment tomorrow. The flight was not long, and it was only memorable because it was the last time he got a headache from casting a mundane spell.

Vrric arrived at the helioarc and waited a moment outside. It was not that he was avoiding Revkin, but he wanted to savor the moment. He knew that once he entered the helioarc his life would begin to change. Again. Vrric stood out on the branch and watched the bats flap impossibly along in the dusk. He fingered the vines that Revkin had neglected to remove from the helioarc. He breathed in the cool night air. Before long, and unbidden, his thoughts turned to Herance's face. To her aching beauty. He finally realized just how long he had been standing outside. He turned and entered the helioarc, looking around mildly for Revkin.

Revkin was sitting in Vrric's tiny room drinking a bit of mead. He was slowly spinning the geode book end between a finger and the desk. "Ah, you are back from the big meeting. How did that go? Or should I ask if you are going?" Revkin took a small sip.

"Yes, of course. Not only does Hulgert need me. Not only did the Queen, our ruler, ask for my help. But, and I know you may not believe this, but I think I might be in love." At that Revkin smiled widely.

"Love? You had best be careful of that, Vrric. You know what love leads to, don't you?" Revkin's voice hovered somewhere between humor and tenderness.

"Happiness?"

"Would that it only brought that! No, that is not to be feared. What love brings is contentment." Revkin's voice began to swing towards humor. His smile began to warm his cheeks. "And you know what contentment is, don't you?"

"Eternal happiness?" Vrric was a touch confused by his mentor's line of questioning.

"Hah! Contentment has nothing to do with happiness. No, no, my apprentice. Contentment is the opposite of ambition. The complete opposite. And if you begin to strangle your ambition, you will lose that delicate edge that I have been trying to hone on you." Revkin's smile was large and warm. He took another drink before speaking again. "But, seriously, I do want you to promise me something."

"Of course, anything." Vrric wondered how deep into his cups Revkin was. He sat upon the edge of his bed, perched to face Revkin.

"Never let your ambition slip like I did. My contentment source, unlike something as noble as love, was the drink." He swirled his glass lightly before taking another sip. "Elange tried to warn me of contentment, but I would not listen. He explained it thoroughly, told me anecdotes and horror stories. He tried his best, but I thought that I could have both contentment and ambition. I was wrong." He took another drink. Vrric began to wonder how content Revkin truly was. Revkin inflated his chest and then let out a slow breath.

"That is not why I am here, though." Revkin swept his arm loosely around the tiny room. "I need another, different, promise from you. While you are there, in the desert, you must begin to prepare yourself mentally for what lies ahead. I figured you would agree to Vanelia's request, and to be honest, I am very proud of your progress. You have improved most quickly, Mudfoot, and I probably do not state how impressed I am with you nearly enough." Vrric thought, maybe pettily, that he had never heard Revkin say how impressed he was. "In fact, I believe that you are at a turning point of your education. A stage that I cannot help you with. I need you to promise me to use this journey of yours as a vision quest." Revkin's voice gained slightly in volume and power. He always spoke through his diaphragm when he was feeling dramatic.

"Vision quest?" Vrric had read the term before and even had a vague idea of what it meant, but he wanted to know what Revkin's definition was. Chiavel had told him that the *way* Luftens tell a story is often much more telling than the words themselves. Vrric found that he paid more attention to others' choice of language than he used to after meeting Chiavel.

"I know that you are on another quest, beholden to the Queen. Your duty truly lies with others. But, before you return, you have an obligation to yourself that you must perform. For a period of time, no one can say for how long, you must live in solitude, which means you may only talk to animals. Also, you may sleep only under the stars, drink only from streams, eat only fruit and maybe the occasional cactus button and, most importantly, you must find your glyph. That one idea that encompasses you, that embodies your spirit. It may be an animal, or a rock formation, or a tree or a river or an idea. An imaginary beast. The stars in the sky or the soil below. It could be something from a different realm, from the Yavens. It can be yourself, or a piece of you. Even a lowly toenail. Anything. You must find some symbol, something that calls forth the idea that you must remember, that which defines your future. Each of us has something that destiny has laid before us. That which pleases it when we approach and angers it when we depart. The idea of a path that we cannot see, only feel, as we push against its inertia. Like crawling along a confluence of helioarc branches, lost amongst the leaves, climbing from one limb to another, from one tree to another. Only when you burst back out into the light can you see where you are headed. Only then can you realize which tree you are climbing. This is what the vision quest should do, provide that space and time to step beyond your path to see with clarity where you are and where you are headed. That future direction, that lengthy goal, that is the idea you must find for yourself. What will remind you of how to best crawl through the leaves? What will help guide you through the dense foliage, help you avoid a catastrophic fall? This will be your glyph, this idea, this reminder. Then, and only then, you may find your chosen name, Mudfoot. When you return we will, of course, continue your training. But, if your story of your revelation is true, I will willingly call you by whatever name you desire. If, however, what you tell me is false, I will know, and you will stay Mudfoot." Revkin took a long draught of his mead. He stared at the tiny amount left in the glass, swirling it vigorously.

"How will I know?" Vrric was going to say more, but he was quickly interrupted.

" 'How will I know?' That is always the question, isn't it?" Revkin smiled and finished his drink. "It is the worst kind of knowledge. It is the kind of knowledge that you will only know after you thought you knew. Maybe several times, you will think you know. But once you do actually know, you will realize that the others were false. By then, however, you may have already made the wrong decision. But with this quest, with naming yourself, you will have your entire return trip to decide which is the true choice, so you should not worry about choosing incorrectly. I need one more promise from you." Vrric had lost track of how many promises Revkin had extracted from him this evening.

"Have I ever told you no?" Vrric sounded more critical to his own ears than he had meant to be.

"Of course not. You are a good soldier, Mudfoot." Revkin laughed briefly. "I want you to find Elange. If at all possible. It would probably be best if you met with him before embarking on your vision quest, but I am not even sure which eshram he is currently in. Therefore, all I can truly ask is that you look for him along your other path, the Queen's path. There are things that he can explain that I never found my voice for. The insanity of mindtraps, the creation of syllables, the Minora syllables, and especially of quests.

He has this way of telling the truth without making sense. And I mean Truth, with a capital 'T', the proper noun. He has the most perceptive mind that I have ever had the pleasure of knowing. If there is a living Luften who could help you with something as amorphic and chaotic as a vision quest, it is Elange." Revkin sat back in his chair and nodded to himself. Vrric had a million questions in his mind, so he picked the largest mystery.

"What is an eshram?" Vrric wanted to ask more but he did not know enough to form good questions. He had heard Revkin mention them before, but had never really gotten a true understanding of what they were. Just vague images. While his mind was wandering, Revkin stood and stared at his empty glass.

"We should head into the parlor. There, I will tell you all about eshrams." Revkin wandered out of the room, leaving Vrric sitting on the edge of his own bed. He stood up and slowly followed Revkin's spoor. By the time Vrric turned the corner, Revkin was finishing pouring the second glass.

"Here. You will need this." Revkin handed a glass to Vrric and kept the first clutched in his right hand. They sat in opposing chairs, facing each other. "There is, of course, no limit to chaos. Therefore, there is no limit to the thought-forms that may be encompassed by syllables. Therefore, there are more than eight elements. There are more than eight effects. There are even more spheres of influence. There might be, if one were powerful enough, even be more levels of power. The Majora syllables that you have been studying are but a section of chaos. Used in conjunction, they can cover over ninety percent of what you would typically need to do. It is only in those rare instances where one feels compelled to step outside of the norm, out of the taught magic and into the intuitive magic. One can be compelled by necessity or even curiosity, but one thing is for sure. If they are to find a Minora syllable on their own, then they must be compelled by a powerful force. Do you know what a mindtrap is?" Revkin was jumping all over the place, conversationally speaking, and Vrric was having some difficulty in fully comprehending the intent behind the words.

"Mindtrap? You have spoken about it before, but no, not really." Vrric himself took a large draught from his glass.

"It is the essence of insanity. A circle that cannot be broken, because it leads where it ends and it starts again where it stops. The mind is truly an amazing landscape. Much learning is circular, I will agree with that. In the proper functioning mind, however, as the circle comes back towards itself, the idea delves deeper, turning the circle into a spiral. With this method, one can keep increasing new knowledge while filling in previous ideas with greater detail. The problem that the insane have is that when circle comes back to itself, their minds pop back to their original position. Something in the swing back towards the origin makes the original idea gain in magnetic strength. Most Luftens can feel this happening and can will the circle into a spiral. Those who cannot... Well, they end up in eshrams." Revkin's eyes were glazing slightly. Vrric had a few choice words for the state of Revkin's mind, but kept them to himself. "You must keep your learning moving up or down, Mudfoot, not just around and around. But I am losing track. The reason I mention mindtraps is because they are the only way to reach certain breakthroughs in reasoning. Sometimes you must circle around a mystery for a while before understanding can be achieved. Just make it a spiral before you get stuck."

"I think you are stuck in a mindtrap right now." It just popped out of Vrric's mouth. He was not trying to be rude, but Revkin kept covering the same ground. To Vrric's surprise, Revkin burst into laughter.

"True, completely true. I think I have worked myself up a little too much. I apologize." Revkin finished his mead off. Vrric worked on his own glass a little. "Well, you will be leaving soon. You must spend tomorrow preparing, gathering and packing. Tomorrow night I want you to have a list of unresolved questions. Anything that you have been thinking about, anything. I promise you, here and now, that tomorrow I will answer anything that you ask directly, without any subtlety, to the best of my abilities. Now, it is late and you should get some rest. Soon you will be thinking of how comfortable your tiny cell was when you are out in the elements, traipsing across the desert." Revkin laughed heartily again.

The weight of the day began to settle on Vrric's shoulders, but his heart was light. He left his mead and conversation with Revkin and headed back to his tiny cell. He had planned on making a list before turning in but instead capitulated to his desire for rest.

Vrric awoke later than he ever had since he arrived under Revkin's tutelage. He felt thoroughly energized and ready for whatever the day had in store. He only hoped that he would feel that way on the day that he left for the desert. He felt that if you could start a journey in an optimistic mood, then you had a much greater chance of ending near the destination that you had aimed for. He truly believed that steering life took a telescopic view of destination. The sooner you can make an adjustment in your direction, the least amount of energy it will take to make that adjustment.

The daylight hours slid by incredibly quickly, and Vrric enjoyed the packing immensely. He packed his backpack and his saddle bags before he packed any books. They seemed like such an unnecessary burden. And yet… yet, Vrric felt like he should take something to study, something to keep himself learning on the road. He wanted to drown out the mind-numbing drone that permeated everything on a long journey. Especially one that had such an unknowable destination as some well in an uncharted desert. He rearranged his backpack a minimum of four times, trying to find the perfect balance. Once the items were chosen harmoniously, they had to fit together in the most comfortable way possible. Vrric had no illusions as to how much of this coming adventure was going to be walking and how much was going to be resting. He had vowed to visit a cobbler and buy the most comfortable boots he could find. Suddenly there was only enough time for boots or to chat with Revkin. As much as he wanted to pick Revkin's brain some more about magic, he knew how much of this journey would be spent on his feet. The boots won over curiosity. Besides, he was unsure of what else they could discuss after spending so much time together.

The time had finally arrived. Vrric gathered all of his gear and headed out towards the royal helioarc. The goodbyes were mercifully quick. After all, at this time, they both believed the trip ahead to be brief. Vrric floated down towards the ground, to the mud, to travel on horseback. He figured he might as well get used to the slow mode of travel. It had been quite some time since he had been in a saddle, so he flew around briefly before landing. He knew that he was stalling. He was spiraling. He was feeling the wind flow through his hair. He felt a sense of freedom that an escaped convict feels. Vrric hovered there next to the horse, above the mud, lingering in the moment. Finally he settled on the ground and slapped the saddlebags over the horse's back. After making the appropriate adjustments and cinching everything tight, Vrric mounted and tapped the horse's ribs lightly with his heels.

The horse trotted along towards the helioarc as if she took the same path every day. It was a nice steady pace. The smell of the horse infiltrated Vrric's nose. He made himself look forward to the time when it was so familiar to him that he could no longer smell it. It would come quicker than he had hoped.

When he arrived at the royal helioarc, the guards were waiting for him. He dismounted and handed the reins to the closest one. The sled ride in the trunkway was incredibly quick. He flowed through different sets of guards as he was wound back into the bowels of the helioarc. He ended in a room that he had never seen before, and then he was again in the presence of the Fluen. She seemed to glow.

The room was large and square with a large square table in the center of it. The walls were covered with colorful tapestries. Vrric thought they showed a preponderance of military scenes. The center table had tall, straight-backed chairs flanking all four sides of it. They were tall enough that Vrric figured that when he sat down the chair's back would reach higher than his head. None of them had any arms, and they were made with a thick dark wood in long plumb lines. The backs were broad vertical stripes, symmetrical exchanges with chunky matter and nothingness. They were cushioned in leather but they looked uncomfortable. What really drew Vrric's attention, however, was the table. It was edged with a wide brim of wood with a smooth dark finish. The center of the table, covering about three-quarters of its area, was a huge topographic map. It seemed to be all of the Luften realm, with some of the Fluen and Pyran realms on the sides. At the far end, where Vanelia and Herance were gathered with their heads bent, the map trailed off into a flat drab area. Vrric wandered off towards them to get a better look. It was not until he was almost across the room that they finally looked up.

"Ah, you're here. We were just examining the map." Vanelia smiled at Vrric. He bowed his head to her and then to Herance. Staring at the near end of the map, however, he could not but notice that it was devoid of any detail.

"Not to seem a pessimist, but what exactly are you examining? There does not seem to be anything there." Vrric smiled back at Vanelia but her grin was slipping slightly.

"Actually, we were discussing how to travel to the Northern Desert, not where to go once you arrive there. Thank you, however, for your clever observations." Vanelia sat down into one of the chairs and motioned for Herance and Vrric to do likewise. As Vrric sat back into his own chair, he realized how wrong he was in his initial assessment of them. The poofy leather was the most comfortable thing he had sat on in quite a while, maybe ever.

"Now, you know how compasses work, yes?" Vanelia was looking right at Vrric. It took him a bit off guard. Did she mean *how* they worked, or just what their predicted outcome was? He guessed, correctly, the latter.

"They point towards the Northern Desert?" Vrric's voice, unconsciously, formed the sentence into a question rather than statement. His arm errantly pointed towards the bland end of the map, without any thought.

"Exactly. Which is how your quest will begin, headed towards the desert. But the problem that other expeditions have found is that the further a compass gets towards the center of the desert, the less reliable they are. There have even been accounts of the needle just slowly spinning in a circle. So you see, the tool that will get you into the vicinity of your goal will cease to work the closer you get to it." Vanelia waved her hand ineffectually in front of her.

"Maybe we should work up to the desert. Show Vrric the path through the Luften lands that you were showing me." Herance smiled at Vrric and then lowered her head to stare at the relief map in front of them.

"Well, Vrric, we are here at the center of the map. The first leg of the journey will be down the Ariel River. She flows down westerly for almost half the way to the beginning of the desert until she arrives at the Iltrolin pools just before the Plyraxus Falls. It should only take four days to ferry down there. Here you will have to skirt past the falls to the confluence of the Ariel and Yadel on horseback. There will be another ferry waiting for you there. After re-entering the river, you should be able to make it down to the midland fork, here, in another two days. You will then have to travel the rest of the way by land." Vanelia was pointing at a blue ribbon on the map with a long pointed baton. She bounced the stick off her hand several times while staring at Vrric. "This is where the compasses shall prove helpful. The journey through Ruyogn Canyon should only take about a day. The Valley of the Caves will take several days, maybe five or so depending on whether you decide to contact someone in one of the eshrams. You might find good information there, but you might not. Many that take refuge there are notoriously unreliable when it comes to directions." Vanelia was pointing at the last semi-defined area on the map. Everything west of the valley was just flat yellow sand. At least that was how it was represented on the map.

"What is an eshram?" Herance sat back in her chair. "You mentioned that earlier but I never caught what it was."

"Well, some experiments in magic do not end well. Sometimes a mage will hurt themselves or someone nearby. Cutting them or burning them or attempting to teleport and leaving half their arm stuck in a rock. Otherwise intelligent mages die all the time trying some incredibly foolish things. Apparently these are the risks that accompany wrestling with reality. Much of the time, however, the damage is not physical, but mental, or something even deeper. The newly mad can sometimes be healed if they are given some time away from society. Eventually they can come back, and while not always completely normal, they can usually cope with reality enough that they no longer disrupt others. They congregate together, segregated from those that are unafflicted, sometimes for the rest of their lives. Where they stay while they are not sane enough for society is at the eshrams. They are villages of necessity, not of opportunity. They spring forth in one area, around a few of the more coherent Luften mages, gaining in members until the size becomes unruly in that harsh environment and they dissipate again into dust. Of course, some of the crazed live as hermits, but most of them belong to one or another of the shifting eshrams. If you really want to know, though, Vrric here could probably answer you more correctly. I am not a mage." Vanelia leaned back in her own chair, waving towards Vrric. The baton lay lifeless in front of her at the flat end of the map.

"To be honest, I have yet to visit any of them and do not really know much about them. Your description, Vanelia, is as good of an explanation as I have ever heard. However, I do have a resident of one of these eshrams that I need to speak with. While I could speak with the mage before or after our visit to the desert, we may as well seek him out on our way through the Valley of the Caves. Just in case he could give us some more clear directions to the center of the desert. That is where we are headed, yes? The well is somewhere in the center of the Northern Desert?" It was Vrric's turn to rest his spine against the supple leather chair.

"That is the only direction I can steer you in." Vanelia stared back at Vrric as a thick silence settled over the room. Vrric wondered if he should have added something to her story about eshrams. He wished he knew anything interesting about them to tell.

"So, basically, after the Valley of the Caves we are on our own?" Herance's pale blue eyes flickered back and forth between Vanelia and Vrric.

"No, not on your own. You requested five other warriors, I believe?" Vanelia was looking at Herance, who nodded in acquiescence. "Then there will be seven of you all together, and the guards should be able to carry most of the provisions and equipment. We can even send some extra horses with you if you like."

"But alone as far as directions are concerned." Herance was staring at Vrric when she spoke. He felt like she had expected him to know how to get to the well. He wondered briefly what Vanelia had told Herance about himself.

"That does seem to be the problem—no one knows how to get there." Vrric laughed nervously. "I think the greater question would be, 'Does the well even exist?' I mean, are we just setting off on a fool's errand?" The Queen gave him a scathing look.

"It does exist! It must." Vrric's chair suddenly became uncomfortable. "Listen, I understand that you both are embarking on a quest at my behalf. If you are unable to find the well before your provisions dwindle, just come back. You will be rewarded either way, trust me." She kept staring at Vrric. He felt a warmth creep into his cheeks. "The important part is that you believe. You must believe or you will never find it. You need to have your full hearts into this quest. Let me know now, right now, if you have doubts about the existence of the well. Or even if you think that you will be unable to find it. Just say so, and I will let you leave here. There are no reprisals." Vanelia's eyes were too intense to stare back at. Vrric looked over at Herance before responding. She was looking intently at Vanelia.

"We are fully committed, Vanelia. Vrric is just expressing the doubts that we are all feeling. For myself, you know that I cannot spend more than two moons on this errand as I have others to complete. As for the reward... You know that my only reason for being here in the Luften realm at all is an opportunity to visit your Temple. I would not be assisting you if I did not think it would eventually assist me. I, however, cannot speak for your mage." Herance had turned from Vanelia during her talk and faced Vrric at the end.

"Of course I believe in the quest, Vanelia. It is just that so few have ever journeyed into the desert that… Forgive my questioning, my queen. I know that you have chosen me for my steadfastness, and I hope that I have not diminished your decision." Vrric's face felt hot under his skin.

"Truth be told, you were chosen for your discretion and versatility more than for your steadfastness. However, I believe that flows heavily through you as well. I could not have asked for better adventurers for my quest, and I am honored that both of you are going. I have chosen some of my most accomplished guards to protect you on your journey. It is high time that all of you were introduced. Are there any more questions about the route?" Vrric could think of hundreds of questions but, unfortunately, Vanelia would be unable to answer any of them. So instead he shook his head at her, smiled at Herance, and hoped that the guards had a map detailed enough at least to get them to the Valley of the Caves. From there, he knew, there were no answers.

"That is fantastic. I have been waiting to meet the entire team." Herance smiled warmly at Vanelia. Vrric began to feel comfortable again, but even more than that, he felt an appreciation to Herance for so easily soothing the situation with Vanelia. It made him think that she had diplomatic blood coursing through her. He, obviously, did not.

Vanelia stood and walked towards a set of large, rectangular doors directly behind her chair. They were opposite the doors that Vrric had entered through. Where his doors had been solid but stately, the ones that Vanelia approached were thick with black iron filigree. She opened the doors with a small flourish.

In walked five Luftens that Vrric would grow to know all too well. While traveling on an arduous journey you could learn things about those trapped along with you that you would rather never had known. However, he did end up liking something about everyone. There were some that he would know for the rest of his life. Vrric would look back on this meeting as a turning point in his life. Even at the time he felt a heavy weight of importance that stuck to everything.

First introduced was Gyllhelon. She had jet black hair pulled back into a tight pony tail. She was tall and lithe, almost willowy, and Vrric would have called her beautiful if he had not just met Herance. The long blade that was lashed to her leg was slightly curved, but looked a little too narrow in breadth to be called a true scimitar. The hilt was long and straight, and her left hand rested lightly upon its end. She gracefully held her hand out to him as they were introduced. Her fingers were long and narrow but had a hidden strength, like the claw of a dangerous raptor.

After Gyllhelon came Torpalin. He projected a menacing figure to Vrric. Not through demeanor or facial expression, but just because he was so huge. He had muscles that bulged from places that Vrric had never seen before. He seemed to have muscles on his muscles. He was tall, but because he seemed to have no neck, it made him appear like he was slightly hunched over. His muscles made his arms stick out away from him, bent at the elbows as if they were unable to stretch out. He had light brown hair and was smiling, with a deep and soothing voice that emanated way down from within his barrel chest. Sticking out from his belt was a large, double-bitted, half-moon, axe. Thick, branded leather hoods covered the blades, protecting Torpalin's arm from accidental amputation.

The middle Luften in stature and order was Haswyxe. He had chestnut brown hair and a boyish face. No one would call him handsome, though Vrric could not pinpoint one particular feature that gave him his homely air. His teeth never seemed to meet in the right places, and when they did, they crashed up against each other a little. His nose had been broken several times, flattening itself a little too wide. There was even a cut in an eyebrow that made a line of scar tissue separating a small island of brow that had long ago been separated from its peninsula brother. Nothing that specifically detracted too much, but the combination made one give pause while speaking with him. On his back was a long bow with white fletched arrows reaching out from the top of their quiver. A broad short sword also hung low at his side in preparation for close-quarter combat.

The fourth Luften to shake Vrric's hand was Escha. She was the shortest derlian in the room and of a somewhat thick build. Her dark auburn hair was more closely cropped than Haswyxe's was. It looked as if she carried an assortment of knives rather than any one large sword. Tight deerskin leggings hugged her thickly muscled legs leading down to tailored leather boots. Vrric would later learn that she was something of a loner, but racked with a nervous energy. A scout by nature, if you will. And she had a weird twitch that would run through her hands while talking. She would stand there, waving her fingers in some repetitive tic, and talk animatedly about whatever had currently captured her imagination. She was the nicest Luften that Vrric had ever met, though. Pure of heart in a slightly childlike manner. She, too, carried a bow. Her fletching, however, was made of brown-and-black spotted hawk feathers. While she had a thick staff tied to her pack, Vrric had a feeling that she used her hidden knives more often.

Finally, and maybe most importantly, Vrric was introduced to Malghain. He was a ruthless fighter. A killer, really, with a killer's instincts. But he was to save Vrric's life more than once. Vrric thought that the most amazing thing about Malghain's looks was that they were perfectly average. He was a little taller than most, maybe, but nothing that would make him stand out. He had a light brown mane and a closely cropped beard. He looked strong, but he was much stronger. He seemed quick in movements, but he was much quicker. He was one of the fastest derlians that Vrric had ever had the privilege to watch move. But he did not *seem* like he was dangerous. You could have seen him walking past you every day out in the street, but you would never be able to describe him if you were asked to later. Vrric thought that might be some of Malghain's strength. The fact that he was perennially underestimated made his skills that much more impressive. All of his victims in the battle field seemed to be ultimately surprised to be losing to one such as him. It was almost embarrassing. He carried a sword at his side, as unremarkable and free from filigree as he was. At his other side sat two daggers of differing size. One was as long as Vrric's forearm while the other was a little more than half of that. There was one tied to his right calf and another, much smaller one, attached to his left forearm underneath his baggy sleeve.

Handshakes were given and names were traded. They all laughed and commiserated about future pains. It was a grand meeting by all accounts, and Vrric would remember it fondly for cycles. It was, in epic proportions, the calm before the storm.

But time passes by mercilessly. Soon they were leaving Vanelia and the palace behind. Soon they were floating down the Ariel river on a low barge. Vrric learned how to play a multitude of card games on the ship. As long as no money was involved, most of the participants could be counted on for a modicum of honesty.

They passed the pools and the falls with only one major incident. While camping at the Iltrolin pools, there was an incredible thunderstorm. It did not tax the campaigners much as they had warning of the storm for quite some time and were well prepared for it. In fact, it was only notable for what happened to Vrric.

He was mesmerized by the lightning. Whereas it kept others awake because of its noise and intensity, it kept Vrric awake because he needed to be amongst it. In the night, in spite of the pouring rain, he rode his horse to the nearest hilltop. There, he dismounted and tied his horse to a small bush, away from as many of the taller trees as possible. Vrric, however, discounted his own safety and climbed to the top of the hill. It was there that he could best see the lightning. It struck down into the valley with quick, powerful bursts of light. The sky seemed as black as the abyss, but when the lightning would strike it would seem like noon. He could clearly see all of the objects around him, the trees, rocks and shrubbery, but there was no color. The lightning, it seemed, only illuminated in black and white. It was there, safe amidst the carnage, that Vrric felt the tug of destiny.

"I need to find the syllable for lightning." It sung in his mind. It would not let him go. There was a chant in the back of his mind that would not slow. It repeated itself to himself. Beckoning him to solve its mystery. His mind cast back to when he was first in Revkin's cell trying, but failing, to place lightning amongst the known elements. He had a burning desire planted in him at the Iltropin pools, in his center. He needed to find the syllable for lightning. He saw himself, years later, confounding his enemies by having elements at his disposal that they had never imagined. It was not a true depiction, certainly not a vision of the future. More of a caricature of his future self. As he would imagine his adult self while he was a child. Not a focused image to be sure, but compelling much the same. As he headed back down the hill, grateful that none of the lightning had decided to strike himself or his horse, his mind fixated on the idea of harnessing it. It was an irresistible image. Vrric realized that his vision quest must include lightning. If not, it had to be an imposter of the type that Revkin had warned him about. The storm disappeared quickly and allowed Vrric some time to brush his horse dry—mostly. He, himself, felt like he was steaming from the moisture burning off of his clothes just like his horse was steaming from its own body. Sleep was difficult to reach, but necessary to have.

Leaving the pools, the horses walked placidly down the twisting hillside towards the waiting ferry. It was almost boring except for fleeting, but beautiful, images of the falls. The ferry was swift and efficient. The horses even seemed to know the way through the Ruyogn canyon. The days crawled along, chewing through the vast distances, until the inevitable happened. They got completely lost. It happened just after they entered the Valley of the Caves.

It took four days to even find their first eshram, called Tlimpid. The denizens were shy and unhelpful. Finally one ancient Luften, with hair that was white and wispy, pointed them further north. Luckily the compass was still mostly working.

They traveled north for another two days. The heat was beginning to affect them, even when they were lucky enough to be traveling next to a streambed that carried a trickle of water. Their compasses were beginning to disagree slightly. Right now they were merely a couple of degrees off each other, and the team all hoped that the compasses' degradation in usefulness would begin slowly.

At last, when some in the group began debating the usefulness of hunting in such a barren place, they found the eshram of Algathia. They gathered together in a tight little knot, looking up at the various dark holes in the cliff walls. Unlike Tlimpid, Algathia had no terraces or real roads. There were just footpaths up into the black holes of the mountain. Vrric was not even sure how many caves were camouflaged amongst the junipers and scrub brush. Instead of visiting random caves and bothering the hapless inhabitants, as they had in Tlimpid, they opted to walk through the valley floor and hope that some of the bolder denizens would approach them. It did not work out as they had planned, but it worked out better than they had hoped. They came upon a small well in the center of town.

Everyone joked that they had found what they were looking for, that they were in the presence of the healing well. But the jokes rang hollow since they all knew they were nowhere close to the real well. There was a small look of desperation on each of their faces while they joked about having finished their quest. About already being able to head back to Ariellyna and the Queen. Towards home.

However, the water at the well was quite refreshing. Several citizens of Algathia came to fetch water while their small troop surrounded the well, though none would let on if they knew of Elange at all, let alone where he might be located. They decided, by a unanimous vote, to wait out the rest of the sun at the well. There was a small arc of stones to rest upon that had the advantage of being covered by the shade. Some voted for it because they were tired and some because of the day's heat. Vrric voted for it because he had felt bad about bothering the Luftens in Tlimpid. It was all the same vote in the end. He had hoped, even if it was a foolish hope, that they would happen to run into Elange. Maybe Elange would have heard about their arrival and about their asking for his whereabouts. Then he might show up just to get rid of them if nothing else. And, for some unknown reason, Vrric had the idea that Elange would know about the well. The thought nagged at him until he gave in and felt it to be true. All that he really wanted was to get some directions to the well. Any directions at all would be preferable to what they had now.

Whether it was fate or luck, Vrric could never know for sure, Elange eventually came down to the well with a bucket to provision his cave with water. Vrric did not recognize the Luften, but felt tingly in his presence. There was a sensation of magic vibrating through him as if he were casting a minor spell on the stranger.

"Do you know the mage Elange?" It was Gyllhelon who spoke up first. She stayed seated, however, and kept her voice even and quiet, having learned earlier that many of the denizens of the eshram were excessively shy. They would turn and walk away rather than speak to someone who startled them, and just about any movement could startle them.

"Who wants to know?" The speaker sounded quite gruff and wore baggy brown robes patched with small rounds of leather throughout. The leather patches were dyed all different colors, but covered with the same shade of dust. It gave a paradoxical image of differentiation and similitude at the same time. It made Vrric's eyes squint involuntarily.

"I am Vrric, and my mentor is Revkin. I am traveling through this valley while on a vision quest... amongst other goals." Vrric was unsure of how to introduce their whole quest and everything it entailed.

"Wait, hmmm. Revkin... Wait. Ah, yes. The drunk. How is Revkin?" Elange would bob his white bearded face while not talking, but his head would stay perfectly still and he would stare up and over everyone else's head while he spoke. He looked very serious when he spoke. Before Vrric could reply, he spoke again. "Okay. I see. You, you and you." He pointed a gnarled finger in a stabbing motion towards Vrric, Gyllhelon, and then Herance. He hopped from one foot to another while holding out his bucket. Gyllhelon slowly reached out her hand to grab the bucket. She went to fill the bucket from the well, and Elange turned to walk back up one of the trails into the rocky dust.

Vrric and Herance followed Elange up the trail. He set such a slow pace that Gyllhelon quickly caught up to them as they were following the winding twists that made up the roads of the eshram. At one time, about halfway up the hillside, he stopped in the middle of the path. Vrric was staring at the ground while walking, to keep his feet from the rocks in the road, and almost ran into Elange.

"Wait. The sun burns the eyes, yes? It brings blindness to its lovers. But necessary, yes? It gives sight to the others." His dark eyes flashed at Vrric. Then he turned and walked upwards again. He did not move quickly, but plodded along as a derlian to the gallows.

They walked past several caves along the path. There was rabbitbrush, both grey and green, there was some mustard, a little sagebrush, and there were rocks. All sizes of rocks. The small little rocks that stick in your shoes and find their way under your feet. They were too big for sand, but too little for stones. There were those rocks. There were also the stones and the sand. There were a lot of cobbles, and every once in a while they would walk by a boulder, but that was rare. Finally they stopped at Elange's cave. He stopped and motioned towards the opening. "The mouse enters the hole."

Vrric and Herance ducked into the dark cave, but Elange stopped Gyllhelon before she could enter. "The cat waits outside alone." Then he followed Herance into his own cave.

When Vrric entered, he was stunned by the blindness. Herance ran into him as he stopped and let his pupils adjust to the dark cave. Laughing nervously, he found a spot on the floor to sit on the vast rug. There was a little nook further back into the cave that appeared to be a bedroom area. Other than that, though, there was just this room. There was a wall that had small crates of kitchen utensils—pots and pans and metal plates, it looked like. There was a stack of four flat-topped chests, piled atop each other in a corner all the way to the ceiling, with their looped rope handles hanging lifelessly from their pine coffin sides. Vrric and Herance sat on the opposite side, which had the carpet and small pillows. He was paranoid to sit on a pillow just in case that could offend Elange. The third direction had the nook at the end of it, and the fourth, of course, held the open doorway, which Elange's figure stood in the middle of, looking taller because of the backlight. Over the doorway was suspended a curtain rod, with the curtains pulled open to either side of the entrance. Herance sat down on a pillow, looking at Vrric as if she thought he was crazy.

"Pillows, yes." Elange sat down on a pillow of his own. "Let you tell me of Revkin." Elange waved at Vrric.

Vrric sat in silence for a moment, wondering what Elange meant. He soaked up a little time getting a pillow under himself. "Well, I am his first pupil. And he…" Vrric was quickly interrupted.

"No, no. What's he do?" Elange motioned again.

"Well, he has a lucrative retainer with Queen Vanelia. In fact, we are on a quest…" Elange broke in once more.

"No, no. I mean creation. What does he create?" Elange was staring intently at Vrric.

"Well I, ah… I do not know." Vrric was unsure of what Elange was really asking for.

"It is nothing, is it not?" Elange kept his eyes on Vrric. "Greatness was not meant for Revkin. His problem was that he never thought he *was* great. He spent the time and the energy becoming great. He, in my eyes, earned to be called great. However, no matter what I tried to tell him, he never allowed himself the pride to think he was great. That is what truly stifled Revkin, not my pattern of teaching. You see, Revkin never believed in pride. In his world there was arrogance and vanity, there was bragging and cockiness, there was pompousness and ego and even hubris. Especially hubris. Never even close to existing was pride. I do not know who took that from him. I surely hope it was not I." Elange was suddenly extremely lucid. The intensity in his eyes began to fade slightly while he was staring down at the carpet. Then, for no reason, it would flare up again. "There could be no other way, you see. That is the problem with what has happened. No other way has happened. You are stuck with happenstance, which rarely makes one happy. Then one mistake begets regrets, which makes one prone to secrets. Does he still drink?"

"Yes, he does. Sometimes it is better when he is drinking, other times it makes things worse." Vrric felt uncomfortable discussing Revkin's drinking while not in his presence. Vrric had not even had an honest conversation with Revkin about his drinking, so he felt shy about expressing his opinions to Elange.

"Wait. You see. Dream not for want of ambition. Learn not for reasons of redundancy. Only the original love, that selfish master. Personal betterment. For the sake itself, it is its own reward. Make yourself grander, however you feel fit, every day. Revkin chose another path. Amaze me." Elange stopped abruptly again. While Vrric's mind attempted to understand the nature of Elange's request, his thoughts were interrupted. "Why should you live? If you die, if I kill you, what does it matter?" Elange sat back on his pillow from his half-crouched position. Vrric had not realized how close Elange had gotten to him. "Amaze me."

Vrric could not for the life of him, and for all he knew that was completely literal, think of something amazing that he could do. He could not think of any spell, any trick any conundrum that would amaze a wizened old crazy hermit mage. He could sense Elange's impatience mounting, however.

"I am trying to find the syllable for lightning." It just burst out of him. He had merely been trying to think of anything remotely like what Elange had asked about Revkin—creation.

"Ha! Yes, wait." Elange began laughing hysterically for quite some time. At first Vrric's cheeks pulled upwards in humorous commiseration, but after a while he found himself shrugging his shoulders at Herance. Finally Elange regained control of himself.

"I myself, yes, tried such a feat. It was my sixth extra syllable, sixth Minora. It proved difficult for me. So much so that I decided to remove myself to here so I could work on it full time. How could it be that you, too, are interested in the same ideas? Coincidences are unbelievable, are they not?" Elange began laughing again. "Too unbelievable to be real..." Vrric began to wonder if having access to magic that few others did was worth the risk. Elange was clearly broken in some fashion or other. The conversation also made him wonder how many others knew a syllable for lightning and whether or not it was the same syllable.

"If two mages know the syllable for lightning, is it the same syllable?" Vrric figured he may as well ask since he had the opportunity.

"Ha! Quick mind. Is magic's derlian representation of manifestation universal? If I learn the meaning of Tec as De, do I harm or protect? You are asking into the heart of the Majora/Minora debate. You see, the Majora we all know. We all know it the same. It is the four-by-eight matrix of agreed upon symbols of syllables. It is the same. If I use De, I harm. However, the Minora are different. Individual even. Each mage must find their own extra syllable. If I knew the syllable for lightning, I could not teach it to you. I could, if I wanted to help, if I were able to help, attempt to shuffle you down the same mindtrap slide that assisted me to find my individual syllable, if I had been able to find it. Yes. But you would have to slip your own slide and come to your own deepening and your own conclusion. The mindtrap is an individual thing." Instead of staring above Vrric, Elange was staring at the floor. His eyes seemed to be bulging slightly.

"What is, exactly, a mindtrap?" Vrric knew that he would soon have to steer the conversation to the well, but he could not help himself from mining an available vein.

"Exactly, ha! Lokinheparc!" Elange waved his hand towards a copper tea pot and floated it over to his waiting hand. It landed flat upon his palm. "Nudepito!" Vrric felt heat radiating from Elange's hand. "The problem with 'exactly' is that it is wrong. A mindtrap is not a singularity but a process. It is the road that one travels to hopefully arrive at a great creative idea. First a tiny seed of the idea germinates. Roots burrow into the mind. But it has no actual answer, see? You begin to reel with the implications. Each branch reaches for the sun, each twig, each leaf, but none of them ever make it. You see? If I ask you a riddle, one that has no sense to make. I ask you, 'How do trees chew their food?' Your mind says no. The answer is no. You know there must be something, however. You have seen lightning. You know it exists. You know there is a chaotic pathway that leads from here to there. How to summon it? How to make lightning shoot from my hands as easily as they shoot fire? I know it exists. I know, but I cannot do it. You see. There is a giant impetus that must push one forth into learning the senseless riddle. That impetus is walking through the mindtrap. You will become obsessed with the attempt at knowledge. That obsession will override your normal mind functions. You will only think of one thing. For weeks, for moons; maybe longer, maybe never. Forgetting to eat, or to bathe. The sight is not pretty. Your mind spirals around that little plant of an idea, unable to escape its orbit and only able to move up or down. You will want, at brief times of lucidity, to quit and give up. But the impetus that proves necessary is the tenacity of the trap. Finished. Completed. Glorious ecstasy of accomplishment. Eventually, however, you get to one that never gets solved. Then you end here. Do you want to be here?" Elange had poured the hot tea while he was talking. Vrric thought it was interesting that the more lucid Elange's diatribes were, the less he bobbed around while talking.

"Not yet." Vrric smiled at Elange, and Elange began laughing again. He sipped his tea gingerly.

"No. Not ever. The trick is to stop attempting them before the one that you get stuck on. The finisher, the ender. No one knows, however, how many one can take. You always think you have one more in you. At least I did. There have been rumors of a denizen of an eshram finally figuring out their mindtrap and being able to re-enter society. So maybe there is hope yet. Yes?" Elange took to not looking at them any more. He sipped his tea in silence for several long moments.

"You, though. I see the aural glow around you differently. You are not as us mere mages, are you? You speak with a purer form of being than we do. Not mere mediocrity, no." Elange began to smile again. It must bore you to listen to such drivel.

"No. Of course not." Herance answered immediately, but looked nervous. Her eyes darted back and forth while she bit her lip lightly. Vrric was unsure of what conversation Elange was referring to, but it was humorous to see the effects.

"How are you called?" Elange stopped swaying and stared straight above Herance's head.

"I am Herance. Actually, we are on a quest to find a well. In the middle of the desert. Vrric, would you like to explain our quest?" Suddenly Herance looked nervous.

"Well…" Vrric attempted to verbally rescue Herance, but Elange would have none of it.

"No, no. You must be serious. How are you called by those who know you?" Elange began bobbing his head again.

"My real name is Clerin. And you are correct. My true quest is that I am a messenger between Belegs." Herance, no—Clerin. Clerin sat there with her back perfectly straight, staring right at Elange. Her eyes did not twitch towards Vrric. He was watching them intently to see if they would.

"That was too easy, Fluen. What if I am not harmless? What if I am the enemy, lain in wait? What if I am not even me, not even Elange?" He laughed again, but it was mercifully short this time. "The true question, however, is why they need an intermediary. Why must an unreliable—no, not even unreliable, but chaotic—why would a chaotic, short-lived, young Fluen girl with questionable abilities and loyalties be the best messenger? They can speak amongst themselves, you know. Ha, but I guess there is little secrecy in that. So what do you think the message is that its necessary vessel is you?" Elange seemed to have a sudden lucidity wash over him.

"That! That is none of your business. It is none of his business. And it is even none of mine!" Clerin was up on one knee grasping at something at her belt. Vrric had a chill fear spray through his veins that she was trying to get a weapon. He tried to stand, to grab Clerin and somehow stop her from attempting to hurt Elange.

"Narkinderarc!" Elange screamed, and Clerin flew against the rock wall behind her.

"Nardepiarc!" Vrric cast out of reflex. He surely did not mean to use an attack spell. But before he was done speaking, Elange was glaring at him.

"Eqetecderpri!" The flames shooting from Vrric's hands parted around Elange. He could feel the heat that was rebounding from Elange on his hands. He did not feel heat from casting the spell though, so it was an odd sensation. Gyllhelon burst in with her sword flashing before her.

"Stop!" It was Clerin. She walked/crouched into the center of the room with her hands up. "Stop. We are all friends here. There is no need for this." She seemed to be breathing heavily. Vrric realized that Elange had not cast anything life threatening. He could have easily hurt them, thought Vrric. "I apologize for overreacting. I should not have moved with such swiftness or animosity. We were merely conversing with one another." With Clerin mostly standing in the cave, with her hands outstretched, there was so little other room as to force the other three in the cramped space sit down.

"It is I who should apologize, young lady. Of course that was a sensitive subject. I should not pry where I am not needed or heeded. My curiosity gets the better of me sometimes. I have so few visitors." Elange bowed his head down so low that his chin almost touched his chest.

"I, ah, should be leaving." Gyllhelon stood and somehow managed to make her crouch look like a bow. She left before sheathing her weapon.

"We do have one other item we need assistance with. We are attempting to enter the desert to find a well at its geographic center. If you have ever heard of such a well or even have advice on finding the edge of the desert, any advice whatsoever would be appreciated." Vrric decided to make the plea right then, to avert any other conversation.

"Ah, yes. Something else." Elange settled back more comfortably onto his pillow. "The good news is that I, like many here, have heard of such a well. I wish I could tell you where it is. But I know not if it exists, let alone where it could be found. What I *can* tell you about, however, are the Vijen and the Tlana. Two unique spirits, one good and one evil. Well, one that is sort of neutral with mostly harmless mischievous tendencies and one that is evil." Elange began to laugh again, but luckily was able to gain control of himself quickly. "The Vijens are seldom seen. They appear as trees that shuffle quickly along with their snake-like roots. They speak in riddles both long and deep. They drip leaves of gold. The Tlana wear the leaves and fly in beautiful spirals. They congregate where malice coalesces, swooping by on golden wings. Beware! They can induce doubt and paranoia in healthy adults. They can work disastrous results with a group that is thirsty, tired, beaten, lost, and still searching for some forsaken well. They are to be the least trusted. They are masters of disguise, however, so take notice of any of those you know that fly, but not normally so, even for a split second." Elange rocked back and forth slightly.

"Would it be safe to say that we should head towards the center of the desert?" Vrric knew he was just fishing but could not help himself.

"Yes, for a while, but then what? Your compass will not abide by the laws that normally govern it. The sun seems to be directly above for over half of the day. The stars refuse to spin as normally required of them. What could I tell you? You will either find the well or you will not. More precisely, the well will either find you or it will not." Elange began to laugh again.

They sat in silence for a while. At least, Clerin and Vrric sat in silence. Elange kept giggling off and on, staring at the floor. In retrospect it was probably not for that long, but it seemed to last forever to Vrric. He glanced at Clerin before drawing a breath. He was unsure of what he was going to say, but he was interrupted before he began.

"Wait, though. Wait. I have something for you. For both of you." Elange stood in a stooped crouch. He waved his hands about slightly while staring at the floor. He went to the stack of chests and pulled off the top two. He bent over and began rummaging through the third chest, humming tunelessly to himself.

"Aha!" He clutched a small leather bag to him and shuffled back to Vrric. "Here, this is yours. When you search for your glyph. When you seek your new name. Take this stone and put it in the side of your mouth, between your cheek and gum. You will salivate, yes you will. Drink all that you create. Both literally and metaphorically. Be the snake that swallows its own tail. It will increase your awareness of yourself. Of the awakening of creating, yes." He stuffed the bag into Vrric's hands and tottered back to the stack of chests.

Vrric stared into the supple bag, and it stared back into him. There was a little stone the shape of a large almond resting in the bottom of the bag. It was opaque with a deep green hue and splashes of a finer, paler green, in flower shapes. "For how long do you leave it in for?" Vrric was feeling a little nervous staring at it. What was it?

"Oh, yes. Maybe one hundred. Count to one hundred in your head. Do not worry about what happens. It is you that you will be feeling, not the stone. It just increases the intensity of your focus of you. Here!" Elange held up what looked like a small chunk of iron ore. At first, Vrric thought it was another type of rock, but all of its edges were just too ragged.

"This metal warms when in the proximity of the eternals. It was chipped off a rock that fell from the sky. I do not know how long its powers will last, because nothing in this world lasts forever. The only things that last that long are the eternals, and they are from a different world entirely, heh. It would be wise for one in your position to be aware of them and their servants. They want you to believe they believe you are on par with them. But behind closed doors, when they think they are only amongst their own kind, their true feelings of superiority come to the light. They seem like they are not sneaky, the Yavens, but it is only because they are sneaky so slowly that one derlian lifetime is not long enough to take notice of it. You may not see the lightning flash if you are not facing the right direction because it happens so quickly, but also you do not notice the glacier moving because it happens so slowly. And they can both destroy a village given enough energy." Elange gingerly placed the small chunk in Clerin's hands.

"I cannot thank you enough…" Clerin was cut off quickly, but Vrric still had time to wonder how he had not thanked Elange yet.

"Don't, please. Do not. I am old, I know what is happening to me. Do you know that I was King Hulgert's personal mage for over thirteen cycles? I will leave this world with plenty of fond memories, despair not. I no longer can abide by trinkets, though. These things I have kept only because of their nostalgia, not because I use them. All I ask is that you use them, yes." Elange nodded at them.

"Thank you." Vrric could not help himself, but Elange would not let him continue.

"It is time for me to eat." Elange looked back and forth between them. "I eat alone."

"Of course, of course. Take care." Vrric rose in a low stoop. He raised the little leather bag in another attempt at giving thanks and shuffled backwards out of the cave. As he was leaving, he saw Clerin lean over and whisper something to Elange. He giggled furiously as she walked away from him.

Popping out into the fresh air was invigorating, if a bit shocking. Vrric felt as if he was leaving a different type of world. Like disembarking from a large ship after a long sea voyage. Yes, the fresh air felt like being back on land. Gyllhelon smiled at him as he stomped around trying to get feeling back into his feet. Clerin popped out quickly, looking slightly flushed. She immediately turned and began walking down the slope towards the rest of the party waiting at the, unfortunately, mundane well.

"After you." Vrric waved Gyllhelon on in front of him.

"I would rather bring up the rear. Officially, my mission is yours and Herance's safety." Gyllhelon waved Vrric on in front of her. Rather than argue or protest, Vrric picked his way down the hillside behind Clerin.

They walked in silence, carefully picking their way down the rock-strewn path. When they arrived, they were all greeted eagerly. As Haswyxe put it, they had all assumed Vrric was getting directions to the well from an old mentor. Once it was explained that they were no closer to the goal of their quest than before, the mood became somewhat more somber. They filled all of their waterskins and canteens with water and headed towards the exit of this particular canyon and into the next. Always descending, always heading towards the desert. The rocks in the road seemed to get smaller the further they got. And the canyon walls diminished in height the closer they got to the valley's exit.

****

It took three more days before they reached the last eshram. They filled up with water there, cramming every vessel they had and burdening their horses until their knees shook, for maybe it would be the last time they would see liquid, and they looked out over the vista. They were still up somewhat from the desert floor, but the path downwards had a gradual sinusoidal curve of switchbacks towards the flat sand. Vrric stared as hard as he could at the horizon, but was thwarted by the sheer vastness of the Northern Desert. He could see nothing in the distance. Nothing but shades of brown. The troupe had attempted to gather some discernable intelligence about the desert, about the well, about anything really, but those who would speak to them seemed to know nothing, and most would not even acknowledge their existence. Vrric was hesitant to begin walking down towards the desert floor. He felt an odd nervousness about it, like a general must feel ordering his troops across a river. Vrric felt exposed, that they were all completely exposed, that when they rode out there, into the open, whatever was waiting for them would pounce.

"Well, this is where it really where it starts, is it not?" Torpalin said. He had his shirt off, and his chest was already glistening with sweat in the heat even though it was still morning. It seemed as if heat was wafting up from the desert, like it was giving them a taste of what was to come.

"Yes, we should get started." Clerin was looking at Vrric when she spoke. Vrric could not understand why he was hesitating, so he decided not to.

"Of course. Hope everyone is as comfortable as possible. It will only get worse from here." Vrric was not sure why he used that to rally those around him, but instead of pondering its melancholic tones, he kicked his horse lightly. At a brisk walk, the steeds began to descend onto the desert. The group had decided to keep the horses for as long as they could, figuring that the extra speed and endurance of the animals would outweigh the amount of water they might drink or oats they might eat. They assumed they had about fortnight's worth of rations with them, which was considerable considering the size of the group. Tonight, thought Vrric, should be a new moon. The night skies would only be lit by stars. He wondered briefly if they should have discussed the visibility of a campfire before embarking into the desert, but then figured they would have plenty of time for conversation during the trek.

Conversation was actually quite limited, however. Clerin rode for a while next to him. After quickly, and quietly, thanking him for not mentioning anything about herself to the others, they had little to say. Vrric wondered if Gyllhelon had heard much from standing guard outside, but Clerin did not want to talk about more about the subject, and instead changed it.

"Did you know my horse is named Riverlightning?" She had a small mischievous smile on her face when she said it. "Since you are so interested in lightning, I thought you would get a kick out of that." She laughed cutely, staring away from Vrric, then at the end she glanced out of the side of her eye to see if he was watching.

"Wow, that is a strange coincidence." Vrric figured she could call her horse whatever she liked as long as she smiled at him like that. "Did you name him?" He felt himself blushing slightly. It was odd, because there was absolutely nothing embarrassing happening to him.

They chatted for a while, but soon the heat took the moisture from their mouths and with it the breath from their lungs. Plodding further into the desert, they attempted to keep the sun on their left cheeks, but the sun did not seem to want to help them. The compasses were beginning to shift oddly, pointing in different directions than each other and spinning slightly when held still. Every once in a while, Vrric would fly up above the caravan to scan the horizon, but he could not see anything in the distance but sand. Soon the sun was setting over the far horizon, and a somber encampment was swiftly made.

The campfire was a small issue at this point. They all agreed that the first night was the least dangerous. Haswyxe made the first night's meal, and Vrric was pleasantly surprised with the quality of it. He had thought that Haswyxe would be a horrible cook, but he ended up being one of the best. In fact, the worst cook ended up being Gyllhelon, not counting Vrric. Though it was difficult for him to be an impartial judge of his own cooking.

The days bored into Vrric's mind as mercilessly as the sun did. The time seemed to melt upon them like cool liquid wax. Soon they were covered, but did not remember it happening. They were, as Malghain put it, as lost as a salmon cut off from its spawning pool by a beaver dam. They could not just wait for the next heavy rain to jump over, however. Unable to find the scent of their destiny, they wandered as logically as they could. Frustratingly, the sun seemed to just spin above them. It would make a wide arc, then duck behind the far horizon. At their encampment, they would lay themselves out based on however it seemed that the sun had landed. Every night they laid out in the same geometric form. And every morning the sun rose in a random direction compared to their earlier orientation. There was no rhyme or reason with the stars, either. They would spin in that same shallow arc in the sky, and then dart off at dawn into oblivion. They could only tell time by the diminishing rations and the tiny notches that Escha dutifully carved into one of her arrows each night. The food seemed to be shrinking fast, even though everyone had been on half-rations for the last several days. Even worse, the common consensus was that each "day" was getting shorter on average. It seemed to them that the time between sunrise and sunset was fluctuating in length. The nights, since they had no stellar way of telling time, were watched by whomever could stay awake. They would take turns rousing each other from a fitful sleep, without ever knowing exactly how much time was left of their watch. Vrric cursed himself for not thinking of an hourglass before packing for this journey. He consoled himself with the thought that even if they had an hourglass, it would probably work about as well as their compasses did. Every time he flew up to take a look around he could not see any objects at all amongst the flat brown sand.

Much to Vrric's dismay, they did not run into any of Elange's Vijen. He even began to hope of meeting with the Tlana to break up the monotony, but that did not happen either. Eventually, their spirits began to sag. The thought that they would somehow stumble across the healing waters waned. They began to admit defeat.

It started as a low grumble amongst the more recalcitrant members. What started with Escha and Torpalin quickly grew to all five of the guards. Clerin finally had everyone pull out what they were carrying one evening as they gathered around the tiny fire. It was the first fire that they had for four "days." They had been trying to conserve the meager wood supply and eating only dry rations.

Vrric stared morosely at the pile. He knew that they were almost out of wood, but for some reason he had thought that they had more food left. The only good part of the pile was the water. They had enough musty, leather-tasting water that they would probably starve before they died of thirst.

"You cannot argue with that." Torpalin's deep voice broke the silence.

"See, this is what we were worried about." Escha added her opinion.

"I hate to admit it, but we do not have that many rations left." Haswyxe looked poignantly at Clerin. She stared at him for a moment before glancing over to Gyllhelon.

"The timing of when to head back is not up to us." Gyllhelon kept her eyes lowered to the small pile.

"It looks like we should head back or start killing the pack animals." Malghain spoke dryly without any prompting.

"If you are to head back, I should take a side trip. I don't feel that I would take too many rations from you." Vrric waved his hand towards the group. He had not mentioned it before, but thought this would be the perfect spot for a vision quest, lost between the realms in the middle of the desert. As hungry as he was, he thought it would not take long before he would start seeing visions.

Everyone was looking at Clerin. Vrric immediately realized that his little statement put the onus of when they would head to Ariellyna back onto Clerin. Feeling sheepish, he started to speak back up, but Clerin waved her hand to cut him off.

"We cannot head back yet. I'm sorry..." She paused and raised her hand again to cut off the chorus of interruptions that looked to ensue. "...But we must try a little longer. However, I know this has been strenuous, so I suggest we wait here for Vrric. We can cut into a dune to make a hill for shade and, if we must, we might have to kill one of the pack animals. We probably should have done that a while ago, when we had enough wood to make the sacrifice worthwhile, but there is no use worrying about lost opportunity. How long do you think it will take you?" Clerin steered her pale blue eyes towards Vrric. He realized how much they reminded him of lightning.

"Three days, at most." He did not know how much time it was supposed to take and thought that three days was cutting it close, or not even long enough, but he knew that everyone wanted to head back. It was no longer just the heat. He knew that everyone was beginning to be afraid of starving to death on their way back, if they could find their way back. They were ready to quit the quest. He realized that Clerin wanted to deflect some of the decision to delay the ending of the quest back onto Vrric, which did not bother him in the least. His only concern was being able to have his vision in time. If nothing else, he thought to himself, he could come back early and have his vision quest later.

"Could you make it two?" Torpalin was smiling, but his eyes looked narrow and hard. Vrric hoped that it was the blinding sunlight that made him squint.

"I will be as quick as I possibly can." Vrric made himself grin back at Torpalin in what he hoped was a jovial looking smile.

"Good. I am not trying to speed up your process uncomfortably, but look at me." He tapped his massive chest with his forefinger. "You could fit two Clerins in me." He pointed his finger over to Clerin. The wide-eyed and comically panicked look he had on his face was enough to burst everyone into laughter, and it was a much needed release. It had been a while since they all had shared a good laugh.

"I will tell you what, Torpalin. While I am away, you may have my rations. I am only allowed to eat fruit on my quest, and since we have nothing of the sort, I shall be going without any food at all. Just some water." Vrric was still smiling widely.

"Really? You all heard him, didn't you?" Torpalin was smiling, but he was also squinting his eyes again. Vrric thought it was probably a good idea to give Torpalin a little extra food.

The next day, Vrric wandered off on his own. He did not want to get lost, but felt he had to be far enough away that he could not see, hear, or otherwise sense the others at all. He flew off into the distance until he felt he was far enough away, and then floated back to the sandy floor. He hoped he would be able to find them again afterwards. If not, he was unsure of how many days he could fly without food before weakening.

Vrric sat there for a while, baking in the sun, trying to meditate. He could not seem to clear his mind. Every time he got close to relaxing, the unbidden image of Clerin's face would come to focus in his mind. He would try to call lightning strikes into his mind's eye, to imagine their forking flash sear across his closed eyelids, and her pale blue irises would form from the flash.

Vrric stood and wandered for a while, figuring that maybe he was not exhausted enough. Sweat poured out of his forehead, his temples, and his scalp. It seemed to stream out of every pore in his body. He walked until his feet started to shuffle into the sand. He shuffled until he made two twin trails that disappeared over the horizon. When he looked back, it was like he was being followed by two large, invisible but straight, pythons. Finally he got bored of shuffling and sat back down. The sun was relentlessly straight overhead. He wondered if the others were able to actually dig a hill for shade. It seemed that there would never really be a time where the sun was at enough of an angle that a mound of sand could create enough shade for one derlian to take refuge in, let alone all six of them. So they probably just made a shade bivouac out of the tents, swords, and whatever wood was left.

Vrric sat and crossed his ankles on his opposite thighs and closed his eyes again. As he tried to clear his mind, a bead of sweat broke free from his eyebrow and poured into his left eye. Once the first drop carved a trough in the dust pasted to his face, a small stream began to flow.

Vrric got to his feet angrily and wiped the pouring sweat from his brow. He started to wonder if this was the wrong way to go about a vision quest. Maybe he should be in a shady forest, munching on blueberries or something. Maybe he should be near a slowly flowing river, listening to the babbling that it brooks. Maybe he should be at a beach near the giant ocean or a high mountain near the snow or a quiet cave underground. He thought maybe he was trying to force the visions. Maybe he should just find the group again and they could head back towards Ariellyna. He knew that they would all be happy with that decision. Well, probably not Clerin. He walked for a while longer, baking in the hot sun. He thought about pouring all of his water over his head to clear his mind, but dismissed the errant idea as foolish.

Vrric figured that he had not been truly trying yet. He knew that no one had a true vision the first day, or at least that is what he gleaned from talking with Revkin and Elange. It was just that he had been lost out in the desert for over a week already. Calming himself, he sat back down on the sand. He closed his eyes and focused on his breathing. He stayed that way for quite some time, just breathing. His mind was completely chaotic. No matter how he tried, he could not calm the constant flash of incongruous images. So he did not try, he just breathed. When the sweat attempted to blind him with salt, he just wiped it away. When the sand began to crust too heavily in his nostrils, he just blew his nose. When his throat began to constrict with the hot dryness, he just took a drink. He did not worry about keeping calm or about achieving meditation. He just breathed.

The images that flashed through his mind were jumbled but had a sort of awkward pattern. Flash through lightning, flash through a river, flash through diving into a pool, flash through Clerin's eyes, flash through a cave, flash through a hole in the clouds into a bright blue sky, flash through the sparks flying away from Kaihlu's hammer, flash through falling off a cliff, flash through a dark well in a bright desert, flash through flying through a clear blue sky, flash through Clerin's eyes. He did not worry that the images made no linear sense. They did not even make a jumbled sense to him. They were all so much that they almost seemed like nothing. The blur in front of him, through him, ebbed and flowed. He drank water and wiped sweat from his brow. Most importantly, he kept his eyes closed and just breathed. Time flowed through him until he felt the sun begin to fade. The slight change in temperature attempted to rouse him, but he would not let it.

Instead he rummaged blindly through his belt pouch until his fingers found Elange's stone. His mind briefly tried to rebel, to make him think better of it, but he knew what he felt. He grabbed up the stone and held it for a while, letting the jumble of images flash through him. The stone felt cold and smooth, almost inviting, but he waited quite awhile. He wanted to start as the sun went down, so he waited with his eyes closed until the coolness coalesced around him. He waited until his eyelids no longer glowed red, but there was still some light in the world around him. He kept his eyes closed, he kept his breathing rhythmic, and he slipped the stone into his mouth.

Immediately he began to salivate. He followed Elange's instructions and swallowed his own saliva. But it kept flowing. It was disgusting, really. It tasted of metal, almost of blood. The tinny taste made his teeth tingle. He could feel it down in their roots. It was if each tooth separated from each other tooth, with his saliva seeping between them like streams of mercury. He held his head upward to be able to swallow it all. Finally, after what seemed to be an age, his mouth stopped producing saliva. He waited for a while to make sure that the surge did not begin again. When he felt safe with the dryness of his mouth, he spit the stone back out into his hand. Keeping his eyes closed, he slipped the stone back into his pouch. He never did count to one hundred.

The tiny red stain that played upon Vrric's eyelids filtered from the fading sun began to become brighter. A little green line began to spiral behind his lids, making spiderwebs of patterns. The green turned yellow as it widened until it was a thick rope. The background red began to pulse lightly, deepening then lightening. Another thread of green began to spiral around the thick yellow rope. Finally the green and yellow spun with each other like giant glowing cogs of gears. All to the rhythm of the pulsating red. It became too much for Vrric to handle with his eyes closed, and he finally opened them. To his relief, the entire world did not swirl like his eyelids did. In fact, he began to feel normal again.

His hands began to push themselves into the soft hot sand. It was oddly relaxing. He would grasp a pile of sand in each hand and slowly let the sand sift out. Without a thought, he began to make two small mounds, one on either side of him. He stared forward and sifted the sand as the sun went down, for he was afraid of closing his eyes again. The stars began to quickly appear, with no moon in sight. He thought it should be darker, but the stars filled the sky with a light blue aura that bathed Vrric. He stopped building sand hills and laid back. The stars moved oddly, falling down out of his vision towards his upturned feet. Except he would follow them with his eyes, and so he was unsure if he was making them fall down with his rolling eyes, or if they were actually moving. As he kept moving his eyes upwards, back to the beginning, straight above him, the stars would start moving back towards his feet. They would not move individually, though; they shifted as a net. Individual stars would shift and wave, but held somewhat together in small groups, as if was they truly were a net, resting on a restless ocean surface.

While he was playing with the stars, a blackness began to move across the sky. He could not see the clouds even though, logically, he knew that was what the darkness had to be. It was more like the stars were being swallowed into nothingness. A small wind began to rise. Vrric watched the blackness moving across the sky with a benign trepidation. He thought about trying to meditate again, but his mind was racing too quickly for him. He could not slow it, focus it, or even seem to steer it. His will was still his own, but it seemed unable to slow his careening thoughts. The sky was getting dark, and the wind began to gust. Bursting forth and then ebbing. It seemed that a storm was brewing.

He wondered what the others were doing, if they were trying to set up tents before the storm hit, or if they were bedded down under the stars as usual. The desert had been hot and horribly dry and dusty, but it had been fairly pleasant at night, if a bit too cool. They had yet to weather a storm here, and Vrric was beginning to wonder if he should try to find the others. All he had on him was the leather bag filled with water and his clothes. A flash of fear shot through him for no reason. It was chilling, and the fact that it seemed to course through him for no reason scared him even more. Suddenly he jumped to his feet. He was not sure if he had heard something, maybe something so quiet that it only reached his unconscious. He spun around wildly. He could feel the blood pumping hard through his veins. He could feel a panic forming, though he could still not understand why. The blackness was almost complete.

Just then a burst of lightning struck a faraway dune. Vrric thought, though he could not be sure, that he saw a figure next to where the lightning struck. His perspective seemed out of whack, and he could not tell if the figure was near or far. Once it was dark again, he tried to make out if there was another derlian in the distance or not, but he could barely see his hand in front of face. Then the rain starting pouring. The drops were large and fell with great force. Vrric hunched his head against the beating rain.

The lightning struck again, much closer this time, and it seemed to last longer. Vrric could swear that he saw a shadowy outline of a derlian this time as well. The figure seemed to be moving towards him along with the lightning. The panic flowed through him like a river, but he could not seem to move.

A third strike brought the lightning to the dune hill next to Vrric. It also brought the figure. The strike lasted so long that the figure was completely visible. Just before the night went completely black again, Vrric saw the figure leap into the air. He wanted to leave, to run, to hide, but he could not even move his arms or shift his feet. His heart pounded in his chest so hard that he could feel his blood pumping through his veins. An incredible urge to urinate was, luckily, stifled by what small willpower was left in him. His head felt light and empty, while his feet felt like lead. He began to wonder if the figure moved by jumping. It did seem to move very quickly. He could not seem to even turn his head to the side, though he truly wanted to. He wanted to leave the hillside before the next lightning strike. He wanted to be with the expeditionary force, with sturdy warriors ready to defend him. He just wanted to find the well and head back towards home. He did not really want a vision. He did not want to be afraid anymore. He did not care if Revkin called him Mudfoot for the rest of his life. Most of all, though, he just wanted to be with Clerin. To look into her lightning eyes and speak of nothing.

Just then something fell in front of him. He did not even stagger back, but stood there staring into darkness, looking for what could have hit the desert floor that hard. "Move! Why don't you move?" The yelling seemed to come from right in front of him. The air seemed warmer in front of him than behind him. Like he was facing a campfire. "Hunting is not hunting if the prey just stands there." Vrric wanted to close his eyes again but was worried that the kaleidoscope colors would return. Just then the lightning struck next to Vrric. The faintest of sounds, "Ellie..."

There in front of Vrric, lit up like it was on a stage, was the most beautiful derlian that Vrric had ever seen. Vrric could not tell what race the derlian was, maybe a mixture if that were possible. He could barely tell that it was male, though if it had been wearing baggier clothes Vrric might not have been able to tell that. His hair was so pale it was almost white. It was perfectly straight and hung judiciously down his back. He wore a small wire tiara to hold his hair back with a striking blue gemstone centered on his forehead. He wore a tunic over a tight jerkin with a wide black leather belt cinched at his waist. Black leather also covered his feet and hands. It was the stranger's face, however, that caught Vrric's attention. It was smooth and androgynous with cheeks that looked gaunt, but not unhealthy. Looking into his eyes, though, was like looking into the night sky. They were infinitely black with glittering cruel stars in their depths. They froze Vrric to his core. Then the flash was over.

Then the pain began. It felt like he was stabbed in the gut with a jagged blade. Not that Vrric had ever been stabbed before, but the pain was so excruciating that he assumed it was like being stabbed. His mind began to thaw a little.

"Nartecgepri!" The pain in Vrric's gut eased for a moment.

"That's better. You want to live, do you not?" Another, but much quicker, bolt of lightning struck near the dune Vrric was on. Just then he saw the derlian's gloved hand arc towards him. It slowed as it struck Vrric's stone shield, but it did not stop. The blade, or whatever it was, grazed him. Reflexively, he struck out with his fist at the derlian. To Vrric's eyes, he struck the derlian. However, it felt like punching a piece of paper. There was no jarring resistance, no shock traveling up into his arm. He wondered briefly if he actually missed, but was struck again by the derlian as the sky turned dark once more.

"Eqedepiarc!" Vrric shot a burst of flames directly at the derlian, but the flames seemed to shoot right through him. Vrric began to panic about how long his shield was going to last. He began to fear for his life.

"Mekkinlufsfe!" Vrric tried to shove the derlian away from him. He did not hear anything for a moment and hoped that the derlian was gone. "Narliderpri!" Vrric whispered to himself. A warm tingly sensation washed over Vrric as he healed himself. He got back up to his feet.

Another bolt of lightning lit the sky. A faint whisper occurred, "Ellie... ellie," and Vrric was astounded at the sight in front of him. It was as if the derlian was coalescing right in front of him. It seemed about twice as large as normal, but with thin spaces between itself. Then it shrank into itself and thickened back up. Vrric could not believe what his eyes were showing him. He wondered if the stone was still controlling his vision, or if he was just groggy from the fight, but the sky quickly grew black again and he was unable to be sure of what he thought he saw in those few short moments. Then the pain came again. It tore through his gut like a shark. He did not know what to do, how to escape.

"Mekkinderpri!" Vrric flew straight upwards. He needed to get away, get somewhere safe. He looked down at the desert, hoping to find a campfire or some evidence of his friends. He stopped and hovered for a moment, trying to see anything through the pitch blackness, anything at all. He felt something grab his right foot. Suddenly a sharp pain shot through his right calf. Another bolt of lightning shimmered in the sky, and Vrric could clearly see the derlian hanging on to his foot with its left hand while slashing at his leg with its right.

Vrric kicked wildly at the derlian's hand but could not seem to dislodge the iron grip. He could feel the blood seeping out of him. He felt that he was getting weak. The derlian kept on gripping and slashing. He knew that he was casting too many spells, much too quickly. He was expending his will like he was in a sprint and not in a long distance run. "Lumdepito!" There was a flash as the derlian's glove caught fire. It did not fall, however, but flew up and stabbed him in the thigh while the flaming glove kept gripping his foot. Vrric panicked and dove straight down. He did not know what else to do. He was getting weaker and weaker, so he figured if he had to die, so did his attacker. They plummeted together like eagles in coitus.

It seemed to take forever, but they finally impacted into the ground with a great thud. Vrric's mind was as blank as his body was limp. The last of his shield had exploded into tiny bits of sand. He was bleeding heavily and felt charred around the edges. It was all he could do to keep conscious. His chest rattled and labored to bring more air into his lungs. It felt like there was a belt wrapped around his chest that kept getting tighter and tighter. It kept him from being able to speak. Finally, with expending great willpower, Vrric was able to squeak out a word. "Loliderpri!" It almost made him pass out. With the effort spent, he leaned his head back into the sand. He did not know what became of the derlian, nor did he care. He just hoped that the derlian had somehow died. He, himself, was almost ready to just die, if it would end the pain. The pain, fear, and struggle. Almost.

Vrric kept his eyes open to keep from passing out, but he could see nothing in the pure blackness. In the back of his mind, as if someone were whispering from the past, a single word began to repeat again. "Ellie, ellie, ellie." Vrric did not know what it meant, or if it was even audible. He thought again, briefly, about the effect of the stone on him. He was so tired and hurt and out of sorts that he could not tell if he felt weird. Well, he knew he felt weird, but he could not tell why. The quiet chant began to become more insistent. Vrric wished he knew what it meant.

Another burst of lightning lit the small dune. Vrric thought he had landed on a different dune, but he had no way of knowing. If he was in a different area, the lightning seemed to be following him. Just before the night went back to black, he saw the derlian coalescing again. Gloves and boots flew in from opposite sides of the dune. In a flash the derlian was glaring down at Vrric. While he was trying to figure out whether or not he was seeing what happened correctly, the stranger began to laugh. The laughter sounded hollow in the sudden darkness.

"Yes! That was fantastic. You, my friend, are fantastic. I was worried at first that you had no fight in you, but you proved me mistaken. Take comfort in the fact that I will remember you for ages. Unfortunately for you, the game is over and I must feed." With that, an incredible searing pain began to creep up into him again. It began in his feet and seemed to travel in small tendrils, like it was traveling through blood vessels or nerves. Vrric heard a horrific screaming and realized it was him. Suddenly air flowed into his lungs as if poured by buckets. He yelled until he was hoarse. He knew it was not happening, but it felt as if a giant millstone was slowly grinding up his body, from the feet up. After the pain had crept up into his legs, his feet felt numb. Like they no longer existed.

He drew in another huge breath and began to scream when he thought of the chanting. When he thought of the chanting, he thought of lightning. When he thought of lightning, he thought of the stranger. When he thought of the stranger, he thought of Elange speaking of evil in the desert. Every time he was able to shake off the stranger, another bolt of lightning came and the stranger re-coalesced. The stranger was lightning. The lightning coalesced. The chanting called the stranger. No—the chanting called the lightning. The stranger was the chanter, before he coalesced. So he *could* coalesce. The lightning was called by the chant.

Vrric drew in another huge breath. The pain was at his crotch. It was excruciating beyond all of Vrric's imagination. He knew that once the pain reached his diaphragm, he would be unable to speak again. Ever. With every last bit of his willpower, with every last bit of his strength, with every last bit of his being, for his being was about to be over, Vrric turned his scream into a word. "Surdeelearc!" The pain ripped through his entire body as the lightning shot from him. In the flash of blinding light, Vrric saw the shock and surprise on the stranger's face for the briefest of moments before the face shattered backwards. Vrric curled into a fetal position and vomited. He was crying and heaving when he, mercifully, passed out.

Vrric did not expect to awaken, but the rising sun seared into his brain and drew him from the dark, safe void that was his dreamless sleep. He immediately vomited again. He tried to roll onto his knees, but was unable to do more than roll away from the vomit. Just then he realized that he still had knees. And even feet. He then noticed that he was covered in light flimsy things, but he still did not open his eyes. He tried to let out a triumphant laugh but it just came out like a croak.

"He's awake! Hey Escha, get Clerin, Vrric has finally woken up." Torpalin's booming voice filled Vrric's aching head. Soon his large face was filling Vrric's blurred vision as he painfully squinted his eyes open. "You will not believe this, Vrric. We were looking for you, after we heard the screaming during the storm. You would not believe the lightning last nigh... Well, of course you would. We saw you. In the sky... Well, we came to try to find you after you plummeted in a ball of fire. And we did finally find you just before the dawn, covered in these golden leaves, but we were unable to wake you. Clerin cast a healing spell on you, but we still could not rouse you. Once the sun was fully up, however, we could see where you led us. You will not believe this, Vrric, but..." Torpalin's soliloquy was interrupted.

"Vrric, you're okay." The relief in Clerin's voice was obvious. He really wanted to open his eyes wider, to be able to see her fully, but the light was too bright with his eyes as they were. His head throbbed horribly. "We found it, Vrric. We found the well!"

Vrric was unable to speak, so he smiled wide instead. Torpalin was right, it was unbelievable. He had survived, found the syllable for lightning— "Ele" —*and* they had somehow found the well? He had truly begun to think that it did not exist, that it was a some sort of myth or even a hoax. All he needed now was to find his name and he would never have to hear the word mudfoot from Revkin again. Through all of his bodily aches and pains, his complete mental drain and his brain's anguish, he felt amazing. It was just wonderful to be alive.

"Call me Feyazki." He did not know why he said that. The impact of what the name meant swerved around him deftly. Mercifully. The reality of implication was hidden beneath his dazed state. It had just come to him, and he had spoken it aloud. Then he had heard himself naming himself. That made the implication a reality. Like telling yourself that there is no monster under the bed. It aids the belief to give voice to a pleading command. All children know that instinctively. He felt change happening, and it felt deliciously healthy.

"Feyazki... are you all right?" Vrric had no idea who spoke, though it sounded like a male voice. He smiled as he closed his eyes. Mudfoot began the slow unraveling of disintegration. Nothing kept that needed to be gone. But nothing gone that needed to be kept. He grinned mutely as sleep overtook him once more.

Chapter 12

After the taking of Parthia's tower, everyone began to treat Trela with deference. Her counsel was sought out for issues small and large. She was not sure, but she thought it was beginning to get to Iventorn. Not that he would show it, though. They had picked up two smaller warpacks after the taking of Parthia. In public, he showered her with praise, and she could only guess what he said about her in private. Right after they had the second warpack swear fealty to him, Iventorn had Cavish invite her to a private dinner. She had insisted on bringing Knill which Iventorn, luckily, had anticipated and agreed upon beforehand.

Trela and Knill left Tumu in their tent when they headed to Iventorn's large marquis tent. Tumu spent most of his time between their tent and Lishean's, though he still would not speak with Trela. Technically he was still a ghulzan, but Knill kept trying to buy his freedom. Lishean, however, was not letting his seer leave easily, but he was giving Tumu much more latitude. Trela and Knill walked slowly to be able to communicate along the way. They had a lot to talk about, but they did not really speak to each other, just held hands as the last of the sun's rays peaked over the low-lying hills in the distance. She enjoyed the quiet walk even though she knew there was much for her and Knill to work out. It was a relaxing walk, like the calm before a storm.

When they finally could see the large white marquis tent in the distance, Trela thought she recognized the guard in front of it. It seemed to be the guard that she had hurt in front of Lishean's tent so long ago. She was having a tough time remembering his name. "What is his name?" Trela pointed to the distant figure.

"How should I know?" Knill seemed a little snappish. Trela hoped this was not how he was going to act in front of Iventorn.

"You know, the Pyran there. I broke his arm." Trela was trying to let Knill know that she sensed his testiness by being testy herself. She knew this was not the best system, but she did it out of habit more than anything else.

"Yes, I can see him." Knill took in a deep breath and let it out slowly. "His name is Nylse."

"See, was that so hard?" Trela realized that she sounded cruel. She did not even necessarily want to be. So she stopped. Knill had kept walking for a second, so he kind of spun around a little as she pulled his arm to a stop with her. "Listen, tonight is very important to me. Iventorn is up to something, I can feel it. Please, just help get me through this evening. We can do whatever you like afterwards."

"Of course, of course. I'm sorry. It's just Tumu, he… Well, I will talk to you later about that." Knill gave her a weak smile.

Trela nodded emphatically, though she was not sure what he was talking about. They started walking in silence again, hand in hand. Finally, they were standing in front of Nylse. His arm looked like it had healed nicely. Much as her wounds from the tower were also fading. It is amazing how quickly you can heal with a little magic and an ameliorator who is skilled with herbs.

"Iventorn is expecting you." Nylse said stiffly.

"Thank you, Nylse." Trela lowered her eyes for the briefest of moments at the end of her short sentence, at his name. It worked as well as she had hoped, for he smiled at her slightly and held the tent flap open for both her and Knill to enter.

Trela ducked in first, and Knill followed close behind. The tent was brightly lit by a myriad of oil lamps. Cavish was already holding the reception area curtain open for them. Trela was not sure, but she thought Cavish gave her a warm smile as she strode past him. As she entered the sparse room that Iventorn's seated form dominated, she bowed slowly and deeply. She intended on giving Iventorn every scrap of respect that she could. She wanted him to feel important, more important than she. She knew that she could only usurp Iventorn if he felt her to be harmless. She stayed in her deep bow until Iventorn spoke, and much to her pleasure so did Knill.

"Rise, rise. You embarrass me with your humility. The hero of Parthia should not show so much obsequiousness." Iventorn's smile showed all of his teeth, but it did not reach his eyes. His deep, dark, black eyes. They glinted like wet onyx. Iventorn waved his hand towards Cavish, who came back into Trela's view and stood next to Iventorn with his hands clasped loosely in front of him. Trela and Knill stood loosely in front of Iventorn. She had to consciously avoid assuming the parade rest position.

"You have made quite a name for yourself here, Trela. The entire camp is abuzz with whispers of your prowess. Yes…" Iventorn's eyes squinted hard at Trela.

"It was your leadership that led the army into Parthia. I was merely in the right place at the right time." Trela was unsure of what Iventorn was getting at.

"You should not sell yourself short, you truly were heroic at the battle. But it is good that you understand the conflict this brings forth. It shows intelligence that you noticed the harbinger before the calamity. The issue, as I see it, is how to agree upon what happens next. To put forth a collective face for the transformation that is to come." Iventorn was speaking over tented fingers, staring hard into Trela. She was still not quite sure what he wanted from her.

"Thank you for your praise. Coming from such an accomplished leader as yourself, it really means a lot." Trela felt she was expected to speak, but she also felt that she needed more information from Iventorn before she could really say anything. Certainly before she could suggest something.

"Enough!" Iventorn suddenly stood. His height and demeanor were truly imposing. Trela felt as if she were frozen in her spot. She could not move. If he attacked, she would just stand there and get killed. "I have worked too hard and too long to lose this warpack! Do you understand?" He had strode to her in one large step and hovered over her, glaring down at her.

Trela could not think. Her mind was numb. It was if a spell was being cast upon her, to turn her to stone. A long, slow, wordless spell that emanated from Iventorn through pure willpower alone. "Yes, sir," she heard herself say.

"Do not 'yes, sir' me! I will not lose half my warpack to you. I do not want to lose even one Second, or a small contingent. Or even one Pyran. Do you understand? I will kill them before I let them leave me. In fact, if pressed, I will kill you before I let you take anyone from me." Iventorn's bald head was beaded with sweat.

After a long moment of silence that he stared unblinking into Trela's face, he turned and sat heavily back into his chair. He kept his head turned to one side, not looking at Trela directly.

"However… however, they would follow you. Against my wishes I would lose at least half my warpack even if you were to just walk away. They are even speaking of you as the Kriishan. You see my problem?" Iventorn sounded quiet, almost bleak.

"I am following you, however. You lead this warpack, Iventorn, everyone knows that." Trela was stunned by the turn in the conversation. She was used to Iventorn yelling, or even being ice cold. She was not used to him looking haggard and sounding bleak.

"We realize that you will eventually lead a warpack, Trela. We just do not want it to be this one. We are not trying to stifle your destiny..." Cavish spoke up quickly but, with a look from Iventorn, he quieted back down just as fast.

"We are going towards the Northern Desert, Trela. We are going to cup the edge of it and then head back towards Agoge. As you know, every warpack must swear fealty to Qizern every three cycles. I can put it off for no longer. You, however, will not be with us as we approach Agoge." Iventorn's black eyes bored into Trela.

Trela did not know what to say. Her heart was pounding in her chest. She was getting used to the community that the warpack had given her. She did not want to leave Lishean or Estfale or even Cavish. She felt like she had just been setting down her roots.

"I suppose you want me to sneak off before then?" Just saying it out loud terrified her.

"Not only that, but you must enter the desert. You must leave to a place that no Pyran would want to go. No one must follow you, understand. No one. After we are gone, and I mean long gone. Many days must pass. After we are gone, you may reenter the Pyran lands and begin building your own warpack. I will sing your praises to every Pyran I see, even Qizern. But you must not decimate my warpack." Iventorn was glaring at Trela, and it seemed as if she could feel the weight of his gaze pressing down upon her. And with that weight came the realization that she had very little choice outside of open rebellion. She wondered how many of Iventorn's warpack really would follow her if she advertised her leaving. It was a dangerous thought, but it was oddly enticing.

"Why can I not continue to serve under you? I mean, I have helped you grow your warpack, yes? I have been a good soldier for you, yes? How can I just disappear? What will you tell the others?" Trela realized that she was showing some fear and frustration, but she could not seem to help it. It was as if the rug was being pulled right out from under her. How could she start a warpack with just her and Knill? Did Iventorn truly expect her to begin from scratch? She wanted to start yelling, but held back. She knew that she needed to keep herself in check around Iventorn and Cavish. She did worry about what the others would think of her, though. Would they call her a deserter? Iventorn may say now that he would sing her praises, but once she was gone who knew what he would really tell his warriors? Certainly not Trela.

"I understand this is unfair, Trela. It pains me to do this to you. I would truly enjoy you working loyally under me and gathering more warriors for my warpack. And I know that you would. I have ultimate faith that you would never betray me. That is what makes my own betrayal so difficult. You must realize, however, that this is my only honorable option. All other options that I have mulled over have been much more grisly and did not involve speaking with you beforehand. I know it will be hard for you, trust me. You will feel an urge to take matters into your own hands. I caution you against this desire in the strongest possible terms. I will be watching you and will not hesitate to strike if I feel you are going to compromise my warpack. I would rather be torn apart by my own warriors then to see them turn their backs on me. Trust me." Iventorn stood back up and walked towards Trela.

"I trust you." Trela felt an itching in her fingers. She wanted, more than anything right now, to be clutching the hilt of something. Just gripping a dagger or sword would have made her feel much better about staring back at Iventorn. Even without that small crutch, however, she was able to meet his gaze without blinking. It made her proud of herself.

"Good. I do not mean to overstate an obvious point. I am not attempting to scare you. I just want you and me to part on good terms. On agreed-upon terms. Trela… Do you agree, as you say, to sneak off into the desert as our arc reaches its apex? Do you agree to take only yourself and the Gaen? Do we have a deal?" Iventorn spit into his hand and held it out for Trela.

"Deal? A deal implies that both parties receive something of value. What you have offered me is an ultimatum." Trela glared back at Iventorn, though she doubted her eyes could put much weight upon him.

"Then do you accept my ultimatum?" Iventorn's hand was still stuck out in front of himself. His saliva was slowly sliding down his palm. It made Trela's skin crawl. She felt as if she had no choice, however. So she spit on her own hand and grasped his.

"You have completely betrayed a loyal servant." Trela tried to glare at Iventorn, but she felt like she was just squinting. He finally let go of her hand.

"Yes, we have covered that. I believe I have already apologized. You. Little Gaen." Iventorn waved a long hand at Knill. "You be careful in the desert. You just might encounter Delubayn." Then he turned and sat back down. He waved at them nonchalantly. "We are done here, you may go."

Trela felt a rage begin to build up in her. She decided to leave before she did or said something foolish. She did not bow on the way out. Not to Cavish and certainly not to Iventorn. She just turned and stalked through the reception area curtain, without even checking to see if Knill was following her. She stormed past Nylse without saying a word. She was halfway to the tent before Knill spoke up.

"Stop, Trela. We have to talk. I know you feel you have been betrayed, but you must listen to me." He grabbed her elbow to slow her down.

"I *have* been betrayed! This is not just a feeling, just some imagined slight." Trela glared at Knill and felt her face get hot with anger. Where was this when Iventorn was destroying her? She felt that she was unable to bear his burden of betrayal. She wanted, more than anything at that moment, to kill Iventorn. Not in a fair fight, not in front of others, but to sneak into his tent at night and slit his throat. He did not deserve an honorable death. Knill must have sensed her overboiling rage.

"Tumu had a vision of us in the Northern Desert. There was another Pyran with us, one that Tumu did not recognize from the warpack. I… I was worried it might be Synde." The words stopped Trela in her tracks.

"What?" She turned to face Knill. So she could see his facial expressions.

"Well, you should hear Tumu tell it. I will end up adding my own interpretations on what I remember his words to be." Knill looked sheepish.

"So you think this… this betrayal is from destiny?" She was calming down but still removed her elbow from his weak grasp.

"All I am saying is that it could be. I am certainly not saying that Iventorn did not betray you, he definitely did. And I am certainly not saying that he is just a pawn of destiny. Iventorn knew exactly what he was doing, and he knew that it was wrong. But I did not expect to be thrust into the desert on the same day that Tumu had a vision about it either. Let us just speak to him before you decide what action to take." It was as if he had looked into her vengeance-filled mind. "He is waiting back at the tent."

They walked back to their tent rather briskly. Trela wanted to think that destiny was involved. Just the thought soothed her rage—a bit. She was worried, however, that Knill knew that. Would he tell her a lie just to make her feel better? She was not sure either way.

Iventorn had given her a better tent after Parthia. It was larger than the tiny original one they had, but still somewhat cramped whenever there were three derlians in it. When they entered, both Trela and Knill sat at the entrance and removed their boots. Since Tumu was not visible, she assumed he was behind the bed curtain. She yelled at the back of the tent for him, but he was not forthcoming from behind the veil.

"Let me get him," Knill murmured to her. He said it like a secret.

Knill briefly disappeared. When he reappeared, it was not with Tumu. "He says that he is not worthy to have you gaze upon him. He says that he was shown that you are the Kriishan, so he must speak to you through me." Knill nodded towards her but had his head cocked backwards to listen to Tumu. Trela was not sure for whose benefit Knill was speaking, but she nodded back to him anyway.

"Ask him if he can sit with his back to me. I would like to hear from him rather than through you." Trela spoke loud enough for Tumu to hear her as well. "I wish to converse with you, Tumu."

There was a small rustling for a bit. Knill leaned out of her vision to speak quietly with Tumu. After some time Knill straightened and pulled the curtain to one side. Tumu sat stiffly with his legs crossed in front of him. His hair wildly stuck out under his rumpled hat. It made it so she could not see any part of his skin, not even his ears.

"How were you shown that I am the Kriishan?" Trela spoke quietly but intensely. She did not want to seem eager, but she always enjoyed affirmation.

"I was shown in the same way I am always shown. A vision so powerful that I dream while walking and must lie down to avoid falling. The dream fills me so completely that I forget that there is another such thing as reality. It seems incongruous that anything else exists except what is before me. That is how I know what is truly real. From there I know what the future holds. I am taken to the future and held there. Sometimes it is as if a large hand is gripping the back of my head, turning it towards whatever I am supposed to see. Sometimes I attempt to look away, but I am unable twist my head. I am held in the iron grip of destiny. Much like you, yes, much like you." His laughter had a slightly ominous tone to it. "But to answer your question, I was shown a taste just before you and Knill arrived. That is why I was so shaken up by your sudden presence. I had always felt like I had known, like it should be a truth, that you were the Kriishan. But I did not truly know, I was not specifically shown, until now. I saw you leading an army across the Dekhan plateau towards Agoge. I saw you locked in combat with Qizern himself. I did not witness you destroying him, but I saw you later… You were standing out on a balcony, arms raised over the triumphant crowd below. They were all shouting your name." Tumu paused briefly. Whether for effect or to take a deep breath, Trela was not sure. "But this was not the vision that you came here to listen to. Yesterday I had a much more important vision. It involved you and, of course, Knill. You were both alone together in the desert, wandering and thirsty, abandoned. There you met a strange Pyran. You will be overwhelmed with excitement at the meeting. On the way to a great well, your small group will be attacked during a lightning storm. The stranger will be killed. I felt that very surely. I know that this will greatly upset you, and so I have been trying to figure a way to speak to you. Some way to bring this up. You see, derlians only like knowing the future when great things happen to them. Unfortunately, most of my visions show terrible things. It is my burden." Tumu grew quiet. Trela waited until it was obvious that he was not going to speak again before breaking the silence.

"Tell me of the stranger. Who shall we find that excites us so?" Trela wanted him to say Synde, though she knew that he did not know who Synde was. Then again, she was afraid of him saying Synde, if they were truly unable to stop the death.

"See? What is the first thing you ask of? No, the good things should be left as a surprise. You should ask me of the well instead. You should be curious of the myriad menagerie that you encounter there." Tumu chuckled to himself quietly.

"What? You did not mention a well." But maybe he did. "You certainly did not mention a menagerie." Trela was unsure of why she would feel annoyed if Tumu sounded like he was enjoying himself. But it seemed to be happening anyway.

"There will be one who speaks to Belegs, one who controls lightning, and one you already know. They will join you on your quest if you join them on theirs. It is through the efforts of the group that the struggles of each individual will be more easily overcome. You will find something greater than everlasting life at the well. You will find companions." Tumu chuckled quietly again.

Trela was beginning to wonder about Tumu. He spoke about things as if he made sense. She was finding it to be obnoxious.

"What if we circumnavigate the stranger, head straight to the well, find these companions, and then find the stranger on our way back? Then we could all protect the stranger from whatever danger you have foreseen but failed to mention." Trela spoke before thinking.

"You have more chutzpah than most, I admire that. No one else has asked me how to circumnavigate my own visions. But think of all the good things I saw as well. Do you truly wish to bypass destiny, to trick her? What if your new destiny is less glamorous than your current one? What if, because of actions against her, you are prevented from defeating Qizern? Your future is not a house made of timber, but of cards. You should think long and hard before jostling the foundation. Please, I should get back to Lishean." Tumu breathed heavily for a moment.

"Of course." Trela stood there staring at the back of Tumu's head.

"Could you turn around, Trela?" It was Knill's request, not Tumu's.

"Fine." Trela turned and walked out of the tent. She did not feel like playing these little ghulzan games. She stood off to one side of the tent, staring up at the moon. It was only after Tumu was gone that she realized that she had lumped Knill in with Tumu in her mind.

The days flew by and soon the warpack was at its apex towards the desert. In truth, Trela was glad that the time had come. She did not like knowing she was leaving while being unable to tell anyone about it. She and Knill had to prepare in secret, and it made her blood boil. No matter her destiny, she knew in her heart of hearts that Iventorn was just getting rid of her. There was no noble idea behind his decision. No hidden altruistic urge. It was pure, selfish malice. Trela wanted to complain to Lishean or Estfale or even Dartsyle, but she did not. Instead she kept her word to that snake Iventorn. They had everything apportioned and packed before nightfall, loosely hidden by their empty shell of a tent. They sat on their full packs and had their last conversation as followers of Iventorn's warpack. It was trite, as conversations engineered to kill time often are. She enjoyed every moment of it, however.

Once the various fires amongst the camp slowly died down, Trela and Knill popped out of the tent to assess the night air. The moon was about half full and high above them in the sky, making the camp around them glow slightly. The pale blue light seemed brighter than it should for the moon only being half full, but Trela attributed the feeling to her nerves. She was sure that Iventorn would leave a large hole in the sentry fence on this night. She and Knill could probably leave with torches held high, and yet there would still be no official witnesses.

"It feels like a good night for traveling. I bet we can make some pretty good distance tonight. Maybe we could start to make our sleep switch immediately." Now Knill spoke jovially about her idea of sleeping during the noon heat and walking during the night in their desert trekking. The first time she mentioned it, though, he had a very different opinion of it.

"If we leave quickly enough, we might be able to rest a little before dawn. Maybe sleep into the hazy morning hours. We could belt our eyes closed." She now referenced the practice of covering your eyes with their wide traditional leather belts. Not the most effective procedure, but better than nothing. Knill had been as unappreciative of that idea as he had the first one. Now, though, he laughed. She enjoyed that.

They left shortly thereafter. They spent the time in a bustling frenzy of tying and retightening their gear to their steeds, speaking only in businesslike clips of monotone instruction. They worked smoothly with each other. They were completely without sparring egos to slow them down into herky-jerky arguments. Efficiency was the standard of elegance that both parties adhered to. Trela always took pride in the simple achievements of life.

They were guided by some vague sense of pull in a specific direction, drifting. Synde used to call it "being guided by your gut."

Trela liked to believe in that more than that they were just wandering around blindly.

"Iventorn mentioned something before we left. Something about Delubayn?" Knill asked in a whisper as they were riding. "He mentioned that I might encounter it?"

"Well, maybe you will. Maybe you won't." Trela did not feel up to the conversation. This, unfortunately, made them proceed in silence.

They seemed to cover a lot of ground before the sky started to lighten. Trela found a little place to hobble the horses while they napped as far into the day as they were able. It was a little before high noon that they could no longer even feign sleep. She laid there with her eyes closed for a while as Knill tossed his little body back and forth, but she could take it no longer.

"Well, since you are up, I guess I should get up as well." In truth, she was having just as difficult a time sleeping as he was and surely could not blame him for her being awake. "Want to see how much distance we can get in before nightfall?" She tried to sound chipper. She did not fool Knill, but he was kind enough not to mention it.

They had traveled for what seemed like forever. They were hopelessly lost. Trela was seriously considering just heading back towards the Pyran realm. They could not find a well or even any strangers. She finally realized that she could not trick destiny because she did not know where anything was, including herself, or how to get there from here even if she knew where everything was. She had reached a state of hopeless resignation when there was a loud crash which woke both of them from the deepest depths of sleep back into their tiny tent. The jolt sent Trela's heart racing, as if she was dreaming she was falling and woke up right before impact. Knill sat bolt upright next to her. They both had a thin veil of sweat about them.

"What was that?" It popped out of Trela's mouth.

"I don't know either." Knill smiled over at her.

She pulled out a long dagger and left the tent in her shift. She squinted into the close darkness and tried to make her eyes focus with conscious thought, but it was not working. As she stared off into the darkness, a large shadowy figure rushed out at her. She was shocked by the image; for some reason it reminded her of Nolt. The motion of the head, or maybe the sag of the shoulders. The shock, however, took over and she stabbed wildly at the figure as it came at her. Just then she was able to see the face that was leering so close to her own. It was Synde. She knew it was. The truth of it struck her very center and created a harmonic vibration within her—shaking its way out. Her arm, however, would not be tamed by her will. There was too much momentum, both physical and emotional, to be overcome. Luckily for Trela, it was Synde, and he knocked her blade out of her hand with a blur of motion. She grabbed him in a bear hug when she was in complete control of her limbs. He broke her grip and lifted her up and away. He stared into her face as she exclaimed, "It's you. Synde, you came back." He put her back down, gently, at arm's length from him. His blond hair even seemed trimmed the same way it was the last time she saw him. And the bright green eyes were definitely Synde's.

"I do not know you." He stepped back and a small hint of fear crossed his face. Trela did not think she had ever even seen that miniscule of an amount on his face before.

"Of course, you do. Its me, Trela. I'm the Kriishan. You're the one who told me. You." Trela was beginning to feel panicky. Her chest would not expand enough to let her breathe. She pulled the leather pouch she wore around her neck and poured out the white stones into his hand. "You left me these. Remember?"

"No, I… I don't remember anything. I know that I do not know you. Or even you." Here Synde pointed at Knill. "But I also have this feeling that I do not know me. You say 'Synde,' and it does not ring a bell. I cannot, however, tell you what the correct answer is. I am… at a loss." He staggered back one step, and then two. Trela felt as if she were dreaming. She pinched her wrist to see if she were asleep and then wondered the wisdom of that saying. As if dreams could not include self-inflicted pain.

Knill had turned his attention down at the ground, looking for the dagger, Trela presumed. "Did he have a scar? You know… something identifying?" Knill was talking over his shoulder at them.

Trela tried with all of her might, but could think of nothing more identifying than the fact that he looked just like Synde. Exactly like him. She had never seen him out of his clothes, not even at a swimming hole. He never bragged about wounds. "Do you remember anything about yourself? What village did you grow up in?

What was your military rank? Do you know who Qizern is?" Trela stared into his eyes as she asked those questions. Looking for any clue of recognition. A tensing of the muscles around the eye. Nostrils flaring or throat swallowing. Anything at all. She saw nothing, however. Nothing to indicate that anything she said, not even just one measly noun, registered in his mind. It was like conversing with a statue for all she could read from his facial expressions.

"Aha!" It was Knill, delighting in his find. "Here it is." He picked it up gingerly and walked it over to her.

"How did you defend yourself? You must have had training." Knill's interruption helped clear her head. She decided to reason with Synde.

"Yes, I feel that I have had training." Synde spoke emotionlessly.

"But you cannot remember who trained you? You are a Pyran, are you not?" She could feel herself getting flustered. Why would he be here if he was not Synde? Why would there be such a coincidence? It did not make sense.

"I feel that I could be a Pyran." The more monotonous he became, the less like Synde he seemed.

"Where were you, just before the crash of lightning? Where were you this morning? You remember that much, do you not?" Trela tossed the dagger lightly between her hands. Sometimes she would spin it in a slow arc before catching it again. As she stared harder at Synde, she thought she could hear a type of low chanting in the background. It was rhythmic, almost soothing. She decided that she just had to know if he was Synde or not. She would pay any price for that knowledge, was willing to make a dangerous mistake. She threw the dagger at him with all of her might. It spun so quickly that it was just a shiny blur to Trela. But he caught it. CAUGHT IT. Not just dodged. Not blocked. But plucked it from the air, like a girl picking a ripe pear.

"You have got to be Synde. There is no other living Pyran who could do that. Let me ask you a question." Trela took a deep breath while she studied his face for a negative reaction. Instead, the slightest smile, for the briefest moment, passed his lips. There was almost a lascivious hunger to that smile. But then it was gone, and she could not rightly recall its true dimensions later.

"Please do." He stood perfectly straight with his arms relaxed at his sides. The dagger dangled loosely but comfortably in his hand.

"How would you describe 'being guided by your gut'?" Trela wanted him to describe something that he spoke about passionately and repeatedly enough that he should be able to do it without being able to remember very well, yet she would easily be able to tell if this Pyran in front of her was really Synde.

"One of my favorite subjects, listening to your gut. We should sit and talk about that through the night. Do you have any grog?" His smile was wide and showed much teeth, but the warmth never reached his cheeks, let alone his eyes.

"You have got to be Synde." She did not want to, but she had to repeat herself. It was quieter and with less emphasis, but it was an affirmation of what she truly wanted more than an absolute belief. She needed Synde's training and knowledge, of that there was no doubt. More than anything, however, she felt she needed his wisdom. She wanted to feel as if she were making the correct choices. And nothing would make her feel better than the sight of Synde nodding in agreement at a decisive action of hers. She wondered again if she were sleeping. It would explain so much.

"You must be hungry." Knill started to kneel by the cold fire pit after the suggestion of drink. Even though he rarely drank, he enjoyed it when others did.

"Yes, I can say that. I am hungry." Synde was not looking at him, but at Trela. He still held the dagger easily in his hand.

"You really do not remember what happened to you yesterday?" Knill had stood back up and was walking towards Synde while he was talking. Towards Synde's back.

"It is as if I am newly born." Synde was smiling sweetly at Trela. She had yet to move towards the dead fire, unlike Knill. Synde had not moved yet either, so she felt obliged to wait.

"That does not distress you? I would be terrified." Knill stopped behind Synde.

"Maybe I am a naturally calm Pyran... I would not rightly know." Synde's voice took on a slightly ominous tone. "Smells like a storm." He lifted his nose in the air and sniffed the wind. There seemed to be a pulse in the air to Trela, with a small repeated harmony thrumming in the background. Like a gang of hummingbirds behind her head, beating their wings furiously.

Suddenly there was a strike of lightning behind her, loud and bright. She naturally spun to look, her heart pounding in her chest. She thought she saw a tree in the distance. When she turned back, Synde was looking at her oddly. With a flash, he threw her dagger back at her. Her reflexes took over her body and threw her to the ground out of the way. She looked up at Synde from her prone position but he just stood there in front of her. So she slowly got up.

"I hope you weren't trying to teach me how to catch a dagger." Trela laughed nervously.

"That was quick. Kudos. This should be entertaining. You know, so many derlians give up too soon. Too quickly, the entire hunt is over. With nothing left but the feeding. You, however, seem to have a tenacious grip on hope and audacity. Almost a kind of hubris in the face of what you should expect. You do know what to expect, do you not?" Synde held his arms wide and walked slowly towards Trela. There was no menace or malice in his movements, yet every nerve screamed aloud at Trela.

"You are not Synde, are you?" Trela quickly hopped from foot to foot. Then, more deliberately she took a low crouch. She wished she had paid more attention to where the long dagger of hers had landed. She did not know how much it would truly help, but even the weight of it in her hand would make her feel less frightened. She needed something solid to hold on to. As she glanced back, she noticed it sticking out of a tree trunk, vibrating slowly.

"I guess you are capable of abandoning hope after all. What a shame." The pyran dropped into a low crouch himself. Seemingly unburdened by the worry that he had no weapons at his immediate disposal. Or at least his visible disposal.

Trela was not feeling anything close to hubris at that moment. She did not know what was happening to her, simply could not figure it out. It made no sense. In the natural scheme of things, it even seemed unfair. This was not a battle that she had marched to be at. Not something she had woken up prepared for. It was merely a violent stranger taking advantage of her lack of forethought. *How evil*, she thought, *how cruel.* She screamed at the cruelty of fate in her mind. Cursed it soundly, or rather, silently. It would have been fantastic to run into Synde here, in the desert. It would have made such a difference in her life. It was, however, not to be. Luckily for Trela, Knill reacted first.

"Aaiigh!" The sound seemed torn from his throat. Trela wished he had not screamed aloud, because the Pyran spun around at the noise. Knill's falling stick was interrupted by the Pyran's sure hands. They stood there, for a full moment, frozen in mid action. Opposing forces equally matched. She turned and ran from the stasis. She jumped over the detritus in her path and yanked the dagger from its shallow wooden sheath. Turning back, she raced towards Knill and the stranger to see their stasis come crashing around them. Around Knill would probably be more accurate. The thick stick had been forced back into Knill's face, and he was being slowly pushed towards the ground. For some reason the Pyran was only using one hand to push down at Knill. The other was held high and out of the way, as if the Pyran was consciously trying not to use it. She only had two more steps. One last leap. Contact.

Trela felt the dagger pierce into soft flesh. She had achieved slipping the dagger under the Pyran's upraised armpit. The blade went straight for the top of his lung. It was a killing blow, and Trela was incredibly proud to have achieved it at full speed. Lishean would have been proud of her as well. To her satisfaction, the Pyran was knocked sideways and fell to the ground with a mighty thud.

Trela knelt by Knill, making sure he was not hurt. He was staring wide-eyed over her shoulder, however. When she was undeterred, he pointed behind her. She turned in her kneel-crouch pose to see what Knill was seeing.

The Pyran was pulling the dagger out, slowly, right behind her. He was standing full height, indeed seemed to be taller than before. Without a moment's hesitation, Trela spun at him with her left leg held high. She was able to round-house into the dagger hilt. The blade jerked violently out of the Pyran's armpit, slicing a large gash as it exited sideways. No blood exited, however. There was no spray, no gush. The Pyran groaned mightily and clutched his perforated flesh, but was still standing through the pain.

Trela did not pause. She used her open palm to flatten his nose against his skull. Her left hand swung in a wide haymaker towards his gaping wound. She knew that was the key. She had to keep working the original wound. Hit him where it hurts. She connected with his arm, which pushed into his wound. She could tell by his grimace. But it was not enough to keep him reeling. He swiped at her with his fingers extended as if he had claws. She was unable dodge since her right arm was extending towards his nose again, but thought she could take the blow.

It felt as if he truly had claws! Trela felt her neck and the top of her chest split by four long streaks of fire. It was luckily only a flesh wound, probably not too deep, but it made her howl in pain nonetheless. She was blinded momentarily by something. Whether by rage or by pain, she was unsure. Her right palm connected soundly with the Pyran's face again. The jarring induced by the irregular shape of his eye socket was absorbed easily into her arm via her palm. She felt as if her wrists were too small to follow through with her fist in a knock-out, drag-out fight such as this. In her heart, she knew the loser of this fight was going to die. She gave her all in a frenzy of panic, but the Pyran struck back with a force that could not be matched. Trela felt the blow to her stomach lift her off the ground slightly. She tumbled backwards onto the dusty ground.

It seemed to Trela like there was a boulder sitting on her chest. She wanted to breathe, truly, but could not muster the strength to inhale. The sounds from outside of her body diminished like the sun dipping under the horizon. She could only hear her own blood pumping in her own ears. A humming or chanting sensation pulsated through the rhythm of the blood. She tried to stand but felt strangely ineffectual. It was as if she had been turned into a turtle and flipped on her back. She struggled there, spine curved in imitation of hard shell, rocking back and forth, trying to get her outstretched limbs to find purchase on something. Anything could have provided the momentary stability required to find balance. But Trela flailed, breathless, helpless, in front of the Pyran. He had gone back to clutching his wounded arm with his good one. But he was smiling as he looked down on her. It was as if the pain did not faze him. He was debilitated in a sense, but not slowed down by it. She took in a ragged breath.

Suddenly the dagger point appeared through the Pyran's chest. Trela had been unable to see Knill charging from behind the Pyran, nor had she been able to hear him, but she noticed the effects. The Pyran howled like an animal. More like a giant moose than a small wolf, but the wildness of nature was captured instantly in that scream. He shook sideways, and Knill was flung off into the dark night, howling his own pain and fear.

Trela was finally able to breathe and staggered up just as the stranger was landing on his knees. He was reaching and twisting behind him, trying to grasp the dagger. Trela ran at him and kicked his face with all her might. To her satisfaction, he fell over backwards and landed on the dagger hilt. The length of the dagger showing in front of his chest was about the same that is still in his chest, Trela thought. She could not understand how he was still thrashing about. She did not dwell on the dilemma either. She grabbed a nearby branch from the ground and began swinging while trying to stay out of the thing's reach. She was not really causing any damage, but mainly keeping it on its back and letting the dagger work its simple magic. The hole seemed to be getting larger as the struggle continued, but Trela was unsure. Every once in a while she got a good hit in as it struggled to get back up. Knill rushed back into the fray with a large rock and half flung, half dropped it on the stranger's head. The blow seemed to daze the stranger briefly, but soon it was up and swiping at Knill. Trela dropped her ineffectual branch and jumped upon the dagger's hilt protruding from the stranger's back. With a mighty downward wrench, she was able to tilt the dagger almost thirty degrees. The stranger bellowed and began to flail wildly. Trela yanked upwards with all of her might, sloping the dagger in the opposite direction. As he shook back and forth violently, she managed to hang on, twisting or jerking on the long dagger every chance she got. She was scratched a few more times during the struggle, but nothing like her first wound. Finally, as the stranger seemed to be losing energy, she pulled sideways on the dagger, attempting to widen the wound, and the dagger sliced straight through the stranger's body. A burst of golden leaves exploded upwards at Trela. She instinctively swiped uselessly at them. When they settled, the Pyran's body was gone. It was as if it never existed. Trela fell upon the pile of leaves, exhausted. Knill soon staggered over. From behind them, somewhere, came a deep rumbling voice.

"Shoo. Shoo! Be gone foul stench!" Trela swung her head around attempting to see what new horror was descending upon them. There was only the tree. It shook and shimmied, but was just a tree. Trela stood up, dagger in hand, and walked towards the tree, thinking that whoever was speaking was standing behind it. It was then that she realized the tree had not been there when they had made camp. At least she thought that it had not been there before. She stopped, nervously, in front of it.

"Fly, smoke, fly! Leave our presence with your non-corporeal form as well as my leaves. Good riddance." At this the tree shook vigorously.

"Are you talking?" Trela had meant the tree.

"Bravo and welcome. We had heard of your coming, and so we sent me out to investigate. Just in the nick of time, it seems. Our roots run through the entire desert, us Vijen. Nothing happens here without our knowing." The tree shivered.

"Nick of time?" Trela still clung to the dagger, though she was not sure why.

"You are mighty, yes! You are quick and strong. You know how to kill derlians well. Yes, you are well trained. But, and I say this with the deepest respect, you would have been destroyed if we had allowed that Tlana to use its lightning. No warrior has ever beaten a Tlana with full powers. Mages, rarely. Warriors, never. With the deepest respect." The tree shivered again.

"Well, if you truly crippled that creature to help us overcome it, I thank you with the greatest gratitude." Trela bowed deeply to the tree. She did not understand anything that had happened since she'd been so rudely awakened. Not in the slightest. Synde, the real Synde, used to tell her to be gracious when she did not know what was going on. Being gracious, he said, disarms your enemies while hugging your friends. Everyone wins.

"Truly. We would not sow discord with the Kriishan. The times have begun to become rapid, yes. Importance so close to importance. Such times are essential to future time. It is during these times that the future is most malleable, yes, most ductile, yes. We feel the lines being drawn in the sand, even though they are not being drawn here in the desert. Do you feel the quickness of the times?" Trela had been staring at the tree's leaves. They looked golden with the same intricate veining pattern as the leaves lying on the ground behind her, though she had examined neither.

"All times are quick to me, Vijen. Tell me, did you turn the Tlana's body into leaves?" Trela hoped that she had the names pronounced correctly.

"Ha, no. No, the Tlana may not be destroyed. They have the same claim to the desert as the Vijen. However, since they are so foul, they are not allowed to affect things. They are smoke, yes. Only when a Tlana has stolen enough leaves to sew to itself may they affect the physical world. Funny, yes, listen to this. They sneak up on us.

They dance seductive dances. They preen and parade, so comical. They will do anything for the leaves, so they may spread their mischief beyond the whispering into derlians' dreams. However, leaves fall because it is their time. They cannot be coerced. We, the Vijen, hold on to them for as long as we can. Using them to bring us life from the very air, from the sky itself. Then, when we are unable to hold them any longer, one will drop to the desert floor. The Tlana, if one has been hovering nearby, will swoop upon it as if it were payment for their efforts. Whatever those efforts might have been. They will then go to more of us, another Vijen you see, and try whatever they were doing when the other leaf fell. Cause and effect, so comical. They can feel life, the Tlana, but since they are not allowed to participate, they do not understand cause and effect. You, though, you do not need this knowledge. What knowledge do you seek?" The tree leaves all pulsated in the wind, but none of the leaves fell. Trela looked back at the pile of leaves that used to be the Tlana and saw them blackened and sinking. They must rot incredibly fast when not being used as skin, Trela mused.

"I need the wisdom to be Kriishan. I need Synde. Who is supposed to tell me how to lead by my gut?" Trela was not sure of what the tree had meant, but wanted to keep it talking.

"The trick is to lose focus with everything around you. Let it blur to background status. Only then do all details gain equality—lost in anonymity. With that conscious disconnect of your constant unconscious choice of what you are paying attention to at any given moment, comes an ability to feel even the slightest tug of destiny. It is what is used by generals overlooking a battlefield. By staring with unfocused eyes over the entire scene, overall patterns can be realized in the tug between armies. The sinusoidal wave demarcating where one army pushes forwards and another pulls back and vice versa until one wave crashes down upon the other. It is these natural patterns, unseen to the focused eyes, that derlians, being a part of nature, follow with their unconscious. If one can understand those patterns intrinsically enough, then the immediate future of the shifting lines of momentum may become apparent. This sight is what you must cultivate if you are to be a great leader. This sensitivity to the ebb and flow of natural energies. Does that help you? Do you feel more wise now?" The tree seemed to be drooping slightly.

"No. I guess I… I just want to be assured of victory." Trela looked up into the fibrous branches. They almost glowed against the black sky.

"Ha. We all wish to be assured. Rest assured that nothing is permanent until it happens and then… then it is already done and there is no going back. You can be assured of who you are, Kriishan. That should be more than enough to keep you warm at night. Who else knows who they are? Think of poor Knill. What destiny does he pursue? Who is he? Does he know what role he will play? You should be less concerned with assurances and keep looking towards gaining skills and wisdom. Knowledge of what difficulty you will face is impossible to tell you, even for a seer, but we can tell you that it will be difficult. Does that help you? Do you feel more wise now?" The tree shivered again.

"No. You are not telling me anything." Trela began to get a little frustrated. She was still not over the fight, and she could almost feel the adrenaline slowly ebbing from her veins.

"What do you wish to know?" The tree shook sprightly.

"How do I find the companions I am supposed to meet here in the desert? Where are those who can help me defeat Qizern?" Trela attempted to recall what Tumu had said. She had been focused so much on the stranger that her mind was a blank for the rest of the conversation.

"Good. See, you are becoming wise as we speak. Walk towards us, through us and straight beyond. Walk the rest of the night and the day tomorrow. They are waiting for you, though they do not know that is why they are waiting. You must not drink from the well." The tree fell silent.

Trela tried to cajole it into speaking again. Finally she turned away in disgust. When she turned back, the tree was gone. She panicked briefly about where the tree had been until Knill made a line in the direction they needed to travel in the sand. They finally agreed upon the direction the tree was in relation to where she was standing and could get to the business of packing. She almost forgot about her necklace, but mercifully the pale stones glowed softly in the moonlight. She gingerly picked the necklace up from the trampled ground and blew the dust off of it. She fingered the stones as she stared up at the moon. She had wanted so much for Synde to be alive. She would have believed anything. It was not her senses or skills that had saved them. No, it was only the tree, the Vijen. If she and Knill had been alone, they would have died. Trela promised herself not to let her guard down like that again, not even for the promise of Synde. She kissed the necklace and replaced it in her pouch.

They mounted and left a relatively clean camp in record time. This was especially impressive because of how dark it was, but they were both worried about more Tlana, so they worked quickly. Trela decided to wear her necklace instead of carrying it. As they were leaving, Trela began complaining that Tumu had gotten everything wrong. "This was nothing like what Tumu said. Nothing." She would shake her head over and over.

"Maybe Tumu is not a very good seer." Knill finally replied to her. The quip was enough to take her mind off of the almost deadly encounter and enable her to proceed in peace.

They traveled until dusk the next day without seeing anything. Trela kept her worries to herself until the darkness started to descend. They were both exhausted from the lack of sleep, the fight and now the ceaseless travel. Just when she began to feel defeated, however, they crested a rise and saw fires in the distance. They could not tell exactly how much further the fires were, but just the sight was enough to make Trela sigh audibly with relief.

The rest of the distance was covered with a zeal that even infiltrated the horses. They almost galloped down the sides of dunes and scarcely slowed down on the way back up. Trela knew they only had so much time to get to the fires before whoever lit them decided to retire to their tents. She need not to have worried, however, for they arrived long before the fires were put out. As they neared the light, a small town began to appear in the starlit darkness. There were little low buildings as well as the random fires spread in a rough circle. Trela wondered briefly what was at the center of that circle.

As they got closer, Trela thought she could hear a cry being taken up through the shanty town. "Visitors. More visitors." She was not sure if that was what they were really saying, but it sure sounded like that.

When they finally arrived, there was a welcoming party formed to meet them. At least Trela hoped they were a welcoming party. When she felt their horses had walked close enough she decided to address the small crowd.

"I am the Kriishan, the rightful ruler of the Pyran realm. I am looking for warriors here, to help me claim my right. I have spoken with a seer and even with the Vijen in the desert, and they both say there are warriors here. Who will join me?" Trela was too tired to care if her message fell on hostile ears. She figured by tomorrow, after a good night's rest—she hoped—everyone in town will have heard about her. Then, maybe, whoever she was told would help her would step forth. If not, then she would have to seek them out more aggressively on her own. If, however, this town was full of Tlana, or something of the like, she was ready to die. She was just too tired for finesse.

"We cannot leave." "We cannot help." "We are tied here." "We do not know you." "There is no one here who can join you." "We need to be near the well." "We cannot leave the waters." "Sorry." "The well is our life." And so on and so forth. Not one helpful face in the group. She could not tell exactly what they were afraid of, but one thing was for sure: none of these derlians would be leaving the well.

That was the fascinating thing. There were Luftens and Fluens and Gaens and even Pyrans. They were all huddled in this shanty town, living peaceably amongst each other just so they could all be close to the well. Trela had never even seen a Fluen before. In fact, she had barely even heard about them. She could tell you nothing about them, as a race. Here, though, everyone was represented. And they all had a similar creepy quality about them. It was almost as if they were empty. Like a full suit of armor that moved and talked, but had no one inside. It made Trela's head hurt to try to figure it out, so instead she allowed herself and Knill to be shuffled to a meal and a place to put their tent. She decided to sleep rather than ask any probing questions.

When they awoke, Trela and Knill realized their tiny tent was surrounded by derlians. Luckily for her, or unluckily for Knill, she had not changed the night before, but had slept in her traveling clothes. She opened the flap and stood out in the blinding sun, blinking at all of those around her. Most of them had the vacant stare that she had seen the night before, but there was one group that stood out from the rest. The group did not have the same gray-brown look that the rest of the derlians wore. She walked over to them.

"Are there warriors amongst you?" Trela asked them bluntly. What sleep she did get did not seem to help at all. The town, such as it was, was already getting on her nerves, and she had only just arrived. She could not put her finger on why it bothered her, however.

A derlian with a huge chest, light brown hair, and a large axe stepped forward. Trela was unsure if he was doing so to block her access to the others or just because he was their leader. He looked like a Luften, even though he was gigantic. In fact, they all looked like Luftens. Except maybe one of the females in the back of the pack. "We are all warriors here." He thumped his chest lightly. The motion was so natural that it made Trela smile a little.

"Excellent. I have a need for great warriors. A sage spoke of your presence, your importance, and your need. I have come to trade my assistance for yours. I am Trela, the Kriishan and future queen of the Pyran realm." Trela did not know why, but she felt that this was the group she needed to bring back to Agoge with her. She threw caution into the wind and bowed her head towards the group in general. "I place myself into your service."

The large luften laughed and began waving his hands in front of her. "We have no need..." His friendly banter was quickly interrupted by a female in the back.

"Wait, Torpalin. Stand down. Let me speak with her." The strange lady from the back walked through the group towards Trela. The warriors parted before her like blades of tall grass.

The young lady took Trela's elbow and gently led her deeper into the drab enclave. They walked for some time, steeped in silence. After winding their way back for a while they stopped in front of a nondescript building. They entered, and the world turned black as the door swung shut behind them. As her eyes adjusted, Trela could barely make out the bleakness. The small table was rough hewn lumber. The bed looked incredibly uncomfortable. There was a small ivy plant in a large vase, struggling to climb up its supporting stick. She did not know why ivy would be chosen instead of a plant that bore edible fruit. Seeing the struggling bit of nature merely added to the bleak ambiance. The entire room reeked of a sort of desperate sadness.

"My name is Clerin Toswin. I heard your plea back there and it piqued my interest. I'll be blunt. We need to find the Luften temple. The Queen has assured me that she knows where it is, but I worry that the King is the only Luften who truly knows the location. I know that it is somewhere between here and Ariellyna. I must give my message soon, but I must also bring some well water to the Luften King as quickly as possible. You see…" Clerin paused for a conspicuous time before Trela decided to interject.

"You will not believe your luck, Clerin. I happen to know the location of the Luften temple," Trela lied. "We can meet with the King there, and you would be able to give the water and the message on the same day." Trela was not fully sure of why she had lied and continued to lie. "Then we can make the quick march to Agoge. There I will defeat Qizern. After that, I will give you the resources you need to get back to your homeland in comfortable style. Sounds easy, does it not? Trust me, Clerin. We can make this work for all of us." Trela thrust out her hand, knowing that she needed to seal the deal quickly. To her eternal delight, Clerin grasped her hand quickly and firmly. In fact, Clerin appeared very relieved that Trela interrupted her. She did not even explain why she needed the temple or why the King could not lead her there. Not until later in the conversation.

"Now." Trela paused for a quick breath. "You will have to tell me of your traveling companions. All of their strengths and weaknesses." Trela did not want Clerin thinking about the actual deal. Especially not about the location of that temple. She figured that if she could get Clerin talking about her companions, it might distract her long enough for her to forget specifics. She just wanted Clerin sidetracked long enough for her to convince her own warriors of the deal. Trela had found that, in general, derlians were most easily distracted when they were discussing other derlians. Except, of course, if you could get them to talk about themselves. "My companion is named Knill and, as you may have noticed, he is a Gaen."

"I had never met a Gaen or, for that matter, a Pyran. At least not until I arrived here, in the middle of all this nothingness. And the denizens… they sit here doing nothing with nothing. Passing through the days like ghosts. Their little village moves around at night, while everyone is asleep. Nothing more permanent than these horrible shacks will move with the village is what I am told. So there can be no agriculture, no stone buildings. Nothing but this gray." Clerin waved her left arm wildly. It made her seem cute somehow. "I would die without any color. At the very least, I would end up killing. See if any of these gray wraiths bleed red." She grinned at Trela. Something about her smile was so naively heartwarming that Trela felt an unbidden urge to protect her. From what, she did not know. Clerin suddenly stopped and stared at Trela's neck. "What a lovely necklace. Are those pearls?"

"I... I don't know." It took Trela by surprise. "What are pearls?"

"They get grown in oysters in the sea, but they are very rare. Yours seem quite large." Clerin's eyes glowed with a soft appreciation. Trela found herself liking Clerin in spite of herself. If they were in the Pyran realm, amongst warriors, she might look upon Clerin as flighty. Here, however, she was a breath of fresh air and information. Unconsciously she touched her necklace. "Well, I..." Trela was thinking about the necklace, and Synde, but floundered before finding the right question.

"Of course. You wanted to know about my companions. How foolish of me to ramble on." From there, Clerin proceeded to ramble on. Trela enjoyed a bit of campaigning gossip at times, but she had not been prepared for the deluge she received. In truth, her mind began to wander. No one specific idea took hold of her attention. It was more as if she floated upon a myriad of tiny ideas. They bubbled about her, jostling for attention, but none of them standing proud of the background noise. Then something Clerin said snapped Trela from her irreverent reverie.

"There was so much lightning over the sky that, even though he was several hilltops away, we could see him and the Tlana fighting amongst the clouds. The lightning would burst, and their silhouettes would be the only dark images in the sky. It was stark. Stark." Clerin's hands were widespread in front of her large eyes. Waving slightly, as if she held them out so rigid that they vibrated with the intensity of the energy it took.

"Did you say he was fighting a Tlana?" Trela racked her brain to recall whom Clerin was speaking of. She knew a name had to have been spoken at the beginning of the story, but she could not think of it.

"Yes, our mage, Feyazki. Do not let his youth trick you. He is a powerful mage." It seemed that Clerin smiled unconsciously at speaking of the mage. Trela did not understand why Clerin would speak of age. Clerin herself looked as if she should still be escorted by elder family members, and Trela knew that she could not look aged either. The most common attack on her claim of destiny was her age. "Youth should not attempt to lead, but try to listen." She had heard such phrases her entire life. *Maybe the Fluen is used to smiling at older derlians and one so young must be powerful indeed to attract her gaze.* The words came unbidden to Trela's mind. She was not sure of their validity, but they made her smile.

"You say he defeated a Tlana with no help. No one else was there. Nothing else was near? Not even a tree?" Trela was trying to remember how far away from the fight Clerin had told her the rest of the party was. She wondered how trustworthy their testimony to that fight could be, being so far away. She thought for a moment and then came to the conclusion that it did not matter if he was powerful enough to defeat a Tlana all alone. What mattered was that others believed it. Stories such at these could be nursed into legends. She decided that she would get the truth from the mage himself. Rather than concerning herself with details, she let Clerin finish telling her stories. Trela felt good, almost as if she were drunk, but she knew it was just the destiny that inebriated her. What were the odds that she would find another derlian who had been attacked by a Tlana? What were the odds that she had found one that defeated the monster by himself? What were the odds that she would find a small commando unit out here in the middle of the desert? The middle of all this nothingness, as Clerin had put it. Astronomical. The feeling was euphoric. How could she not believe in destiny? The joy threatened to burst within her.

After the euphoria wore off, Clerin was still talking. Trela found herself nodding in unison with Clerin and finally could take no more. It was as if the energy was beginning to seep out of her, weakening her. Trela yawned and stretched, hoping that Clerin would notice. Or at least that the yawn would be infectious. But there was no such luck. Trela listened dispassionately for a brief while longer when she heard something unexpected.

"What was that?" Trela was not quite sure what she had missed.

"The Gaens? I was just mentioning the Gaens that are here as well. By the well, ha." Clerin's eyes lit up briefly as she laughed at her own joke.

"No, I meant the name. Did you say Croy?" Trela did not realize that she was holding her breath.

"Yeah, the Gaen's name is Croy. And his wife's name is Ilana." Clerin lifted one eyebrow briefly. "Does that mean something to you? Does your Gaen know him?"

Trela was too shocked about Croy to say anything about Clerin's comment on Knill. She was unsure why everyone kept giving her ownership over him. They had not even mentioned the word "ghulzan" during their desert trip.

"No, he doesn't. Well, maybe he does; I am not sure. I, however, have spent some time in Serif and... well... I know a Croy Sie'tin. It would just be the most bizarre coincidence if it was the same Croy." Trela paused for a moment and let the idea sink into her head. It took some time, but the euphoria snuck its way back into her. She was incredibly excited to think that Croy would be here, in the middle of all this nothingness. And yet, she was scared as well. He would not be happy with her. In fact, he might even blame her for Nolt's death. Truth be told, she kind of blamed herself for Nolt's death. Her mind began to race so fast that she did not realize that Clerin had started speaking again.

"...since their last names are not familial, I do not really pay attention to them. You know, I never thought about it, but what if married Gaens had different vocations? Belonged to different guilds, you know. Would they have different last names? And what about children? Do the children have last names? The whole system is too confusing." Clerin was still smiling at Trela. It gave her the impression that Clerin was assuming that she had been listening to everything. That, however, had been far from the truth for some time now.

"Oddly enough, married couples often have different last names. Maybe more bizarre, the children do not have any last names at all. They take neither parent's name and will only get one once they graduate from their apprenticeship." Trela was somewhat surprised at how quickly the simple knowledge came to her. "As a matter of fact, my Gaen friend has no last name either."

"Ah, friend." Clerin looked slightly smug. Trela was sure it was supposed to be a knowing look, but it appeared smug to her. Of course, Trela had to admit to herself that it was a sensitive subject for her. She almost broke the small patch of silence before Clerin spoke up again. "How did you come to spend time in Serif?"

"I lost my mentor very near there and... well, I spent some time there before finding my way back to my homeland." Trela had decided to be as vague as possible concerning the Gaen realm. "Please, you must show me this well."

To Trela's delight, Clerin immediately acquiesced. "Of course. Follow me to your gateway to adventure." Clerin laughed lightly at her little joke as she turned to leave the shack. The light burst towards Trela as the door opened, and she thought more soberly about the statement. Clerin's body grew unnaturally skinny in the blinding light outlined by that open door. It made her seem even taller than normal. Trela quickly followed her outside.

They wound their way through the drab landscape, past the dilapidated shanties, and finally approached a small stone circle that Trela realized must be the well. Sitting next to it she could make out a female Gaen, an ancient-looking derlian that she could not determine the race of, and Croy. He locked eyes with her as she approached. He immediately stood and then wavered unsteadily, briefly. His arm rose towards Trela. He pointed his index finger at her and fell to the ground. It was all done in eerie silence.

Clerin paused in her shock, so Trela was forced to run past her to get to Croy's crumpled form. The female Gaen, however, beat Trela to his prone body. Trela knelt on the opposite side of his body.

"You must be Trela." The Gaen's voice was taught with emotion. "Do you know who I am?" She placed some wadded clothing underneath his head.

Trela thought for longer than she needed to. There was only one name that the Gaen could be known by. Trela just did not want to say it. "You must be Ilana." Trela braced herself, though she was not really sure for what. She just knew that her stomach was in knots.

"Do you see this? Do you see how you have wrecked my Croy? Nolt was his best friend." Ilana stood quickly with her hands clenched at her sides. The militant stance looked so odd on her that Trela was almost comforted by it. She could certainly fight this Gaen. It was the emotional outburst that she could not deal with.

"Now calm down, Ilana. I did not kill Nolt." Trela stood slowly herself. She kept her arms loose at her sides, just in case, but she made a conscious choice to not make any threatening overtures.

"Really? Are you saying that your foolish attempt at escape did not directly cause Nolt's death? Do you expect me to calm down because you did not slit Nolt's throat with your own hand? You may as well have, you know. If you had never arrived at Serif, he would still be breathing. If you had never tricked Croy into taking care of you, teaching you and nourishing you, he would still be alive. More importantly—most importantly—if you had not left the way you did, if you had not rushed out of Serif without explaining anything to anyone, he would still be alive. His blood will never leave your hands, do you hear me? Killer. Murderer! How can you live with yourself? How can you continue breathing knowing that you caused, directly caused, a beautiful, innocent Gaen's death? Answer me! What makes you so special that you could run off and leave his corpse bleeding, alone in a tunnel? Why are you so unique that the death of innocents does not affect you? Does not bother you? Answer me! How could you leave him as his last breath rattled in his bloody lungs?" Ilana finally lowered her voice. "Nolt is dead now. Forever. Do you not feel any remorse?"

Trela wished that Ilana had struck her. When the tirade began, she promised herself that if Ilana swung at her she would not block or dodge or even flinch. Instead the words flooded her; drowned her. Her chest felt as if it were being constricted by metal bands. She could not breathe. The worst part of it all was that she knew Ilana was right. It was her stubborn pride that had made her chafe in Serif. It was her dream of destiny that pushed her towards escape. But escape from what? What in Serif was so heinous that she had been unable to stay? Midway during the diatribe Trela could feel the tears well up in her eyes. Ilana was correct. No, Ilana was right. Right! Which meant that Trela was wrong. She had been able to suppress the memory of Nolt's death by keeping herself supremely occupied. The quest to become Kriishan. Iventorn's warpack. Knill. Knill was the greatest distraction of all. But not anymore. The image came roaring back into her head, unbidden and unwelcome. It was the first time in a long time that the image came to her while she was awake. It could not be shaken. The horror dripped down her spine like ice water. Then it turned into a cataract. She could feel nothing but the rushing cold inside her. She could not run, could not escape, could not even move. Trela did not feel like herself. It was if she were someone else, shocked by the truth being spouted from the enraged Ilana. She could feel nothing.

Trela's stomach heaved as a powerful sob racked her. The breath escaped her suddenly open mouth as she had escaped Serif. Trela tried with all of her might to control herself, to stay stoic. Another sob was ripped from her quivering diaphragm. She almost doubled over. She felt ill, poisoned. If someone stuck a knife in her at that moment, she would probably not even have noticed. If she would have, it would have been a grateful relief. An escape from those words. An escape from her own thoughts. An escape from the horror of the image of Nolt's bleeding, arrow-struck body. The way his eyes had widened. How the blood had flown from his mouth like the hateful spittle that shot forth from Ilana's. Trela just wanted darkness. She wanted to be empty. She wished her mind to be wiped clean. To no avail, however. Her wishes were like whistling past a graveyard. Useless to yourself, while at the same time showing anyone within hearing distance of just how much fear you were carrying. And who would come to comfort her? Was there anyone within hearing distance who would take pity on her? Not Knill, he was too far away. Not Clerin, she was too stunned to move. Certainly not Ilana—her anger was still palpable. No, the voice she heard as she quickly regained control of herself was Croy's. Like that of her doting father's. The shame of it all racked through her a little more as she realized it was him who reached out to her. But not for too long. His soothing magic was that strong. Not magic in the sense that he had cast a spell, but it was a type of magic all the same.

"I'm sorry. I'm so sorry." Trela could think of nothing else to say. Truly, there was nothing else she could say. Her arms dangled uselessly at her side.

"That is a start." He paused for a small moment and almost smiled with one corner of his mouth. "You know that I tried to have the 'jin who killed Nolt demoted? At the very least. However, I got the 'They were just doing their jobs speech.'" He laughed softly.

"They *were* just doing their jobs, Croy. That is why you received that speech." Ilana's voice came crashing down at no one in particular, or maybe everyone in particular. Trela's stomach tightened again, but part of it was annoyance, if not actual anger.

"You are correct, Ilana. Only I should bear the guilt for Nolt's death. I know that you do not believe me, but I am sorry for that. It was a mistake. I would tell you that it was done in the folly of youth, but I am still very much living the folly of my youth." Trela brushed at her clothing half-heartedly. It was more about ending the conversation than it was about getting clean. She realized that she could not be near Ilana for any longer. "Thank you, Croy. Goodbye, Ilana." She walked away without looking back.

Trela had never before let another make her feel that badly about herself, and she vowed that she would never feel like that again.

The attack had been shocking in its severity, but it also strengthened her against future attacks through a more basic understanding of her feelings' roots. She had not fully grieved, though she had thought she had. She had not truly examined her feelings of guilt, regret and sorrow. They were like poisons, not like the daggers of anger that she understood so much better. She had thought that ignoring these things was the same as solving them. So she learned that day to recognize the pressure building up within her and to let it out in smaller doses over larger amounts of time. She learned to do it privately, every night before falling asleep if she had to. She would mull over the day's weaknesses and aches, the day's poisons. She would decide how to best avoid them in the future. It was the same explosion, but in such slow motion that nobody really noticed. It kept all mountains as molehills.

Trela realized that she did not really know how to get back to where Knill was waiting. She walked in the direction she thought it was until she was far enough away from the well that she was sure they could no longer see Ilana. She decided to sit down on a low stone wall in the shade. For a brief moment she wondered why the stone of the wall and that of the well could move, but the villagers were unable to keep any crops with them.

"You did not mention there would be conflict. If you did not want to talk to them, we could have left without seeing them." Clerin's voice caught Trela by surprise. Not only because she had forgotten that Clerin was with her, which she had, but also because her voice was congenial. Trela naturally assumed that everyone in hearing distance of the well during the exchange would consider her a monster. Much like she considered herself one at that moment.

"Well. I had wanted to talk to Croy. To be honest, I did not realize that Ilana would be there, or that it would be she who held such a vehement grudge. To be even more honest, I would like to not speak of this anymore." Trela felt drained. She felt old. The catharsis, if that was what it was, left her completely devoid of emotion.

"I understand." Clerin placed her long-fingered hand over Trela's. It was soothing, cool, and dry. Trela appreciated the weight of it over her own small, sweaty hand, and appreciated the sentiment behind it even more so. However, she knew she could not afford the luxury of feeling better at the moment. She had to talk to Knill. She needed to get him to convince Croy to come with them when they all left. Trela could not say why or how, but she knew that Croy was essential to the mission. Not necessarily with Clerin's mission. But with the mission of her own destiny. She felt it as much as she felt that Clerin was important. As much as she felt the mage who fought the Tlana was important. She could not say how she knew any of this, just that it felt true to her.   "I must speak with Knill. Can you bring me back to the others?" Trela felt a tiny loss of connection when Clerin pulled her hand away.

"Of course. They should be just over there." Clerin pointed in a vague direction, but Trela was not paying much attention. She was grateful that Clerin led the way in silence.

In a few short moments they reached the group. Clerin was suddenly boisterous with her fellows, explaining how Trela would lead them to the temple. Trela took Knill's hand and led him off to the shade of a nearby building before anyone could speak to her.

"I need a favor from you, Knill. I think you are the only one capable of accomplishing this task." Trela took a deep breath. She did not know how to proceed.

"Meaning that you could not get the Fluen to do it?" He was smiling, but the statement caught her off guard. She realized suddenly that she had always assumed Knill would accomplish whatever she asked of him. That was probably because he always did. She was caught between feeling proud for Knill and shame for herself. She swallowed the latter emotion, knowing that she had felt enough shame on that day to last her the rest of her life.

"I need you to convince Croy to leave this place and travel with us." Trela knew she should express her pride in him or try to ease into her request, but she was too tired to banter with him just now.

"What? I mean, did you already ask him?" Knill looked a little taken aback, though he did not ask about Croy. He must of heard that the Gaens were here from Clerin's warriors.

"No, I… I wanted to, but I was unable to get around Ilana. When you convince him, you should take him aside and speak with him privately. Please? For me?" Trela knew that she was using the wrong voice. She had a sudden image of herself wheedling her father.

"Of course, Trela. Of course." Knill was looking down as he started to shuffle away. Trela knew that he would try, truly, but it did not seem as if his heart was in it. Before he fully could turn away, she grabbed his face with both hands and planted a kiss straight on him. When their lips parted, she held him for another second, staring into his eyes.

"Please. For me." Trela's voice was low and husky as she spoke those words. The effect on Knill was astounding. His face bloomed into a wide smile.

"Of course." The words had not changed, but the intent, the energy, had morphed into something much more intense. She let her hands drop, and he trotted off in the direction of the well.

Trela sighed and waited. As the time flowed by, her original dour mood crept back upon her. By the time that Knill returned, she felt that it would be bad news. Her prognosticating skills were, unfortunately, quite correct on this issue. Knill explained how he had tried. He had removed Croy from the well, and thereby Ilana, as she had advised, but nothing he could say would convince Croy to leave Ilana.

Even though Trela had known the possibility of this outcome, she was truly saddened. When she had heard that Croy was here, she thought it was a sign. A good omen from the past that would help ensure her success in her quest against Qizern. She had trouble not thinking of Croy's refusal to join her as a curse. She knew, however, that she could not face him again. Not after Serif, after Ilana, and after she had sent Knill to do her job for her. No, she had to write Croy not only from out of her quest, but out of her life as well. A heavy sadness fell over her heart as she headed back to Clerin and the group. They decided to leave the next morning.

Trela was beginning to worry that she would not be able to find the Luften Temple. She kept hoping to find some trace of the royalty that Clerin had said were supposedly waiting for them at the site. There was not even campfire smoke on the horizon. Nothing to lead them towards their destination. No signs to follow, no footprints to track. She also began to worry that if the King was not lucid and the Queen did not know where to go, that they would not be waiting for them at the correct spot. Which meant, unfortunately, that even if she could find the temple, they would not know they had found it without the royalty there to prove it. For all she knew, they could be standing above the temple right now. Yes, Trela was beginning to worry.

They had been traveling for a fortnight. At least that is how long it seemed to Trela; the desert had a way of bending time. Their meager provisions from the village were not holding out. They had finally found foothills to a canyon to land that almost looked green. Not quite, mind you, but close. There were juniper bushes and sagebrush, some straggling mustards. No grass yet, though. Their mounts were nibbling on the last of the oats that Clerin's party had brought with them originally. There was certainly nothing around them for a large herbivore to survive on. The entire party was overjoyed last night when Escha had killed one little rabbit. Trela knew that their morale hung on finding a big game animal. She had been trying to steer them towards the more verdant Luften lands, but was unsure if they had truly left the desert.

"You do not know where you are going, do you?" The whisper came from Knill.

"Whatever gave you that idea?" Trela hissed back at him. She swiveled her head in a quick panicky arc, looking for any prying ears. It was funny the first time he had said that to her. It was even amusing the last couple of times. Now, however, the joke was getting stale. "You should be helping me, not mocking me. I have half a mind to let the others cook you. They have been talking about it, you know. Torpalin especially. I keep sticking up for you, though. Don't know why I bother." Trela tried to smile, but it felt strained.

"Why did you tell them you knew where it was? We could have just gone back to Ariellyna and met their Queen." Knill sounded pained.

"Well, we are nowhere near Ariellyna either. We are nowhere near anywhere. We are... nowhere." Trela trailed off slightly. "Even if we could just find some village to purchase some cheese, or something."

"Yes, but then being lost would be their fault. Not ours." Here he looked deeply into Trela, as if he were trying to read her thoughts.

"I am not keeping a score, Knill." She felt exasperated.

"Well, I believe some of them are. I fear you might be correct about Torpalin. I thought he was eyeing me earlier, but I wrote it off as my own paranoia. No doubt he was mentally sizing up how many steaks he could carve from me." When Knill laughed, it was contagious. It was one of the things that Trela enjoyed about traveling with him. She laughed with him, too, briefly.

"Your point is well taken, Knill. I will, from here on out, put all of my energies towards solving the problem. And, therefore, solve the problem. You see, I was only using about half of my energies earlier. But now, thanks to your stirring speech motivating me beyond my own capabilities, I will actually try to find the temple." Trela felt her mood change as she spoke, though she did not want it to. It was somewhat eerie. It was as if the words she had been speaking were making her feel worse, but she could not stop herself from speaking them. She knew about halfway into her speech that if she did not stop herself, she was going make her own outlook gloomier. And truly, if there was one derlian who did not need to be gloomier at that moment and time, it was Trela. The words came out in spite of her meager efforts at stopping them. She felt as if she were losing against the tide and being sucked out to sea. She could see the shore receding but could not figure out how to bring it closer. She wished Knill would say something else funny. She even promised herself not to say anything afterwards, just to laugh. He did not, however. He just stared at her with those eyes of his.

Chapter 13

Croy told Knill no. Firmly and repeatedly. He admired the young Gaen's tenacity, but he could not leave Ilana alone at the well. Knill finally realized that he would not convince Croy, and he gracefully bowed out. Croy did not want to, but he ended up liking Knill. It was much the same with Trela. He had every reason in the world to hate her, but he could not. She was too bright-eyed. Too full of the youthful optimism that he had at one time, not so long ago, relished in himself so much. Of course, all of Croy's bright-eyed daydreaming had not amounted to much and, if he were honest with himself, neither did he. It was just that he enjoyed the simple things in life too much. Other than practice axe-fighting with the other 'jin hopefuls, he would have rather hiked on a hillside, or spelunked deep into the caves. He preferred going to rare, seldom-trafficked places with good friends rather than doing the same thing over and over in search of some form of perfection. It was his curse. However, he also did not think that others should be stifled in doing what they wished. Maybe it was because he was "just" a farmer that he did not feel a need to impose his will on others. But he could not just leave Ilana for some foreign adventure, even if the meals would have gotten better once they re-found civilization. His internal argument continued after Knill had left.

Lemniscate had been correct about the shanty town moving towards some raw materials after Ilana joined. They had taken an abandoned shack that still moved with the town and were able to fix it up a little for the first few days. Soon, however, they were moved back towards the center of the desert, where nothing grew and the only living creatures to be seen were the carrion birds, soaring high and lazy upon the updrafts. Croy was unsure of what they fed off of.

They had lived quietly during the moons before Trela and Knill appeared. Croy had enjoyed talking to the myriad of derlians who had come there over the ages. They all joked that they could see him aging, but he knew that he had not been there long enough for that to be true. In all, he found a simple and comfortable life there, amongst the eternal youth and his one love.

Ilana was angry that she had not been given a choice as he had, but it seemed that she had finally come to grips with that. She did truly enjoy the well water. She would drink several times a day, some days. It would leave her in a pleasant stupor for about an hour each time. Croy stayed by her side for the first few days as she stared at the wood ceiling of their little shack, drooling slightly. Now, though, he preferred to let her enjoy the water on her own. He would wander the little town, speaking with anyone who would come out of their little shacks. It was pleasant. Not exciting, but pleasant. He missed walking the lush valley with his sheep, but the pining was manageable. It was not until he saw Trela there at the well that he started having dreams again.

The first one was simple and elegant. It was almost like a normal dream except for the feeling of importance upon waking. He was a leaf, taken alight upon the wind. He fluttered over the landscape until he reached a gorge. There, he fell slowly in. The wind then switched direction and blew him along the gorge. With the canyon walls flying past him, he slowly descended towards the river at the bottom. He woke up before reaching the water, however.

The second was much like the first, except that he was now several leaves being blown about by the wind. In the third dream he was leaves and flower petals all jumbled up in the wind. He never reached the water, however. In the third dream it seemed that he was heading towards a cave in one of the cliff faces, rather than falling towards the river. The fourth dream brought insistence through velocity. The fifth dream he became a gale with twigs and small branches amongst him. Always heading towards the cave in the cliff. He began to become uncomfortable with the dreams. He started trying to stay awake longer and to rise earlier. He would attempt to position himself such that the morning sun would burst through a hole in their shack's wall and keep him from sleeping in.

To no avail. The dreams got more and more frenetic as the days wore on. Eventually he became a tornado that tore about the trees on the hillside before forcing the debris that was him through the gorge and into the cave. It always ended in the cave. He knew the cave was a destination, but he did not think it was his. There was an unshakeable insistence to his dreams, however. He constantly thought about them while he was awake and he dreamed them while he was asleep. There seemed to be no escape.

Eventually, he went back to the well to speak with Lemniscate. For some reason he felt ashamed to bring the dreams up to begin with. He thought that Lemniscate would think that Croy only spoke to him when he needed advice.

"You never did tell me how many derlians choose death over an eternity stuck in this desert." Croy smiled at Lemniscate as he approached.

"I suppose you have held off from drinking for long enough. The rate is quite high actually, though not done through withdrawal. No, most of those committing suicide do it here. Through the well." Lemniscate had a small, wry smile on his lips as he spoke to Croy.

"You mean they drink so much that they die?" Croy sat down next to Lemniscate so that both of their backs were towards the sun.

"No. I mean they throw themselves into the well. The body flares on fire and disintegrates about a third of the way down." He broke into a full smile.

"How do you know they disintegrate? You could be drinking their rotten bodies." Croy smiled back.

"You can see their bodies shrink to nothing as the fire consumes them. But your point is well taken. Truly, I have only watched three as they fell towards their doom. You wanted to know quantities, though. About thirty-five percent commit suicide in the first sun cycle. Then another thirty percent in the next ten cycles, bringing the total to about sixty-five percent. After that, though, it is usually more than a century before you see many-slash-any more suicides." Lemniscate was smiling and nodding to himself at this point. There was a long silence.

"How old are you, if I may ask?" Croy was trying to keep the conversation going.

"I am one of the originals. I was a Yaven. In fact, I knew Lembin before it became a Beleg." There was a bright glint in his eye. Not quite mischievous, but something akin to it.

"Seriously? I never would have dreamed… I cannot believe it." Croy tentatively reached out and touched Lemniscate's arm. It was a purely unconscious reaction. It was as if the touch would prove that Lemniscate was real, that what he said was true. "How have you…? You must have found the well."

"True, it was I who found this well. I begged for it. I screamed for it. You see, we thought we would be the same, but in a different place. We did not even know the concept of aging. We knew death, we even knew suicide; but we had never even heard of aging, could not imagine it." Lemniscate bowed his head towards Croy conspiratorily and whispered, "There may even be more than one well. Who knows? The desert is full of secrets. Do you think there is more than one Vijen? Is there more than one Tlana that ravages the land?"

"I do not know about the well, for I had never heard of it before. But I believe there are more than one Vijen and Tlana. In fact, we entered the desert to find the cause of the increase in Tlana activity." Croy kept his voice low though not quite at a whisper.

"More activity, yes. But more Tlana? There may be, my decaying friend, but I have never encountered a derlian who has seen two of either at the same place or time. Makes you wonder." Lemniscate used his normal volume at the last sentence. What made Croy wonder, however, was the usage of the word "decaying."

"Do you think they came into being at the same time as the well?" Croy kept an eye on Lemniscate's facial expression as he asked the question. Nothing shifted to indicate anything, at least nothing that he could pinpoint.

"I do. I think they came into being at exactly the same time. But that does not really answer anything, now does it?" His face wrinkled up as he smiled towards Croy. Croy was still nervous about broaching the subject of dreams, so instead he continued to lead Lemniscate where he wanted to go. Each derlian, when truly interested in a subject, needed only a few words, a few nudges of encouragement, to keep them happily talking.

"What do you think there was before Yavens, since you were a Yaven yourself?" To Croy's pleasure Lemniscate's face lit up.

"I call it the Is. The point of destiny is to capture the Is. The Is is not conscious, no. But merely a shadow Pattern. A thoughtform of a blueprint, created by its own catharsis of its existence rather than something that chooses. For all choices were made at its inception. Time is not fluid, no. It came at once, but we are too frail to notice. It is like a large cut gem, with us gliding along one faceted edge. What looks like the end to us is merely another edge beyond our perception. This scales to individuals as well. When you were born you saw your entire gem. That is why babes scream at inception. It is too much knowledge to hold. The first scream is knowledge of predestination, which causes madness. It is that or amnesia, yes? What do you think every living thing chooses? Amnesia or insanity? Everything capable chooses amnesia. Then, over a lifetime of crawling all over our individual gems, we can finally see it all in its grand finality only after the wisdom of experience has strengthened us. Only then do we get to see the gem as a whole, right before we die. That is how the Is sees its own Pattern, but it does not die. Destiny is knowing which way to crawl along the gem—how to use the allotted time to learn linearly what we already know intrinsically. At least that is my belief. But you did not come here to talk of philosophy, did you? You have a specific question, do you not? You have dreams that you can not shake?"

"How… how could you know that?" Croy was shocked but intrigued. The ancient one might actually be able to help Croy if he already knew what was going on.

"I know many things I should not, haha." Here he stopped, so Croy resumed.

"Well, I have been dreaming of wind taking me to a cave along a canyon wall. Nothing makes sense—there are no derlians, not even me. I am merely the debris caught up in the wind." Croy was not sure how to explain the urgency, the insistence of the dreams. The few sentences taken to explain the dreams did not really do anything to explain how the dreams felt to Croy.

"You are being shown the Temple of Air. Not for yourself, no. But for another, to be able to show yet another. Such are the silken threads that tie us together. Do you want them to go away?" Lemniscate's smile was one of pure enjoyment, pure pleasure.

"Well, yes. Especially if they are not for me." Croy had a small hidden worry that Lemniscate could just make them stop. That is what he wanted, however, so he was not sure why he felt any worry.

"There are two ways to stop them. You may accomplish what the dreams wish you to do, or you may drink from the well. One is your destiny. One is such the opposite of your destiny that your gem will crack and be forevermore less beautiful than if it had no cracks. The choice, as always, is yours." Lemniscate stood abruptly. "Take the time to listen to yourself, Croy. Or else." He started to walk away, towards the closest shack.

"Wait! How am I supposed to know? Wait!" Croy stood, but did not chase Lemniscate down. For his part, Lemniscate ignored Croy and entered his own little shack without looking back.

Croy did not spend a lot of time at the well, however. He did not feel that it was his destiny to drink from it, so that decision was easy. He forced himself to stand and head back to the little shack that he shared with Ilana. The difficult decision lay inside the shack. It lay with Ilana. He was not sure how to converse with her. How to explain that he could not stay trapped here with his maddening dreams. He almost went back to the well and drank, just so that he would not have to break her heart. But he did not.

Croy opened the door, and with sweating palms and heavy heart said, "We have to talk."

Ilana was curled up asleep, however, and Croy could not summon the courage to wake her. Instead, he lay down next to her and placed his arm around her. Within moments he was asleep. And dreaming.

The wind started slowly, swirling Croy's scattered debris into a corporal form. He was next to a large tree that seemed to be the source of all the leaves. He quickly spun into a funnel shape and twirled towards the same cliff edge. The wind was insistent but not as violent as some of his recent dreams. He was able to watch the grass bend to and fro in the light breeze. He watched the flowers nodding towards him as he spun. Croy enjoyed the gentle flight over the edge of the cliff. He dropped towards the river, but not too far down. As he was floating through the gorge, he was able to look around with ease. He saw the different trees lining the top of the cliff walls. There were even a couple struggling sideways out of the cliff face. He could even see some reeds swaying to some other breeze way down at the bottom of the gorge. It was beautiful and serene, so unlike his last few dreams.

He hovered momentarily as he approached the cave in the cliff face. He could spin around and look in all directions as he floated there, like a hummingbird. He looked at the different colorations in the cliff, the striated veins of rock layered upon each other through time. There was an odd orange stripe on the opposite cliff face, directly across from the cave. He soaked everything in slowly, serenely. The wind began pushing him towards the cave opening, and he let it guide him. In the other dreams he would wake up as he was scattered across the cave floor, dripping in sweat. But this time he gently wafted in. He swirled in the large entrance for a moment before being led deeper into the cave. The slowly narrowing passageway twisted and turned for some time. Croy did his best to keep track of what direction he was heading, but the occasional twisting confused him. When the tunnel finally forked, however, the wind slowed so that he could hover there. After a moment, he shot into the left passageway. He started speeding up as the tunnel shrunk in size. He came to another fork, hovered again, and then shot to the left again. The pace began to quicken. There was yet another fork in the tunnel, but this time he shot to the right without pausing. There were two more forks, first to the left and then lastly to the right. He had stopped spinning, but was flying so fast that it was still difficult to tell where he was going. Finally, he burst from the small tunnel into a large circular chamber.

There was strange writing or symbols of some kind all over the floor. In the center was a circle, with three spirals spinning off from it. He hovered in the center of the room, over the circle, spinning too fast to recognize any but the largest symbols carved into the rock. Not that recognizing a triangle on the wall above the tunnel as he was whipping around could help him understand why any of the symbols were there. Croy had not noticed any light in the tunnels, yet he could see. It was as if every part of this cave had a low background glow, and he attributed that to the fact it was a dream. Most of his dreams had the same low-level background light around everything. But now that he was in the circular room he noticed another light source. There was a hole through the rock above him, and he could see blue sky in the distance. It was while he was looking up through this chimney that the spinning slowed. Before he could look around the room for more detail, however, he shot up through the chimney. He flew at break-neck speed until he popped up into a small ring of trees. The sky was a clear bright blue, ringed with pointed conifers, and he shot up through them as well. There was not a cloud in the sky as he went ever higher. He almost began to panic when he woke up with a start. Ilana was sitting close by staring at him.

"Can't sleep?" She asked with a wry smile.

"Ilana, I have to leave you." Croy just came out and said it. "It's not you, it's this place." He smiled weakly.

"I know. I know. It's okay."

"It's just that I have something I need to do. There is an urgent…" Croy stopped and stared at Ilana.

"It's okay." Her face, sheening slightly with the sweat of the day on her, looked as youthful as he had ever seen it. The air, humid with perspiration, made her hair curl around her. She looked radiant.

"What?" Croy was stunned.

"I've known. I can tell. I am not happy about it, but I understand." She reached out and touched his cheek lightly with the back of her index finger. "I love you more than anything in this world, Croy."

They cried and kissed and held each other until nightfall. Neglecting sleep, they talked through the night. As the sun came up, they entwined deeper and slept. Croy had a deep, restful, dreamless sleep. It was not until afternoon was fading towards evening that they stirred.

"I need to go to the well. Will you come with me?" Ilana was already tugging him up towards his feet. They got dressed and left the tiny shack, walking towards the well. The moon was low on the horizon and looked large and bright. The sun was at its opposite, lazily falling behind far away dunes. It appeared larger than the moon, with reds and yellows streaking through the distance.

There was no one at the well, so Ilana expertly lowered the bucket into its opaque depths. While Croy was looking around, slowly waking up, he saw Lemniscate leave his shack to walk over towards them.

"How are the both of you today?" Lemniscate's voice sounded thin, almost old.

"Good, good." Croy did not really know what to say. Ilana was busy filling her cup with water from the well.

"Any decisions?" The ancient derlian looked expectantly at Croy. Croy was not sure if he should refer to him as an ancient Yaven instead. But no, he supposed that Lemniscate was truly a derlian.

"I have seen the path to the Luften Temple. Clearly. Completely. I... I have decided to catch up with the others." Croy was not sure exactly why, but he stared down at his own feet as he spoke.

"I told them you would, but they never listen..." The whisper was so soft that Croy was not sure he heard it. He glanced up quickly to see if Lemniscate was speaking, but did not catch him in the act.

"If you feel that is the best decision, then it must be." Lemniscate seemed to be smiling a little, but Croy could not be sure.

"Well, I am terrified to go. I do not want to leave Ilana and am worried that I will be unable to make it back here. You know, the shifting sands, the moving well." Croy looked back down at the ground.

"It is very difficult to find the well. And, truly, most derlians do not make it back here for a second time. For you, however, I feel it may be different. You never know who the desert takes a liking to." Lemniscate nodded towards Croy and then turned towards Ilana. "You may have tomorrow to rest, but I will expect you here at dawn the next day." He then nodded towards her. Before Croy could interrupt him, Lemniscate turned and walked back towards his shack.

Instead of yelling at Lemniscate's back, Croy turned towards Ilana. "What…" He pointed towards Lemniscate's receding form. He had wanted to say something more coherent, an actual question even. He was not even sure what to ask, however.

"You are not the only one who takes advice from the ancients. As you slept, I came and spoke at length with Lemniscate. He is a wealth of arcane knowledge. He has promised that he would teach me the histories. The true, complete, Histories. He knows magic, he knows Yavens, and most importantly, he understands dreams. I can learn more from him than spending a thousand cycles in Larelt. Don't you see? This is my chance to truly learn. Learn at the feet of the oldest and one of the wisest of all derlians." Ilana was beaming at him.

Croy was shocked, almost stunned. Not because of Ilana's windfall. That was perfect. It made each member in the small struggle the winner. No, he was shocked at his own ego, his own self-centeredness. He had thought… No, he had been worried about what his decision would do to Ilana. He had been worried about whether or not his decision was the correct one. Whether or not his decision would destroy him, or destroy Ilana, or destroy them both. But it was not just his decision. It was not just his life. He had almost drowned in his own narcissism. He was just happy that his decision coincided with Ilana's. No, he was more than happy—he was elated.

"That is fantastic, Ilana. Truly fantastic." And he truly meant it.

They went back to the shack, and Croy pretended to pack while Ilana drank her well water. He collected his meager belongings, a walking stick, and what extra food they had. He kissed her lightly before heading out.

"I love you." Her voice was soft, yet heavy.

"I love you, too." Croy walked out of the shack and in the vague direction that Trela and the others had headed out so recently.

They had decided that he should travel at night to avoid the heat of the day. As he was leaving the shantytown, he began to worry. He was on his own, completely alone. Wandering through a desert that kills many more than it saves. He kept his feet moving forward, but he was not sure where forward was headed. After what seemed like forever, he turned back around and made to shuffle back towards the town. Maybe he would try some of the water. Ilana seemed to like it. She was right with another aspect, too. Who could be more wise than an original Yaven-derlian? The stories that Lemniscate could tell! Yes, maybe going back to the well would be for the best. As he lifted his head up to find the torchlight in the distance, however, he could sense nothing. No flickering lights. No murmuring sounds. He stood there, petrified, and peered vainly into the distance. He thought about following his footsteps in the sand, but became concerned that they would lead to nowhere, or just fade into nothing. There was a small wind behind him. His paranoia made him assume it came up for the express purpose of erasing his tracks. Instead of letting his fear get the best of him, he turned back around and headed in his original direction. There was nothing else to be done.

Croy walked at night and tried to make rudimentary shade shelters during the day from his extra clothing. It did not work very well, but he managed several fitful hours of sleep a day. The desert, for its part, was very kind to him. He did not find any Vijen, but he also did not run into any Tlana. Soon, much quicker than it took to find the well, he saw some low hills in the distance. It had been difficult to tell at first since they only hid the lowest of the stars. After a while, though, dawn began to lighten the sky and erase the stars into a deep blue. Instead of trying to make a sunshade as usual, he began to jog towards the hills. He though that if he could just reach the hills, then he could find a much cooler shelter.

Croy could not make it all the way there, try as he might. With the hills still a tantalizing distance away and the sun almost a quarter into the sky, he decided to rest. He took his walking stick and jabbed it into the sand and hung his rags off of it to make a small square of shade on the ground. Tucking himself up into a small ball, he lay in the shade and rested. And dreamt. It was his first dream since the vivid dream of the Luften Temple.

There was no wind this time. No leaves. No chasm. Just blazing heat. There was sand as well, just as in the desert, but it seemed thicker, more dense somehow. Croy looked around and realized he was in a giant pit. No, not a pit; an arena. When Croy looked up he saw a huge teeming crowd. They were all screaming and waving their arms. The arena was elliptical with hard stone walls. Against the walls, hanging and propped, were various weapons glinting in the hot sun. A figure stood at each of the foci. The figures were vague and hazy, with only their relative size different enough about them to tell them apart. The large one was preening to the crowd, lifting its arms to the deafening roar. In its right hand was a huge, broad, and bright sword. The small one seemed to be backing away slowly, looking around warily. In its right hand was a slender but longer sword.

The larger figure swung back around towards the smaller one. With a great roar it leapt forward and slashed mightily towards the other. The smaller one quickly parried, holding its sword with both hands and tilting it at a canted angle to help with the deflection. The larger figure used the deflection to swing the sword back around in a large arc. The smaller one parried again, but this time pushed the larger sword away from it in addition to the block. Instead of slowing down, the larger figure spun in a tight circle, swinging the broad sword wide as it came back around. The smaller figure ducked the steel and thrust forward quickly. The larger figure dodged but seemed to be thrown off balance.

They fought back and forth for some time while Croy tried to move. He seemed to be frozen in place, unable to turn his torso. Finally, it seemed that the larger figure was beating down the smaller one. The smaller figure had fallen backwards, holding its sword above it, with one hand on the hilt and the other one against the flat side of the sword. Blow after punishing blow rained down upon the sword from the large figure. It almost seemed as if the smaller figure was being pounded into the sand like a nail into soft wood. The slender sword suddenly cracked and split. The tip of the large sword sunk into the sand close the prone figure's head. The crowd went wild. The smaller figure quickly curled up and rolled away from the larger figure, who was again preening to the crowd. The roar was deafening.

The smaller figure jumped up and pulled something from its sleeve. In a flash, a dagger flew across Croy's vision and struck the large figure in the back as it was waving its arms towards the crowd. The large figure dropped to the ground amongst hollow silence. The smaller figure raised its arms towards the crowd. To silence. Croy blinked once... twice... Suddenly, the crowd burst over the railing of the arena and ran across the dense sand towards the small figure. Croy had thought they were there to congratulate the victor, but they attacked the figure instead. In a frenzied orgy of violence, they tore apart the figure in front of Croy. He awoke with a scream.

Croy was drenched in sweat, and even though the day was still hot, a cold chill ran through him. The sun was low in the sky and was becoming slightly colored. He wiped the sweat off of himself with the rags he had used as a sunshade for his nap. The image of the fingers of the small figure being pulled off, the arms being snapped back at the elbow, the rage-filled screaming—it was all too much for him to bear. He would have gladly had another repetitive wind dream. As he wiped himself down, he closed his eyes and thought of Ilana's smiling face. It took a little while, but he was finally able to purge the bloody images from his mind. Instead of allowing himself time to think, he packed his belongings and trudged towards the hills.

It took a complete day of hiking in the hills before Croy saw smoke from a distant campfire wafting in the sky. He had no idea if this was the group he was looking for, but it was his only direction. Of course, they were on mounts and he was on foot. So once he knew what direction to head, he would get a running start, cast a low-powered flight spell and zoom through the air for a couple of minutes before beginning his decent. Whenever he felt like he was starting to fall again, he would try to slow himself down and drop to the ground as gently as possible. He would then walk for a while, dizzy and weak, until he felt better enough to attempt another leap. He wished that he could appreciate the amazing sites more as he zipped right above the occasional treetops, but it took all of his energies to keep himself from crashing. One time, after taking what seemed like forever to hike to the top of a ridgeline, he cast another spell and glided completely over an entire, though small, valley before having to land on the opposite hillside. At the beginning of his glide, he was able to appreciate the flashing green-grey of the scrub underneath him, but his attention was soon diverted.

It took another two days before Croy was able catch up with Trela's party. It was at the end of dusk, when they had settled down and started another fire. He was high above them and it felt like half a world away, but he could see figures moving against the flickering light. He was incredibly tired but knew that if he could actually make out the shape of derlians against the tiny light, then he should be close enough for one more glide.

"Nukinderpri!" Croy rose slightly and tipped his body down towards the fire and began to slowly glide. He had used Mek a couple of times earlier, but he felt too tired to try that powerful of a spell this time. As he was gliding he felt himself pick up speed. He wanted to try to slow himself down, but he knew he would not be able to cast another spell until he had slept. He pointed himself straight at the glowing fire and rather than braking, he focused all of his concentration on lift. He was plummeting at an amazing speed, and he could feel himself passing out. His vision narrowed, his mind became cloudy, and his body grew numb. When they realized that he was coming, they all jumped up and scattered about, but Croy could not stop himself. Mercifully he lost consciousness just before he crashed into the fire.

When Croy came to, it was morning. He was in a small tent, but he could tell it was morning because the sun made the dirty canvass glow. Trela was sitting next to his prone form, but she seemed to be sleeping while sitting up. Her head had lolled into an uncomfortable-looking position towards her left shoulder. He wanted to shake her gently awake but was racked with a violent coughing fit instead. She almost fell over at the commotion.

"Croy? Croy! You're awake. We were worried you had put yourself into a coma." Trela unconsciously wiped some saliva from the corner of her mouth.

Croy explained how he had caught up with them. He explained his dream in the desert. Finally, he explained his dreams of the Luften Temple. Trela was ecstatic.

"Wait here." She ran out of the tent.

Croy waited for a while wondering if he could get some food soon. He felt too weak to get up and leave the tent. The air seemed to be getting thicker, stuffier, by the moment. The tent was getting hotter with each of his exhales. Just before he was about to break down and leave the confining tent, the flap opened up. Trela pushed in a Luften before entering herself.

"This is Feyazki. He has agreed to help us find the Luften Temple. Tell him your dreams of the Temple, of the gorge. He will fly the both of you around until you can locate it, then you can come back and show me where it is. Then I can show Clerin." Trela was smiling widely as she glanced back and forth from Croy to Feyazki.

"Wait, wait. Why do you get to show Clerin where the Temple is?" The Luften named Feyazki narrowed his eyes at Trela.

"Do not worry, we will think of something heroic for you to do for Clerin." Trela smiled back at him.

"I... I did not mean that, I..." Feyazki looked somewhat flustered.

"Of course not, nor did I. Listen, we are wasting valuable time. The sooner we are able to find the Temple, the sooner we will be able to get back. Here, Croy, I have brought some iron rations for you. Tell Feyazki of your dream." Trela handed a couple of small dried and salted pieces of meat over to Croy. He was so overjoyed at the thought of food that he glazed over Trela's avoidance of what, exactly, they would all be getting back to.

Croy nibbled on the jerky while explaining the gorge in as complete detail as he could muster. He explained the starting tree, the gorge itself, and the river. He even explained the orange stripe in the rock at the gorge. Everything that he could think of that would help them find the cave. Feyazki appeared to be soaking all of the information in.

"Since I *whispered* to Vanelia's mage, I have been scouting a little each day, looking for the royal pavilions. Or any other derlians, really. There is a small river towards the rising sun that we could check out. Are you a mage?" Feyazki smiled at Croy.

"Well... yes?" Croy smiled back at him.

"Croy is still in training. That is why we need your help." Trela touched Feyazki's arm lightly to make him look at her. "And your silence."

"No problem. I just thought that you needed my assistance because I know the area better than anyone else in our party. Did you not fly here?" Feyazki turned to look back at Croy.

"A little. I suppose it was more like gliding." Croy felt the small heat of blush flow into his cheeks.

"How long have you been in training? What power level can you cast?" Feyazki's eyes seemed to light up a little.

"The perfect time to discuss this would be during your scouting mission, don't you think?" Trela looked a little strained.

"Oh. Sure. Come on, Croy. I will show you the river." Feyazki stood and held out a hand to help Croy up.

"Thanks. Thank you. Thank you both. I am truly indebted to both of you." Trela gushed to them.

"You are not indebted until we return successful," Feyazki said while pulling Croy up. Croy laughed lightly along with him.

"*If* we return successful," Croy retorted.

"No! You must be successful. Any other thoughts are a waste of energy." Trela looked hard at Croy and then shifted her gaze over to Feyazki. "Failure is not an option."

"You are going to get along great with Queen Vanelia." Feyazki was grinning.

"What, why?" Trela was looking annoyed and just a tiny bit puzzled.

"Nothing." As Croy and Feyazki wandered away from the tent, and away from all of the other tents, Feyazki whispered conspiratorially to Croy, "Do not mind her. It has been a difficult trip."

"Yes. It has been a difficult trip for us all." Croy felt a thousand times better just being out of the tent and into the breeze. The sweat was leaving a salty cake upon his skin as it dried, but he did not mind. It felt good to be in the bright sunlight without all the fine sand blowing around.

"Eqekinderclo!" Feyazki's voice was strong and confident. While it was the spell itself that sent tingles through Croy, the way that Feyazki spoke it sent chills along with them. *That is what a mage sounds like*, thought Croy. The Blind One was always insistent with his voice, and truly, he was powerful. But this Luften spoke in a way that suggested magic was second nature to him. That it was as natural, and as simple, as walking. Croy wondered if one race could apprentice under another. The swift feeling of flight, however, took his mind away from the fanciful and up into the air.

The feeling was amazing. Though Croy could not affect their direction, or even their speed, he could feel the magic coursing through him. The feeling was so potent it was as if he, himself, had cast the spell. It seemed that every bit of him, every tiny piece, was vibrating to the same frequency. His heart was beating at a ferocious pace. It was like pure excitement. He did not know whether to laugh or cry, but more than anything, he wanted to be able to feel this on his own. More than any other time in his life, he truly wanted to become a master magician. To be able to make himself feel the magic coursing through his veins. It was that powerful.

Croy was flying next to Feyazki in the same horizontal position, with face forward and arms flat against their sides. He put his hands out in front of him to help part the wind. It felt more streamlined but he did not move any faster. Whenever Feyazki would turn, he would roll slightly towards the curve. This, somehow, made Croy list in that direction as well.

They flew in silence, darting over the landscape at breakneck speeds. Croy watched the ground slip by underneath them with fascination. Soon they came upon a small stream, and Feyazki slowed down a little as they began to track over the water.

At first, the banks of the stream were shallow, but they soon began to rise above the water. The foliage began to take on a lush, verdant tone. The scrub brush gave way to dogwood and even a few willows. Croy was not sure at what point the stream turned into a river—he could not point at a particular transition area—but eventually they were flying over a full river. He squinted into the wind as he tried to look for landmarks. The banks of the river rose steadily as they flew towards the distant hills.

A small gorge rose up from the water. The walls rose slowly compared to their horizontal velocity, but they rose relentlessly. Soon the walls rose into a full canyon. Feyazki had been flying low over the river, but as the canyon walls got higher, he began to rise towards the top.

"Does any of this look familiar?" Feyazki tried to yell quietly.

"The river needs to be deeper," Croy yelled back, unsure if his words made sense. Feyazki seemed to nod, and they shot forward with even greater velocity.

Suddenly they had to bank sharply back and forth as the canyon twisted and turned. As they straightened back out for a moment, Feyazki took them up and out of the canyon entirely. They flew that way for a short while, gradually following the river's windy path. As the scenery was whipping past below them, Croy suddenly thought he recognized a tree.

"Stop here!" Croy waved frantically towards Feyazki. Once he had Feyazki's attention, he pointed repeatedly at the rapidly fading tree. Croy felt a gut-wrenching deceleration as they slowed, stopped, and then reversed direction back towards the tree. They alighted near the tree with a quick gentleness.

"Do you recognize this?" Feyazki walked over to the tree and placed his palm flat against its round trunk.

"I… I think so. The leaves… they look familiar." Croy knelt down and picked up a handful of leaves and dropped them, watching them fall. It was the vision. The line of sight from the tree to the cliff wall was as familiar as his own feet. He walked with an ever-increasing speed towards the cliff. He was almost running as he reached the edge and skidded to an abrupt stop. He peered over the edge to the other side. He had begun the dream here so many times. He was sure that this was the place. This was the starting point.

"Go ahead, jump." Feyazki thumped Croy so hard on the back that he fell forward. He pin-wheeled his arms frantically but to no avail. As Croy fell, Feyazki jumped off the cliff edge next to him. They both floated over the middle of the river at the height of the cliff. "How much further back down the river do we go? You mentioned an orange rock formation?"

Croy laughed a little nervously at what he supposed was meant to be a joke. It felt like his heart had skipped a beat. Since Feyazki was not speaking of the incident, however, Croy did not speak of it either. He felt too embarrassed. "Yes, it was like a scar on the rock. It should be on this side of the gorge." Croy pointed to his right since he was facing downstream. "Across from that will be the correct cave." He then pointed across himself, towards his left. "Go slowly downstream and we can check out each of the caves that we come across." Croy had tucked his feet under him as if he were sitting on cushions. He figured he may as well enjoy the ride.

There seemed to be more caves in the cliff face than had appeared in his dream. Croy knew that the cave was not too far from the top of the gorge, so they could ignore the lower caves. They spent longer than seemed probable and were getting close to heading back towards the beginning tree when he noticed the stripe.

"That looks like it." He waved Feyazki towards the oddly colored rock.

They stared at it in silence for some time. Feyazki would look back over to the other side of the cliff and then swing his head heavily back to the stripe. Croy knew what Feyazki was thinking. It was the same thing that he was thinking. There was no cave on the opposite side of the gorge. He knew what he dreamt, though. Croy knew what the orange stripe was supposed to look like, and this was it. He did not want to speak about it. He felt that any conversation would jinx the entire mission. His own head swiveled back and forth between the two cliff faces. The face with the stripe and the blank face. Finally, when he sensed that Feyazki was going to break the silence, he waved over to the blank face, opposite the stripe. Rather than spoil anything Feyazki scooted them closer to the rock wall. As they were getting past the midpoint of the river, they began to shake lightly. To bob up and down in the air rhythmically. It was enough, though, to make Croy nervous enough to stand up while they were flying. As if that would have helped at all.

"I… I'm getting weak." Feyazki turned quickly and flew them to the other side. Straight as an arrow, with no wasted distance. Once over the striped cliff's face, safely over solid ground, they dropped lightly to the grass.

"What happened?" Croy was panting more from fear than from exertion.

"I don't know. It was as if my spell was ending. Just fizzling out as if I was trying to extend it past its power level, you know?" Croy did not know.

"What do you mean, 'past its power level'?" He smiled at Feyazki.

"Well, each power has so much duration it can muster up. So a level Nar spell should last greater than a level Nu spell. But of course, the difficulty rating of the rest of your syllables will also affect the length of a spell. Usually, though, you have a feel for how long a common spell may have. I cast flight fairly often. I use the Clo suffix less than Pri, but still often enough to have a feel for how long each power level should last under normal circumstances." Feyazki was looking seriously at Croy. Croy thought that he might be looking a little tired as well.

"Meaning?"

"Meaning the spell should have lasted longer. I think. It failed as if it ran out of time, however, rather than as if it were being countered by another mage. I am not sure how to further interpret the information. So… what do you think?" Feyazki smiled at Croy.

"I think the cave is there. I think we will have to fall at a trajectory such that if your spell gets dispelled, or runs out of time, or whatever, we will drop through the illusion and land inside the cave. I think that the same force that is disrupting your magic is making us incapable of seeing that particular cave. And I think, unfortunately, that we will have to physically enter the cave, the correct cave, without a shadow of a doubt, before we can head back to the main encampment." Croy tried to look as serious as young Feyazki was looking back at him.

"I agree with much of what you think. I must point out one small discrepancy, however." Feyazki was still smiling.

"What is that?" Croy felt his face involuntarily wince at the thought of the imagined tirade that Feyazki was to deluge him with. It did not happen.

"Can we throw rocks at the illusionary wall before we fling ourselves at it? It is not that I don't trust you, but…" Feyazki's smile took on a sheepish tone.

"That is a fantastic idea. Do you have a sack?" Croy found out quickly how ill equipped they were. No rope, no pouches, not even any more rations.

"Narkinderclo!" Feyazki's voice spoke out into nature. It was not in conflict with nature, not challenging or even strident. But on par with nature, certainly as equals. Croy always had a difficult time separating out the "bending reality to your will" hubris from the… well, he was not quite sure what. There really is nothing more prideful than forcing nature to do something other than it would normally do. The world's normalcy being the most basic definition of nature. Somehow Feyazki made magic seem as if *it* were a part of nature. Since magic is possible and all that is possible is part of world, and with nature being comprised of the world's possibilities, it made some perverted sense to Croy that magic should be one with nature. It was not until Feyazki that he realized that he had the problem to begin with and, at the same time, the way around it presented itself. It was like getting an exercise problem and the solution at the same moment. Croy enjoyed the sensation and vowed not to let the ease of learning cloud his retention.

They flew down to the riverbed, careful to stay well clear from the anti-magic shell, and filled up Croy's shirt with rocks. He held the bottom hem of his shirt out while Feyazki piled on the driest rocks they could find. Once his shirt was at capacity, they flew through the air again. Careful not to get too close, Feyazki brought them a little higher so they could throw the rocks from farther away.

With Croy's hands being used to corral the rocks, Feyazki got to throw first. He peppered the side of the canyon with stones for a while, throwing completely at random, it seemed. The stones would bounce off the cliff wall and clatter back down to their river. Each time one bounced back with a loud echoing thwack, Croy grew more disheartened. He could only thrust out with his chin in a general direction to try to guide Feyazki. Oftentimes even that seemed to be ignored. Croy began to wonder about Feyazki's commitment to the vision. He supposed that it was difficult to stay committed to somebody else's vision, however, so he kept his thoughts to himself. When the rocks got low enough that Croy could hold his shirt with only one hand, he held up his other to stave off Feyazki taking any more.

"Let me try a little bit. Could you float upstream a little?" Croy was intently staring at the cliff face, trying to recall where the cave entrance had been. "Now down a little." They started to float back downstream. "No, not downstream, just down. You know, vertically." They went nicely back upstream and then lost altitude slowly. "Good! Here is good."

Croy let fly with a couple rocks, three, then four. They all bounced ungracefully off of the seemingly solid stone wall. "A little more downstream... There... Hold!" When the idea had come to Croy, it had seemed perfect. It answered all the components of the riddle nicely. It was not until he started throwing the rocks himself that the doubt began to creep up. He would stare at the cliff until he was sure that he was staring at the cave. He would then throw rocks. It would take three or four before he could even hit where he was aiming. Then, to his disappointment, the rock would bounce off of solid stone. With the last few rocks staring at him from his shirt, he had Feyazki take him back to the orange stripe. He stared at the stripe for some time. It looked completely familiar. This had to be the spot. Croy gripped a stone in his right hand and slowly turned around. Without opening his eyes he threw the stone as hard as he could and he waited for the thwack.

"That was amazing! Do it again." Feyazki was staring in disbelief at the far wall.

"Where did it go?" Croy was elated.

"I don't know. I was watching it... Do you see that dark outcropping about a quarter of the way down from the top and right... there?" Feyazki was standing behind Croy pointing his arm down Croy's nose, towards a dark outcropping.

"Yes. Yes, I think so." Croy wanted to throw another rock.

"Let your eyes drift straight up just a little bit to the grey patch. That's where your rock disappeared." Feyazki was patting Croy on the back. "Here, let me show you." Before Croy could protest, Feyazki picked up a rock, wound up, and threw mightily at the grey patch. Even though he knew what to expect, it still seemed shocking to watch the rock penetrate the cliff face. There was no noise afterwards. It was an odd feeling, not hearing any noise after the rock disappeared. It was the unsatisfied anticipation of missing what typically followed. Croy threw the remaining stone, but it merely bounced off the cliff face.

"That is amazing, truly. I'm flabbergasted. No offence, but I was beginning to have my doubts. About the invisible cave, about your sanity, about the mission in general… Let's grab some more rocks so we can feel real comfortable with where the cave is." Feyazki's smile was disarming and infectious.

They flew down and re-armed themselves. After pinpointing where they thought the cave to be by loosing more stones, Feyazki flew them high into the air.

"Did you want to rest for a moment? Maybe recast the flight spell?" Croy suddenly got a little nervous looking down at the river. For no real reason he then said, "Sorry."

They dropped like stones. After what seemed an eternity, Feyazki pushed them furiously towards the cave entrance. Croy positioned himself to strike the cliff face, or even the cave if they were lucky, feet first. He had his teeth gritted together, waiting for impact.

Before they struck anything, there was a sudden feeling of cold water being splashed over them. Croy was well above the river, so he knew it was not really water. But the sensation was definitely cold and somewhat viscous. Like stepping out of a hot bath into a wintry, fogged forest. Thick with haze and the distant call of wolves. The sideways thrust being provided by Feyazki halted. Croy could feel the magic drain from him. Like the draining of possibility. They flew in a quiet soft arc, hurtling towards the cold hard cliff carried by inertia alone.

And fell into a cave entrance. It was incredibly painful, but no bones were broken. They lay there in silence for some time. There was no illusion on this side of the cave. They could look straight out at that orange stripe on the other side of the gorge. Sound, however, did not seem to travel as easily as light. The constant roar of the river was strangely absent on this side of the illusion.

Croy stood and slowly looked around while Feyazki threw their rocks back out of the cave. Once he was satisfied that it was the cave he saw in his dreams, he walked back to Feyazki and smiled and nodded. It seemed too quiet to speak inside the cave. Croy was vaguely gesturing towards the entrance, or exit from this direction, when he first heard it. It was a rushing noise. At first he thought they could hear the river again, but it began to get louder and louder. There was almost a whistle in it, but lower. Like blowing over the mouth of an empty jug. Croy was stunned motionless. There was no reason for the panic welling in him. There could be plenty of logical, harmless explanations for the noise. But the fear was increasing exponentially. Croy turned his stunned face towards Feyazki. He was backing up and crouching, then running. Then jumping. Before Feyazki had fallen from view, Croy had backed up as far as he dared. There was wind blowing by him, faster than he could run. It was like the hot breath of a ravenous canine, warm on his neck.

The cool shock of fresh air greeted Croy as he burst from the cave. The gust belching forth from the cave pushed on his back. Then ruffled his hair. Then the pull of gravity took over all sensation. As he was plummeting, he tried to remember the flight spell. He had just used it yesterday. Was it only yesterday? Bits of it came to him out of order. There had to be a Kin in it, he was sure. Probably a Der as well.

Someone yelled something. Though Croy could hear it, it sounded like gibberish at the time. It was only later, when Feyazki and he could laugh about the whole incident over a drink, that he learned what was yelled. "Fall away from the cave! Push out!" Feyazki yelled from the river. As Croy came crashing down into fast-moving waves, he realized that they were still under the influence of the anti-magic shell. The river was mercifully deep for how quickly it was moving. Time slowed as he tried to get his bearings under water. He kept his eyes closed and frantically tore towards what he thought was up. He paddled and struggled, but his clothes weighed heavily on him. After what seemed an eternity, Croy burst the water's surface. He gasped happily at the air and just floated for a brief moment, treading water. He caught sight of Feyazki a ways ahead of him struggling towards the right side of the canyon walls. Croy began to struggle in that direction also. There did not seem to be many rocky beaches or sandbars where they were, unlike further downstream. He swam with the current and began to catch up to Feyazki.

"Give me a boost," Feyazki said while treading water and floating downstream with Croy. "Hold me up for a moment." Croy got up under Feyazki, gripped his waist, and heaved while kicking furiously with his feet.

"Mekkinderclo!" There was something desperate in Feyazki's voice. They shot up out of the water quickly and up past the walls of the gorge. It was a long slow arc once they topped the gorge. They landed rather roughly at the top, but Croy was just happy to be out of the water. They lay there on the grass breathing heavy and looking at the clouds for quite some time. To rest after such a surge in activity makes the respite that much more enjoyable. It was good to just be there on dry stable land and to breathe.

"What was that? I haven't been that afraid since... well, since my fight in the desert. Which was more recent than I care to think. But there was nothing there! The cave was completely empty. We didn't even walk through any of it. All we saw was the antechamber. That wind... there was something terrifying in that wind. How about you, Croy? When was the last time you were that scared?" Feyazki lay on his back, panting lightly between sentences.

"There was a time, not so long ago, that I would have said never. Now, however, it happens more frequently than I wish." Croy smiled towards the clouds. Though he did not say it aloud, he was thinking of that carriage ride with the Blind One. That first ride. It was more terrifying than the fight that started it all. The one after finding Trela... the one with Synde. Croy's mind began to wax nostalgic when Feyazki rolled over on his side to face Croy.

"But there is usually a reason, right? I get terrified, not often but enough to know the experience, and there is always a reason. I tip my chair too far back on its hind legs, and I'm toppling over. I'm under water and running out of breath, where screaming my fears aloud will rob me of any precious air I have left. I'm high up in a tree on a windy day and unable to cast a flight spell. I'm running from a Pyran with a sword. Any number of things. Reasonable things." He rolled back onto his back. "I was really terrified."

"I think it was the Temple. We are dealing with things that directly conceived us. The powers of those... of that... it's all unimaginable. I don't know about you, but I am completely out of my depth." Croy laughed lightly.

"You and I both, Gaen. You and I both." Feyazki sighed deeply. Though Croy did not think there was much that the young Luften could not do, he could certainly understand the feeling of inadequacy. Croy often felt inadequate and so was unperturbed by the feeling. He assumed otherwise about the mage. Incorrectly, though he did not realize his error until later. "You know, besides Knill, you are the first Gaen I have ever met. No offense, but I somehow expected something more menacing."

Croy laughed aloud. He curled up gasping and slapping and laughing aloud. The phrase was not even that humorous, but it was like a sudden release. It was slightly confusing, like a juxtaposition of logic, but without any riddle in it. It felt good to laugh.

Feyazki was back on his elbow, looking at Croy. He had a large grin on his face but questioning eyes. Like he was ready to be in on the joke but was still unsure as to what it was.

"That is probably the most inapt word to describe me that I have ever heard. I just… It has been a difficult trip." Croy was back on his back, panting from laughter rather than exertion or fear.

"Yes. It has been a difficult trip for us all." As Feyazki said it, he burst into a short-lived but seemingly sincere laughing fit of his own.

After a short, enjoyable rest, they flew back to the others. Their trip back to the main camp was quick and uneventful. They circled the camp slowly before alighting comfortably in the midst of the gathered crowd. Trela hustled over to them before anyone else could speak to them.

"Success?" The word was whispered so that only Croy could hear. He was not even sure that he heard it versus reading it upon her lips. He smiled and nodded slightly to her.

"We will all have time to meet and greet later. I need to speak with Clerin and, of course, Croy and Feyazki." Trela waved her hands at the small mob as they began to clamor around the new arrivals.

As they headed towards the tent that Croy had woken up in earlier that day, he thought he could hear someone asking where they had been. It was a well-disciplined group, however, and even though emotions were high, they all went quietly back to whatever they were doing before Croy and Feyazki had arrived.

The tent did not seem as stifling as it had in the morning, but with four of them in there it did seem pretty cramped. Croy sat cross-legged with his back against the far wall, and the others filed against the remaining three walls. Trela chose to sit in front of the entrance flap. Croy was not sure, but it seemed that she was intentionally blocking the exit, or maybe the entrance. The other derlian, Clerin he thought her name was, sat to his left. He thought she might be a Fluen, but he was not quite sure. She was definitely not a Gaen or a Pyran, but he could not be sure that she was not a Luften. Croy caught sight of her pale but luminescent blue eyes right before Trela began to speak. He knew he had met her briefly at the well, but he certainly did not know her.

"I believe that introductions are in order. Croy, this is Clerin Toswin. She is the Fluen that we are taking to the Luften Temple. And Clerin, this is Croy Sie'tin. He is an old Gaen mentor of mine." Croy was not sure about the "old" adjective, but he was tickled that Trela had used the word "mentor." "As promised, we have finally pinpointed the Temple's location, with the help of Croy and Feyazki, and we should prepare tonight for our journey. It will take at least a full day to trek there unless…"

"You have found it? For sure?" Clerin interjected. Her head moved upwards just as her torso pushed forwards slightly. She glanced quickly at Croy, but then stared, smilingly, at Feyazki.

"Definitely." Croy was not completely positive, but he was as positive as possible without actually speaking to an actual Beleg.

"Unless?" Feyazki was smiling at Clerin even though he was speaking to Trela.

"Well, Clerin, is there any reason that all of us should go to the Temple?" Trela had an inscrutable half smile on her face as she glanced between Clerin and Feyazki.

"Not that I can think of. There is safety in numbers, however." Clerin had settled softly back against the tent wall.

"How many derlians do you think you can fly at once?" Trela was looking at Feyazki.

"Maybe… five?" Feyazki's answer came out as a question of its own. "It is a fair distance. I could always make stops along the way if we wanted to take more."

"I was thinking that Feyazki could fly you to the Temple. With, of course, several others for protection. After you deliver your message to… to the Luften Beleg, we will figure out where to meet up with Vanelia." Trela had turned to Clerin.

"She is coming?" Clerin's forehead scrunched into a cute picture of confusion.

"I had figured that if she brought Hulgert since he knows where the Temple is, if we were having difficulty finding the Temple, maybe…" Trela floundered for a second.

"Was she supposed to meet us at the Temple so soon? I had completely forgotten. There were certainly no signs of any other derlians around." Feyazki had a curiously crooked smile on his face, and Trela looked at him with a relieved expression.

"Maybe what you found was not the Temple." Clerin looked forlorn.

"That was definitely the Temple." Croy had seen that exact cave in his dreams. It had to be the Temple.

"Have you ever been to a Temple before? The Gaen Temple maybe?" Clerin was fixing her ice blue eyes at Croy.

"Well, no… but you should have felt it. There were even illusions protecting it. The feeling… it… it… Feyazki, help me here." Croy looked beseechingly over to him.

"There was certainly something there, Clerin. Whether or not it is the Temple that you seek… We will not know until you visit it yourself. Which, by all accounts, will be as soon as tomorrow morn. I think Trela has the right idea. We should fly a small contingent over to the Temple, let you investigate, then meet back here to decide what would be our best next move. Now, who do you think should travel with Clerin?" Feyazki looked around the tent, seemingly open to suggestions from anyone.

"Croy has more specific information about navigating the caves. He has dreams." Trela smiled conspiratorially at Clerin. "So he should go. Feyazki will, of course, have to go. That just leaves two spots open." It was Trela's turn to look around the tent.

"Well, we should bring you for protection, and… do we need a fifth?" Clerin also glanced about. Her eyes were like nervous birds, ricocheting as soon as they landed.

"I am certain that I could fly four in one shot." Feyazki interjected.

"You will probably not even need me with a mage such as Feyazki to protect you, but I agree to come along. Just in case." Trela spoke to Clerin alone. "Then it is settled. We four shall fly to the

Temple tomorrow after breaking our nightly fast. Everyone should try to get some good sleep tonight. It will surely be a busy day tomorrow." This she spoke to all of them.

"Is this a secret?" Croy popped out his question before Trela had time to stand and end the meeting.

"Surely not. This is our mission, and all the others are fully aware of it. Of course, the danger is celebrating tonight. They will insist and you... all of us... must be strong enough to refuse. In fact, it may be much easier if we do not mention it right away. We could bring it up tomorrow before we leave. We will celebrate when we have accomplished our mission and not a moment sooner. Agreed?" Trela turned a hard eye on her companions.

"Agreed!" They all spoke at once. And, truly, they were of one mind. It was difficult, however, to suppress the urge to celebrate. Croy was feeling giddy already. After all, the hard part for him was already over. Wasn't it?

Trela and Feyazki left together, talking animatedly. Clerin looked around, nodding to herself for a long moment. It was not until she stood that Croy remembered the dreams. He stood to stop her with his hand outstretched, but he did not touch her. The gesture was enough.

"Trela is correct. I have dreams." Croy smiled awkwardly and sat back down.

"What do you mean, dreams?" Clerin sat herself next to Croy, turned to look at him. As if she were sitting side-saddle.

"The Luften Temple. Or what I think is the Temple. When I dreamt of its location, I dreamt of a maze comprised of various tunnels that lead to its heart. I did not take any other paths, only the one, so I do not know what other things might lurk, scattered about in the bowels of the Temple. And believe me, there is a terrifying horror that..." Croy paused for a moment, trying to gather his wits. Would she feel the terror that he had felt if she was delivering a message? What if the Temple wanted her there? He suddenly realized that the information he needed to impart was not what he was talking about.

"I was going to tell you that we, Feyazki and I, were compelled to leave. The compulsion manifested itself through a feeling of terror that, for some reason, I have yet to completely cleanse from my system. I was using you as an emotive outlet, rather than giving you the information you have waited so long to get."

Croy was not sure why he suddenly got embarrassed. And he certainly did not know why he gave voice to his thoughts so readily. Something about her made him put his guard down.

"Sometimes an emotional description is more detailed, or at least more compelling, than a factual one. I am a strong believer in whim, Croy. You should describe your communication in whatever way you feel most comfortable. No apologies." Clerin smiled warmly at him.

"We were probably compelled because we were not supposed to be there. Not like you. The feeling itself was a kind of rushing. Like falling from a cliff or being pulled by an undertow deeper into unconsciousness. There was a wind that accompanied the rushing. Everything led to the mouth of the cave. The exit. You will know the panic when you feel it, whether or not you recall my words. I can only hope that you are stronger than I, or Feyazki for that matter, if you are faced with such a compulsion. However, we must assume that you will be welcome in the Temple. If so, then you must take these turns into the cave system: Left, left, right, left, right until you reach the circular chamber. There are symbols carved in the floor and a small patch of sky above. You will know it when you feel it." Croy nodded at her.

"Left, right, left, left…?" Clerin was squinting at him.

"Left, left, right, left, right. Whenever there is a branch, there are two ways to go." Croy began to look around for some writing utensils.

"A map would be fantastic." Clerin followed Croy's gestures as he searched in vain.

They eventually left to find Clerin's tent. Croy wrote the verbal instructions and sketched a rudimentary map for the cave system on a scrap of vellum for Clerin. They talked for a little while longer before he excused himself. It was getting late, and he was still fighting the urge to celebrate. Croy did not know it, but Trela and Feyazki were already alone in their tents. Tomorrow would have started out as a fine day indeed, but no one remembered to tell the rest of the companions what had been going on. What had been decided in their absence.

Chapter 14

Clerin awoke with sunlight illuminating her little tent. She became fully awake instantly, without her usual lingering shades of dream and lethargy. She must have been getting used to sleeping with the vial around her neck. Though there were no birds within earshot, the sunlight conveyed the image of their birdsong. That she was coming close to delivering Lembin's message was enough to buoy her spirits.

She got dressed in the same crusty breeches and jerkin that she had been wearing for most of her trip through the desert. After stepping clear of the tent door, she attempted to beat the previous day's trail from her clothes. A mighty cloud came up, but she felt none the cleaner for it.

Clerin meandered over to the breakfast fire to stand next to Vrric. No. Not Vrric, she thought to herself, but Feyazki. She understood the practice, but it was not greatly adhered to in the Fluen realms. Besides, most of the mages that she knew were much older and had already changed their names by the time that she had met them, so her experience with a mage in name transition was basically nil. Even though she thought of him as Vrric, she needed to remember to call him Feyazki.

"It's a beautiful day for a flight, is it not, Feyazki?" Clerin hoped that it was not obvious she was trying to use his name in a sentence.

Escha was handing Vrric a plate of grayish gruel. Torpalin and Haswyxe were milling about, eating while talking and standing. The flames in front of Clerin crackled merrily. Vrric smiled shyly at her.

"Yes, it is gorgeous out here. Fine temperature. It will surely be a pleasurable flight." His eyes darted back to his gruel after speaking.

"Flight, eh? Where you goin'?" Escha looked pointedly at Clerin.

"Yeah? Are we finally going to be heading home?" Torpalin took several steps towards the fire.

"Now… we can not confirm, nor deny…" Vrric turned to face Torpalin.

"On whose orders?" This came from Haswyxe. He, too, headed towards them.

Clerin felt a short-lived, but sharp, pang of panic. Though she knew that this situation paled in comparison, she felt what she imagined to be the same emotion that a ship's captain would feel at the start of a mutiny. *Why had they ever followed an order of mine?* What is it that makes some derlians take orders from others? Did Clerin grow complacent in the glow of Vanelia's authority? A borrowed authority at best. The question struggled deeper into Clerin and would have lain fruit if the chaos around her had not intruded.

"I'm sure that Trela will…" Vrric was immediately interrupted. Again.

"That is what I am talking about. This is it exactly. Why is that Pyran in charge? Who put her in charge? Did you? I don't recall voting on it." Torpalin was poking his thick finger into Vrric's chest.

"Listen, she is not in charge. No one is in charge. We just…" It was Clerin's turn to be interrupted this time. But the voice came from behind her.

"She is correct, I am not in charge. No one is. We had, maybe unfortunately, come to a group decision, and these two did not feel comfortable in speaking for the group as a whole. In fact, we are still missing one of those members, the older Gaen, Croy. Since we have three-fourths representation, however, let us get to your questions. One, we have found the Fluen Temple, and we are going to take Clerin there today. This will close one more chapter on our shared adventure. The next goal would be to return to Ariellyna. Two, we found what we *think* is the location. We will not know for sure until Clerin can enter the Temple. We had thought that, rather than get your hopes up and maybe dash them to pieces… Well, we thought to postpone the anxiety by postponing… Let me be the first to apologize to you. It was a complete oversight." Trela leaned dangerously over the fire with her right forearm extended. Torpalin only hesitated a moment before clasping hands.

"It has just been so long since we've heard anything… Anything about what we're doing or where we're going." Torpalin spoke while looking down at the fire.

"Understood." Trela nodded sincerely at Torpalin for half a breath and then began again. "But at least you can look forward to the Queen's just rewards."

"Actually, we are on a kind of retainer. But I am sure that she will throw in a bonus of some sort. Some hardship

500

compensation." Escha stared up at Trela. She had served up another plate, but had not handed it to anyone yet.

"Oh, yes. I am sure she will. I should have mentioned it earlier, but it just came to mind… My revolutionary warpack pays quite well. In bonuses, that is. Not so much in retainers. Or even in per diem, really." Trela eyeballed each of the three, briefly but securely, before breaking into a smile.

"Recruit on your own time. We have business to attend to." Vrric gave Trela a strange look. Clerin was not sure if it was a glare or not.

"Of course. I was thinking, maybe, that after you flew us to the temple you could come back and get the others. And the equipment… and animals. How many trips do you think it would take?" This time Clerin was sure that Vrric was glaring at Trela. It was Torpalin who answered, though.

"Oh, no need for that. We can follow behind. At least our horses are well fed." He smiled at Vrric.

"Are you sure? It could take most of the day." Trela shot questioning glances to both Torpalin and Vrric.

"No problem at all. We have been getting lazy camped here." He nodded at Vrric.

"Well, that's all up to you. I am glad that it is settled, however." Trela laughed and pulled back. Clerin thought she was turning to go when Haswyxe spoke up.

"Who will guide us to the rendezvous point?" He seemed to be smiling to himself a little.

"I will." It was Croy. And even though they had spent much of last night discussing the intricacies of his dream tunnel, Clerin felt a sudden pang of worry that he would not be accompanying them as previously planned. Her hand unconsciously touched the crude map in her breeches pocket. "I have seen the temple myself. It will take a good day to get there on horseback, but a manageable day."

Croy stood in front of Torpalin smiling, Trela slipped away quietly, Escha handed her a heavy plate, and Vrric pulled her away from the group. She could hear Croy and Torpalin bantering logistics in the background while Vrric whispered to her conspiratorially.

"You are not going to believe this, but I owe Trela a silver head." They had found a small log to share. Clerin was about to chastise Vrric. For what, gambling? She was not sure herself, but instead he continued. "Last night after we left, Trela and I got to talking. I was sure that the *best* thing to do today would be to ferry us back and forth to the temple site until everything was transferred. It would probably take until a little in the afternoon, if I flew as fast as possible. I would probably exhaust myself, but then I could rest the remainder of the day. I even told Trela that would be ideal. You know, for the common good." Here Vrric paused to look around. Once he had satisfied himself that there were no other derlians within earshot, he continued. "But then I started to complain about it. I tried not to. And, really, I was just venting that I felt like a pack animal sometimes. I didn't really think it was a big deal. But then she bet me a silver head that she could get the others to agree to go on horseback instead. That she could make them insist upon it. I did not believe her at the time, so I figured it was an easy bet."

"You shouldn't be gambling with strangers." Clerin laughed with him.

"Jealous?" Vrric's comment caught her off guard. He was looking at her with such intent that she felt a blush coming on.

"No, I was thinking of the old quote, 'A fool and his money are soon parted.' " Luckily he laughed at that.

They kept the rest of their conversation benign and cordial. In truth, they did not have much time for socializing anyway. Camp was hastily being taken down around them.

"Lumkinderclo!" It sounded like a thunder clap. They shot into the air with the speed of an arrow. The rocks and shrubs below them passed with a dizzying blur. The wind seemed so powerful that Clerin eventually just put her arms in front of her face. It was too difficult to communicate with the others anyway. The trip seemed to take a long time, but she knew it had to have been less than an hour.

They landed lightly on the plateau of a cliff. It seemed peaceful and idyllic. There was lush grass everywhere and some scattered trees in the distance. They waited briefly for Vrric to get his breath back.

"I should apologize for my tactical error of not explaining our progress to the troops sooner. I had not realized how thin the morale was getting." Trela looked from Clerin to Vrric.

"What? Oh, that was not your responsibility. Don't worry about that." Clerin had lain herself down on the grass.

"That was something I promised myself that I would keep an eye on." Trela was looking down.

"Well, if you promised yourself, then you should only have to apologize to yourself." Clerin watched the wispy clouds. They were all quiet for a while, each lost in themselves.

"So we should be right above it." Vrric was standing over Clerin's head like some giant.

"But I didn't see a cave. I don't sense anything." Clerin stood a little too fast. She was about to root around for the stone that Elange had given her, about to realize that she had forgotten it back at her tent, but Vrric was too excited to be interrupted.

"It is all hidden by illusion. Come, let's gather some rocks and I'll show you. Narkinderclo!" The two of them floated gently into the air and then wafted down into the gorge, leaving Trela alone on the small plateau. She was not sure if she was imagining things, but she thought she could smell the river, even at the top of the gorge. It was not long before they were at a small bank gathering fist sized stones.

"What are the rocks for?" Clerin held a pile of them in her arms.

"To show you the illusion." They shot up into the air. For some reason it felt odd to be flying with her arms pinned in one position. Being able to move her arms did not help Vrric fly them at all, yet she felt like her mobility was inhibited in some way. It did not make logical sense. They hovered about four fifths of the way up the cliff, facing a solid rock wall. Vrric reached over and grabbed a stone.

"Watch where this lands." Vrric hurled the stone at the wall in front of them. It finally thunked against the wall and fell back into the river.

"Hold on a moment." He turned and stared hard behind them. Then they floated sideways briefly. He picked up another rock and threw it. This one also struck the wall. After several tries and adjustments, the rock finally did what it was supposed to do. It disappeared into thin air. Clerin had only been paying half attention when it happened, so she made him do it again.

"Here, I want to try." She shoveled the remaining rocks over to Vrric. It took her four throws, but she finally got a stone to disappear as well.

"So how did you get in? Fly?" Clerin was watching the cliff face rather than Vrric.

"No, no. Magic near the illusion just… dissipates. Croy and I had to fling ourselves towards the cliff with the right trajectory and then just… fall. Luckily for you, I should be able to toss you through the illusion much like we did with those rocks." His smile had a manic tinge to it.

"Toss me?" Clerin glared at Vrric.

"You know. Telekinesis." Vrric tossed his remaining stone up and down in his hand.

"You said that magic does not work near the cave. I do trust you, don't get me wrong, but are you sure you can even fly and use telekinesis at the same time? Show me with a boulder. Use magic to toss a rock that weighs as much as I do through the illusion." She did trust him, but was nervous just the same.

"If I keep casting flight spells, we may have to wait for me to rest up again." He looked at her askance.

"We can wait until Croy and Torpalin arrive if you like. I want to see you do it with a boulder." Clerin was standing straight backed with her arms crossed over her chest. She was unsure if that posture had the same effect while floating above a river.

"All right." Vrric lowered them towards the river. As they hovered above it he intoned, "Nusidgesfe!" They skimmed the surface of the river until he suddenly perked up. "I have it, hold on. Mekkingearc!" A boulder smaller than Clerin's torso lifted from the river, dripping. They all flew back up to the same level they were before. Vrric eyeballed the cliff face for a moment before throwing his small stone through the illusion. Then, smiling, he sat down cross-legged. She was not sure why that should look odd compared to him standing in thin air, but it did. The boulder hovered in front of his face as he concentrated on the cliff. Finally, without warning, the boulder shot off towards the rock wall. It traveled perfectly horizontal before arcing in a low ellipse. About three-quarters of the way across the arc sharpened into a true parabola. Vrric crouched forward when that happened to watch the boulder fall. Amazingly enough it disappeared without a sound.

"Not bad, not bad. Do you need a rest?" Clerin's heart was pounding ferociously in her chest. She had been putting off thinking about what she had to do. She had just been traveling from one place to the other without a thought to how close to her goal she was getting. What if the Beleg did not want to talk to her? What if that pure panic Croy spoke of made her leap blindly into the river?

"No, I don't think so." Vrric was standing again.

"Do you want to inspire confidence in me or not?" Clerin's mind came sharply back to the task at hand.

"I feel great. And we should do this before I lose my feeling as to where the entrance is. Don't forget to roll the boulder back out. It did not feel like a place that enjoyed littering." He gave a warm, if somewhat weak smile. That did not instill confidence either.

Clerin nodded and sat cross-legged in front of him. "Narkinderarc!" Her mind was spinning too fast for her to think of something clever to say. So she stayed quiet. She concentrated on breathing and closed her eyes. She exhaled through her lips, loosening them. She tried to keep her face muscles relaxed. Then… movement. It was worse than just falling. It felt like her skin was being pulled behind her. She kept her eyes closed but uncrossed her legs and held an awkward crouch. She kept thinking of her forehead smacking into the top of the cave. Her head was pulled down so far into her neck that she looked like a frightened turtle. Then… freefall. She had not been sure how she would be able to tell when she was no longer being propelled by Vrric, but she sure felt the change. The wind whistled by her ears. She rotated slightly. She wanted to stop holding her breath, to take one more lungful, but couldn't. Then… impact. Into the face of the cliff. Luckily she had her feet facing the cliff when it happened. She plummeted like a stone. She thought she could hear Vrric yelling something in the distance, it was probably something useless like "sorry." She drew in a deep breath before the river crashed into her.

Splash! Clerin went under into the fast, and thankfully deep, waters. Though her clothes hampered her, she was naturally a strong swimmer. She struggled for a few moments before finding which way was up. Soon she had breached the surface and could breathe. And scream obscenities.

"I am so sorry, I just feel awful." Vrric quickly lifted her from the river. The wind gave her a chill while she wiped the water and a what seemed to be a cycle's worth of dirt from her face. "I don't understand what happened. I saw you hit the exact same spot as the boulder." Vrric truly did look stressed. Clerin thought about her crusty, travel stained body.

"Lower me back into the river. I may as well bathe." The words were meant to be consolatory, but they sounded mean to

Clerin's own ears. Rather than replying, however, he dunked her again.

Clerin did her best to clean herself with all her clothes still on, floating stationary in the swift current, head just above the water. It was actually nice but she had a hard time not glaring or muttering. There were certainly no herbs, or incense or oils, but she quickly felt refreshed and cleansed. Cleansed enough to commune with a Beleg.

"One more chance is all you get." While it was not necessarily meant to be consolatory, it sounded more harsh to Clerin than she had meant it. Vrric was silent the entire flight, brow furrowed in either consternation or concentration. For Clerin's part, she tried to think of nothing. There was a genuine fear that this would happen again. There was a genuine fear that it would never work. That there was no temple. That, even worse, there was a temple but that Linchon did not wish to commune with her. The wind chapped her face while leaving her hair and clothes feeling soggy. There was no happy medium.

Vrric had brought up a boulder and a variety of rocks. He tossed them all at the cliff face and they all disappeared. It was maddening to watch.

"I swear you hit the same spot. I..." Vrric looked even more distressed than earlier. Clerin wanted to help but her mouth would not listen to her.

"Obviously not." She took in a deep breath to gain control of herself. "It is fine. Really. We should try again before I lose my nerve."

Clerin sat cross-legged in front of him again. "Narkinderarc!" Instantly there was movement. She could feel the flying, then the falling, just as before. She held her breath, lowered her head and kept her legs in front of her. She could not believe she was letting him try again.

There was searing pain in her ankle as she landed. Her body flung forwards even as her feet seemed attached to the cave floor. Her arms instinctively thrust forwards, scraping into the stone. Luckily for her, her head bounced off her shoulder as she rolled into the crash. She lay there for some time, mildly crumpled. Finally she rolled up into a sitting position. She scooted herself so that her back was resting against the cave wall and rubbed her aches. Nothing seemed broken. She sat there, in pain, for some time. It was not until she realized that she heard no water did she finally stand. No wind came, no panic came. In fact, there was no noise at all. She just realized that she could not hear the river. The eerie silence, her beating heart, and her shortness of breath combined to remind her of playing hide-and-seek as a child.

It took her a little while but she finally got the boulders rolled out of the cave. The rocks were much simpler. She then pulled out her crude map. Before opening and reading it, she closed her eyes and said to herself, "Left, left, right, left, right." She opened her eyes to the map and, gratefully, saw that she had the correct directions in her head.

As she walked deeper into the cliff she realized that she was surrounded by an eerie light. The very stone itself seemed to give off a faint glow. She stopped to scratch at the walls. She was startled out of her curiosity by the sound of a distant wind. As she walked further on the sound faded back to silence.

The passageway twisted oddly. Clerin would have described it as the tunnel in the soil left behind a traveling worm. There was a certain ebb and flow to the arcs of the tunnel that was organically comforting. After a while she reached the first fork. The passageways branched slowly away from each other. The right path had a gentle upward slope to it and soon curved sharply. The left led downwards. The stone wall that separated the two tunnels was radiused inwards like a hitching post, worn thin in the middle by countless wrappings of rope. She walked deeper into the narrowing tunnel.

Soon Clerin reached her second fork. She knew that it was left again, but she checked her map just in case. This time the tunnel sloped up. She went forward with a little unfounded trepidation. This temple seemed so much different than her previous experience. She had known that was a temple immediately. Besides her mother there to guide her, there were guards surrounding the entrance. It was obvious and simple. She just needed to follow the path lain before her, and she would find Lembin under all that water. As she got to the next fork she thought that, arguably, the same could be said about her present situation. It seemed much more confusing this time, however. There was definitely a different confidence level this time. They had told her that Lembin wanted to speak to her. Maybe that was it. She was just not sure if she was wanted here. She did not know the message she was to give. She did not really know the derlians that helped her to get here. And she did not even know if this was a temple—the Temple. *What if the only thing at the end of this tunnel is a hibernating bear, grumpily awakening to my disturbance?*, she thought. That was followed quickly by, *How could I have forgotten Elange's stone?*

At the last fork she had taken the right tunnel without thinking. Now, staring at a tunnel she might have to crouch in to avoid bonking her head, she checked the map again. It could not truly be called a map, since the tunnels not taken just truncated immediately. It made Clerin feel better to think of it as a map, however. She stared at it hoping to make this fork the large and roomy right tunnel. But it was clearly marked left. She bent her head as she walked onward. Though it was a small tunnel, it was mercifully short. Soon, she was at her last fork. Her last choice. One more chance for her to shirk all responsibility and run laughing in the wrong direction. In truth, there was not much of a choice. She felt that the vast majority of her life was made up of "choices" such as these. She was not sure if it was better or worse than the alternative. At least the right fork was the larger one this time. And it headed upwards as well. She took a deep breath and started walking through the last tunnel. All she could hear were her own footsteps.

The tunnel seemed to brighten as she walked. The color sharpened as well. From a dull green-yellowish glow to more and more white light. Pure light. Clerin turned one last curve and saw the source. Before her was a circular room and at its center was a pillar of light. She squinted and shielded her eyes so they could adjust to the change. Though the pillar itself glowed, there were dark fissures that enveloped it like a choking vine. And they moved and shifted under her gaze. Inky lightning strikes cut across the surface. They would fall into a cohesive pattern, then disappear as soon as she began to sense it. The pillar's light seemed to be pushed through its skin only to be broken by the cracks casting incomprehensible shadows upon the walls and floor. The pillar did not seem to pulse so much as shiver as she approached. The tunnel walls flared out towards the room's entrance, like a trumpet horn. Unconsciously, Clerin began to disrobe. She looked around her briefly, nervously, then continued with her gut feeling. Maybe Vrric had miscalculated, but if Linchon had made her fall into the river just for a ritual bath, she did not want to upset it any further. She was just thankful that the gruel she had for breakfast did not have any meat in it. Would she have had to vomit before entering? After she had a small bundle of her wet clothes, she tried to tuck the pile away but ended up just placing it on top of her boots. She grasped the vial with her right hand and stood there for a moment. It took her some time before she could bring herself to remove the vial. There was nowhere to hide anything in the tunnel, so she stopped trying. She walked back towards the circular room, but then hesitated.

"May I enter?" Clerin stood at the threshold. She knew this was the Temple. She knew the room ahead of her contained a way to communicate with a Beleg. All doubt of whether or not Croy knew what he was talking about fled from her mind. Along with her willpower. She was terrified to go on, but knew she must.

The black fissures coalesced into an infinitely interlaced honeycomb shape across the entire surface of the pillar. Clerin watched them for a moment, then watched the shadow spinning on the wall. Suddenly, a horrific wind whipped up behind her, flying towards the pillar, pushing on her back. She half-stepped, half-stumbled into the room and the wind died down instantly. Looking at the floor she noticed that the cracks in the stone floor made the same type of archaic looking letters as she had seen in Lembin's temple. She wished there was some way to compare the two. In all her time with Wil, she had never even thought to ask about a written Yaven language.

Clerin stood and looked briefly around the room at the symbols on the wall. She barely realized the shape of a triangle above the tunnel that she had entered through before the pillar began shifting its pattern again. The honeycombs fell away to the random lightning strikes and cracks.

There was a distant whistling. A pitch so high that she wondered how it was audible. A gentle breeze began to circle around the room. It was a slow and pleasant wind, wafting through her hair. It seemed to be moving clockwise, so she began to walk in that direction. The lines in the floor tried to spell something but she could not read it. She stared hard at them for a moment, then stared at the pillar. Its cracks shaped themselves into the same geometric similarities as the floor. The wind increased in speed until she was almost running. The whistling dropped slightly in pitch, but gained in volume. She did not know what to do. In a panic she yelled, "Lokinderpri!"

The wind doubled in velocity and ferocity. She left the stone floor and spun around the pillar, orbiting like the moon. Phase locked and unable to turn away she watched the fissures shimmer and dance.

They shifted so quickly that colors began sprouting from the white light. Clerin could see the light diverge into its rainbow then, as if an upside-down prism were held up to it, converge back into white. Though the rainbow seemed to take up more space, the diameter of the light stayed constant. It was an illusion that occured with choice and the appropriate feeling of space. Through this faux dynamic pulse from all colors to all white came a sense of a question. It was a general question, Clerin felt. The most basic one of all: presence and purpose. As she whirled in ever tighter circles, she yelled desperately, "Linchon! I have a message from Lembin!" The wind increased, the pitch lowered and gained in volume. "Linchon! I have a message from Lembin!" She yelled it over and over. It became a chant, an anchor amongst the maelstrom. She did not know what else to do.

She stopped in her orbit while the wind continued to run past her. She was facing the glowing pillar, her arms outstretched in a vain but instinctive attempt to slow her angular velocity, but she was no longer spinning either. Her hair streamed horizontally in the wind but everything else of Clerin stared straight forth. The column wanted her to look down. All of its honeycomb edges sagged downwards, as if being drug by their own onerous weight. This made the leading corner of the honeycomb pull into an arrow shape, pointing at gravity. And the light itself was pulsing downward with a stripe of brightness. A jagged stripe with half-arrows pulling from a parachute of half-hexagons. The stripe was of such an intensity that she could only compare it to the sun. The column wanted her to look down. So her eyes followed the pulsating light downward to a small dark hole. Her eyes became transfixed...

That is why she did not see it coming. Unless, of course, there was no visual cue with what was to happen. Either way, she felt distracted when it started and was at least mildly grateful for that. Later she would describe it like being stabbed. Cut open. But it was much more than that. Being cut implies that you were whole. To Clerin, she was of two halves. Maybe split into right and left sides. These halves, or sides if you will, then were pushed in opposite directions, separating in the third plane. The inside of Clerin, as far as she could sense, was hollow. No guts or blood or organs came gushing out. Nothing but a scroll. The scroll did not even bounce upon the stone floor before being sucked down into the hole.

The pain was excruciating, but lacked a certain... substance. It was only painful because it had to be. There was no malice to it.

No malevolence. It was like being eaten by a bear or drowning in a river. She floated there, her two halves drifting independently, trying to scream. The seam of her cut, the slice itself, did not hurt. That was another way it was unlike being stabbed. It was the disconnect itself that was painful. The one half missing the other and vice versa. Like an empty glove across from a cold hand, both unfulfilled. She ached. Every last piece of her ached. It made her confused. Was she missing something? Was she gaining in numbness what she was losing in pain? Were they two sides of the same coin? Could they be separated? Could she be separated? But, still… no malice.

But, still… no scream. Sure she was whole. What can half of infinity be? The same? No, of course not the same. But, still… infinity. She had to be whole. But she could not remember. Was she different from what she was? Was her other side the same as her? No, of course not the same. But what if it was thinking the same thought at the same time? Always and forever. *Would she not be the same as I?* thought Clerin, *Which half would I be anyway?* She tried to peer around to find the half that she could barely remember being a part of.

Then came the malice. She felt her self thrown, crushed, burned, pierced and sliced. And sliced. And sliced. Ad infinitum. Each piece so tiny, with so much surface area that even though they came from a finite source they could still represent infinity. Each piece in so much pain that they would scream forever, making a finite torture infinite. If she could scream.

But all that happened in a flash. The pain ended and the sifting began. Each piece gladly told its story. Clerin's entire life, told from an infinite number of angles. Many with such minute differences as to be indistinguishable. At least to Clerin. It all zipped by, some parts lingering more than others. The most, by far, were the memories of Lembin's temple. Each split second of each split section was examined. Clerin had no sense of time for this segment of her experience. If she had to choose off of feeling, she would say decades. She knew that not to be true, however. At least, that was not how the world of the living marked the passage of time.

Clerin awoke on the cold stone floor. She shivered and held herself closer. Wanting to be done, she stood and headed back to her clothes. Standing in front of her was her father. He was gesturing widely, his hands circling some unseen girth in front of him. He shimmered slightly when he looked up at her. She wondered if he was an illusion.

"Father, is that you?" Knowing full well that an illusion, and definitely an hallucination, would answer affirmatively. But he just gestured up towards his face. She stared at his lips as they mouthed something. Three words, over and over. "Lotion goat's cart." Clerin sounded it out before realizing that it must be four syllables, over and over. He wanted her to cast a spell. It took her some time but she finally realized he wanted her to commune with spirits.

"Losidtotarc!" Clerin gave it her all. She had thought about using Nu, to try and go above and beyond what was asked of her, but the day seemed long already and she was unsure of what else might come before the sun set. Then she realized what the spell really meant.

"Are you dead, Father? Why are you here?" Clerin was wondering if she should have cast Clo at the end of the spell. What if he was not the one she needed to speak to?

"I'm afraid that I am, my little derling. It was an event of vengeance, of nemesis. It happened recently but quite painlessly, I might add. We have larger problems that lay before us, however. You must take Lembin's message to Gorbanax and Gunzgak. You MUST. After that, and only after that, you must take Linchon's reply message to Lembin. Do you understand? The message may not be delivered to only one Beleg. Think of the imbalance." Her father's shimmery ghost arms rose as if to grip her shoulders.

"But I thought I was done. Lembin did not mention taking the message to the others." Clerin felt tired. Her father's ghost howled. Whether it was in rage or in pain, she was unsure.

"Lembin did not fully respect the impact that its message has had upon Linchon. Communication works in two directions, not just one. There must be discussion amongst like minds. Decisions may be made. The reply must be as thoughtful as the original message. You must take the message to Gunzgak and Gorbanax. All of the Belegs must be aware. These are hidden matters only to those who are below the being of Beleg, all of the others. You are hereby charged with this quest. What say you?" Her father's ghost peered into Clerin.

"I suppose… I suppose I have no choice in the matter." Clerin felt defeated.

"It is good to realize these things. Certain deepenings of understanding may lighten the burden of living. You know your quest? No confusion, no failures?" He sounded angry to Clerin.

"I know my quest. You do not need to put a geas on me to ensure my loyalty." She was looking at the ground while speaking. She was unawares.

"Good. That is what we like to hear. This, unfortunately, is Linchon's reply to Lembin." He punched her in the stomach, his fist sinking through her skin, past her muscle and viscera and into the middle of her. She stared down at his forearm protruding into her. The pain felt real, but it seemed somewhat fake if she could just keep her mind set on thinking that it was fake. Then her father's ghost dropped a scroll into her. "You still have the original message. That is the one you are to give to the others first. Give them this one second." Her father's ghost pointed at her stomach.

"What if they peek at that one first? I am certainly in no position to stop a Beleg from doing anything it wants." Clerin's hands unconsciously clasped her belly.

"They should know the natural order of cause and effect. I am just asserting to you the natural order so that it will appear natural in you as well. The messages are not the only thing that Linchon is worried about them peeking at." Here he paused. His head cocked to one side and an eyelid fluttered lightly. "I must beg your pardon, but my time is nearly up. Destiny is currently waiting for more than one Toswin." His lips continued moving, but she could no longer hear him. He faded quickly from sight with one arm raised as if to wave goodbye. Clerin raised hers vainly in reply.

It was densely quiet. There was not a trace of wind. No pillar; nothing was spinning. There still appeared to be a shaft of light beaming into the center of the circular room, but it did not have much intensity. Clerin finally realized she had been staring at the wall behind where her father's ghost had been and jerked back into reality. She cleared her throat quietly to make sure she had not been struck deaf. In a daze, she wandered into the tunnel over to where her clothes were piled and picked them up. Oddly enough she felt safer in the large room, so she returned there to re-dress.

Clerin sat down in the shaft of light and pondered what had happened. The apparition sounded too angry and clipped to be her father. However, he had said things like "derling" to her, which would only be known by her father. Or, at the least, a close member of their family. As a matter of fact, she would rather that it was not her father's ghost at all. More than anything she did not want him to be dead. She started crying for the thought of him but ended crying for the thought of her. She was so incredibly tired and just wanted to go home. She wanted to sleep in her own bed and wake to the smells of breakfast cooking and her father's soothing voice. She curled up on the stone floor, using her arm as a pillow, bathed in a shaft of soft light. Her mind wandered between her own self pity and wondering whether or not her father had actually died half a world away. It had seemed so fake. The apparition did not "sound" like her father, but sounded like a direct mouthpiece for Linchon. Even with her mind awhirl, and as uncomfortable as she was, she slept soundly amongst the peace.

When she woke, nothing in the room had changed, which made it difficult to estimate the passage of time. Her muscles complained as she stood, but she definitely felt better for the nap. As she headed back out towards the river, she dug the map back out. It was doubly useless on her return trip, yet it intriguingly made her feel better.

Clerin paused as she neared the exit. Staring across the gorge to the other side of the canyon, she noticed an odd orange stripe in the rock strata. She knew there was a raging river at the bottom of the gorge, but she could not hear it. It was strange what was hidden from one realm to the next. One would think that the senses would align with one filter or the other, but they did not. Into this quiet chaos Clerin yelled back into the cavern system, "Best of luck, Linchon!" And she meant it. She only hoped that Linchon felt the same towards her.

Clerin took a running leap and jumped out as far as she could. The realm of sound came crashing back to her. As she hurtled downward, the sounds of the wind and the river became all encompassing and swallowed her up mere seconds before the water did.

The water was a shock, but it was a relief as well. The world grew quiet with the impact. She slowed to a stop almost immediately and was able to swim upwards to the river's surface quickly. From there it was a loud struggle to reach the far bank with its small but adequate sandbar. She pulled herself from the wet and collapsed for the second time that day. She laid there until a shadow crossed over her, darkening her day briefly. She sat upright immediately.

"Clerin?" It was a question shouted from above.

"I'm here!" Clerin hopped up and waved her arm vigorously. She assumed that it was Vrric but could not be sure from her angle. Truly, she would have smiled at any friendly face at that point. The figure dove down to her.

"You are lucky that I spotted you, I was just heading back…" Clerin hugged Vrric, interrupting him. She did not know why, but she needed the derlian contact. For his part he squeezed her back. The silence was golden.

"I'm sorry, I… It has been a long day. I am looking forward to you flying me up to some peace and quiet. I would kill for a glass of wine." Clerin separated herself from Vrric and smiled up at him.

"Well, I am sure that something to drink may be arranged, but you are going to have to do without the peace and quiet. You have been away for quite some time and much has happened. Vanelia has arrived with Hulgert. They showed up with another Luften and a mage valet shortly after you entered the Temple. They are awaiting you and the elixir, I believe." It seemed that no matter the news he brought, he always smiled. And when Vrric smiled at her, it had some real warmth behind it. She thoroughly enjoyed it.

"We mustn't keep royalty waiting." Clerin smiled back at him.

"Nukinderclo!" They shot upwards past the canyon walls, back across the river, and over towards a group of white tents. All of them were in the tall, rectilinear marquis style, with scalloped fringes and all manner of flags and banners aflutter. Vrric brought them high over the camp and then slowly down into the center of it. Everyone on the ground gathered around the new arrivals. There was Trela, of course, and Vanelia, who was definitely showing now. Hulgert was strapped into a chair. Chiavel was with them as well, and one other Luften that Clerin did not recognize. She was shocked to see that Chiavel was there, and a small, unexplained tingle floated through her as she laid eyes on him.

"Clerin, you have finally arrived." Vanelia, dressed from head to foot in stark white, strode past Trela to extend her hand to Clerin. She took it in her own and made a small curtsey while kissing Vanelia's white glove. It was somewhat complicated, and Clerin was tired. She could sense Vanelia's impatience and decided to beat her to the punch.

"I have the vial with me, Vanelia. We have been successful at the well." Clerin produced her oversized necklace and showed it to all who gathered around. "Now we shall see how successful the legend is." The group made the short shuffle over to poor Hulgert.

Vanelia stepped behind the king, presumably to help administer the elixir. Clerin leaned towards the old man, her hands clutching the tiny vial. As she looked at Hulgert, she realized how far gone he was. His eyes were dense, foggy cataracts staring blindly forth. His skin was a thin velum, stretched so tight that there were spots Clerin was afraid she could see right through. His head did not even twitch as she approached. Vanelia was whispering encouragements to Hulgert, but he did not move. There was no indication that he even realized that he was outside. If Clerin concentrated, truly narrowed her focus and concentrated, she could see his chest rise and fall ever so slightly. That was all that could be said of King Hulgert at that moment.

Vanelia's impatience peaked when she pulled Hulgert's head back. His mouth automatically widened towards Clerin. She took the stopper from the vial's neck slowly. Intently. She refused to be rushed by Vanelia's impatient aura. She held the vial with both hands as she tilted it towards the King's open maw. She did not want to spill even one drop of it. If any liquid even fell into his shaggy beard, she thought she would be forced to attempt to retrieve it. She only intended one drop to fall from the vial. More than one certainly leapt into the king's mouth, but less than five. Clerin immediately righted the vial and stoppered it back up.

There was nothing. Not one of the derlians present even blinked. They all waited, holding their breath. Until the moment stretched so far that it became too thin to hold Vanelia back. She screamed and brought her fists down on the back of Hulgert's chair. Right there, right while Clerin was staring at him, his eyes cleared. He blinked once, then coughed. Everyone grew quiet again as a spasm wracked through him, forcing him to curl up into the chair as he coughed. He was still bone thin and frail, but his skin seemed more opaque. By the time he had gained his senses and finished coughing, his cheeks seemed to have gotten some color.

"Where… where am I?" The voice was quiet but steady. It had the hum of a healthy baritone. Then a great cheer erupted amongst the small group. This seemed to confuse Hulgert further. "Where am I!?" He yelled and stood up right in front of Clerin. She staggered back as he began to swing his arms about wildly. "Who are all of you?!"

"Hulgert. It's me, Vanelia." As her hands grazed his shoulders to turn him towards her, Hulgert's defensive posture instantly softened. "Who are all of these derlians? Why are we at the Temple? How long have I been..." He straightened his spine as he looked at her.

"What do you last remember?" Vanelia patted his arms warmly.

"Falling off of a horse." He looked somewhat bemused at his own words.

"That can't be. That was over a cycle ago. You were healthy then." Vanelia looked around for corroboration. Chiavel nodded seriously to both Vanelia and Hulgert, but Clerin could not tell if he meant it or was just helping Vanelia.

"I remember that we were having a picnic. We were about half staff that day. You were there." Hulgert pointed his finger menacingly at Chiavel, then just as quickly stopped. "I was riding Old Red while you were riding Moonglow. We had broken away from the rest of the group, remember? We were each looking..." Hulgert turned his body towards the sun as a reference point. "We were each looking this way at the most curious tree when suddenly Old Red bolted upright. I remember being thrown... but not landing." Hulgert shook his head and stared at his feet.

"I immediately screamed for help. Chiavel was the first to respond. He did what he could, but we needed to get you to a real mage. No offense." Vanelia lamely offered as an afterthought. "We finally got you back to the royal helioarc and had all of the best mages come to help heal you. Euclodia herself even cast a healing spell upon you. It was quite some time after that that you started to get ill. Don't you remember any of that? Anything beyond the horse accident?"

Hulgert looked around at the others briefly. As if gaining help from them somehow. "I can remember that picnic like it was... like it was yesterday. I have no recollection at all of getting ill." He looked down at himself, as if checking to see if he was currently ill.

"You were dying. You just got a little sicker each day. We... we cured you." Tears welled up in Vanelia's eyes. "We all cured you here. Now. Finally."

It was then that Hulgert noticed Vanelia's growing belly. He did not say anything aloud. He merely paused for a moment. For too long of a moment.

"This is Clerin. She is the Fluen that brought the elixir from the well back to us." Vanelia gently turned Hulgert towards Clerin while she spoke.

"You are saying that I am cured through water from the well at the center of the Northern Desert?" Hulgert had a strange monotone voice when he said it.

"Yes, is it not amazing? I told you that we tried every magician in Ariellyna. What else was there to do?" Vanelia smiled warmly at Hulgert.

"What else indeed." Hulgert then looked up at Clerin. "It is certainly a pleasure to make your acquaintance. Your services to the Kingdom will not soon be forgotten. And who are you?" Hulgert pointed over to Vrric.

"That is Feyazki, a new mage in our employ. He escorted young Clerin here. A student of Revkin's, I believe." Though she did not phrase it as a question, Vrric nodded back to her. "This Pyran is Trela. Clerin and Feyazki met her at the well and she has accompanied them back here. You know Chiavel of Largon, of course. And Sempere over there as our mage valet. And the others? I sent five warriors with Clerin and Feyazki..." Vanelia looked over to Clerin.

"The others are walking here from our base camp. They include the five warriors—Gyllhelon, Torpalin, Haswyxe, Escha, and Malghain—Knill, a Gaen traveling companion of mine, and Croy, another Gaen who we met up with at the well. They should arrive later in the afternoon." Trela grinned widely at Hulgert.

"Well, that is foolish. Sempere! We need you to find the others and bring them back here. Which way was your... base camp?" Vanelia looked over at Trela.

"They should be following the river, on this side of the bank, from back down there." Trela pointed downstream.

"To think you are making them walk uphill." Vanelia looked over at Clerin like it was her fault.

"Here, let me show you the way." Vrric intercepted Sempere before he reached Vanelia. They walked away from the group talking quietly.

"Well, that is a lot of derlians, do you think…" Clerin was not sure what she was about to say, but she was interrupted before her mind could get there.

"That is what Sempere does." Vanelia placed a heavy inflection on the word "does." "Besides, he has Feyazki to help him."

"Every play has different characters. And an actor to play their part." Trela stepped next to Clerin's side, effectively drawing Vanelia to herself and cutting Clerin from the conversation.

Clerin was unsure to whose benefit the action was intended, but she was grateful that Trela interceded just the same. Instead of worrying it over, she turned and watched Vrric and Sempere fly away. She walked a couple of steps forward just watching them disappear into the distance.

"Don't think like that." Chiavel was suddenly beside her, strolling slowly.

"What?" Clerin had trouble even recalling what she had been thinking about.

"Oh, it's just a phrase." He laughed somewhat quickly.

"I don't understand." Clerin stopped walking.

"It's just something I say when others are quiet. Don't take it personally." He laughed again.

"Then why would you say it?" Clerin decided she should take it personally.

"If someone is staring pensively off into the distance, walking away from the group, then they aren't thinking about you, are they? They are thinking of something secret. Especially if they are watching another leave." His smile finally became genuine.

"Oh, that. That's nothing. I was just staring off. Not thinking about anything, really." Clerin looked into his brown eyes. "Did you just say you wanted me to be thinking about you?"

"I thought I was being more adroit, Herance." His black hair shifted in the breeze.

Clerin laughed and started walking back up towards the others. She had forgotten the fake name she had given him when they first met, it seemed so long ago. It was funny that he remembered it. She was unsure of what she thought about Chiavel, though. Of course, there were a lot of things she was unsure about at that moment.

"Do you think the elixir stayed potent because of you? I mean, do you think you will have to continually wear that, or do you think you can hand it off to Vanelia now that you have brought it back from the desert?" Chiavel's little chuckle sounded a bit nervous.

"I had not really thought about it. I guess I had assumed that we would heal Hulgert and that would be the end of it. I will probably just hand it off to Vanelia." Clerin stopped because Chiavel had stopped.

"You could hand it off to another, if you wished. In fact, there may be quite a bit of money in it for you if you did." He smiled at her again, and she examined his countenance with renewed interest. His cheeks kept the smile, but his eyes had something more serious in them.

"You do not understand. Vanelia sponsored the expedition, the elixir is rightfully hers. Besides, I do not need more money." Clerin lied a little at that last bit.

"You are obviously not thinking about the amounts that I am, but no matter. What do you think it would do for a healthy derlian? Like, say, if you let me taste a drop." Clerin's own cheeks felt sore in sympathy for Chiavel keeping his smile up for that long.

"Well, I do not know. What if it was poisonous to a healthy derlian?" Clerin was not feeling nervous, per se, but felt like she should continue walking back towards the group. She had a hard time just turning and leaving, however.

"Think of what it did to Hulgert. It took him from death's door to complete coherency. Do you not think that it might increase the senses and sharpen the wit?" Thankfully, he had finally stopped smiling.

"You do not chew echinacea root if you are healthy…" She could not tell if she trailed off or if he interrupted her.

"Ha! Roots do not really help. That is all in the mind." He tapped his index finger against his temple. "I know you would not have wanted to waste it on a healthy derlian, but you have now used it. You were probably also worried that it might be poisonous, as you just suggested. Or even worried that it would do nothing, that it might just be normal well water. We now know differently, though. If it was poisonous, it would have put Hulgert out of his misery. Instead, it offered him new, fully coherent life. We now know that what you carry around your neck works. It works greater than I had even dreamed." His smile came back, but it seemed somewhat hollow and insincere. Then she realized he said that "he had dreamed."

"This is all academic. It is not mine to share." Clerin turned to walk back towards the group when Chiavel grabbed her by the arm. It was not a tight grip. He did not squeeze her and there was no physical pain, but it was alarming nonetheless. Clerin was not used to such impropriety.

"How many drops do you think you have left?" He immediately released her arm as she turned towards him. That was not enough to soothe her sudden unease, however.

"I said no." Clerin crossed her arms in front of her. Part of her wanted to charge back up the hill but somehow that seemed like losing. He glanced up at the hill and back at her several times.

"Of course. Please accept my apology, I was not trying to make you do anything you do not want to. I was merely overcome with emotion. The ah… the effects of the elixir were astounding, and my curiosity got the better of me." He bowed his head to her. She waited briefly, not knowing what to do. Finally she realized that he was not going to look back up until she said something.

"I accept your apology. Now let us see how healed Hulgert really is." Clerin started walking before he could say anything else. Her anger began to ebb as they walked up the hill, however. Words, after all, were just words.

"How did you find the well?" Chiavel seemed back at ease.

"I do not believe we did. It was more like the well found us." She laughed lightly. "Vrric had wandered off alone and ended up in a huge fight with… something unnatural. When we went to find him, we found the well."

"You mean Feyazki, don't you, Herance." They both laughed at that.

"Please, don't mention that to him. It has been a while since I have made that mistake." She did not really care if he told Vrric or not. More importantly, she did not think Vrric would care. She was curious, however, if Chiavel was the type of derlian to say something after being asked not to. She glanced sidelong at him. He was smiling back at her.

"Don't worry about me. Luckily for you, I am one of the few that knew him as Vrric before he became Feyazki. Or at least one of the few beyond his humble upbringings. I did not even know about his name change until earlier today." He was staring at the grass in front of him as they walked, only occasionally glancing over at her.

"Humble upbringings? You know, we have been traveling together for what seems like forever and he never mentioned his upbringings." She had never thought of Vrric as vain, but she had never really thought of him as humble either.

"Did you ever mention your upbringing?" He glanced back behind them.

"Sure. I mentioned my lineage when I explained why I was in the Luften realm." His glance made her look back as well but she could not tell what he was looking at.

"What if you had no lineage? I myself always mention that I am from the branch of Largon. Do you know what the branch of Largon is?" Chiavel smiled over at her.

"Well, no… But I know that it means that you are part of a larger clan. Probably a clan with some influence, or else why would you mention it?" She was not sure why he was talking about himself suddenly.

"Exactly. It is my lineage. And, as you say, it is a lineage with some influence and therefore comes with some privileges. Even if you do not know the name I am dropping, you know that I am dropping a name. What if, however, you did not know your lineage? Or maybe your lineage was embarrassing. Even the most obnoxious village drunk may have some progeny who will grow up to achieve some level of respect. Maybe not even an obnoxious drunk, but a well-meaning, poor dirt farmer. It is those types of derlians who will never mention their lineage. Their silence is not often noticed. That is why I pay extra attention to such silence. You can often learn more about a derlian by what they do not mention, than by what they do." He glanced back once more.

"What silence?" They had arrived at the top of the hill, and Trela had wandered towards them without Clerin noticing. The sudden addition of another voice lightly startled her.

"We are talking about Feyazki's lack of lineage," Chiavel stated dryly. They stopped where they were, leaving Vanelia and Hulgert plenty of space to speak to each other without fear of being overheard .

"Who cares about lineage? That Luften fought a Tlana single handedly. And won! Or so I hear. I will take capability over lineage any day." Trela smiled between the two of them.

"That is because you have no lineage." Chiavel smiled back, but Trela narrowed her eyes in response. He turned towards Clerin, "Do you know how I know she has no lineage?"

"Well…" Clerin was wary of annoying Trela.

"Because I pay attention to what derlians don't say." He turned back towards Trela. "Do not fret, however. I sense plenty of capability in you." With that he broke away and walked towards Vanelia and Hulgert.

"Can you believe his nerve?" Trela focused her narrowed eyes on Clerin.

"Well… can you trace your lineage?" Clerin did not mean to say it, it just sort of popped out of her mouth.

"I am the Kriishan. That is more than enough for me." Trela cocked her head slightly. "To be honest, I had not realized that you cared that much about things like that."

"I don't. We were just having a conversation." Clerin waved ineffectually towards Chiavel.

"Good. Because here comes the rest of the riffraff." Trela pointed behind Clerin. As she turned around she noticed a large dot growing larger in the sky. Vrric and the other mage must be bringing all of the others back at once. She felt a twinge of guilt at thinking "the other mage," but for the life of her she could not recall his name. "Be careful of derlians selling things. Especially themselves." Trela waved behind her as she headed down the hill leisurely. Clerin watched from where she stood.

The group grew steadily closer until they filled up the sky. The nine of them looked like a flock of giant birds. They landed in a graceful herd about half way in between Trela and Clerin. Trela turned as they passed overhead and trotted after them. They all paused as they got used to solid ground and the instant chatter was trivial. "The other mage" bowed towards the others and flew off again. Trela swept through the rest and they all began walking behind her, towards the royalty. As they passed, Clerin could hear bits of Trela's strong voice.

"… had to come down to see my warriors. Make sure everyone had a pleasant flight …" And on, ad nauseam. Clerin had the sudden insight that if there was one derlian who sold themselves as much as Chiavel did, it was Trela. She watched the crowd go by, staring down, thinking of Chiavel and Trela.

"It's good news, I hope." Vrric had walked over to her. "Your smile. It must mean good news." Vrric himself wore a large grin.

"I was just thinking how derlians are quick to notice their own faults in others." She was glad he stopped by to talk to her. The voices of the others cascaded down the hill at the two of them.

"That doesn't seem like a great reason to smile." They both started to walk up the hill. Taking their time.

"The characters involved made the realization amusing. Remind me to tell you sometime." She felt like she might be able to relax soon. It was a good feeling. "The elixir worked. Hulgert is as good as new."

"Unbelievable." They caught up with the others almost immediately. There was a large circle surrounding the rejuvenated King. The sounds were indistinguishable but definitely jubilant.

Everyone was congratulating each other and laughing and hugging. Soon some bottles of mead were opened. Clerin was astounded by the warriors' reaction to the news of Hulgert's health, but she should not have been. It was not just their beloved King's sudden consciousness, but the end of a mission. The successful completion of a quest. Suddenly Torpalin was in front of her. In a flash he gripped her waist in both of his huge hands and lifted her high above the others. Just as quickly he spun away again. There, right in front of her, stood Croy. He held out his hand to her. Though she was not sure what he was doing, she grasped his hand with hers.

"Congratulations. You have delivered your message, have you not?" He shook her hand heartily.

"Yes, though I fear it is not the end of my journey." His eyes commiserated with her but he stayed silent, so she continued. "And, as you can see, we have healed the Luften King."

"I had heard something to that effect. How did you do it?" Their hands parted, and Clerin straightened her back again.

"We brought him the elixir from the desert. You know, the well water." She pointed into the far distance that they had traveled.

"He has drunk from the well? But… he's nowhere near it. That's no decision." Croy narrowed his eyes at Clerin. She could not tell what he was talking about.

"It was the only way to cure him. Look." Clerin waved her hand towards where the king was standing.

"It's poison." Croy hissed.

"What do you mean? Look." Croy grabbed her arm with such urgency that she could feel it bruise.

"We need to speak to them. The King and Queen, we need to speak to them. Away from all this. Please, we must speak to them quickly." He started to pull her towards them and, though she tried, she was unable to wrench her arm free. He held up both his hands in front of himself. "Please."

Not knowing what to do, she left Croy at the fringe of the small gathering and waded to the center. After worming a bit closer to Hulgert with happy smiles and good-natured nods she bent over to whisper to him. "The Gaen needs to speak with you." He looked at her intently. Clerin could not keep his gaze and instead glanced over to Croy. Hulgert followed her sightline and stared hard at Croy. Croy made drinking motions with his thumb and pinky. Hulgert looked back at Clerin.

"It is not good news, is it?" His bright eyes smiled up at her.

"It does not appear to be, sir. I mean, sire." His face even seemed to have less wrinkles than it did before. It was amazing. He nodded briefly at Clerin.

"Cover for me." He stood, grabbed a bottle of mead from Malghain, and tottered away from the crowd. She did not see where Croy had scampered off to. It was some time before Vanelia realized that Hulgert was not just wandering off to relieve himself.

"I wonder where Hulgert is?" Vanelia questioned aloud.

"I… I believe he is paying his respects to all of the valiant members of the party." Clerin smiled to Vanelia.

"He does not pay respect to others, others pay respect to him." Vanelia snapped at Clerin.

"I am sure she means that he is speaking with each of them individually. I believe he wants the clearest view of this momentous occasion, so he is conducting private interviews with his subordinates. Only with each piece of story told separately can he decide the true history of what has just happened. Please, your glass seems to have emptied itself again." Chiavel waved a hand towards Malghain who was commandeering another bottle. Malghain dutifully poured a healthy amount of mead into the Queen's glass and then walked over to Clerin.

"You look a little too serious for the levity of the evening. Also, you seem to have lost your glass. You know, that may have something to do with…" Malghain's voice died when the King burst back amongst them. He looked old and haggard.

"I need… I need another drop." Malghain flowed away from Clerin as the King shuffled towards her. "But just one. I need to think clearly for my decision." Hulgert knelt before her with his mouth open like a baby bird. As she stared at the top of his pate while she fumbled for the elixir, she could see freckles grow into liver spots before her eyes. The sight of it made her panic even more.

"Wait! Wait, you should decide before you ingest more!" Croy came crashing towards Hulgert but was tackled by Malghain before he could reach him.

"Now, Fluen!" Hulgert spread his arms dramatically.

"It's poison!" Croy managed to choke out audible enough to reach all present. There was not another sound to be heard beyond Croy and Hulgert.

"I know its poison! I've already taken it, though, haven't I? I was not given a choice to begin with. It's already too late." He turned his ragged brown eyes towards Clerin. It somehow appeared that his snow-white hair had grown longer, but thinner. "Now, before I complete my metamorphosis, give me my poison." Every pair of eyes laid heavily upon Clerin. She could hear Croy struggling against Malghain, but it sounded far off. She could not refuse Hulgert, however. Her choice was swift. She gave him the drop he requested.

The effects were almost immediate. He stayed on his knees panting, face straight up towards the darkening sky, and with each breath he grew calmer. His face plumped healthily from the skeleton it had sunken to. His cheeks grew ruddy. His hair seemed much less disheveled and slightly thicker, maybe even darkening a bit in color. Clerin was not sure how much was real and how much was a trick of the eye. As he stood, she resecured the vial.

"You have doomed yourself." Croy would not be let up until the King nodded to Malghain.

"I appreciate your zealousness, Gaen. I know you mean well. But, as I have said before, I was doomed before I even— unconsciously mind you—partook of the elixir the first time. Why don't you explain your hysteria to the others?" Hulgert grumpily took a half-full glass from Escha and finished it in one gulp. Escha dutifully went off in search of more.

"The water from the well is two distinct things. First and foremost, it is the most powerful healing elixir known to derlians. Secondly, it is a slow poison. Well, not necessarily slow, but a couple of days. I have been told that there is no known cure for the poison, other than itself. So, as long as you can drink a little water every couple of days, it will heal its own poison enough to keep you alive. If you can drink a little water a couple times a day, you will not even feel the effects of the poison. And, in fact, be in the best health of your life." Croy spoke for everyone to hear, but he was speaking to Vanelia. It struck Clerin as very considerate of him.

"That's why they couldn't leave the well. No one would tell us…" Everyone turned to her, and Escha grew silent as quickly as she had spoken up.

"In the village that accompanies the well, there is an ancient derlian. One of the originals, if he can be believed. He attempts to guard the well to give newcomers the option of forever living near the well for the rest of their lives or not tasting of it at all. He was lax in his duty when my Ilana drank from it, and now that it was my turn, I too have failed to give adequate warning. I thought we were just finding the Luften Temple… I did not realize…" Croy grew suddenly sullen. Clerin suddenly realized how little time Croy had spent with them.

"What worries me more is how I got sick in the first place. The poison will kill me much less quickly than my own original sickness." Hulgert stood there with fists clenched.

"Is that your decision then? Do you want to find the village by the well?" Croy asked of Hulgert.

"No… no, that decision is not made yet." Hulgert looked slightly nervous. He turned to Clerin. "You may transfer your burden now." He held his open hand to her. Clerin felt the stares of the others upon her. She reached around her throat for the vial's tether.

"What of the legend? The elixir should only be held by a Fluen." This time it was Vanelia who spoke up. Clerin paused in mid-motion.

"The legend's constraints are based on the fact that the elixir only works temporarily. Each time the elixir was brought back by a Luften, its powers only worked until the water ran out. So the legend became more complicated to encompass the ephemeral attitude of the healing. If Croy is to be believed, the healing is temporary even if I drink it straight from the source, with no intermediary whatsoever. Is that correct, Croy?" Hulgert did not remove his eyes from Clerin, whether he was speaking to Vanelia or to Croy.

"That is what I was told by the guardian of the well. Not that he is a very good guardian." Croy looked at Vanelia as he spoke.

"You see, even Croy agrees. No magic is permanent." In a chorus, though muted and not coordinated, Vrric, Croy, and the mage from Largon all spoke under their breath. "No magic is permanent." Hulgert shook his hand gently at Clerin. Once Clerin realized that no one else was going to say anything, she handed over the vial. She had not thought to ask anyone about the waters, but had simply filled the vial. There had been several denizens that had watched her dispassionately and said nothing. She spent a moment attempting to figure out if she should feel bad about herself. Hulgert spoke up before she came to a conclusion.

"Set up camp. We will stay here until I have made my decision. Unfortunately, I do not know how long that will take. Good evening to you all. You are all heroes of Ariellyna!" Hulgert raised the vial high and everyone cheered. Chiavel followed Hulgert and Vanelia to their large central marquis tent that had been set up while Clerin had been communicating with Linchon.

Clerin turned around and headed over to Croy and Malghain.

"You are not hurt, are you?" Malghain's question was directed towards Croy.

"No… no. Nothing but my pride." Croy's laugh sounded slightly forced.

"I would apologize, but the King's safety is a top priority." Malghain smiled warmly.

"Think nothing of it… but. But, you know, I had the King's best interests in mind." Croy's smile looked a bit forced.

"I do now. Very often I work reflexively, you know." Malghain kept his smile.

"I do now." Croy laughed.

Escha appeared with a full bottle and a bevy of empty glasses. As she began to parcel them out, Clerin leaned over to her. "Where is Feyazki?" She took the filled glass that was offered to her.

"You too, huh? I think he slipped away with Gyllhelon. They left down the hill when Hulgert and Vanelia went back to their tent."

"Oh. Maybe they are waiting for the other mage to come back with the pack animals?" Clerin took a deep drink.

"Yes. Maybe they are." Escha had a small nervous tic in her cheek periodically. Sometimes it made her appear to be winking. Clerin assumed this was one of those times.

Clerin peeled away from the small group as they started discussing the probability of having to journey back into the desert. She had started heading over to where Trela, Knill, and Torpalin were conversing, but found herself wandering down the hill instead.

The sky was turning from dark blue to black. Since the moon had not yet risen, it was getting dark quickly. She walked a ways before noticing something in the sky. There appeared to be several flying horses heading towards her. They were fully saddled and were carrying the tents and the last of their meager provisions. Without thinking about it, Clerin moved off to the side so that the horses would have plenty of landing room. She ended up standing by a spiky, gnarled blackthorn tree, staring up at the spectacle above her. A few more moments passed before the beasts landed. They were rolling their eyes and snorting heavily as they made contact with the ground. They began trotting up the hill when Gyllhelon appeared on the other side of them. She put herself in front of them and calmed them while they were still prancing about. She softly petted their noses and whispered to them.

"Do you need any assistance with the rest of them?" Vrric's voice startled Clerin. She had been paying so much attention to the horses that she had not seen him and the other mage walking up the hill together.

"There is only one more load. So, no, I do not need any help." The other mage, the mage valet from Largon, stopped in his tracks with his arms crossed in front of him.

"Then why don't you head up to the camp and I'll go get them." Vrric stopped as well.

"Because it is my job. The Queen would never let me drink if you were out fulfilling my duties. Let alone what Chiavel would do to me. It is fine, I will rest after this last trip." The mage turned around to face the direction he had come from.

"They have already retired to their tents. Truly. I can fetch the rest of the horses and equipment. It is no big deal." Vrric put a friendly hand on the mage's shoulder.

"Why do you wish to help anyway? This is what I get paid to do." The mage turned towards Vrric.

"Magic is a gift. I enjoy using it to help others." Clerin could see Vrric's teeth as he smiled.

"There is a fine line between helpfulness and servitude." The other mage was not smiling.

"What do you mean?" Vrric lowered his arm.

"I mean that others' complacency on the extent of your gift makes charity turn into a menial job. Servitude." Now the mage smiled. "Do you get thanks for your gift?"

"I know that others appreciate my efforts." It was Vrric's turn to cross his arms over his chest.

"They may say the word 'thanks,' but… trust me, they are apathetic to your assistance. They take it for granted and assume you will always be there helping them. You see, that is why I choose to get paid for my gift. At least then I don't feel so bad when others are complacent about my helpfulness." The mage put his hand on Vrric's shoulder. "I appreciate your offer. I do. I actually know what effort and energy is needed to cast spells. However, it is my job to do, and I would not feel right letting you do it for me. You have already helped me more than enough. Narkinderpri!" The mage lifted smoothly into the night air. Vrric watched for a couple of moments and then turned to walk up the hill, towards the others. Then he saw Clerin.

"Have you been there the whole time?" Vrric sounded incredulous.

"Yes. I was…" She started to say.

"Why didn't you say anything?" He still had his arms crossed.

"There wasn't really an opportunity." Clerin felt her cheeks flush. "I wasn't eavesdropping."

"I don't know what else you would call it." Vrric started walking up the hill.

Clerin was flustered. She had not meant to be offensive in any way. "An accident," she called out after him. She had to trot to catch up with him. "Feyazki, please, I really did not mean to overhear your conversation." He stopped beside her.

"Maybe, maybe. Either way, I am more annoyed about my conversation with Sempere than your eavesdropping. So… you have nothing to worry about, okay? I'm just… I apologize if I said anything to upset you. Everything is fine." He patted her shoulder in a friendly fashion and then started back up the hill. She kept pace with him.

"Well, I certainly appreciate your helpfulness." Clerin kept quiet after that, not sure if she should have even said anything. So she spent the time memorizing Sempere's name.

When they arrived at the main camp, it was bustling with effort. The pack animals had been unpacked and most of the available tents were in the process of being set up. Clerin broke away from the silent Vrric and found a couple of glasses and a bottle of mead. By the time she had filled them and found Vrric again, he was speaking quietly with Gyllhelon. Clerin approached and cleared her throat loudly.

"Here, you both look like you need a glass." Clerin handed all of it over and then wandered off to see if her tent was amongst the ones already here before she could be brought into their conversation. She had intended on drinking a little with Vrric but thought it would be rude to interrupt them, especially considering what had just happened with Sempere. Besides, she could not seem to get used to the taste of the Luften drink. What she wouldn't give for a glass of simple, delicious wine. She looked amongst the pack animals for a while but could not locate her tent.

"I am still awaiting my tent as well." Haswyxe spoke from behind her, startling her somewhat. "Hopefully that other mage will show up soon with the other horses. It's already too dark to set up very quickly. I helped out Torpalin with his tent hoping he would help me with mine."

"I think Sempere should be back soon." Clerin spoke while still rummaging around.

"I knew I had heard that name at some point this evening, but could not think of it for the life of me." He chuckled quietly. That made Clerin smile. She was not about to mention her own struggle with that name, however. "Feyazki was right next to me when they began to fly us, so I just paid more attention to him. Familiar territory, you know."

So they chatted until Sempere arrived with the last of the animals. Both Haswyxe and Torpalin assisted Clerin with her tent, setting up the small shelter in record time. Others were circled around the fire and the invitations to join were warm and tempting, but she was simply too exhausted. She begged out of being social and immediately crawled into her tent. She was under the blankets and almost dreaming when she finally realized that she had not helped any others set up their tents.

The sun was not long in the sky before the camp was awakened by the sounds of screaming. Clerin paused long enough to dress before she joined the general chaos. She followed the sound of hysteria, knowing full well where it would lead. The screams were coming from the largest tent at the top of the hill. They had to be Vanelia's. Which meant that something had happened to Hulgert. Clerin hoped that it had happened quickly, whatever it was.

Clerin saw two derlians disappear into the confines of the tent before she reached the front of it, but she was unable to tell who they were. She halted there with Croy, Escha, and Haswyxe as they all had reached the entrance simultaneously. Haswyxe held his hand in front of them and paused for a moment in front of them.

"We don't want to trip over each other in there. Assistance?!" He yelled back at the tent.

"No combat!" The answer was yelled back from somewhere in the tent. Clerin was not positive, but she thought it may have been Malghain's voice.

"Escha, proceed with care." Haswyxe nodded towards the tent, and she quietly disappeared behind the cloth. He kept his hand extended towards the rest of them. They were quickly joined by Gyllhelon, Torpalin, Knill, and Vrric. All running in from different directions. Haswyxe straightened his spine slowly and positioned himself in front of the tent entrance. The mood grew from panic to one of curiosity as the screaming stopped. They all had an idea of what had happened but none would speak it aloud. As if voicing it could make it true.

Eventually a disheveled Vanelia appeared in the darkened doorway of the tent. "He drank too much elixir during the night. He… it might have been purposeful. I do not know… He did not discuss his intentions with me." She made shooing motions towards the group. "There is nothing to be done. Go… make breakfast."

Rather than scattering individually, the group shuffled down the hill in one unit. They went straight to the largest firepit from the evening and began fire preparations. The talk was minimal and cooperative in nature. They worked efficiently with the same calm stoic exterior imprinted on each of their countenances.

Eventually Trela, Sempere, and Malghain filed out of the large tent and shuffled towards the fire. They were handed food as they arrived and then split to eat in solitude, as the others had previously done. The solitude was no more than a stone's throw away, but it was separate none the less.

Chiavel finally appeared from the tent but Vanelia never did. It was her absence that weighed upon the group. They knew the grieving that must be going on in there. It kept them in quiet, close solitude with each other throughout the day.

That night they finished off the rest of the mead but there was no celebration. Vanelia never left the tent, at least not that Clerin saw. Chiavel brought her food but said that she would not eat. Clerin was not even sure of how Vanelia relieved herself, probably a chamber pot. She went to bed early and peacefully awoke to a quiet morning. She had not wanted to participate in the hushed nighttime conversations.

As Clerin wandered towards the breakfast fire, Trela approached her. "When do you think you will be heading home?" She had planted herself directly in front of Clerin, forcing Clerin to stop or circumvent around her.

"No good morning?" Clerin stopped and crossed her arms.

"Of course, please forgive me. Good morning." Trela truly sounded chipper. It made her wonder if Trela's apparent moods were genuine or not.

"Good morning." Clerin did not uncross her arms.

"I trust you slept well last night?" Trela smiled at Clerin. As Clerin nodded, she continued, "Torpalin actually cooked this morning. Not that I ever would have guessed, but he is fairly adroit with eggs. He can leave the yoke soft but cooked, if that is how you like it." That was one reason, out of many, why Clerin was grateful that Vanelia had caught up with them. It had been quite a long time since she had tasted an egg.

"I am unable to leave for home. My quest has been broadened to visiting the Pyran and Gaen Temples." Clerin was unsure of how long Trela would be able to draw the small talk out, but she had already gotten tired of it.

"And how do you think you will find the Pyran Temple?" Trela was grinning broadly now.

"I had planned on asking you." Clerin was unsure of why, but Trela's happiness was slightly grating. She wished she had let Trela stay abrupt.

"Excellent, that will make convincing Feyazki easier." Trela spoke so softly that Clerin was unsure of what she heard. "Excellent, you are a great boon to the team. I look forward to traveling with you. Rest assured, I do know where the Pyran Temple is located." Trela seemed to speak from her diaphragm this time.

"Well, you certainly led me to this temple." Clerin finally uncrossed her arms.

"Yes. I certainly did that. Please excuse me, I must speak with Gyllhelon before entreating Feyazki. You will find that most of the other Luftens have agreed to accompany us. If you could put in a good word to Croy, I would appreciate it. He seems to respect you. And, really, you have got to try Torpalin's eggs." Trela bowed deeply to Clerin and then left. Clerin stood there for a moment, not truly understanding their conversation. Then the smell of cooking breakfast reached her and she decided it did not really matter. If she was forced to find the Pyran Temple anyway, there was no other group of derlians that she would want gathered around her than these.

Chapter 15

Vrric had agreed to help Sempere bring the royal branch back to Ariellyna and return with as many provisions as he could carry. He was unsure as to exactly how he had been talked into even entering the Pyran realm, let alone flying equipment and food back to them. He was beginning to think that Trela could sell dirt to a Gaen. He tried to remember what she had said to convince him but could not think of a single detail. He was approximately halfway back from Ariellyna and had stopped to rest. It had taken him three days to get this far. Unfortunately, he had assumed he could fly more stock than was really feasible, and it was cutting down his daily distance capacity. He lay down in the shade of a large, bushy elder tree and contemplated the leaves and tiny white flowers above him. Soon it would be noon and he would have to try to sense Croy's beacon. Vrric found that it was much easier to sense the direction it was coming from if he was not actively doing anything. Therefore he had taken to resting each day slightly before noon so that he would be rested up to fly once he was able to sense it. After his mid-morning and mid-afternoon rests, he had to gauge his flight direction as best he could. Vrric had not specifically mentioned the other rests to Croy during their brief exchanges, but he figured that they knew he was not flying continuously throughout the day. He had almost slipped into a nap when he heard the first tentative wisps of Croy's telepathy, his *whisper.*

"Feyazki... Feyazki... Feyazki..." It was so quiet as to be almost subliminal. Vrric waited in repose for a couple of moments before responding. It slowly grew more insistent.

"Eqefintotarc!" Vrric spoke quietly to himself and envisioned Croy sitting with his eyes closed. Since Vrric was responding to Croy, he could use Arc. Croy himself was using Sfe and just broadcasting the name Feyazki to everything in a quickly fading radius. The sense of direction was imparted by how the radius passed through Vrric. With the general direction and the knowledge of Croy—the magical essence of Croy—Vrric was able to focus his telepathy straight to him. Though he did not need to envision what Croy was doing, like sitting with his eyes closed, Vrric felt that it helped him focus the spell. He would have to remember to ask Croy what position he was usually in while he broadcasted his beacon. In truth, he felt sure enough of the general direction and was probably within a close enough range that he most likely did not need Croy's beacon to instigate communication, but it could not hurt and he had thought it would be a good exercise for Croy. Before he had left to re-equip the party, they had practiced the telepathy at close range several times, and Vrric felt that he knew Croy's magical *signature* enough to get a lock on him at this distance, especially with Croy's open willingness and attention. However, he did have to use a much larger power syllable for the spell than he would have liked since Croy's direct communication to Vrric "piggy-backed" on his spell, not on Croy's own broadcast that he had just previously cast. Though there was little likelihood of eavesdropping, they did not want to take too many chances. "Good day, Croy. I trust you are well."

"Yes… and you?" Croy's voice sounded clear and strong.

"Fine." The only problem with helping Croy exercise was the small talk. Vrric hated small talk, especially when it drained his flight energy. He etched a small arrow in the ground so that he would not forget the nuance of direction that he had picked up.

"Everyone wants to know how far out you are." The question was asked tentatively. Even though it was worded as a statement.

"Maybe tomorrow. I was too ambitious in deciding what to bring." Vrric wasn't quite sure, but he knew he was getting close.

"That is excellent news. Everyone is eagerly anticipating your return." Vrric thought that meant, "Everyone is ready to leave and are being held up by you," but he kept his thoughts to himself. He apparently waited too long in silence because Croy piped back up. "We all really appreciate your efforts in this. Don't… do not feel rushed. Especially because of anything I say."

"No problem, Croy, don't worry." Vrric felt himself sigh and hoped that was not translated through the *whisper*.

"Travel safe." Croy's voice sounded a little farther away. Vrric was unsure if it was the spell fading that quickly or if Croy was speaking to others while he was communicating with Vrric.

"Thanks. Talk to you tomorrow, Croy." Vrric ended the communication. He lay there for quite a while, dozing slightly, before he gathered up enough strength to restart his journey.

It took another day, but Vrric finally found the river and soon thereafter spied the tents in the distance. He unconsciously sped up like a horse heading towards a barn. It was early afternoon when he finally touched down. Everyone gathered around him and greeted him enthusiastically. They were all in good moods. They had accomplished great things together. They had overcome adversity together. They were in between missions and fully provisioned. The feeling was fantastic and, best of all, utterly communal. They stayed put one more full day to let Vrric bask in the feeling with them.

The day was greeted by a boisterous Trela. She (and Knill) had made a large breakfast early in the morning and woke the camp by banging pots together. Vrric forgave her the rude awakening after his belly was full. They passed around a giant jug of mead. It was too early in the morning, but Vrric drank at first to be social. He ended up drinking more heartily than he had anticipated. He was ready to just relax the day away, but Trela had other plans.

They had foot races. Vrric begged out of participating and got to watch that one. He was amazed to see Gyllhelon's long stride outpace all of the others. They had an axe throwing competition which Torpalin won, of course. Though Malghain came in a closer-than-expected second. They had poetry recitals and juggling. They had long jump competitions and push-up competitions. They tested every aspect of strength, speed, and agility. They tested each other in archery, in which Escha narrowly bested Clerin. Trela even showed off her knife-throwing skills by knocking various objects out of Knill's hands. The mead was kept low and steady while the competition was kept fierce but friendly. It was a day that Vrric felt good about everyone. Each of them. Later, when one of them would say something stupid or do something mean, Vrric would think of them on this day, and he would forgive whatever menial annoyance they had caused him. He truly felt closer to all of them after the sun disappeared.

The next morning, however, was completely different. Trela still made breakfast and woke everyone by banging pots together, but that was where the similarities ended. Vrric was not feeling well when he woke up and was not feeling much better by the time he was swaying on top of a horse's back. The day dragged long.

The next eight days also dragged long. Spirits were still up and everyone was getting along, but the monotony of horseback eventually drilled into Vrric's skull. He spent his nights trying to figure out ways to fly ahead of the pack. Maybe a scouting mission? But what would he really be scouting for? They had no agenda that he could figure out. As far as he could tell they were just traveling towards the Dekhan Plateau. Towards Agoge and Qizern. He had no idea of what the plan was when they got there. Could Trela really just walk up to Qizern and challenge him to some duel? Unfortunately, she was very touchy if asked about her plans. Vrric gave up after their first evening around the campfire. Clerin, however, seemed to enjoy being told to mind her own business.

The traveling was easy for the first three days as they followed the river, but then the relative forest gave way to scrubland rather quickly. It did stay scrubland, though. No matter how far they delved into the Pyran interior, they never found the shifting sand dunes that covered the central Northern Desert. It was dry and hot and parched and rocky, but at least there were no dunes. Rabbitbrush and juniper sadly dotted the landscape, while the mustards would dry up and roll around in the constant wind. It was bleak and desolate, but at least there were no dunes.

It was the end of the eighth day, just when dusk was turning from blue to black, that they noticed the firelights in the distance. Escha was first to spot them, but they were eventually noticeable to the entire party. They were certainly far off into the distance. Vrric was not quite sure if they could even reach them in a full day's ride. But Trela was unnerved enough that they lit no fires that evening, eating only salted meats and stale, unleavened bread. She did allow, for the first time in eight long days, one bottle of Luften whiskey to be passed out amongst the group. It wasn't quite enough to do the trick, but it mellowed them all and made sleeping next to an unknown group of fires more palatable.

Dawn seemed to arrive early and Vrric had difficulties getting out of his sleeping bag, let alone his tent. By the time he joined the group, breakfast had already started cooking. The fire was placed behind a boulder and was merely coals. There was not even a wisp of smoke rising from it. Trela herself served Vrric. She let him finish his food at his own pace before walking over to talk with him. She handed his dirty plate over to Knill without looking at him and smiled widely at Vrric.

"I believe I know the warpack on the other side of the valley. I was able to scan a couple of the standards, and even though I was unable to find the leader's flag, I think I know who it is." She was sitting in front of him with her knees almost touching his. But not quite.

"Warpack?" Vrric was vaguely familiar with the term, but was not quite sure what she was getting at.

"Yes. Knill and I traveled with Iventorn's warpack for some time. It was that pack that we left when we entered the desert to find the well. I think they are waiting for me." She leaned forward slightly.

"You mean… waiting to kill you and take your body back to Qizern?" Vrric began to get a sinking feeling in his gut.

"Maybe. But maybe they are waiting because they realize that I am the Kriishan. Maybe they are waiting to join up against Qizern's oppressive rule and to become a force of history." She touched his knee lightly.

"Maybe they are not waiting for anything. Maybe they are just camping." Vrric worried about Trela sometimes. She always assumed that everything that happened was part of a grand scheme of destiny. He was not positive that she wasn't correct but had not been convinced that she was right either.

"And maybe they are from a different warpack entirely. We will not be sure until we parley with them." She patted herself on the knee. "I will need you to fly the both of us and… Clerin… and… Malghain over to them after Clerin has finished eating."

"What? Shouldn't we all ride over to them? There is safety in numbers, you know." Vrric felt that he could escape if pressed, but he was worried that he would have to abandon the others if it came to that.

"Not against a warpack of that magnitude. If they decide to kill us, it will not matter how many we bring to the slaughter. No. We cannot afford the time. Nor can we afford the element of surprise. If we fly over to them, with a Fluen and a Luften mage and a mean-looking foreign warrior, it will be a much more impressive spectacle than a meandering dust trail slowly heading towards them. A dust trail that would last all day long. We must have the upper hand during the parley. We must look exotic and powerful. This meeting is very important to me, Feyazki. I need a warpack to march upon Agoge." There *was* a desperate need on her eyes. And truly, he had known that she would ask him to do foolhardy things on this journey. His worry was not that it was foolhardy. His worry was that it was stupid. Unfortunately, there was only one answer that he could really give her.

"So it begins. Let me make sure I have everything I need." He smiled as he nodded to her.

"Of course. Make haste, however. Remember, there is no need to take your tent down or to pack up. We will be returning here after our parley. And Feyazki… Thank you." Trela nodded back to him before she turned away.

Vrric sat in his tent for several moments, savoring the stillness. The only thing he truly needed to grab from the tent was a small dagger that he hid in his boot. And he was not sure that he actually needed that. The dagger would not be very useful if it came down to combat, much less useful than his magic. More than anything he had wanted to meditate. Since he did not have enough time, he made do with breathing in the close warm air trapped in the tent. It felt good to be surrounded by the claustrophobic canvas before he had to fly over a possibly hostile army. He waited for several more peaceful moments before exiting.

Malghain, Knill, and Trela were conversing next to the hidden firepit as Vrric walked up. He felt good that they were still waiting on Clerin, or at least that they were not waiting for him. He looked around absently for Croy.

"Greetings, Feyazki. I trust you are well rested." Knill held his hand out for Vrric to shake. Vrric shook his hand heartily. Though they had never spoken much, Vrric found himself liking Knill. He always seemed earnest and nice. "We would not want you getting tired on your trip over the warpack, heh." Vrric realized that Knill was feeling him out.

"I am feeling tip-top, not to worry, Knill. Though I was wondering if I could ask Croy a favor before we left. I was hoping to have a small shield cast under us before we flew and did not want to use up any unnecessary energy." Vrric cocked a questioning eyebrow at Knill. It seemed to him that Knill was the type of derlian who was happiest when they had an errand of some sort. It would also give him another chance to gauge Croy's abilities.

"Of course. That is an excellent idea. Give me just a moment." Knill was gone in a blink.

"That is a good idea. Do you feel that Croy is up to the task?" Vrric had expected the question to come from Trela, but it was Malghain who spoke up.

"We should not be in the air for too long, and he will have the rest of the day to recover. So, yes, I feel he will be able to accomplish what we need. If we face an all-out assault on us then it will be a different story. In that case, however, I think a retreat would be more in order than testing his protective capabilities." Vrric smirked, and Malghain laughed.

"I prefer the term 'retrograde offensive' to retreat." Trela chimed in. Though she sounded jovial, there was something hard and steely in her gaze. Like she was angry that he would even mention the word "retreat." It unnerved Vrric momentarily. Luckily, Clerin arrived just then.

"Looks like we are all here, though I am still not sure why I am necessary." Clerin smile warmly at Vrric, but her eyes grew tighter as she turned to Trela at the end of her sentence.

"As I explained earlier, you are my Fluen princess." Trela stayed jovial.

"My family is barely considered part of royalty, I am certainly not..." Clerin was unable to finish her thought.

"It is a figure of speech, my dear. They will not know the difference. The reason I have asked you to accompany us is that none of those Pyran warriors over there have ever set eyes on a Fluen before. Your mere presence will unnerve them and put them off guard. Not to mention what your beauty will do to them. I will need every advantage that I can get during this upcoming meeting and first impressions are essential. Why is Malghain coming? Just look at him." Trela turned towards Malghain. "Look menacing, Malghain."

Vrric was not really sure how he accomplished it, but suddenly Malghain looked menacing. He did not have a scowl, per se, but his eyebrows arched and furrowed nicely. His lips were tight and pulled slightly upwards into a cruel, but subtle, sneer. His feet were shoulder width apart with his left foot slightly forward. His hands, though still at his sides, were stiff with energy and tension, appearing almost claw-like. The tension translated into a slight bend at his elbows. And while his torso seemed slightly lower to the ground, he was certainly not stooping. Each item, taken separately, would have seemed comical. But, somehow, all put together on Malghain's form, they cumulated into a very menacing image.

"Is that not fantastic? Malghain knows how to follow orders. Both of you could learn from him." Here Trela looked back and forth between Clerin and Vrric.

"But why not Torpalin? Surely he could look as menacing as Malghain." Clerin stood with her back straight and her arms across her chest. "No offense, Malghain."

"None taken." He was instantly back to his relaxed and casual demeanor.

"Torpalin does not have the mental acumen to be truly menacing. I do not need truly murderous capability, which Torpalin does have, and I admire him greatly for it. And besides, there are many Pyrans who have the imposing structure of Torpalin. Cavish comes to mind... No, what I need today is truly torturous intent. I am not completely positive that Malghain is sick enough to have that in his heart, but he can certainly appear to be that sick, which is all I need." Trela looked from Clerin to Malghain. "No offense, Malghain."

"None taken." He looked amused.

Trela lifted her right index finger and opened her mouth wide and... stopped. Her eyes glanced between Clerin and Vrric for a split second before she closed her mouth and slowly lowered her hand. She took a deep breath and put on a large, seemingly sincere, smile.

"I would like to take this moment to express my true appreciation and gratitude for all of you assisting me today. This may be one of my most important parleys in my life and will certainly be the most important one to date. Today I must convince whoever is leading that warpack to give their power over to me. I must convince that leader to step down... to take commands from me... and to tell all of their followers to do the same. I am going into this very delicate and, to be honest, scary situation blind. I do not know who leads that warpack. I do not know what their proclivities and desires are. I do not know what their worries or fears are. I have no intelligence on the enemy. In short, I have no leverage." Trela looked somberly at each of them. "Scratch that. *You* are my only leverage. I have chosen each of you to accompany me today for specific, individual reasons. Please trust in my decision and play your part. I will be eternally grateful to each of you if we are successful."

The silence began to stretch. All Vrric could think about was what would happen if they were not successful. The horrible unbidden image that crossed into his mind was of him escaping through his magic, and their death screams and accusations following him hauntingly. Luckily Clerin spoke up.

"You have my full support. My only concern was that my support would not amount to much." Clerin reached out and took

Trela's hands in her own. Something shimmered in Trela's eyes, but she was smiling widely.

As they were all professing their loyalty to Trela, Knill finally returned with Croy. They all stood there nodding for a brief moment before Croy took Vrric aside. They did not walk far, but far enough not to be easily overheard.

"You asked for my assistance?" Croy glanced up and then back down.

"Yes. I want you to cast a shield underneath us before we fly over the warpack. Just in case." Vrric touched Croy's shoulder so that he would look at him. "I would cast it myself, but I am trying to save my strength just in case something happens over there. I need your help, Croy."

"Well, I have never cast a shield spell before, you know. Not really." He smiled weakly.

"Do not worry. I have faith that your spell will work fine. We will only need it to last a little while." Vrric was a little worried that Croy's lack of confidence was going to affect his casting ability. "In fact, I can see if you can come along with us, if you like. It would be great to have another mage with us."

"No, do not worry about that. I already offered to come along but Trela was adamant that she only wanted 'ones.' " Croy was looking down at his feet as he spoke.

"Ones?" Vrric did not understand what Croy meant.

"Yes… One warrior, one mage, and one diplomat. And herself, of course. I told her that she should have one of each race and she agreed, but said that she did not have access to a good Gaen warrior." Croy glanced up at Vrric. "Knill was livid, let me assure you. He really wanted to accompany her today." Vrric wondered what that would look like. He could not recall ever seeing Knill even remotely angry before. They both stood in silence for a moment.

"Do you think you could cast a Nar spell? We would want effectiveness more than duration. Do you know how to tilt the power pillar?" Vrric decided to plunge ahead.

"Uhm… yes and no." Croy chuckled quietly. "I will certainly try the Nar level, but I have never tilted a pillar. To be honest, I did not even know you could. I thought effectiveness and duration were intertwined."

"Well they are, but you can make a weak Nar spell last a long time or an extra strong one last momentarily. It is as if you have two cups with one amount of liquid to share between the two. Tilting just pours more water in one of them, leaving the other more shallow. No matter. Just cast it normally, then." Vrric was already regretting bringing up something complicated.

"What... what element should I use?" Croy rubbed his hands together slowly.

"I would use air, since we do not want it visible or bulky. I would also avoid Sfe and just use Clo. Maybe make a large rectangle on the ground. Then we can board it and I will take it with us as we fly." Vrric tried to sound light.

"Okay... So, Nar... tec... luf... clo." Croy counted on his fingers as he spoke the syllables aloud to himself. Vrric was starting to worry that the entire idea was a waste of time. "I think I have it." They walked back over to the others.

Everyone waited in silence for several moments watching Croy stare at the ground before Vrric cleared his throat loudly. Croy's head snapped up. "Just over here?" He pointed vaguely a couple of steps away from the group.

"Sure. That looks perfect." Vrric was beginning to wish he had never mentioned the idea.

"Narteclufclo!" A whuff of dust appeared over the location. Vrric felt a surge of magic when the spell was cast and it caught him off guard. He walked over to the invisible shield and stepped up on it.

"That is almost a hand high, Croy! That is fantastic! I almost wish we were going into battle with this." Vrric was stunned. He walked around it to find its edges, and it was certainly large enough for all four of them to stand comfortably. He not only felt better about asking Croy to do this for them, but he felt much better about Croy as well. The Gaen might actually make a decent mage one day. Especially if he could gain any confidence. Croy beamed with the praise and then staggered slightly and vomited. Knill was instantly at his side comforting him.

"Everyone up. We do not have a lot of time." Trela was shooing Malghain and Clerin up on to the shield. Once she was aboard as well, she stamped her feet approving on the invisible floor. "This is perfect, Croy. Every day you amaze me a little more." She nodded to Vrric that they were ready. "Farewell, Knill. We will be back before you realize we're gone."

"Do not anger Iventorn unnecessarily. Remember that Cavish, as nice as he seems, will attack you first when he is ordered." Knill raised his hand to shade his eyes from the morning sun. It made it appear like an uncoordinated salute.

"Lumkinderclo!" Vrric raised his voice above the others. He tilted the power pillar ever so slightly towards duration and made sure to grab the excellent shield within the confines of his flight spell. They began to rise slowly. The others sat down upon the invisible slab. He had grabbed them all within the spell so they would surely not fall off, but he assumed that they must feel more comfortable sitting while moving on an object. It's funny how they all would have been laying prone had he just been flying them through the air. They were all quiet for some time as Vrric gained in speed and altitude.

"What did he mean by 'Cavish will attack you first?' " Malghain asked Trela after they had reached a nice, consistent cruising speed.

"We had an argument last night. We both agreed that if a surprise attack were to happen during the parley, it would come from the bodyguard, not the leader. Our assumption was that this is Iventorn's warpack, and so Cavish would be the bodyguard. I thought he would attack you first. You know, bodyguard against bodyguard. Croy thought he would attack Feyazki first. To try to neutralize the magic threat as quickly as possible. Knill, however, was adamant that Cavish would attack me first. I tried to argue that Cavish and I had become friends during our time together and that would make him hesitant to attack me." Trela had turned herself on the shield to face Malghain.

"In my experience, whether or not someone likes you has little to do with hesitation in combat. Especially if the individual is a professional. Especially if they are under orders. Hmmm… Your Knill might be right. I will have to rethink my strategy." Malghain rubbed his chin.

"Rethink your strategy?" Clerin joined in the conversation.

"Yes. I would have originally agreed with Croy. The bodyguard will usually go for the mage first. Especially if it is a surprise attack. So I was prepared to protect Feyazki first." Malghain glanced up at Vrric. "But now that I think it over… You are going to try to impress upon them your destined right to lead the warpack, yes? The, ah… Kriishan."

"Of course. I need a warpack to march upon Agoge or else Qizern will not take me seriously enough to grant the duel." Trela glanced between Malghain and Clerin. "It is my destiny. I am the Kriishan."

"Of course, you are. Nobody is disputing that. We are all here because of that, yes?" It was Malghain's turn to glance around for support.

"Yes." Clerin and Vrric spoke at the same time. Whether or not they actually believed was beside the point. The reason they were all there was definitely to support Trela as she asserted her own belief.

"The issue is whether or not Iventorn believes it. Because if he does not believe, he will need you removed before you can speak to his warriors. And, therefore, he may have his bodyguard attack you before Feyazki. He may figure that all he has to do is neutralize you and the rest of us will collapse. Yes. Your Knill may just be correct." Malghain smiled at Trela.

"Stop calling him my Knill." Trela narrowed her eyes at Malghain.

A great cry rose up from beneath them. Vrric glanced down to see that the warpack had finally spotted them. No one had loosed an arrow yet, but their intensity was becoming palpable. A group was gathering underneath them and attempting to follow them. A separate group was trying to run before them, while a third group was coalescing near the large marquis tent on the far hill. The news seemed to be traveling fast, almost as if they had been expecting it. The little flying group was barely halfway to their destination and already it appeared that a good quarter of the army was mobilizing. It was disconcerting at the least, and if Vrric was honest with himself, becoming a little frightening.

"I almost wish they would shoot some arrows up here so that we could see how well Croy's shield works." Vrric laughed a little as he spoke.

"Do not tempt fate." Malghain turned swiftly towards him.

"I thought we had fate on our side." Clerin smiled back at Malghain.

"I am fate!" Trela spoke so forcefully that all the others fell silent. "But, no. There is no reason to flirt with disaster. Feyazki, maintain your altitude until we get to the large marquis tent. Only then should we lower ourselves into their range." It was quiet for some time before Clerin spoke back up.

"You need a standard. Some symbolic flag that will alert your allies, and your enemies, to who you are." She smiled softly to Trela.

"You are right, Clerin. That is the best idea I've heard yet today. I definitely need a standard." She clasped Clerin's shoulder comradely. They all fell back into brooding silence as they flew along. The warriors below them crowded the hillside like angry ants. Vrric wished he could tell their mood, but did not want to take his attention from flying them and their shield. So he dared not cast anything else and did what all the mundane had to do. He waited and hoped for the best.

Finally they arrived at the tent. Vrric held them hovering over it at a high enough distance that they could not be struck by arrows. Or, at least, that was the hope. No one below them tried, however. There was a low, unintelligible roar of shouting that drifted up to them. The hill was thick with Pyrans. Vrric looked at Trela, waiting for her decision. They had never discussed the problem of not being able to reach the ground. They had not planned for being mobbed long before they were able to parley with anyone. Vrric was getting nervous.

"Take us down. Slowly. If we are immediately attacked, then do your best to fly away. With all of us. If we are not attacked… I will dismount first. Let me speak for a moment before disembarking. If I get immediately attacked, then do your best to fly away. Without me. There is no way to fight a whole warpack." Trela looked only at Vrric.

"What do you think the odds are that they will attack?" Malghain spoke up from behind.

"I had originally thought only about twenty percent. But now… Maybe fifty-fifty?" She glanced back briefly.

"Wait. You thought there was a twenty percent chance that we would be massacred before even getting a chance to parley? You never mentioned that." Clerin's voice was loud and accusing.

"I was afraid you would not come if I explained all of my fears to you." Trela did not look at her.

"You got that right." Clerin did her best to bore holes in the back of Trela's head with her eyes.

Trela kept looking at Vrric. She took a deep breath in and let it out slowly. Then she nodded to him. She was ready. Vrric began their decent somewhat slowly, keeping a sharp eye for any arrows. Part of him wanted to stomp his foot to see if the shield was still holding up, but part of him would rather not know. He was not sure how fast he could fly them away, but every nerve ending was primed for flight. The adrenalin made him somewhat queasy. Still, no one attacked. The crowd dispersed beneath them, leaving a small circle within which to land. They were still yelling, but Vrric could not make any of it out. They got to approximately shoulder height from the ground when Trela raised her fist, palm facing towards Vrric. He stopped their decent. Vrric decided that the yelling was joyful, not angry. Or else they would have been shredded by now.

"Who leads this warpack?" Trela yelled into the crowd. All four of them were standing on the shield. She turned to them and pushed downwards with her palms flat at the ground. Instinctively the other three sat. Trela faced towards the marquis tent, her feet floating at face level for much of the crowd. She spread her legs in a wide stance and held her arms above her for a brief moment before sweeping them down. "Silence!" The crowd continued to make some noise, but the effect was astonishing nonetheless. "Who leads this warpack?"

"I did." A tall muscular Pyran stepped to the front. He had white hair and a wispy beard, but despite his obvious advanced age was still muscular enough to look dangerous. His blue eyes flashed back and forth amongst the four of them. He broke into a smile when they came back to Trela.

"Lishean!" Trela jumped down from the shield and immediately ran to the old Pyran. The crowd began yelling again. Vrric did not know what to do, but since Trela had dismounted and had not been attacked, he assumed they were being welcomed. He stood up, lowered them to the ground, and stepped off the shield. Clerin and Malghain stood up and stepped off as well. Vrric wondered if he was going to go deaf because of the thunderous crowd.

Soon the old Pyran was clasping Vrric's hand in a crushing vice grip. Vrric hated to think of what it would feel like if the old Pyran were not so jovial. He quickly moved on to Malghain and then Clerin. Vrric could not tell what was being said, but was soon being motioned to follow Trela. They walked in single file through the roaring gauntlet straight up to the large white marquis tent. The crowd parted before them nicely but closed back in behind them disconcertedly. There was no way to escape before being grabbed by hundreds of Pyrans. They truly were in the middle of an army.

As they entered the tent, the noise from the crowd died down somewhat. There was still some shouting, but it seemed more diffuse and farther away. More like individuals passing a message than an entire crowd speaking at once. Vrric sensed, however, that the Pyrans were still surrounding the tent. They had just grown quieter.

The air was much warmer in the tent. Vrric would have described it as "close." The tent floor was covered in rugs but was devoid of furnishings except a round table ringed with wooden chairs in its center. He had been expecting a bed off in a corner or something more domestic, but the tent was obviously only used for meetings.

Lishean smiled at them all and motioned to the chairs. Trela sat almost directly opposite of Lishean. Vrric assumed she did that on purpose to keep the conversation open to all, but he was not sure if there were any Pyran customs that governed these things. The rest attempted to fill the circle, though it was a little unbalanced. Vrric had expected to parley with more than one representative. There was not even a bodyguard in the tent. Lishean was either confident in Trela's motives or else he was supremely confident in his own abilities.

"Excuse the warriors, Trela. We have been waiting half a moon for you to arrive and many were beginning to lose hope. Tumu foretold of your arrival here, and even though he was incorrect about the timing, it is astonishing that he got the right location. I must admit that I was beginning to lose hope as well. Not in your return to the Pyran realm, of course, but that Tumu was mistaken as to where and when your return would occur. I will have to congratulate him." Lishean smiled a little to himself.

"You have all been waiting here for my arrival?" Trela looked a little astonished.

"Of course! Tumu has been your loudest trumpet. Iventorn attempted to make it appear that you and that little Gaen had stolen off into the night like ashamed thieves. It was Tumu who spoke of your need to commune with vast magics in the desert. He explained that when you returned you would be ready to take up your proper title." Lishean had been leaning forward to speak more intimately with Trela. He leaned back in his chair as he continued.

"Iventorn was livid. In Iventorn's warpack there can be no leader but him. He had spent his entire career building up that warpack. There is a dangerous fire that burns in Iventorn. Eventually, he even tried to have my Tumu killed. Luckily for me, he thought it was too politically dangerous to do the deed himself. Or more accurately, to have Cavish do it for him. No, he chose someone young and inexperienced to do the job. I was returning to my tent from..." Lishean paused for a brief moment and spread his hands before him on the table. "Well, when I returned, I saw this Pyran skulking outside of my tent. He took so long building up his courage for the murder that I was able get behind him and place a blade between his ribs before he touched the tent's canvas. He died so quietly that Tumu's sleep was not even disturbed. Of course, Iventorn banished us the next day. He could not have us officially accusing him of anything. To his shock and dismay, however, almost a third of his warpack left with us. I am not sure why, and who can really divine what goes on in that Pyran's mind, but he did not attack us. He may have thought the battle would be too costly. We were allowed to leave, though, and for that I will always be a little grateful. We wandered for some time, picking up stragglers from other warpacks, until Tumu had his vision." Lishean leaned towards Trela again. "You can tell me something truthfully, yes?"

"Of course, Lishean. Speak freely." Trela leaned forward a little as well.

"You are the Kriishan, aren't you? I mean, this is not some wish for power or some crazy quest for vendetta against Qizern, right?" Lishean did not blink. Neither did Trela.

"As surely as I breathe before you, I have always known in my heart that I am the Kriishan. I know that this is my destiny. But do not just take my word for it. Why would Qizern raze an entire frontier village if he were not afraid of who was born there? Why would Synde throw away his career and... give his life... if he did not believe? All of these derlians around me, from every other realm, believe as well. Most importantly, however, is Tumu. You know Tumu. You know his powers. How could he foresee our arrival here? Right here!" Trela tapped her forefinger on the table for emphasis. She had looked a little choked up when she spoke of Synde, but her eyes were bright and clear as she spoke to Lishean. "This is not just some crazy vendetta. This is my destiny. I have no other path I can walk. I have no other place to go. I need this warpack, Lishean. And from what you have been telling me, they also believe."

"If I let you leave this tent and speak to the warriors out there… the die will have been cast, you understand? There will be no turning back. Either you die at the end of this, or you kill Qizern. There is no other option for you. I take my life very seriously. I take those warriors' lives outside of this tent very seriously. I will not risk all those lives if I do not think you understand the gravitas of the situation. You have convinced me of your own beliefs. My worry now is that you feel you cannot lose. You keep saying this is your destiny. That may be, but if you make foolish choices with those warriors out there… well, you will have killed a lot of young potential. Needlessly. There will be an incredible amount of bloodshed because of you claiming to be the Kriishan." Here Lishean held up his hand to stop Trela from interrupting him. "Maybe bloodshed is what destiny wants. I certainly lay no claim to know what destiny wants. That is *your* claim. You claim to be so certain that destiny wants you to kill Qizern that you will sacrifice hundreds… No, not hundreds. You are willing to sacrifice thousands of lives just to get the chance to kill one Pyran. These are not your lives to give, you understand. Qizern is an obnoxious ruler, but is he really that bad? Is he so bad that you will take the blood of thousands onto your hands? Are you prepared to look at a battlefield after the fighting is over and see the field of bodies that your destiny has wrought? You must choose carefully, and you must choose now. Once you leave this tent, the blood will be inevitable. Rivers of it, Trela. Parthia was nothing compared to what Qizern will throw at you. I have met him. He has no compunction about destroying others' lives, none whatsoever. Does your destiny give you the stomach to finish the job that you will start once you leave this tent? I want you to think beyond what you know as your destiny. I want you to think about what this truly means. You are not just killing one evil Pyran, you are killing thousands of innocents as well. That is, if you can even kill Qizern, or if we ever even get to Agoge. He is an amazing warrior, you should know. He started as a gladiator before winning his freedom. He went straight from there into a warpack and worked his way up through the ranks. He may be a horrible King, but he is a prodigious killer. This…" Lishean spread his hands over the table in front of him vaguely. "…is going to be terribly difficult. I do not wish to scare you, or to deter you, or to bore you with my speech. I merely want you to comprehend the enormity of what you and hundreds, and eventually thousands, of your followers are about to embark upon."

As soon as Lishean had finished speaking, Trela opened her mouth to voice her answer, but Lishean raised his hand to silence her again. "No. Think about it. I mean no disrespect, Kriishan. But I am an old warrior and have seen countless horrors and sorrows. Please… indulge me. Placate me. Think about it. As for the rest of us… who would like a drink?" Lishean stood up and wandered to a corner of the tent. Vrric had not noticed the couple of casks tucked away when they had first come in, but he was certainly glad for their existence now.

Trela, for her part, stood and carried her chair over to a corner of the tent. Like a scolded child she sat facing away from the others. Vrric wondered briefly if Lishean had belabored the point so much that he had offended her. He came to think that the more noble of the options was taken, that she had removed herself only so that they could speak and share the grog more freely.

"So who is this Tumu?" Clerin asked as a tankard of grog was passed to her.

"He is my ghulzan seer. He is the most amazing seer I have ever witnessed. In fact, if it were not for Tumu being so adamant about Trela being the Kriishan, we would not even be here. It is only my trust in Tumu that has brought me to this precarious position." Lishean laughed and passed another tankard over to Vrric. "How came a Fluen to follow a Pyran?"

"Well… let us just say that our quests are currently overlapping." Clerin drank heavily from the tankard. Vrric had not realized that her mission was secret until that moment. He made a mental note to lock it away.

"Your statement provides more questions than it answers, but I will not pry. Today you are amongst friends. I hope you are able to relax. I have just never seen a Fluen before. You do not look that different from a Luften, if you ask me." Lishean looked slightly uncomfortable. Embarrassed maybe? "You are a mercenary are you not? Trela has promised you riches, correct?" He turned his attention to Malghain.

"Yes. She promised me all the gold I could eat!" They all burst into raucous laughter. The tankards were moving in opposite directions, and somehow Vrric ended up with both. He took a mighty pull from one and passed it to Clerin and held on to the other for a moment. He watched her drink, and there was a small line of dark amber that had escaped her lips and trickled down her neck.

"But you. You are not enticed by riches, are you?" Lishean turned towards Vrric. "How did Trela convince you to leave your home realm and fight in the Pyrans'? You cannot really be that interested in Pyran politics, can you?"

Vrric glanced over at Lishean. "To be honest, I am not sure why I am here. Everything has happened so quickly." Lishean eyeballed him for a moment before glancing back at Clerin.

"No matter what you do or where you are, you should know what your goals are." Lishean held his hand out waiting for the tankard of grog from Vrric.

"My goal is to gain in strength and power each day. The only way to do that is to exercise, correct? So I suppose I am here to test myself." Vrric took his drink and passed it over.

"You seem like a nice derlian… but there is something dangerous about you. I can't put my finger on it, but…" Lishean trailed off as he took a swig of his own. Vrric thought it was supposed to be a compliment, coming from someone as rough and weathered as Lishean, but he was not quite sure.

"He single-handedly killed a Tlana." Malghain spoke up suddenly. "Or at least survived its attack. We never did find a body. If there is something more dangerous than that, I have never heard about it."

"Tlana don't really exist, do they?" Lishean looked over at Malghain. For his part, Malghain stared his dead serious eyes back at Lishean and barely nodded.

"Well, then… Here is to having you on our side." Lishean raised his tankard in a rough salute and said, "Here, here!"

Malghain raised his own tankard and said, "Here, here!"

Vrric glanced over to Clerin. She was wiping the grog from her neck with delicate fingers. "Here, here," she spoke quietly to him.

"I believe we have stalled enough. Trela, come have a toast and tell us your decision." Lishean stood up from his chair and waved Trela over.

Trela stood and brought her chair back over. She stood behind it, rather than sit down on it. Though she took Lishean's offered tankard, she did not drink. Malghain passed his tankard over to Lishean. Everyone stared at Trela.

"There is nothing I can say. Of course, I do not want to cause carnage. I do not want one drop of innocent blood to spill. How could I say otherwise?" Trela was looking directly at Lishean. "But my hands are tied. I am the Kriishan and this is my destiny. War must be had and I must begin it. Believe me, Lishean, if I thought for one moment that I could stride over the Dekhan plateau, walk right into Agoge and battle Qizern alone, I would. I truly would. But that is not the Pyran way. He will not accept my challenge until my warpack is at his doorstep. Even then I fear that he will avoid it for as long as possible. I believe that he is such a coward that we must lay siege to Agoge and be on the verge conquering her before Qizern will grant my duel." Trela laid her tankard on the table and crossed her arms in front of her. "You speech did not deter me. It could not. I know my destiny as much as I know myself. All your speech did was cloud my conscience."

"Maybe for now, Trela. But you will see that my speech actually clears your conscience. Preparedness is always beneficial. That is why we have minds—to imagine the possibilities that we must prepare for." Lishean smiled at Trela and raised his tankard towards his lips. "To the Kriishan!" He took a mighty drink and passed the tankard on to Vrric.

"To the Kriishan!" Clerin picked up the tankard in front of Trela and took a drink.

"To the Kriishan!" Vrric spoke heartily and drank heartily as well. It was as if a dam broke. No, not that catastrophic. It was as if a clog in a pipe had been suddenly pushed forwards, allowing the water to freely flow again. The mood in the room, and in Vrric himself, was getting lighter.

"To the Kriishan!" Malghain toasted Trela as well.

Vrric held the tankard he had finished drinking from out to Trela. She paused a moment before picking it delicately from his hands. She stared at the tankard for some time in silence before taking a small swig.

"To the Kriishan!" Finally, a smile appeared on her lightly stained lips. She looked around the table briefly. "I should have brought Knill with us. He would have really enjoyed this." She took another swig and laughed out loud. "I thought there was a good chance that at least one of us was going to die today. You know, Lishean, I had convinced myself that this was Iventorn's warpack."

"Well, there you are mightily mistaken. It is your warpack. All you have to do is walk out of this tent and speak to the warriors who have waited for you here." Lishean grinned widely and took another swig of his own.

"Feyazki, I need you to raise me up and project my voice. I want this to be a day that each of those warriors out there remembers well into their old age." Trela handed her tankard to Clerin. Vrric refused Lishean's offer of one last gulp.

"Of course." Vrric was not exactly sure of what spell to cast to make her voice available to all, but deafening to none. His mind raced as he stood. *Fin or Sid? Luf or Tot?* It was times like these that he wished he had the time to sit back with his spellbook and really research the nuances between the syllables. Or even enough time to decide exactly what effects were most likely to best resolve the situation. Figuring out what to aim at was half the battle.

Trela opened the tent flaps with a flourish. The cry seemed slow coming up, but soon the crowd realized that she had emerged. Vrric was worried that a flight spell would require too much active concentration, so he decided upon a stairway and podium made of solid air.

"Lift me up, before they get more agitated." Trela's eyes flashed to Vrric from the crowd.

"Eqemorflufclo!" Vrric felt a little dizzy at the end of the spell. He doubted that he needed the time afforded to the power Eqe, but did not want to have to worry about Trela talking for longer than the spell might last. Better safe than sorry, he felt, even if he was only densifying air. He knew that he needed to save the majority of his strength for the communication spell.

"I'm not flying, Feyazki." Trela looked tense.

"Stairs. I've made stairs from the air, much like Croy's shield. Except, of course, these will not be able to protect you from anything, hah. I thought you might like the solid feel under your feet. Plus, the spell was less taxing..." Trela shook his hand to stop him from talking.

"This will be great. Thank you. Will you be able to amplify my voice?" She stared intently into his eyes.

"I will make sure that even Knill can hear." Vrric felt he was exaggerating a bit. Trela laughed in a way that hinted of disbelief.

"Don't deafen anyone." She tapped is cheek lightly. "How tall are the stairs?"

"About four luftens tall. A podium should stop you as well. There is a small platform at the top. Try not to pace too much." Luckily she laughed at that.

"Wait until I have reached the platform. I do not want them to hear me panting up the stairs." Trela nodded to Vrric, as if answering her own question. "Wish me luck." Her eyes glowed with an internal intensity that seemed unnatural. The dull, wild yellow irises seemed to burn. They seemed to be looking through Vrric, however, focused past him into the distance.

"I'll wish you better than luck," said Vrric, "I wish you destiny." Trela nodded again, turned, and began walking up the invisible stairs without a stumble. As she walked slowly up the stairs, she extended her foot forward so she could feel when the stair turned vertical. She walked stately that way, with her arms held straight down and her spine held straight up, flowing from step to step. The crowd roared in response to seeing her. When she got to the top she raised her hands dramatically.

"Surfintotsfe!" Vrric's scream was immediately lost in the noise of the crowd. He fell to his knees and dry-heaved. A part of him was amazed that no grog escaped him at that moment. The other part of him was grateful. All he had to do now was hold it together. Some fine tuning and minor tweaking, but once a spell like that was cast, the energy output to control its effects was akin to holding the reins of a horse headed back to its own barn. He sat back on his heels and watched Trela. He could see the side of her face and could make out her grin. He wondered what her eyes looked like as she stared at the multitudes below her.

Trela dropped her hands to her sides, making a sharp cracking noise. The entire hillside hushed immediately. Her head swiveled back and forth as she surveyed the crowd.

"Fellow Pyrans, thank you for gathering. I know that each of you have your own individual priorities. Loved ones far away awaiting their meager stipend from what you can spare each moon. You far away, fighting for income, spending your time out in the cold, sleeping on the hard ground. These are not favorable conditions. These are not stable conditions." Trela paused for a moment before continuing. She eyeballed the crowd, making sure they were all paying attention. "You need one large campaign. You need to be able to fight for something you believe in. You need to make the rest of your life's income in one fell swoop. You need to be part of a revolution.

I am that revolution. *Because I am the Kriishan.*" Trela's last sentence was a quiet whisper. Vrric was watching her as she was talking and did not think her mouth moved.

"But why is this so? Why do half your wages go to Agoge? Why does Qizern have such a huge palace, filled with every luxury our lands contain? How come you have no say in this?" Trela paused again, but this time for dramatic effect. "Qizern uses your hard work to increase his own wealth. He pits you against each other, using one warpack to threaten another if they do not follow his arbitrary rules. He wants you to be separate and small and suspicious of strangers. This is why he does not want you here, today. This is why he has forced me out of the Pyran realms. Twice! *Because I am the Kriishan.*" Vrric was positive that her lips did not move on that last sentence. "Qizern has been busy, however. All of his efforts since he has come to power, over thirty sun cycles ago, havebeen to increase the tributes flowing to Agoge. He has squeezed more from the farmers under threat of seizing their lands. He has squeezed more from the merchants under threat of seizing their wares. And he has squeezed more from you, the warriors, under threat of death. He uses war as a tool to divide and conquer. Not a real war. Not something that he would have to come down from his stone throne to squelch. No, he uses the constant skirmishes between rival warpacks to keep the populace in a state of fear. *Because he is an antoshan.*" Vrric suddenly realized that he could hear her thoughts. Which meant they *all* could hear her thoughts. He had cast the spell too deeply. He had been trying to place Trela's voice in all of their heads, in an attempt to keep the volume the same for each of them, but had somehow amplified more from her than just her speech.

"We need warriors in our society. They should be the most exalted. It should not be the only vocation, however. Warriors should not be used to cow the rest of the populace. We should be fighters, not herders! Our skills should be used to keep the peace, not for keeping the fear. Our skills should be used for order, not carefully constructed chaos. Are you not tired of peasants looking upon you with fear and loathing? Are you not tired of being reviled? *Answer me!*" Suddenly, the crowd began to shout in assent. At least it sounded as if they were agreeing with her to Vrric. Trela let them shout for a moment before raising her arms to quiet them again. "I am, too. We need to re-instill the nobility that rightfully belongs to warriors. We need to re-instill the honor that rightfully belongs to us.

But this will take courage, for there is only one way to restore these things. There is only one way to relieve the pressure and fear that Qizern has placed over all of us Pyrans. There is only one way to start over. And that is to put your trust in me. *Because I am the Kriishan.*" Trela paused again to look over the crowd. Vrric was not sure what she was looking for, but each face that he could see was turned upwards in rapt attention.

"Would you rather not see your monies go towards new roads? Would you rather not be paying for aqueducts and clean water? Don't you think your tributes should be used to pay for healers in every village rather than more gladiator fights in Agoge? That is what I believe. I believe that the reason tributes are collected is for the collective good. To achieve some sort of parity. To make our realm a little more equal. To allow those not living on the Dekhan plateau to enjoy some of the same opportunities that those nearest the King enjoy. The village that I grew up in did not even have cinnamon or paprika or sesame seeds. The only spices we could get delivered were salt and maybe a little pepper. Our only healer was an herbalist. We had to protect our own livestock from wolves. And yet… yet, half of our food was taken by Qizern's tribute collectors. How could the roads be good enough to remove our livelihoods, but not good enough to bring us the simple luxuries of life? That is unfair. That is cruel. There is much more to the Pyran realm than the Dekhan plateau and Agoge. If we are all one community that must pay tributes to one cause, that cause should benefit the entire community! That is what I believe. *Because I am the Kriishan.*" The crowd yelled at all of her questions, but Vrric found it impossible to tell what they were yelling.

"Don't you think that every Pyran should be held accountable for the same laws? Don't you think that every Pyran should have the same opportunities? I know what you believe in and what you believe in is right! Qizern is not concerned in what you believe in. He is not interested in the welfare of your loved ones. He is not even worried about whether you live or die. He thinks of you as his ghulzans! Are you a ghulzan?" The crowd roared. "We must remove Qizern from power, for he will not listen to our concerns. *Because he is an antoshan.* The march begins tomorrow. Tomorrow we rise at dawn. Tomorrow we turn towards Agoge. Tomorrow we shall start the wave that will come crashing down upon Qizern and the entire Dekhan plateau. Tomorrow we begin our journey. But today… and tonight... we celebrate!" The crowd roared again and kept roaring. Trela stood over them, with arms raised as if she had won a race, and they just screamed. The Pyrans pounded sword against shield to create a rolling thunder. They stomped their feet and thrust their spear butts against the ground. They beat their chests and howled. They were deafening with their wildness. And oh so softly, Vrric could hear, "*I love you. I love you all.*" Trela just stood there, atop Vrric's staircase made of air, and basked in their madness. Vrric had the sudden feeling that Lishean was correct. There would be bloody carnage.

Even though the time seemed to pass in slow motion, Vrric knew that Trela stood there for a long time. The warpack surrounding her never seemed to tire or fatigue. Vrric had closed his eyes after a while, which somehow helped him shut out some of the noise. "*I love you. I love you all,*" rang back and forth through the crowd.

He felt a hand on his. Trela was pulling him upwards, to his feet. Vrric ceased the spells rather than letting them dissipate on their own. He certainly did not want any other Pyrans climbing around on invisible stairs. Quickly, their little group walked back into the tent they had emerged from so recently. The yelling continued unabatedly.

Trela took Vrric aside. "I do not want you flying for a while. You should communicate with Croy and let the others know to meet us here."

Vrric nodded. He knew that it would take much of the day for them to get here, but did not want to fly horses back and forth either. He wandered away from the group and sat in a corner of the tent. There was certainly enough strength in him to cast one more tiny spell, but he was not feeling well. He sat there listening to the chaos outside the tent for some time, building his strength.

"Mekfintotarc!" Vrric hoped that it would be powerful enough to reach Croy, but he was wary of casting too powerful of a spell at this point. Besides, the communication link only had to stay open for a moment.

"Feyazki?" The voice of the *whisper* was faint, but sounded like Croy.

"Come meet us here. All is well. You will be received kindly." Vrric concentrated mightily.

"Thank goodness, we were all worried, Knill especially. We were going…" The voice faded out. Vrric's spell should have lasted a little longer, but once he realized that it must be Croy, he somewhat gave up on it. It had already been a long and strenuous day and it was barely noon. He was sure that Croy would not take offense.

Vrric waited in his corner for a little while longer before rejoining the group. The warriors outside had found drums and the chaotic yelling was beginning to take shape and form. Vrric had always been warned as a child as to how violent and primitive the Pyrans were, but there was something in the drumming that appealed to him. He had thought they were all herders and nomads. It was interesting to hear Trela speak of villages and palaces.

"What is this about broadcasting my thoughts?" Trela caught Vrric before he had the time to sit down.

"What?" Vrric had shuffled over to the table thinking only of how societies paint each other.

"I hear you placed the megaphone to my mind instead of just in front of my mouth." Trela's eyes flashed. Lishean handed Vrric a tankard, which he gratefully took.

"I was trying to regulate volume to each individual, so I magnified your voice more telepathically than just by placing a megaphone in front of your mouth." Vrric took a mighty swig.

"What if I had thought something horrible? What if I had even paused and tried to list out the different things to say? It could have been a disaster." Trela was still glaring at Vrric even while she took the tankard he extended.

"Then they would have known you as a false prophet." Malghain chimed in, smiling. "You know…" He snapped his fingers a couple of times while staring at the tent's ceiling. "An antoshan."

"The only reason I mentioned it, Trela, was in support of your claims. You spoke what you thought. Purely. To me, that signifies that you truly believe you are who you claim to be." Lishean was sitting across from Trela and was trying to catch her eye. Vrric was doing everything he could to ignore her stare. "In fact, the only non-spoken thoughts that we heard seemed to be unspoken to avoid hubris. You truly believe you are the Kriishan, don't you?"

"I already told you that, Lishean." Trela's temper was still high, but at least she had stopped trying to bore holes in Vrric's skull with her eyes.

"Yes, you spoke those words to me. And yes, I mostly believed them. You have very earnest and emotional eyes, Trela. However, I am an old pessimist. I have been told some outrageous lies by some very earnest and emotional Pyrans before. To me, being able to hear your thoughts solidified my belief in your belief. That was why I had mentioned it. To show you what a happy accident your Luften friend has given you. To be honest, I am not sure how many who heard your speech realized that those were thoughts. We were close enough to see your lips, but most of the warriors were not." Lishean matched her stare's intensity. "You should be thanking Feyazki, not berating him."

"You still cannot say that I am the Kriishan, can you? No matter that you know that the warriors out there believe or that I believe or even that Tumu believes. You, yourself, do not believe." Trela's stare did not diminish in intensity.

"Some derlians believe in destiny, Trela. I envy them that. Truly I do. I, however unfortunately, believe there is too much chaos in this world for any one invisible plan. To me there are thousands of invisible plans all vying for dominance. Is it not enough that I have assembled this warpack for you? Is it not enough that I have staked my own reputation on your claims? Not even just my reputation, but my own life? I believe that you believe. That is enough for me. Why is that not enough for you?" Lishean broke his gaze with Trela to take a small swig. For the first time today, Vrric thought that he looked old, truly old.

"You are correct as usual, Lishean. I apologize for my improprieties. Your efforts up to this point are greatly appreciated and I am sure your continued efforts will be equally as indispensable." Trela's eyes lost their icy grip and she smiled warmly at Lishean. "Now. Do you feel it would be proper to meet them all? I was thinking that it would be good for them if I met each one individually and learned their names and specialties."

"Learned? There are literally hundreds of pyrans gathered outside of this tent." Lishean looked at her askance.

"Well… heard, then. Do you think we should bring them into the tent one by one and I could hear their names and specialties? We could write down their name, specialty, and what warpack they originally came from. That way, it would be easier to split them into appropriate regiments. During which they could take their oath of obedience." To Vrric it sounded horrible, but Trela was smiling at the prospect.

"Yes, that would be good for the warriors to all meet you, but do you think you can keep it up? As I said, there are many…" Lishean was quickly interrupted by Trela.

"I insist, Lishean. I wish to meet those who have waited here so long for me. It is the least I can do." Trela was nodding to herself. Vrric was not sure if she was insisting for the warriors, or if she was insisting for herself. She had seemed oddly bothered that Lishean would not call her the Kriishan. To Vrric, it did not matter. One title was much like another. He wondered why Lishean would not just say it to her almost as much as he wondered why it bothered her so.

"I will procure some parchment and a quill." Lishean stood to leave.

"I'll come with you." Vrric stood with Lishean. He was not sure where he was going or what he would do, he only knew that he could not sit there while the endless Pyran parade shuffled past, swearing fealty to Trela. Though they had just re-entered the tent, he felt like he needed some air.

"Sure. Maybe I could introduce you to Tumu." Lishean patted his back warmly as they left the tent.

Vrric followed Lishean through the carousing crowd. Many of the warriors saluted or struck their chests with their fists as the two meandered through the camp. Lishean was obviously well known and respected throughout the warpack. He soon stopped in front of a small, unassuming tent.

"This is our logistics tent. I'll just pop in to get the parchment, then I can show you to my tent." Lishean smiled at Vrric.

"Actually, I think I will wander around the camp. It has already been a long morning and I would rather just…" Vrric was not really sure what he would rather just, but Lishean mercifully interjected.

"Of course, of course. Feel free to… to wander. You and Trela arrived from over there." Lishean pointed over Vrric's left shoulder. "If you are waiting for anyone in particular." Lishean winked at him and patted his shoulder before ducking into the small tent.

Not knowing which direction to head, he walked in the direction that Lishean had pointed. His head was still fuzzy from all of his earlier spellcasting, but that did not explain his confusion with Lishean. Vrric could not figure out what he had been talking about. Why would he wink? It just added to the fuzziness surrounding Vrric's mind.

Vrric wandered in more or less a straight line and eventually reached the edge of the encampment. There were still some Pyrans about, but the tents and cold campfire pits had finally ended. He found a large boulder near a tree and lay down on his back in the shade. The rock was hard, but refreshingly cool. It felt good to let all of his muscles relax. The air seemed less stuffy away from all of the others. He closed his eyes and just breathed. He had not meant to, but he quickly drifted into a dreamless sleep.

"Feyazki! There you are. Croy has been trying to find you." Vrric awoke with a start. The shade had moved away from him and he opened his eyes to the blinding sun. He sat up and shaded his eyes to look around for the voice. "We arrived almost an hour ago." It was Gyllhelon. Her dark hair blocked the sun as she stepped closer.

"I… I must have dozed off." Suddenly, everything ached. Not just his muscles from sleeping on a rock, but his bones as well. A headache began to throb in his temple. He must have moaned unconsciously.

"Oh. Are you all right?" Gyllhelon bent over him. "Nuliderto!" She placed a cool hand on his forehead, and Vrric immediately felt better.

"Thank you, I… I didn't know you knew magic." He hopped up in front of her.

"Any good warrior knows some simple healing spells. Don't worry, it will wear off soon and you will be feeling as bad as ever." Her laugh lilted through Vrric.

"Well, again, thank you. I feel much better now. I suppose that everyone is waiting for me." He laughed sheepishly.

"Trela is still meeting with the warriors, so Escha and I decided to help Croy find you. Haswyxe and Torpalin are setting up our camp next to the main Pyran camp, while Knill and Clerin stayed with Trela. I think that is everyone." Gyllhelon's eyes looked up in thought as she tapped her finger on her chin. "Oh, Malghain is helping Haswyxe and Torpalin, I think. At this point, the camp is probably finished. Do you want to head back there?"

"Sounds good. I can always contact Croy and Escha if they are not there. Do you know the way back? I sort of wandered out here." He laughed sheepishly again.

"Follow me." She turned and walked towards the main encampment. Vrric could not help watching her lithe form for a moment before walking after her.

They wove through a maze of tents which were mostly deserted. Though the closer they got to the center of the encampment, the more Pyrans they had to dodge. As the way became more crowded, Vrric struggled to keep up with Gyllhelon. She wove deftly between the Pyrans milling about. She eventually realized that he was falling behind and reached back. He grabbed her hand and she practically dragged him behind her. He felt like he was bumping into others along the way but somehow the crowd would part in front of her. They finally burst out of the crowd into their own small camp. Gyllhelon was laughing as she drug Vrric into the calm. Vrric could not help laughing with her.

As they stopped, he realized that Clerin was standing there with her arms crossed. "So that is where you have been. You should let Croy know you're okay. He's been worried." As she turned to leave, Vrric dropped Gyllhelon's hand. Vrric nodded to the Luften warriors that were gathered. Then he headed to a corner so that he could *whisper* to Croy.

The party lasted into the night. Trela allowed the entire pack to sleep in at their leisure. It was not until noon that the warpack finally mobilized. Trela joked later that evening that by the time the last of her warpack had started moving, the front of the warpack was beginning to stop to make camp. In truth, they did not make it incredibly far, but they all traveled until sundown. There were no parties the second night. Nor the third, or the fourth. Vrric figured that Trela was trying to iron out the logistical nightmare of just moving that many warriors about. Even though they had plenty of food, she had scouts hunting game in shifts. A smooth pattern was developing. Eventually, however, the inevitable happened. Trela's scouts caught site of another warpack. They were not sure who led the pack nor how large it was, but there were too many Pyrans and too much movement to be anything else. Trela only allowed covered cooking coals that night. No fires and no drinking. That evening she gathered the others for some consultation.

"I need to see it for myself." Trela had barely waited for them all to sit down before speaking.

"No, absolutely not. What if you were captured? It's too dangerous." Knill half stood up, looked around at the others nervously, and then sat back down.

"That is ridiculous. How do they know we are here?" Trela was pacing in front of the group.

"I think the more obvious question would be, how do they not know we are here? We have not been discrete, Trela. Tonight is the first night we have even attempted to hide our presence. We have been hunting, cooking, and clambering about for days. If our scouts found them, then how could their scouts not find us?" She stopped pacing when Lishean spoke up.

"We should send a more trusted scout, for a night mission. Purely for reconnaissance. I would bet that they are more prepared than you think. Maybe even dug in." Malghain interrupted Lishean but was looking at Trela as he spoke.

"Well, if they are prepared for us, it will be a dangerous mission. Have you found any favorites yet, Trela?" It was Lishean again. Truly, Trela had been trying hard to get to know her warpack. But there were many hundreds of them and it had only been a few days.

"I'll go." It was Escha who spoke up. She raised her hand to silence the room. "It should not be a Pyran. If a Pyran is found snooping around their encampment, it will be known that they are a scout. They will be captured and tortured before we know it, and the enemy will find out everything the scout knows. However, if a Luften is caught near their encampment, they will not immediately assume that they're an enemy scout. We are still close enough to the border that I could be wandering the forest for my own innocent reasons." It was quiet for a moment as everyone digested her suggestion.

"They might make the same assumption about you that they would make about a Pyran. You cannot be sure they won't torture you as well. I know how tough you are, but... Well, nobody withstands torture for long." Torpalin was looking at Escha as he spoke. Rather tenderly Vrric thought.

"I think Escha has a point here. Not only is she an incredible scout, whom I trust to be able to give me reliable intelligence, but I also think that her being a Luften lessens the chance of her being associated with my warpack." Trela was looking back and forth between Torpalin and Escha. "What, ah, what would make you comfortable about this, Torpalin? We could send Feyazki with Escha..."

Vrric was not sure that he wanted to go. Nor was he quite sure why Trela would be worried about what Torpalin thought. In his mind, Trela should be asking Escha what she was comfortable with.

"No, if I go, I go alone. It will look suspicious with the two of us. Besides, I do not want to responsible for anyone else's well being." Escha looked around the room quickly. Almost wildly. "I work alone." She had dropped her eyes and her voice at that last sentence.

"Does anyone have any objections? Torpalin?" Trela glanced from Escha to Torpalin.

"No objections. Just concerns." He smiled weakly.

"Good. Eshca, Lishean, Knill and Feyazki—I need to speak with you for a moment. The rest of you are dismissed. Thank you." Trela began pacing again as the others stood to leave. She waited until they had all left before she spoke again. "Is there anything I should know about? You know..." Her eyes darted back and forth from Escha to the door.

"No, don't worry about that." Escha blushed slightly as she waved her hand dismissively.

"Well, I am here if you ever need to talk. I don't mind and I don't pass judgment. My only concern is my subordinates' contentment and happiness. Happy warriors perform better, it is that simple. Speaking of which... Feyazki, have you figured anything out yet?" Trela suddenly turned to Vrric.

"Figured out what?" He asked her quizzically.

"That's what I thought. Don't worry about it, take your time. We're here for you." She nodded at him briefly. "Now, I've asked you to stay because I need you to help Escha."

"I told you I work alone." Escha spoke up defensively but stayed seated.

"Of course, I will not be sending him out with you. I was hoping for something more covert. We need to know if you run into trouble. We need to be able to check in on the encampment with you. We need... I need to know whose warpack that is, especially if they are lying in wait for us." Trela had hunkered down so that she was eye to eye with Escha. She turned towards Vrric. "Can you enchant something for Escha? I want to be able to see what she sees. I was thinking of a spyglass, or something."

"How long would it have to last?" Vrric wrinkled his brow attempting to think of what he could cast.

Trela stood back up. "Would you take any assistance getting to the encampment? Maybe a little flight, or a horse?" She was looking directly at Escha.

"No. It has to be on foot or else I might be noticed. I… I just don't trust anything else's stealth. Horses are notorious for making noise. If I flew, all they would have to do is look at the sky and watch the stars black out as I soared above them. While I might be able to ride a horse for an hour and then dismount, I might not. We do not know where their pickets are or where their scouts are. In fact, they could be watching our encampment right now." Escha looked to Lishean for moral support.

"She has a point," Lishean said dutifully.

"Then the enchantment will have to last a minimum of five hours. Do you think you can do that, Feyazki?" Trela looked pointedly at Vrric.

"I can try, but that is a tall order. One, I have never cast an enchantment like the one you are requesting, and two, I have never cast an enchantment that lasted that long. The biggest problem is that we will not know how long the enchantment lasts until it stops." Vrric answered as honestly as he could.

"You are the one who bested a Tlana, are you not?" Lishean hardened his eyes at Vrric.

"That was a completely different situation, but if it makes you feel any better, I did not know what I was doing then either." To Vrric's surprise, Lishean burst into laughter.

"No, no, not better. But I guess I believe the story a little more." His laughter quickly faded. "It just seems that if you can do something that amazing, you could enchant a simple spyglass. You are a great magician, are you not?"

"What weapon are you most comfortable with?" It was Vrric's turn to harden his eyes at Lishean.

"Knives. Then short swords, broad swords, and long swords. I can do all right with axes, the smaller the better, and I am okay with a mace or club. My worst weapon is probably the staff." Lishean was counting off his fingers as he made his list.

"What about archery? How good are you with a bow and arrow?" Vrric asked pointedly.

"Ah, well. I never took up the sport. A short bow won't pierce armor, and everyone knows that longbows are too unwieldy to be used in battle. One volley and then you're cut to ribbons." Lishean looked amongst the other warriors for support.

"What if I asked you to hit a condor with a long bow? While it was circling above you in the sky. What would you tell me?" Vrric leaned closer.

"I would tell you to leave the hunting to farmers." Lishean seemed to be in good humor.

"How can you not kill a large, slowly floating carrion eater? You are a great warrior, are you not?" Vrric smiled back at Lishean.

"So you are telling me to find another mage to accomplish what we need? One who is skilled in enchantments?" Lishean was smiling at Vrric.

"I am just telling you that enchantments are not my specialty. If there is a mage in the warpack who can cast this better than I, then certainly call them to the tent." Vrric was not sure how his little example had backfired.

"At the risk of changing the subject, how many mages are in the warpack?" It was Knill who spoke up. "I only recall a handful of warriors who declared themselves mages."

"There were not many and they are almost all exclusively war mages, meaning they can throw a little fire and probably know some simple healing spells. But certainly none of them said that they specialized in enchantments." Trela sighed. "This is all academic, really. You two can argue your different merits tomorrow. Right now, I need Feyazki to muster his strength and cast his longest-lasting enchantment ever."

"Of course. I'll get the spyglass." Lishean paused in front of Vrric before leaving the tent. "Truly, I meant no offense." He was still smiling. For the first time since Vrric had met Lishean, he felt completely annoyed by him. For his part, Lishean looked totally at ease and in a good mood, which only annoyed Vrric more. He breathed deeply and let it out slowly. There was no real reason for him to feel aggravated and he knew that he had to calm himself before casting the spell.

"I need to think about what I am going to cast." Vrric went over to the far corner and sat down to clear his head.

"You do that." Trela patted his shoulder as he walked by. "Now Escha, here is what I will need from you…" Trela huddled conspiratorially with Escha. Vrric closed his ears to them and concentrated on his breathing.

Vrric went over all the different syllables in his mind. Should he use Fin or Sid? Should he use Hep or Pan? Or even Tot for that matter? He wanted to cast the spell on an object, but wanted the effect of the spell to be seen back here at the tent. Seen by all, or at least by Trela, not just by him. He wracked his brain trying to come up with something, all the while trying to calm himself and gather his strength. Five hours?! He had never even cast an enchantment that lasted over one hour. He tried to think back to Revkin. To anything that might help him. But he could think of nothing that his mentor had said that would aid him in this.

Finally, Lishean re-entered the tent brandishing a brass spyglass. He stood by Trela and Escha until Vrric got up and walked over to them. "Here you go. I'll be waiting outside." He handed the spyglass to Vrric and nodded forcefully at him, with a slightly furrowed brow. Vrric was sure that it was meant to be reassuring. Mercifully, he then left the tent.

"Is there anything that I can do to help?" Trela looked him in the eye. Vrric merely shook his head. There was nothing anyone could do to help.

Vrric sat down in front of Escha and crossed his legs. He smiled at her. For her part, she smiled quietly back. It was nice and quiet inside the tent. He laid the spyglass in his lap and breathed deeply. He closed his eyes and rubbed his hands together for a moment. Once they tingled slightly he stopped rubbing and placed them on the cold brass. He took one more deep breath. "Surfinheptorefarc!"

Vrric had not realized that he had passed out until he woke up. The tent walls glowed slightly with the rising sun. He had a pounding headache and for a brief moment wished that Gyllhelon was there with a small healing spell. He raised his head to look around and let out an unconscious groan. Before he laid his head back down, he caught sight of Croy's beaming face.

"You're awake, good." Croy hustled over and squatted next to Vrric's prone form.

"I wish I were dead." Vrric blurted it out before he thought about it.

"Oh. That happens to me sometimes when I cast something over my head. Hold on a second." Vrric could hear Croy drawing a breath. "Mekliderto!" Croy's small hands touched Vrric's forehead, and he instantly felt better. He was even able to tentatively sit up.

"What happened? I… I don't remember anything." Croy handed him a waterskin, and Vrric drank greedily while Croy filled him in.

"Well, Knill came to fetch me after Escha had left. When I arrived you were lying on the floor right there and there was a glowing circle situated above your chest. It was a pale light blue and large, about the circumference of a cooking fire pit, and it just sat there flickering for what seemed like forever. Trela said that it was the spyglass's view itself that hovered there. She said that when you passed out, the circle appeared above you and they could see the side of the tent in the circle. Knill walked in front of the spyglass and they could see his legs. Trela was so excited that she covered the spyglass and made Escha leave at once. They were unsure as to how long it would last, you see. Trela had thought that it was based on how many images were sent over, which is why she covered the glass. They were still arguing about it by the time Lishean brought me here. I agreed with Knill that it had to be time based, not the amount of information shown. Either way, it stayed blank until Escha finally uncovered the spyglass. We also argued about whether to try to wake you or leave you as you were. I wanted to cast a healing spell on you right then, but I was heavily outvoted. They were all worried that anything we might do to you would interrupt the spell. Maybe they were right, we'll never know. I did straighten your legs out for you, which did not seem to affect the glowing circle at all. It took at least a couple of hours before Escha uncovered the glass and real images appeared in the glowing circle. It was amazing. At first it was just a dizzying blur of trees and leaves. Then she steadied the glass to look into the distance. The image would be out of focus as she shifted the focal point of the glass and then it would snap into sharp relief. It was like I was looking through the spyglass myself." Croy took a quick break from his storytelling as he accepted the waterskin from Vrric. Before

Vrric could think of anything to say, however, Croy jumped back into it.

"At first it was just spotting campfires. Trela madly took notes as to how many Pyrans were around each fire. They asked me to *whisper* to Escha so that they could direct her movements, but I… I couldn't. After walking along one side of the picket, Escha started to move closer to the encampment. The images would be jumpy and blurred for a while and then she would use the spyglass again and everything would come into focus. We would be looking at the ground and then, suddenly, we would be scanning tents in the distance. Escha scanned each tent looking for insignia and nothing seemed marked. She finally made it around to the back of the encampment—it was up a small hill—and began scanning the fires and tents up there. Suddenly, Trela screamed. She was yelling at Escha to go back to a particular tent, but of course Escha could not hear her. From what I could gather, it seemed that she had seen a large marquis tent that she recognized. Escha never made it all the way around the encampment, but doubled back after reaching the end of the treeline on the hill. It was on her way back that she focused back upon the tent in question. Lishean swore aloud, and even Knill seemed to recognize it. It appears that lying before us was Iventorn's warpack. This meant nothing to me, but it is the same warpack that Trela and Knill traveled with. The same one that Lishean left, taking many of its warriors with him. It was, apparently, not unexpected but it cast a pallor over the room. The concern is that Iventorn knows about Trela and is waiting for her. The greater concern is that he knows she is here and has dug himself into the hillside. Lishean does not think he will attack but will force Trela's hand so that he may keep the advantage of defense."

"Well, then, we should not attack, correct? If all you say is true, we should just skirt his warpack and not engage beyond a simple skirmish." Vrric squinted his eyes at Croy.

Croy nervously licked his lips. "The attack will begin any minute. I stayed behind to make sure you would recover."

"What? That doesn't make any sense. You just explained why we should not attack." Vrric jumped up and felt no ill effects. He would have thanked Croy again for the healing spell but he had too much on his mind.

"Because I thought it was foolish. But I do not make the decisions." Croy looked down.

"What about Lishean? Surely he is not so headstrong that he would make a tactical error like that." Vrric made sure that his belt was tight and his boots felt comfortable

"Strategic error." Croy corrected quietly.

"What?" Vrric asked.

"Nothing. Look, Lishean did try to talk her out of attacking. He made quite an argument, as well. He said it was pride versus common sense. Knill also argued against it. Clerin and the Luftens stayed out of the fight. Trela would not be deterred, however. She said that her first victory in battle must be against Iventorn. She was adamant."

"Do we have horses? I want to save my strength." Vrric walked out of tent and was astounded. There was only the one tent left up in the clearing. A couple of small groups of older Pyrans were loading the last of the pack animals. Croy ran over to one such group while Vrric unhobbled their horses. He mounted his and waited for Croy to finish speaking with the Pyrans.

"How long ago did everyone leave?" Vrric did not think it could have been too long since there were still some rolled up tents lying on the grass.

"Dawn. They left right before dawn. Trela made them tear everything down in the dark and left different groups to pack the rest. The last warrior group left almost an hour ago." Croy mounted and Vrric dismounted.

"Never mind, we will have to fly." Vrric ran his fingers through his hair. He really did not want to cast a flight spell before going into battle. Croy clambered back off his horse. "How far do you think you could get us?"

"You mean flying? I don't know. I just cast that healing spell." Croy looked down at his feet. "I don't think I could get us all the way there, but… maybe halfway?" Croy squinted at Vrric as if he were staring towards the sun.

"That would be great. You get us halfway there and I'll take us the rest of the way. Who knows, maybe you'll be able to get us the whole way there. That shield spell you cast for us on our way to this encampment was sure impressive." Vrric tried to give Croy a confident smile. He figured he would have to cast a flight spell at some point, but he was trying to save up as much strength as he could.

Croy took a few deep breaths. He looked up briefly at Vrric and then put his head back down. "Narkinderclo!" They both shot up in the air with such ferocity that Vrric was stunned into silence for a moment.

"Wow, Croy, wow. This is amazing. You are getting better at casting Nar spells. Very impressive indeed." And Vrric was actually impressed. Croy, however, was concentrating too hard to talk. He smiled at Vrric for a split second then turned his head back to see where they were going. They flew in silence with Vrric occasionally throwing out compliments.

Vrric was worried that they did not know where they were going since Escha had the spyglass covered during her travels. Soon, however, they saw trails of smoke lifting towards the sky. After that, they were able to see actual fires. Eventually, Vrric could see a hill in the distance that appeared to have swarming ants crawling all over it. At the base of the hill was a short plain skirted by a wispy line of trees. He realized that all Croy really needed to know was the general direction that the warpack was headed.

"You can do it." Vrric did not want to be distracting, but only encouraging. The battle was closer to their starting encampment than he had thought, but he had not really expected Croy to get them all the way there with one spell. "We are going to make it." Vrric watched the edge of the trees get closer. It was soon obvious that Trela's warpack was against the treeline and covered the small plain. They had thrust a ways up the hill, but certainly not halfway up. "We are almost there." The clamor of the battle reached them a while after the sight of the hill, but its violence was much more difficult to ignore. The cacophony rose to a deafening roar as they closed upon the active battle. "Here, here. Land just over there." Vrric pointing to a medic station near the treeline. "You have done it, Croy! We have made it." Vrric thought the landing would be a bit rough, but Croy held everything smooth until they reached the ground. Vrric was jubilant. He was astounded at Croy's efforts and strength. As Croy sat heavily on the ground, Vrric stood over him and cast, "Mekliderto!"

"Thank you, I needed that." Croy looked up happily at Vrric.

"It is the least I can do." Vrric was still speaking to Croy when Clerin ran up. She was wearing a white nurse's apron.

"Feyazki, Croy, you have finally made it. We were worried that you both would not arrive in time. I am supposed to tell Feyazki to get in touch with Trela as soon as you arrive. And so I have." Clerin smiled to both of them. "She is near the front a little to our left from here. She is trying to enact maneuvers through bugle calls, so you should be able to spot her by looking for the buglers."

"Will you be traveling with me?" Vrric looked over at Croy who was still breathing heavily.

"I think my skills will be better served here." Croy looked somewhat sheepishly at Vrric.

"You did fantastic getting us over here." Vrric looked at Clerin. "He flew us straight over here, fast as a diving eagle." Vrric patted Croy on the shoulder, and then looked back at Clerin. "Is there a horse available?"

"Well, you can take Riverlightning, but you must promise to keep him safe." Clerin looked serious. Vrric had forgotten the name of her horse until she mentioned it. He was not used to naming working animals, but that was probably because he had never really owned any.

"I will protect him with my life." Vrric placed his hand over his heart.

"That is what I like to hear. Come, I have him hobbled over at the other side of the medic tent. Croy, we will need you at the surgeon's tent. There are too many wounded to be able to heal with magic, so you will probably be anesthetizing amputees. There are hardly any healers with this warpack. You would think that would be a priority." Clerin talked while she walked, forcing Vrric to keep up. Croy looked a little dejected as he headed towards the large white tent. Vrric was unsure which was worse, causing injury to an unknown "enemy" or being overwhelmed trying to heal friends. He tried not to think about what Trela would soon be having him do.

As they stopped next to the horse, Clerin suddenly looked pensive. She looked beautiful dressed in white with her hair glowing in the morning sun. Quickly, she kissed him and just as quickly she blushed. "Keep safe." Before Vrric could reply, she turned and headed back to the front of the medic tent.

Unable to think of anything to yell back at her, he unhobbled her horse and mounted. As he started to ride towards the churning mass of Pyrans, he suddenly wished he had not promised to protect the horse. The odds of him not flying at some point today were effectively zero. To begin with, he wondered how he would find the buglers from the ground.

The horse began to gallop across the short plain, and soon he was coming up to the rear lines. Vrric tried to veer the horse slightly to the left as they closed the distance to be a little closer to where Clerin had indicated Trela was located. He had to slow the horse to a walk as he started to pass Trela's back line of warriors.

Eventually he started making out the bugle calls. Trela was obviously trying something. The horse was able to trot a little as the warriors began to shift around to the time-honored calls. Vrric was unsure of where any of her cavalry were located, as he was on the only horse he could see.

He was able to find the buglers and therefore Trela's command center long before he was able to find combat. There was a tiny circular tent that stood to the right of the buglers that had a flag flying upon its central pole. He steered towards that until he saw Haswyxe approach. The horse had to stop due to the pedestrian congestion that surrounded Trela, the buglers, and the tent. Haswyxe took Vrric's reins from him.

"I am glad to see you, friend. Trela is beating her head against a brick wall here." He nodded behind him towards the hill.

"Guard him with your life." Vrric patted the horse's neck as he walked past Haswyxe. He thought that he heard Haswyxe mumble, "Must be Clerin's horse," but he could not be sure. Instead of turning back, he wormed his way towards Trela.

Vrric saw the back of Trela's head as she was speaking towards Lishean. He reached out his hand to touch her shoulder but his wrist was suddenly grabbed by Malghain's iron grip.

"Oh, sorry. I did not realize you had arrived. Trela!" Malghain gave Vrric a quick grin as Trela whirled around. He made sure that she saw him gripping Vrric's outstretched arm for a split second before he let it go. Trela nodded to Malghain in acknowledgement. He, for his part, relaxed his stance and wandered a few paces away. Not far enough away that he could not be next to her in an instant, though.

"Feyazki, finally! I thought Croy would never awaken you." She glanced between Vrric and the small circular tent behind him. Not many times, but she had a nervous look to her.

"We came as fast as we could once I had regained consciousness. In fact, it was Croy who flew us the entire way here. We..." Vrric was suddenly interrupted.

"What? Of course we can speak privately. Come, enter the tent." Trela waved her hands towards the little circular tent. Since

Vrric could not see anyone else that she was talking to, he nodded to her and ducked through the tent flap.

The tent had a small circular table attached to its central pole that cantilevered out the length of a tall Luften's arm. There were several maps laid out on the table that had various wooden markers representing different military divisions. They represented the enemy as well as friendly forces. Vrric quickly realized that Trela was using the pole piercing their table as the peak of the hill that Iventorn's warpack was currently dug into. A couple of chairs were placed around the table. There was one chair on its side at the back of the tent. Everything in the tent seemed designed to make it seem even smaller than it already was. Vrric scooched over to one of the chairs. He turned and waited for Trela to enter since he could not get much further into the tent than he currently stood without rearranging the chairs.

"I need another way of communicating with my troops." Trela walked the other direction of the tent and flopped herself unceremoniously into the first chair she found. "I don't know if my warriors can hear the bugles on the front line. Everything takes so long before I can tell if something has changed or not that I am tempted to call off the order. But I don't want to give them conflicting orders. So I wait and wait to see if the maneuvers are working, but I can't tell if they are working from here. Do I weaken the lines elsewhere to give them the support they need to complete the maneuver? So I bring my second cavalry back from a wide flanking maneuver to help the infantry. They somehow hear the bugles and take off immediately, even though they are farther away. The infantry finally blows a hole in the line I was trying for before the cavalry can arrive. Then I had to resend the cavalry out to skirt the hill. I know my name is being cursed out there. I need better communication, Feyazki. I need a spellcaster next to each lieutenant who can communicate with every other lieutenant, and I need to be able to reach each of those spellcasters instantly and collectively. And I should have a view of the battlefield, Feyazki. A big, broad view, where I can tell if my calculations are working. I was thinking about how we flew over to my warpack on an invisible shield. Could you make us invisible, if we were above the battle?" Trela had tightened up her sloppy appearance during her little speech. Vrric swung a small chair around to sit on it backwards as he looked at Trela.

"Well, we could try to camouflage ourselves. I could try to make us the color of the sky, or the clouds. That would be one spell to cast that affects only us. But they might be able to see us if the shades are not just right." Vrric paused long enough to invite the question.

"Why can't you make us invisible?" Trela did not disappoint.

"To truly erase us from all of the warriors below, I would have to cast a spell on each of them. Not necessarily individually, but each of them as a collective whole. There comes a point where the spell becomes too large to cast." Vrric watched Trela's nose wrinkle up in concentration.

"But what about Croy's shield, or the stairs you made? Those items were invisible to a large number of observers, were they not?" She squinted at him a little.

"Well, yes, but they were made up of air. Which is invisible to begin with. So they kept their properties even when they were densified." Vrric was not sure if what he was saying was completely true, but it sounded good enough to him.

"So why is air invisible? Or glass, or water? What makes a material able to allow sight to pass through unhindered?" Trela was looking down and may have been thinking aloud for all that Vrric could tell. He waited quietly until her head came back up. After all, he certainly could not answer her questions even if they were not rhetorical. "You think about that. There is an answer here somewhere."

"Not to burst your bubble, but all of this is purely academic. We can work on different types of communication and reconnaissance when there is not a battle raging around us. You have to win this particular battle, Trela. Now. Then you may use the lessons learned here to make a more efficient effort at the next battle." Vrric felt himself getting impassioned and breathed deep after speaking.

"Oh! I have a plan to finish this battle. It is simple and should be effective. Would you like to hear it?" Trela perked right up.

"Please." Vrric stood up with Trela as she stepped up to the map table.

"You are going to take these units here, here and here. I am going to take these units over there and there. We will have the cavalry, which should finally be in place over here, charge up this portion of the hill. That will put them directly behind Iventorn's command tent. He does not like these little mobile tents, unlike me. This cavalry shall be my anvil. You will charge straight up here and hold. You are my knife, cutting his army into manageable pieces." Vrric watched Trela's finger impassively, but inside, his mind was reeling. Trela placed a hand comfortably on Vrric's bicep. "Do not worry. Lishean shall be with you, delivering all of the orders. Forming the warriors into a manageable, defensible line. But you, Feyazki. You are my knife." She squeezed his arm before letting it go. "I will take my contingent, come crashing up the hill at this angle, and... wham!" Trela's fist sent the little wooden markers careening around the tent. "I am the hammer, Feyazki. I just need you and Lishean to hold the line for fifteen minutes. I will crush Iventorn myself, or he shall vanquish me. Either way, the battle is over and I can forget about my useless buglers." She loudly dusted off her hands and stared at Feyazki. "And that... is that."

"But what happens after the fifteen minutes? Even if you crush Iventorn, Lishean's line will only last so long." It was not that Vrric did not trust Trela, but he was nervous.

"The plan came to me after one of our feints. I noticed that Iventorn's warriors fought bravely when they were being attacked, but that they became lackluster when it was their turn to go on the offensive. His warriors are well positioned to win, but they do not have the heart or the will to crush us. I finally realized that it was not the warriors who want to destroy me, it is Iventorn who wants to destroy me. If I remove Iventorn from the battle, I will remove the battle from his warriors." Trela stood and scooted the chair back behind her. "I just need enough time to strike hammer on anvil. Give me that time, Feyazki. You must help Lishean help me."

"Of course, that is what I am here for." Vrric took Trela's outstretched forearm.

"Promise me that you won't die today." She gripped his arm firmly.

"I promise. Not today." She let go of his arm. "You have to promise, too." Vrric was unable to keep hold of her arm.

"Thank you, but I can't make that promise." Trela turned and left the tent.

Vrric stood there stunned for a moment. Trela was always stating that she was destined to kill Qizern. If she was destined to kill him, how could she die today? She did not look nervous, but was she losing her nerve? Vrric took his time leaving the tent, it puzzled him so.

As he left, he was almost deafened by the buglers. They were apparently still useful despite Trela's negative attitudes towards them. Malghain was already waiting for him.

"Come along, we've got to meet up with Lishean. He should be at the second skirmish line along the hill base." Malghain pointed off into the distance. "Trela had certain zones set up around the hill to facilitate the bugle calls. We are heading to zone five," he said with a shrug. "His regiment is the only one currently seeing action I hear. We gained some ground up over to the right in zone eight." He again pointed off into the distance, but in a different direction this time. Vrric was not sure, but that may have been where Trela began her hammer swing on the maps in the small tent. "It has been quiet over there for the last half hour or so. I'm not sure why Iventorn has not pressed an attack. There were a couple of times, while troops were shifting around, that the lines got pretty thin in spots. But… nothing. Do you think they are lying in wait for us, just hoping we'll do something rash?" Malghain had slowed while talking and stopped at his last sentence. He placed his hands on his hips.

"Well, I certainly I hope not, because if they are, we are going to play right into their hands. Trela has a different theory as to why they are not attacking aggressively. I just hope that she is correct." Vrric had momentarily halted next to Malghain, but just as he stopped, Malghain began walking again. They walked the rest of the way in silence. Vrric wanted Malghain's opinion on Trela's theory, but could not figure out a way to sneak the question in while they were walking. Eventually Vrric noticed the slope of the ground changing. The line they were approaching was definitely up the hill a little ways.

They were getting close to the skirmish line when another bugle call rang through the air. Their line began to slowly move backwards. The gap between the two lines grew until you could lay three pyrans down end to end between the warriors, or almost two rods. If Vrric was looking uphill, the line of skirmish was to his left. Everyone looked tense. However, Iventorn's warriors did not come crashing down the hill at them. No spears were being tossed after them, no arrows. It was truly curious. Vrric had a hard time deciding who was more correct about the enemy's actions, Trela or Malghain.

He was going to engage Malghain in some deeper conversation about it when Lishean found them.

"Feyazki, you've arrived. You were out cold last night and I was worried that you would sleep through the entire battle." Lishean clasped Vrric's forearm hard, but in a friendly way. "So why are you over here? I figured you would be with Trela."

"Trela has orders for you." Malghain spoke before Vrric could open his mouth. He handed Lishean a folded piece of paper.

Lishean opened and read the orders. Vrric studied his face for a sign of what he thought about the orders, but it stayed inscrutable. After enough time had passed for Lishean to read the orders several times, he crumpled up the paper and handed the wad back to Malghain.

"She thinks that'll work, huh?" Vrric was unsure if Lishean was talking to him or to Malghain. Lishean turned to another Pyran who was standing close to him. "Grab Hulwein and Ashkar and any buglers who are next to them. We are going to have to consolidate before the offensive." Then he turned to Malghain. "Did she mention a timeline?"

"No. Just that you are to give the signal before your attack. I am not sure what she would do if she were not prepared by the time you gave your signal." Malghain spoke plainly.

"Probably attack anyway." Lishean laughed to himself for a second. "Don't worry. By the time we get the extra warriors up here, she'll be ready enough to get impatient." Lishean turned to Vrric. "Well, I do appreciate her letting me use you both. I figured at least one of you two would be her bodyguard."

"Why do you think Iventorn's warpack is not attacking?" Vrric decided to ask Lishean point blank.

" 'Ours is not to reason why, ours is but to do or die,' " Lishean intoned.

"Spoken like a true warrior." Malghain nodded to Lishean.

"It just seems…" Vrric was interrupted by Lishean.

"I know what it seems like. But what am I to do about that?" Lishean poked his finger against Vrric's chest. Then, just as quickly, he stood back and looked apologetic. "Listen, my honest opinion puts the odds at almost even. If you were to flip a coin and let Trela choose the side… Yeah, I'd say about fifty-fifty. The problem is, if she is wrong, we get crushed first. She may be able to meet up with her cavalry and escape, but we will be hit from both sides. I don't know about you. You might fly, or turn invisible, or who knows. But us…" Here Lishean pointed his finger back and forth between himself and Malghain. "We will not be walking away. These orders, if she is incorrect, are suicidal. Even if she is correct, she must still find and kill Iventorn quickly." He smiled at Vrric. "However, I have faced worse odds under commanders that I have held in less regard."

Just then a small group of Pyrans came upon them. The four looked dirty and tired. Croy marveled at the difference in facial expressions from the warriors at the back, or even the middle, of the battle than that of those operating at the front. Vrric hoped that they had not heard all of Lishean's speech and vowed not to provoke him again about Trela's orders while there were subordinates about. One of the four was carrying a bugle. Lishean turned towards them.

"I want maniples B and F to fall in behind us here. We will also want cohort sixteen to consolidate to our right. Quickly!" Lishean shooed the bugler off and turned towards Vrric.

"There are approximately forty warriors per cohort, and two to four cohorts per maniple. I also have a maniple already here under my control. We are going to try to hold a line an eighth of a league long for a minimum of fifteen minutes. Just to give you an idea of what our situation is." Lishean smiled at Vrric. Then the cry of the bugle pierced the sky. Lishean waited until the echo faded before continuing to speak. "Tighten your armor and ready your weapons. We are heading out when the reinforcements arrive." Lishean raised his arm to point up the hill. "Meet me at the head of the column. The die is almost cast."

Vrric and Malghain walked up the hill, towards the farthest penetration of Trela's warpack. His mind raced, but he could not think of how to express anything, so they walked in silence. Malghain, for his part, merely looked grim and determined. Vrric only hoped that he looked half as determined as Malghain did.

The further along they walked, the more of a stir they caused. When they finally stopped, warriors gathered around them. They all wanted to know if there was an attack planned, how many reinforcements were coming, what other areas were seeing action, which direction they might be attacking, whether or not one of the cavalry units was helping, how their wounded friends were doing in the back lines, where Lishean was at; there were even rumors that there was a Yaven somewhere on the field. Vrric would not even have known where to begin with all of the questions, so he stayed quiet. Their arrival certainly increased the energy and agitation of the area, and not just with Trela's warriors. Iventorn's warriors, a short spear throw away, began milling about and making preparations. Obviously something was afoot.

"Lishean will notify you when he gets here. That is all I can say." Malghain looked like he was getting annoyed with the crowd. Vrric had never seen Malghain get truly angry, and he almost wanted see it happen, just to experience it. Common sense got the better of him, however.

"Back to your posts! Lishean will be here soon. Reinforcements are coming. You all need to get back to your posts and follow the chain of command. You know we are not allowed to tell you anything." The words just fell out of his mouth. Vrric realized that he had been traveling with warriors for too long if he had picked up on their lingo and mannerisms. Malghain wordlessly smacked him playfully on his back.

Eventually Lishean did arrive. Soon afterwards the reinforcements also arrived. The chaos kept Lishean busy for some time. Vrric and Malghain waited patiently for him, trying not to be jostled by the crowd. Finally, Lishean approached them.

"Well, this is it. If anyone has any second thoughts, now is the last time to voice them." Lishean smiled at both of them. They, of course, did not voice their concerns, as he knew that they wouldn't. "Good. I want you both at the front line with me."

Lishean turned and motioned to his bugler, who ran off a little distance but stayed silent. He then, without another word, started walking the last hundred steps to the front. Vrric and Malghain dutifully followed him. They stood there a moment looking out around them. It was like they were a peninsula surrounded by a sea of enemies. All of their warriors were behind them. There was an eerie quiet on the battlefield. Iventorn's warriors peeked out nervously from behind their small wooden bulwarks. Looking further up the hill, Vrric could see their evolution into packed soil ramparts. It was at least as bad as he had feared. He wondered briefly why they should look nervous. He glanced behind himself to check on Trela's warriors. Though some looked nervous, they all looked excited. At least she commanded a higher morale than Iventorn. Lishean let out a howl. The bugler behind them began blasting his horn. None of the warriors moved. Lishean walked over to Vrric conspiratorially.

"I have given the signal to Trela. She and the cavalry should be moving slowly into position now. We will give them a few moments and then make our charge. I will need you to clear a swath." Lishean winked at him.

"Clear a swath?" Vrric was unsure of what Lishean meant.

"Yeah, shoot a stream of fire through their line. Use a seismic tremor to make a crevasse and swallow them whole. Rain hailstones the size of horses on them. I don't know… Do what you do." Lishean squinted at him a little. "Should I be nervous? You are making me nervous."

"Do not worry about me, Lishean. There is no call to be nervous." Vrric hoped he sounded less nervous than he felt. He had not realized that Lishean was counting on him to provide the impetus behind the charge.

"Good, good. I don't like to be nervous." Lishean then turned towards Malghain. "He is your ward. Do not fail."

"If I fail, you will have two burials to preside over." Malghain smiled reassuringly to Lishean, then over to Vrric. Vrric, however, was not reassured.

They waited awhile in silence before Lishean spoke up. "Make your move, Feyazki." He stepped sideways away from Vrric. At this motion all of the warriors surrounding them moved away and gave Vrric room. Only Malghain stood close.

Vrric breathed in slowly and exhaled loudly. He refused to think about the Pyrans in his path. He thought of it as merely blowing open a locked door. He took one more deep breath. "Eqedepiarc!" He raised his hands and shot a pillar of flame forward with a diameter equal to Croy's height. Vrric held it for a full thirty seconds, waving it back and forth to create the widest swath possible. The screams of the wounded were drowned out by a great cry of triumph behind him once the fire sputtered out. Vrric felt weak but was able to jog next to Malghain as the charge surged forward. The surge was able to get a fair way up the hillside before they met resistance.

Vrric was happy when they slowed down since he could then just shamble along in the middle of the pack. The roar of the battle came back with a vengeance. A deafening amalgamation of sounds assaulted Vrric. The clang of metal striking metal mixed with the screams of the wounded and the war cries of the strong. Trela's warpack unit was still pushing forward, however, and Malghain half drug and half prodded Vrric to keep them from being trampled.

The surge was finally halted about halfway up the hillside. Vrric was not sure if they were up far enough, but he needed a little more time before being able to cast a large spell again. They basically just stood in the middle of Trela's warriors, Vrric catching his breath and Malghain glancing about nervously. Lishean could be heard screaming orders nearby.

The warriors finally began to edge forward again, but it was slow going. Innumerable minutes passed before Vrric could finally begin to catch his breath. Malghain and he would shuffle forward for a moment, and then stop. In this fitful manner the warriors made a slow progress further up the hill. Vrric started thinking about what power level of spell he could cast without making him useless for the rest of the battle. As he stood there pondering, a commotion arose at the head of the column.

The edging forward halted while the commotion grew louder and louder. The clanging was so loud that it reminded Vrric of his time with Kaihlu in the forge. Though he could not afford to, he lost precious seconds to a fit of nostalgia. Eventually, though, Vrric could make out what the commotion was. There was a score or so of heavily armored warriors with battle axes pushing their way down the hillside. They walked close together and swung their axes in unison to an erratic rhythm. Once they contacted Lishean's unit, they left behind a trail of dead and dismembered in their slow but implacable wake. Vrric was stunned into silence as Lishean's front line began to crumble before his eyes. He numbly watched the heavy infantry creep towards him.

"Feyazki. Feyazki!" Vrric thought it was Lishean's voice that made up the frantic cry, but he could not be sure. Vrric held his forehead for a moment attempting to gain focus.

"Nuliderto!" It was Malghain. Instantly Vrric felt revitalized. He was unsure of how long his feeling would last given the low power of the spell. He tore his eyes away from the murderous vision approaching them and searched his mind for the most devastating spell he could cast.

"Get behind me!" Vrric yelled at Malghain. He needed a clear shot at the heavies. Malghain looked hesitant to remove himself from between Vrric and danger. So Vrric yelled again, "Get behind me!"

"Retreat! Retreat!" Vrric again thought it was Lishean yelling. He never dreamed that he would hear Lishean speak that word, however. Especially not to his troops. Suddenly Trela's warriors parted before Vrric and rushed past him, behind him. Vrric widened his stance and took a deep breath. Malghain's simple healing spell still had him feeling strong. After a mere moment, there were no Pyrans between Vrric and the glinting steel wall rushing towards him. They had gained a fair amount of speed when they heard the retreat signal.

"Lumdeeleclo!" Vrric screamed the word, and behind the scream rolled thunder. A bolt of lightning shot forth from Vrric's outstretched palms. It struck the lead heavy in his steel breastplate. From there it shot lightning to his left, to his right, and straight through him to the warrior behind. Each time the lightning struck a warrior, it would split into three smaller streams and strike more warriors. The lightning pulsed back and forth through the steel clad warriors, striking each one more than once. Though it seemed to take an incredibly long time, Vrric knew that it only lasted a moment. The smell of burnt hair filled the air as the warriors all crumbled before Vrric. Vrric himself crumbled to his own knees.

The silence was deafening. No one moved from either warpack. Weapons hung limply in hands while every face was glued to the smoking carnage in front of Vrric. The stench of burnt—no, not quite burnt, but of cooked flesh—filled the air with its pestilence. No one spoke or screamed. There were no last moans or cries from the pile. Even the normally raucous ravens, used to their own small battles over the carrion, had grown quiet. All of the hair on Vrric felt as if it were standing straight up. He glanced around him and noted that Malghain's hair looked quite lofty as well.

Suddenly a new commotion began. Iventorn's warriors began tossing their weapons on the ground. Though Vrric could still hear traces of battle happening in several far off directions, none who had witnessed the lightning were fighting. It was a sea of grim, somber faces that stared at Vrric. They conveyed a feeling that was not fear so much as a hollow dread. Like a child playing mischievously who had just been back-handed by an adult. They were not truly hurt, but there was a shocked seriousness that now clouded their spirit. Their accusing eyes filled Vrric with an odd pang of guilt. Truly, any one of those warriors in front of Vrric, alive or dead, would have killed him without a second thought. There was no reason to feel guilt over death at a battlefield. That is not what the sea of eyes spoke to him, however. The clang of dropped weapons continued.

Finally, it was Lishean who stepped between Vrric and the charred pile of flesh and blackened steel. He spoke in a loud clear voice.

"We accept your surrender and we accept peace. We, too, shall sheath our swords. Right now, as I speak, Trela is locked in combat with Iventorn. One will conquer the other. I say we leave our fate to that outcome. If Iventorn kills Trela, we will happily join your warpack at the lowest rank. But…" Here Lishean raised his arms and raised his voice. "If Trela vanquishes Iventorn, you shall all swear fealty to Trela, the Kriishan!" Many cheered from Trela's camp, but few were boisterous on the opposite side of the skirmish line. In fact, though some picked up their dropped weapons, most merely sat down. But all of them, and all of Trela's still standing warriors, sheathed whatever weapons they had in their hands.

Lishean lowered his arms and walked over to Vrric. "How do you know they are in combat?" Vrric whispered.

"I don't. In fact, I doubt that they actually are. But we have to buy her the time she needs to be the hammer, now don't we. This way we can all stop fighting and let destiny decide. After all, isn't that what Trela wants?" Lishean whispered just slightly louder than Vrric had.

"Well… I hope she wins." Vrric smiled at Lishean.

"Me, too. That is why I need you and Malghain to head over to zone eight. If you have to interfere—be discrete. By the way, you didn't disappoint, that was impressive. And you saved a lot of lives today." Lishean pointed over the pile of dead towards the sitting crowd behind. He patted Vrric on the back and then turned to walk in the opposite direction.

Malghain took Vrric's arm and spoke loudly. "They're going to need your skills at the medic station." They hobbled off a little ways. They walked through their own side even though there was a small truce. Once out of sight from Lishean's battalion, Malghain stood and walked quickly.

"You did not even sound convincing back there. The Pyrans are going to think you're taking me to the medics because I'm weak, not to heal others." They slowed to walk at Vrric's pace, which was slower than Malghain's.

"Good. Most importantly they think that we are going to the medic station. Making others believe they are seeing through a lie makes them believe in what they think is the truth even more. They can feel the smarter for being misled as well." Malghain turned his head and looked Vrric up and down while they were walking. "What do you care what they think we're doing, anyway? There is not one Pyran at that battle who does not fear that you could kill them. Their respect is yours, whether or not you need to go to the medic station. In fact, I may have made them respect you more by making you appear more mortal. Nobody likes a show off. Or are you concerned because you really do need to go to the medic station?" Malghain stopped, forcing Vrric to stop as well. "How are you feeling, tell me honestly? If you are remotely feeling woozy, we will go to the medics and leave Trela to her destiny. I would cast another healing spell on you, but I don't think it would help much and I need to stay sharp."

"I'm fine, really. I am walking a little slow so I can catch my breath, but there is nothing to be nervous about." Vrric started walking again. "You know, I believe that is the most I have ever heard you speak in one spiel." They both chuckled. It got them both going again, but the downside to Vrric's short spiel was that they walked the rest of the way in silence.

Amongst a cleft in the hillside, much smaller than a dale, they came upon a natural amphitheater that held a large ring of Pyrans. Trela's cavalry occupied the left side of the bowl's rim. In the center of the ring were two individuals. Trela and a lanky, gaunt Pyran that Vrric assumed was Iventorn. They had arrived too late to affect the outcome of the contest. Iventorn was lying in the center of the ring with a long dagger embedded in his right thigh. Trela was standing over him with a short sword held outstretched towards his head as she circled around him. He was begging her to kill him.

"Don't make me a ghulzan. Just finish it, you trickster! Lop off my head and show it to the crowd. That may go a long way in erasing the memory of these fine warriors who witness it. Let them forget how you threw a dagger from your boot to bring me down instead of besting me sword to sword. Yes, let my blood be the grog of amnesia for them." While Iventorn's right hand held his leg just above the protruding dagger, his left curled and opened in front of his throat as he spoke.

"I will not kill you, Iventorn. You have to do that yourself if you want to escape your fate." Trela circled slowly.

"I… I can't do it. But I… I can't be a ghulzan. Please, just kill me." Iventorn's voice was becoming soft and hard to hear.

"I will not kill you, Iventorn. If you cannot honorably kill yourself, then you will be mine until you can break your geas. You know the honor code as well as I. You *will* be my ghulzan." Trela stopped in front of him.

Then something happened that Vrric had not expected to see. The wiry, dangerous-looking Pyran wept. He fully doubled over into a fetal position and wept. Great heaving sobs wracked his body. Vrric had never before witnessed such a thing.

"What a culture," Malghain said dryly.

Chapter 16

Though, all things considered, it was a fairly small victory, the celebration was epic. Trela did not want any hard feelings from anyone. Some used the cover of the celebration to desert during the long night. Rather than mete out the typical harsh punishments, she let them go. More than numbers, she wished loyalty, and she would rather know sooner than later where her warriors' passions lay.

Trela wanted the warriors who had waited for her return to feel as if they were being rewarded, so she gave them the typical spoils of the enemy dead. The equipment of the friendly dead went in their usual order of family, friends, acquaintances and, at last, persistent strangers. Strangely enough, no one claimed the steel plate armor that Feyazki had shot lightning through. Trela was thinking of specifying a cart to carry it around with her. There was a blackened sunburst pattern on each breast plate and back plate, but no dents or other visible damage could be detected in the metal. She thought they could make frightening symbols of her warpack's power. Charred marionettes. However, she also had a small worry that the cart full of empty armor would have a demoralizing effect on the warpack and she did not want to risk that. She figured on camping on the hillside for the next couple of days, so she had some time to truly mull over the situation before coming to a decision.

Trela also did not want the newest members of her warpack to feel downtrodden. She did not allow the common, if not quite typical, spoils of the surviving enemies. Approximately seven-eighths of her entire current warpack at one time or another took orders from Iventorn. They all knew each other or, at least, knew of each other. Trela needed assimilation more than anything else at that moment. Later on, when her warpack destroyed a warpack that had no previous ties to her, the spoils would be reaped en masse. However, she could ill afford to enrich the warpack in that way, at that moment. The only ghulzan taken during the battle was Iventorn himself.

Which meant that the burden of the night's celebration was solely born by the warpack's diminishing coffers. Trela knew this was unsustainable, but what else could she do? There needed to be an immediate reconnection of old camaraderie in addition to new bonds of shared hardship. It was true that the only promotions she was planning on handing out the next day were being given to her original followers, and the only demotions were to be amongst the vanquished. It was also true that she planned on keeping many of Iventorn's lieutenants, if not the majority of his Seconds. The next couple of days would be spent with her meeting with her entire warpack, a cohort at a time. It would reinforce her current knowledge of the original warriors and it would give her the opportunity to familiarize herself with the new ones. Other than that, it would be just drills, drills, and drills. They obviously needed to work on their coordination. Also, she felt that shared hardship (and shared enemies) brought warriors closer together than anything else. She would willingly make Lishean provide the two.

Lishean had chided her for not posting any of her warriors to guard the pickets through the night. Trela explained how she did not want any warriors in her warpack who did not want to be there. That she would not abide by even the most gently persuaded conscript. She truly thought that those who harbored loyalty for Qizern were better off sneaking away into the night which, in her mind, had the added benefit of making her own warpack stronger. As Feyazki had put it last night, "You fold metal to remove the impurities, not to force them back in."

That left only three mysteries for the morning. How to fix the communication problem on the battlefield? How to make the next battle fill their coffers? And where was Cavish? Trela could not say why that third question bothered her so, but something about it gnawed at her. The first mystery would best be investigated by speaking with Feyazki. The second question was best answered with Lishean, some of the Luftens, and maybe even Clerin. The third mystery was easily enough pursued but was difficult for her to execute. She would have to speak with Iventorn. She knew she would have to talk to him eventually, and she truly had a terrible urge to humiliate him, but she thought it best to let his new status sink into him a little before speaking with him.

The night, however, was not to be spent in contemplation, but in celebration. Her warpack was unused to fighting under her, and they had been outnumbered. The enemy had been dug in and expectant. The battle was uphill, but it was also mercifully brief. Trela knew that was because many fighting against her were not unsympathetic to her cause, but she still felt elated. Her first victory! She partied way too hard and stayed up way too late. It was not until noon the next day that she even woke, and it was much later before she dared to appear outside her tent.

***

It was a fortnight after their first victory and Trela's warpack was camped along the edge of the Delphin forest, a gorgeous wood outfitted with silver firs. They had made no progress on the coffers front. Trela wondered if she was just wandering around blind. Feyazki had been training two dozen warriors in the art of casting telepathy spells—*whisperers* he called them—and she was eager to try them out. She, of course, still had her buglers and her war drums to fall back on, but she felt they were making good progress on that front. All she needed was a good excuse to use them.

Trela got her wish before they were forced to find a town. There had been enough hunters amongst them, and the Delphin forest had been fruitful enough that her warpack's diminishing coffers were not yet noticed. As they were skirting the forest, her scouts noticed that another warpack was tracking them. She was concerned at first since they reported that the warpack flew two flags. One for its leader, a black lion rampant on a backdrop of orange, and one with Qizern's bright red warhorse on sea of light blue. She did not recognize the warpack's personal insignia but wondered just how closely linked to Agoge it was. She wanted more time to practice and many more warriors under her own banner before she began actual battle with Qizern's forces.

Trela sent messengers through her warpack searching for those with direct knowledge of the black lion's insignia. Once enough had been found, she called a closed meeting with her most-trusted counselors, what she had taken to calling her Privy Council. She needed to know whether the warpack had a direct communication line to Qizern, or if they flew his flag merely to avoid trouble. Many commanders flew the King's flag more out of concern for their own safety than out of any particular loyalty. She did not allow any grog during the meeting, but promised those who provided useful intelligence much drink afterwards. It was a tactic suggested by Lishean, but it was her idea to bring them in one at a time, to hear their individual stories without the others. Then the counselors would allow them to argue any and all discrepancies together. Those who produced the least amount of discrepancies would get the most grog, thought Trela.

The first warrior to enter was called Pliney. He asserted that the commander of the black lion's warpack was named Ugoth and that most of the warriors were from farming villages near a town called Inkuik. Pliney said that the warpack consisted of almost ten maniples, just a little less than Trela's. He stated that Ugoth liked to use cavalry flanking maneuvers with a strong mid-column infantry. Dartsyle laughed and said, "Who doesn't?" That slowed Pliney down a bit, but not by much. He continued to describe Ugoth's warpack and fighting style in some detail. At the end of it all, he smiled warmly to Trela and said, "Now that I have told you everything I know about Ugoth's warpack I... well, I hate to be crude, but I heard there was a reward for the information." His eyes darted to the pile of small casks that Lishean had placed conspicuously at the end of the counselors' table. Each tiny cask had only three or four tankards worth, but there were eight of them all jumbled together.

"Intelligence." Trela narrowed her eyes as his widened. "There is a reward for intelligence, not information." She made a shooing motion and had Torpalin show him out. "We will speak to you again in a moment, don't wander off."

Torpalin returned with a Pyran called Yongle the Younger. He asserted that the commander of the black lion's warpack was named Ilhomen and that most of the warriors were from farming villages near a town called Anshale. This time the warpack was comprised of upwards of fifteen maniples, just a little more than Trela's. Once he stated that Ilhomen liked to use his cavalry to flank the enemy while engaging them with a strong central infantry, Trela stopped him.

The counselors quickly moved through the others. Only the third, sixth, seventh, and tenth warriors agreed upon the name of the commander, where the warpack had formed and its approximate size. Trela ran through those four individually one more time, probing them for their succinct opinions. Then she brought them in front of her counselors and hashed out the discrepancies. It was amazing how quickly Pyrans would get honest when confronted with another's knowledge. Basically, they each knew very little. She allowed them one tankard of grog when they were together, then let them each have a tiny cask as they left.

From the amalgamated consensus, Trela had found out that the commander of the black lion warpack was named Rewista and that the warpack had formed somewhere around the Oplet lakes area, maybe seven sun cycles ago. They all stated that her ties with Qizern were tenuous at best, and that his flag was probably being flown as a warning, an indication of hostility, rather than of loyalty. And the four had all agreed that the warpack was of a similar size to Trela's, but everyone in camp probably knew that. Scouts were notorious for leaking general information such as that. As for Rewista's strengths as a commander, the accounts were too varied to figure out what her tactics might actually be. They had all mentioned that she did not rely heavily on cavalry, but that was as close as they got to agreeing to anything.

After the meeting was over, Trela sent out four scouts, including Escha, to bring back actual estimates of Rewista's warpack composition. She wanted to know if they did not have many horses in the warpack. If so, she was determined to find a way to exploit that knowledge. She, herself, liked a balanced warpack.

Once it was confirmed that the black lion was short on horses, Trela made her plan. First, she had some of her warriors strip the forest edge of usable saplings. She wanted an arsenal of lances. Second, she moved her warpack down from the forest into the nearby open grasslands. She would need lots of room to maneuver. Third, she broke her chain of command up into smaller pieces. She decided to split each maniple of her cavalry into two, so she took some of the *whisperers* from her infantry and embedded them with the cavalry. She was willing to trade a more cumbersome infantry for a much more mobile and deadly cavalry. Fourth, she had to choose sub-lieutenants to lead each of the split-halves of the cavalries. And she had to decide which cohorts stayed together and which were moved to the less-experienced leader. It was a process that turned out to be much more difficult and time consuming than she had originally thought it would be. Finally, they set up minor defenses and chose the pickets. Trela was going to make Rewista engage her.

The next morning, the warpack rose early. Trela had banned alcohol the night before and ordered meat to be served at every breakfast this morning. She felt it was going to be a grueling day and wanted each of her warriors to be prepared. It did not disappoint.

About two hours after sunrise, the other warpack approached across the grasslands. The bulk of the warpack stayed about a league away, while a group of five approached. They stopped about midway between the two warpacks. Trela had picked Feyazki, Estfale, Gyllhelon and Zira. She wanted some foreigners, but more

Pyrans than Luftens. She also wanted more females than males. This was her first negotiation with a female commander and she did not want to appear to be controlled by some male. She had wanted to bring Clerin, but she felt her entire entourage should be combat appropriate. Not that Clerin could not hold her own in combat, but she just did not look mean enough for Trela to take her. That was why Trela chose Zira instead. Zira looked mean enough to cover for all five of them.

As they rode towards the enemy, Trela stared hard at the opposing warpack, trying to see if they had any horses. It appeared that they only had one cavalry maniple way off in the distance, while Trela had four. Their horses trotted the little distance to the parley, as if they sensed the tension.

"Are you the one who claims to be the Kriishan?" There were five warriors in front of Trela and they all stayed on their horses. The one who spoke was in the middle, much like Trela was in the center of her group. She had four males with her. Trela wondered who was gaining the upper hand.

"I am the Kriishan, yes. No other may make that claim." Trela spoke up and extended out her right arm. "If you join me now, I will make you a Second under my command."

"I would not be flying the red horse if I wished to hand over my warpack. Your confidence precedes you. I sure hope it is not just hubris. Every warrior has a plan in mind until they get hit. Well, I am going to hit you. I am going to hit you so hard that all your plans will rearrange. And then what will you do?" Rewista had short dark hair and fierce light brown eyes, backlit with the intensity of a raptor. She held her helmet in her left arm, and Trela tried to memorize the look of its dark blue plume.

"I will give you one more chance to surrender your warpack. I am destined to fight Qizern and you are merely in my way. If you do not capitulate now, I cannot guarantee your personal safety." Trela felt she could not back down from Rewista.

"I would rather kneel in the sand." Rewista referred to the ancient practice of beheading a vanquished commander.

Trela interrupted Rewista. "But if you would like a duel instead..." She needed her warpack to know that she had tried to avoid an all-out battle, so she hopped off her horse and drew her weapon. "I will fight you here, to the death, for both of the warpacks. If you win, you will double the size of your warpack and prove that I am not the Krüshan, but merely full of hubris. If I win, however, your warpack joins up with mine. All at the lowest rank. Do we have a deal?"

"We have nothing of the kind." Rewista did not budge from her saddle.

"Fight me!" Trela screamed into the morning air. She waved her sword above her head. A roar came up from her own warpack behind her.

"We will settle this in a civilized manner, with our warriors. We are commanders, are we not?" With that Rewista turned and rode back towards her warpack. Her four silent warriors turned their horses and galloped behind her.

Trela re-sheathed her weapon and climbed back on her horse. She and her four silent warriors galloped back towards her own warpack. She did not feel that the parley went well, but she was unsure of how she could have changed it. She thought that maybe she should bring Lishean to the next parley. He would be honest with her about her speeches. Plus, he was one of the few Pyrans under her command that had good experience with these types of things. It was certainly food for thought. She just naturally liked leaving the command of the warpack with him while she was away.

Trela galloped all the way back to her warriors. They cheered when she arrived. Their blood was up. They were excited for combat. But Rewista never attacked. Her warpack stood across the field and waited, much like Trela's. But unlike Rewista's warriors, who knew why they waited and what her plan was, Trela's warriors began to get restless. They were ready to repulse an attack from a warpack five times their size if they had to. They were not ready to stand there all day, doing nothing. Not even a half-hour had passed and their morale was back to square one. Trela realized that she should have attacked immediately, but she had not anticipated this. She had assumed that Rewista was ready to attack, head on. She could not wait any longer, however.

Once Trela fully realized that Rewista would not attack, she gathered her Seconds, lieutenants, sub-lieutenants, and even captains. She outlined her basic plan and gave them new cascade orders. Her basic plan consisted of where her infantry units were going to aim and where the various cavalry groups were to aim, in very broad terms. She had decided to try out cascade orders during this battle and had briefed them all on what to do. A typical cascade order ran like this: First you charge where you're aiming at. If they begin to yield, push forward from the center and then widen the column for stability. However, if they do not begin to yield, then fall back and circle clockwise around the preceding cavalry subgroup to attack further up the enemy's flank. That would trigger the cavalry subgroup behind the attacking group's cascade order, which would be to flatten out and hold ground, rather than push towards their own aim. She made every other subgroup hold ground rather than fall back and circle around. She was certainly hoping to use Feyazki's *whisperers* to offer more dynamic commands, but they had yet to be used in a battle. She was also using the trumpets for dynamic commands, but wanted a set of passive cascading commands to each cavalry subgroup just in case they had difficulty hearing the trumpets during the melee. More than anything, she did not want her forces to just sit there on their horses because they were unsure of what to do next. The whole point of cavalry, to Trela, was to constantly keep stirring the pot, to keep the chaos running high. Rewista must not be able to tell what was happening around her. For it was in frustrated confusion that most commanders could be made to make a fatal error.

After dispersing her cavalry she consulted with Lishean. She wanted him towards the rear, handing out orders to the infantry and the archers. She felt that she needed to lead the infantry in this battle, to be the spearhead, as it were. She would keep Feyazki nearby, not only for protection, but also because he could instantly switch between all the different *whisperers* in her warpack.

"You cannot be on the front lines, swinging a sword, and still think you have enough extra capacity to command. It cannot be done. One of the two will suffer. If your focus is not on the warrior right in front of you, how will you parry his blows? If your focus is to survive your personal fight, how will you be able to strategize what to do with cavalry subgroup D2? How will you even communicate to Feyazki what you want him to *whisper*? Shall you shout above clanging din of sword upon shield? I understand that you want to lead the warpack by deed as well as word, and that is a noble want trust me, but you are spreading yourself too thin. Listen to reason. Do not let your personal pride turn into hubris." Lishean looked a little frustrated at the end of his speech. Trela had been ignoring him until the word "hubris." Did not Rewista herself just warn Trela of the very same thing?

"You worry too much, Lishean. Once we have broken their front lines, I will fall back and begin commanding my warriors in earnest. I will only be at the spearhead for the briefest amount of time. All of my warrior groups, cohorts, and maniples have their main orders and their cascading orders to hold them through until we make a puncture." Trela spoke quietly to Lishean, making sure her words had no hot emotion in them. "The warpack needs to see me break their front lines, Lishean. They need to know their trust in me is well founded."

"These 'cascading orders,' as you keep calling them, are complete rubbish. They have not been tested, and I think they will cause more confusion than they will eliminate. Let us try one new trick at a time. This battle, try your cascading orders and hang back to try your *whisper* trick if they do not work. Set up your mobile command post and roll out your beloved maps. In the next battle you can try to fight with one hand and command the entire warpack with your other." Lishean was not calming down.

"Your concern is noted, Lishean, and your advice is appreciated. I have decided to lead the infantry at this battle, however. I will make sure to fall back as quickly as I may, but you are not going to change my mind. All you will accomplish is angering your Kriishan." Trela could not afford a long, drawn-out argument. The warpack was ready for battle, and there had already been too many delays.

"I would rather have an angry commander than a dead one." He turned and walked into the warpack, disappearing quickly into the fold. Trela knew that he meant well and that she would have to soothe him over after the battle. For now, though, she needed to get to the head of the infantry.

Trela turned to her other counselors for support. They all stared hard at her. She realized that she would have much soothing to do after this battle. She sent Clerin, Croy, and Knill to the mobile medic unit. She knew it was frustrating Knill that she continually removed him from the front lines, but she would not be able to forgive herself if something happened to him. Escha, Estfale, and Malghain were dispersed amongst the cavalry units. That left Dartsyle, Gyllhelon, Torpalin, Haswyxe, and Feyazki amongst her infantry group.

Trela wanted to give Rewista the chance to engage, so she started the infantry with a slow march to the thunder of her war drums. She kept the pace at a walk as they crossed the meadow. The other warpack just waited for them patiently. The steady beat of the drums kept her heartbeat up and eventually her warriors began to beat their swords against their shields in time with the drums as they marched. She felt the morale picking back up. They were marching in step, heading towards battle as a single unit. There was no more waiting, no more wondering. The fighting was to begin soon.

As they approached at a slow jog, however, the center of Rewista's warpack caved in. Her warriors walked backwards as Trela's neared. Trela slowed her warpack's advance, knowing it must be a trap of some kind. Eventually she stopped her advance, and Rewista's warpack halted. About six Pyrans could have laid head to foot in the distance between them. Just then a cavalry sub-group flew past the front line in a blur. Trela cursed the over-zealous lieutenant who broke ranks too soon. Trela pondered briefly before giving the signal for her cavalry. Something was definitely afoot with Rewista's warriors. The trumpets blared.

As the rest of Trela's cavalry shot up the sides of Rewista's infantry, they rushed forward and attacked. Trela barely had time to lift her sword before the battle had begun. It quickly became chaotic and she had a moment of panic in the confusion. She could not figure out why she would be nervous, but her stomach was becoming more nauseous by the moment. Suddenly, Feyazki was next to her.

"They were hiding halberds, Trela. They just decimated Nylse's cavalry unit." Trela hopped back from the fighting to better speak with Feyazki. The sub group that rode by must have been Nylse's. He had something to prove ever since she had broken his arm. Lishean had argued against giving him any responsibility whatsoever, but she had overruled him. She could only hope that Nylse's folly would be beneficial to the warpack as a whole.

"Call them off. All of them! The trap isn't for the infantry, it's for the cavalry. Swing all the horses to the rear of the warpack. I'll have to figure out what to do with them in a minute." Feyazki was already ignoring her and *whispering* to the cavalry. Trela hoped that they got the warning quickly enough. A warrior crashed through the line and came screaming straight at Feyazki. She was able to pierce his side before he could reach his target. As he fell to the ground, one thought repeated itself in her mind. *Lishean was right.* Over and over, it repeated.

They fought that way for several moments, infantry against infantry. Finally, Feyazki had contacted each of the cavalry units and approached Trela for new messages. She fell back when she realized he was ready again.

"Tell Lishean to use all the archers. Go over our heads. He is no longer in any danger of striking the cavalry, and we shall hold our ground here." Trela made sure he got the message and then turned back to the front line.

Torpalin had carved out a small buffer around him, so she sidled up next to him. "We go no further than here. Keep the line here." He turned to Gyllhelon on his right and conveyed Trela's message to her.

Luckily, Lishean did not wait long before unleashing the longbows, even though he despised them. They arched high overhead and fell towards the back of Rewista's warpack. Lishean was obviously worried about striking any of Trela's warriors. It made Rewista's warriors redouble their efforts at the front line, pushing Trela's back a little. Feyazki approached again, and so Trela pulled herself back. Another volley of arrows darkened the skies briefly and gave her an idea.

"Have Lishean find all the shortbow archers who can ride. They should be escorted by the more experienced of the cavalry, of course. I want them to ride beside the warpack, out of halberd range, and fire into the ranks of warriors. I want a constant circuit on both sides. If the enemy runs out to meet them, do not engage, but skirt around back to our warpack. I do not want any of our cavalry engaging Rewista's infantry. We cannot afford whatever she is trying to trick us into." Trela patted Feyazki on the shoulder so that he knew she was done giving her instructions. She then ran back to the front line to fight amongst her warriors. A third wave of arrows passed overhead towards Rewista's back line.

Trela was enjoying the front line work. Swinging a sword felt honest to her. As a commander, she was always trying to think up ways to confuse her opponent, to catch them off guard. That strategy led to what one could consider underhanded tactics. She trusted her warriors completely. There was no doubt in her mind that if her infantry stood toe to toe against Rewista's, they would eventually wear her down and win. And it would be a good, honest win. Her warriors' lives, as an aggregate, as a warpack, were her responsibility, however. And the quickest victory often sheds the least amount of blood. Therefore, she was willing to put archers on horseback and harass Rewista's flanks. She hoped it would make her opponent feel unarmored. Naked. She needed Rewista to get frustrated.

Soon arrows were flying from Rewista's back line. The flew over both warpacks at the front, but came down somewhere in the middle of Trela's infantry. She hoped that they had the foresight to be prepared with their shields. They had certainly had enough warning. Another wave from Lishean's longbow archers passed by. It made Trela wonder if her arrows were being successful, and whether or not Rewista's arrows were successful. She surely did not want to be wasting arrows if they were just being blocked. And if they were not being blocked, then were her own warriors being decimated in return? Trela stepped back from the front line to ponder the effectiveness of trading volleys of arrows. She looked around for Feyazki, to see if he could contact a *whisperer* in the middle of her infantry and maybe glean some intelligence.

Trela caught sight of Feyazki a little further back into her warpack. He appeared tense and was staring up at the sky. She started walking towards him when another thick mass of arrows came flying over from Rewista's warpack. Suddenly Feyazki raised both his arms and shouted something that was immediately lost amongst the din of battle. To Trela's astonishment, the arrows burst into flame as they flew overhead. A quick, bright, and consuming flame. She could not tell what happened to the arrowheads since they were so small, but she assumed they were less dangerous without their shafts and fletching attached to them. She quietly thanked fate for bringing such an imaginative mage into her destiny. Instead of interrupting his defensive vigil, she yelled to the warriors immediately surrounding her.

"Brothers and sisters, now is the time to press our attack. Follow me to victory!" Trela turned and ran back to the front line. She was not sure how many could have heard her in the deafening battle, but enough followed behind her that she was able to pierce into Rewista's line slightly. She ended up near Torpalin again. When he saw that she was pressing forward, he gave a mighty yell and swung his axe in a continuous X in front of himself. Dartsyle was suddenly at her left arm, piercing a warrior's stomach with a powerful thrust from his blade. Trela felt elated. They were not gaining much ground, but they were gaining some.

The slow, hard push took longer than Trela had wanted. Try as they might, they had difficulty moving the front line. It seemed that every time they gained a couple steps forward, they got pushed back at least one. The effort not to lose ground was all consuming. She did not disperse any more orders or check up on any other portion of her warpack. She could not even watch the arrows overhead to make sure that Feyazki was still immolating them. Her only communication was between Torpalin on her right and Dartsyle on her left. And even that was mostly non-verbal. Eventually her mind became as numb as her swordarm. She finally allowed herself to admit that they were going to have to switch with fresh troops.

That was when it happened. Rewista's trumpets blared into the open sky, and the fighting at the front line began to slack off. Her warriors were still defending themselves, but they had stopped pushing forwards. Trela's own warriors sensed a coming lull and began to ease up. Eventually there was a small distance between the two warpacks. The fighting had come to a standstill.

Trela waved to her own trumpeters. They quickly signaled an end to the merciless arrows. Trela waited for some time before the warpack in front of her parted and Rewista herself strode forward. She had the same silent warriors around her that she had brought to the parley. She did not say a word. No kudos and no threats. She merely threw her sword down in front of Trela.

"Kneel in the sand." Trela spoke the words of condemnation as coldly as she could. She wanted to strike fear into Rewista.

If it worked, Trela could not tell. Rewista's face stayed completely emotionless as she knelt down on both knees. She held her hands behind her back in supplication. After staring quietly at Trela for a long moment, she bent her head forward. Ready for the blade.

"All of you. The Seconds as well. Kneel in the sand." The other four pyrans knelt in front of Trela with hands held behind them and heads bowed. The two warpacks had opened up a small circle between them, around the group, giving Trela plenty of room behind the kneeling warriors. She walked behind them swinging her sword. She spoke loudly, to reach as many ears as possible.

"Mercy is for the weak, is it not? The vanquished, by custom and by law, have given up the right to existence. Look upon your commander! See how she bows her head. This is to save you. This is to stop the bloodshed, to stop the arrows, to stop the cavalry, to stop the axes. This is to put an end to a losing argument. Is this weak? Is admitting defeat and paying the ultimate sacrifice weak? Look upon your commander in her defeat! See how she peacefully accepts her loss for you. She is willing to die so that you may live. This is her mercy to you. This is her gift to you. Her life... is your gift... is her mercy." Trela kept walking as she was talking and circled back around the kneeling warriors to stop in front of Rewista.

"And that is the ultimate in strength! No commander has ever shown more strength than when they are kneeling... vanquished before their foe... waiting to die. I have a different idea of custom and law. I believe there is strength in mercy. I believe in cooperation. I believe in being given more than one chance." Trela stabbed her sword into the soft soil between herself and Rewista. "Raise upon one knee and kiss my blade. Swear fealty to me as the Kriishan and I shall let you live. Honorably. For you have shown great honor to your warpack today by offering up your life for their safety. And so I do not take any ghulzans today. When the Kriishan says 'kneel in the sand,' it is for fealty, not death." Trela grew silent. They all did. No one made a sound or even moved. All eyes were fixated on Rewista. Trela did not know if she would kiss the blade or insist on becoming a ghulzan, or even insist upon being beheaded. Maybe she would attempt to grab the sword and attack Trela. Her head stayed bowed for quite some time, making the air dense with anticipation, while Trela stood motionless and quiet in front of her. Trela wondered briefly if she was marking Rewista for a later assassination by allowing her to betray Qizern and the customs of old. Of course, it was either that or kill her now in front of her warpack.

Rewista slowly pulled one knee up in front of her and kissed Trela's sword. She did not look up at Trela, but spoke quietly to the sword in front of her. "You are truly the Kriishan. My life is yours."

Though the words were spoken quietly, all those around heard her clearly. Much to Trela's surprise, Rewista's warpack erupted into applause. Rewista stood and stepped back with her arms open. "My warriors are at your command."

Trela was confused at first. It was not until later that Rewista explained it was all a test. Trela had to prove her skills as a commander, a warrior, and as an agent of destiny. When Trela asked, "How did you know I would not kill you?" Rewista replied, "I had no such knowledge, only a strange trust in my heart. But I will tell you this. If you had killed me then, every one of my warriors was ready to destroy you and only you. And your back was towards them all."

The victory was fulfilling, it truly was. Trela felt like she had proven herself to her own warriors and to Rewista's. She had begun to gain more confidence in Feyazki's *whisperers*, even if she was losing confidence in her cascading orders. The addition of Rewista to the warpack was also incredibly fortuitous. Though Trela had quite a ways to go before she fully trusted Rewista, her acumen as a leader could not be questioned. Rewista had a rare mind for strategy. She understood the mind of a warrior with a crystalline clarity and could get them to do the most menials tasks with gusto. Rewista could never replace Lishean, but she was one of the few who could come close. Her warriors were incredibly loyal, and she fully shifted that loyalty to Trela. The humility and obvious intelligence that she showed during the warpack's transition gave her the respect and loyalty of Trela's warriors as well. Truly the victory was advantageous for Trela in many different ways. It was after that battle that Trela made her standard. It was a lightning bolt about to be shot from a bow. She made them both silver and placed them on a field of deep green. This was also the time she started wearing her crimson cloak more conspicuously.

The victory did nothing to alleviate her funding problems, however. Since Rewista's entire warpack enthusiastically and passionately joined with Trela's, she could not just strip them of all their possessions. There were not even any deserters, or at least none who were noticed. None to speak of. No, there were just more mouths to feed.

When Trela dreamed of leading a warpack across the Pyran realm, cutting a swath to the Dekhan plateau, she had not imagined the difficulty of boots. Socks and boots plagued Trela like Qizern never could. A warpack like hers was always on the move, always walking. If they stayed in one place for too long, they would destroy all of the wildlife in the area. They could denude a forest faster than goats could ravish a hillside. The logistics of keeping the warpack fed and shod were simply... mundane. It was incredibly difficult and it took all of her resources to just keep them going. She walked the razor's edge of success or failure. But there was no glory to the trials and tribulations. There was a certain mediocrity to it that wore her down. Trela was as loyal to her warriors as they were to her. She would do anything in her power to protect them, to keep them safe and happy, to provide for them. And that was what logistics came down to. That was what leadership came down to. Providing for your crew.

The next three warpacks that they came across were simply absorbed. They were small, about a quarter the size of Rewista's, and they came without riches. They arrived hungry and without socks or quality boots. One, poorly led by a Pyran megalomaniac named Hylth, had scarves and burlap sacks wrapped around their feet. Not all of them, but many. Trela was not one to kill a warpack commander who immediately surrendered and swore fealty, but Hylth made her want to. She felt that any leader who abused their own troops so mightily should suffer as badly as if they had been defeated on the battlefield. Maybe more so. In fact, it was Hylth who pulled Trela from her rut. He was such an obviously inept leader that Trela began to study what made him so. What was it about him that disgusted her so?

Hylth was short and wiry. He kept closely trimmed and meticulously shaped facial hair. His dark hair was kept short in the classic Pyran military style. There were no obvious scars, no disfigurements, not even one conspicuous mole. He seemed handsome by typical standards, even including his short stature. In fact, there was only one physical feature that Trela could think of that bothered her. He always had a ready smile on his lips that never seemed to reach his eyes. It was the smile that first set her on edge. There was a silent condescension to it. It was as if he were thinking superior thoughts while you were speaking. Or, at least, what he felt were superior thoughts. He always seemed to be on the verge of saying something cruel. Some obvious point that was only kept silent because he used his incredible self-control to overcome the urge. Trela also didn't like his laugh. It was a deep, throaty, almost conspiratorial, "heh-heh-heh" sound and his eyes would dart around to measure who was laughing with him and who was silent. Trela was sure that he kept tabs on those types of social interactions, to see who got the joke and who did not. As if a lack of joining in the cruel laughter meant that a warrior did not understand what was being said. As if it were impossible that one could understand the wit but not be amused by it.

These slight foibles of individual personalities Trela usually ignored. If Hylth was just annoying to her, she would just ignore him. There were many that she felt were needed and welcomed in her warpack that she did not necessarily like. There were many that were unnecessary—the fat and the gristle of the warpack—that she fully tolerated with a heartfelt smile. She understood that many ingredients, though tasteless or even repugnant if eaten on their own, could have a pleasant effect upon the whole dish once properly cooked. And even ingredients that everyone enjoyed, like salt or sugar, could become obnoxiously overpowering if taken in too high of dosages. Trela felt that it was necessary to have a large variety of personalities mixed amongst her warpack. She felt it made her warpack as a whole more resilient, gave it more ductility, more strength. She was generally concerned with her warpack as a whole, as a separate living and sentient creature. The individuals that she did not interact with much did not affect her, one way or the other, so long as the warpack as a whole was healthy and thriving.

That was what really bothered her about Hylth. He was a vector who carried a disease from his own decimated warpack to infect her own. That thought was also what made her embrace mundane logistics. That realization was what pushed her from being a great warrior, into being a great leader. She had always cared greatly about the overall mood of her warpack. She had always been hyperconscious of the morale of her warriors. Some commanders cared greatly about who drank too much or who was sleeping with whom. Some were even vocally predujidiced against the loves of those like Dartsyle and Rewista. Trela had always been very liberal about these things, believing that, as long as it did not affect the warpack as a whole, derlians should be allowed to be derlians. Only so many of them really needed mothering, and she certainly filled her brig when she needed to. She never allowed fights to induce schisms into her fighting force. She was not negligent. But it was not until her examination of a diseased warpack, one that was on its deathbed, that she moved beyond the idea of warpack morale as a collective consciousness and fully to the idea of the warpack as an individual organism. Something that needed to be tended and cared for in the broadest sense. Hylth gave her the realization that a group of derlians could have their morale infected, as with a disease. More importantly was her next realization. It was more of a deepening than a realization. It was a leap of consciousness that enabled her a fuller understanding. To nurse a warpack back to health she needed to use logistics. That was the healing spell. That was the medicine that could cure Hylth's disease and improve the warpack's immunity to future outbreaks. With that realization, Trela threw herself into study with a fervent desire. She first needed to understand the disease completely, then she could begin to examine the magic and medicine at her disposal to cure it. For Trela, logistics were mundane no more. She could not afford them to be.

Trela knew that she did not like Hylth personally but was not exactly sure why she felt that he was the vector. Even though she was loath to spend any time with him, she knew that she must. She invited him to a private meeting. A little one-on-one, a tete-a-tete. To make it less awkward, she decided to speak with him over a meal. That way she could always eat or drink while he was blathering on. It would give them something to discuss during the odd silences that occur during meetings of disparate derlians. To Trela a meal was, conversationally, much like the weather. An innocuous subject to broach when nothing else could be thought of. She decided to have the meal at the meeting tent. It was a bit large but nicely situated between her tent and her cook's.

Hylth arrived in good form. He was barely early, cleaned up, well groomed, and carrying a large jug of grog. He smiled ingratiatingly as Trela opened the tent flap. She did her best to ignore it and smiled back.

"May I come in?" He bobbed his head quickly.

"Of course." Trela backed out of the way, to the side, and swept her arm in front of her. In her mind she could hear herself, *That was why I opened the flap,* but she did not allow the thought to come further into her mind.

Hylth took a few quick steps past her and then slowed to gawk around at the tent. Maybe gawk was an unfair word. He looked around room and at the ceiling appreciatively. "This is nice. A little plain perhaps, but certainly vast." He nodded to himself. "Do you have all your meals here?"

Trela almost laughed as he asked that question, but luckily it just came out as a quiet grunt. "No, no. This is the meeting tent. Sometimes I have large meetings here. Sometimes small." She looked around the tent as well. She had not realized how grimy the edges looked. It amazed her how many times she could enter a tent without actually looking at it, examining it. It was such a daily, mundane experience for her. She wondered how long something small, like a stain, would go unnoticed. Then she wondered how long a small tear would go unnoticed. "Kolaf! We are ready!"

"Would you care for a glass of grog first?" Hylth shook his jug.

"Sure, sure." Trela sat down at a long table across from the small one that had place settings on it. Hylth dutifully picked up the goblets from the other table and brought them over. While he filled them with a sour-smelling grog, Trela drummed her fingers on the tabletop and cursed herself for being unable to think of anything besides the weather. She did not want to start grilling him until he had a finished the main course. She wanted him to be off his guard and a little lazy before she tried to glean how he had ruined his warpack. "How about this heat, huh?" She inwardly cringed after she listened to herself.

"It has been brutal, hasn't it? Saps the strength right out of your warriors." He handed her a goblet that was filled to the brim. She waited until he had a drink of his before she sipped her own. "Luckily we don't have to walk, do we?" His smile had an air of sweet innocence. It was almost cloying.

"Yes, I guess most of the officers do ride." Trela made a mental note to herself.

"Most? What is the point of being an officer if you are forced to walk with the rest of them?" He took another drink.

"Them?" Trela was trying to get used to his way of wording things.

"You know... the warriors. Them." He squinted at her sideways. "To properly follow orders, a grunt must know they are a grunt. To properly give orders, an officer must know they are an officer." He paused for a moment, waiting for her to speak. "These lines may be somewhat illusionary. I mean, the greatest warrior is not always the greatest leader. Therefore, it can seem like a paradox to have a Pyran whose station as a warrior is lower giving orders to someone who is greater. You see, these things get confused if they are allowed to mingle. There is an inherit separation here. The reason a great warrior will follow a poor warrior, who happens to be a great leader, into battle is mostly due to habit. It is buttressed by this separation. They follow the other because that is how things are done." He paused again. Trela had never heard a speech such as this. It was a fascinating glimpse into Hylth and his warpack. She could have listened to him ramble on for hours like that. Therefore, during each of his pauses, she merely sipped her grog. She decided to give him as much rope as he desired. "Have you ever seen a trained dog?" Trela nodded. "When you give orders to a dog, do you ask it a question first? Do you give it the treat first? Do you start out by patting it on the head?" Trela shook her head. "Of course not! That would confuse the issue. Things are done in the proper order, or the trick will not be completed correctly." He paused again and tilted his head again. This time in the opposite direction. "You are judging me, aren't you? I have watched the officers in this warpack, and they behave the same here as they would anywhere in this realm. They ride horses during the long march. They eat their meals together more often than they do with the warriors they command. In fact, did you ride a horse today?" He paused for a long, long time. Trela knew she could not hold out on him this time, no matter how much she drank.

"Yes. I rode today. Not only that, but I rode with my inner circle." She took another drink. The grog he had brought had a tasty vibrancy that belied its first impressions.

"You see? You understand how things are run. Instinctively. That is why you are a good leader." He looked relieved after she had spoken.

"I am trying to be." Trela nodded at him. Luckily, at that moment, Kolaf arrived with the food. Trela waved a hand towards their seats. She was not sure whether the gesture was for Hylth's benefit or Kolaf's.

They all moved to the small table at the same time. It could have been a disaster, but Kolaf quickly placed what he had been carrying and dodged back out of the way to get the rest. Trela would have to remember to thank him for his suave professionalism later. He was very skilled at his chosen vocation, which made her job that much easier. Truly, he was one of the many hidden members of her warpack who were vital to its smooth function.

Hylth and Trela silently poked around their plates until Kolaf returned. He placed the rest of the food between them and bowed to Trela. "If you care for anything else, just holler." His bright smile looked almost out of place in his old and weatherworn face. Trela immediately felt embarrassed at the thought. Quietly they filled their plates with Kolaf's various offerings. Hylth was the first to break the silence.

"So does that mean he will be listening to our entire conversation?" Hylth's smile looked slightly worried.

"I've never had a reason to question Kolaf's discretion. Believe me, he has overheard much more important conversations." She had not really thought about it before, but it was true. Kolaf either had the tightest lips in the warpack, or he was half deaf. Since he was always prompt if she needed him, Trela assumed the former. The thought made her wonder about how many in her warpack could overhear her if they chose. Many of the warriors had off-duty tasks, like Kolaf. The tasks were not necessarily servile, but somehow they gave the warrior an air of invisibility. She made a mental note to keep better track of her hidden warriors.

"How do you like the grog?" Hylth barely looked up from his food.

"It's excellent, truly." Trela paused for a moment. She knew there were Pyrans who could tell all about the hidden flavors of grog. Some could even tell which herbs were used and where they were grown. Where it was bottled, in what cave it was aged. She had never been a connoisseur, however. "Where is it from?"

"The cellars of the Guard captain of Loipaln. We overran the city one night during a harvest festival." He snorted derisively. "Stupid farmers didn't even know what hit them. It was pretty useless, as hauls are considered, but the captain had a cellar full of bottles, casks, and amphorae of some of the finest grogs I have ever had the pleasure to taste." He lowered his voice conspiratorially. "I still have a wagon pull the remnants around for me, but I've transferred it all to leather bags so its less conspicuous."

"Oh, I meant 'where was it aged?' " She smiled a little and took a sip. It was incredibly good, there was no denying that. "So... what did the citizens of Loipaln do to your warpack?" He stopped laughing. "I mean, what was their transgression? What led to the sacking?" Truly, she had not meant to offend.

"Why did you sack Parthia?" He leaned back but kept his hand forward touching the stem of his goblet.

"You would have to ask Iventorn for the reason, but I do not believe it was fully sacked. From what I recall, we left the citizens unscathed." She took another sip.

"Well, I never said we sacked Loipaln, for that matter. But trust me, Iventorn's warriors took their fair share away from Parthia. Besides, you should be congratulating me on taking from one of

Qizern's servants and bringing unto you." He lifted his goblet in a small salute.

Trela thought about it for a moment and realized that it was the farmer comment that made her think he had attacked Loipaln unprovoked. He was correct in his assertion that he never said he stole, or gained his "fair share," from any of the non-warrior civilians. But it was the way he talked about it. His disdainful language. She had to keep in mind that she did not like him and that tainted what she imagined his motives to be.

"To the fall of Qizern." Trela raised her goblet to follow Hylth's salute. He had almost placed his goblet back down.

"To the fall of Qizern." He raised his goblet again and took a deep draught. They ate in silence for a while. "When did you realize you were the Kriishan? Do you just wake up one day and say, 'I should try to kill the King of the Pyrans?' "

"The feeling of destiny pervades my entire life. If there was a time when it did not exist, its slow fade into being makes it impossible to discern any real starting time. But in answer to your question, though my grandmother spoke of it often, it was not until Synde that I knew there was no turning back." She was prepared to continue, but was interrupted.

"Ah, Synde! Yes, I met him once. He could convince a wolf that it was a sheep. He was a master of the mind. 'The Will will overcome,' he used to say." Hylth smiled but there was a small sourness to it. Her first impulse was to ask about Synde. She had spoken to so few that had met him. Her instincts, however, were directly opposing. And his smile... his words... She felt the tripwire on her shin and she froze. She needed to back up before the trap sprang.

"Yes, he did say that lot." Trela took a sip of grog to gather her thoughts. "But I am more interested in you. How did you come to command a warpack?"

This seemed to take him by surprise. His mouth froze in mid motion. He leaned back with his goblet and stared at her briefly over its rim. He was not silent for long, however.

"I guess you could say that I inherited it from my father." He took a sip but kept hold of the goblet. "He was a great warrior and a respected leader. I was his favorite son and he took me all over the Pyran realm." He took a deeper sip and then replaced his goblet. "I was never a great warrior myself, so I strove to become a great leader. I learned all I could from him and his lieutenants, but they did not have the understanding of strategy that I craved. So I begged him to send me to the Academy at Agoge."

"Isn't the academy where all the Guard get chosen from? Isn't it run by Qizern?" Trela picked at her food like a bird, having gotten sated during their earlier moments of silence.

"Yes and yes, but do not be concerned. The Academy has seen many many Kings, and will continue to do so. That is where I met Synde, you know." He smiled and gave her a small wink.

"How long were you there for? You obviously did not become one of the Guard." She was unsure of what his game was.

"For a full five sun cycles. Oh, I became adequate with a sword, but certainly not Guard material. I was there for the learning. Did you know, they have a detailed account of every major battle ever waged on the Dekhan plateau? Troop movements, weather conditions, geography—all meticulously detailed. They even have many lowland battles documented as well. And the maps! You would love the maps. We even had a war room where we could move mock troops around a large topographic model. Yes... those were the best cycles of my life." They both took a drink during his pause. "Eventually, however, my father was unable to keep up with the payments. He never had a mind of how to hoard resources. He was like a river, instead of a lake. Resources flow in and they flow back out just as quickly. I was forced to return to assist with the warpack, rather than complete my studies."

They had finished eating, but Trela did not want to call Kolaf back yet. She had not gained the information she needed from Hylth. She needed to probe a little further.

"And how were the warpack's affairs handled when you came back? Did you... did you take over from your father?" Trela had heard of fathers refusing to send their sons to academies, since the son often tried to usurp them shortly upon return.

"No! No, of course not. He would have none of that. Even though he did not have two coins to rub together, he refused to allow me to make decisions. To make any modifications to the way that the warpack was run. He refused to realize his failings." Hylth took a mighty draught. "I tried to explain it to him, again and again, but he would not listen to me." The emotional twinge in Hylth's voice was faint, but noticeable. The quietness started to gain in density, like a thick fog.

"Well... what were his failings?" Trela felt like she needed to keep him talking.

"I think he misunderstood the role of a leader. He was such a skilled warrior, and his warriors respected him so much, that he could not separate himself from them. He was not only amongst them, he was one of them. They were family to him. More so than his actual family. And that led to his ultimate failing. He could not say 'no.' It was impossible for him." Hylth finished his goblet and set it back down on the table with a quiet thunk. Trela quickly finished hers and started to refill them both as he continued. "If a lieutenant asked for swords or axes, he gave them. Whether or not their existing arms could be sharpened back into usability. If another asked for more arrows, he gave them. If someone asked for extra food for a feast he not only gave them the food, but gave *all* of his warriors enough extra for the feast. Regardless if they were involved in the original festivities. And the grog! He gave away rivers of grog. And not only that..." Hylth barely hid an unsightly but quiet burp behind a hastily raised fist. He took another quick drink. "Not only that, but he refused to sack villages. He was always concerned about what the farmers would think of him. I mean..." A little laugh escaped his stained lips. "How are you supposed to support all those warriors? How can you keep everyone happy all the time?" He cast his eyes down in a brief moment of brooding. "Especially when you cannot even afford your own son's education." He looked up at her with wet eyes. "That is what stung the most, I think. I came back from Agoge, two cycles away from graduation, to join his rundown band of jolly old Pyrans. No one wanted to change their ways, curtail their expenses. They had all been adventuring together since their youth! It is like a cart, being pulled down the same road a thousand times, stuck in the ruts of its past. And when my father had his... accident... well, they just did not want to follow me. They did, out of loyalty, but not out of loyalty to me. Out of loyalty to my dead father." He sat back, spent. Trela took a deep drink and tried to think of something soothing to say.

"I am sure there are many warriors..." She was interrupted.

"No. No there are not. But thank you for trying, Trela. Truly, running into your warpack has breathed a new hope into me. Your beauty has not necessarily been sung about, but you have your curious charms. And I am fully flattered that you have asked me to dine with you. In fact, your interest has rekindled my own spirit." He smiled warmly to her and raised his glass. "To Trela. To us."

"What do you mean? What do you think this dinner is?" She was caught up by his use of the word "curious," but she could not be angry about that now.

"Why, to get to know me better, what else?" His grin became more knowing.

"I eat with all the warpack leaders who are absorbed. I ate with Rewista." Trela could feel adrenalin pushing through her veins and breathed through her nose to calm herself.

"Yes, I have heard those rumors as well. To be honest, I wasn't sure if I had a chance. Apparently you straddle both sides of the fence..." He may have been stopping there, he may have been continuing, but Trela could take no more.

"You are wrong. You are dead wrong. This meal is about learning why your warpack is in the worst shape of any I have ever seen. I have no interest in you whatsoever. I do not dabble in the other side of the fence, as you put it, but yes, in fact, Rewista has a much better chance at bedding me than you ever would. At least she is a leader highly respected by her warriors. You are reviled by all!" Trela immediately felt ashamed for losing her temper. This entire evening was supposed to be a clandestine intelligence gathering opportunity. She had shown her hand and thrown that all away in a moment's loss of self control.

"So, it's the Gaen, isn't it? Or one of those Luftens. You just don't like Pyrans, do you?" Hylth stood and angrily grabbed his jug. "You should watch who you make enemies with." He stormed out, showing his own emotional loss of self control.

Trela sat back down. She didn't even remember standing. She took another drink of Hylth's excellent grog.

"Be careful around him. I am not one to spread talk, but the noise from his old warriors is that he killed his own father to gain control of the warpack." Kolaf had snuck up behind her. "Snuck" was probably too strong of a word, Trela thought to herself. She had just not noticed him.

"I would bet money on it." Trela motioned for Kolaf to join her. As he sat down, she handed him her goblet. "Please, you should enjoy the fruits of your labor." He did not pull a plate of food to him but took a swig of her grog and smiled at her. "In fact, if you know of anyone from Hylth's warpack, I would love to speak to them. Not only do I need to finalize my opinion of why he is such a terrible leader, but I think I need some dirt. He has outlived his usefulness, and I have angered him. He needs to be banished at the least." Trela smiled warmly to Kolaf. "If you are unable to find the right warriors to speak with, at least point me in the right direction. You are one of my most trusted warriors, Kolaf. I probably do not express my appreciation enough." She had almost said "most trusted servants," but she had wisely checked herself.

"Your trust is not unfounded, Kriishan. I am a true believer and have been since your speech on the invisible stairs. But even if I was not a believer, I would do my best to help you put down that dog. You are correct. He is reviled by all." Kolaf raised the goblet to her.

Trela did not have a chance to present evidence at any sort of court martial against Hylth. Once the inquiries became serious, he stole away in the middle of the night, leaving his tent and belongings, even his wagon of grog, all behind. Trela had little doubt of his guilt, even before he absconded. Unfortunately, there was not much direct evidence. Hylth and his father were alone when the accident happened. There had been no witnesses. By all accounts Porthlac was incredible on a horse. And the accident did not just happen on any horse, but on his trusted warhorse, Clodhopper. Hylth's story was that the horse almost stepped upon a snake, reared up, and threw Porthlac off. Unfortunately, his neck was broken upon his fall. There were oddities, however. The area they were riding in was not known for harboring snakes. Clodhopper was trained to kick and step on derlians, which horses are naturally loathe to do, let alone small snakes. And, most odd, was the position that Porthlac was found in. Though his skull was not fractured, nor his face bruised or bloodied, his head was turned at such an extreme angle as to be looking behind himself. This puzzled many of those who saw it, but Porthlac was also an incredibly strong warrior. The odds of a weakling such as Hylth killing his own father in such a violent manner seemed low. So Hylth was given the benefit of the doubt. The fact that Porthlac was much beloved by so many was the only reason that the warpack stayed together under Hylth for as long as it did. Somehow, in the space of four moons, he had taken them from barely but comfortably surviving to the precipice of ruin. And they had sacked three villages in that time. The warpack was ready to revolt or disperse by the time that Trela had come along.

The talk was not what made Hylth flee, however. He knew that many others did not like him and he did not care. It was not being scorned by Trela or having all of the rumors flying around him again. No, it was chance advice from Croy that had sent him packing and solidified Trela's feelings of his guilt. Croy mentioned watching his Gaen mentor, the Blind One, speaking to the dead of Synde's ragtag refugee warpack. He spoke, in full hearing of Hylth, of how the dead could be coerced into speaking their story. Of telling truths of how they met their end. All at the meeting agreed that was a capital idea. Several of Hylth's, or it should be said Porthlac's, warpack swore that they knew where his body was buried. Hylth argued that it was far away and a waste of valuable time. Trela did not mind spending the time, however. Especially if it would lead to the truth. To her, this was a magical balm for what ailed Porthlac's warpack. This would cure them immediately. Though they were small in number compared to the rest of her warriors, Trela knew that putting that extra effort here, for them, would buy her extra loyalty from the entire warpack. Plus, she had invested time and energy into this mystery and had become curious herself. Hylth was gone by the next morning.

That should have been that. He was obviously guilty or he would not have run. But Trela wanted all in her warpack to be fully healed before continuing. She felt that the mystery of Porthlac needed to be solved. So they went in search of his grave.

Trela decided to make the search into somewhat of a quest. Not necessarily a quest to find the truth about Hylth—she believed she already knew that—but a quest to find the truth about warpack's disease, as she had begun to call it. She stopped riding her horse if the journey was difficult. She began to eat her meals with different warriors each night. She traveled amongst them and told dirty jokes. She spoke passionately with the lowliest members, those she had previously thought of as servants. She still had meetings with her Privy Council, yes. She still left Lishean in charge if she left the warpack for any length of time, or with Rewista should Lishean accompany her. She did not become an invisible warrior in her own warpack, lost amongst equals. But she did do her best to take the time to listen, to laugh, to experience all that her warriors wished to share with her. She was not necessarily one of them, but she was certainly accessible to all of them

What Trela discovered was amazing. The "servants," as she had deemed them, knew much more about her and her inner circle than she did about any one of them. They knew everything. Little secrets that she deemed too small to notice, or too well hidden to find, were talked about openly. Like whether Feyazki was riding with Clerin or Gyllhelon. Or if Elzie had visited Lishean during the night. The gossip never stopped, especially where the Privy Council was concerned. They waged bets on whether or not Tumu would ride that day, or if Torpalin would cut himself, or when Escha would return from a scouting mission. The daily life—the mundane, boring, rote existence—was laid bare for all to see and discuss. There were no secrets in the camp. At least not from the servants.

There was one who knew it all. Every bit of gossip, every bit of conjecture. One who understood a warpack's disease better than any other. One who understood that the cure was logistics. He was the ultimate servant in the warpack. He was the hub of all communication, all food, all shelter, all boots and socks, all tacks and harnesses, all things that make a warpack operate. He was the hub of logistics. He was the quartermaster, and his name was Wesduin.

Trela began conversing with Wesduin when her quest to prove Hylth's guilt began. She had certainly known of him and had even spoken with him several times before. But she had not sat down and had a real conversation with him. She had not gotten to know him. To her incredible shame, she had not even contemplated his importance. He was a servant doing a job. A boring job at that. How could counting socks be honorable let alone exciting? What she quickly realized, however, was how lucky she was that Lishean had chosen such a competent Pyran to be in charge of her logistics. She began to wonder if Wesduin was more important to the smooth operation of her warpack than she herself was. He was absolutely essential.

He first explained what he did. What his routine was. He broke it down into simple steps. Which was how he did everything—simple steps.

"I have fifteen wagons under me." Wesduin spoke of everything under his purview, under his auspice, as his own. It did not matter who ran the warpack, he was the quartermaster. "If we are going to settle in one place for a moon, I will unload them all. If we are going to camp for week, about five will be unburdened. If we are just staying the night, only one gets unloaded. I call her my 'satchel.' She's got a bit of everything on her or at least anything that might be needed in a jiffy. I refill her as she dwindles. I'm not one to leave her wanting, but I like to keep her lean enough that I can find what I need." He referred to anything that moved and carried something as "she." Even the draft animals, regardless of their actual gender. "I have a wagon just for boots. More important than swords, boots are. I've seen warpacks destroy each other with rocks and even their bare hands before, but I've never seen them march for long without boots. I have a wagon for soaps and detergents. Personal and industrial, depending on your needs. One cannot call themselves civilized without soap, nay. Note, however, that the soap wagon needs to be refilled much less than the others. We'll go moons without anyone touching it and then, when we settle next to a warm river, voom! We are all out of it. Everyone's clothes and arses are clean all at once. I've got a wagon just for cooking utensils. Pots, pans, kettles, cauldrons, and the like. I've got three for food and one for water. Sometimes these are empty, of course. You can watch the nervousness and anxiety build as they dwindle. You've never seen such wide and rolling eyes as when there's nothing on the food wagons. I've got one for extra tarps, tents, blankets, and pillows. I keep a nice heavy canvas tarp over that one, even if its not looking like rain. You never know. I've got a heavily laden one with extra arms. From quivers of arrows, to swords and halberds. Even covered with a heavy tarp, I carry a barrel of oil on that one. Nothing worse than rusted metal. I've got one for extra armor; most of it is leather but I gather as much metal as possible after a good battle. The warriors are supposed to be in charge of their own arms and armor, pounding out the dents and sharpening them up and the like, but you know how they can get. One's got extra clothing. Mostly socks and cotton shirts or leggings, but sometimes I'll hand out tunics or jerkins. The medics carry their own supplies, but I've got a wagon full of bandages, utensils, and cots, just in case. I've got all your meeting tables and chairs on one. You are welcome. I've got tools and extra wagon pieces, wheels, spare boards, and what have you on another. The last one carries the firewood. I carry everything for myself on my own horse so you don't have to worry about that. And I am just the quartermaster master. We keep picking up warpacks and we absorb their quartermasters as well. Some, like that rat Hylth, have nothing and are just a drain on our resources. That warpack appears to have been absorbed haphazardly. Mingling in various maniples and cohorts, wherever they may be needed or at least welcomed. But others, like Rewista's warpack, are almost completely whole; separate while absorbed. They follow her and she follows you. Her quartermaster has several wagons of his own and keeps his own warriors outfitted nicely. Grand fellow, Sezal is. Quick as a whip and kind enough to offer inter-warpack loans without a ledger. Reminds me of myself when I was younger."

And on and on. Wesduin was the rare type of Pyran who did not appear to need to breathe while he talked. He obviously loved his work. And it was only because he was so skilled that it seemed like he did nothing at all. He never stopped moving though, much like his talking. He would fold a mountain of shirts while extolling the secrets of waterproofing canvas or how to properly grease an axle. Trela joined in to help, of course, but while listening she would find that one of her shirts was folded to his five. If she tuned him out, she could get much more done, but that defeated much of the purpose of their talks. He had such an absolute enthusiasm for logistics, it could not help but rub off on her a bit. And that, more than any absolute knowledge, was what she really needed.

They found Porthlac's body less than a moon after they began. Trela had not allowed her warriors to sack anything along the way, but she did let them hunt. Their supplies were dwindling, much to the chagrin of Wesduin. Trela did not want combat along the way. She did not want any distractions, any side adventures. She needed to follow this through, to spend her time with Wesduin, and to get a full understanding of warpack life sans the war. Somehow it felt like being with Iventorn's warpack and having Lishean yell at her each morning for holding her dagger wrong. It felt like being with Synde's band of refugees and having him show her how to roll her wrist while striking under an opponent's shield. It felt like beginnings. It felt like learning. There was something acutely awkward about it all. No combat, just boots. Trela truly found a passion for logistics. She had found the medicine, the cure, for warpack's disease.

Though Croy remembered the spell, it was Feyazki who cast it. Though no one was surprised by the outcome—Hylth had torqued his father's head violently while Porthlac filled his canteen at a stream—there was some surprise at the vitriol that Porthlac's shade exuded. It demanded a promise from all within hearing to exact revenge upon Hylth if anyone ever saw him again. After listening to the shade's stories of Hylth, all agreed to the pact.

Chapter 17

Croy quickly adapted to the regimented lifestyle of the warpack. Sleeping, eating, and working at the same times of day, every day, reminded him of living underground. It was comforting in a small way. He was happiest when there were long stretches of routine between the battles.

He had been given a horse after the owner died during the battle with Rewista. Her name was Crusher, but Croy had taken to calling her Buttercup. She was a sturdy warhorse, bred for strength not speed. She was a chestnut brown, with dark markings on her forehead. Her trimmed tail and proud mane were a deep, glossy black color. Best of all, she was trained to be steered by using only his knees.

During the respites of routine, Croy rode about half the time and walked the other half. Sometimes it would depend upon who he was traveling with. Tumu, for instance, rarely rode a horse. Since Tumu was often in the company of Knill, whenever Croy wanted to chat with Knill, he would often do it on foot. Other times it would depend upon how tired he was or how tired he thought Buttercup was. She liked to browse on her own time. She would start eating at a small clump of grass or a bush—she loved gorse—and the whole warpack would walk past them. Eventually she would be satisfied, and he would hop on so they could catch back up with the front of the pack. Actually, Croy quite enjoyed watching the warriors march past as he patiently waited for her to sate herself. The warriors, for their part, seemed to enjoy marching past him. He always had a friendly smile for them as they had one for him. At least, those who were not staring at their own boots as they plodded onwards usually had a smile for him. He was quickly becoming a fixture amongst the routine of the warpack.

One morning he was riding next to Clerin. Even though he was not old by any stretch of the imagination, Croy felt a fatherly protectionism towards Clerin. He had felt similar to Trela, but after watching her in combat he had come to the realization that she did not need his feeble skills. Clerin probably did not either, but there was a certain demure daintiness to her that was lacking in Trela. Today, however, he was not attempting to dole out advice or commiserate with any foibles. He was trying to gain information that only she could provide.

"So you don't see them as figures, and you don't hear them... I don't understand how they communicate." They were riding slightly off to the side of the main marching column.

"It's hard to explain. First of all you have to realize that I have only communicated twice with a Beleg. My mother has spoken with Lembin many times, and she probably has quite a different impression of their communication than I do. I could never get her to adequately explain her experience before I had mine. And then... it was too difficult to talk about at first. I left for the luften realm soon after my first communication, so I never did get the chance to compare notes." Clerin was silent for a while as they rode along. Croy was wondering if he should have even brought the subject up. "That is not what you asked about, however. I guess I would say that they force thoughts upon you and that you then have to interpret them. Just being in their presence causes discomfort that can border upon pain. I always seem to be disoriented and overwhelmed. Most often their communication is a series of visions. Flashes of symbols and fleeting images. I guess at one thing the images seem to mean to me. Then I guess another. Correctly guessing the meaning of their visions seems to be the only thing that makes the pain subside. Then new images appear and so on. Finally, their will is communicated to me. That seems to be the only way to end the ordeal." Clerin's smile was weak and her hair hid part of her face.

"I only ask because I have been trying to figure out my dreams." Croy had not wanted to tell her the root of his curiosity. Not due to any mistrust—Clerin was probably the kindest of any of those that Croy had met outside of Serif—but more due to Croy's own feelings of security. It was just something he had not wanted to say out loud. Clerin had seemed too distraught by his prying, however, which is why he blurted out his thoughts. "I was wondering how things could be revealed. I mean, true things. The way you describe Beleg communication seems similar to some of my dreams."

"Do you think the Belegs speak to Tumu? Do you think all sight must come from one source?" Clerin looked comfortable to be speaking of something other than her own ordeals.

"Not necessarily. That is why I wanted to hear how they communicate from someone who knows. Truth exists without the Belegs. Finding the truth unconsciously may be much like communicating through a wormhole—it just finds you if you happen to be on the other side." Croy took a breath as he tried to gather his thoughts. But it was like herding cats: they did not obey long enough to queue up. "Your description seems close to my truth."

"But all dreams are like that." She took a quick breath. "Do you have dreams that do not impart truth?"

"Yes... they seem more coherent, though. They are like walking along a familiar hillside, looking for lost sheep." It was Croy's turn to pause. "The ones that mean something have a different feeling. Like the images appear with purpose, but are much more disjointed. Forced maybe."

"Of all the Gaens in the entire world, why do the Belegs choose you? If Tumu happens to carry a wormhole of truth around him, how come yours is a conscious effort by beings greater than ourselves?" She did not look at him as she spoke.

"I could ask you the same thing. Why do the Belegs choose you?" Croy thought about her words for a moment. "I never said the Belegs speak to me. I never said that the Belegs do not speak to Tumu, either. I do not understand how truth comes to Tumu. Believe me, I have tried to find out. I do not think Tumu understands. I do not think that Tumu wants to understand. But I do know that the Belegs have chosen you. You are the only derlian I know who has spoken with them. You are the only one I can ask these questions of."

"I seem to be a vessel to them, more than one to communicate with. A messenger perhaps. Or maybe a harbinger. We do not share ideas. We are definitely not equals. When my mother spoke of communicating with Lembin, it was about translation. Lembin needed her, and those like her, who could take the images and turn them into words. It seemed like there was give and take. With me, it seems different. It is more like take and take, and it is only in one direction. They take what they want and make me take what they want to give to others. I am just a vessel." Clerin was beginning to look pensive again. "Linchon was definitely angrier though. Linchon did not ask for me, did not request my presence. Linchon did not want to be given the message that Lembin made me take."

"Why do you think I dreamed of the location of Linchon's temple?" This was the crux of Croy's curiosity. He, like Clerin, felt like Linchon had not wanted to be found. But the way was shown to him. Shown in a dream.

"I do not know. That is what I cannot argue with." Clerin paused for a brief moment. She took a deep breath and let it out with a quiet sigh. "When I communicated with Linchon, I cast a spell. It was... like a compulsion."

"What?" Croy froze in stunned silence. Luckily Buttercup was not so affected. "What did you cast?"

"It was an apparition. Linchon set up a way for me to communicate with an apparition." Clerin had her eyes closed. Croy was not sure but he thought he saw her eyes flutter with suppressed emotion. "The spell was Losidtotarc. Try that next time you are dreaming."

"What was the apparition?" Croy knew he was prying, but he was unable to stop himself. He should have found a way.

"I am not talking about this anymore." Clerin shook her head slightly. "I... I have things to check up on." With that she kicked her horse and trotted away from Croy.

Buttercup naturally wanted to keep up with Riverlightning, but Croy reined her in. He needed to let Clerin be. The guilt of driving her away almost made him forget their conversation. Losidtotarc, he thought to himself. He did not want to think of it too hard, to accidentally cast it. But he wanted to think of it enough that he would not forget it. Softly, casually, over and over until he felt it was memorized. He was not sure that he could even cast a spell in his dreams. He never felt like he could control them, or himself in them. He always felt more of an observer than a participant in his dreams. He would have to try, though. It was his only lead.

Croy kept Buttercup towards the back of the warpack for the entire day. There was a small feeling of guilt that pursued him. He had not meant to drive Clerin away. In fact, he was a bit confused as to what he had done. He promised himself that the next few times he spoke with Clerin he would let her pick the subject.

Each night as he lay to sleep, he would think to himself, "-sidtotarc, -sidtotarc," over and over. He did not know what power level he should use, but he was sure that Lo would not work. No, the only reason that worked for Clerin is that Linchon wished to communicate with her, had willed it so.

Each night was another night without dreams, however. Not even a simple one that held no message. He had hoped to just dream of Serif, or Ilana. To slowly move up in significance until he would be able to try Clerin's trick. But there was nothing at all—pure blackness. He went to sleep and then just woke up; it felt like he blinked. Worst of all, the sleep was not as restful as it usually was. He awoke each morning still tired with sandy eyes.

This morning he had decided to talk with Knill and Tumu, so he walked next to Buttercup. They spoke of nothing for a while, reminiscing about Serif. Tumu would ask questions about the underground life during lulls in the conversation. Croy was not sure if he was truly interested or if he was being gracious. It was definitely appreciated.

"Tumu, what is Delubayn?" It was a question from Knill that made no sense to Croy.

"Who told you that word?" Tumu looked as shocked as Croy.

"Iventorn. He warned that I might find it in the desert, but I found nothing in the desert." For some reason, Tumu smiled at that statement.

"I believe Iventorn was just being mean. But you never know..." Tumu thought for a moment. "Delubayn is uniquely Pyran. Simplest, I think, it means 'unrequited love.' It has more connotations than that, however. There is a measure of angst and betrayal involved. More like if someone has led you along and then, without warning, dropped you for selfish reasons, and you feel a mixture of anger, frustration, and hopelessness afterwards. I think... I think that is what Iventorn would have meant by Delubayn. He was saying that Trela was using you."

Croy watched Knill for a few moments, but Knill did not react. "Is she using you?" It came from some hither unknown mischievous impulse. It just popped out.

"How should I know?" Knill's voice sounded much less downtrodden than his words.

Croy realized that he was steering them towards a dangerous path. For no reason. He needed to change the subject, so he broached what he wanted to learn. He decided to change the subject to Tumu and his gifts.

"So you have dreams and you are not asleep when you see these things. I don't understand how you can prophesize the future." Croy was holding Buttercup's reins tightly as they walked.

"I see images in my head. Quick and fleeting when I am alone. But, sometimes I see images around other derlians and the images are so large and luminous that it pains me to look at them." Tumu looked at his feet. He often looked at his feet, however.

"Like Trela?" The question came from Knill before Croy could ask it. Meaning that Knill already knew the answer and was just prodding Tumu. Croy often wondered what conversations they had already had. It made him feel like the odd one out, as if they were repeating themselves for his benefit. It seemed somehow... scripted. Almost rehearsed.

"Yes, exactly. She is too bright for me to look at. It is like staring into the sun." Tumu smiled down at his feet. "That is how I know she speaks the truth. That she is the Kriishan and our efforts will not be in vain."

"So you know that she will win?" Croy got his question out before Knill could steer the conversation. He figured that if Tumu was going to soothe Knill's fears about Trela, he would have already done so.

"No. I do not see that part of the future. I only know that she is the Kriishan." His right hand touched his face briefly. "You would think that being the Kriishan would guarantee her defeating Qizern, would you not?"

It was Croy's turn to contemplate. "That is always how it is defined to me. When I ask a Pyran, the answer is always that the Kriishan is the good ruler. How can one be a Kriishan without ruling?"

"Ah, there is some confusion in that answer. The correct response to, 'What is the Kriishan?' should be, 'The one who is meant to rule,' not necessarily, 'The one who ruled who was good.' That is a different idea, one which predates your earlier question." Knill broke in and answered for Tumu with his quick, insistent voice.

"Which earlier question?" Croy's brow furrowed in puzzled concentration.

" 'Is there Truth greater than Belegs?' That is not exactly what you said, but it is what you meant, yes?" Knill smiled warmly at Croy. "You want to know who shows Tumu the Truth, with a capital 'T'. You think that this will help you decipher who shows you the Truth." Knill stopped, bringing Croy and Tumu to a halt. "You say that you were shown the location of the Luften temple?"

"Yes. Its exact description was burned into me during a dream." Buttercup immediately began grazing during their brief hiatus. "During several dreams, actually."

"Why should I believe you?" Knill's smile grew larger. "Why would you finding the cave entrance not be considered serendipity, or luck, or coincidence?"

"The description was so complete that we were able to locate it even though the front of the cave was hidden by illusion. It... it just looked like a cliff wall." Croy was unsure of where Knill was going with his line of reasoning.

"How do we know that you did not use magic to sense the entrance?" Tumu piped in. "That is what derlians always ask me. They have an understanding of magic and wish to assume that my visions stem from something they understand."

"Well... we were not even able to fly through it. It negated magic itself and was undetectable. Though, if I think about it for a moment, the negation of magic is what made us assume that we had the correct location." Croy paused. "But we never would have known if I had not seen that exact location in my dream. Every single little detail was the same. Well, except for the illusion of the cliff wall. In my dream I could see the cave entrance."

"So... I have to trust you that you did not use magic. I have to do this since I was not personally there and could not try to sense if magic was being used." Tumu looked up at Croy.

"That brings me to my earlier point." Knill interrupted before Croy could answer Tumu.

"Which earlier point?" Croy was thinking about the trust that Tumu brought up. He wondered how often derlians questioned Tumu's gift.

"That fate and destiny are beyond the purview of the Belegs." Knill clapped Croy on the shoulder and got them walking again. "That is what you want to know, is it not? The Belegs are our Creators and, as such, are the largest and most profound conscious force in this entire world. Everything that exists, everything we see and hear and taste, these all come from the Belegs. The Belegs made all of that stuff on purpose. We derlians are merely short-lived, ignorant, chaotic shadows of our ancestors, the Yavens. We, today, have none among us who can remember where we came from. We have been breeding a form of chaotic dilution, making us shadows of the first derlians. The Yavens themselves are mere shadows of the

Belegs. That makes us shadows of shadows of shadows. But there is more, is there not? What about the unconscious forces?"

Croy suddenly brightened. "Were the Belegs destined to be the Creators of our world?"

This stopped both Knill and Tumu. They all stood there for a moment as the question sank in. The silence was thick and heavy, but not necessarily uncomfortable.

"Exactly, Croy. Exactly." Knill was grinning ear from ear. They stood for a while, grinning at each other. Finally they began walking again, in silence. Eventually Croy could take no more and shattered the quiet.

"So, what do you think destiny is?" He was trying to bring the conversation back.

"Well... I'll tell you what I thought it was before meeting Tumu." Knill nodded towards Tumu who, naturally, was staring at the ground while they were walking. "I call it 'stream theory' and it has nothing to do with forces, conscious or not. I do believe that the idea and search for destiny brings us closer to our most perfect selves." Knill paused a moment to collect his thoughts. "We all enter this world with a set of affinities. We are all born with inherit pluses and minuses. There are those who are born strong, some who are born smart, and others born beautiful. Some are born with all three. There are many, many other traits, of course. But let us say that someone born strong decides to never exercise and only read math books. They may become a great mathematician through perseverance and industriousness. Let us say this derlian has a brother who is born smart, but weak. The weak brother only enjoys climbing. He pushes himself to the limit and eventually becomes an amazing climber. What have they overcome to do and be what they wish? They have overcome friction. At birth, there is a certain path of abilities that you may have inherited in you. During your first cycles, this path is etched deeper by the experiences you encounter before you have any control of your surroundings. Soon, you are as a stream, meandering about down a mountainside by the eternal tug of gravity. Moving against one's natural abilities is like a stream attempting to cut a new bed amongst the soil. It can be done, surely. And many times it must be done to avoid disaster. But the further along the stream flows, the more difficult it is to change direction. And the hardness of the soil, or even stone, will affect and deflect your path. There are certain items that are beyond our control. Some that we must flow around. There are some desires, some dreams, that are so inherently at odds with our natural abilities that it is as if we are trying to flow the stream uphill. We all know that streams do not flow uphill." Knill paused briefly.

"Imagine, now, that the brothers trade dreams. The strong brother wishes to be a climber and the smart brother wishes to be a mathematician. Will they each flow further down the mountain due to less inherent friction? My belief is yes. Not only will they flow further, but with greater ease. They will be able to chart their course more consciously and more poignantly. The reduction of friction is a great boon to life. This does not mean you should do what you do not wish to, if you happen to be good at something you hate. Part of your inherent affinities *are* your desires. You should listen well and often to your own desires so that you can understand their true geometry and meaning." Knill paused briefly again. "My belief is that Trela follows her stream with the least amount of friction that I have ever witnessed. Ever. And I have been a student of this theory since I could reason. It is what originally attracted me to her, and it still amazes me. She flies down her mountainside as if it were made up of clouds. Every obstacle in her path is swallowed whole without so much as a hiccough. Every pebble seems as smooth as ice, there is so little friction. It seems impossible for her to turn in an incorrect direction because every turn seems meant to be."

They walked in silence for a little bit. Croy thought about Knill's theory. His own stream, he felt, was full of crashing waves and inconvenient curves. Full of jagged stones, branches, and fish poop. There were times when he felt he was trying to force his stream sideways, away from the gentle pull of gravity. As if he could defy gravity. But something unheard nagged at him about the theory.

"I know you stated to listen to your desires, but if the weak brother wishes to only climb rocks, won't he be miserable doing only math?" Croy knew the rub lay in there somewhere.

"There is no reason he cannot do both, is there? But that is not your question and not my answer." Knill grew quiet and furrowed his brow. "I think friction and destiny have little to do with happiness. There are many great derlians who are not very happy, and many happy derlians who are content to sit in a small pool and not flow anywhere. Is that their destiny? Surely, I do not know."

They walked in silence for a while longer. Croy wanted to say that chasing desire may not always make one happy either, but he could not think of a way to work it in. And besides, he had desired Ilana, chased her, caught her, and was happy while they were together. Now that they had parted, maybe forever, he was sad about it, but was he unhappy? Could he never be happy again? He knew the answer to that question. He was oddly afraid to voice anything, however. For some reason a part of him felt that he was being cruel to Ilana if he felt happy. Still. Even after all these moons. But a larger part of him knew that was completely absurd. He could not live the rest of his life unhappy. And even if he could, he doubted Ilana would want that. He surely wanted her to live the rest of her life happy. So his mind circled back to desire. Did chasing desire make one happy? Instead of pursuing this new line of thought with Knill and Tumu, however, he wished to finish the earlier one. The one that all three of them had begun together, even if the other two had already discussed it.

"And you, Tumu? What do you feel that destiny is?" Croy thought it would be better if he heard Tumu's version, so that he could make a similar revelation to what Knill had made when he first heard it. If he heard Knill's version first, the revelation would seem a mere shadow of the one that Knill had experienced. He had not, however, taken into account the vast amount of time the two had spent together, building and refining their respective worldviews. Being able to communicate efficiently because they knew the exact definitions of the words that the other was using. Words could increase in meaning when experiences amongst friends added shared nuance. Outsiders of a group often have difficulties in full comprehension even when speaking the same dialect. It was not something that Croy had fully considered at the time, but would think about much later.

"Let me say that I agree with Knill in many aspects. But I do believe there is something more. Some type of unconscious pattern. It is like..." Tumu paused and looked up from the ground. "Have you navigated by the stars?"

"No, I have lived most of my life underground." In the pause Croy felt he should add something. "I do find the stars very beautiful."

"Hmmm. Clerin explained it quite adroitly to us one evening. Apparently, if one is educated in the matter and knows the time of season and makes careful measurements, one can navigate at sea by using only the stars. I myself have noticed how the stars spin throughout the sun cycle, but I have never left the Pyran realm. The pattern of the stars varies over vast distances, much further beyond their seasonal shifts. I hope to witness this myself one day. So, even though I have explained nothing, this is what destiny is to me. There is an unimaginable vast pattern, far off into the distance. It varies with distance and time, but it is also somewhat cyclical. It is not conscious, or at least not so that any derlian could recognize. The unfathomable complexity of meaning shines through the darkness of mere being. A glimpse is insight and inspiration. A wide-eyed examination, filled with the tumult of effort, is... is what I do. I believe it is what you do as well. The recognition of pattern is not magic; no, it is almost the opposite of magic. It is the other side of chaos. They may be of the same coin, but they are completely different images." Tumu took a quick breath. "When the Belegs made this world, they made chaos intrinsic with it. They shattered the barrier of the Void and mixed the elements. I used to think that, at that very moment, they also engrained something into the sky. Into the ground. That a vast pattern was etched upon everything the moment it burst into existence. If one looked close enough and hard enough..." Croy waited for Tumu to continue.

"You said, 'used to believe.' " He tried to verbally nudge Tumu.

"Well... were the Belegs destined to be the Creators of our world? That says it all. If there was a pattern that led to Truth before our world sprang into existence, then what etched that? The further back you look, the more hazy it becomes." He paused for another moment. "Why Yavens? Why were only four elements given realms and life? How could the Belegs evolve into being—but only once? Was the Void first, or is it just the distances between existences? I mean, how is nothingness a boundary? It seems simple and easy for me to begin everything at the Belegs. Both chaos and order. They created us and the world, end of story. It becomes impossible to think of what created them. My mind... has nothing to grasp a hold of. Nothing to evaluate or to even grip. I am lost at sea and unable to glimpse the stars." Tumu shook his head and stopped speaking. They all walked in silence for quite some time.

Much later, during the battle of Unaqa at the cliffs of the same name, Croy had some time to speak with Feyazki. As they were resting amongst the archers at the top of the cliffs, Croy posed the very same question to him.

"Were the Belegs destined to be the Creators of the world?" They had not quite been speaking of destiny, but Croy had wanted to segue into the topic for some time.

Feyazki snorted, somewhat derisively. "Of course not. Don't be absurd."

"But..." Croy had not expected the turn of conversation and was a bit stymied by it. "Someone had to create this."

"And they did. Just because it has 'always been' does not mean that it was supposed to be that way. All great events, in hindsight, appear to be planned. But that is only because you already know their outcome. Just because we do exist, does not mean that we need to exist. Or that we needed to exist. It is just that it is impossible for us to imagine not existing." Feyazki smiled at Croy. "I believe you are confusing truth with reality."

Croy thought about it for a moment, since he did not want to appear foolish. "If truth is not the basis of reality, then I do not know what is."

"You are correct. But they are not mutually exclusive nor, necessarily, overlapping." His eyes went up to the sky for a moment. "If there are infinite worlds, must there be another one just like this one?"

"Well, if there were infinite worlds, then... yes. There should be an infinite amount of everything." Croy smiled to himself.

"You know there can be an infinite amount of odd numbers, correct? Is there not also an infinite amount of even numbers? Is there not an infinite amount of negative numbers?" Feyazki was nodding to Croy slowly. "You see, they are all infinite, but they do not overlap at all. You can perceive one of them, and not the others, but still understand the truth of infinity. You are just missing the reality of it."

Croy thought for some more. "So, are you saying that any four Yavens could have become the Belegs?" Croy decided to skip the analogy and stick to the real dialogue.

"Not any four, no. There is certainly a delicate balance in that power shift... power sharing?" He squinted uncertainly. "No, they needed to be at the peak of their power. They each needed to bring to the table what the others were lacking. I believe it is much like a complicated puzzle, where all of the pieces must fit together in perfect harmony for something like that to happen. I do feel that they were not necessarily the only four that could accomplish that, if others were given the chance. I also believe that, afterwards, they did something to prevent others from accomplishing what they already had. And finally, I believe that they did not need to create our world. I believe they created it out of a weakness born of loneliness. They could have filled that loneliness by allowing other Yavens to become Belegs. Instead, however, they chose to create us. They chose pitiful shadows to watch and play with, rather than equals to contend with. They chose pets."

"So there is no destiny greater than the Belegs?" Croy felt that Feyazki was close to deriding the Belegs and he was unsure of how it made him feel.

"Chaos is greater, but it disagrees with destiny." Feyazki quipped much too quickly to be serious.

"Maybe I am asking the question incorrectly. I dreamed the location of the Luften Temple. I do not believe, and Clerin does not believe, that Linchon wished to be found. So, I feel that I was given a verifiable truth that may have been above and beyond the will of a Beleg." Croy decided to get to his point.

"But not necessarily beyond the desires of all Belegs. Was not Clerin's message sent by Lembin?" Feyazki pursed his lips.

"If Lembin could find Linchon, why would a messenger be required?" Croy was trying to stay on track.

"Hmmm. There are too many unknowable variables with this reasoning. We could not say for certain if Lembin could find Linchon, if they could communicate or—most importantly—why the messenger was needed at all. You raise a good point, but you will not be able to win this argument in this way with our current available facts. I think you had more of an argument with your first question." Feyazki looked thoughtful. Croy hoped to bring the conversation back to that first question. Maybe, this time, Feyazki would not just dismiss the premise immediately. They were interrupted, however, and the conversation would have to wait.

"It is time." Escha had been watching the fighting down on the valley floor below. Her understanding of subtle infantry movements and cavalry maneuvers made her timing impeccable. Croy was always amazed at how she could tell when, and even where, a line was going to break, sometimes minutes in advance. She tapped her spyglass on Feyazki's knee. "They will start to run the gauntlet in less than three minutes."

Feyazki stood quickly, Croy less so. They had been trekking up to the top of the cliffs since morning because Trela was afraid that any use of magic would give away her plan. She had been so concerned about anyone being seen at the top of the cliffs that Escha was the only one allowed near the edge until the gauntlet started.

Trela's plan was simple. She would fake a rout into the chasm below, drawing Astydle's warpack after her. The boulders would seal off any escape and the arrows would drop upon them like a summer's rain. Trela had tried mightily to absorb Astydle's warpack through other means. Talks, threats, bribery, begging, and cajoling. Astydle was a complete loyalist and the warpack was just as steadfast. Unfortunately for Trela, Astydle was a mastermind of strategy and tactics. It was rumored that the warpack had never lost a major battle outside of the Dekhan plateau. It had taken Trela a fortnight to position herself for this battle. She had done her best to keep all of her movements small enough such that her aim was indecipherable. She had only explained her plan to her Privy Council. Even the archers now upon the cliffs had not been told about their position until this very morning. It all came down to these last few minutes. Soon Croy, and everyone else, would find out if Trela's ruse worked. Or if there was subterfuge from the other side.

Feyazki crouched along the cliff wall to avoid any chance of being seen. Croy followed him. They positioned themselves at the far outcropping above the neck of the canyon's mouth. Croy kept his left hand against the rock wall to keep himself steady. It felt comforting to be touching stone.

Escha was back at the edge of the cliff, laying on her belly with her head hanging over the precipice. Croy could not see the spyglass but she was holding something in front of her. Time slowed to a crawl as everyone was ready, but waiting. Was the bluff called? Did Astydle not pursue Trela's retreating warpack? Croy began to wonder if Escha had misjudged the time, but then she rolled over onto her knees and waved her hand frantically at them.

"Lumkingeclo!" Feyazki's voice rang strong and true.

"Mekkingeclo!" Croy's voice sounded more hollow to him, but it was impossible to tell the differing power levels since the cliff opposite them immediately exploded into a dry avalanche. The noise was deafening and the air quickly filled with dust.

The archers sprang quickly into action and began loosing their arrows blindly into the dusty chasm below. Feyazki and Croy both pulled back away from the edge. Croy could not imagine how Feyazki felt, since casting just a Mek spell had instantly tired him out. He had come such a long way, but still had so much further to go. He sat rather clumsily next to the cliff wall that rose above them. Though the stone was comforting, his stomach felt mightily queasy.

"Their fate is sealed." Feyazki smiled wearily as he sat next to Croy. They breathed heavily together in silence for a short while.

Eventually Escha walked over. "Why did you not just crush them with the rocks? Seems like a waste of arrows to me."

Feyazki looked over at Croy, giving him the chance to answer. Croy, however, had been thinking along similar lines. He smiled weakly to Feyazki indicating that he had no answer.

"One, Trela wishes to trap the entire warpack. If we dropped the rocks directly upon them, some of the pack might have escaped. Two, Trela wishes them to surrender, not to kill them all." He looked as if he was going to continue, but Escha interrupted.

"From what I hear, Astydle does not surrender. And if Astydle does not, none of them will. This will be a fight to the last warrior." She seemed to be frowning at Feyazki. Croy could not particularly tell, however, since she often seemed to be frowning to him. Even when she was in a good mood. He had a hard time reading her emotions. Feyazki just took it in stride.

"Three, intentional death takes the most amount of energy of any magic. Some of the boulders may have crushed some of Astydle's warpack. But that was by accident, not design. It would be... serendipitous." Feyazki took a breath that seemed labored enough to prove his current level of exertion. "If we had intentionally dropped the boulders into the middle of the pack, the spell would have been much more difficult to cast. Even without using the syllable De, the stones would know the intent. And it would have sucked more energy out of us than we would have been prepared to give. It can be like a siphon if you are not careful. It can suck a derlian dry and leave them a mindless husk."

Escha thought for a moment in silence. "What if you did not know? What if I lied to you and made you cast the spell while there was still the majority of the warpack underneath the falling boulders?"

Feyazki thought for a moment as well. "I am not positive, but I would not be willing to risk my mind for such a dangerous experiment. I think it would drain the amount of energy that casting De would, at least for the amount of derlians who were crushed." He thought for a moment. "I do feel a little more drained than expected." His brow furrowed quickly before his eyes suddenly widened. "That is not what you did, is it?"

"No, of course not." She laughed easily. "But you never know..." She was going to say more, and Feyazki was going to angrily interrupt her. Neither got the chance, however.

The feeling started just as Escha started her retort. It was a feeling of dry, cold water splashing against Croy's face. Like a shock of some sort, like a gasping of breath. His heart leapt in his chest and began to pump furiously. As if he were running up the path to the cliffs. As if he were a child who had just realized they lost their parent in a crowded bazaar. As if he had leaned a chair back too far and started to fall. It was a feeling of surprise that kept him from reacting. Escha started speaking and the feeling eased somewhat. Then the solid stone that they were sitting on fell away.

Croy's legs naturally sprang downwards as their purchase dropped. As if he could jump up and avoid falling. Escha screamed like an attacking owl. Feyazki closed his eyes.

"Narkinderclo!" The word passed from Feyazki's lips in slow motion. Drawn out and distorted. It seemed like time stopped as they levitated in place. There were five archers floating there with them. Seven stunned faces stared at Feyazki. All the others plummeted to their doom. Almost an entire cohort of archers.

They were still falling, but they drifted slowly downwards and outwards. Gliding to the ground on the far side of the boulders. Unfortunately, they had glided off course and were a small ways away from the boulders. Croy thought that the avalanche spell must have taken more out of Feyazki then he had first supposed. Or maybe Feyazki wanted the battle to die down a little before rejoining. Croy was happy either way. They had landed in the trampled waste where the warpacks had first engaged each other and waged their pitched skirmishes before Trela led Astydle's warpack into the canyon's maw. Into her trap.

"Thank you, thank you." The surviving archers were overjoyed. They probably knew in their hearts that it was only proximity that saved them, not intent. They were too ecstatic to care, however.

"Do not thank only me, warriors. If I had not recognized the sheer terror on Croy's face, we would have all fallen upon the mages below who were so intent upon our demise." Feyazki clasped his shoulder with a weak grasp but firm hand. "How did you sense the spell from so far away? I felt nothing."

"I... I don't know." And he didn't.

They walked slowly back towards the giant pile of rubble at the mouth of the canyon. Both Croy and Feyazki were too tired and shaken up to fly them all back. The sun was high in the sky and they would not find shade until the canyon. Croy often got homesick when it felt too hot. He sorely missed the dim cool of the underground.

As they neared the pile of boulders, a small sense of foreboding entered Croy. It was definitely not the icy chill that he had felt on top of the cliffs, but it would not go away. It was certainly less intense than staring at the carriage with the Blind One in it. As they approached, the air was still thick with dust which Croy attempted, but failed, to peer through. The sense did not increase as they drew closer, which made him think that he was being paranoid or that he was still feeling some diluted fear from atop the cliff. But it would not fade, either. He finally decided to voice his concerns.

"Feyazki, I..." And that is when it happened. As if they were waiting for his cue. The dry cold water crashed upon Croy again.

A wild, gray-haired, and bearded mage appeared directly in front of them. Croy was not sure how he had bypassed Escha. He had red robes with wide black stripes and more scars on his face than teeth in his head. He screamed unintelligibly and swung a short heavy staff at Croy's head, a cudgel really.

Croy's arm automatically flew up to protect himself, just in the nick of time. The staff struck his arm so hard that his arm was flung into his face, and he dropped to one knee. After the brief moment of searing pain, his arm felt numb.

"Nardepiarc!" Flames shot from the end of the mage's staff, over Croy and into the archers behind. The screams told Croy the story of what happened, so he did not need to lose precious seconds glancing backwards.

"Mekdeelearc!"   Lightning shot forth from Feyazki's outstretched hands.

At the same time, however, the mage was intoning his own spell. Croy strained to hear, but it sounded unfamiliar. A bit like "Nutelderkha," but he could not be sure. The mage disappeared faster than the lightning appeared.

The mage reappeared towards the boulders a little ways away. He was facing away from Croy, but swung his cudgel out in front of him as if he were striking someone. It would have been a cruel blow had it landed. The Pyran then looked around and spied Croy. He began to run at full speed, screaming at the top of his lungs, cudgel held high.

"Mekdepiarc!"   Flames exploded out of Feyazki's hands. Before they struck the Pyran mage, however, he disappeared.

And reappeared close by, swinging his skinny club dangerously. Aimlessly. He quickly got his bearings and began charging Croy again. And Croy began to wonder if they were just being worn down. Could he be so quick that he was tracking what they were doing and responding? Before they had struck first? Croy suddenly realized that the mage in front of him would dodge whatever was thrown at him, no matter how potent.

"Lodepiarc!" Croy shouted with bluster. The flames that shot forth from his hands were pitiful and short lived. But they glowed bright and roared loud. Much to Croy's satisfaction, the Pyran mage disappeared and did not feel the meager heat. Croy felt sure that he had guessed the mage's game correctly. Only once they were tired and getting sloppy would the mage truly begin to press his advantage. Until then, everything they threw at him would just wear themselves down.

Another burst of flames engulfed the space the mage had so recently occupied. Croy began running towards Feyazki, who obviously was still trying to catch the mage. He had to explain himself to Feyazki without letting the Pyran know that they were on to his tricks. The mage appeared screaming off to Croy's left. "Lodepiarc!" It was a natural response and took very little energy. The mage disappeared, and Croy started running again.

The mage appeared near Feyazki, who shot a massive pillar of flame at him. Of course, the mage disappeared before the fire reached him. Croy was having a hard time catching up with Feyazki.

It almost seemed that Feyazki was trying to get away from Croy. They all ran around haphazardly for some time.

The mage appeared next to Croy, but before he could shoot his tiny spell to make the mage disappear again, the cudgel came down upon his shoulder. Croy instantly fell to the ground. It was lucky, too, because suddenly lightning shot over him where he was just standing. Where the mage was just standing. But the mage escaped that as well.

Croy picked himself up and gripped his right shoulder with his left hand. "Nuliderto!" The warmth cascaded through his hand into his arm. He paused for a moment as fire was flung near him. This time it was the mage who cast it. Croy was not sure where he was aiming, but it did not appear to be at Croy. He breathed deep and closed his eyes. The mage was going to wear them down. He did not know how long Feyazki could keep this up, but even the minor spells that he was casting were slowing him down.

Croy had an idea as the mage swung and hit Feyazki's leg. He kept his eyes closed and spoke as softly as he could, with as much force as he could muster. He wanted the spell to be able to last a while. "Mekdepito!" Croy jumped about and pinwheeled his arms about him. His throat let out a wordless yell as he spun. He could feel the hot fire within him, waiting to be unleashed. And then, from out of nowhere, the mage appeared right in front of Croy, swinging his cudgel wildly. But not before Croy's whirling palm touched the mage's cheek. Boom! The shock blew Croy backwards onto the ground and blew the mage in the opposite direction. Dazed and confused, Croy lay there for several moments before his hearing began to return with a high pitched whine. Eventually a dark shadow was cast over him. He squinted up to see who it was. Though he did not think that it would be the mage, a wave of relief washed over him as he realized it was Feyazki.

Feyazki reached down to grasp Croy's hand and pull him up. Croy felt weak, and Feyazki seemed to be favoring one leg heavily, but they managed to get Croy upright. "That's the second time you have saved me today, Gaen. I owe you." Feyazki smiled large and brightly.

Croy grinned weakly back. He could not count the times that Feyazki's prowess had kept him safe. "Let's just say we are even."

Grisly as it was, Croy was glad that Escha had decapitated the mage. He did not want to think about the body disappearing suddenly. The three of them sat down on the trampled battleground and passed Escha's waterskin for a while. None of them wanted to head back to the larger battle just yet.

Escha, Feyazki, Croy, and the surviving two archers, Hygen and Urwst, made themselves as comfortable as they could amongst the strewn rocks. The sun was still high. They wasted some time in silence.

"How do you shoot lightning?" Croy spoke mainly to break up the monotony as they started moving again.

"It is a spell like any other. Lightning has a syllable for its unique element." Feyazki and Croy were walking behind Escha but in front of the archers. The archers huddled together and spoke in whispered tones.

"But how does your mind know what it is?" Croy felt that he could barely understand typical spells. "I feel air constantly. There is soil under my feet and water all around. Even though I cannot touch fire, derlians' experience with it is vast. Metals, woods, even the mind... these are all elements that I have daily contact with. I can examine them at my leisure. Inspect every aspect of their nature. They are common." Croy paused for a second. "No, not just common. But constant." He smiled at Feyazki. "But lightning... That is the definition of ephemeral. You cannot hold it or experience it in any way. I have seen it several times in my life during the wild spring storms that would crash against the hills around Serif. But I know Gaens who have never even seen it at all." He paused again. "How do you know enough about it to be able to translate a syllable for it?"

"Well... you are right about the Minora. It is difficult to explain how a syllable comes to represent an idea. Especially one that is not taught to you." Here Feyazki stopped and looked at Croy. The archers stopped behind them, unwilling to accidentally eavesdrop. "I learned it from another. The syllable came to me as an enemy attacked me with it. I experienced lightning like very few because I felt it coursing through me. I felt it killing me." He took a ragged breath. Croy had never seen him look so weak. "If I had not learned how to use it, I would have died that night. There was no other alternative. So... I learned."

"And what about that mage's... disappearing? If I told you I heard the syllable he used, could you learn how to cast it?" Croy knew that he himself would be unable to cast it, but was curious about a mage of Feyazki's skills.

"I doubt it. There are certain ways a Minora syllable can be learned. The way of the learning is just as, or more, important than the actual syllable itself. I spoke with Elange, my mentor's mentor, about the Minora. He was of the opinion that it could not be readily taught. Or, if the concept was taught, the syllable may be completely different, or the effects may vary. He felt that the Minora were very personal and not readily transferable. The fact that the syllable may not even be the same..." Feyazki looked thoughtful as his mind wandered to the past.

"I don't understand. All the magical syllables are the same. Even amongst the four races." Croy furrowed his brow.

"Yes, that is true. Much like our language is all the same. However, the Minora are a bit different. If I was able to teach you how to cast lightning, and you were able to learn it, then the odds are that you would use the same syllable as I did. I would probably need to teach you the way I learned, for that is the only way I personally understand lightning's mindtrap. That would certainly be a painful process. However, say that you learned lightning on your own. Say you were walking along and maybe saw it in the air and had a deepening of understanding of it. Maybe you were struck by it. A different syllable may have been shown to you, been etched into your mind. The syllable you learned then may not be the same as mine. At least that is how I understand it. I have limited experience with the Minora." Feyazki kept his eyes looking towards the mage's body as he spoke. Almost wistfully.

"Some mages may spend a lifetime not knowing any Minora, so I would say that you have quite expansive experience with it." Croy paused for a moment. "At least compared with most."

"You know what the main difference is between us?" It came out of nowhere.

"Skill?" Croy asked quietly.

"Yes, but why?" Feyazki was smiling kindly.

"Practice? Time, energy, and a lot of natural talent?" The line of questioning made Croy nervous.

"True, but... no. What truly separates us is confidence." His smiled widened into a grin. "You could be a great mage one day, Croy. Truly."

Croy was going to continue the conversation, for he was building himself up to ask the burning question. He was worried about being shot by lightning, but wanted to gain skill as a mage. He wanted to learn some Minora. His fear kept him from speaking his wishes, but his desire made him keep talking. Now was not to be the time to overcome himself, however. He had taken too long.

"Boring!" Escha suddenly began brushing her pants with her hands. "You two can speak of this at any time. I understand that we are all tired and no one wants to fly us over the boulders, so I suggest we start climbing. We need to reach the warpack before nightfall and there is no telling how far the battle has raged. Up, up." Escha waved her arms at the lot of them. It may Croy think of the phrase, "mother hen." At the thought, he felt a little wistful and nostalgic for his farming past. As a consequence, he was the last derlian not moving. Escha glared over him for the brief moment it took him to regain his bearings.

After Unaqa, Croy began staying back to assist the physicians during the battles. He started because he thought it would be a great way to gain confidence. He figured the constant use of small magic would give him the faith in his capabilities that he needed to attempt large magic. And he enjoyed the way it made him feel about his work. He caused no harm to others; he only helped, he only healed. But the deeper reason that he kept coming back, the real reason he endured the sights, sounds, smells, and emotions of the medical tent, began with Nochiel. Nochiel was an amazing Pyran mage. She would never admit it, of course, because she only knew how to do one thing with magic. She never flew, or threw fire, or spoke with the dead. But she could heal like none other in the warpack. Even Feyazki's great natural talent and hard-learned skill could not match her in that one realm. She had a saying when she defended her specialty against those obsessed by throwing fire. "Giving life and dealing death are of the same Rank."

Nochiel was older and kept her wavy brown hair quite short. She was oddly tall and a little broad with large hands. She had a serious countenance and sometimes hummed to herself while she worked. She was like a giant Gaen.

It was from Nochiel that Croy began to really learn. He knew he needed to become an expert in something. Learning from Feyazki had been haphazard at best. He seemed to know so much about every subject that it was difficult in knowing where to begin, what questions to ask. And he was always in meetings or on the battlefield, so it was difficult to gain enough time for a full lesson anyway. Feyazki was certainly the most powerful mage in the warpack and he seemed to genuinely care for Croy, but Croy needed something more focused. And there seemed to be little more focused than Nochiel. She did not care for any other type of magic. She did not seem to care for any other type of life. It was rare to see her outside of the medical area, even for her meals. She was the focused expert that Croy needed.

During the down times, she taught him the nuances of healing. The spell could be spoken the same way a hundred times, but have different levels of efficacy. Verbally there was only one spell with different power levels, -liderto. But mentally—what was focused on in the mind during the casting—there were many different spells. She taught him that if the patient was bleeding profusely, he needed to imagine the blood coagulating. Thickening and hardening into armored scabs. That would not be the end result, of course. At best the bleeding would halt enough for the physician to begin suturing. But it was like "following through." "Have you ever fought with swords?" she had asked. "When you swing, and you are trying to penetrate thick plate armor, you must 'follow through.' You not only swing until you connect, where you know the sword will be stopped, but you swing as if cutting through soft fruit. You need to push all the way through to the other side. You want the tip of the sword to come back around and strike your own heels. That is how to swing a killing blow, and that is how to cast a healing spell." She taught him that if the patient had too high of a fever and was going to burn themselves out, to think of icy mountain peaks. She taught him to think of being drunk while casting anesthesia spells. "As drunk as you have ever been. Drunk enough to fall over while attempting to walk. Drunk enough to awaken with strange bruises." She taught him to think of a small brush fire while disinfecting a wound. To think of a desert breeze while clearing liquids from a punctured lung. To think of antidotes while healing livers and streams while healing kidneys. Even how to conjure lava in his mind while cauterizing amputees. She taught him that it was the nuance that made the spell effective, not the word. "The mind must sift chaos for the desirable outcome. You must think the nuance as you speak the word to guide your willpower through the limits of eternity. Only by pressuring your will can your will pressure reality. Visualizing nuance is the key." He began to spend the majority of his time in the medical tent, learning as much as possible.

As he spent more time at the tent, there were those who began to recognize him, to pat him appreciatively on the back as they walked by. It made him feel welcome in a foreign realm. Many of the Pyran warriors were happily simple in much the same way that Gaen farmers were. It produced an odd mixture of nostalgia and comfort in the face of the exotic violence he witnessed. It made him realize that simple derlians had more in common with those of other races than they had with the extraordinary of their own race. He saw the personalities of Belg and Nolt and even Greshcly repeated amongst this foreign warpack. Over and over. He could tell by a Pyran's smile that he would act like an old schoolboy friend or another of his. Croy could predict behavior, trustfulness, jovialness, sensitivities, and even levels of integrity. All by gauging how that Pyran matched up with a Gaen that he had known back in Serif. The system only began to break down once the personality became more unique. He had not known a Feyazki or a Trela in Serif. Maybe, if he had known more 'jin, he might have recognized a Malghain. But Torpalin... Torpalin was as predictable as stone. In this vein, he began to talk to the most ordinary of the extraordinary. She was a nurse alongside of him and seemed to be out of her depth at times. But she always seemed at ease. She was always gave an aura of confidence, even when she did appear to be out of her depth. She was Trela's Fluen princess.

"Were the Belegs destined to be the Creators of the world?" Croy asked Clerin as they were resting between waves of wounded.

"You haven't cast my spell yet. Or you haven't dreamed." Clerin smiled at him. "Or both."

"Well... one precludes the other." Croy smiled back. "And I don't really have a lot of control over the first. But you did not answer my question."

"I was avoiding your question with a bit of diversion. But, if I had to answer with my own opinion, it would be that no, they weren't necessarily destined to do it." She paused and looked serious for a moment. "But I believe that someone was."

"So, you feel that a Yaven from each of the four realms was destined to create our world?" He had not expected her answer.

"I am not even sure I would go that far. I feel that someone was destined to create our world, as you say. I am too feeble minded to be able to say anything beyond that, however. I can think of no other reality than what is before me, therefore it seems that all of this is destined, or else something else would have happened. That is the problem with destiny, is it not? If you are destined to accomplish something, then do you have to try to accomplish it? I mean, if it is planned out to happen for you anyway, why put in all that effort? If you are destined to fail, then it does not matter how hard you try, does it? There is no winning with the concept of destiny." She took a breath. "I do feel that the world needed to be created, though. Therefore, I feel there was a universal compulsion, which I would call an unconscious force of destiny, to make the necessary world. I do not know if I feel that the world needed to be created through my own hubris at existence, though. I think every living thing would say that the world was destined to be created..." Croy let the pause linger, hoping she would continue. She did not.

"Well, if you are of the opinion that it is the act that is destined, but not necessarily the actor, then you need to try to accomplish it. You should try your absolute hardest, or else someone else will accomplish your destiny in your stead." Croy was merely trying to understand Clerin's meaning, but he felt like he had stumbled upon something else. She suddenly laughed quite heartily.

"Wow, yes. Yes, indeed." Clerin continued to chuckle to herself. "If Lembin had not helped to create the world, then another would have. Lembin would be sitting in the Fluen Yaven realm with this odd feeling of emptiness, unknown to any of us, while another would be hiding deep in a temple." She paused for a moment. "What if, and I am just speculating here, but what if Lembin was not destiny's first choice? What if another was supposed to accomplish that destiny, but failed? And the other is sitting in their own realm with an odd feeling of emptiness, while Lembin... Well, maybe the other would not have been afraid of becoming a Beleg. Maybe there would be no self doubt... no self hatred..."

"Belegs cannot feel doubt, Clerin. They are the Creators." Croy smiled to himself briefly. "How could someone that powerful feel regret?" he thought.

"No. No, of course not. I was thinking of something else." Clerin looked like she was thinking somewhere else, not just something else. The wistful look in her pale blue eyes made Croy think of Ilana for no good reason. And that took his own mind somewhere else. They sat in silence for some time.

"What if... what if our happiness depends upon how close to our destiny we become?" She still looked far away.

"I can't think of a better question." And he couldn't.

Another wave of wounded arrived and they went their separate ways. Clerin would be at the front of the line. Cleaning wounds, dressing minor ones, and performing the hectic duty of triage. Since she could cast simple healing spells seemingly all day long, she was perfect for intake. Those with large gashes then went to another mage for anesthesia, and then a physician would sew them up. It was the truly damaged and dying that Croy and Nochiel would see to at the back of the line. If the skirmish was small enough, he would be able to go over the sutures to keep their scarring down. If the battle was large, he would have to make some triage decisions himself. There were some that nothing could be done for and there were others that there was not enough time for. Unfortunately, magic was temporary while wounds were permanent. At least until the body's natural healing process could take over. Some things were past the natural healing process, however. Someone could be kept alive without a liver or a heart for some time, but they would eventually succumb, no matter how much magic was spent. So it went with amputations. Sometimes the bones were too crushed to repair or just too much meat had been left on the battlefield. Croy had a hard time with amputations. He knew that the warriors were glad to be alive, but... there was something about cauterizing a stump that crushed his spirit. The stench was awful and the magic draining, but it was speaking to the warrior when they woke up that really bothered him. There were times when they still felt their limb and would argue with him. Tell him that nothing was wrong because they could feel their toes wriggling. Some even got angry with him. It was heart wrenching.

The learning, however, was priceless. Within days of his tutelage, he began to feel more confidant. Within weeks, he began to feel more powerful. It was now several moons, and he began to feel like an actual mage. The Blind One had opened his eyes to magic. Ilana taught him to believe in himself and his destiny. Feyazki showed him the inexhaustible limits of chaos that true power could achieve. It was Nochiel, however, who taught him the actual skill of magic. It seemed so simple, but it was the most profound gift he had ever been given by another. It would not have been possible without everything before it, he knew that. If the Blind One had not begun his training, he would not be able to cast anything. He would still be a simple farmer and Ilana would still be by his side. Each day he tried not to think about that, but that faraway look in Clerin's eyes had somehow brought the painful twinge back. It was the gaining of skill, the healing of friends and strangers, that pushed his past back into the quiet depths of his mind. If he was to be honest with himself, that was the true reason for his need to focus.

"Are you daydreaming again, Croy?" Nochiel's voice brought him around to the present.

He looked down at the frightened Pyran held down in front of him. Eyes wild with pain and fear. A wooden spoon clenched between crooked teeth. Sweat beading on his stripped skinny form. He was almost still a boy, but had a huge gash along his left side and a small crying slit on his right. It appeared to be a puncture wound at his liver.

"The puncture first and then the slice?" Croy's voice went up slightly in pitch as he posed his question to Nochiel.

"Yes. The stab wound is killing him. As nasty as it looks, it would take hours for him to bleed out from that gash." Nochiel nodded to Croy as she spoke.

Croy placed his hands over the slit. "Mekliderto." Croy had his eyes closed. He thought of the sword tip being pulled back out. He thought of the thinly cleaved liver pressing itself back together, sealing back up. He thought of the split skin throwing ropes from one side to the other, pulling the hole closed tight. He thought of the blood getting thicker, caking in a small pile on top of the Pyran's quivering stomach. He thought of the scab solidifying and densifying. He thought of all these things, from inside to out, in the moment it took him to speak that one word. He willed it to be.

"Good, good. I am glad to see that you are learning to pace yourself. We have plenty more wounded. Let a physician suture him before casting anything on the gash." Nochiel spoke between working on her own prone patients. She always seemed to be everywhere at once. Looking over shoulders to make encouraging comments, then continuing seamlessly with her own rapid work. As quickly as the warriors could be laid down, she would heal them. Croy did his best to keep up.

The next body to be laid in front of him shocked Croy to his core. It was Haswyxe. Unconscious and ashen, it looked as if he had been slashed a hundred times. Croy swallowed hard and tried to decide where to begin. He thought about asking Nochiel for assistance when she appeared behind his shoulder.

"That one is too far gone. Send him off." She waved her hand towards those bearing the stretcher. They hesitated for too long. "What is it?"

"Clerin asked us to bring him to the Gaen. She said he would know what to do." The old Pyran nodded towards Croy.

"Well, she is wrong. There are too many other wounded to be wasting our energies like this. Maybe if the Luften were the only patient in the tent." Nochiel trailed off and waved her hand towards the old Pyran again. The Pyran just stared between Croy and Nochiel, waiting.

"I... I would like to try." Croy spoke downwards.

"Look around, Croy." She waved her arm in a wide circle. "Saving this one will mean killing ten others. This is not the time to become irrational."

"But... he is a friend." Croy suddenly felt sheepish and small. He had never argued with Nochiel before.

"Then pick them out. Pick out the ten you will leave to die." Nochiel placed her hands on her hips. "I will not allow you to walk away from all these others. You will not just let the last ones in the tent perish. You cannot just say it was their destiny because they arrived late. Their blood must be on your hands." Her voice bore into Croy. He felt timid, as if the Blind One were berating him for not understanding something simple. "You point to ten different warriors. Then I will allow you to heal this one. You must choose."

"I will heal him and then the next ten. None need perish." Croy was not sure what to say. There was no way he could point to a Pyran and tell Nochiel to let them die. From the sternness in her voice, he felt she just might.

Nochiel lifted Haswyxe's gray hand and let it drop back down with a thud. "You are wrong Croy. This will take a mighty effort. The tent is rapidly becoming full. Who knows how many more hours of combat there will be? This is a simple choice of triage. Do not make it more difficult then it needs to be."

"What if I was not here? What if I was out on the battlefield with Feyazki? Then how many would die because the tent was filling up? If I am sick and spend the day in my tent, am I to blame for all of the wounded here who do not survive?" Croy felt himself raising his voice, so he consciously brought it back down. "I do not choose who gets lain before me. This is a friend, and I cannot let him die."

"No, Clerin chose to lay this foreigner before you. You are here right now. You are not sick and you are certainly not on the battlefield. You must... no, we must—we *all* must do what we can to save as many as possible. The old adage, 'The needs of the many outweigh the needs of the few,' is true in many instances. But it holds no more truth than when spoken in this tent." Her voice softened.

"I owe this warrior my life." The words just slipped out. He knew he needed to say something that a Pyran would understand. He needed to convince Nochiel to let him do what he felt he needed to do. So he lied to her. It was not as if he wanted to harm any other Pyrans, especially the wounded lying and groaning around him in the tent. But he knew Haswyxe. Though they had not had many heart-to-heart conversations or shared their philosophies of life or cried on each others shoulders, Haswyxe had been there from the beginning. From the desert. They had gotten drunk together and told jokes and ribald tales to each other. They had laughed together and shared food and trekked countless leagues together. Croy was a simple Gaen who believed in a simple construct of loyalty. Those you knew deserved more effort than strangers. It made his bile rise to think this, to realize this. It was selfish and cruel, he knew. It was who he was, however. And nothing could change that about him. So, straight to his mentor's face, he completely lied. There seemed no other option.

"You will do what you must, but you disappoint me, Croy. I thought you had more character." Nochiel spoke softly but stared straight into him. Croy had never seen her so demure. Demure was not quite the right word. There was no shyness to her look, but it was soft and quiet. "You will have to speak to the friends of the first ten Pyrans to die in this tent after you pass out from exertion. You will not escape that." With that she turned and bent over her own patient. Croy realized that something broke that day. Something he did not know had existed and, even worse, something that could not be fixed. He could not think about that during the moment, however. He looked down at his dying friend and concentrated at the task at hand.

Croy's hands quickly palpated Haswyxe's body. His mind began to inventory the long litany of injuries. Most of it appeared to be cuts, which meant that blood loss was the major problem. Haswyxe also had a broken tibia and what appeared to be a fractured skull. Nochiel had taught him to always be wary of head injuries since something as simple as swelling could destroy the greatest of warriors. Croy felt what he needed to do and in what order. He was unsure of how much energy to put into the spells. He wanted to prove to Nochiel that he could still be helpful afterwards so he could not cast them too powerfully, but if they failed to revive Haswyxe, then all would be for naught. He would be tired and his friend would be dead. He felt time slipping away from him.

Croy bowed his head and ran his stubby fingers over Haswyxe's skull. He felt for the fissure and traced its extents. The blood had already caked. "Mekliderto!" He imagined water being sucked into dry desert sands. Rains evaporating before they fell and clouds disappearing into the clear sky. Croy knew that the first thing that needed to be resolved was any brain swelling or hemorrhaging. He was unsure of how bad it may have been, but decided on casting a Mek level in lieu of casting a different spell to find out. That was his first spell. "Nuliderto!" He thought about the one time he saw a bridge being built over a chasm, in fast motion. The ropes shot over, back and forth. The large wooden beams being felled across the span. Finally, all of the little cross-beams and planks being placed to complete the deck. He thought the skull fracture would not take too much effort since it was so small, but he wanted to be sure of a clean set. He then went to the leg. The physician who had sewn up the previous boy's gash was waiting at the leg. Croy nodded to him, and the physician grabbed the foot with one hand while pressing sideways on the knee. With a sickening crackling sound, the leg appeared straight once more. "Mekliderto!" Croy cast a stronger bone amelioration spell than he did for the skull due to the amount of damage. For his fourth spell, his final spell, he took a deep cleansing breath. This would resolve the issue one way or another. He wanted this last spell to be a combination of re-sanguination and a healing of all the gashes, slices and cuts. He let his breath out through his mouth with slow deliberation. He breathed deeply in once more.

"Eqeliderto!" His mind raced. The images poured over and through him so quickly that he was barely conscious of them. Rivers, streams and gushing water. The split skin pressing itself together from the inside out. Ropes and spider webs gripping and pulling. It was all a blur. The headache was immediate and insufferable. He vomited on the floor and dropped to his knee. Time slowed to a crawl.

Suddenly Hasyxe was coughing. His lips were flecked red with blood. Nochiel was standing over Croy admonishing him. She was complaining about something in specific, probably the vomit. He was sure that she would not be happy about him casting an Eqe spell. More than anything he had to rise. He must stand and show her that he could continue to heal others. He must!

Slowly and shakily, he stood. He clutched the small wooden table that the bodies were moved on and off of. It felt as if the room were swaying, but he knew it to be himself that was in motion. He looked at the old Pyran. "Remove him from the room." And he pointed at Haswyxe. Croy could not be more specific than that. His mind could not find the correct words to use. Language itself seemed foreign. He then kicked what dirt he could onto the small pile of vomit that lay at his feet. He nodded to the physician, who brought the boy back to the table.

"Loliderto!" It was not much, but the gash had already been sutured. The cat gut held the skin together, Croy just melded it a little. He might have used Nu if he was not feeling as horrible as he was, but he did not feel that he was short-changing the wounded warrior.

Croy took as much time as he could between patients. He was sure that Nochiel noticed. But he did not stop, he did not pass out. It was, by far, the longest day of his life. Longer than the days filled with trepidation and the Blind One in Rycher. Longer than the day he left Ilana, longer than his gliding flight to find Trela again. Longer even than the day he met Synde and Trela that first time. But he did not pass out.

As he had worried, things were not the same between Nochiel and him. She was pleasant and helpful, they were still friends, but it just did not seem like the same warmth was there. Soon afterwards she declared him just as skilled as she was at healing. He knew it was a lie, but he felt that he should no longer ask her questions about the art. He did still ask her advice about difficult patients and she freely gave it.

After several moons had passed, Croy wondered if there ever was a time where there had been more warmth. Maybe the past has a way of appearing more congenial. The lens of nostalgia can distort many things. Maybe they had always been this way, and it was wishful thinking that he had ever thought otherwise. The rhythm of the warpack became comfortable again. They laughed and joked about little things, but did not speak of Haswyxe. Maybe the warmth had returned and Croy just did not notice it because it was so gradual. He was happy with daily ritual again at any case. And that was what mattered to him.

Haswyxe became much more friendly when he was around. Always quick with a smile and a handshake. He seemed to be around less often, however. The warpack was a large entity and Trela was marching further and further into the depths of the Pyran realm. There was not much time for any of them anymore.

Croy was very rarely alone with Trela. She was usually incredibly busy with some aspect of planning or commanding or facilitating the warpack in some way. There was an odd night, when the others had retired to their tents, where he found himself alone with her. He wanted to talk about Nolt or Synde, but did not want to distress her. He wanted to speak of Serif and to know whether or not she enjoyed her time there. His mind churned in the awkward silence.

"Were the Belegs destined to be the Creators of the world?" It just popped out.

"Of course. And I am destined to be the Kriishan. A world without destiny is a dry colorless husk." Trela drank mightily from her tankard.

Chapter 18

Clerin enjoyed working at the medic tent. She enjoyed being on the front lines of something. She had no knack for destruction so she opted for the opposite, though her ability to cast healing spells was a bit stunted. She could cast Lo and Nu and sometimes, rarely, even the level of Mek but had never even attempted the power level Nar. She found, however, that with a steady breathing pattern she could cast a small spell every few minutes throughout the entire day. She was not sure if Olwinn would be proud, but many of Trela's warriors were quite grateful. She never cured anybody and was certainly not capable of being in the back assisting the physicians like Croy. But she had a quick smile for every warrior, no matter how ghastly their injuries. She used a delicate touch while applying bandages and spoke in meaningless, soothing tones. The inanity of her words went unnoticed by the wounded. They would smile up at her and tell her how beautiful she was while she cooed sweet nothings down at them. It was amazing how a "there, there" or an "everything is going to be just fine" would loosen up the tension in their faces. A quick, small, healing spell, and they would lie back down on their stretcher or cot with a satisfied sigh. As if she had just completely healed them. It amazed her how many of the wounded just wanted comfort, any comfort at all. Sometimes all she could do for a warrior was to hold their hand and wipe the sweat from their brow to allow them a peaceful passage unto death. Was it enough? How could she say?

The worst part of her job was triage. She wanted to save everyone. She felt that if a body was brought to her, it was her responsibility to make sure that it kept breathing. But they were not all brought to her in good enough shape. Some died as they arrived, some soon after. These felt terrible to Clerin, but there was nothing that could be done. Even worse was when they were brought in such numbers that those normally savable needed to be set aside. She could only send so many at a time to the back. That was cold implacable truth. In slower times she would send the most heavily wounded back first. During the most inundated times she would only send those she deemed savable. The others died at the front, denied access and, at best, were comforted as they left the world. Those were tough decisions. How does one decide if someone is unsavable? Worst of all, however, was the borderline. There were times were she sent too many wounded in and Nochiel would send some back out. And there were times when Clerin had decided that one warrior was unsavable and kept them out, only to have that warrior linger. Linger almost long enough to be sent back later, once they had cleared more room... but not quite. She had one such warrior, a Pyran so young that he was incapable of growing a beard, who showed up with a sucking chest wound. He rattled and spat blood. He was unable to sit up. She cast her small healing spell but the tension stayed in his face. She was sure that he would die within minutes. Positive, in fact. So she set him aside, sent the largest group she could to the back and let the others groan and wait for available physicians. She made her rounds and then went back to the dying warrior. But he wouldn't die. He just laid there, rattling and wheezing, bleeding copiously, but he kept a shaky white-knuckled grip on the world. Finally they were able to receive another batch. Clerin felt she needed to give the young warrior his chance since he had hung on for so long. Plus, most of the others left in the front were not too seriously injured. Certainly none as close to death as this one. He died right as they lifted his stretcher to carry it to the physician's table. She might have been able to save him had she sent him in there during the first batch. Might is a funny word, though. He also might have died on the table. She would never know. Her hesitation may have killed him but it may have saved another. Every one of those she had sent in the first batch had survived. Whichever one she had chosen not to send, in his place, might have died. But were they all that close to death? Surely there was one who would have survived until she was able to send in the next batch? Wasn't there? She could never know. That was the crux of it, that was what she hated about triage. She could never know what would have happened if she had chosen differently. But, she supposed, that was the trouble with life itself.

However, the vast majority of her time in the warpack was not spent near the medic tent. The entire culture was built around combat. Daily exercises, practices, sparring, and drills abounded. The word "war" was directly in their group description. But it amazed Clerin how little fighting there actually was. She was grateful for it, truly, but it surprised her just the same. When she was growing up, she had heard how horribly violent the Pyrans were. How they would throw deformed babies off cliffs. How the soil was fertilized by the blood of their warriors. How they would force their children into pits with wild dogs to fight for food. All of these horrible images that Fluens used to describe a race that they had never met were... false. The combat, and the medic tent in particular, would always be a part of her memories of the Pyran realm. It was that powerful of an experience, that those images could never fade from her mind. They spent an inordinate amount of time preparing for battle, however. Clerin realized that was the major motivator. It brought them together in a way that nothing else did in this barren landscape. They traded stories of battle, gave strategic advice about battle, and, most often, reminisced of battle. It was the bonding experience, however infrequent, that drew the family of the warpack together. There were those who had been in other warpacks together, ages ago, who could wax nostalgic about faded commanders. Others had been at the same battle but on opposite sides. They would trade what they noticed from their own perspective, to weave a more detailed tapestry of the actual event. What amazed Clerin the most was that there was almost no animosity, no grudges. What happened in other warpacks, in other battles, was... well, if not forgotten, it was certainly forgiven. In the Fluen realm, families may sometimes get together at one gathering and force themselves to lie about how much they enjoyed each other's company. But in the Pyran realm, it really was all about family. It was about friends so close that they were considered family. It was as if the entire realm were one huge, sometimes fractious, clan. They were all related in some sense. In the Fluen realm the hierarchy of royalty was based upon which Yaven you could trace your family to, and woe be to one who could not trace their name back that far. Lineage was everything, and it separated them into neat, tidy, understood packages. What it mainly seemed to do, however, was separate those who were planned from those who were accidents. To be an orphan in the Fluen realm was to be doomed. The Pyrans did not even seem to know the word "bastard." They were all bastards in some way, with half the populace running around from town to village, battling themselves along the way. Here it was inconceivable to treat a child differently just because they were unsure of exactly who their father was, or that their father was off at war. And maybe had been gone since conception. The entire community took care of their young as if they were their own, no matter their provenance.

As she got to know the Pyrans and their culture, so they also became curious about her. She spent time with different warriors, sometimes even eating outside of Trela's Privy Council. She did her best to understand the Pyran culture and the warriors themselves, but there was somewhere else she was hoping to spend time. Vrric rarely seemed to be alone. Oftentimes he was with Trela or Croy. Sometimes with other Pyran mages, teaching the *whisperers* and whatnot. Many times he could be seen spotted walking with Malghain discussing Ariellyna. These did not bother her in the slightest. For some reason, however, his time spent with Gyllhelon did seem to bother her. It was not as if they spent an inordinate amount of time together. And it was not as if she, herself, did not get to spend any time with him. It just seemed that whenever she felt like talking with Vrric, he was with Gyllhelon. It was the timing of it.

The warpack had been camped in the same spot for almost a week. They were at the eastern edge of a forest. Clerin thought it was called Yaniqua. Somehow they had traveled in a giant circle from the Unaqa cliffs, where Astydle's warpack had been crushed, and had come round to the opposite side. The forest was lush and verdant, which kept the camp well fed.

Clerin and Vrric walked along a shady path, away from the others. It was mid-afternoon and the sunlight splashed through the leaves. There was a large field of heather off to one side that was simply breathtaking. Clerin, unconsciously, kept attempting to steer Vrric over to the field.

"I hope that Trela lets us stay here awhile, Vrric. This is the most comfortable encampment I've experienced since leaving Ariellyna." Clerin laughed quietly to herself.

"You are the only one who still calls me that." Vrric stopped and smiled but kept his eyes downcast.

"Does it bother you?" She did not think of him as Feyazki, but thought that she had gotten better about calling him that.

"No, not here. Not while we are alone." He kept his eyes down.

"But elsewhere..." She felt like reaching out for his hand but instead they started walking again.

"I am not sure how it is done in the Fluen realm, but a Luften mage changes their name once they have left their mentor and become a full mage. It's a symbol of the life left behind. Of a new beginning. No one here knows me by any other name than Feyazki." They walked in silence for a moment. Then Clerin slowed to a stop.

"That is not how I know you, however. I met you when you were Vrric, and that is always how I will think of you. When someone says Feyazki did this or said that, my mind translates it to Vrric. When I think of how nice it would be to go for a walk with you, I think of how nice it would be to walk with Vrric." Clerin paused for a moment. "Does your real name give anyone power over you? Does it embarrass or humiliate you?"

"No, none of that. It's more a sign of respect. No, that's not right either." Vrric chewed on his lip briefly. "It is an acknowledgment of the change within me."

"Maybe it is because I only knew you as a mage but I don't feel that you have changed. Remember when Vanelia first introduced us? You seemed so much younger then, but you don't seem like a different derlian now." She smiled up at him.

"Yes, Herance, I do recall." They both laughed. "That seemed so long ago, before the well. Before my vision quest, before the eshram. Before my fight with the Tlana." He face grew serious. "That is what did it to me. The lightning. I do feel different than I used to. That moment... that survival... the learning of a new element... it did change me."

Vrric had a way of suddenly smiling when he was serious. To Clerin it was almost magical. He would be staring at his feet, sometimes at hers, and suddenly his head would lift and at the same time the smile would grow on his face. They happened at the same rate, the smile and the lift, so it seemed that they were linked together. By the time his face was looking straight into hers, he would be pleasantly beaming. He usually had some nonsensical joke that he was overly proud of, but not this time.

"You know, I told my mentor about you after that first meeting. I tried to explain how striking your eyes were, but was unable to find the perfect words. I..." Clerin interrupted.

"Try now." He stood there looking slightly stunned. "Tell me how striking my eyes are." Clerin came from a land of poets. Boys would surround a girl and attempt to outdo each other with flowery praise of her beauty. The constant attention from strangers, that oftentimes felt wholly disingenuous, began to weigh on her. When she was back there, before all this began, she wondered what it would feel like to be anonymous. To be invisible. But here, now, she was tired of that. She did not want to be ignored by everyone, all of the time. Only by those she did not care for.

Vrric was quiet for some time. He was not staring into her eyes, like a brazen Fluen boy would be, but staring up and over her right shoulder. He was painting from memory instead of gazing at the landscape before him. Clerin was unsure if that made her happier or not.

"They are the color of lightning. Not the afterimage burned into your eyes once the flash has ended, tinged with red, yellows, and bright greens. Not when you close your eyes and see the fading image slipping down and to the side, then suddenly centered again. No, they are the color of the strike itself. That one instant that is so fleeting that one can never be sure if the memory of the color is as accurately vibrant as the reality. Somehow that is captured within you. Within your eyes." His voice was quiet.

Clerin had no recollection of thinking about it, no forethought whatsoever, but she immediately raised herself on her toes and leaned in for a kiss. It was motion of pure impulsiveness. He kissed her back and she held her arms around his neck. But then it felt like he pulled away.

"Thank you for that bit of home." She did not know what to say, but doubted he would understand what she had said. Her calves felt stretched so she lowered herself back to the ground. "Sorry, I wasn't trying to..." There was a sudden terrible embarrassment that entered her.

"No, no... don't be sorry. I enjoyed that very much." He smiled warmly but did not lean in for another kiss.

Clerin was slightly out of breath. Her chest heaved as she inhaled. Though she could feel herself blushing, she kept smiling at him with her lips slightly parted. Waiting. Waiting... But she could wait no longer.

"Well, I'll try to keep the name straight." She laughed nervously. Did she miss something? Did she misunderstand something? She was unsure as to what had just happened.

"No problem. Like I said, it doesn't bother me when we are alone." They started walking again. "At least you don't call me Mudfoot." He mumbled it so quietly that Clerin was unsure if she heard it correctly.

As her confusion about Vrric grew, she began to think of Chiavel more. That was just as useless, however, so she attempted to put that out of her mind as well. She tried to think of Fluen boys that she had flirted with in school. They all seemed so young in her memory, like children really. She felt that she had grown and changed a lot during her journey. But how long had it really been? Was she really that much older? Had she actually changed that much? She sometimes wondered if she should take on a new name as well. That left the multitude of Pyran warriors that surrounded her. There was certainly no lack of interest. Oh, there were some who would not give her the time of day, some who would not even speak to her just because she was Fluen. They were a quiet minority. The vocal majority showered her with compliments. Whether they had been wounded and under her care, or if they just hovered about the medic tent, there were always some around. She could not always tell if it was because she seemed exotic or if it was genuine interest. To be honest, she did not really care. They were entertaining flirtations at best. She did not allow herself any actual diversions.

And that brought her back to Trela. For a while Clerin had been lax about attending any Privy Council meetings. They were not always the height of entertainment, even with the amazing cooking of Kolaf. At first she had played hooky with Vrric. He was often needed at the meetings, however. So eventually she had begun wandering off on her own. She decided to bring herself back into the fold. It just so happened that Trela was alone on that particular evening.

"Where's Knill?" She had barely popped her head into the tent when the question came unbidden to her lips.

"That's it? 'Where's Knill?' Whatever happened to 'Hello, Trela, how are you?'" Still, Trela was grinning as she spoke. She left her maps upon the tall table and walked over to Clerin. She shook her hand a bit roughly. "What brings you here?"

"Well, to be honest, I'm not very sure." Clerin thought hard about what the actual issue was. "I'm tired of not being chased."

"From what I hear, you've been nothing but chaste. Do you bring me gossip?" Trela moved back towards her maps.

It took Clerin a moment to realize what Trela had said. "No, no... Not chaste, but chas*ed*." They both laughed.

"Then let me reiterate: from what I hear, you're nothing but chased. A lot of my warriors think that you are the 'bees knees' as they put it, and there is quite a buzz about. All you have to do is to pick one and check it out. If you don't like it, pick out a different one. Trust me, you'll get bored with the variety before they stop chasing you. There's something about a warpack on the move..." Trela spoke with her head down, pushing small polished stones around a map.

"Well, but they're not... I don't necessarily want to be chased by everyone." Clerin spoke quietly to the floor.

"And I told myself I wasn't going to drink tonight. Ha!" Trela moved over to a shorter table with some goblets on it. "Have you had any of Hylth's grog? It is fantastic." She poured a full goblet for each of them. "So, who is it? Feyazki?" She looked Clerin in the eye. "That is my first guess. Prove me wrong and shock me."

"Probably." Clerin took a drink. "Yes, if Vrric chased me I would enjoy it. I just... I don't know if I would let him catch me." Trela was silent for a little while.

"Sometimes I wonder why they call us the fairer sex." She smiled warmly at Clerin. "So you don't really want to be chased by the multitudes who are willing, and you are not sure if the desired chaser would be allowed a successful hunt. Does that sum it up?"

For this, Clerin was embarrassed. She did not want to say it aloud. And had not even let herself dwell upon it for any length of time while she was alone. She took another sip. She took a deep breath.

"I hate to admit this, but I would prefer it if he didn't chase anyone else." She stared into her goblet.

"Well... to be honest... that doesn't sound very fair at all." Trela kept her warm smile. "But I like you, Clerin. I truly do. You hear so many horrible rumors about Fluens growing up, and I must say, you have squashed every last one of them. No other warpack has a Fluen princess. None but mine." It was Trela's turn to take a drink. "I will do what I can."

"No, no... please don't. Just saying it out loud is enough for me. I would rather not have any outside interference." Clerin thought about it long and hard. It seemed odd that she could think about things lightly while alone with all the time in the world, but it sometimes took speaking things out loud, to another derlian, to think hard about them. "I think, actually, that I do not want to be chased. The Fluen realm is just so different. There is so much emphasis on poetry and song that every time you turn around there is some young troubadour exclaiming your beauty to the sky. I have had times where they practically surrounded me, each compliment more unbelievable than the one before. More emphatic, more flowery, more convoluted metaphorically. They swoon before you in droves. But do any of them mean it? Any of it? Professing love is to Fluens like sharpening a sword is to Pyrans. It is a type of practice, the honing of a skill. The sincerity is difficult to gauge. Here, however, there is an overabundance of sincerity, but no one knows how to project it. Part of me carries a distaste for the empty poetry of my youth, but part of me... I think part of me misses it. The truth is that I want both, or neither. I guess the truth is that I want some truth. Even just a little bit." She took another sip. "How did you come to be with Knill?" Clerin had been wanting to ask the question for some time. They were the only two, that she knew of, from different realms who were together. She felt her right eyebrow lift quizzically. With a monumental effort, she forced the errant brow back down to rest in plane with its sister.

"That is a question with two answers, one simple and one... not so simple." Trela paused for so long that Clerin thought she would not divulge her answers.

"What is the simple answer?" Clerin smiled warmly to assuage what she imagined were Trela's fears.

"Knill pursued me from the beginning. From my very first day in Serif. No matter that he was a Gaen and I am Pyran. No matter that he is younger than me. No matter that I rebuffed his advances as cruelly as I could." Trela took a deep draught. "He is the reason that I was able to escape from Serif. He left a life of ease as a future physician holed up amongst his own kind, following in his father's footsteps, for... this." Her hand encompassed the room but the implications were much larger. "Now he is adrift amongst strangers in a realm filled with violence and conflict, with only Tumu and Croy to talk to."

"And you." Clerin smiled again.

"Yes, of course. And me." Trela's tone began to have the low droning quality to it of someone who knows they are defeated. Or maybe just resigned.

"And what about the not-so-simple answer?" Clerin burned to ask if Trela loved Knill. It took all of her willpower not to blurt out the question. She needed to be gentle in her probing.

"Well, that is the entire issue, isn't it? I am in here with my maps, or in council." Her hand holding her goblet pointed a finger at Clerin while she took another drink. "While he is doing... what? I could not tell you where he is right now. To be honest, I had not even been thinking about him until you arrived and asked me."

"Do you love him?" Clerin could not help herself. She felt the conversation slipping away.

"Of course. Of course, I do." The words fell immediately from her mouth. "But leading a warpack keeps me very busy. The time demands are enormous. How can the Kriishan be allowed to be in love? I keep thinking that after I defeat Qizern, I will have more time for Knill. Maybe."

"So, basically, you are following your destiny and Knill is following you." Clerin spoke softly and did not try to look Trela in the eye.

"It is more complicated than that." Trela did not continue, however. She did not try to explain the complications.

"I think that is my fear. That Vrric is following his own destiny..." Clerin trailed off. Trela did not speak either. The silence stretched to distortion. Clerin liked and respected Knill. She did not want to appear to be disparaging to him or to his loyalty. She felt she needed to clarify her fears to Trela. Instead of doing that, she decided to clarify her wants. "I want to be following my own destiny. A destiny that is large and beautiful. Challenging but endurable. One that appears ordered behind the chaos, like shadow puppets at the bottom of a rippled lake. But more than that, I want a destiny that includes another's. I want destinies that collide. That meld like soap bubbles. That are all encompassing." Clerin lowered her voice. "And I want the other destiny to have the same desires as mine. They need to feed off of each other like a moebius strip of starving cannibals."

Trela's laugh was musical.

Clerin spent little time alone. When she found herself in that state, she wandered off to find another derlian. She would trade cheap jokes with Torpalin or philosophize with Croy or dance near the fire with Zira to the pounding rhythm of the Pyran war drums. There was a touch of unconsciousness to it. She had never liked being alone as a child. It was not necessarily interaction that she needed. She used to sneak into her father's study while he was writing and just sit quietly in a corner. The gentle scratching of her father's quill was soothing to her, especially when mixed with the crackling fire during cold winter nights. She would play with her dolls, making them speak their stories only in her head so as not to disturb his important work. But it was not all unconscious.

When she was alone in the warpack, her mind would turn to the Belegs. It would turn to the messages inside her. There was a burning urgency to unload that which she carried. But there was nothing she could do to speed up the process. Even worse, she was becoming concerned that Gorbanax would not be the last message. When she first communicated with Lembin, she had thought it would be a quick journey. She had figured on a short trip to a foreign realm, a warm welcome by the royal branch of Areillyna, a quick sojourn to the Luften temple to deliver the message, and then a leisurely return to the home she was so familiar with. But that was not what happened. Not even close. Now she was trapped on the opposite side of the world, with several messages that may or may not be deliverable inside of her and no end in sight. It was difficult not to despair. She wondered when she would ever get back home. But that was not what really bothered her.

Clerin thought she could feel the messages. It was in the space between her stomach and her lungs, just under her heart, but centered. When she was alone and it was quiet and still, she could feel them there. They were a little warm and vibrated slightly. The effect made her nauseated. She had not noticed the sensation when she just had Lembin's message in her, so maybe it was just Linchon's. It unnerved her to no end.

It was so subtle, however, that any amount of distraction made the feeling disappear. Even when alone, if Clerin were concentrating on something or physically active, she did not notice it. It was the slow quiet times. Times when, in the recent past, she would have called herself bored. It got to her the most when she was trying to sleep. If she was not sufficiently tired, once in her cocooned bedding, the warmth would begin. It would start as a pinprick and slowly expand into a small sphere the size of a eyeball. Then it would begin to vibrate. That was when the nausea would begin. If left unchecked, the sphere would grow to the size of a fist and shake violently. She had stared at her stomach, expecting to see something under her skin, any sort of movement, but the sensation was never visible. So she would concentrate on something. She would think of all the things she learned at the medic tent. She would bring each face, wounded or healthy, that she had seen that day into her mind's eye. She would remember old conversations. She would do math in her head, or imagine Trela's colored stones shifting about her maps. Anything would do. Finally, after making herself world weary, she would fall into a peaceful sleep. She did not have dreams like Croy had. Nor did she endure visions like Tumu. It was just this low level of constant discomfort. Either that or blissful distraction.

So she kept herself busy. In a warpack the size of Trela's it was not difficult. There was always something to do. Some meeting to attend. Some assistance to provide. She spoke to no one about her feelings. In fact, she spoke to no one about the Belegs. They all knew that she was seeking the various Temples. The story of her communing with Linchon was known by all. But Clerin found that the Belegs were thought of differently in the various realms. In her realm, Lembin was thought of as a kind of great-grandparent. A kindly, if misunderstood, ancient relative who only wants the best for their progeny, but finds it difficult to communicate seamlessly with the youth of today. Not quite doting and certainly not doddering, but well intentioned and well thought of. There was a touch of nostalgic normalcy to the way Fluens spoke of Lembin. Here, Gorbanax seemed to be thought of only as a cruel creator. A fickle child who was always on the verge of growing weary with their toys. Even the name was whispered as if Gorbanax would somehow hear and punish. Croy did not speak of Gunzgak like that, and the Luftens seemed to have forgotten that the Belegs even existed. But the Pyran realm included a mixture of awe and fear that surprised Clerin when she had first heard it. The reverence was nice to hear, but everything else seemed an impediment. Few then, even though they all knew she had communicated with more than one Beleg, would bring the subject up. And Clerin, for her part, never brought it up herself. Her goal was not to examine these things. It seemed that there was nothing she could do to divert, or even to speed up, her destiny. No, her goal was merely the sweet and simple succor from discomfort that gentle distraction brought.

So Clerin found herself going to all of the meetings of the Privy Council. At first she stayed quiet. She was merely there to relieve her discomfort. She sat near the back and listened to the arguments. She was not a warrior, only a diplomat's daughter, so she felt that she had nothing to contribute. She expected the conversations to be about military strategy and tactics, and sometimes they were. Most of the time, however, they were more mundane. Vrric took an entire meeting to brag about the cohesion of his *whisperers*. Torpalin discussed how he felt that the morning exercises lacked enough strength training. Dartsyle argued that they did not involve enough stretching. It seemed that each individual had their pet project, their pet concern that they spent grueling hours on trying to convince the others of its importance. Much of the meetings were a waste of time, a boondoggle, a mere distraction. The problem was that if they got important, if there was real strategy being discussed, she felt out of place. When Trela began discussing troop movements, Clerin could actually feel her eyes glaze over. It was not as if she were not intelligent enough to understand strategy, but she just had little interest. The jargon involved, especially in a foreign realm, was difficult to follow. It appeared that every Pyran was born with an inherit instinct for how large a maniple was, or which side of the halberd was used to unseat a warrior from their horse. She preferred discussing the healing arts to the martial, but the only time that subject was discussed was if there were issues with supplies. The minimal effort it took to ignore the meetings was still enough of a gentle distraction, however, so she continued to attend them.

Clerin was quietly ignoring a meeting when she realized a diplomatic question was being discussed. Her ears pricked unconsciously and she instantly tried to recall what she had been ignoring just a few moments before. It appeared that the warpack was running low on resources. This was a perennial issue for Trela during these meetings, at least for the last couple of moons, which was probably why Clerin had been ignoring it. The conversation that brought her out of her distraction appeared to be about a nearby village. Some wanted to attack the village since it was considered fiercely loyal to Qizern. Gain some non-perishable food, coin, bandages, tents, and other badly needed supplies. Others felt there were too many civilians in the village. It amazed Clerin that there was such a thing as too many civilians. The idea that there was some crucial ratio of warrior-to-civilian that made it acceptable ransack someone's farm seemed incongruous. She immediately gained interest in the argument.

"All I am saying is there is at least half a garrison stationed there. And not in a well-guarded keep or tower, but just amongst the villagers. They have a strong, standing militia and have been loyal to

Qizern since before he usurped the throne. It would not only send a strong statement to Qizern but it will also replenish our diminishing supplies. And not just any supplies, but shields and axes and arrows. Our scouts tell us that there are even a few members of the Guard amongst the garrison. This is a perfect mission. To steer away from this is to shirk your duty to your warpack." The speaker was a young Pyran that Clerin did not know very well. She thought his name was Droc, or some such. He was tall, had hawklike, piercing eyes and was always voting for combat.

"I am a scout and have seen the village with my own eyes." Escha stood with her fists clenched unconsciously. "There may be a militia there, but I did not detect any portion of a garrison, let alone any actual Guards."

"And how would you even know what a Guard looks like, Luften?" A different Pyran, Clerin thought her name might have been Nesrut, stood and glared at Escha.

"I was with Escha. There were no Guards." Yarsurle did not stand.

"How long were you there for? Maybe you just did not see them. Maybe they were hunting, or out for a walk, or maybe they were just indoors." Droc had his arms crossed over his chest.

"Is there a better target? A purely military target?" Escha spoke up again.

"We are in the middle of nowhere." It was Nesrut again. "There is nothing around here but farming villages. I understand the hesitation, but this village is the most militant and most loyal to Qizern in the remote area."

"Aren't we near the Yaniqua forest? What about Dun Oengen?" This was Lishean. The best thing about Lishean, Clerin thought, was that all the Pyrans listened to him. He was almost more revered than Trela. It certainly seemed that he was more respected.

"That is a suicide mission. Why would you even bring that up?" Clerin did not recognize the Pyran speaking. She was quite shocked that any of Trela's warriors would speak to Lishean like that.

"Iftrin is correct. Dun Oengen is a star fort with five points surrounding a central keep. Each point holds a guard tower. At the top of each tower are probably three to five warriors, depending on the fort's alert status, and conceivably a ballista and/or a small catapult that could fire over the crenellated walls. We all know the purpose of a star fort is that each tower can direct archery or small siege engine fire to the base of two other towers. In this way, each of the towers can protect two of its brethren. That is a forty percent coverage rate, not including the tower protecting itself. Therefore, we would have to attack each tower at once. And to keep anyone in the courtyard from being alarmed, we would have to be incredibly discrete and incredibly coordinated. It is pure madness." This was Droc again, and many of those present were nodding their heads in agreement. "Plus there is only one road that passes Dun Oengen. They would see the warpack from leagues away and button it up tight. I'll say it again. Madness."

"There is the Thieves' Passage. No way a warpack could take that path, nor even a maniple, but maybe a small strike force with a heavy cohort for backup." Yarsurle's quiet voice rang through the silence.

"That is also madness, but even if it were to work, it still solves nothing. There is no way to attack the fort by surprise. And there is no way to take the fort by force. It is too well defended. I say we take the village." Droc just would not back down.

"We get them drunk." Clerin surprised herself by speaking. "We have a small unarmed force arrive at their front gates with a wagon full of grog. Hylth's grog. Make some pretense of a local festival or celebration or something and get them to drink it. It should not be too difficult to convince warriors to drink. Another force takes this Thieves' Passage, with the backup trailing behind. Once the warriors are drunk enough, the force attacks the towers, quiet and coordinated. The force then gains entrance to the keep's gates and the rest of the warpack can walk through the front door." She had stood while talking though she was not sure why. It made her face Droc while she spoke. There was a frustrated look in his eyes, almost angry, that Clerin did not understand. Unconsciously she wiped her sweaty palms on her breeches.

The room was silent for some time, all eyes on Trela. She stood in front of them all, leaning against a table with her left arm across her stomach supporting her right arm. Her right hand covered her mouth, making it difficult to ascertain her thoughts. Her brow was furrowed, indicating that she was thinking heavily.

"What do you think?" Lishean broke a silence that no one else could.

"I think Droc is right, it is madness." There seemed to be a collective sigh of relief amongst the gathered warriors as Trela started to speak. "However, I cannot attack a farming village full of civilians. We need supplies, and more than that, we need to replenish our coffers. We have spent too long wandering about and not enough time in combat. Real combat, not fighting some dirt farmer." She smiled a bright and confident smile. "I think the time is ripe to show Qizern that we mean business. That I am coming and he had better get prepared. The only way to do that is to be daring. Fortune smiles upon the bold, my friends. If we are unable to take a fort, we will be unable to march upon the Dekhan Plateau. And if we cannot do that, we may as well all go home." Trela paused for a moment. "I must ponder this plan. You are to speak nothing of this to anyone outside of this Council. I will need some time to decide that this is the best course of action."

As the warriors began to shuffle out of the tent, Trela stopped Clerin. "You stay. I need to speak with you."

It took a while for the tent to clear out. Nobody spoke as they left, but Droc stared hard at Clerin as he walked by. She was not sure, but she thought she detected some animosity in that stare. Trela waited for a moment after the last of them left.

"Where did your idea come from?" Trela looked at Clerin a little sideways.

"I am not sure, what do you mean?" She was not sure why, but Clerin would have felt more comfortable if there was another derlian in the tent.

"If there is any way to avoid attacking Yuwalt, I must take it. If there is any way for me to conquer one of Qizern's forts, I must take it." Trela had her arms crossed in front of her. It took Clerin a slight moment to realize that Yuwalt must be the name of the village. "I am just curious how you came by the idea. Of getting them drunk. Is it something that happened in your realm, maybe a legend of old? Or is it something made up, like a children's story? Or, and this is what I am really asking, did it just pop into your head? You do not often offer advice during these meetings." Clerin thought long and hard about the question. She could not think of any other source.

"It... it just came to me. I just thought it and spoke." Clerin was getting nervous. She had never been questioned about the origin of her ideas before. Trela stood there, arms crossed, and stared at her. Hard. Then, suddenly, she smiled.

"Excellent. I am glad that you thought about your response. I will assume this is the guiding hand of destiny. I have one other question for you. This one is difficult." Trela took a breath. "I want you to wheel the wagon up to the front gate. I want you to present the grog to the warriors of Dun Oengen. What do you say?"

"But, why me?" Her pulse quickened at the thought.

"You are perfect. One, you are a foreigner with foreign ways. Two, a princess like you can afford to drop off a wagon full of grog. Three, and this is the real reason, you can be incredibly persuasive. If I were a young, virile male and you were standing in front of me, begging me to imbibe some of your free grog, there is no way I could refuse. Just smile with those dimples, and they will all line up for a draught." Trela's smile made her own eyes sparkle. Then, almost under her breath, she added another. "Four, destiny wants you to be the one."

"Let me consider it." Clerin wanted to say that she was not a princess, that she doubted she had magic drink inducing dimples, that she was just not that persuasive. And, if she allowed herself to think about it too much, the largest worry for her lurked in the back of her mind. That if they smelled a trap, she would be the first one killed. But she said none of those things.

"Of course. I will give you until tomorrow evening, before the next meeting." Trela patted her shoulder as she prepared to leave.

Clerin wandered the camp alone. She did not feel like talking to anyone, but she did not want to sit alone in her tent, either. As she walked, she pondered her situation. She felt like an ant on a leaf in the middle of a raging river. What could she do but cling to her leaf and hope that the sound that thundered in her ears was not a waterfall? Nothing. She did not have Trela's steadfast belief in destiny. Sometimes bad things happened to good derlians. There was no argument for that. Where was the destiny in the death of an infant? No, she could not assuage her fears by assuming she was meant to speak at that meeting. On the other hand, what *had* made her speak? She had never spoken at a meeting before. Oh sure, she had whispered a joke to Vrric or answered a direct question, but she had not really given any unsolicited advice. Not that she even thought it was advice. Why did she speak? There were certainly times in other meetings that she thought up amazing plans but kept quiet. Sometimes another would say almost exactly what she was thinking, as if she had broadcasted her thoughts through telepathy. Sometimes the idea would fall away unconjured. Forgotten from the realm. But now here, with a not-so-amazing plan, she had stood and spoken aloud. There was no reasoning. Of course, why did she do anything? When someone spoke and she thought she had something clever to add, what makes her say it aloud? As she wandered through the camp, she wondered how much of her life was truly conscious. How much was rationally thought through? When was the last time that she spoke that she sounded each word in her head and rearranged them to her liking before speaking? Speaking amongst friends was a reaction for Clerin. A reflex. The spontaneity was enjoyable, and sometimes the most insightful things popped into her head and out of her mouth, but not always. She decided to find someone to talk to. She was starting to feel angry that Trela had put her in this position. She did not want to be an ant on a leaf.

Clerin went to find Vrric, to ask him if he thought about his words before speaking, but he was not in his tent. Afraid of finding him with Gyllhelon, she wandered towards Croy's tent. If there was a derlian with whom she could have a serious talk with, it would be him. The thing that she thought she loved most about Croy was his constant earnestness. She felt certain that he would attack any given subject with brave naiveté. In fact, he was so earnest that she even doubted that he could lie.

Croy was outside of his tent, alone, staring up at the stars. Clerin thought she detected a smile on his face. He looked so peaceful that she almost walked away so as not to disturb him. He must of heard her coming near.

"Well, hello. I didn't expect to see you tonight." His ever-present grin warmed his weathered face.

"Did you think about that before you said it?" Clerin decided to jump in head first. "Did those exact words walk slowly through your mind before you decided to speak them?"

"Uhm, no. I just spoke them." Croy cocked his head at her. "Why do you ask?" Clerin sighed audibly.

"I spoke at the meeting earlier this evening." Clerin was going to continue but was lightly interrupted by Croy.

"Ah yes, the 'get them drunk' plan." Croy's grin was somewhat infectious.

"Well, after the meeting Trela took me aside and asked how I thought up the plan. I told her that it just popped into my head, and now she thinks that destiny speaks through me." Clerin sighed again.

"To be fair, Trela always thinks that destiny speaks to her through various derlians. And the way the wind shakes the leaves in the trees and the patterns of birds flying overhead and the rhythm of horse hooves while she's riding. She is obsessed with destiny." His head tilted back to examine the stars once again. Clerin thought about the last time she had spoken with Croy and felt that Trela was not the only derlian who was obsessed by destiny. "So what is the problem? Are you worried that if the plan fails she will blame you?"

"No. Not until you mentioned it." They both laughed briefly. "She wants me to deliver the grog."

"Ah. I have always thought it is easier to believe in destiny when your own life is not on the line. And how do you feel about it, your plan?" He was nodding slightly to himself.

"Well, I just spoke the words. Trela wanted to know if the idea came from a legend or children's story. I told her that they just popped into my head, and that was enough for her. My problem is that all my words just pop into my head. How am I to differentiate between saying something as I think it and actual destiny?" Clerin explained her problem as succinctly as she could.

"Hmm. That is a little different. When you said she assumed it was destiny because the words 'popped into your head,' I had a different image in my mind of the conversation. She actually asked you if you had heard of the plan earlier in your life?" His stubby fingers rubbed his stubbly chin.

"Yes." She could think of nothing else to say.

"Then maybe she is not as flippant as you believe. Did she give you reasons as to why she wanted you to deliver the grog?" He still looked thoughtful.

"Besides saying that destiny wanted me to do it?" Clerin paused for a brief moment. "She said my dimples would convince them to drink, and that being a foreigner would make them question me less."

"You do have a disarming smile. And, to be honest, being foreign is an advantage. They have no idea of your Fluen customs." His finger began to tap his chin. "So what is your fear? Why have you come to talk with me about this?"

"My fear is that they will figure out that I am just a distraction, a fraud. Then they'll kill me—if not worse—beforehand and be prepared to destroy Trela as she tries to take the towers. You know she will not trust another to do that. Then, after she has been killed, the entire warpack will be whipped up into a frenzy and foolishly attack a well-defended and prepared keep. Then all of those derlians that I have become so close with in the last several moons will be horribly killed. Then all of our dead bodies will be tossed into a mass shallow grave to be dug up and tossed around by forest animals. And it will be all my fault." Clerin sighed once more. "That is my fear."

"Wow." Clerin did not expect it, but somehow Croy's grin became wider. He barely contained his mirth. "All I can say is wow." A small chuckle escaped his tight lips.

"You are not helping, Croy." Yet, somehow his mirth was contagious. Against her strongest wishes, she began to smile.

" 'Our bodies being tossed about by forest animals?' Where does that even come from?" It appeared as if he was struggling to keep a straight face but losing. He clutched his stomach as he laughed.

"That is the problem. I don't know!" Clerin was not sure if she was laughing at herself, or because Croy was laughing, or just to release the unbearable tension that had built up in her. They both laughed for a long moment. Amazingly enough, it calmed her completely. It was just what she needed. She felt her anger fading with her fear.

Clerin was not sure if she would have agreed to deliver the grog if it had not been for Croy. What if she had found Vrric and he had warned her away? What if she had found no one and worried herself into not accepting the challenge back in her own tiny tent? There were so many permutations, so many variables, that may have swayed the decision. But only one thing had happened. She had found Croy, and he was in a good mood. Maybe Trela was right. Maybe it was destiny.

The warpack was camped along the eastern edge of the Yaniqua forest. They had been attempting to find the Thieves Passageway, the rough pathway that wound through a narrow spot in the forest. Clerin was not sure how large it was at its beginning, but was told there were locations where only two warriors could walk abreast. It seemed, however, that finding the entrance was going to be difficult. Trela admitted as much during the meeting.

"As you may have heard, we passed the main crossroad to Dun Oengen today. That means that we are getting close to the entrance to the Thieves Passage. Though many know if its approximate location, there are none amongst us who will admit to knowing its exact location. Since we are getting so close, tonight will be our first night of iron rations." There were audible groans from the warriors present. "I understand your concerns, but I cannot risk the smoke or glow of any fires. If I thought I could keep warriors from smoking their pipes, I would ban that as well. We need an upper hand for this battle, and our only advantage is surprise. If they even get a whiff of our presence we will be unable to penetrate the fort's defenses. After this attack, Qizern will be on high alert. This will be our last chance to catch the enemy unawares. Unawares... Think long and hard about that. We are going to attempt to capture each guard tower without raising the alarm. Then we need to storm the gear-housing, which should consist of a murder-room above the blood-room. While the gear-housing should be easy to enter and holds the counter weight mechanisms that lift the portcullis and lower the drawbridge, it has a ceiling of interwoven metal slats that will stop weapons from passing easily from underneath but allow boiling oil to drop unhindered. Also, being closer to the holes in the slats than those below in the blood-room, those above the slats will have a much easier time jabbing spears or pikes and shooting arrows through them. From the countless heroic epics we have heard as children, you know that we cannot head straight for the gear-housing. We will have to pick the lock, or use magic, or break down the heavy oak door to the murder-room so we can fight the guards on their own level. But first things first. We must be able to take the towers unawares. Do we have any suggestions?"

"I thought your princess was going to entice them to drink themselves unawares." Droc spoke with heavy sarcasm.

"We could start a forest fire. That should keep them occupied." Clerin did not see who was speaking.

"You are going to need five strike teams with five members, including a mage who can fly, a spy who can pick locks, and three warriors. These strike teams must hit each tower at exactly the same time and be perfectly silent." This was from Estfale.

"We could make stuffed dummies and place the uniform of an unconscious guard on them. Each tower taken would have the dummies propped up so the other tower guards would think nothing was amiss." This was from Dartsyle. "It would be like the story of Hengfir and Telinder."

The room broke out into raucous laughter. Though Clerin had never heard the story, she figured it was an improbable children's tale. The laughter merely solidified her belief.

"You are not helping." Trela spoke to no one in particular. Or maybe she was speaking to all of them.

It took another two days before they found the Thieves Passage. The entire camp had been eating iron rations for the last couple of nights. The nights were warm enough that the lack of fire was not a physical discomfort. Still, the camp felt empty during the dark nights. The warpack as a whole was experienced, and any complaints there might have been did not reach Clerin's ears. The excitement and expectation of the impending battle seemed to overshadow the small hardships. The thought of attempting to storm a keep made her nervous, but it actually seemed to calm the majority of the warpack. Clerin supposed that this is what they did.

The plan was simple but maddening. Trela had decided to only use one strike force to take the towers. Evidently she was going to attempt the stuffed dummies. Clerin did not like that one bit, but Trela did not feel she could trust five different strike forces to not raise an alarm. Or maybe she did not think they could perform the correct timing. Either way, Trela, Vrric, Malghain, Estfale, and Jalin were the only strike force. Jalin was a tall and lithe Pyran spy. Clerin did not know her, which was not a surprise since she knew so few, but Trela seemed to not know her either. Lishean and Dartsyle had spoken highly of her skills during one of the meetings. Clerin supposed there were few warriors' opinions that Trela trusted more. Jalin had long lanky arms and legs that were roped with distinct muscles. Not huge bulky muscles like Torpalin had, but they were incredibly well defined. They would ripple under her black clothing as she moved.

Clerin was to be accompanied by Dartsyle and Serghno. Serghno was a short and slightly fat Pyran mage who seemed pleasant enough. He had a mustache that was short over his lip, but curled upwards in a waxy crest at each side of his mouth. He would stroke his mustache when he laughed or seemed nervous. Clerin would have felt more comfortable with Croy, but it was decided that the only foreigner should be her. She did admit that a Fluen with a Gaen and a Pyran was a bit much, but she trusted Croy. This Serghno was probably a more skilled mage—he certainly had many warriors vouch for him during the meetings—but Croy would have been more familiar. The grog was supposed to be prepayment for giving sanctuary and protection to the three of them, and they figured having only one foreigner with them would help sell the story, that having an exotic Fluen princess would add that bit of mystery so necessary to a good lie. Would a Pyran pay for un-rendered services with a cart of grog? Probably not. Would a Fluen? Who knew? Trela was willing to bet that not one of the Pyrans in the fort had ever even seen a Fluen before. Her hope was that that mystery, that niggling doubt of what would be acceptable and normal for a Fluen to do and to act like, would be enough to convince a group of warriors to get drunk on free grog. Clerin was beginning to have her doubts, however. It somehow seemed like Trela was punishing her for not letting them attack the helpless village. As if that were Clerin's fault. In her heart of hearts, she knew that was a foolish idea, that she was just scared out of her wits, but there it lurked. The real trick to the whole plan would be to get the tower guards to participate in the drunkenness. Those few would be the key. They would not be allowed to drink on duty. Clerin racked her brain trying to figure out a way to get them to imbibe.

For his part, Lishean was to lead the warpack up the main road and arrive just when Trela was opening the gate. There had to be enough time for Qizern's warriors to get drunk, but they wanted to make their attack long before dawn. The timing was critical even if the exact moment of attack was impossible to foresee. Unfortunately, as was often the case, Tumu was of no help. Getting the warpack through the forest without alarming the fort was going to be a difficult chore. Another, much smaller contingent of two cohorts was to filter its way through the Thieves Passage led by a Pyran named Kryhir. The plan was to have Lishean wait about twenty minutes away from the fort, so the timing of when Vrric could *whisper* to them to start marching was critical.

The sun would set in a little less than an hour. Dartsyle held the reins of the wagon team, leading them through the large open swath of road. Serghno was sitting in the back of the wagon with the grog, they had repoured the grog into casks to make the wagon look more impressive. They had already been riding for almost an hour, deep into the heart of the forest. Though the road was wide, the canopy of the trees still stretched out and covered it. The spotted light waved with the branches in the wind. The trees were small compared to those in the Luften realm, but they were large and lush by Pyran standards. If not for Clerin's nervousness, the ride would have been incredibly peaceful and relaxing. It was truly beautiful.

Her clothing, however, was making it difficult to breathe. Trela had dressed Clerin herself. They had spent almost an hour while Trela made her try on various undershirts with different jerkins and bodices. Clerin felt sore from so much poking and prodding and stuffing and tightening of laces. Trela had put her hair up, took it back down, tried braids and combed them back out. Clerin was unsure of the exact look Trela was going for. Trela would cram her into something and then stand back, squint at her with her forefinger tapping on her chin, then shake her head and start over again. She ended up deciding upon incredibly tight doeskin leggings stuffed into tall black leather boots, with a white cotton shirt and a low vest clamped over her stomach which caused her the breathing issues. The top of the vest was wide open and the shirt had laces that Trela spent an inordinate amount of time getting to the perfect looseness. Clerin wanted nothing more than to undo her vest for the ride and breathe normally, but was afraid she would never get it back to its proper position.

They turned around a bend, and the road began to wind upwards. They followed the gentle rise for another half an hour and Clerin tried to soak in all of the breathtaking views. At the crest, off the road a ways, stood the impressively huge stone fort. If Clerin had to describe it, she would have used the word fortress instead of its shortened cousin. There was a wide circle of treeless land around it, clearly demarcating the perimeter of defense. The path leading up to it was beaten ground that was amazingly free of ruts. They were supposed to be arriving at dusk, so they were slightly early. Dartsyle stopped the cart.

"Should we wait here?" He glanced over at her.

Clerin looked around. There was nowhere to go but backwards. They were in full view of the fort, and she could almost imagine the tower guards staring at them with spyglasses. She wished she had realized that they were nearing the crest, but she had not been paying attention to the road.

"No. We must continue. At least we are only a little early." They were almost twenty minutes early, she thought, but she felt that there was nothing she could about it now. There was certainly no use sitting here, stopped in the middle of the road, arousing suspicion. Dartsyle looked from Clerin to Serghno, as if checking for confirmation. For his part, Serghno merely shrugged his shoulders, and so Dartsyle flicked the reins.

As they turned towards the stolid stone structure, Clerin got a full view of the portcullis. It was gigantic. She estimated that seven warriors could easily walk abreast through the opening it covered. It was so tall that a warrior on horseback could have another warrior sitting on their shoulders and not have to duck. Though she was too far away to see it, the steel was three fingers thick with a bottom of spear-heads to pierce anyone unfortunate to be under it as it fell. There was so much confidence in the portcullis that massive wooden doors were wide open. Clerin could see into the courtyard as they approached the gate.

"Halt!" A wary guard shouted at them. Dartsyle had begun to rein in anyway, so the order was a bit redundant. They were about a hundred steps from the gate. The three guards who had been near the portcullis approached them. Two looked wary, one looked bored.

"Who are you and why do you approach Dun Oengen?" The other wary guard emphasized his questions by shaking his spear at the words Dun Oengen.

"My name is Herance, a visiting Fluen on a diplomatic mission. I must speak with your commander." Clerin had thought it sounded weird to state her race in the opening, but Trela had insisted. It appeared to have worked since they all stood there staring for a moment. Eyes wide open and jaws slack. Even the bored one. "Now!"

They hopped up in unison, but only one of the wary ones took off towards the portcullis. He stood in front of it, gesticulating and talking quietly to another guard stationed at the interior. That guard soon ran off.

"You are quite a bit away from home, yeah?" The bored guard did not look so bored anymore.

"Am I to discuss my dealings with a sentry?" Clerin made herself keep her eyes above his head. It had been a while, but she had been well trained in the subtleties of hierarchy. Her spine was as straight and rigid as one of the keep's stone towers. It is the little things that exude confidence. And it is confidence that asserts your height in the hierarchy. The silence was uncomfortable but she did not have to endure it for long.

The portcullis made a horrendous noise as it slowly rose. Clerin figured it must be raised several times a day, so she could not fathom the sound of rusty iron grating against stone. She wondered if there was another, smaller entrance to the keep somewhere else along its walls.

Three warriors came riding under the gate and out of the keep. They were in triangular formation, so Clerin assumed the point was the leader. However, they were not in dress uniform, so there was no distinguishing insignia on any of them, at least none that she could distinguish. The horses stopped in front of the wagon team, which left some distance between Clerin and the commander. He would not lower his status by dismounting, however.

"I am Lieutenant Uriels, acting commander of Dun Oengen. I understand that you are on a diplomatic mission. May I inquire as to what that is?" He was stiff, to be sure, but he did not know how to lock his spine. At least not on a horse. He was quite short as well, which may have affected Clerin's view of him.

"You may inquire whatever you please. My name is Herance, from the House of Ilhillim in the southeastern coast of the Fluen realm near the Vatlisi river delta." Clerin had been afraid to speak anything true about herself, in case there had been any rumors about Trela's warpack, so she chose the House of a distant cousin. Of course, if they had heard any rumors, it would only have been about her being a Fluen, not about where she was from. She took the precaution anyway. "I would like to purchase a week's protection within your walls."

"I had meant my question to be my inquiry." Uriels narrowed his eyes at her.

"I am offering this entire wagon of various fine grogs for the week of protection." Clerin did not want to provide any information to him she did not have to.

"I thank you for your interest, but I am not sure from what protection you seek." His horse danced sideways, but he kept his gaze on her. Clerin decided there was no use in stalling further.

"I have come to speak to your wondrous King, the one called Qizern. I have messages for him from mine own House. These are not messages for lieutenants. Even those in command of such formidable keeps as this one. I am to meet another before I travel to the Dekhan plateau and am, unfortunately, quite early. This quaint custom of yours in having roving bands of marauders killing and robbing each other has quite unnerved me." Clerin did her best to impersonate her mother.

"Warpacks. They are called warpacks. And they are not robbing each other." Dartsyle kept his hands tightly gripping the reins and his eyes staring at the back of the horses' heads.

"Humph. A pleasant name, to be sure." Clerin glanced sideways at Dartsyle. She made herself look as disdainful as she was able. "And I thought I told you not to speak unless spoken to."

"So... you wish to stay one week in our keep. And for payment you will provide this wagon of grog?" Uriels was looking less suspicious.

"Not the wagon, just the grog. And I expect a room to myself. My servants may share a room." Clerin pointed behind her towards Serghno. It appeared that none of the guards had noticed him until that moment.

"Do you mind?" Uriels waved his hand towards the wagon.

"Not at all." Clerin watched him as he rode his horse slowly around the wagon. No doubt attempting to do arithmetic.

"It is, of course, our custom to open a cask or two for the first night, then another on the last. I must feel that I have the loyalty of each of your warriors, not just yourself." Clerin had been unsure of how to broach the subject, and Trela had been no help. "Unless you are one of those types of commanders who hoards all of the profits made off of his warriors."

"No, of course not. Besides, there are at least sixteen casks here. What if three are spent on the warriors?" Uriels was smiling broadly.

"Or four or five?" Clerin smiled warmly at him. She now had to cut a hard corner in her demeanor. She knew it would be difficult to perform without anyone noticing but it was easier, for her at least, to switch from hard to soft than from soft to hard. "You cut an impressive figure, Lieutenant. I certainly hope I do not drink too much tonight." She giggled slightly as she watched him swallow hard.

The lieutenant and his two warriors led them into the keep. The three on foot followed the wagon. The portcullis came crashing down behind them.

The vast courtyard was open and inviting. There was an ambulatory underneath the catwalk that ringed four of the towers. The remaining section was purely the gatehouse. Clerin had not conceived of the size of the fort from the outside. Surely it was massive, but she had only really seen one edge of it. Once in the interior, the scale of it boggled her mind. There were three low buildings near the back wall. The barracks, she assumed. There were rows of gardens and another, taller building in the middle. It would have been called a citadel, but did not seem so defensible. It could have been called a tiny palace, but did not seem so extravagant. Clerin figured this was where the officers stayed. The front third of the courtyard was open and the soil was packed hard by countless drills. Just behind them, the massive gatehouse cast its massive shadow over the courtyard. The mass of the structure made even the shade feel thick. The colorful sunset was no longer visible once inside the stone walls.

"Let me show you to your quarters." Uriels dismounted smoothly.

"You two—stay with the wagon." Clerin wanted to have a reason to get back out to the courtyard.

Uriels was sweating a little and had a squatty mace tied to his short waist. He had a comically large keyring with many clanging keys that he fumbled around. Finally he unlocked the door to the citadel with one of them. Clerin was not sure why it would need to be locked. She could only assume the commander did not trust his own warriors. The downstairs had several open rooms with couches and tables and chairs. Clerin thought she could see a dining room in the distance with the archway to a kitchen beyond. They turned the other way and walked down a long corridor and up some stairs at the other end.

"All of the sleeping rooms are on the second floor. I'll put you in the room next to mine." He smiled over his shoulder at her.

"That will certainly make me feel more safe." Clerin kept her voice interested.

"Here it is. These are probably simple accommodations for one such as you, but they are the best you'll find out here." He was nodding his head like a porter at an inn.

The room itself was not bad. Clerin had not spent a night in a real bed for an incredibly long amount of time, so it took a monumental effort to keep her countenance bored. She had to remind herself that the only way she would be able to sleep in this room was if the overly gracious Pyran behind her died. If not, she doubted she would be able to profess her innocence and would, at best, be sleeping in the brig. She tried not to think about what could happen at worst. There was a small desk with a stoic chair. There appeared to be various writing utensils on the desk and a half burnt candle. There was another much more comfortable looking chair in the far corner. Then there was the bed. Simple and sagging in the middle, but to Clerin's mind it looked fantastic.

"This will do nicely. Thank you so much for your hospitality." Clerin smiled warmly at him.

"And, if you like..." He was looking down at the floor. Clerin decided quickly that she did not want to hear what she might like. Afterwards she would wonder what he had planned on saying.

"I will need to see to my servants and my wagon." He looked a little downtrodden to be interrupted, so she touched his arm as he turned to lead the way out. "Thank you lieutenant. Truly. You don't know how much this room means to me." She widened her smile for him. He smiled back and led her back the way they came.

It was dusk outside and a couple of fires near the barracks were getting started. Clerin wanted to start drinking now, but knew that after supper would be the best time. They would be full and relaxed with no more chores to fulfill. That would be when she started her plan. She hoped they had some musicians in the fort. For some reason she felt like dancing.

Clerin felt better standing, so she hovered around the wagon. Dartsyle and then Serghno took turns finding the nearest toilet facilities. Each time they came back with a small group of warriors to show off the wagon full of casks. Clerin would ask who among the group were musicians or sang. Then she would check for dancers. Finally she would ask about side skills. Juggling, knife throwing, handstands, or gymnastic tricks. Though she admired storytellers greatly and wished to be considered one herself, she left them out of her inquiries. She needed performance artists to push the festivities. She needed each warrior to lower their inhibitions enough to drink. She needed a raging party.

"You know, musicians get first refills," Clerin giggled.

Soon word spread throughout the fort and warriors were walking up to see the Fluen and her wagon full of grog. Clerin smiled and flirted with every one of them. Young or old, ugly or handsome, short or tall, male or female, warrior or mage, officer or grunt, it did not matter. It was an atmosphere she was attempting to build between them all. An atmosphere of excitement and energy. She knew she had several hours to get an entire fort intoxicated to the point of dereliction of duty. Trela and the entire warpack were counting on her. She was starting slow because she knew that her slow crescendo would take all the energy she could muster before the end of the evening. She did not think the typical musical rhythm of rise and fall to rise higher would work as effectively. No, she planned on a constant rise until the moment that Trela walked through the gate. Originally she had thought to begin in earnest after supper. To save her energy in anonymity for another hour or so. But that was not to be.

Soon a crowd began to form around the wagon. Some industrious warriors had brought over half a dozen oil-soaked torches to brighten the area. The moon had yet to rise, and even when it would, it would be barely gibbous. The chatter was gaining in volume and they had yet to drink a drop. Clerin was flush with excitement.

"Warriors! I know that you are all anxious to meet our new guest and welcome her to Dun Oengen, and you will all get a chance tonight, I promise, but we need to finish preparing our food, secure the gate, and finish rotating the on-duty guards before we can even eat." Uriels glowered at his troops. They did not appear to pay him any heed. He then looked beseechingly at Clerin.

"To your duties! The quicker they are completed, the quicker we can eat and the quicker we can open these casks of grog!" Clerin raised her arms wide, and to her surprise, a cheer ran up from the small crowd. They soon dispersed.

Uriels was looking nervous. "You should not promise..." But Clerin would not let him finish.

"I am so excited. I have not felt this alive since leaving my own realm. Please, you must enjoy this evening with me." With that she grabbed his hands with both of hers and spun them both around in a circle, laughing all the while. "Tonight will be magical."

Uriels lost his despondent look. It quickly turned into a smile. He nodded emphatically to her. "Yes. Yes, I surely hope so."

The meal passed quickly. Clerin did not know what their normal routine was, but tonight seemed to be out of the realm of normality. They gathered around the wagon and all sat on the hard-packed ground. Clerin, Dartsyle, and Serghno were brought food from several different kitchens. Clerin was not sure if she would have been allowed to wander away, the crush of derlians was getting so thick. To Clerin's great relief, Dartsyle entertained them with war stories as they ate. He, of course, omitted anything recent from his recounting. It gave her the chance to eat, which was difficult with so many eyes upon her. But she knew she needed to throw herself headfirst into the festivities, so she needed to fill her stomach to absorb some alcohol, breads mainly. She ate as much as she was able without making herself feel bloated. She would be worse than useless if she ate too much. Serghno told a story as well while she rested. He had odd mannerisms, with quick jerks of his hands and head. He reminded Clerin of a chicken sometimes. Then his story came to a close and there was a moment of silence.

Clerin left her empty and half-empty dishes behind a wagon wheel and leapt to her feet. The warriors in front of her stayed seated and watched with heads tilted back. It reminded her of her Telling, so long ago, and of the children in the front, rapt with attention. It gave her confidence and set her on the right path. This was, more than anything, about entertainment. The warriors here were stuck by the side of a seldom-used road in the middle of a forest. She imagined that the boredom built up in them must have been crushing.

Clerin flung her arms out in front of herself and then opened them wide. Inviting all of them in. They smiled. She spun and placed her hands on the wagon, bent over slightly and then sprang up and over into the wagon, doing a handstand in the middle and landing lightly on her feet. They laughed. She again opened her arms to them again, grinning.

"Fellow derlians, I am here for but a moment and then I will disappear. I come bearing gifts, a whole wagon full of gifts. But more than that, I come bearing me. I wish to be shown the infamous hospitality of the Pyran warrior. I wish to delight in your skills and abilities, no matter how trivial. I wish to hear your music and sing loudly to your songs. I wish you to teach me what only Pyrans know. I wish to see your strongest warriors shirtless and gleaming in the firelight, juggling tree trunks with their bare hands. I wish to dance with each of you in the flickering firelight, while all of nature in the forest is shaken awake with your wardrums. But more than any of that, I wish to drink. Do you wish to drink?!?" They cheered. It was a thundering, relentless cheer. The warriors erupted onto their feet. Clerin tipped the uppermost cask to them. It was shifted to the side and was carefully, but quickly, opened. She tipped another cask, and another. Soon four large casks rested on the ground and had grog being scooped out of them. One for each Beleg, Clerin thought. One for each race. One for each of us.

The queues began, wildly enthusiastic but civilly ordered. The voices of a hundred private conversations melded into one living tapestry. Soon the drums started. They were faint and scattered at first, like horses on the opposite side of a valley. The sound gained in breadth and depth until it was a herd thundering across the plain. It crescendoed into a stampede, and Clerin was the wind whipping through their manes.

Clerin hopped down from the wagon. She had wanted to stand behind the casks and drink in between filling others' tankards like Dartsyle and Serghno. The enthusiastic energy needed to be spun into a tornado, however. There was no time to let it falter into a summer breeze. Clerin began spinning with her arms spread and feet stomping out a rhythm that, though different than any individual drumbeat, fit enticingly between them, complimenting them. There were several frustrating moments where Clerin felt alone and gawked at. She forced her smile to stay intact. She did not allow herself to flag and kept her energetic rhythm. Though it felt like a long time, it was truly brief. Soon a warrior joined her. Then another. Quickly the packed dirt floor was being trampled by a score of wildly dancing warriors. Most of them held grog in some vessel or another. Arms held high to avoid spilling, faces split into grins. Clerin allowed herself to be lost for quite some time. It was glorious.

The festivities went through several stages, and Clerin danced through them all. It was dark and the vast majority of the warriors in the keep were well inebriated. There were no signs of the drinking slowing, but Clerin suddenly realized the towers were untouched. The realization started a quiet panic in her. She made her way over to Serghno.

"This is fantastic, everyone is here. There are three different enclaves besides this one. Look over there, that drum circle has broken out their own grog." He handed her a full tankard. "And over there..." She interrupted his praise.

"I need you to fly me to each tower. I need ten waterskins filled with grog so I can drop off two at each tower. I need these now." Serghno looked stunned for a brief moment but quickly nodded and hopped into action. He soon had the skins filled and stoppered.

"Leave six here and we'll come back for them." Clerin wished to start at the furthest towers, to leave as much chance as possible to go unnoticed. At least to go unnoticed for as long as possible.

"No, no. They may be gone by the time we come back." He tied eight skins around his ample frame to his sagging belt. She carried the other two, one in each hand. As they walked away from the firelight, she became grateful for his quick thinking. Now they could skirt the interior of the courtyard without having to re-engage with the main revelers. They left Dartsyle in charge of the casks. She left him with her full tankard as well.

They got to the bottom of the first tower. Though the roar of the drums echoed off the courtyard wall, the overall sound seemed quite muted compared with dancing directly in front of the musicians. Coupled with the darkness of the corner they were in, it made for an eerie feeling.

"Do we both go up?" As Serghno asked the question Clerin realized that she had not thought about it.

The quiet and darkness made her wish for company. So many things could go wrong. But she did not want fear or discomfort to make her decision. As she thought about it, the image of both of them floating over the parapet wall, him with eight skins tied to his portly frame, struck her. She thought it would look like they were trying to get the guards drunk. At best. She thought about leaving the extra skins on the ground, at the base of the wall, but the image in her mind did not gain in integrity.

"How will you know that I am ready to fly back down?" Clerin's mind raced over all of the implications.

"Just step back over the edge. You'll float down like a feather and when I see you I can control your decent more directly." He seemed very sure of himself, with the tips of his mustaches wriggling with his smile.

"I won't just plummet?" She stared hard at him but could find no trace of worry.

"No, I will set it up as a featherfall for the constant background spell and then add the flight on top of it." His smile broadened farther. "Trust me, I will not let you fall. Even if I thought I could explain the mistake to Feyazki, there is no way that Trela would let me live if you plummeted."

Clerin thought about that for a moment. She imagined Trela getting the news, after the attack failed due to the tower guards being completely sober, and imagined her reaction. Clerin was not positive that Trela would kill Serghno, but felt assured that the punishment would be bad enough that he would do his best to keep her safe. More importantly, Serghno looked as if he believed that Trela would kill him. His smile held a serious look in his eyes.

"Okay. Send me up." Clerin took a deep breath.

"Narkinderto!" Serghno touched Clerin with his palm. Clerin did not start floating, however.

"Isn't that a flying spell?" She raised one eyebrow.

"That was just the featherfall. Jump." He stood back. She jumped and it took about tens seconds for her feet to touch the ground again. She smiled broadly. "Now for the flight, Mekkinderarc!"

Clerin felt herself soaring upwards. She gripped her skins with white knuckles. Almost as if they were ropes that could steady her. She popped over the edge to see three bored and disinterested guards. At first they did not notice her, staring begrudgingly out beyond the keep's walls.

"Good evening, gentle warriors. I trust your watch has been uneventful?" Clerin wanted to gauge their vigor.

One turned quickly around, left hand at his chest while the right fumbled for his short sword. The other two laughed and mocked him. Clerin noticed dirty bowls lying around the turret. They had already been fed.

"Nothing staring back but the moon." One of the guards stepped forward. "You must be the Fluen that everyone has been talking about. You brought the wagon of grog." It was more of a statement than a question.

"I have done more than that, my friends. I have brought you some grog as well." Clerin held out the skins as they looked back and forth to each other. "This is an evening of celebration and I cannot abide by any such strong warriors missing out." She kept the skins held out in front of her and slowly walked towards them.

"Much as we would like, we are under direct orders not to drink tonight." It was the one who had fumbled with his sword that spoke. The other two only showed hunger in their eyes. He was on her left, and she started to zero in on him.

"What happened? Did you say something rude to your commander?" She paused between each sentence to give them a chance to reply. "Get caught doing something? Get caught not doing the right thing? Or does the lieutenant just not like you three?" Her arms were getting tired but she refused herself the luxury of lowering them.

"No... no, nothing like that." The guard almost stammered. She let the skin touch his chest. He made no move to stop her, but made no move to take the skin either.

"Then why is he punishing you?" She pushed the skin in her right hand against another guard's chest. He reflexively grabbed hold.

"He's not. It's just that it is our turn." His arms stayed motionless. Clerin took her newly free right hand and brushed a lock of his hair from his face.

"No one has to know. It is just you three up here, is it not? They are all drunk down there and wouldn't notice if the keep were on fire. All you have to do is remember to toss the skins over the side of the wall before dawn." Clerin cocked her head just slightly and took a deep inward breath. Her left hand pushed the skin into his chest. "You need to open this so that I can have a drink."

He glanced at his two companions. One stood cradling the other skin while the other stared blatantly at Clerin. They were of no help to him. He looked a little apprehensive and licked his lips. "Yes. Of course. Just so you can have a drink."

Clerin laughed and let go of the skin. His hands quickly grabbed it, brushing lightly against her as he did so. She winked at him. "You don't mind if I drink from the skin, do you?" He fumbled with the stopper for a moment then offered the skin she handed to him back to her. She took it and tilted her head back. She kept her tongue over the hole so as not to drink too much. She needed to drink enough that the skin had some air at the top of it, however. She left a little grog on her lips to color them and give them a sheen, even though she figured it was too dark for that trick to work. "That is just what I needed. Now you." She thrust the opened skin back into his hands. He looked nervous but did not glance at the other two guards. He drank prodigiously, with several large gulps.

Clerin smiled and nodded at the others as they too began to drink from the other skin. They offered her a drink from hers and she laughed while she took it. Though she used her tongue-block maneuver each time and only took little sips, she soon began feeling the grog as it piled upon her earlier drinks.

"Now we have a little secret. Don't tell anyone I was here and remember to toss the skins over the edge before dawn." For some reason she blew a kiss at them before she hopped over the side. They rushed over to see her floating down but luckily Serghno was not in sight. She turned and looked upwards, waving at them. They waved ecstatically back till she was about halfway down.

"What took you so long?" Serghno's voice whispered from the darkness.

"I had to make sure that they drank enough that they will finish off what we gave them now didn't I?" She peered at the direction his voice came from.

Serghno stepped out, staring up at the tower she had just drifted down from, and handed her two more skins. "Well, we have four more towers, so try to be quick about it."

Clerin felt good. As good as she had in a while. It wasn't just the grog, either. She had accomplished her mission and gotten all of the tower guards to drink. Each time they resisted until she poured on her charms. In truth, that was what really made her feel good. It made her feel powerful. A smile, a word, a pose, a light brush of a finger. She had started feeling like she could make them leap from their towers had she wanted to. She started feeling that maybe she did have magic drink inducing dimples. She walked back to the wagon thinking that she might even be able to get into the gatehouse. Trela had been adamant about her not even trying. That was Trela's job to accomplish. But Clerin was feeling so powerful that she thought they just might open the door for her. She had to try.

At the wagon, however, she ran into a very drunk Lieutenant Uriels, and her priorities changed. She decided she just needed to keep everyone happy and the party going for as long as possible. And that meant keeping Uriels happy. She needed to do all that without getting talked into going back to his quarters to see his sword collection or any such nonsense. Trela would just have to get into the gatehouse on her own.

Chapter 19

Vrric, Trela, Malghain, Estfale, and Jalin were concealed in the brush near the end of the Thieves Passage. Jalin was a slender but toned Pyran spy. Vrric did not know her, but both Lishean and Dartsyle spoke highly of her skills. Trela took their trusted advice and brought her along. Jalin's muscles were not bulky, but so well defined that you could see them move individually under her tight clothing. It made Vrric feel out of shape just looking at her.

The sun would set in a little less than two hours. Trela had wanted to arrive early to get into a good position. They were at the edge of the forest, but still had a few layers of trees in front of them. There was a wide circle of treeless land around the fort, clearly demarcating its perimeter of defense. They had found the perfect brush to hide behind, such that they could also see the main road that led to Dun Oengen. It was a large, empty swath cut through opposite side of the Yaniqua forest. The trail entered their vision from the upper right and continued its beaten path to the barely visible portcullis. They were facing the first flat side of the pentagon clockwise of the entrance. They were also well situated to be able to observe the tail end of the Thieves Passage on their left side. Unfortunately, now they had to wait in silence before Clerin's distraction was supposed to arrive at dusk. Estfale and Jalin were talking quietly amongst themselves. Malghain was peering through his small spyglass at the fort. Vrric was so bored that he lay on his back in the shade of the trees. He was not sleepy he told himself, just bored.

"I am going to check the other side of the fort." Trela whispered to Malghain. The quietness of it pricked up Vrric's ears.

"Okay. Let's go." Malghain lightly shook his leg.

"No, no. Just me. You don't need to come. I'm just getting a little restless. Thought I would see if there was an easier way to breach the walls over there. I'll head over by the quaking aspens across the way. Stay and rest." She patted the air in front of her.

"Who will protect you?" Malghain narrowed her eyes at her. Vrric was fully sitting now.

"I will protect me." She started to sound annoyed.

"You know that the fort is completely symmetric about its entrance." His eyes loosened a little.

"You can never have too much reconnaissance." Trela tried to loosen Malghain further with a smile. "I'll be very careful and keep my distance."

"Protection just means you are important, not that you are not capable. What I offer is no dishonor." Malghain did not move, but every muscle seemed primed to lift up and follow her at a moments notice. All she had to do was to say the word.

"I thank you for your offer. Know that my refusal of your assistance is no dishonor to you." Trela stood and Malghain stayed seated. Vrric lowered himself back down. Once enough time had passed that Trela should be safely out of earshot, he spoke.

"You know nothing will get her ire up faster than offering to help." Vrric kept his eyes lightly closed.

"Well, she should know that nothing will get my ire up faster than running off alone." Malghain's voice sounded rough, but Vrric could tell he was more worried than annoyed.

Trela returned to the small group just before sunset. Soon the cart began to rumble into view. Vrric was peering through his spyglass, through the bushes, at the keep's monstrous front gate. Clerin, Dartsyle, and Serghno's wagon stopped a ways from the keep. Clerin and Dartsyle waited patiently at the front of the wagon until three guards approached on foot from the keep. Serghno appeared to be lounging in the back. Vrric could not figure out their interaction, but eventually the portcullis lifted and three warriors emerged on horseback. He found himself holding his breath as they silently spoke. Trela had given strict orders against casting any spells. She was paranoid, and maybe rightly so, that any magic sensed near the keep might raise an alarm. Then the attack would need to turn into a rescue mission. The talking seemed to take forever but eventually the horses turned back and reentered the keep with the wagon following close behind. He had not been too worried about them getting a wagon full of grog into the keep. Nor did he think it would be difficult to make them drink. *The trick will be to get the tower guards to drink*, he thought. In any case, watching the wagon enter the keep was a great source of relief for Vrric. It must have been for the others as well since a collective sigh rose as the portcullis fell. The real waiting had just begun.

Lishean and Rewista were to lead the warpack up the main road and arrive just when Trela was opening the gate. There had to be enough time for Qizern's warriors to get drunk, but just enough. The timing was absolutely critical. Unfortunately, Tumu was of no help. Getting the warpack through the Yaniqua forest without alarming the fort was going to be difficult. Another much smaller contingent of two large cohorts was to filter its way through the Thieves Passage led by Kryhir. Vrric had not spoken with him much, but he was well respected amongst the warpack and had been attending regular meetings.

An unbearable amount of time passed. Finally, the dark over the keep was beat back by the orange glow of a bonfire. A few voices could be heard murmuring above the distant crackle of the fire. They waited patiently. Then another fire threw its glow over the keep's tall walls. As over an hour passed, Vrric began to wait impatiently. Finally, a chorus of babble began to overflow the walls in a steady stream. Like the froth of an overboiling pot. He began to scan the top of the walls with his spyglass. The tower guards were disdainfully watching the fires in the courtyard rather than keeping an eye out for danger, but they were certainly not drinking yet. He had to remind himself that the night was still young.

Another unbearable amount of time slipped by. Vrric had propped his spyglass up so that he could lay his head on a log and watch the closest tower. He had watched them somewhat disinterestingly on and off for the last half hour while doing his best not to nod off when suddenly a figure flew into his view. It looked like Clerin was flying up to the tower with each hand carrying a waterskin, hopefully filled with grog. Vrric sat up and focused his spyglass. Clerin was definitely floating up there at the tower, handing over a skin. She placed her arm around one of the guard's shoulders drunkenly and appeared to be laughing. Her other arm snapped up with another uncorked skin. The guard did not hesitate in taking a drink. She stayed up there for a full ten minutes in all. She appeared to be animatedly telling a story, occasionally hanging on a different guard. Vrric even thought that she looked directly over at the bushes they were squatting in and winked once, but he banished the thought as folly. She eventually floated away back down to the courtyard. Vrric noticed her on another tower a little while later. That turret was further away, so he could not see what was going on as well, but he knew what was happening. Vrric had known that sending Clerin was a genius move. And Trela's Fluen princess had come through for her. It could have been Serghno's idea, or even Dartsyle's, to fly from tower to tower, but there was no way that any male could have pulled that off. *And,* Vrric thought, *there were very few females who could have pulled it off either.* But in his heart he knew that it was Clerin's idea to begin with. It just sounded like her. The image of her laughing and holding a full, bulbous skin came to Vrric, framed in the circular orbit of the spyglass. But it was images of their past that filled him with nostalgia. Was that the right word? *The best part is that she does not even have to act,* thought Vrric. That was just who she was. Effervescently smiling, gesturing with the skin and laughing. He could almost see her dimples from here. It made him realize that there were few derlians in any realm who were more enjoyable just to chat with than she naturally was.

They waited another hour for the peak of the party to pass. Another half hour for the guards to get tired of listening to the quiet. Vrric had *whispered* to both Lishean's group and Kryhir's, and they were in first position. The main warpack was still at least a twenty minute march down the main road. This was going to be the most dangerous time for the advance teams. They would have to kill all of the tower guards before giving Lishean the signal. Then they would have twenty minutes to break into the gear-housing and raise the portcullis. And they had to do it all undetected. If any alarm was raised, they would not only be endangering themselves, but also Clerin's team. Kryhir's two cohorts were closer, maybe five to ten minutes away. But his contingent was too small and was not to attack unless there was an emergency. Mainly they were there to seal off any escape routes. Even though Vrric would have liked a shorter lead time, he understood that they could not risk the larger forces coming any closer while the tower guards were still alive. The possibility of raising an alarm was just too great.

They got all of their gear that they were taking with them situated comfortably before beginning their slow walk out of the bushes. *The worst part about moving amongst the trees quietly is how long everything takes,* Vrric thought. Each foot needed be slowly lowered gently onto the forest floor, muffling each snap of a twig under his own boots. And everything seemed too loud as he was trying to sneak. Each breath seemed to rattle the nearby leaves with its ferocity. It was as if his own senses increased tenfold while he was trying to subterfuge another's. He had to consciously breathe with his diaphragm just to calm his lungs.

They had decided to take the tower just clockwise from the front gate and rotate clockwise from there, finishing at the opposite side of the gate. Vrric had felt it was somewhat riskier since it was so close to the gate and had argued against it. If any of the guards were still sober, it would be those in control of the gate. They would not have to backtrack this direction, however. And Jalin had brought up the benefit of only having the enemy in front of them, not having to worry about any tower guards behind them. In the end, it was the fastest route. They were all afraid that any one of the guards laying about in the courtyard could look up at a tower and notice them at any time. Speed was the essential element, so Vrric was easily outvoted.

They reached the treeline and paused. The open dash to the keep's stone walls was almost a quarter league. Vrric took out his spyglass and scanned the closest tower. He could not see anyone standing. He checked the tower closest to the gate, their target tower, and could see no one there either. He wished that they were already passed out, laying prone and dreaming heavily. He hoped they were at least sitting down. A Pyran guard may not be paying attention to their surroundings, but the slightest unauthorized movement caught in the corner of their eye may catch their attention quicker than an owl can swoop upon a fleeing mouse. He was afraid that any of them could be standing during the strike force's sprint. Vrric lowered his glass and realized that each of them were spying on the towers. Trela seemed to notice the others put their glasses down, quickly checked the two nearby towers, and then gave the signal for them to move forward. Vrric wondered if she would have stood there with her spyglass up all night if he had not lowered his. It was her call, however, and he did not begrudge her for her style.

The others dropped into a dead run as Trela lowered her fist. Vrric took a precious moment to collapse his spyglass before charging after them. He tried to run as quietly as he could but his breath rattled loudly in his chest. He wished he could just fly them over to the keep. They would end up flying soon anyway. The dark uneven ground came up to meet his feet unexpectedly at times, jarring his thigh bone up into his pelvis and making his knees ache. Worst of all, his backpack bounced uncomfortably against his kidneys. He did not know what to do with his collapsed spyglass, so he kept it clenched in his fist while he pumped his arms. It was times like these that he felt out of place amongst the warriors.

The first to reach the walls was Jalin. Then Malghain, followed closely by Estfale, then Trela, and Vrric brought up the rear. They quickly all had their backs against the cold stone walls of Dun Oengen. Since it was in his hand, Vrric extended his spyglass and pointed it straight up. Unfortunately, their position, while it was great for hiding them from the guards, afforded little visibility of the towers. Trela raised her fist again and quietly led the small group along the wall to their targeted tower. Once there, she pulled out a small dagger for her left hand and unsheathed her short sword for her right. Vrric quickly stuffed his spyglass into his pack. Once everyone else had armed themselves, Trela nodded to him. He knew what to do.

"Mekkinderclo!" Vrric said in a quiet whisper that barely escaped his lips. All five of them rose quickly up into the air. He reduced their speed as they neared the wall's parapet. They hugged against the tower's wall as it jutted up beyond the main wall, keeping it between them and the courtyard. He slowed them to a crawl as they neared the crenellated tower's parapet. His heart beat forcefully in his chest.

Trela squatted while they were rising. At first Vrric was unsure why, but quickly took the hint and gave her some extra height before stopping them all. She then uncurled and raised herself slowly as if she where crouched under a window on the ground, until she could just barely peek over the stone. A huge grin splashed across her face. She crouched back down and faced the rest of them. She lifted her pinky, ring finger and middle finger from the hilt of her dagger, indicating that there were three guards. She then pointed at Malghain with her dagger and pointed to her left, then pointed at Estfale and pointed to the right. She tapped her own chest and, of course, pointed towards the middle. She sheathed her short sword and made a repeated lifting motion with her right hand.

Vrric raised all five of them quickly above the parapet and then dropped them back down. Trela ran in a low crouch to her intended victim. He was laying prone on his back with his arms and legs akimbo. He stared as if in a trance. She kept her dagger in her left hand as she charged ahead. Then she made a small hop as she reached his feet and turned slightly in mid air. When she landed she had her right hand covering the sleeping guard's mouth, and with her left she jabbed the dagger under his chin straight into his brain through the back of his throat. She crouched there with her arms stiff, not moving but pushing hard against the tower's roof, for about ten seconds of death throws, though it seemed like much longer. As the guard twitched his last, Vrric marveled at Trela. He had seen her be a commander and she did that quite well, but he had not really realized how deadly she was. She stayed stiff until Malghain and Estfale had finished their business, then removed her dagger and wiped it clean. Vrric was stunned for a moment and almost forgot his duties.

Jalin was already busy setting up the dummies on the tower's roof. This was the brilliant addition to the scheme and why they needed the entire keep to be completely inebriated. Vrric had laughed out loud when it was mentioned, thinking it was a joke. Hadn't someone brought up a children's story when Clerin first mentioned the grog? The dummies were very rudimentary, mainly consisting of straw filled clothing on a stick. The plan was to set up a few at each tower and add the helmets from the dead guards on top. The guards, however, did not have any helmets on, so Vrric started gathering their cloth hats to add on top. While Vrric and Jalin fixed up the dummies as best they could, Trela retrieved her spyglass and peered out at the other towers. She stayed in the middle of the turret, presumably to avoid anyone noticing any reflection of firelight that might glance off the lens from below.

"We'll only put the dummies up if the guards are standing when we attack." Trela whispered to them. "They might be passed out at the next turret over as well, but I think I saw movement on the one after that. We should proceed with the utmost caution." Vrric and Jalin both nodded in agreement and started stuffing the half-assembled dummies back into their packs. He wished she had mentioned this plan sooner. She then motioned for Malghain and Estfale to huddle. "If any of the guards on a turret are on task and doing their duty, we will not be able to spy on them before our attack. Rather than picking which member of the strike force attacks which guard, I will split the turret rooftop into zones." She backed herself in a crouch towards the exterior parapet of the turret until her back was against the cold stone merlon behind her. Her voice was a quiet whisper but was heard clearly by Vrric. "We will model the zones after our attack here. Malghain, you will take zone A, to my upper left. Estfale shall take zone B, to my upper right." Trela stuck her arm out at the naming of each zone, just to avoid any confusion. "Feyazki shall follow Malghain to my lower left in zone D, and Jalin shall take the lower right zone, E. Zone C shall be the center and that is my zone." *Follow Malghain*, thought Vrric, *easy enough*.

Vrric flew them over the tower parapet on the exterior side of the keep's defensive wall. He dropped them below the main wall's parapet and then flew low until they got to the next tower. They took it much the same way they took the first tower. There were just three guards asleep with empty skins surrounding them like discarded children's playthings. The violence was swift and brutal.

Trela crept over to the crenellations and spied upon the next tower over. She kept her spyglass well within the tower's parapet. After biting her lip for a moment, she quietly laid down some further ground rules.

"No one can look into the courtyard. I do not want any movement to be visible from below, and the only way to do that is to treat this portion of the turret as quarantined." She made some frantic gestures towards the courtyard. "No reflective spyglasses but mine. I shall be the only one to examine the next turrets. The only time we can chance being visible from the courtyard will be when we top the parapets. The only Pyrans who should have a chance of seeing us at all will be the guards we are overtaking. And that is only because we have no choice in that matter. Vigilance is our enemy."

Malghain looked at Trela and then back at Vrric. "Are there guards visible at the next tower?" His eyes narrowed slightly and he seemed to be gauging something besides their next skirmish.

"There are at least two guards milling about on the next tower over. I really had been hoping that every tower would be as easy as the first." Her smile looked more embarrassed than weak.

They flew low along the exterior stone wall. Vrric flew them slowly to keep their flight as smooth as possible. Once they reached the tower, they stopped and hovered low. Trela pulled out both of her weapons and the others did the same.

"Zones." No sound actually came out of her mouth, but the caricature of the word left no confusion. They all nodded. Vrric lifted them straight up alongside the rough wall. He felt a moment of vertigo as they topped the parapet and he set them back down a little jarringly. Then there were Pyrans in front of them.

Trela slashed at the front guard's throat with the sword in her right hand. A spray of blood cut his scream into a quiet gurgle.

She swiveled on her right foot, bringing her left from the rear position to the forward. He stopped in his tracks, dropped his weapon and gripped his bleeding, silent throat with both his hands. She lunged as far as she could with her left hand and slipped her dagger under the incapacitated guard's ribcage and pierced a lung. He fell forward against her. In some brave, half-crazed attempt to strangle her, he removed his hands from his own throat. Once he stopped staunching his throat, however, he became more limp.

Malghain slashed at his guard's throat with the sword in his right hand. It cut through to the bone in the back, dropping the guard in front on Vrric. He lunged to catch the guard in a panic as Malghain swung towards another guard. He sat hard under the weight of the dead guard as he caught the body.

Vrric looked over to his right and his blood froze. Another guard was running full tilt for the parapet wall. It looked as if he was meaning to jump into the courtyard and he had a roar slowly building from his lungs. Estfale and Trela both started running towards the errant guard. She dropped her sword on the wooden floor and tossed her dagger into her right hand from her left. Just in front of Vrric's eyes another dagger spun into view. It must have come from Jalin, but he had been too slow to notice. With a quiet but solid thunk, it sunk into the guard's back, making him arch back. The low roar turned into a small cry as the guard began to tumble. Trela tossed her own dagger to the floor and leapt head first at the guard's legs. She tackled him and rotated, somehow placing her body under his, silencing his fall. Estfale jumped on the guard a split second later, placing his hand over the guard's mouth.

It was all over in just a few quick moments. They all froze in silence, waiting for the alarm to be raised. It had all seemed so loud, especially the cry. Vrric kept his eyes on the trapdoor that led down into the turret for the first few seconds, concentrating on the quiet. Malghain was crouched next to it, his sword at the ready. His muscles looked as taught as a bow string. Trela and Estfale were still tangled up in their guard. Vrric stared up at the stars. It felt good to sit there and pant for a while. The stars seemed especially bright that night. He wondered briefly if Clerin was looking up at the at the stars at that very moment. If they could both see the same scene without being able to see each other.

Once it was realized that no one had heard the ruckus, Vrric and Jalin began removing the dummies from their backpacks. The stars looked like a net of diamonds, but he could sit there no more. Malghain and Estfale were removing the various guards' headgear. It was not until the calm afterwards that Vrric realized there were four bodies. He wondered why there were four. Did it mean that the next tower over will only have two? Or did it mean that there was supposed to be four on each tower and another guard would show up for the first or second tower and raise the alarm at any moment? He did not like inconsistency. He tried to think of it logically. The extra guard was most probably just a friend who had come up to share the free grog with his mates. Unfortunately, "most probably" was about a fifty-fifty chance in Vrric's mind.

Trela knelt somewhat near the parapet edge, but far enough away not to be seen, and pulled out her spyglass. She stared at the next turret for some time. The dummies were set up and everyone was sitting around waiting for her to move. Vrric could feel the time slipping by. He knew he was already going to have to cast another flight spell as it was. He sidled up next to Trela.

"What are you doing?" Part of why he was so quiet was to not alarm any guards in the keep. The other part, however, was due to Trela's trancelike state. He did not want to startle her for fear of reflexive reprisals. Somewhat like awakening a somnambulist.

"I'm making sure that no guards show up." Her voice was just as low.

"Well, eventually, the guards will detoxify their blood enough to stumble awake." He smiled at her, but she did not smile back.

"Fine." She put her spyglass away and nodded to him.

"Mekkinderclo!" They quickly popped back over the parapet and dropped behind it. They flew over to the next turret, hiding themselves behind the exterior wall as they had before, and found it completely deserted. It worried them all to no end. Someone should have been up there, and if they weren't, they could show up at any random time. There was just no way to judge what type of schedule they might be on. It was discussed whether or not they should block off the trapdoor that led down into the tower so the returning guards would be unable to spot them. It was dismissed because it might alert the guards a little sooner.

They left the turret immediately, knowing there was no use for them to be wasting any more time up there. They swooped upon the last turret before the gate and found three sleeping guards, just like at the first two towers. And the outcome was as swift and as satisfying as those two had been. Trela spied upon the tower behind them one last time before turning her attention to the gate. This time she did not take so long.

Vrric examined the opposite direction. The large gate house seemed to be a separate building connected to the towers by the continuous perimeter rampart walls and catwalks. It was a little squattier, maybe rising one story above the catwalks, whereas the towers rose two stories. But mainly it seemed thicker and made of a darker stone. The feeling of thickness stemmed from the massive buttress walls extending into the courtyard.

There was a door at the end of the catwalk that Trela motioned to, showing that she assumed it to lead into the gear housing itself. If Vrric remembered correctly, it was the room above that they needed to attack first. Unfortunately, there did not appear to be an exterior door at that level.

Vrric contacted Lishean's and Kryhir's *whisperers* to let them know it was time to start marching towards second position. Then he flew the tiny strike force over to the door on the catwalk. It did not seem as if they were noticed. Vrric felt somewhat exposed near the gatehouse. The firelight from the courtyard below flickered a dim but wild orange. While Jalin was picking the lock, Trela crouched next to him.

"I want you to suck all of the air out of the room above this one." Trela pointed upwards and inwards.

"What?" came his eloquent reply.

"I want you to suffocate all those guards." She waved her hands towards the target again. "I figure it will be the quietest way to take the gate."

"Well I just... I've never actually..." Vrric struggled to find his words. Then something occurred to him. "Why didn't we do that to the tower guards?"

"I thought it would be more difficult in the open air." Trela furrowed her eyebrows at him. "Besides, we did not have to. Here, however, we have no choice. There is no door to the upper level and there is no way we can survive a frontal assault in the gear housing. Why do you think they call it the blood room?"

"Okay, okay. I just need to figure out what to cast." Vrric sounded impatient, even to himself.

"No problem. Take your time." Trela patted his knee. It was somewhat matronly, but he was not positive it was meant condescendingly.

Jalin soon had the door unlocked. After she had apologized about three times for taking so long, Vrric thought that he was ready to cast his spell. He had decided to use De to move the air instead of Kin since the main object of the spell was to kill those inside, not just to move air around.

"Now, it is not this adjacent room you need the air removed from, but the room above, correct?" Vrric asked Trela. She nodded emphatically. "Eqedelufclo!"

Vrric's strong voice carried farther than he would have wished, but that was not the worst of it. There came muffled cries from inside. Vrric kept concentrating on his spell, since he thought he should keep the air out for at least a minute. He did not know how long the guards could hold their breath.

Trela opened the door and rushed in, with Malghain and Estfale right behind. The interior was horrible, but they could not stop to the think about it. With the door open, the screams of the three still alive in the gear housing were definitely less muffled. Trela immediately threw her dagger at the one standing in the middle. Though the dagger struck him in the chest, it did not seem to slow him down much. In fact, it seemed to make him realize that they were under attack. Trela quickly drew her shortsword and parried his battle axe. Though he was wounded from the dagger, it still took her a couple of swings before she connected a good blow. As he dropped to one knee, she finished him off. Malghain and Estfale dispatched their guards quieter. Vrric walked into the room but was immediately stunned into inaction.

There was blood covering the floor, which made it difficult to maneuver around. It was dripping down the walls, slowly descending from above. There were bodies up above laying on the woven metal slat ceiling. It looked as if... Vrric tried to calm himself for a moment, but he got sick anyway. It looked as if their skin had been removed. As if their organs and blood just exploded from out of the muscles and bones that had contained them, shredding the skin open as they did so. It was all oddly lit from below since the torches in their sconces at the upper floor had all been snuffed out. Those below cast strange shadows through the woven slat floor. Vrric had thought the carnage on a battle field was rough to look at, but he had never seen anything like this. As he looked around the gear housing, he saw Estfale and Jalin also getting sick. The only derlians not to vomit were Trela and Malghain, and even they looked quite green.

"I knew this was called a blood room, but..." Vrric knew that Malghain was trying to lighten the situation, but he was not in the mood for gallows humor, not about a horror that he had caused. Luckily, Trela cut him off with a wave of her hand

Trela had Jalin relock the door they came in through, and then checked the opposite door. The floor was a horrible mess, but all they could really do right now was try not to slip in it. She then took one of the torches from a sconce and began searching for the way up into the murder room. Vrric was stunned enough that he was simply waiting for orders. Trela seemed to have found some metal rungs attached to a wall making a rough ladder. There was a steel trapdoor above the ladder that would have looked like a gate if it was standing vertically. She climbed up the rungs and pushed up on the trapdoor, but it would not budge. She climbed back down and went over to Jalin. They huddled quietly for a moment. Suddenly, there was a loud banging at the door they had all just come through. Trela passed the torch off to Jalin and motioned her to the ladder. She then cautiously approached the door.

"Hey, Inthuka? Glisnute thought he heard a commotion. We just want to make sure everyone is okay." The door handle rattled as someone from outside was trying to get in. Everyone stood silently and looked at Trela. "I know it's protocol to lock the door, but it's me, Lorca. Glisnute and I were walking around the courtyard and thought we heard something." Trela quietly walked close to the door but stood just off to one side. "Inthuka?!" The door seemed to rattle a little under the Pyran's blows.

"Inthuka has passed out. We're fine in here, just got to drinking and got a little rowdy. Thanks for checking." Trela lowered the pitch of her voice, but Vrric did not think it was deep enough to be mistaken for a male. The three they killed down in the gear housing were all male. There may have been a female up in the murder room, but there was no way to tell at this point.

"How did you get grog up here? After the issue with the towers, the Fluen was forbidden to come near the gate. You should know that." The door rattled again.

"No, no... It wasn't her. I brought up some myself." Trela looked nervous, but kept her head. The worst thing that could happen, in Vrric's mind, was that the guards took Clerin, Dartsyle, and Serghno hostage before Lishean arrived. He figured that Trela was trying to deflect blame from them.

"Who are you, anyway?" Trela stayed silent for too long. Vrric held his breath. What could she answer? This Pyran might know all the guards stationed in the gate tonight, but he might not.

"No... You'll just tell the lieutenant that I snuck grog in here. I'm not losing rank for something as benign as grog." The guard certainly seemed persistent.

"Listen here. We are not trying to get anyone in trouble, we just need to make sure you are all safe. Just open the door and let us take a look around." The banging on the door became more insistent.

"We were specifically told not to open that door for anyone. Everything is fine in here, go back to the party." Trela motioned for the others to get the bodies up against the door. The scarce furniture in the gear housing made it difficult to block the door with much. Jalin was jamming a chair diagonally against the far door, with the back of the chair snug underneath the door handle. Vrric was worried about the noise they were all making, but it did not seem like this ruse could be kept up for too much longer anyway.

"Just open the door for a second. I'll just poke my head in, no one will get in any trouble." Vrric thought he could hear a second voice quietly speaking in the background.

"I told you, we are under strict orders. How do I know that you are not the enemy?" Trela's voice got slightly deeper.

"Wake Inthuka. Now!" The door shook violently as something rammed it. "It is going to be so much worse for you if you do not open that door. Just open the door, and I promise no one will ever know that you snuck grog up there. I give you my word." Another bang rocked the door.

"You are going to have to get the lieutenant. I cannot open the door for just you. We are under strict orders and I would rather get in trouble for drinking on the job than for opening the door just because someone bangs on it." Trela was biting her lip in between speaking. Vrric thought that was a bad sign.

"Are you serious? You actually want me to bring Lieutenant Uriels over? He will bust you down to permanent kitchen duty. You'll never be a guard again!" Trela's chest heaved as she took a deep breath.

"I told you, I will only open this door for Lieutenant Uriels." The door banged one more time then got quiet. Trela put her ear to the door for a moment.

"Quickly, the lieutenant will bring a key. We must pile everything we can up against the doors. Feyazki, can you freeze the locks? Or melt them? Or turn them into solid steel? We need to buy enough time for Lishean to arrive." Trela turned towards the ladder. "Jalin, how is the lock?"

"It was trapped, so it took me a lot longer to pick than I had hoped. But you stalled long enough that I have it open." Jalin's voice paused. "It is a horrible mess up here." She was already up in the murder room, relighting the torches. She seemed to be moving delicately across the slick slats. Vrric could only imagine how one less coordinated than her would fare up there.

"Feyazki, how are the locks coming?" Malghain and Estfale had finished piling the meager furnishings in front of the doors.

Vrric's mind came back to the task at hand. He had thought about using Tec, but decided that destroying the lock mechanism would buy them more time. "Nudehepto!" He peered into the dark mechanism. "I think I have melted the steel enough that a key will not work, but the lock is still engaged. Here, Malghain, try to open this door." Vrric ran over to the opposite door with the chair jammed under it and cast the same spell.

"The thumb latch will not even budge. Great work, Feyazki." Malghain smiled over at Vrric. Due to all the blood dripping on him from above, his visage looked ghastly. Vrric was afraid that they all looked ghastly, but there was no time to worry about aesthetics.

Trela walked over to the portcullis gears to inspect them. There was a wheel with large spokes resting horizontally on the upper gear. She peered around underneath to find the ratchet latch that would keep the wheel from spinning in the wrong direction. Once she found it, she released it so that it would be ready.

"Estfale. Malghain. I will need both of you to raise the portcullis. We will wait until they truly try to break the door down before doing anything to the gate. I want to keep them confused for as long as possible. The only way we will survive the night is for Lishean to show up before the guards enter this room. Time is of the essence. Feyazki, Jalin and I will wait up in the murder room. Once they break through the doors, whether or not the portcullis is raised,

I want you two up there with us. We will try to get Feyazki to finish the job if need be. No heroics, do you hear? The only way we will survive in the murder room is if all five of us are up there. Understood?" Estfale and Malghain nodded in agreement. They hovered around the wheel as if itching to begin turning it. Vrric wondered why she did not just have him raise the portcullis, but he was getting quite tired and decided not to question her gift.

"What about Clerin?" Vrric walked over from the other door towards the ladder to the murder room.

"Get up into the murder room, find the deepest darkest corner, and squat there until the guards come. Then you can *whisper* our situation to Serghno." Trela squinted at Vrric as if trying to solve a puzzle, then her face softened. "Our best defense for those three is to keep the guards occupied here. It has already been what, ten minutes? Lishean will arrive in no time."

Vrric went up the ladder like he was ordered, but could not calm his fears. They were completely defenseless out there, especially Clerin. Vrric and Trela's group were at least barricaded where they were supposed to be. Jalin was squatting by a window looking through her spyglass towards the main road. Vrric got to experience the slippery metal slats first hand as he attempted to join her.

Time slowed to a crawl. Each second seemed to lasted a minute. Vrric *whispered* to Serghno, but got no response. He tried not to worry about it and instead concentrated on making the time fly by. He wished for Jalin to suddenly look down from her spyglass and say that she could see the warpack in the distance. But that was not what happened.

Eventually a loud banging shook the door. The good news was that it had taken much longer to get the lieutenant than Vrric would have thought. Maybe the lieutenant had been drinking also? Trela hopped and stepped over to the door, but was careful to stay out of its direct line.

"Open up! This is Lieutenant Uriels." The door bounced under his heavy fist.

"How do I know that you are who you say you are?" Trela tried to lower her voice again.

"Are you trying to worry me? There is only one reason you would not open this door for me." There was a scraping sound, like metal against metal. Trela glanced over to Estfale and Malghain. They were standing there with their arms on the spokes of the wheel, feet braced at the ready, and their eyes staring fixedly on her. Waiting for her signal.

"We are under strict orders not to open this door for anyone." Trela bit her lip waiting for the reply. The scraping sound grew more frantic.

"Who gave you those orders? Did I give you those orders? What have you done with the lock?!" The door rattled back and forth on its hinges.

"There... there was a fire." Trela moved a little further from the door and drew her dagger.

"You are done! Do you hear me? You die tonight!" There was a small pause and a shuffling noise. "Break it down!"

A deafening thud emanated from the door. They had some sort of ram with them. It could not be too large since they got it on the catwalk, but that thought did little to ease Vrric's mind. Trela gave Estfale and Malghain the signal and backed towards the ladder. She was about halfway between the door and the ladder, about the same distance as to Estfale and Malghain. The chain slowly began to wind its way around the drum.

The door shook mightily with the next blow. Vrric hoped the door would last five more blows, but he was not sure that would be the case. He thought he would wait for them to break through before casting anything. He positioned himself to get a clear shot at the door in a moment's notice since he did not know how much time he had. The portcullis continued its agonizingly slow ascent. Estfale and Malghain were moving quickly around in a circle, but the chain was so long and went through so many gears and steel tackle that every revolution only moved the portcullis a couple fingers' width higher.

The door visibly bounced with the next blow. "Hurry, they are raising the portcullis. Sound the alarm!" A trumpet blared into the night. Vrric hoped that Clerin's group had made it to safe ground before the alarm. He also hoped that Lishean's and Kryhir's warriors heard the trumpet and were speeding their way through the Yaniqua forest. If the alarm was raised, they would not need to worry about stealth. He was about to *whisper* to them to increase their speed, but lost his concentration at the next blow.

"Feyazki, the portcullis! Everyone up, up into the murder room. The door will not hold." Estfale and Malghain leapt away from the wheel and ran to the ladder. The ratchet held the portcullis partially lifted. Estfale and Malghain rushed towards the ladder without any weapons in their hands. Trela stood between them and the door.

"Nukinheparc!" Vrric wanted the portcullis to raise quickly, but did not want to tire himself out. He was glad that the warriors had gotten it half raised before he had to cast anything.

The door made a sickening cracking sound when it got hit again. Vrric had a perverse urge to stare at the door, but he kept his eyes on the spinning wheel of the winch. He could feel and hear at least one of the warriors tromping on the metal slats. He knew that he would have to cast something large when the guards broke through and hoped he had not squandered his energy earlier.

The door splintered into shards. As the first wave of guards rushed in, Malghain, staring at Vrric, yelled an urgent order for Trela to duck. She immediately dropped prone onto the slippery floor. "Eqedepiarc!" Flame shot over her, through the open trapdoor, and struck the three guards who had gained entry. It was suddenly completely silent. Trela picked herself up slowly, without making any noise. Vrric slumped against the wall. He had a raging headache and felt a tingly numbness in his fingers, toes, and the tip of his tongue. He was not sure if he would be able to cast another spell, but at least the portcullis was fully raised.

"I told you they had to have a mage in there." The words were whispered urgently, but rang loudly in the quiet. The whispering that came afterwards was much softer. Strain as he might, Vrric could not make any intelligible words out. The pounding blood in his skull made listening difficult.

Vrric watched dully as Trela startled a little to the movement above her. It made her stand on wobbly legs. Jalin had a bucket and was making her way as quietly as she could towards the far wall. Some of his flames still licked the wooden walls. She finally got over to the small fire and started pouring water on it. There was a hiss from the steam and the room got just a little bit dimmer.

"Now!" The hollow sounding yell came from the back of the catwalk, outside. The lieutenant must have realized that the front line was going to take heavy casualties. Like many a leader, he chose to give orders from behind. The guards began pouring in. The first ones ran straight across, allowing those behind them to gain entrance. It was only until about ten guards had entered that they tried to turn towards Trela's small group.

Trela threw her dagger at the first to rush her. It protruded ghastly from his throat. At that she turned and began climbing the ladder as if her life depended upon it.

Malghain and Estfale were at the front, thrusting spears through the slats in the floor. As Trela reached the upper rung, Jalin's strong hand grabbed her wrist and literally pulled her up through the small opening. Jalin then dragged her away from the opening and dropped the trapdoor with a clang. She frantically worked the lock to the only entrance to the murder room, while Trela ran to a side wall and grabbed one of the heavy thrusting spears hung from hooks embedded in the wall. Vrric turned to look out of a window slit as she ran to the front line to join Malghain and Estfale.

Again the sounds of trumpets blared into the night. This time, however, there was an answering call. It was too far off to tell distance and the room's construction made it impossible to tell what direction it came from. But it signaled that reinforcements were on their way. Vrric grinned maniacally and breathed through his diaphragm. All they had to do was keep the portcullis up long enough for the rest of the warpack to arrive. The replying trumpets had the effect of pausing the combat for just a second. The mental calculation did not take long as both sides knew what the sound foretold, and the fight was quickly rejoined.

The guards redoubled their efforts, but so did the strike force. Vrric had been hoping that the sound of the approaching warpack would cow the guards, to make them think twice about pressing their attack, and at least once about surrender. He had known his hope to be irrational, but was frustrated to see it dashed so quickly. Every time a guard fell, another took his place. Jalin soon appeared by the others with another spear.

Vrric watched the fight with a detached fascination. Estfale appeared to be well skilled in the spear, making jabbing thrusts to actually wound a guard. He would spot his target, track for a second, and then, THUNK—the spear would strike as quickly as a snake. But in between actual thrusts, he would leave his spear partially exposed into the blood room and swish it around, like he was stirring a giant pot of stew. This would back the guards up just a little. Long enough for him to take aim at another guard and—THUNK.

Trela glanced over at Estfale a couple of times and then starting swishing her own spear down into the blood room. Immediately, one of the guards struck the wooden shaft of her spear with an axe. Vrric could feel the horribly jarring vibration from where he was and watched as the spear dropped through the slats in slow motion. She tried to run to the back wall to grab another spear. As quickly as she moved, her boots slipped on the slick metal slats, but somehow she did not fall. The rest of her way to the wall seemed agonizingly slow, however.

Before he could get up to help, his mind felt a sharp tug. His spell to raise the portcullis was still in effect. The short time from when he had cast it had not dissipated it, even though he was no longer concentrating on it. He now realized that some of the guards had reached the gear and were desperately trying to release the ratchet. In his haste, he simply cast another spell. "Nukinheparc!" He used it to keep the ratchet engaged, rather than keep the portcullis up.

Suddenly, Trela was above them, jabbing her new spear at them. Since they had not been paying attention to her, she was able to kill the first guard she aimed at and gravely wound a second. The other two took their attention from the gear and tried to jab back at her with their own spears. Vrric figured she had the gear under control.

He glanced over to the trapdoor. Jalin was attempting to hold off a small group of guards by herself. Jabbing with her spear and hopping nimbly back and forth to avoid getting stuck in the foot. There were many guards down there, and Vrric wondered how long she could keep up her dance without slipping.

A loud trumpet blast pierced the night sky, followed almost immediately by a different one. They were both so loud that Vrric could not be sure which one came from inside the fort and which was from Trela's warpack. At least he hoped the second blast came from the warpack. Off in the distance a third blast could be heard. It was definitely from farther away than either of the first two. Vrric glanced from Estfale and Malghain near the entrance, to Trela above the gear and Jalin at the trapdoor, and marveled at how they all danced. It looked like they were madly churning butter while dancing a jig on hot coals. He knew what he had to do. He crawled his way to align the trapdoor with the entrance below. He took a deep breath. Took another, then let out a deafening scream.

"Mooove!" Everyone in the room stopped and peered around for the briefest of seconds, trying to ascertain where the voice came from. Those in the murder room had the advantage of knowing the voice and could tell the direction much easier. Malghain and Estfale both flung themselves in opposite directions across the slats. Jalin rolled smoothly out of his way. He did not know what Trela was doing. "Lumdepiarc!" A huge cylinder of fire shot past the warriors and immersed the floor below. It lasted a full three seconds. Once it was over, there was a molten hole in the slats where the fire cylinder had penetrated. The steel was red hot around the opening. The bodies of at least fifteen guards were still burning on the floor below. The far wall had caught on fire and the slatted floor began to sag, even under Trela. The air was thick with black smoke and the smell of burnt hair was nauseating. Vrric vomited and fell over, face first, onto the slats next to Jalin.

The roaring in his ears would not let him pass out into sweet oblivion. The blood-soaked slat under his cheek was beginning to coagulate, maybe due to the heat still traveling through the metal. The thought of soft, molten metal made Vrric think of kind Kaihlu, wearing his thick leather apron, pointing at the red hot metal of pig iron as it flowed through the sand molds on the floor. The rivulets like a mother sow suckling her many young. The way that Kaihlu laughed and would slap Vrric on the back. He had always seemed so happy, so robust and full of life. Vrric wondered what he was doing right then, at that very moment. It saddened Vrric to think that he had broken Kaihlu's heart. It saddened Vrric that he was going to die here, surrounded by Pyrans, so far away from the forge that he had spent his adolescence in. It all seemed so long ago, and he found himself wondering why he had even left. That thought made him think of Clerin's glowing blue eyes. It felt like his face cracked as he smiled a little at the thought of her. He couldn't let her down. And he couldn't let Trela down. He tried to sit himself up.

"They are here! They made it!" It was Jalin from somewhere beside Vrric. A flood of relief washed over him as another trumpet blast filled the night sky.

There was fire creeping up the front wall. He stared at it while sitting with his back against the back wall, not really comprehending what it meant. Suddenly a huge guard loomed up in front of him. Vrric took a moment trying to figure out how he had gotten up the ladder, not really comprehending what it meant. It was an almost fatal pause. Searing pain shot through Vrric's left shoulder. It felt like molten steel was being poured into him, through him. All he could do was scream. He tried to think, but all he could think was pain. He tried to see, but all he could see was pain. And when he tried to speak, to bring forth any spell that could save him, all he could scream was pain.

The guard slowly removed his sword. He was grinning, grinning widely. "I have the mage!" His right arm pulled back for the killing thrust. His left foot lifted for the lunge. And suddenly blood poured forth from his mouth as a thin blade of steel pierced through his chest to poke out the front. His sword clattered upon the steel slats. His body fell next to it.

Malghain's grin looked somewhat eerie in the flickering firelight. He jerked his own sword from the guard's body. He knelt near Vrric and his hands expertly ran over Vrric's wounded body. Quietly, almost to himself, he cast a healing spell. "Loliderto!" It felt as if a wash of cool water splashed upon Vrric, waking him up and soothing him with mint and aloe. Malghain grinned his odd grin, the blood of others running in splashed rivulets along his face's creases, and Vrric thought how good it was that Malghain was on his side. Then Malghain stood, raised his sword over his head and screamed a terrifying cry at the ceiling. It was half hawk's piercing shrill and half bear's growling roar. Then he jumped down through the trapdoor amongst the stunned guards.

Jalin was next to Vrric, running her own expert hands along his body. She mumbled while doing so, but Vrric was unable to ascertain what she was saying. She turned his head slightly to look behind his ear, felt his throat under his mouth, patted his chest and arms. Finally she squinted at him. "Nuliderto!" Another refreshing wave of mint and aloe.

The frantic sounds of a trumpet came from inside the keep, but instead of a short blast of confrontation, it was a series of trills. They were attempting to make formation in the courtyard, thought Vrric. Though the guards in the room had redoubled their efforts, the lieutenant and their reinforcements were outside waiting for Lishean. Even with the healing spells, Vrric had never felt more tired in his life.

Soon there was audible commotion beneath them as the warpack stormed the keep. It seemed that the few guards remaining in the gatehouse had lost their lust to reach the portcullis, so Jalin was able to leave Vrric to start tossing water on the flames. He sat there and attempted to recuperate. At least the metal slats near the hole were no longer glowing. He felt his eyelids growing heavy. His limbs seemed to be made of lead, they felt so dense.

Once it was obvious that the warpack was gaining ground in the keep, the few remaining guards turned and jumped past the flames to make their exit. Jalin had already used all the buckets of water available to her and was using the couple that were filled with sand by the time that Estfale and Malghain were able to help her. Trela walked gingerly over to Vrric. She knelt by him and placed a hand on his right shoulder to see if he was okay.

"If Clerin is hurt, I'll kill you." He did not meant it to sound that aggressive, it just sort of popped out of his mouth.

"Don't worry. If Clerin is hurt, I'll kill myself." Trela's dry statement shocked Vrric and he laughed heartily, but then started coughing. They were great, racking coughs that shook his whole body. Even his feet twitched uncontrollably. Trela held him to her as his body convulsed briefly, but violently, without even a hand free to smooth his hair or wipe his brow. When he finally stopped, he noticed flecks of blood on his hands. He tried to hide them from Trela. She had further fighting to do, and he knew she could not afford to be distracted.

Another thought came unbidden to his mind, that of the horror show around them. "I am not removing the air from a room again. Never again, so don't even ask." He smiled weakly but could not release her gaze until she answered. Deep down inside, deeper than magic, at least as deep as forging, he needed to be assured this would not happen again. That this was the peak horror of what would be asked of him.

"No, no, of course not. I had no idea that this is what would happen." Her arm swept the room. "I thought they would just fall over dead. Honest."

"Me, too." Vrric was a little lost in himself. Why was this more horrible than engulfing a derlian in flames? Was it the image that he, and Trela, had to deal with? The aftermath? How could what happened after death make that death more horrible? He wanted to ask Trela these things, he wanted a conversation with the one who was responsible for the killings, who started the war, who was commander of the warpack. But he was unable to form the words before being interrupted.

"Are you coming? Lishean is still struggling to enter the courtyard," Malghain yelled from the blood room below.

"Yes, of course." Trela stood and looked around for a moment. "Jalin, come and keep Feyazki company." Jalin strode back over from the front wall, giving the hole in the slats a wide berth. "There is still water in my pack if he gets thirsty. Don't let him leave the room until the fighting is over." Trela patted Jalin's cheek as she headed towards the trapdoor.

Trela climbed down the ladder and strode purposefully between Malghain and Estfale. "Let's make history!"

Jalin was staring out the window, looking at the bulk of the warpack trying to push into the keep's courtyard. The commotion in the courtyard became hushed. Vrric strained to hear what Trela was saying, but could only catch the gist. She was calling out Lieutenant Uriels to a duel. By the roar of the crowd, it appeared that he had accepted and that they approved. Jalin sat on the slats with her back against the back wall right next to Vrric. She handed him a skin half-full of water. She had a genuine smile, one that pulled back naturally to her muscular cheeks. Maybe it was a bit too wide, thought Vrric, but it exuded sincerity.

"This is my favorite part. The clandestine fight is over and the main fight, the grueling hack and slay of the warpacks, has just begun. I can sit back and relax and listen to the swords striking shields from far away. Sometimes it sounds like rain, sometimes thunder. Everyone out on the field thinks they are the reason the war is won. Truly, there will probably be many more bodies out there than there are in here, even with Trela's penchant to stop battle for single combat." Jalin took the skin back from Vrric. "This, however... This is where the war is truly won." She took a deep drink.

"But what if Trela loses to Uriels and the war is lost?" The slight pressure of Jalin leaning on his right shoulder was comforting.

"First of all, she can't lose. She may be tired, she may even be exhausted, but that lieutenant is a weasel, pure and simple. You could hear it in his voice and the way he yelled commands. I'll bet you five gold coins that he has some relative higher up in the ranks. Qizern's entire army is built on stupidity like that. Second of all... there is no second of all." She took another drink of water before handing the skin back. "But the real reason the war is won here is that it would already be lost if we had not accomplished what we needed to. There would be no warpack in the courtyard, no single combat for Trela, no nothing. All those big dumb warriors out there make fun of me for picking locks, but they have no real idea of what

I do. They do not realize my importance, or the importance of scouts, or the importance medics or quartermasters or cooks. Well, they probably realize the importance of medics, but that is only because it involves them directly. A warpack is a giant endeavor, and I am but a small specialist. You, too—you are a specialist. But your specialty is honored amongst the warriors because you cause death."

"What about Trela and Estfale? They understand your importance." Vrric was still tired but gaining slowly in strength.

"Of course. But they are specialists in their own right. Estfale is routinely a part of strike forces and, therefore, sees who those forces are comprised of. And Trela truly has a wider appreciation for the warpack as a whole than any other commander I have fought under." She took another sip. "I believe I gave you the wrong impression. I do not mean to complain at all. In fact, I enjoy my invisibility quite a bit. No, I am just trying to explain that the war is won on the battlefield lastly. There are millions of other tiny things that must fall perfectly into place before the battle even begins. And that these tiny things are often as dangerous as combat. Sometimes more so." Jalin sat the skin on Vrric's legs and stretched over to where her backpack was laying. She grunted slightly pulling it over.

"How does one get to do what you do? How does one become a spy?" Vrric took a sip. If he was honest with himself, he was not even sure what she did. But he was surely not going to voice that.

"Ha! That's a story. To be honest, most of us started out as thieves. You learn how to walk silently, sneak up on your victim, reach over and cut his pouch off his belt without him even noticing. You learn how climb stone walls, fingers and toes jammed into the tiny chinks, pulling yourself up slowly as to not make any noise." Jalin was twisting something up into paper. Her eyes were downcast, staring at, but not concentrating on, what her hands were doing. "It's weird, because as you learn to be a predator, you have to understand prey better than they do. What sound does a house make while settling or creaking in the wind? What sound do I make while sneaking about over the floor boards on the upper story? How do I make my sound appear to be a natural sound, background noise? What is difficult is that the sound I hear that I am making sounds differently to those a room over, or a floor below, or two floors below. Even the type of wood makes a difference. Pine boards will squeak as you cross them much worse than oak. Lodepito!" She said the last word so quietly he barely heard it, soon she was smoking.

"Why do you smoke?" Vrric did not mean to interrupt, but it did not seem as common in the Pyran realm as it was in the Luften.

"Because I don't like to drink." She smiled over at him. Then looked at him a little more closely. "Why is a Luften mage following a Pyran warpack around? Or are the prophesies of the Kriishan well known in your realm?"

"That would be a story as well, if I understood it. The Queen of Ariellyna, of the Luften realm, ordered me to help Clerin find the Luften Temple. Well, I guess it was a request more than an order, but how do you refuse a request from the Queen?" His eyes looked up at the ceiling for a moment, trying to recall exactly.

"That is one thing you don't have to worry about in the Pyran realm. Qizern would never deign to speak to a commoner. But I suppose you are no commoner, are you?" She took a drag. "So you followed Clerin into the desert and... found what?"

"We found Trela, who told us she could lead us to the temple that Clerin was looking for. But only if we promised to help her afterwards." Vrric was not sure why he felt shy about divulging the entire story. He felt a sudden urge to turn the conversation back to her.

"What about the well? More importantly, what about the Tlana? I hear that you single-handedly killed a Tlana. Is that true?" She beat him to the punch, but he was enjoying her leaning on him and realized that the entire warpack must have heard that legend already, so there were few secrets.

"I don't know if I killed it. There was never any body. Just a pile of Vijen leaves. But yes, I single-handedly fought a Tlana and lived to tell about it. It was the most... it was... grueling, the fight was exhaustingly grueling. To be honest, I am not sure how I survived."

"Well, Trela tells the story much better. Both of you flying at each other, lightning shooting across the sky. It sounds very exciting." Her left hand rested lightly on his right thigh.

"I am sure that all of this will sound very exciting as well, once Trela retells it." Vrric waved his hand around the blood-soaked room.

"It was exciting. Near death experiences are often exciting. Or is it just a Pyran excitement? What excites Luftens, Feyazki?" She was smiling warmly, but all Vrric could think about was the room. It was weird. He was sure that he would cause much more harm, kill many more derlians, in the service of a warpack commander such as Trela. But he could not be expected to visit this much horror upon them. He couldn't.

"Do you think they felt pain?" Vrric waved his hand again.

"Personally, I think they suffered less pain for less time than being torched or stabbed five times and left to bleed out. It was quick." She snapped her fingers. "Is it the gloominess in the room? Do you want to head out to the catwalk, get some fresh air?"

"Well, it just... it seems horrible, doesn't it? It seems worse than the other ways of dying." He furrowed his brow.

"Death is death. The beauty of death is that there is no more pain. No more humiliation, no more struggle. It is not the dead who feel that this room is horrible. No, only the living worry about those aesthetics. This is how the room is affecting *you*, Feyazki. You shouldn't feel bad for what happened in here. Could you imagine the bloodshed that would have occurred if we had been unable to secure this room? The amount of bodies outside in the courtyard, the amount of bodies laying at the foot of the keep's walls? That would have been much more horrible than this. No, what this is, is *rare*. You never see this, or at least I don't. You were not prepared for it, that's all. You should not be angry at yourself for this. You should not think of this as horrible." Her hand stayed conspicuously on his thigh. She smiled and tilted her head. "You never told me what excites Luftens."

Vrric found himself struggling to his feet. He enjoyed Jalin's company greatly, but could not calm himself from the horribleness of the room. Maybe he did need some fresh air from the catwalk.

"Discovery. I like to think that Luftens are more excited by discovery than by near-death experiences." Even as he said it, he doubted its truth. More than anything, he just needed to get out of the room. He found his mouth struggling to explain as much as his body was struggling to leave. "I need to find Clerin. I need to speak with her." And it was true. That was what he needed. If Jalin had asked him a minute ago, he would have disagreed. But as he heard the words leave his mouth, he knew them to be true.

Jalin snubbed her smoke, jumped up, and slid down the ladder first. From below, she helped him navigate the few rungs until he was on the floor of the blood room. She allowed him to lean on her as they stepped over the charred remains of guards. Soon he was at the door, staring out at the catwalk. He breathed in deep. The fresh air was wondrous.

"Sorry, I think you were right. The gloomy room..." He trailed off as he tottered out.

Chapter 20

Once it was obvious that the warpack was gaining ground in the keep, the remaining guards turned and jumped past the flames to make their exit. Jalin had already used all the buckets of water available to her and was using the couple that were filled with sand by the time that Estfale and Malghain were able to help her. Trela walked gingerly over to Feyazki's limp body. She knelt by him and placed a hand on his unwounded shoulder to see if he was okay.

Immediately his eyes popped open. Once he recognized her, however, his eyes narrowed slightly. "If Clerin is hurt, I'll kill you."

Trela was completely taken aback. She had not expected the vehemence in his voice. And, unfortunately, he was probably the one derlian who could accomplish his threat.

"Don't worry. If Clerin is hurt, I'll kill myself." It just popped out of Trela's mouth. Luckily, Feyazki laughed heartily, but then started coughing. Great racking coughs. Trela held him to her as his body racked violently for a good twenty seconds. When he pulled his hands away, she noticed flecks of blood on his fingers. She swallowed hard.

Trela realized that she had pushed her team too far. She did not want Clerin to be hurt, but Feyazki definitely was. She could not afford to loose a mage of his capabilities. Nor could she afford to loose his loyalty. She needed to be more careful next time. He looked back up at her intently.

"I am not removing the air from a room again. Never again, so don't even ask." Though he smiled weakly, his eyes kept their intensity until she answered.

"No, no. Of course not. I had no idea that this is what would happen." Her arm swept the room in a pitiful attempt to encompass the consequences of her command. "I thought they would just fall over dead. Honest."

"Me, too," came his quiet reply.

"Are you coming? Lishean is still struggling to enter the courtyard," Malghain yelled from the blood room below.

"Yes, of course." Trela stood and looked around for a moment. "Jalin, come and keep Feyazki company." She wanted more than anything to have him jump out onto the catwalk and shoot a pillar of flame into the face of the enemy. She knew that was not going to happen, however. She also knew how selfish it was for her to even want that. "There is still water in my pack if he gets thirsty. Don't let him leave the room until the fighting is over." Trela patted Jalin's cheek as she headed towards the trapdoor. She had done it unconsciously and hoped that Jalin did not consider it condescending.

Trela had wanted to drop down through the hole in the slats for a more dramatic exit, but she was just too tired and there was too small of an audience. She climbed down the ladder as the others had done. She had no clue what three warriors could add to help the situation on the ground. Her brief conversation with Feyazki left her feeling mischievous however.

"Let's make history." She spoke to neither Malghain or Estfale but walked between them and past them.

Trela strode out onto the catwalk, threw her head back, and howled as loud as she could. The trumpeters followed her lead, and for a brief moment after that, it was silent on the battlefield. Lishean had punctured the gate and was drawing troops into the courtyard. It was obvious that the keep was close to being taken. She could not let him share in the glory, however. It had to be her victory.

"There has been too much bloodshed tonight. We are all brothers! Should we not be embracing each other instead? Where is Lieutenant Uriels? Come, show yourself. You are certainly not hiding behind your warriors, are you?" There was quiet amongst the ranks and Trela was briefly afraid that she had misjudged the lieutenant. Surely he was the type to lead from behind. Surely he was still alive, bravely urging his troops on with that strong, forceful voice of his. "Surely Lieutenant Uriels has not already perished?"

Finally, a voice raised itself from the opposing warriors. "I am Lieutenant Uriels." It was not quite as forceful as it had been earlier in the evening.

"You and me. In the circle. Now. We shall settle this once and for all." Trela shook her fist above her head for effect. "To the death! "

A great roar rose up amongst her warriors. That she expected. A roar also rose up from the guards in the keep, which caught her by surprise. She thought they would be resistant to losing Dun Oengen over one duel. Either they realized they were not going to repulse her warpack or they had great confidence in their lieutenant. Trela hoped that she had not made an error. He should be fairly well rested, while she was almost spent. It was too late to turn back now, however. Her warriors had cleared a path for her and a circle was forming in the center of the courtyard.

Trela gripped the wood planks of the catwalk and swung herself down. She would rather have leapt off the catwalk for dramatic effect, but could not risk twisting her ankle right before the duel. It only looks good if you land it right.

As she walked through her ranks, her warriors reached out to brush her arms and shoulders. It made her feel good and helped to invigorate her. They began to chant her name and bang their swords against their shields. With each step more energy flowed into Trela. It came from all around and was almost dizzying.

She entered the circle and stood near her warriors, waiting for Uriels to appear on the other side. None of the keep's guards were making noise. They all stood in stoic silence as Trela's warriors whipped themselves up into a frenzy. She stood facing the guards, arms crossed, feeling euphoric. Finally Uriels materialized.

He was a short, squatty Pyran, almost Gaen looking. His hair was a little stringy from sweat, as if he had been running with a helmet on. His eyes looked meek, but somewhat wild as they darted around in his head. He had a heavy mace tied to his side but its bulbous head looked too shiny, as if it had never been used. Trela smiled at him while her warriors pounded away at their own shields. She had to consciously think to herself not to get overconfident, he had surely made rank for some reason. The guards stayed silent, and Uriels kept looking back, this way and that, as if wondering where his support was.

Trela strode forward and raised both her arms. Her warriors quieted to a low rumble. "Great guards of Dun Oengen. Know that we feel no ill will towards you. You are not our enemy. We are but a passing storm, and as swiftly as we have come upon you, we shall be on our way. You are not our aim, nor our goal. We travel across this realm with only one aim. Agoge! And we have but one goal. Qizern! He is a callous and fickle ruler who knows only the strength of his sword arm. And I... I am the Kriishan!" Her warriors erupted into a cacophony of screams. She let them howl for a brief moment and then cut them off again with her arms. "We do not relish in bloodshed but require supplies and treasure on our long march. It is the same game that our warpacks have played since the beginning of time. Any of you... all of you who wish to join with me once we leave this keep will receive full amnesty. In fact, even if you stay behind and send intelligence to our hated enemy Qizern," —at this her warpack behind her gave out a collective hiss—"there will be no reprisals. I wish all of you long and happy lives, whether you ride with me or curse me. All except for one." Trela drew her shortsword and pointed it directly at Uriels. "You told me that I was to die tonight. Well, now is your chance to prove yourself correct. If you kill me, my warpack shall leave without raising another weapon. You shall have rebuffed an attack from a warpack at least five times your size. There will be songs sung about the Pyran who proved that Trela was not the Kriishan as she claimed." Trela smiled at him. The more he shrank from her, the more his warriors ignored him, the more energy she felt coursing through her veins. "If I kill you, however, the keep is ours. This is it, Uriels. All or nothing. What say you?"

He looked back and forth across her line of warriors. He glanced behind him, to the right and left. He licked his lips repeatedly. It almost made Trela feel bad enough to call off the duel. The guards were obviously ready to lay down their arms and hand over the keep. Most of them looked horribly hung over. But she knew that it was too late. She had already made her speech and had already made her ultimatum.

"You are a liar and a coward. You attacked us with trickery and deceit, not an honorable assault. You will find that you are merely another deluded antoshan. And... and if I do not destroy you tonight, you will surely be crushed by our rightful and just ruler, Qizern!" He pulled his mace out with a flourish and, truly, some of his guards cheered and banged their swords against their shields. But certainly not a quarter of them, and certainly not that loudly.

They began to slowly circle each other. Watching how the other moved, making obvious feints to see how the other would react. For Trela it was important to concentrate and breath slowly. Her warpack had begun to chant again and it filled her with a huge amount of energy. She wanted to just step forward and thrust her sword into him and be done with it all. But this was practice. Every single combat she undertook was practice for Qizern. Every time she fought a leader in a ring was practice, no matter how skilled, or not, her adversary may have been. She made herself study Uriels. How his feet crossed behind him as he circled. How he swung his mace in wide circles in front of her. How his left hand was held up and open, as if he could block her charge with it. She feinted a thrust, and he swung his mace mightily down towards it, heavily overcompensating.

If he had struck her sword, he would have shattered it. He missed by a prodigious amount, however. She could have slashed him then, as his right arm crossed over and he bared his shoulder to her. She waited though, and kept practicing. He rushed at her with his mace spinning over his head. She dodged and rolled to her right, his left. She stood at the end of the roll as Synde had taught her so long ago and swiped at his thigh. She had rolled too far away to be able to connect. Not only that, but the swipe was a little wide and pulled her slightly off balance. She mentally chided herself for the mistake. Qizern would take her smallest mistake and destroy her with it. Of that she had no doubt. But she kept on practicing, and Uriel's reactions became quite predictable. After a while he rushed at her again, but instead of rolling, she side-stepped to her right and spun clockwise, in a full circle, stretching her right arm to full extension. The tip of her sword slashed his side, and by the feel of it, nicked a rib. He let out a howl of pain and spun around to face her. She feinted a thrust with a short step forward and waited for his mace. Right on cue, he swung mightily for her sword. She pulled the sword back but kept moving forward. His mace barely missed her and her sword. She then made a small hop and lunged with her right foot forward and her left extended behind her. Her sword struck his abdomen just under his sternum. And it sunk in sickeningly far. Trela knew that he would soon be laying on the ground begging for mercy. Rather than that, she drew out the sword, slid her left foot in line with her right, and spun in a quick circle. As she came back around, she gripped her sword with both hands and brought it down as hard as possible. It struck him in the neck as he was sinking downwards. It did not decapitate him, but put him quickly out of his misery. Her entire warpack erupted into cheering.

The guards did not cheer much, but they did not jeer her either. Trela raised both her arms and faced her warpack. Their chanting washed over her like a gentle rain. She turned back to face the vanquished. "Warriors of Dun Oengen." Her own warriors quieted down as she started speaking. "Let me assure you once again that we bear you no ill will. You have fought bravely this night. However, you must bivouac outside of the keep tonight on this fine warm eve. I will allow you to enter the barracks in groups of twenty to retrieve your gear. Once those twenty have exited the barracks, another twenty will be allowed in." There were some grumbles from the audience, but they were quiet grumblings since the night would have normally ended much worse for the guards. Trela had tried to think up a more congenial way of accepting victory but she could not. The first night is the most difficult with a defeated army. There was no way that she could take the risk of allowing them to stay inside the keep. Even if she had thought it was a good idea, she knew that her warriors would question her decision. It was best to make some changes slowly. And, truly, some traditions were there for a reason.

Lishean had lightly chided her again for not posting any of her warriors to guard against deserters throughout the night. She thought of Feyazki's response at the beginning of her warpack's journey. "You fold metal to remove the impurities, not to force them back in." It still rang true to her.

Some Qizern loyalists had stolen away in the night. That was obvious during the light of day. Some more left when she gave them all one more chance at amnesty in the morning. Still, Trela estimated that well over two-thirds of the guards pledged their loyalty to her after breakfast. Her warpack was growing steadily.

They stayed at Dun Oengen that night as well. The next morning they stripped everything from the keep that they could take with them and moved on. The larder was not as full as Trela had hoped, but the treasury was greater than she had imagined. She did her best to downplay the discovery, but handed out a full quarter of the entire treasury to her warriors. That was a lot to downplay, but it had been a while since they had been paid in gold for their service. She wanted loyalty based upon her warriors' belief in her, not in their interest in getting paid. However, being a warrior in the Pyran realm was a profession, not just a philosophy.

Trela's push towards the Dekhan plateau was gaining momentum. The next three warpacks they came across immediately joined up and swore fealty to Trela. They had sought her out as her reputation grew. They were not large warpacks by any means, each only about half the size of Rewista's. Their addition was certainly welcomed not only for the amount of skilled warriors that Trela gained, but also due to the morale boost. The influx of enthusiasm that followed each absorption was infectious.

The next two warpacks were Qizern loyalists. Though not of the Guard themselves, they fought like they were. Unfortunately for them they were of a small size and not led very competently. Still, they were both winnowed down to a third of their original size before surrendering. Their tenacity worried Trela.

The warpack after those two was small but incredibly skilled. They were led by Cavish, and they swore fealty immediately. Apparently Cavish had taken it upon himself to round up the best warriors he knew and bring them to Trela in the shadow of the plateau. She offered to give him Iventorn to be his ghulzan, but Cavish would not take him. Refused to even speak with him. And, unfortunately for Trela's insatiable curiosity, Cavish would not tell her why.

When the warpack arrived at the plateau, it was strangely quiet. Trela had convinced herself that this would be where Qizern would place his army. There were very few paths which reached the top of the plateau that were wide enough for a warpack of Trela's size. She was sure that they would be harassed on the long uphill hike, but there was not even a skirmish.

After two grueling days, they got to the top of the plateau. There were two empty guard towers straddling the main path which was lined with ancient and gnarled yew trees. The towers had been stripped of all furnishings but they did not seem to have been abandoned for long. The grounds still looked kept, there was no ivy climbing the stone walls, and there were even ashes in the fireplaces. Qizern had to know she was coming...

As they traveled further onto the plateau, there were more oddly empty towers peppering the landscape. Trela would make camp near them, just in case they were attacked in the night. She knew they must be empty on purpose, however, and that there would be no night attack. In a strange way, she would rather have fought for every step of the way to Agoge.

Even the landscape was trapped in an eerie silence. There seemed to be no large game for hunting. They were having difficulties foraging as the ground grew rockier and more barren. Tokroak's smoldering peak loomed in the distance. They plodded along for days, eating into their carried provisions.

On the fourth day, her scouts came back with news of a great warpack in the distance. The estimates of its size came back as high as eight times that of Trela's warpack. Trela then realized why the plateau had been so deserted. Qizern did not want to lose any warriors as she wound her way to Agoge. He would just stop her here with an overwhelming force. Only one battle needed to be waged.

Trela was concerned that the effect of the obvious disproportionate force would be devastating to her warpack's morale. She knew that the rumors of its size would already be buzzing through her warriors. For the first time she worried that she would have to set up a rear perimeter to prevent desertion. The feeling was disconcerting.

Trela needed to parley with Qizern before her warpack got any closer to his. And somehow she needed to convince him to allow their single combat before the two warpacks collided. She was not sure how she could accomplish that, but her desperation spurred her thoughts forward at a furious pace. Her destiny had come to this. She knew that the next few hours... maybe days... would be the most important in her life. She felt fear attempt to creep into her spine but she willed it back into her stomach.

Trela decided to take a large entourage for the parley. She wanted to make sure that every contingency was covered. She knew that he would already have a rough idea of the size and makeup of her warpack. Therefore, she felt a stronger impulse to show a large force immediately than to try to lull him into complacency. He would be confident enough already.

Trela brought most of her Privy council with her, with a couple of her lieutenants thrown in for good measure. She stopped well short of bringing the entire general counsel, however. And, of course, she left Lishean behind in case the rest of the warpack needed to be mobilized. She hated always losing her wisest advisor, but who could she trust with the safety of her warpack? He embodied so many of the necessary traits with none of the customary vanities that usually accompany warriors of rank. Somehow he just brought out the right mix of calm determination and loyalty from all of the warriors and could mount an orderly retreat or a massive attack with the same speed and efficiency. The only other Pyran that she trusted enough to be a great commander was Rewista, whom she left behind with Lishean as well.

Their steed's hooves thundered across the plateau. Trela was in the lead, and they rode in a sharp triangular formation. She wanted them to be moving quickly to mask their distance. She was not sure if that would work. Soon Qizern's warpack slowly rose into view.

It was truly massive. If anything, Trela thought that her scouts had been downplaying its size. She was somewhat shocked and dismayed but had truly expected no less. The warpack faded into the distance to her left and her right. Yet it stayed quite thick in the middle, probably twenty or so warriors deep. There was a straight basalt cliff rising behind the warpack, cutting off any hope for her to route them into a retreat. There were more warriors here than there were Pyrans in Parthia, let alone in Trela's old village.

Trela kept her horse at full gallop. There was a large tent several hundred paces in front of the warpack that she aimed for. Qizern's insignia of the red horse over blue flapped in the breeze atop the central pole supporting the tent. Trela imagined that she could hear the fabric snap as it rippled in the strong breeze. She shut her mind to all other distractions. She bent over her horse's neck as they flew across the barren landscape. Looking neither right or left, refusing to glance again at the sea of warriors, staring only at that flag. She needed to clear her mind of negativity. She needed to focus only on the task at hand. *I am the Kriishan,* she thought. Over and over it rolled in her mind, until it became a rhythm, a cadence. Until she finally arrived at the tent.

There was one old, grizzled guard standing outside of the tent. His chest and arms were still thick with muscle, but the hair on his head was white and frizzled in disarray. He leaned on a halberd as he watched her approach. Trela leapt off her horse and then stood there awkwardly for a moment. There was no one to hand the reins off to.

"Looks like you won the race." The old Pyran laughed.

Trela glanced behind her and saw that the rest of her entourage was fast approaching. "I travel ahead because I am not afraid."

"Some do, yes, some do. Some travel ahead because they are afraid, however." The old Pyran smiled kindly. "I do not suggest that you mask cowardice with bravado, young one, but in my time I have seen many that do."

"To be honest, I was focused on my goal, and forgot that my companions were with me. I am here to destroy your master. I am the Kriishan." Trela looked into the old Pyran's deep brown eyes for a moment too long. They were heavily lidded and somewhat puffy on the bottom, making him look somewhat like a sad puppy.

"That is impossible." He looked back into her eyes for a long pause, waiting for a retort that did not come. "I have no master." The sound of hooves made further conversation moot. The old Pyran let the others dismount and held the flap open for the large tent. Two younger guards walked out, blinked repeatedly, then gathered the various horses' reins. Trela and her companions entered the darkness.

There was a large, long, wooden table with chairs set up facing each other. On the opposite side of the table sat a line of warriors, on the near side the chairs were empty. Behind the warriors was a long curtain that split the tent in half. As her companions began to find their appropriate sitting arrangements, Trela noticed that the chair at the center of the table was empty. It was a simple wooden chair, like all of the others, but she figured it must belong to Qizern. She sat opposite the empty chair, annoyed to be kept waiting, in silence. Obviously, Qizern wished to give a grand entrance. She made a mental note to herself not to stand when he deigned to appear, even if everyone else in the room did. *I am the Kriishan*, she thought to herself. She had brought too many warriors with her, however, and half of them had to stand behind those seated at the long table anyway.

The tent glowed with the relentless sun beating down upon it, and soon her eyes adjusted to the interior light. She was about to break the odd silence by asking where Qizern was when she heard movement behind the long curtain. The Pyran who emerged from behind the curtain was less disheveled, but was certainly the same Pyran who had been guarding the tent when she had ridden up. His half of the table stood up as he entered. Much to Trela's pride, none of hers did. Customs and habit are difficult to override sometimes, and she had expected at least some of her companions to stand just because the others did.

Qizern quietly sat down in front of her and smiled. "I trust your travels have gone well?"

"You know why we are here." Trela's voice made the statement sound a bit like a question.

"Let us see... You have brought a tiny warpack all the way across this realm and up onto the Dekhan plateau. You are here to give some ultimatum that I will not grant you because I have a vastly superior force. You will make some harsh comments upon my character and my reign in the hopes that I will become emotional and accept your farcical challenge to a duel. It will not work. You will then proceed to claims of some sort of magical destiny. How I must lay down and die for you. Let you wrest from me what countless of stronger, faster, and smarter Pyrans have failed to wrest from me in the past. Do you think I wish to die? You bring your warriors with you to impress upon me that your threat is serious." Qizern swiveled in his chair, motioning behind him. "I have an entire township of warriors behind me. We are dug in and prepared. The only reason you have even made it this far is because you are such a tiny insect that I did not notice you climbing up my leg. That is what your tiny warpack is to me. Insects. I will crush you as I have crushed all before you. Congratulations, you have gotten my attention. You have forced me to gather my warriors and leave the comfort of Agoge. However, this ends here and now. You go no further." Qizern built a crescendo through his speech but had calmed himself by the end.

"You are correct that your warpack is vastly larger than mine. But there will still be needless bloodshed on both sides. And truly, even those warriors who are in my warpack are still your citizens, are they not? The coming battle is unnecessary. Look at you. You are a giant Pyran, skilled in the arts of swordcraft like no other. As you say, you have vanquished countless foes before me, better matched to your skills. If I am such an insignificant insect, then crush me. In front of all your warriors. In front of all of mine. Wash your sword in my blood. What better way to shame those who have chosen to follow me? What better way to prove that my magical destiny is a farce? What better way to prove to your own warriors that not only do you care about their well-being and safety, but that you are as powerful now as you ever have been. Show them that the comfort of Agoge has not dulled your martial prowess. Show them that you are still the greatest warrior in all the Pyran realms. Destroy me in public, I beg of you." Trela took a deep breath. "Or are you afraid of a little girl?"

Three of Qizern's warriors stood abruptly at her challenge. Malghain and Estfale, sitting directly across from two of them, also rose. Clerin, who was across from the third, stayed seated. Qizern had not taken his eyes off of Trela, not even for a second. Not even to blink. He waved a lazy hand in the air.

"Sit down, sit down. This is what she wants. This is what you want, isn't it? Strife?" All of the warriors slowly sat back down.

"I am not the one who showed up on your doorstep with a warpack. I did not besiege any of your keeps. I have not attacked any of your warriors. In fact, I will not attack any of your warriors. If you wish to avoid bloodshed... go home. It is as simple as that. No matter how you try, you cannot make me into the aggressor here. You speak of wanting to save lives... then save them. I promise you this, if you leave here today and take your warpack with you, there will be no reprisals. I will grant full amnesty to all of your warriors and let you all live long, peaceful lives." Qizern swept his hand through the air again. "If you attack me, however, I will not rest until I have destroyed every last one of your followers. And, if I am able, I will torture them first. I will find out who they love and care for most in this world. Then, when all of your followers have been destroyed, I will stride through this realm maiming all who they loved and cared for. I will obliterate your tiny village... well, what is left of your tiny village. Then I will reach far and wide with my powerful hands. I will reach into the Gaen realm and kill your parents." Here Qizern pointed at Croy or Knill, Trela was not sure, they were sitting so close together. "I will send agents into the Luften realm and assassinate your mentor." He then pointed at Feyazki. "Finally, I will reach all the way across the desert and murder your entire family, royalty or not." He nodded towards Clerin. "Those are my two promises, girl. Do you wish to test me? Is that what you want? Or do you wish to avoid the inevitable bloodshed and violence? The choice is yours. Peace or strife. It is as simple as that."

"I wish it were that simple. I truly do. But I am unable to make that choice. My destiny was laid out before me before I was born. I am not a derlian, though I am still a Pyran. I am the Kriishan. I am an arrow that has already been loosed, Qizern. I cannot turn nor veer, let alone drop from the sky. I am unstoppable, and I know that I cannot die until after I have killed you." Qizern gave a loud guffaw. Trela paused a moment before continuing. "You scoff because you do not understand destiny. Life has always gone a certain way for you, so you think it will continue to do so. You have always ruled with an iron fist and so you believe that is the only way to rule. You have always triumphed in single combat and so cannot envision defeat. It is this hubris that will be your undoing. I am the Kriishan and have been ordained by the hands of fate to defeat you."

"You have just described yourself to me." Qizern guffawed again. "You are the one filled with hubris because you have not tasted defeat. I have. You think you are invincible, but you are not. When you find that out, it will be too late. There will be rivers of blood flowing again upon my plateau." He paused for a brief moment. "You simply cannot win. My warpack is ten times the size of yours. Easily. Knowing I will destroy you is not hubris, but simple common sense. Turn your warpack around. Go home." He almost appeared saddened by the thought. Trela was unsure of exactly what thought, however.

"I cannot back away from my destiny. I am the Kriishan." Trela did not know what else to say. She hated herself for it, the redundant chant, but she had no other answer.

"Then we are at an impasse. The battle begins at dawn." He stood.

"If we repulse your attack during the day, if I am still standing at dusk, will you then grant me single combat?" Trela felt she needed something to bring back to her warriors. Something besides Qizern's promise of vengeance.

"No." He looked down upon her as the rest of his warriors stood with him. "My only promise is destruction. Think carefully tonight. Once tomorrow begins, there will be no more chances. You will not be given another offer of reprieve."

Trela let Qizern and his warriors leave. Her own stayed stoically quiet. She did not say a word either. She knew that now was the time for reassuring speeches. She needed to tell the others that she had a plan and assuage their fears of the carnage in front of them. She knew that if they went back to the warpack in silence, Qizern's threats would spread like wildfire through her warriors. She wondered how many would desert tonight. It was an academic thought, certainly not something she could dwell upon.

Trela stood in silence and so did the others. She left the tent and mounted her horse. So did the others. She promised herself that she would stop short of the warpack to give them a speech. To order them to keep the parley confidential. She promised herself that she would use the ride to think up what to tell the rest of her warpack, but her mind was blank. Qizern's threats were real. She realized that he was fully capable of torturing the survivors. He really could hunt down family members just for punishment's sake. She did not fear for herself. She still believed in destiny and that she was the Kriishan. But... she began to fear for her warriors. She knew that was what Qizern wanted. She knew that he was trying to unnerve her. But...

the beginnings of a niggling doubt shadowed her mind. She rode the whole way back to her warpack in silence and did not think of a single speech.

When she dismounted, with her warriors gathered around, she noticed a piece of folded up parchment jammed under her saddle. Ignoring the clamor of questions from all around, she unfolded the parchment. It said, "Meet me at the tent at midnight. It will be left up all night. Come alone." It was signed "Qizern the Merciless." She smiled to herself. She had thought for a moment that destiny had forsaken her, but no. It was merely lying in wait. She jumped back on her horse and stood unsteadily in her saddle. She outstretched her arms to steady herself.

"We have met the mighty Qizern and seen his weakness. His warpack is large, I will not lie. His warriors are rested and dug in, that is true. But he himself has become soft and complacent in his old age. Destiny has shown me that. All we need do is to remove the head and the body shall quickly wither. His warriors do not wish to fight. I believe they secretly wish us a swift victory so that they may go back to their loved ones in peace. We may fight an entire warpack tomorrow, but we only need to kill one Pyran. Destiny is upon us! I am the Kriishan!" Her warriors erupted into cheering. She did not know if she was lying to them, but she was also unsure of whether she spoke the truth. She did not have the time or the energy for a long speech, however, so she hopped down from her horse.

"Don't go, it's a trap!" Knill was the first of her advisors that she told of the note. He would have been the last if he had encouraged her. Trela was worried that he would react this way, but had been hoping his faith in her destiny matched her own. She let him rant for a while before leaving the tent.

Trela went next to Clerin's tent, but she could hear that Feyazki was in there talking. Not wanting to cause a disruption or to accidentally overhear something she should not, she quickly left. Lishean was worse than Knill. She had to promise not to meet with Qizern before he would even let her leave. That soured her on speaking with Estfale or Dartsyle.

Eventually she found herself in front of Croy's humble tent. It appeared that he was alone and still had a lantern burning, so she asked loudly if she could enter, and he quickly acquiesced. He was sitting cross-legged on his sleeping gear, and she sat down opposite of him.

"What are you doing?" Trela was unsure of how to start the conversation.

"I was thinking of Ilana. I have been working on my *whispering* skills with Feyazki, getting a farther and farther range. But I can't sense Ilana. Try as I might, I am unable to communicate with her." Croy looked down at his stubby fingers.

"Maybe we are too far away, or maybe she is not a mage of Feyazki's capabilities?" Trela suddenly realized how little she had talked to Croy during the campaign.

"Those are both true, but it seems like a different feeling. More hollow, perhaps? It is like, not only do I get no response, but it is as if I am not sending anything out..." He trailed off for a moment before looking up at Trela. "But you did not come here to discuss Ilana with me."

"Unfortunately, I did not. But I should have, Croy. I apologize." She wondered if it would have been better to speak of the note to no one.

"Do not worry, I know my problems are small." When he smiled at her, she detected some real warmth. Somehow it made her feel better about her own narcissism. "Please, do not keep me waiting. Have you come seeking advice?"

"Yes. Yes, I have." She thought she detected a slight grin form on his face as she said that. "I have been given a note from Qizern. He wants to meet me tonight, alone." She paused since she had been interrupted by everyone else at this point. When he did not speak up, she had to think of how to continue. "I feel I must go to this meeting, since it is my only way of truly talking with Qizern. Without an audience, just between us. But... what if it is an ambush?" She did not want to say that everyone else she had already talked to had warned her that it was an ambush.

"Well, I can tell you one thing that may ease your mind. I have dreamt of this." He looked more serious. "You do not die tonight. You do get to fight Qizern in single combat." He took a deep breath. "The dream was very vague, but I am sure it was you and him. Especially since I have had time to ponder it. It was a close and difficult fight, for the both of you. At the end, you pulled a dagger from your sleeve and hurled it into Qizern's back, killing him." He took another, deeper, breath. "Then the watching warriors tore you limb from limb."

"What?!" Trela had not expected that. She was not sure what she had been expecting, but certainly not that.

"Well... I think it was the thrown dagger. When you fight Qizern, you must kill him face-to-face. With a sword maybe." Croy looked a little uncomfortable.

"But, what if that was the only way I could win? There is nothing dishonorable about throwing knives." Trela thought back to the crowd's reaction to her defeat of Iventorn. It made her pause.

"My dreams are not purely literal, if that makes you feel any better. I do not have Tumu's gifts. I believe this one took place in an arena, which surely does not exist out here. I think it means more of *how* you kill Qizern, not just that you win. You wish, more than anything, to win the respect of the warriors, yes? Both yours and his. You do not need to grandstand or to put on a show, but you do need to be cognizant of the final blow. Think of how it will look to the audience before you strike it." Croy paused briefly, then looked down. "All I really meant to say is that you should not worry about this rendezvous. I do not believe it is an ambush."

"No... no, there is no need to back down now, Croy. I have seen your gift of dreams and completely respect that ability. More importantly, however, I believe what you say has merit. You are wise beyond your age, Croy. I thank you for your advice." Trela truly meant that. For the first time since leaving Serif, she thought of how much she might have learned by staying there. She decided to repeat Croy's warning to herself three times. It was an old memorizing trick that Synde had taught her. "To make your muscles remember what your mind knows," he used to say. If Croy saw her killed in a dream due to something she could avoid, she would do her best to avoid it.

"You flatter me, Trela." Croy was still looking down.

"If I can be accused of anything, it is not flattering you enough. You are a powerful asset to my team. If not for you, I would still be wandering in the Luften realm looking for Clerin's Temple. Thank you again." She stood, which had the desired effect of making him raise his head. He appeared to be mildly blushing. "I should stay longer, but unfortunately I must be going. Synde chose you well."

"He had no choice. I was the only one to stumble upon him." He smiled a large, honest smile.

"Then destiny chose you well." Trela smiled back at him. Then she turned and left the tent.

Trela did want to stay and chat, but she needed to pack her saddlebags. If she was to ride her horse to the rendezvous, she would have to leave soon. Originally she had thought about making Feyazki fly her most of the way, leaving her to walk the last bit. She knew that Qizern would realize that she could not walk the entire way, however. That would make him suspicious. She then thought about making Feyazki fly her and her horse. The only real reason she would do that, though, would be if she wanted him for backup. But if he was that far away, far enough not to be seen from the parley tent, then he would be unable to get there in time anyway. She decided to just ride out there. Besides, Croy dreamt that she and Qizern faced single combat amongst their warriors. She had to trust destiny. It had gotten her this far.

Trela packed some extra weapons, some dried food, and a shawl in case the ride back was chilly. She was soon riding out alone into the night. The stars were bright in the cloudless sky, but the moon had yet to rise. Millions of thoughts raced through her mind, none coherent enough to follow. She pondered if Qizern slipped the note under her saddle before the parley, or afterwards. She guessed before, since he seemed so much less pleasant after. She was unsure of which she would have preferred.

Trela rode slowly since she had left a little early. She had not wanted to wait around the camp with so many of her advisors wanting to talk her out of leaving. It was an uneventful ride to the parley tent. There was a small glow to the tent, as if there was a lantern lit in it. She tried to see any shadows cast upon the walls, but Qizern, or any Pyrans lying in wait, must have been behind the light source. She let her horse walk down to the tent, then she dismounted and hobbled her horse.

With one hand on the hilt of her sheathed blade, Trela took a deep breath and opened the tent flap. The table was still in place from earlier, with one lantern sitting in the middle. Qizern was sitting in the same chair that he had before. There did not appear to be any other Pyrans around, but Trela told herself not to get complacent. Qizern rose when she entered the tent.

"I knew you'd come. Sit down, have a drink." Qizern motioned to the chair across the table in front of him. There was a jug of grog and two glasses set on the table. Trela walked over to the table and contemplated whether or not to have a drink. She decided she could, so she switched the glasses and poured his first from the jug. Then she poured hers and sat down. He sat down after her and took a hearty draught of the grog. Trela took a small sip. It was simply amazing.

"I've never tasted grog this good." Trela took another drink.

"One of the benefits of ruling a realm." Qizern smiled warmly at her and took another drink. "Do you know how many cities there are in the Pyran realm? How many towns? How many villages? How many backwater groups of Pyrans one can only call a settlement?" He paused but Trela did not wish to be drawn into such an arbitrary question. "The answer is twenty-three, maybe a hundred, over four hundred, and who knows. This does not include Agoge or anything on the plateau. Do you know how many cities I can personally oversee? Do you know how many villages I can visit each cycle?" He paused again. Again Trela refused to bite. "When something horrible happens in some town, when some tragedy is afoot, who do you think they blame? Do I have any control over the crops along the Verdai hills? Do I make the swamps fetid at the delta of the Istanto? When a guard that I have never met before takes bribes at the expense of our elderly or weak, is that because of me? If I find that guard, I punish him. What else can I do? I keep the peace amongst the warpacks as much as they will allow. I keep the traders trading, and I keep the healers healing. I keep the push and pull of society moving. I am the paddle that churns the butter. What else can I do? What else could you do?"

"I am the Kriishan." Trela knew that was the wrong thing to say, even as she said it.

"You really think it is that simple? You really think that you can do better? That you can just whip every citizen into shape by your mere presence? That they will stop being murderers and thieves, liars and cheats, all because you killed an old Pyran on some plateau that most of them have never even seen? That is absurd." He took another sip of grog. "I had hoped you were smarter than that."

"I would spend the tributes on the citizens. I would make roads, drain swamps, build irrigation canals. I would enforce the laws of the land upon every Pyran, including myself. 'Who keeps the keepers themselves?' " Trela quoted the old rallying cry of the downtrodden. He laughed heartily.

"Oh, yes. Do you know what that means, or are you just parroting poor, dead Synde? It is Pyrans like him who truly make the job difficult. There is nothing like getting stabbed in the back by an old compatriot, Trela. Nothing like it in all the world. And until you experience it... you will never understand." His face had hardened into an ugly frowning countenance.

"Do not speak ill of Synde. He saved me from your wolves and for that... for that you had him murdered! This is exactly what that quote means! You feel that you are above the law because you serve the law. You misuse use the word, however. It should come from the root of servant, not something a waiter does. You mete out justice at your whim, not at the roots of injustice. You use your royal Guard as a private assassination troupe, not to protect the weak and elderly as you suppose." Trela was interrupted.

"I taught Synde everything he knew. I showed him the sword and spear. The thrust and parry. He was a young, adventurous fool when he arrived in Agoge. I took him under my wing. I shaped and molded him. I gave him advancements even though there were others, better prepared, who should have received the promotion. I loved him like my own son. I gave Yaserli that necklace you are wearing. Do you know how expensive pearls are in the desert? And she still left with him..." They each took a drink. Qizern in remembrance and Trela to keep from lashing out. "You have yet to experience the true ugliness of the world. These decisions are never easy. Do you really think that I have not built roads and bridges? You think there are no canals that exist due to my largesse? Do you know how many times I have sent out surveyors and engineers with coffers full of gold, only to be told that it is not enough? They will always need more. There will always be another road, Trela, another swamp to be drained. These are not ideas that you alone have thought up. That is an endless cycle of spending that will bankrupt the entire realm if you let it." Qizern paused again and seemed to calm himself.

"You murdered Synde." Trela took another drink to calm herself but it did not help. "You say that you loved him. Well, I truly did love him. He was a father to me. He taught me the sword and the spear. The thrust and the parry. You... murdered... Synde." Spittle flew from her mouth at his name. It was Trela's turn to have an ugly, frowning countenance.

"He betrayed me like no other." Qizern put up his hands to Trela, showing her his palms. "That is no excuse, I understand. Please... please, let us speak of other things. I did not bring you here to discuss my past mistakes. I... I wanted to explain that you can have the noblest of intentions and derlians will still hate you. You can put every effort forth, every ounce of your energy to helping them. All of them. But the system is... well, it is a beast. It is like being at the head of a fire line. Everyone lined up, handing buckets of water down the line, towards the blaze. Except the buckets have holes in them. And just because you are the one at the well, personally dipping each bucket in and hauling it back out full of life-saving water, all the others blame you as the flames consume their homes. The water just splashes and sloshes on their shoes. They know that you did not put the hole in the bucket yourself, but... Well, they must blame someone, yes? And, truly, who else is there to blame?" Qizern looked melancholy as he refilled their glasses.

"The time has come for change, Qizern. The status quo cannot hold. Grant me the single combat tomorrow. I beg you." Trela did not believe Qizern's innocence. She had seen what he had done to her village. To Synde. To the entire realm. But she realized now, like a blinding truth, like staring straight into the sun: Qizern believed in his own innocence. He believed he was some sort of victim. That was the key that she sought. That was the only thing that could unlock her destiny. And she needed to use the key tonight, while he was drinking fine grog and being pensive. She could not convince the Qizern who had met her earlier in the afternoon to join her in combat, when he was surrounded by his advisors, lieutenants and warriors. His bravado amongst them would not let him take the risk. But this Qizern...

"Yes, the time has come for change." He took another healthy draught. "Join forces with me. You need my experience, and I need your youthful exuberance. I have ruled for so long that I have become jaded towards my own subjects. I understand that. I do. You can breathe knew life into the kingdom. I... my advisors warned me against even having a parley. They told me to launch a full-out assault on your tiny warpack. To crush you quickly and completely." He took another quick drink. Trela was too stunned to blink, let alone speak. "But word of your beauty intrigued me. Before I destroyed you and your followers, I had to at least see you in person. You are... bewitching." He was looking down at the glass in his hands.

"I don't... What are you saying?" Trela took a large drink from her own glass.

"I am inviting you to be my Queen. No more bloodshed. No more turmoil. No strife. You would rule at my side as my equal. I..." Trela interrupted Qizern's speech.

"Are you mad? Have you completely lost your senses?" Trela was too stunned to stop herself. She knew that she needed to cultivate his empathy so that he would not start tomorrow with a "full-out assault," as he had put it. But this was just too absurd. "You do not even know me. What if I killed you in your sleep? That is not even the most audacious thing about this, however. What is going through your mind that you think I would ever, EVER, consider being your Queen?" Trela had to bite her tongue to stop herself. She needed to think of a way to salvage the situation.

"Then just give me this night. If you will do that, I will grant you single combat tomorrow. I..." She interrupted him again.

"You must have countless mistresses amongst your warpack." She forced herself to breathe evenly in an attempt to slow her heart rate. She needed to think clearly.

"Is it my age? I guarantee you that I am as virile as ever." His face curled up into itself. His grin turned into a sneer. A thousand voices began to shout in Trela's head for her to flee. But she still wanted to salvage the conversation. If she could just get him to agree to fight her tomorrow morning, somehow. Without making any promises of herself...

"No, it is not that. You are striking for a Pyran of your age. Muscular and energetic, with a real fire behind your eyes." Her mind told her not to, but her right hand was not listening; she raised her glass to him in a sort half-salute, and she finished off her glass. Trela watched the glee in his face rise. It made her bile rise.

"Then what is it? You are certainly not still... shy? You and the little Gaen, certainly..." He finished his own glass. A thick tongue, slick, red and fumbling, licked his chapped lips.

"It is not that, it is just..." Trela had an almost uncontrollable urge to stand. Just to stand. Maybe, after standing, she could leave. She forced herself to stay seated and cordial. There had to be some way to get him to agree to single combat. She would do anything for that, *anything at all,* she thought to herself. Single combat would save so many lives. But she was lying to herself, she would not really do anything and she realized it at that moment. She couldn't do that.

She wouldn't do that. There had to be another way, she had to think of something else.

"Just what?" His face was still pinched and ugly, but he was smiling at the same time. More voices clamored for her to flee.

"I am the Kriishan. My destiny with you is combat. It is that simple." It all came crashing down. She could not think of anything else. There was no ruse that would convince him. No way to for her to cajole him into single combat tomorrow. Not without lying with him, not without his sweaty, ruddy face grunting above her, not without his wretched breath pouring down upon her. And she just... could... not... do... that. She was the Kriishan. Her destiny with Qizern was only combat. It really was that simple. He suddenly stood. The hair on the back of her neck stood as well. His chair fell in slow motion behind him.

"We are alone here, you know. I know that you did not bring anyone with you. You should not make such ultimatums. Such refusals. It is not healthy for a young girl." His forehead was tilted downwards such that his eyes had to look up to stare straight at her. He glared at her through his brows. The screaming in her head to flee was deafening. "Run," the voices chanted. At the same time, it felt like her blood was draining away from her. She realized that she had been sensing danger. This shift in Qizern's personality. He had seemed almost charming at times. Earlier. Now he just appeared ugly. There was a handsome young boy in her village growing up that was accused of torturing animals. She had not believed the rumors, he had seemed so nice. His face was always smiling and he was quick with a wink. But when the elders confronted him with his crimes, when they cornered him to bring him to justice, his face... changed. It was something in the way the eyebrows and upper cheeks swelled. His face had become flushed and his jaw hung open slightly. Like he needed to bite something. More than anything Trela remembered how his eyes changed. Pupils can either dilate or not, and the iris does nothing at all. But somehow, someway, the light behind his eyes changed. It did not grow dimmer, but it grew darker. At that moment she had realized that the rumors were true. The dissected, or more likely vivisected, animal carcasses around her village came from him. He looked like a completely different derlian. Like he should have a different name and come from a different place. That was how Qizern's eyes suddenly looked to her. They had not grown dimmer, but they had grown darker. She stood but he continued speaking.

"What if I decide I don't like 'no'? What if I decide I am the King? The King does not ask for things, girl. The King takes them!" He suddenly reached out with his right hand, across the wide table, and snatched her left. He yanked her so hard that her arm felt like it would leave its socket. Her pelvis slammed hard into the table edge. She could no longer look into his eyes, they had grown so dark. The chorus in her head kept screaming "Flee!" She suddenly, and without warning, felt a hopeless helplessness descend upon her. Her revulsion almost turning into passivity. Luckily, however, her right hand was not listening. Just as it had finished her grog for her, it snapped up the dagger in her belt and cut deeply into the back of his hand. He screamed so loud that she thought she would be struck deaf. But he let go.

Trela probably could have killed him then and there, if she had been able to think. But the voices kept telling her to flee, and flee she did. Her heart pounded so loud that she worried it was audible. He stood there clutching his hand, screaming at her. She sheathed her dagger and ran out of the tent to unhobble her horse with shaking fingers.

"I will destroy you! I will destroy all of you!" It was the only intelligible sound that emanated from the tent. It was the last words she heard from Qizern that night. She made her horse gallop the entire way back to the encampment. She could not turn right nor left, but could only flee. Her mind could coalesce nothing on her ride. She could only flee. The sickness in her stomach, the fear in her heart, the irrationalness of her emotions... It was worse than when Nolt died. It was sheer horror.

Dawn came quickly the next day. Trela had been unable to make herself gather her advisors last night. She could not bring herself to speak with anyone about Qizern. It had taken her awhile but she did finally fall asleep. When she awoke, however, it felt that it had certainly not been long enough. She felt drained, both emotionally and physically. She found some forward sentries while Knill was cooking breakfast and made sure that Qizern's army was stationary.

After eating, she gathered her Privy Council. She needed to outline her plan. Trela knew that time was of the essence. They could only survive a couple of days, and that would only be if Qizern did not pursue them. She hoped that he was still planning on keeping his losses to a minimum. To stay dug in, as he had indicated in the parley yesterday afternoon.

"We will need a strike force to flush Qizern out. His plan, as far as I can discern, is to hide behind waves of warriors and wear us down. Our plan, in fact our only hope, is to get me to him, in front of his warriors, such that he cannot turn down my challenge. I need this strike force to fly. This will mean Feyazki. I will need Croy to keep an active and robust shield. There is sure to be many mages in Qizern's warpack. Probably thicker wherever he his hiding. Therefore I will need another two mages in our strike force. One to find those on the ground, a senser if you will. And one to keep them from dispelling our flight or our shields." Trela paced in front of the packed tent.

"I can keep others' magic from affecting ours." Serghno spoke up from the back. "And, if there are no other volunteers, my... friend Arnasta can pinpoint where a spell originated from over a league away." Others nodded and murmured. Trela assumed this Arnasta was, if not well regarded, at least heard of.

"Excellent. That will fill the four mage slots. I will need two expert archers, to dispatch those pinpointed mages on the ground. And I will need three warriors to accompany me so that when I reach the ground I will live long enough to challenge Qizern. Lastly, I will need my ghulzan, Iventorn. There will be two more strike forces, to confuse and harass the enemy. One will be made of cavalry and one will consist of infantry. The warpack itself, under the guiding hand of Lishean, shall attack where I think Qizern is hiding. His warpack is weakest in its thickness, we must take advantage of that. He will want to watch the combat, even if he thinks that he can avoid it. We will have our scouts on horseback at the back of our warpack, training their spyglasses upon the enemy. When Qizern is spotted, his coordinates will be *whispered* to Feyazki, and we shall take flight. I wish there was a way to win the actual battle, but I am afraid that the best we can hope for is to corner Qizern. Once we are engaged in single combat, all other fighting should stop. Once I kill him, we will be merciful to his warriors. However, if the unthinkable should happen. If I should fail... you are all to disperse. Retreat fully and without hesitation. Escape the plateau and never speak of your fealty to me to another Pyran for the rest of your lives." The air in the room seemed to get heavier. "But do not fear my faithful followers.

Though we throw ourselves into the maw of the beast, we are destined to be victorious! I am the Kriishan!" The others quickly erupted into cheering.

Trela chose Estfale, Dartsyle, and Malghain to accompany her strike force. She had wanted to take trusty Torpalin or skilled Haswyxe, but she knew she needed to arrive at Qizern's doorstep with Pyrans. So she only took two Luftens and a Gaen amongst her personal guard. Croy was right. Perception did matter. They filled the force with Hygen and Urwst. Everyone agreed that they were two of the most skilled archers in the entire warpack. Plus, they were the only survivors out of the entire maniple of archers that had accompanied Croy and Feyazki on the cliffs of Unaqa. Trela had felt at the time that they had been spared by destiny for some future service.

Once Iventorn was fetched, the eleven grouped themselves back in the council tent. She would need to speak to Iventorn alone at the end of the meeting. She was prepared to offer him release from his geas if he fought well. It was the best way that she could think of to ensure his loyalty. Afterwards, Trela planned to hand pick the infantry and cavalry forces, speak with them individually, and then make her plans with Lishean and Rewista. She hoped to mount her campaign in less than an hour.

Before she could begin her meeting with the strike force, a panicked cry erupted from outside of the tent. Trela rushed out to see what the commotion was. There was a sentry running as fast as he could, screaming unintelligibly. Trela's heart sank. Qizern was not going to wait for an attack to lessen his casualties. He was going to lose as many warriors as it took to crush her entire warpack before sundown. She had run out of time.

Trela ran over to the sentry. She wanted to hear from him exactly what was happening. She grabbed him by the arms in an attempt to calm him.

"Qizern's warpack is on the march." He looked young and nervous.

"Did you see it? Is the entire warpack marching, or just a portion of it?" Trela spoke calmly but forcefully as she let go of him and dropped her arms.

"No, no... It was *whispered* to me. They are moving slowly so far. And I believe that the whole warpack is coming." He looked up at the last sentence, as if trying to remember her question.

"Good. I was worried that Qizern might try to stay out of reach. Check and make sure that there are no contingents being left behind. And then make sure that all of the *whisperers* know of the coming warpack." Trela turned and saw warriors gathering around them. She did not have time for speeches, however. Luckily, part of her council had been loitering around. She grabbed ever-present Knill first.

"Get Lishean. Tell him to bring his most trusted lieutenants here, but that I need to speak with him alone. Hurry!" She then turned and found Yarsurle, he was always near Dartsyle.

"Tell the buglers to sound revelry. We need the entire warpack to finish breaking their fast and to prepare for battle. There is no time to lose." She then turned towards the tent that housed her tiny strike force. There were still many random warriors gathered around, staring at her or at their feet. She drew her sword and held it high to flash in the morning sun.

"Prepare for battle my warriors. We shall bask in the glory of victory by nightfall!" Luckily, those around her began to cheer. She had no other words to say. Instead she strode purposefully, with her sword still held naked in her hand, towards the tent. She did not know how much time she had to prepare, but she trusted Feyazki to get real information from the *whisperers* more than she trusted the sentry. He had trained each one of them himself and should know who was stationed where.

Trela threw open the tent flap, sheathed her sword, and strode in. The members of the strike force were all on their feet, waiting. She motioned for them to sit but only about half did so. The sounds of warriors preparing for battle crashed in upon them from all sides of the tent.

She looked at Feyazki first. "Find out from your *whisperers* what is really going on out there. I need actionable intelligence." He nodded to her, businesslike, and then sat down. His eyes rolled up into his head and he started mumbling under his breath. Trela took a deep breath and turned towards the others.

"We are going to continue as planned. Qizern shall be somewhere near the back of his warpack. We must find him. And quickly. The warpack will not survive until nightfall if we fail to uncover his hiding spot." The rest of them sat down. "You all know your parts, yes? Croy shall be the shield. Feyazki is flight and navigation. Arnasta shall scout all enemy mages, and Serghno shall destroy them. If there are too many, we have Hygen and Urwst to kill them the mundane way. They can harass the ground forces if they are not needed for mage assassination. That leaves Estfale, Dartsyle, Malghain and myself. We will be the ground force once we find Qizern." Trela had nodded to each as she spoke their name. "And also my ghulzan." Trela turned to Iventorn. His black eyes stared back at her emotionlessly. "I want all of you to hear this." Since he was sitting, she leaned over to keep her head at his level. "If you get me to Qizern, if you help me confront him, you will be released from your geas. It does not matter if I die, it does not matter if he will not fight me, or even if he slips away unharmed. If you get me close enough to him that I can yell at him, you are free." She thought she detected a small smile. She stood back up. "You are all witnesses. No matter what happens afterwards, my ghulzan either dies or walks free before this day ends. I will accept no other alternative." Trela had thought long and hard about how best to ensure his loyalty. Part of her wanted to keep him as a ghulzan, part of her only wanted to grant his freedom if he helped force Qizern into single combat, and a small part of her did not trust him enough to even want him on the strike force. Once Qizern started to move, however, she knew it was destiny or death. If she could just reach Qizern, she thought, everything else would fall into place. All she really wanted was that chance. "Now leave me. I must gather my thoughts before Lishean arrives."

They stood quietly and filed out. As Iventorn passed, he paused. "You should have killed me long ago. Now I will only know shame until my death."

"Maybe you do not die today." Trela was taken aback. This was the first he had spoken to her unbidden since he had become her ghulzan.

"No matter how I try, I cannot imagine today not ending badly. There are just too many of them." He touched her shoulder lightly. "Do not worry about any betrayal coming from me. I still value honor more than I fear death." He dropped his hand. "But you know, in your heart of hearts, you have to know... we both die today. We all die today." He waved his hand to take in the entire camp.

"You are more honorable and more skilled than I. You have incredibly deep strength, both physically and as a leader." It was Trela's turn to touch his shoulder lightly. "Do you know why I could best you? Do you know how my warpack could hold off yours until you were forced to fight me? You should have killed me, not the other way around." He stood there silently, staring into her. "Because this is my destiny. I am the Kriishan."

He shook his head, but Trela thought she detected the same small smile creep onto his face. Silently he walked out of the tent. Trela suddenly felt exhausted. She sat down on a chair at the large table and held her head in her hands. She had not slept well last night.

"Don't look so defeated." It was Lishean. Trela had no idea of how long she had sat there motionless with her mind blank. She hoped it had not been long.

"There must be something wrong with your eyes, ancient one. I am undefeatable." Trela smiled up at him but did not move.

"Good. I would rather lose my sight than your conviction. At least on this day." He sat down across from her. "Did you sleep at all last night?"

"Yes. Some." Her smile weakened but did not slip.

"I told you not to go talk with him." She started to protest, but he raised his hand. "Do not worry. I knew that you would, your honor would insist upon it. I just wish your honor was such that we could have ambushed him last night. That would have saved us a lot of trouble today."

"He could have just as easily ambushed me. And believe me, he has less honor than I do." Trela paused for a moment. "I need to lean on you one last time, my general. I will be unable to lead the warpack today. As you well know, our survival depends upon me finding Qizern as fast as possible. And I need you to hold out for as long as possible. I do not care how many of Qizern's warriors you kill. This will not be a test of strength. It is a test of endurance." Trela took a deep breath. She could not tell him that all she truly needed was time. That she needed the battle to last until her last warrior. "What matters most is that we lose as few warriors as possible. A giant phalanx of turtles, bristling with halberd quills. Use the cavalry at first for sortie rallies, but do not let them get caught far afield. If they get cut off from the warpack, they will be swallowed whole. Do your best to hold ground but do not worry about being slowly pushed back. Lean on Rewista whenever you are able."

"Do not worry. I will get you the time you need. Just be as quick as you can." That was exactly why Trela could not find a replacement for Lishean. He could understand what she needed without her coming out and stating it. And, even if it was a selfish need, he would convey his agreeableness. Even more than that, however, was the fact that he always delivered. He was a rare mix indeed.

"You know that you will have first pick of positions once I defeat Qizern. Anything at all, Lishean. Any compensation at all." Trela wanted him to realize how valuable she thought him, but did not want to embarrass him with overflowing praise.

"Just be as quick as you can. We will worry about everything else after you have defeated him." His pragmatism kept him humble.

Trela stood and extended her arm across the table. "To the battle." She said it as if making a toast.

"To the death." He clasped her forearm with his hand.

His retort unnerved her slightly, for he was not one who usually engaged in word play. Did he mean that her battle with Qizern was to the death? This was it, however. Though Trela was loathe to admit it, this might be her last conversation with Lishean. Today might be her last conversation with any one of her warriors. The warpack was sorely outnumbered. "To the victory." She could not end it on a dour note. Lishean laughed heartily.

They unclasped arms and walked out of the tent. The camp was a buzzing hive of chaos. Lishean started barking orders at the lieutenants who now hovered around him. Trela went to find her strike force. There was not enough time to make any of the other forces that she had wanted to create. She would just have to leave her warpack in the capable hands of Lishean. She had no other choice.

Trela found the force at the front line. Several were sitting on the ground and several were stretching. As she approached them, she singled out Feyazki.

"How fast are they approaching?" She wanted to ask him if anyone had spotted Qizern yet, but she knew that he would have told her immediately if that were so.

"Quickly, for their size. Maybe twenty minutes to battle?" He squinted at her. She cursed herself for not discussing strategy with Lishean and his lieutenants more. But she had been concerned that Qizern's warpack would arrive sooner.

"Any word of Qizern's location?" Even though she hated herself for it, she had to ask. He pursed his lips and shook his head. She raised her head and her voice. "Mages, come hither." That left the others still stretching. She waited until they had gathered around, then spoke more conversationally. "How can we track Qizern?"

"Well, it depends upon if he is camouflaged, magically speaking." The statement came from Arnasta.

"You are thinking that if he is camouflaged, you might be able to sense the effort it takes to hide him?" Trela mused.

"Maybe. It depends on how skilled his mage is. More to the point, however, I was thinking that there are different ways of detecting a derlian, depending on how they are trying to hide." She looked from Trela to the others.

"So, how do you find someone who is not camouflaged?" Trela had always been a little curious.

"Well, everyone has an unique signature, their own personal scent. The more I know about you, your personality, your traits, the way you think, the more I can recognize your signature. When I go sifting around looking for you, I can easily distinguish those who are completely different. Like males, or Luftens. It is more difficult to discern from those who are similar, like warriors who specialize in short swords and daggers." Arnasta continued. "The issue will be that there are so many in the warpack who are similar enough to Qizern that, since we do not know him personally, will make it difficult to pin him down. To be honest, it probably would be easier to track him if he were actively being camouflaged."

"What if I knew what was on his mind?" Trela was trying to think of discerning characteristics.

"There are many in the warpack who might be thinking the same thoughts. So the more unique the better. However, it is usually easier if you know the derlian personally than if you can guess what they happen to be thinking of while you are looking for them." Arnasta tapped her forefinger on her chin.

"What if I knew about a recent, unique wound?" Trela was honing in on her hope.

"Someone such as Qizern would almost certainly have had his mages heal him by now. There is probably not even a scar currently." She cocked her head. "What do you mean by recent?"

"He grabbed my arm and I cut the back of his hand last night." Trela looked down when she said it, still somewhat embarrassed.

"Did you wipe the blade? Do you have a trace of his blood on a cloth or boot or something?" Feyazki interrupted Arnasta. Trela could not recall what she had done. In somewhat of a daze, she pulled out her dagger. There, caked a little on the sheath, was some dried blood. It was brown and dull and miniscule, but there was some there. She must have sheathed it wet. Lishean would have chastised her for such a mental lapse had he known. The mages gathered around her, however, were ecstatic.

"Why did you not mention this earlier? Blood is the most traceable of all bodily fluids. It carries more of your signature than any other." Arnasta was grinning from ear to ear. It was infectious, and soon Trela was smiling as well.

Trela unhooked her belt and removed the sheath entirely. She handed it and her dagger over to Arnasta. Arnasta sat down with her legs crossed and laid the items in her lap. She rubbed her hands together lightly before placing them over the sheath.

"Lumfintotarc!" The word was spoken softly. Her eyes fluttered under closed lids. She stayed still for what seemed like a long time. Finally, she opened her eyes.

"Were you able to locate him?" The question came from Serghno, but it was on everyone's mind.

"I believe his is in the back of his warpack. Way down there, to our left." She pointed to her right since she had her back to the advancing warpack.

"Then we ride." Trela turned to her own chaotic warpack and began yelling orders.

They were soon at the far end of her warpack. They all dismounted and handed the horses over to Lieutenant Kryhir. Trela had not wanted to exhaust her mages immediately, but time was of the essence. Luckily or not, the sounds of lock step marching came thundering down to them almost as quickly as they had dismounted. Then the first wave crested the last hill between the two warpacks.

Qizern's warpack stretched as far as the eye could see. Trela wondered why he had not consolidated his forces, but guessed that the warriors to her left would swing around behind them like an old wooden gate. She had known that they would be outflanked but had not fully realized the amount of warriors that would soon be behind them. She was worried that her warpack would not make it past high noon. Lishean was smart to put the more competent lieutenants at the corners. Kryhir was as solid as they came.

The coming march was slow but steady. Trela moved her strike force towards the back of the line so they would have room to set up. They had little time before Croy would need to cast his shield spell. She left her dagger and sheath with Arnasta, in case she needed to cast another seeker spell. Hygen and Urwst had strung their bows and were testing their pull. Malghain, Dartsyle, and Estfale were talking quietly amongst each other, huddled together off to one side. Feyazki and Serghno appeared to be meditating, while Croy looked like he was just fidgeting. Trela was trying not to think about how naked she felt without her dagger. She had her sword and even had a knife tucked into her boot, but she missed the weight at her waist.

"Croy, set up the shield." Trela pointed to the cleared area in front of them.

"Eqeteclufclo!" The dust around the sides of the invisible shield stirred. Immediately afterwards, as if on some cue, the first volley from Trela's archers took to the sky.

They all climbed onto the shield. Croy, Arnasta, Malghain, Iventorn, and Dartsyle sat down in the center as they clambered upon it. The others jumped on quickly afterwards. Feyazki, Estfale, and Trela sat as well, while Hygen, Urwst, and Serghno all knelt near the edges. Another volley took to the sky.

"Lumkinderclo!" Feyazki spoke with a calm but forceful confidence. They followed the arrows up into the air. Feyazki took them straight up at first, far above the capability of any arrow, before angling them towards Qizern's warpack.

The sight was astounding. Trela could see the entire battlefield from their height. Soon after the third volley, the sound of clashing metal wafted up to them. The packs had met. The clock was ticking.

They kept going up, higher and higher. Since they thought they had a good idea of where Qizern was, Trela wanted to avoid being seen as much as possible. Arnasta and Feyazki spoke quietly to each other as the shield began to slide sideways. The cool air made Trela shiver, both from the morning chill and the altitude. She was glad that she had eaten earlier because she was getting butterflies in her stomach. The feeling did not come from excessive acceleration, as Feyazki segued from upwards motion to sideways motion very smoothly. She was getting nervous. It was one thing to push yourself relentlessly towards a far and distant goal. It was another to be on top of it. She breathed in through her nose and out through her mouth as Synde had taught her. Just thinking of Synde calmed her and steeled her resolve. *Today you shall be avenged*, she thought.

After a while, they stopped. Trela cocked an eyebrow towards Arnasta. She had her head tilted towards Feyazki, talking too quietly to be heard over the sound of the wind in Trela's ears. She turned towards Trela.

"We are, as close as I am able to discern, right above Qizern." She still held the sheath and dagger in her hands.

"Then we drop." Trela glanced over to Feyazki. "Slowly." Her hand squeezed the hilt of her short sword unconsciously. He nodded wordlessly.

The descent was gentle but nerve racking. Trela's own warpack was nowhere near Qizern. There would only be eleven of them in the midst of a sea of enemies. Qizern was truly at the backline, so Feyazki steered them towards the open area behind the warpack.

There were several moments of relative calm as they descended. Eventually, however, they were spotted. The warriors on the ground, who had been staring towards the battle lacklusterly, suddenly sprang into action. The first volley of arrows struck Croy's shield dead on. Then they fell back towards their masters, their heavy heads pointing them downwards. Trela watched in mild amusement as the archers scrambled madly away from their own attack. Hygen and Urwst stood near the edges of the shield and began to loose arrows indiscriminately into the warriors below. The second volley was shot above them in an attempt to drop the arrows down upon the strike force from above. Though none were aimed well enough, Serghno cast a quick little spell just in case.

"Nuteclufclo!" They were getting close to the ground, but were still much too far away to jump to their safety.

"Help! I'm losing it!" Croy suddenly yelped. The solid surface under Trela began to feel spongy. She rolled to her feet but stayed in a low crouch.

Arnasta quickly turned towards the nearest edge. Laying prone upon the shield, her fingers gripped the edge, and she had her head over the side. "Narsidtotarc!" she spoke quietly. Serghno knelt next to her, peering over the edge.

"Hurry!" A panicked cry erupted from Croy's throat. Arnasta suddenly pointed and said something to Serghno.

"Eqedepiarc!" Flames shot from Serghno's outstretched hands and engulfed a mage down below. The invisible surface that Trela was crouching upon instantly firmed back up.

Feyazki dropped them a little faster. Hygen and Urwst kept loosing arrows at a terrific rate. Another volley struck the bottom of the shield. Immediately afterwards, the feeling of the shield under Trela simply... vanished. Croy screamed and blood shot forth from his nose. Serghno again engulfed a mage in flames, but the shield did not come back.

"Scatter!" The command came instinctively from Trela, but she was not sure what could be done about it. Suddenly, when they had almost landed, they were all thrown in different directions. Only Feyazki and Malghain dropped straight down.

Trela was flung towards the clearing at the backline. She unsheathed her short sword and swung it mightily with both hands. She decapitated one Pyran, got her sword stuck in another, and went crashing feet first into a third. She rolled on the ground until she stopped in a daze. She quickly realized she was unarmed and tried to leap up to rectify the situation. Unfortunately, she was still too dizzy and she dropped back to her knees. Next to her, however, was the Pyran she had crashed into. He was folded up into the fetal position and was moaning lowly. She crawled over to him to take his sword from his scabbard. He struck her while she was disarming him, but he was too weak to stop her. She wiped a little blood from her nose and stood while using the sword as a cane. She was fully intent upon stabbing the folded-up Pyran with his own sword but realized that there were several unwounded warriors headed her way. She backed away dragging the sword and tried to regulate her breathing. There were three of them at the lead. The only good news was that they did not seem to recognize her. She was just one of many who had dropped from the sky behind their lines.

One rushed at her screaming. His right hand gripped an ugly mace that he held high for the strike. She gripped her sword with both hands and hefted it upwards and to the left as she moved to her right. His mace was too slow and short to hit her, but she was able to nick the inside of his wrist with the tip of her blade. His scream turned into a howl, and she spun around for the kill.

The other two hesitated for that brief moment, staring at their fallen comrade. She continued to back away. Then they both rushed her. She jumped to her left attempting to keep them from flanking her. She swung wildly at the warrior in front of her, but he parried easily. She kept moving and striking, trying to at least wound him before the other warrior could get around them and behind her. She used the first Pyran as a pivot point to avoid the second. They traded slashes and parries briefly before Trela got a lucky strike in on the warrior's thigh. He dropped to one knee, but the other Pyran jumped around him before she could get another blow in. They struck steel and tiny sparks flew off into the air. Trela was still winded from her tumble and could only back away as he continued his barrage. She was beginning to get more time between blocking each of his swings and was beginning to feel a little more confidant when her heel struck a rock. She fell unceremoniously backwards but was able to keep hold of her sword. She held the blade above her with the flat edge supported by her left hand. The Pyran warrior took a wide stance over her and began raining blows down upon her blade. She was sure that he would quickly break the sword and her soon afterwards. She thrust her right leg up as hard as she could. It scraped on his inner thigh slightly, slowing her some, but it had the desired effect once it met its aim. The Pyran fell over sideways.

Before Trela could stand and finish him, however, the wounded Pyran was suddenly on top of her. She raised her sword above her face with the flat side held up as a shield again. Her right hand upon the hilt and her left supporting blade. She grimaced and squinted her eyes, waiting for the blow, but it never came. The tip of a sword flashed through the Pyran's belly and then retreated. When the warrior fell over, Iventorn was standing behind. He paused for a moment, his sword held ready to strike. She tried to read his thoughts, but his black eyes gave away nothing. Finally, he reached down and helped her up.

"Thanks, for a moment there I thought you were going to kill me." Trela smiled weakly.

"So did I." He smiled broadly at her. Then, quick as a snake, he thrust down and pierced the Pyran she had kicked earlier. "We get anywhere near Qizern and I am gone. I am free."

"That's the deal." She stood and peered off towards the main group of warriors. More than anything, she wished she could stumble upon Arnasta. As she tried to pick out individuals, suddenly a bolt of lightning flashed through the crowd. "Feyazki!" She moved towards the line, but Iventorn grabbed her arm. Hard.

"He can take care of himself. We have a King to find." Iventorn pointed with his sword to Trela's left. There, amongst the thick dust, was Qizern's standard flapping lazily in the breeze. "I'll bet you my freedom he is over there."

Trela had a burning urge to rush into the melee to find Feyazki but knew that Iventorn was right. Of all the derlians in her strike force, Feyazki was probably the one she should worry least about. Plus, what she needed from the strike force more than their protection was their ability to divert attention. There was really only one thing that could ensure her warpack's safety and put a stop to the battle, and that was for her to find Qizern. The quicker the better. She let Iventorn lead her over towards the standard. Even if all he did was to stop her from rushing foolishly to aid her strike force, Trela owed him his freedom. She had not realized how strong an impulse she had to help those she deemed as friends. It completely overrode her logic. In fact, Feyazki would probably have had to protect her once she arrived and not the other way around.

The lightning had an amazing effect. Trela had been concerned that warriors would flee Feyazki's magic, but instead they flocked towards it, like moths to a flame. Literally. She assumed that it was Serghno's fire, because there was another bolt of lightning behind it. Trela and Iventorn charged towards Qizern's standard unimpeded.

They swung around to arrive at the group from behind. Since all of the focus was on her strike team, it seemed that no one noticed the two Pyrans running behind the lines. Maybe they looked like scouts with an important message. Trela could not be sure, nor did she particularly care. The important part was that they were close, she could feel it.

As they arrived at the back of the group, she thought she could hear Qizern's voice. It was soft at first, as if discussing strategy, but soon it began to boom orders. Trela smiled to herself. Feyazki's lightning was disconcerting the warpack.

"I don't care how many die today, have I not been clear? We have them vastly outnumbered. We will crush them as quickly as we are able. All of them. I do not care if they have a mage who can shoot lightning from his hands. I don't care if he can shoot lightning out his ass! Get everyone down there and kill him. Bring all of the mages you need, bring all the warriors, all the archers, anyone! I want his head on a pike within the hour. No more excuses, no more concerns, no more wasting my time. You are the greatest warriors in the largest warpack this realm has ever seen. Now stop huddling around my skirts like frightened children and crush my enemies." It was definitely Qizern's voice. "If the girl is with the mage, incapacitate her and truss her up tight. I do not want her able to move a finger the next time she is in front of me. Her long slow torture will keep me satisfied for moons to come."

"With all due respect, sir, why did you not just crush her already? We could have easily surrounded the parley tent, and we would all be heading back to Agoge right now." A small voice on the other side of the group spoke up. Trela could not see who spoke, but she could barely see the top of Qizern's head from where she was anyway. She looked around her and realized that Iventorn was gone. She grew flush with anger but it quickly subsided. She had no right to expect that he would stay and fight by her side once they had found Qizern. She had made the terms of the deal.

"Because I will crush every Pyran foolish enough to follow her. I will destroy every last one of them today. Vengeance will be mine." He had swirled towards where the voice had come from but did not move beyond that.

"Vengeance is not a strategy." The quote came from another part of the warpack.

"My strategy is working. We will conquer them all before nightfall." Qizern retorted.

"You call this a strategy? We are just throwing wave after wave of our warriors at them. We were dug in amongst our defenses! Now we are in the middle..." The third voice was cut off.

"My strategy is winning! And that is what we are doing today: winning." Qizern paused to take a deep breath. "No more questions, no more insolence. You have your orders. Once this Luften falls, we can concentrate on the rest of the fools. Go!"

In a rush, about half the small crowd near Qizern took off towards Feyazki and Serghno, their purple cloaks swaying with their gait. Trela felt a little naked with so many on the move. Several Pyrans near her stayed, so she just stood her ground amongst them, pondering her next move.

Others were slowing peeling away from the group. Trela realized that she did not have much time before she would be noticed by someone. She was not sure what to do, however. If she shouted a challenge to him, he might just have her killed. There were at least twenty warriors in the immediate vicinity. While she stood there immobilized by indecision, a strange commotion began. The crowd began to tighten around Qizern.

"Back up! Back away, or I slit his throat." It sounded oddly like Iventorn.

"Do as he says." Qizern's voice was quiet, almost pensive. The crowd moved away slightly. Since Trela had stayed where she was, she was now at the front of the ring and could see Iventorn and Qizern. Their backs were towards her. Iventorn was taller and had Qizern's forehead gripped with his large left palm. In his right hand was clutched a small dagger pressed against Qizern's throat. Qizern's hands were held wide and well away from Iventorn. They shuffled back and forth a little, but did not turn to face Trela.

"Who controls this warpack if you die?" Iventorn asked as they shuffled.

"If you kill me, your death will be long and painful." Qizern's voice had an undercurrent of calm rage.

"I am already dead, my King." The words were whispered quietly, but Trela heard them clearly. "I'll ask you one more time. Who is your First?" Iventorn raised his voice, but Qizern would not answer.

"I am." A Pyran stepped forwards who was a little older than Qizern, but would not be considered frail by any derlian standards. "I am Tweltas, leader of the Guard."

"Well, Tweltas, if I kill Qizern and make you King, will you call off the battle? Would you give a reprieve to those that fought against Qizern and return to Agoge? Could we end this madness?" Trela was not sure what Iventorn was striving for.

"Kill him!" Qizern shouted quickly before quieting down. Trela assumed the knife was pressed harder against his flesh. She was sure that if anyone managed to kill Iventorn without hurting Qizern at that moment, they would be richly rewarded. No one moved, however.

Tweltas took an agonizingly long time staring at the two of them before answering. "Yes. I will call off the battle if I am made King."

"Traitor!" Qizern had one more short outburst.

Trela took two steps forward. "Or you can accept my challenge, Qizern."

The look of fear and anger that crossed Tweltas's face was palpable but faded quickly. If Qizern accepted and she failed, he would be tortured for as long as Iventorn. Maybe for longer. He was a consummate professional to be able to swallow his feelings so quickly. He did not speak another word.

"You?! Do I not have Guards anymore? How did you get here?" Qizern's arms were still held out and the knife was still at his neck.

"You sent them to go get struck by lightning, don't you remember?" Trela walked so that she was near Tweltas but well out of his arm's reach. "You have a decision to make, Qizern. It should be a simple one."

They all stood there for quite some time. None of the surrounding Pyrans made a move. Everyone was waiting on Qizern,

"Yes," he said quietly.

"I'm sorry, I did not quite catch that." Trela wanted to make sure what he was saying yes to.

"Yes, I accept your challenge for single combat. Now let me go." Qizern started wiggling.

"On your honor?" Trela smiled at him.

"Yes, now let me go." Qizern kept his eyes lowered. Trela nodded at Iventorn. Iventorn released Qizern and backed away. Qizern staggered a little and rubbed his neck.

"Seize them!" Qizern pointed an accusing finger at Trela. "Seize them both and tie them tight." No one moved. "Tweltas, I will forgive your traitorous outburst, you did not know what you were saying. Now get them to the brig so that we can finish this battle uninterrupted."

"You swore on your honor." Tweltas stared straight at Qizern. Still no one moved towards Trela or Iventorn.

"I did not. I never swore anything and did not even use the word honor." Qizern looked around at all of the frozen faces. There was a long pause. "Fine, we shall make the ring here. I will destroy you with my own hands." He pointed at Trela. Then his voice began to raise in volume. "Realize that I consider this a trick and not honorable by any means. I was forced into accepting your challenge. My First has betrayed me and my Guards have failed me. Once I destroy you, my vengeance will know no bounds and will hold all witnesses here accountable for being passive while I was being wronged. Threatened in front of my own warriors and not one will lift a finger? You should all hang your heads in shame." No one, however, hung their heads in shame.

The ring was quickly made. A quiet crowd had begun to gather. Trela could only hope that the fighting elsewhere had stopped. It was certainly quiet and still as far as she could sense. She hoped that word of the challenge would have reached the strike force at the least. With warpacks this large, however, communication was often slow and cumbersome, especially during the din of battle. She wanted to hope that word of the challenge had already reached the front lines, but she knew that was impossible.

Qizern huddled with some of his lieutenants. There were many warriors gathered around the ring, but one stood out alone. There were no Pyrans standing next to Tweltas. Trela pondered this. If she were to lose, this warrior would most certainly be publicly executed. At best. She looked at his fine clothing and weaponry. She looked at her own meager short sword. Without a second thought she walked over to where he stood, separated like a pariah.

"I have come to beg use of your sword." Trela looked him in the eye. He stood there, waiting silently.

"I cannot afford to do that," he finally uttered.

"You can't afford not to. If I lose, you die horribly whether or not you had lent me your weapon." Trela smiled slightly. "If I win, you could be the warrior who ensured it was a fair fight."

"You are correct when you say that I will die if you lose. Qizern will see to that. He will also do his best to ensure that the story of his victory includes my bitter betrayal. However, if you lose and I had lent you my sword, all those present would know of that betrayal. It would be real. They shall spread the word of my villainy farther and faster than Qizern ever could alone. As of now, I have only caused the single combat that will end this battle. That is honorable enough for me." He smiled back. "My reputation is worth a hundred lives."

"What happens if I win?" Trela had not anticipated much difficulty and was not sure what to make of it. "How could I even be here if I was not destined to win?"

"If you are truly the Kriishan, I believe you would be gracious enough in your victory to grant me mercy." His smile grew larger. "And if you are destined to win, then nothing I do or not do will affect your victory."

Before Trela could press Tweltas further, she was interrupted by a Pyran warrior. Though there was an air of greenhorn about him and an exuberant gleam in his eye, he was older than his first impression belied. Before her, held out in his hands, was a magnificent specimen of a bladed weapon. It was a little longer than what she was used to, but shimmered brightly in the sun. It was slightly curved, appeared razor sharp, and had a worn leather grip. Like its presenter, it appeared to have a hidden gravitas that floated just beneath a sprightly surface. The Pyran knelt down on one knee in front of her, his empty scabbard splayed out behind him.

"Please grant me the honor of using my father's blade, Talon. It is one of the few swords in this realm that will withstand the onslaught of Strife." He bowed his head after speaking.

"Strife?" Trela's eyebrows attempted to converge upon her wrinkled brow.

"Qizern's mistress." He did not move. Trela remembered that swordmasters called their swords "mistresses. " It was appropriate that Qizern would call his mistress Strife. And it made some of his previous comments to her make much more sense.

Trela took the sword from him and showed it to Tweltas. "Now this is a Pyran with some foresight." She then turned towards the kneeling Pyran. "What is your name, warrior?"

"Pejal. At your service, my liege." He would only look at her boots.

"I will remember your kindness, Pejal. You have made this a fair fight. I was worried I was going to have to use a dagger." The sword felt perfectly balanced.

"You had better hope she wins." It was Tweltas.

"I wish it more than anything in my life." Pejal stood and bowed at her and then, unexpectedly, he bowed at Tweltas as well. Trela felt odd holding a sword she could not sheath but was very pleased with the heft of it. She turned towards Tweltas as Pejal walked back towards the edge of the ring.

"I thank you for your stubborn pride. For even when you think you are not being helpful, destiny still speaks through you. That is a gift." She made a small bow to Tweltas.

Trela turned and walked towards the center of the fresh ring. She glanced quickly for Iventorn but could not immediately find him. Qizern stood opposite of Trela, glaring at her. Without speeches or words or warning, he rushed towards her with Strife raised high. His barbaric scream was deafening.

Trela easily dodged his wide swing. She began to swing her new sword around, trying to get a better feel for it. She wished she had more time to get familiar with it, but she knew Qizern would not concede that to her. She dodged three different attacks before she felt comfortable enough to parry with Talon. She held it at a sharp angle and used her left hand on the pommel to lessen the strain on her wrists. It felt good. Strife slid down Talon's blade and struck the protective hilt. She snapped her sword horizontally in a quick attempt at a counter strike. Qizern had already danced back. He looked at her more warily after her strike, however.

When he charged her again, it was more controlled. His screams and grunts took on a more focused tone. The gleam in his eye lost just a little bit of its wildness. Trela realized that she had missed her first opportunity. Those first few seconds were when he was at his most overconfident, and he would never be that overconfident again.

Trela parried and riposted. She danced and dodged. She thrust and slashed, but she did not get close to cutting Qizern. For his part he missed as often as she did. They circled each other relentlessly.

Trela's mind wandered to Synde. "There is always a weakness to your enemy," he used to say. "A great warrior will be able to hold their own until they find that weakness." When she asked what that weakness might be, how she could spot it, he laughed. "If there were an easy answer to that, an answer that would work in all situations, then we would all be great warriors. Sometimes, their weakness will be your strength." He had laughed again. "But, more often than not, you will share their weakness. Knowing your own weaknesses, their signs and manifestations, will often give you an advantage over a warrior who does not think during battle. Even if thinking may slow your reaction time slightly. If you have ever fought with a pulled muscle in your lower leg, remember how that felt. Remember how your opposite leg must compensate for your aching one. Remember how shifting your balance becomes ungainly. If you see your enemy favor a leg, that is their weakness. Try to think of what they are thinking during combat. Watch how their bodies move and attempt to feel what they must be feeling." Trela blocked and lunged and wondered what Qizern was thinking. His eyes held a fiery intensity. He watched her move with as much study as she assumed her own face belied. He would try the same strike several times and examine how she reacted. Then, suddenly, after four times thrusting in the same manner, he would flick his wrist upwards at the end of the lunge, almost slashing the side of her face as she frantically batted away his sword with her own.

Trela finally realized what he was thinking. He had realized that she was studying him. Therefore, he was going to build patterns with which she could use. These were not real patterns, however. They were a ruse that made her fall into a response pattern. Then he would counter that pattern hoping her response would be the same. A couple of times he came close to connecting with his razor-sharp sword. She then tried to ignore his patterns, but that brought her back to mere reactionary parries. Mere stimulus-response. That, she knew, was not her strength. She also doubted that it involved his weakness.

Trela stopped circling for a moment and stared at Qizern. He stared back at her with anger in his eyes. There was no sign of crazy, no hint of what she had seen back in the parley tent. Only a hot but controlled frustration. He took a small step to his left. She took one to hers, keeping them opposite each other. He moved his right foot as if to circle back to the right, then suddenly lunged forward with his right arm swinging low, but then snapping upwards in a shallow arc. The arc at the tip of his sword, however, was wide and fast. Trela jumped unceremoniously to her right and lifted both arms while arching her mid-section backwards. It was ugly and awkward move but it worked. The sword tip went slashing past Trela harmlessly. He immediately began to withdraw his right leg back in line with his left but his sword arm was still across his chest. Trela hopped back forwards and slashed Talon down and to the right, but she was a little to Qizern's right and he was able to snap his sword back into parry position. Trela briefly cursed herself for not executing the same move that he just had. His sword had been out of position and would not have been able to block that in time. In her frustration she continued a barrage of blows upon his upraised sword. She was quick enough that he was unable to mount a counter attack and was pushed backwards several steps. Pressing her attack, however, winded her a little and gained her nothing.

Trela had an urge to kick sand towards his face, to throw a dagger, to fall back on some new and unexpected attack, but she knew she must not win by anything that looked dishonorable. Then the idea came to her as he took another wide swing. It was simple. It was destiny. His weakness was his old age. Her strength was her youth. She had to make him expend as much energy as possible while conserving her own. She needed to wear him down until he started to make mistakes. Then, and only then, could she put the full force behind her swings that would be capable of delivering a killing blow. She began to dodge more and parry less. Her own thrusts and slashes turned into little more than strong feints. She kept her footwork light and short, allowing him an illusion of control. She found herself smiling. She almost heard a chant in the back of her head. Some unknowable rhythm. *I am the Kriishan. I am the Kriishan.*

As they danced around and circled each other, it appeared that Qizern was growing older before her eyes. He moved more wooden as each moment passed. His joints especially seemed to get stiffer. Though his knees and elbows seemed to work fine moving up and down, they did not seem to rotate or shift side to side as well. He squinted and grimaced more. Even the lines on his face appeared deeper. The transformation took some time and it was almost distressing to watch. For Trela, however, an opposite transformation was happening. She began to get tingling sensations in her extremities. It did not feel like the tingling that erupted due to a sudden loss of numbness, such as when you sit with one leg over the other for too long and your foot falls asleep. It felt like she was pulling energy from the dirt below her. It felt like each breath had twice as much life-affirming air in it. As if the sun was brighter but not hotter. As if her blood pumped pure nutrients through her. She had not felt this energized since she had decided to escape from Serif. And even that time began to pale in comparison. Each second seemed to pump more energy into her. The rhythm thrummed. *I am the Kriishan.* Yes, that was it: his age. That was the thought, the excuse, the rational explanation for what was happening. That would allow her mind to keep doing what it was doing. That made chaos seem normal, made the irrational rhythm make sense, allowed her the freedom to reach beyond herself for reserves of strength. *I am the Kriishan.*

The look in his eyes somehow grew in intensity. He showed his teeth and slashed his sword in front of him, swinging it around his left side, swinging it around his right, making a giant X in front of him. He took in a large breath and rushed towards her. Trela jumped back but he kept running, so she dove and rolled to her right. Strife came close enough that she thought she could hear it whistle through the wind. She struggled to her feet as he struggled to stop himself before leaving the ring. And there it was, with his back to her, more of the same rhythm. *I am the Kriishan.* She regained her balance and shifted towards him, not quite running, by the time he spun back around. Trela stopped in front of him, watching his chest heave. His breath was ragged and belabored, but his sword was held high and steady. The energy continued to pump into her. She felt that she could leap over him. The thrumming was incredibly loud in her ears. She felt that she could fly if she wanted. *I am the Kriishan,* repeated through her mind, through her body.

Qizern showed his teeth again and began swinging his sword in front of himself again. But she was not pinned against the edge of the ring this time. As he rushed her, she merely dodged to her left. True, she had to almost run sideways to avoid his wide arcs, but it did not take too much effort to avoid Strife. The thrumming rhythm continued to reverberate within her. The chanting in her mind got louder with each passing moment. *I am the Kriishan.*

Trela backed up to the edge of the ring. She needed to parry more but the dodging seemed to be taking a toll on Qizern. Sweat poured from every pore. He kept trying to wipe his brow with the back of his hand. It made his hair seem stringy. And somehow more gray. He seemed to age further as she watched him. He gave a large scream and slashed wildly at her. She again had to duck and roll away from him. She came up in a low crouch, and he kicked a swath of dirt towards her face. She squinted and rolled further backwards. His grunting yell warned her that he was pressing his attack. None of the dirt reached her eyes but she held them to narrow slits, making it difficult to see more detail than his hulking shadow. But still, even half crouched and half blinded, she felt more energized than at any time before in her life. The thrumming was almost deafening. It pounded in her brain with that constant rhythm. She slashed towards him to slow him down a little.

He backed up slightly. He was panting heavily. The tip of his sword drug along the ground. *I am the Kriishan.* It was an unstoppable phrase that thrummed continuously through Trela. He gave a loud bark and slashed and lunged. Then he backed up a little and drug his sword tip. He gave a high pitched scream and slashed and lunged. Then he backed up. He looked ancient to Trela. With each second, with each passing moment, he seemed to age. The thrumming drowned out all other sound. With each passing second, with each moment, she felt more energy pour into her. *I am the Kriishan.*

Qizern began to use both hands upon the hilt of Strife. His bony and wrinkled hands moved in front of the sword as he brought it down heavily from overhead. It was as if he was dragging the sword through the air. At that moment Trela realized that he was ready for death. That he did not wish to be humiliated. Trela easily skipped to the side out of harm's way. Then, as quickly as a snake, she spun in a tight circle, only extending her arms and sword as she came round fully. Strife's tip struck the ground below and stopped. Talon's edge struck Qizern's neck and continued. The decapitation stunned Trela. Though her body hummed with power, she had not anticipated such a decisive killing blow.

The crowd erupted. At first Trela could not tell if it was erupting in adoration or murderous rage. Like with Iventorn standing over her, she doubted that the crowd knew what it would do next. It was merely an expression of passion to be rationalized later. It was an ending. It was a beginning.

Chapter 21 - Epilogue

The fighting was stopped fairly quickly after Trela defeated Qizern. The war drums and bugles caused a theta wave of peace to ripple through the warpacks. Once Feyazki was safe, he was able to *whisper* to Lishean. The enormity of Qizern's warpack meant, unfortunately, that lives were certainly still being lost after he had fallen. But Trela's warriors had been fighting purely defensively to buy her as much time as possible and many of Qizern's warriors were not fully committed to the battle. They had answered the call and were willing to crush the rebellion with overwhelming forces. But they were more hesitant about sacrificing themselves, of pushing into the breach, of leaving their flanks open during a charge. Their hearts were not fully in it. It was a testament to how many were tired of Qizern's rule that there were not more casualties. They fought out of duty and honor, not for their lives and certainly not for the full-throated desire of destruction.

It came as a small shock to Trela that more did not revile her. Oh, they had not thought that she was the Kriishan, at least they would not have publicly admitted that. Most of them had not known who she was, truly. She had assumed that Qizern would have defamed her, made up stories of how she slaughtered children and the like. But his strategy appeared to be the opposite of that. To keep her storyless and nameless, to leave her in obscurity. It seemed like just trying to ignore a problem and hope that it went away on its own. But Trela was not so sure that it wasn't effective. How many warriors would have left his warpack to join her had they known about her? Maybe none but, judging from the aftermath, maybe a sizeable portion. Certainly not half, but maybe enough that Qizern would have been forced into single combat. Even twenty percent would have been a huge boon.

They were at a long row of tables out under the stars. Trela had as many of her original warriors as she could fit filling those benches. There were also many long rows of tables running perpendicularly, far into the distance. Those benches were filled with the Guard and Qizern's old warriors, now hers. She had wanted to mix the warriors a bit more, but Lishean had insisted upon tradition. "Tomorrow they can all mingle", he had said. There were many more tables scattered about, many filled the tents, many revelers just wandering about under the stars. But here, at the spot of her victory, with her chair centered over the prodigious, mostly dried, blood spot from Qizern's decapitation, were her best and most loyal warriors. They were swapping tales of how they had survived the battle.

"I thought we were going to die. Seriously. We were completely surrounded. I had a sword in each hand and just kept spinning them around while spinning myself around. I kept waiting for a spear or arrow or, at the very least, an adventurous sword to puncture me. There was no way that whatever I was doing was being effectual." Malghain laughed as he spun some dried out turkey legs around himself. "Then Feyazki lets loose with his lightning. They all back up a little bit. I'm a bit more crouched now, we're back-to-back, and we are still slowly spinning. They start scrunching in a little and he lets loose again. This is when I realized it was all over. I had no idea how many more lightning bolts he had in him, but I knew it wouldn't be enough. It couldn't be. There was no way that he could cast something like that every minute or so for an hour. Not before they got some spears in us. Then, out of nowhere, he turns and grabs my face." Malghain dropped his partially eaten dinner and grabbed his own face between his hands. His eyes were bugging out so far that Trela almost spewed her grog across the table. "He stares at me like a lunatic, with his nose, I swear, not more than a finger's breadth from mine. I half expected him to kiss me. Then, in a completely serious tone of voice, he says, 'We are going to have to go fetal.' Now I have no idea what he is talking about. I think I might have said something intelligent, such as, 'What?' He then drops to the ground, still holding my face mind you, and he curls up and I curl up and we are cuddling like a couple of newlyweds when, Bam!, he yells out some spell and we are surrounded by a... a shell of lightning. It was amazing. They would bang their swords on it and torch their hands off. Eventually they backed away and we lied there cuddling until the bugles sounded Trela's victory." Malghain looked around while everyone laughed before finally raising his glass. "To Feyazki!"

"To Feyazki!" All those around him shouted and drank mightily.

Trela had never heard Malghain speak so much at once. She had certainly never heard him making so many jokes. She was sure that she had seen him quite drunk before, but could not picture his smiling cheeks like they were at that moment. It was pleasantly shocking.

"I had to cast that lightning-shield spell four times before you finally beheaded Qizern." Feyazki was all smiles himself. "To Trela!"

"To Trela!" All those around him shouted and drank mightily.

It felt great, and that was not just the grog talking. All of those that she felt close to had survived. Trela had kept many of them in the back of the battle on purpose. What would have Clerin or Knill been able to assist her with? She had refused to endanger them. There were others that she had refused to endanger as well; the majority of the Luften warriors and the majority of her Privy Council. Out of everyone in her warpack, she could not afford to lose Lishean. At all. Nor could she afford to lose the likes of Rewista as a military advisor. Though she could dictate little of how a First or Second led their warriors, she had attempted to keep them away from the vanguard. Kryhir's maniples took the brunt of the damage and he had survived by staggering his retreat with unpredictable charges into the face of the enemy. But even those who had come along with her had all somehow survived the carnage.

Croy, Serghno and Arnasta had retreated quickly. Croy cast shield spells and Serghno threw fire while Arnasta navigated the quickest way out. They even had the archers, Hygen and Urwst, with them. They had gone so far out of their way while escaping that by the time they got back to Kryhir's maniples the fighting was over.

Estfale and Dartsyle were flung in a different direction. They had landed in the midst of a small group of Qizern's warriors. Landed was not quite the right word, they had bowled straight into them. While struggling in the pile, they were able to stab those that they had landed on before they were stabbed themselves. They tore Trela's bow and lightning insignia from their uniforms immediately. Bloodied and sore, clutching each other so that they looked like warriors from the front line, they slowly wandered towards Qizern's medic tents. Slowly enough that they never arrived. When the bugles and drums indicated Qizern's defeat they straightened up and ran towards Trela, wanting to be the first to congratulate her.

No one knew where Iventorn was. He had completely disappeared. Trela was not sure how a Pyran of his stature could vanish, but she could not begrudge him anything. She told anyone and everyone that he was released from his geas and was no longer a ghulzan. More than anyone, if it had not been for Iventorn, Trela would not have been able to fight Qizern.

Later that evening, Knill was extolling his logical explanation of destiny, his "stream theory". Trela felt a sudden affection for him that was not in the least bit rooted in what he had done or could do for her, but was rooted in who he was. She truly enjoyed listening to him speak passionately about... anything.

"...each flow further down the mountain with less inherit friction? My belief is yes. My belief is that Trela followed her stream with the least amount of friction that I have ever witnessed. It is what originally attracted me to her and it still amazes me. To Trela! " Knill raised his glass. So did all of the others. He drank the drought in one mighty gulp. Trela stood.

"We are all good at that, stream theory, everyone of us here. Even more so, we have combined ourselves into a mighty, unstoppable river. And where are we now? Where has our river taken us? We have finally reached the sea!" Trela drank her glass in one gulp as well. Those before her cheered wildly. She had never felt better in her life.

Appendix A (Races)

The general race descriptions given below are not absolute and are by no means considered exhaustive. Though rare, there are certainly blond Luftens and tall Gaens. Personality traits are even harder to pin exclusively to one race or another. These generalities are merely provided to assist in getting an overall flavor of the various derlian denizens of the world.

Race: Gaen
Element: Stone
Beleg: Gunzgak

The shortest of the races, the Gaens live in underground cave complexes and against rocky hillsides. They are simple and civilized, enjoying order and structure throughout their lives. They are skeptics and jinxers in general, and therefore are typically the weakest mages of all the races. Their hair is typically quite curly with mostly brown and red coloring. They are stocky bordering on pudgy. They love beer and are excellent miners, and colloquially refer to their coined money as "pebbles." They have a strict caste system based upon vocation. The last name of a Gaen consists of two syllables, the first denoting their rank and the second their guild:

Sie – Peasant	Tin – Farmer
Beo – Apprentice	Lak – Merchant
Ona – Member	Cha – Blacksmith
Mur – Overseer	Wir – Carpenter
Fyr – Teacher	Tul – Stoneworker
Cru – Guild Leader	Sol – Artist
Dea – Assembly Member	Rem – Physician
Ata – Assembly Leader	Jin – Warrior

Vyx – the Guild Lord

Race: Fluen
Element: Water
Beleg: Lembin

The blond, ship-building Fluens live around the Clatsvol sea. Each royal family can trace their lineage back to the original Yaven they sprang from. Their family name carries much weight and responsibility. Bastards are shunned. They are strict adherents to tradition and even call their coined money "crowns" in deference to the monarchy. They are generally tall and thin, with long, straight hair to match. They are great cultivators of wine and masters of all manners of fishing. Magic is a skill much used in the Fluen realm by beggar and prince alike, though maybe not quite as specialized as in the Luften realm.

Race: Luften
Element: Air
Beleg: Linchon

There are two types of Luftens: those who live high in the cities amongst the helioarc trees, and those who shuffle along the ground. This demarcation means more than a family name or a chosen vocation, though those things may dictate where a Luften lives. They are somewhat thin with curly and mostly black hair, though there are also some browns. They are the tallest of the races, but are thicker than the Fluens, making for a more symmetric form. They harvest honey and ferment a deliciously sweet mead. They excel in woodcraft and magic. They are undoubtedly the most focused and engaged of the races when it comes to magic, as it is one of the most powerful guilds in the Luften society. There is a shaky monarchy, bound by a council of Branches, that has gone through so many kings of late that they have taken to referring to their coined money as "heads". There are both family Branches and guild Branches that make up the general council, balancing traditional aristocracy with meritocracy. In theory, at least.

Race: Pyran
Element: Fire
Beleg: Gorbanax

Pyrans are a nomadic race ruled by a caste of warriors. They are short and muscular and many of them travel in warpacks, fighting with each other and living off the land, sending what additional coins they can back to their families. The fighting is considered an art form, with warpacks growing and shrinking more from trading warriors than from actual death. A warpack is typically broken up into smaller units, a cohort having approximately forty warriors and a maniple comprised of two to four cohorts. They generally have straight, light brown hair. They drink grog by the barrelful, and there are more herders than there are farmers, though there are plenty of both. The king or queen rules with complete power, beholden to none. They have mages but they study, almost exclusively, destruction or healing magics.

Appendix B (Magic)

Magic is the art of sifting through Chaos to find a desired possibility, then willing that possibility into reality. A spell is comprised of one word, typically with four syllables: Power, Sphere, Element and Effect. This word defines the desired possibility in its simplest terms. The difficulty of the spell is estimated by adding the ranks of the syllables and then multiplying them by the Power's Multiplier. There are Majora syllables, those that are taught, and there are Minora syllables, those that are individually learned. The Majora syllables are listed below, separated into the four Pillars:

Power	Multiplier	Sphere	Rank	Element	Rank	Effect	Rank
Lo	3	Kin	2	Luf	2	Pri	1
Nu	5	Fin	2	Ge	1	Arc	2
Mek	8	De	3	Pi	3	Del	2
Nar	11	Tra	1	Flu	2	Sfe	3
Eqe	15	Tec	2	Der	3	Clo	3
Lum	19	Li	3	Hep	1	To	1
Sur	23	Sid	1	Pan	1	Kha	1
Tor	27	Morf	1	Tot	2	Ref	0

POWER:
Power designates a spell's effectiveness and duration. These are intertwined. A mage may make a spell shorter to increase its effectiveness, or they may decrease the effectiveness to increase the duration. This is known as "tilting the pillar." This list is simple since the Syllable is mainly defined by its Multiplier.

Lo:
Glyph: ●
Multiplier: 3

Nu: ● ●
Glyph:
Multiplier: 5

Mek:
Glyph: ● ● ●
Multiplier: 8

Nar:
Glyph: ● ● ●
Multiplier: 11

Eqe:
Glyph:
Multiplier: 15

Lum:
Glyph:
Multiplier: 19

Sur:
Glyph:
Multiplier: 23

Tor:
Glyph:
Multiplier: 27

SPHERE:

Sphere designates a spell's action, its sphere of influence. The following descriptions are from Elange's book, *Principles of Grey Magic.*

Kin: Sphere of movement. This Syllable brings your Mind to the Realm of Movement. This Sphere is dependant upon the Element to be moved. This Syllable may be used with any Effect of the Caster's choosing. Movement is defined as changing an object's location through adjacent space over a period of time, meaning the object must move through all intervening space between locations and must take a certain amount of time to do so. Objects cannot be made to disappear and reappear, nor can they be moved through solid objects.

Glyph:

Rank: 2

Fin: Sphere of the Mind. This Syllable brings your Mind to Itself and to Others. This Sphere is Elementally limited for Majora use. The vast main Element to be used is Tot, though Pan occasionally and Der rarely may also be used. This Syllable may be used with any Effect of the Caster's choosing. The Mind is defined as all mental activities including thought, analytics and perception. This Syllable may not be used to affect anything tangible.

Glyph:

Rank: 2

De: Sphere of destruction. This Syllable brings your Mind to the Path of Death, Damage, and Destruction. This Sphere is Polymorphic, but most often paired with Pi. This Syllable may be used with any Effect of the Caster's choosing. Destruction is defined by causing injury to the living and demolishing the inanimate. The type of injury depends upon the Element and Power level, up to and including Death.

Glyph:

Rank: 3

Tra: Sphere of transmutation. This Syllable brings your Mind to essence modifier of Transmutation. This Sphere is dependant upon the Elements to be transmuted. This Syllable may only be used with the Effect of Ref. This Sphere is used to create the only typical five Syllable Majora Words. Transmutation is defined as changing one Element into another. This Syllable may not affect shape, but may affect density and thereby mass.

Glyph: 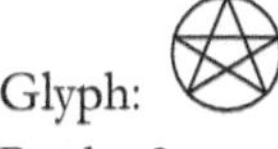
Rank: 1

Tec: Sphere of protection. This Syllable brings your Mind to the Path of Protection. This Sphere is Polymorphic, so most Mages use lower ranking Elements in the Word. This Syllable may be used with any Effect of the Caster's choosing. Protection is defined as the stopping of physical harm/damage from immediately happening. This Syllable may not be used to Ameliorate or Heal.

Glyph:
Rank: 2

Li: Sphere of healing. This Syllable brings your Mind to the Way of Healing. This Sphere only affects living beings and is therefore Elementally limited for Majora use. The vast main Element to be used is Der, though Pan occasionally and Tot rarely may also be used. This Syllable may be used with any Effect of the Caster's choosing. Healing is defined as the temporary Amelioration of damaged tissue. Temporary Amelioration may close wounds, bind bones, reconnect severed arteries, numb pain, and even cure some diseases, but the spell will always wear off. Only time-based cellular reconstruction has long lasting effects on the derlian body, making this Sphere act more as a time accelerant than true Healing.

Glyph: 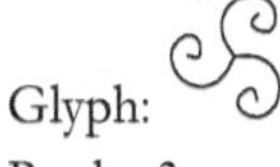
Rank: 3

Sid: Sphere of communication. This Syllable brings your Mind to the way of Communing with Spirits. This Sphere may not be used to commune with a living derlian and is rarely used with the syllables Hep or Pan. This Syllable may be used with any Effect of the Caster's choosing. Communing is defined as transferring thoughts with Spirits. This Syllable is used to summon Yavens and commune with the dead.

Glyph:
Rank: 1

Morf: Sphere of change. This Syllable brings your Mind to the way of Changing Shapes. This Sphere is dependant upon the Element to be modified. This Syllable may be used with any Effect of the Caster's choosing. Change, in this instance, is defined as modifying a purely physical form. This Syllable may not be used to change Elements or the Essence of the object.

Glyph:
Rank: 1

ELEMENT:

Element designates what type of object the spell is acting upon. Its basic constituents, its Essence. Due to the amount of different types of objects in the realms, some of these elemental categories are quite broad, though the first four come directly from the Yaven realms and are, therefore, specifically defined. These definitions are considered intuititive.

Luf: The element of Air.

Glyph:
Rank: 2

Ge: The element of Stone.

Glyph:
Rank: 1

Pi: The element of Fire.

Glyph:
Rank: 3

Flu: The element of Water.

Glyph:
Rank: 2

Der: The element of derlians, of flesh.

Glyph: 
Rank: 3

Hep: The element of metals, salts, and crystals.

Glyph: 
Rank: 1

Pan: The element of nature: plants, animals and wood.

Glyph: 
Rank: 1

Tot: The element of the mind.

Glyph: 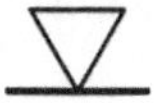
Rank: 2

<u>EFFECT</u>:
Effect designates the target of the spell, the aim. This Pillar is highly
affected by the Power level of the spell. The shapes of these Effects
are intuitive and so are defined simply, below.

Pri: The target of yourself.

Glyph: 
Rank: 1

Arc: A target in a line of sight.

Glyph: 
Rank: 2

Del: The target of a sphere at a later time.

Glyph:
Rank: 2

Sfe: The target of a sphere centered around the caster.

Glyph:
Rank: 3

Clo: The target of a cube placed at the caster's choosing.

Glyph:
Rank: 3

To: The target of your direct contact.

Glyph:
Rank: 1

Kha: The targets are random living objects.

Glyph:
Rank: 1

Ref: The target refers back to itself.

Glyph:
Rank: 0

Appendix C (Map)

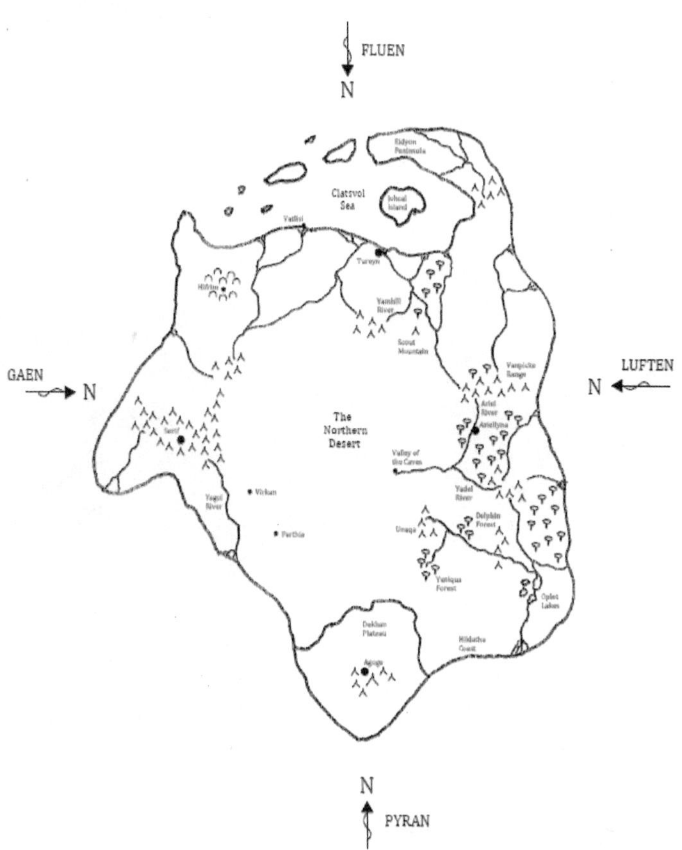